True Blood Omnibus II

True Blood Omnibus II

Dead to the World
Dead as a Doornail
Definitely Dead

Charlaine Harris

GOLLANCZ
London

This collection first published in Great Britain in 2010 by Gollancz
An imprint of the Orion Publishing Group
Orion House, 5 Upper St Martin's Lane, London WC2H 9EA
An Hachette UK Company

A CIP catalogue record for this book is available
from the British Library

ISBN 978 0 575 09689 9

1 3 5 7 9 10 8 6 4 2

Typeset by Input Data Services Ltd,
Bridgwater, Somerset

Printed in Great Britain by CPI Mackays, Chatham ME5 8TD

The Orion Publishing Group's policy is to use papers that are natural,
renewable and recyclable products and made from wood grown
in sustainable forests. The logging and manufacturing processes are
expected to conform to the environmental regulations of the country of origin.

www.charlaineharris.com

www.orionbooks.co.uk

Contents

Dead To The World

Though they'll probably never read it, this book is dedicated to all the coaches — baseball, football, volleyball, soccer — who've worked through so many years, often for no monetary reward, to coax athletic performances out of my children and to instil in them an understanding of The Game. God bless you all, and thanks from one of the moms who stand through rain, cold, heat and mosquitoes.

However, this mom always wonders who else might be watching the night games.

I found the note taped to my door when I got home from work. I'd had the lunch-to-early-evening shift at Merlotte's, but since we were at the tail end of December, the day darkened early. So Bill, my former boyfriend – that's Bill Compton, or Vampire Bill, as most of the regulars at Merlotte's call him – must have left his message within the previous hour. He can't get up until dark.

I hadn't seen Bill in over a week, and our parting hadn't been a happy one. But touching the envelope with my name written on it made me feel miserable. You'd think – though I'm twenty-six – I'd never had, and lost, a boyfriend before.

You'd be right.

Normal guys don't want to date someone as strange as I am. People have been saying I'm messed up in the head since I started school.

They're right.

That's not to say I don't get groped at the bar occasionally. Guys get drunk. I look good. They forget their misgivings about my reputation for strangeness and my ever-present smile.

But only Bill has ever gotten close to me in an intimate way. Parting from him had hurt me bad.

I waited to open the envelope until I was sitting at the old, scarred kitchen table. I still had my coat on, though I'd shucked my gloves.

Dearest Sookie – I wanted to come over to talk to you when you had somewhat recovered from the unfortunate events of earlier this month.

'Unfortunate events', my round rear end. The bruises had finally faded, but I had a knee that still ached in the cold, and I suspected that it always would. Every injury I had incurred had been in the course of rescuing my cheating boyfriend from his imprisonment by a group of vampires that included his former flame, Lorena. I had yet to figure out why Bill had been so infatuated with Lorena that he'd answered her summons to Mississippi.

Probably, you have a lot of questions about what happened.

Damn straight.

If you'll talk to me face-to-face, come to the front door and let me in.

Yikes. I hadn't seen that one coming. I pondered for a minute. Deciding that while I didn't trust Bill anymore, I didn't believe that he would physically harm me, I went back through the house to the front door. I opened it and called, 'Okay, come on in.'

He emerged from the woods surrounding the clearing in which my old house stood. I ached at the sight of him. Bill was broad-shouldered and lean from his life of farming the land next to mine. He was hard and tough from his years as a Confederate soldier, before his death in 1867. Bill's nose was straight off a Greek vase. His hair was dark brown and clipped close to his head, and his eyes were just as dark. He looked exactly the same as he had while we were dating, and he always would.

He hesitated before he crossed the threshold, but I'd given him permission, and I moved aside so he could step past me into the living room filled with old, comfortable furniture and neat as a pin.

'Thank you,' he said in his cold, smooth voice, a voice that still gave me a twinge of sheer lust. Many things had gone wrong between us, but they hadn't started in bed. 'I wanted to talk to you before I left.'

'Where are you going?' I tried to sound as calm as he.

'To Peru. The queen's orders.'

'Still working on your, ah, database?' I knew almost nothing about computers, but Bill had studied hard to make himself computer literate.

'Yes. I've got a little more research to do. A very old vampire in Lima has a great fund of knowledge about those of our race on his continent, and I have an appointment to confer with him. I'll do some sight-seeing while I'm down there.'

I fought the urge to offer Bill a bottle of synthetic blood, which would have been the hospitable thing to do. 'Have a seat,' I said curtly, and nodded at the sofa. I sat on the edge of the old recliner catty-cornered to it. Then a silence fell, a silence that made me even more conscious of how unhappy I was.

'How's Bubba?' I asked finally.

'He's in New Orleans right now,' Bill said. The queen likes to keep him around from time to time, and he was so visible here over the last month that it seemed like a good idea to take him elsewhere. He'll be back soon.'

You'd recognize Bubba if you saw him; everyone knows his face. But he hadn't been 'brought over' too successfully. Probably the morgue attendant, who happened to be a vampire, should have ignored the tiny spark of life. But since he was a great fan, he hadn't been able to resist the attempt, and now the entire southern vampire community shuffled Bubba around and tried to keep him from public view.

Another silence fell. I'd planned on taking off my shoes and uniform, putting on a cuddly robe, and watching television with a Freschetta pizza by my side. It was a humble plan, but it was my own. Instead, here I was, suffering.

'If you have something to say, you better go on and say it,' I told him.

He nodded, almost to himself. 'I have to explain,' he said. His white hands arranged themselves in his lap. 'Lorena and I—'

I flinched involuntarily. I never wanted to hear that name again. He'd dumped me for Lorena.

'I have to tell you,' he said, almost angrily. He'd seen me twitch. 'Give me this chance.' After a second, I waved a hand to tell him to continue.

'The reason I went to Jackson when she called me is that I couldn't help myself,' he said.

My eyebrows flew up. I'd heard *that* before. It means, 'I have no self-control', or, 'It seemed worth it at the time, and I wasn't thinking north of my belt'.

'We were lovers long ago. As Eric says he told you, vampire liaisons don't tend to last long, though they're very intense while they are ongoing. However, what Eric did not tell you was that Lorena was the vampire who brought me over.'

'To the Dark Side?' I asked, and then I bit my lip. This was no subject for levity.

'Yes,' Bill agreed seriously. 'And we were together after that, as lovers, which is not always the case.'

'But you had broken up . . .'

'Yes, about eighty years ago, we came to the point where we couldn't tolerate each other any longer. I hadn't seen Lorena since, though I'd heard of her doings, of course.'

'Oh, sure,' I said expressionlessly.

'But I had to obey her summons. This is absolutely imperative. When your maker calls, you must respond.' His voice was urgent.

I nodded, trying to look understanding. I guess I didn't do too good a job.

'She *ordered* me to leave you,' he said. His dark eyes were peering into mine. 'She said she would kill you if I didn't.'

I was losing my temper. I bit the inside of my cheek, real hard, to make myself focus. 'So, without explanation or discussion with me, you decided what was best for me and for you.'

'I had to,' he said. 'I *had* to do her bidding. And I knew she was capable of harming you.'

'Well, you got that right.' In fact, Lorena had done her dead level best to harm me right into the grave. But I'd gotten her first – okay, by a fluke, but it had worked.

'And now you no longer love me,' Bill said, with the slightest of questions in his voice.

I didn't have any clear answer.

'I don't know,' I said. 'I wouldn't think you'd want to come back to me. After all, I killed your mom.' And there was the slightest of questions in my voice, too, but mostly I was bitter.

'Then we need more time apart. When I return, if you consent, we'll talk again. A kiss good-bye?'

To my shame, I would love to kiss Bill again. But it was such a bad idea, even wanting it seemed wrong. We stood, and I gave him a quick brush of lips to the cheek. His white skin shone with a little glow that distinguished vampires from humans. It had surprised me to learn that not everyone saw them like I did.

'Are you seeing the Were?' he asked, when he was nearly out the door. He sounded as though the words had been pulled out of him by their roots.

'Which one?' I asked, resisting the temptation to bat my eyelashes. He deserved no answer, and he knew it. 'How long will you be gone?' I asked more briskly, and he looked at me with some speculation.

'It's not a sure thing. Maybe two weeks,' he answered.

'We might talk then,' I said, turning my face away. 'Let me return your key.' I fished my keys out of my purse.

'No, please, keep it on your key ring,' he said. 'You might need it while I am gone. Go in the house as you will. My mail's getting held at the post office until I give them notice, and I think all my other loose ends are taken care of.'

So I was his last loose end. I damned up the trickle of anger that was all too ready to bubble out these days.

'I hope you have a safe trip,' I said coldly, and shut the door behind him. I headed back to my bedroom. I had a robe to put on and some television to watch. By golly, I was sticking to my plan.

But while I was putting my pizza in the oven, I had to blot my cheeks a few times.

Chapter 1

The New Year's Eve party at Merlotte's Bar and Grill was finally, finally, over. Though the bar owner, Sam Merlotte, had asked all his staff to work that night, Holly, Arlene, and I were the only ones who'd responded. Charlsie Tooten had said she was too old to put up with the mess we had to endure on New Year's Eve, Danielle had long-standing plans to attend a fancy party with her steady boyfriend, and a new woman couldn't start for two days. I guess Arlene and Holly and I needed the money more than we needed a good time.

And I hadn't had any invitations to do anything else. At least when I'm working at Merlotte's, I'm a part of the scenery. That's a kind of acceptance.

I was sweeping up the shredded paper, and I reminded myself again not to comment to Sam on what a poor idea the bags of confetti had been. We'd all made ourselves pretty clear about that, and even good-natured Sam was showing signs of wear and tear. It didn't seem fair to leave it all for Terry Bellefleur to clean, though sweeping and mopping the floors was his job.

Sam was counting the till money and bagging it up so he could go by the night deposit at the bank. He was looking tired but pleased.

He flicked open his cell phone. 'Kenya? You ready to take me to the bank? Okay, see you in a minute at the back door.' Kenya, a police officer, often escorted Sam to the night deposit, especially after a big take like tonight's.

I was pleased with my money take, too. I had earned a lot in tips. I thought I might have gotten three hundred dollars or more – and I needed every penny. I would have enjoyed the prospect of totting up the money when I got home, if I'd been sure I had enough brains left to do it. The noise and chaos of the party, the constant runs to and from the bar and the serving hatch, the tremendous mess we'd had to clean up, the steady cacophony of all those brains . . . it had combined to exhaust me. Toward the end I'd been too tired to keep my poor mind protected, and lots of thoughts had leaked through.

It's not easy being telepathic. Most often, it's not fun.

This evening had been worse than most. Not only had the bar patrons, almost all known to me for many years, been in uninhibited moods, but there'd been some news that lots of people were just dying to tell me.

'I hear yore boyfriend done gone to South America,' a car salesman, Chuck Beecham, had said, malice gleaming in his eyes. 'You gonna get mighty lonely out to your place without him.'

'You offering to take his place, Chuck?' the man beside him at the bar had asked, and they both had a we're-men-together guffaw.

'Naw, Terrell,' said the salesman. 'I don't care for vampire leavings.'

'You be polite, or you go out the door,' I said steadily. I felt warmth at my back, and I knew my boss, Sam Merlotte, was looking at them over my shoulder.

'Trouble?' he asked.

'They were just about to apologize,' I said, looking Chuck and Terrell in the eyes. They looked down at their beers.

'Sorry, Sookie,' Chuck mumbled, and Terrell bobbed his head in agreement. I nodded and turned to take care of another order. But they'd succeeded in hurting me.

Which was their goal.

I had an ache around my heart.

I was sure the general populace of Bon Temps, Louisiana, didn't know about our estrangement. Bill sure wasn't in the habit of blabbing his personal business around, and neither was I. Arlene and Tara knew a little about it, of course, since you have to tell your best friends when you've broken up with your guy, even if you have to leave out all the interesting details. (Like the fact that you'd killed the woman he left you for. Which I couldn't help. Really.) So anyone who told me Bill had gone out of the country, assuming I didn't know it yet, was just being malicious.

Until Bill's recent visit to my house, I'd last seen him when I'd given him the disks and computer he'd hidden with me. I'd driven up at dusk, so the machine wouldn't be sitting on his front porch for long. I'd put all his stuff up against the door in a big waterproofed box. He'd come out just as I was driving away, but I hadn't stopped.

An evil woman would have given the disks to Bill's boss, Eric. A lesser woman would have kept those disks and that computer, having rescinded Bill's (and Eric's) invitations to enter the house. I had told myself proudly that I was not an evil, or a lesser, woman.

Also, thinking practically, Bill could just have hired some human to break into my house and take them. I didn't think he would. But he needed them bad, or he'd be in trouble with his boss's boss. I've got a temper, maybe even a bad temper, once it gets provoked. But I'm not vindictive.

Arlene has often told me I am too nice for my own good, though I assure her I am not. (Tara never says that; maybe she knows me better?) I realized glumly that, sometime during this hectic evening, Arlene would hear about Bill's departure. Sure enough, within twenty minutes of Chuck and Terrell's gibing, she made her way through the crowd to pat me on the back. 'You didn't need that cold bastard anyway,' she said. 'What did he ever do for you?'

I nodded weakly at her to show how much I appreciated her support. But then a table called for two whiskey sours, two beers, and a gin and tonic, and I had to hustle, which was actually a welcome distraction. When I dropped off their drinks, I asked myself the same question. What had Bill done for me?

I delivered pitchers of beer to two tables before I could add it all up.

He'd introduced me to sex, which I really enjoyed. Introduced me to a lot of other vampires, which I didn't. Saved my life, though when you thought about it, it wouldn't have been in danger if I hadn't been dating him in the first place. But I'd saved his back once or twice, so that debt was canceled. He'd called me 'sweetheart,' and at the time he'd meant it.

'Nothing,' I muttered, as I mopped up a spilled piña colada and handed one of our last clean bar towels to the woman who'd knocked it over, since a lot of it was still in her skirt. 'He didn't do a thing for me.' She smiled and nodded, obviously thinking I was commiserating with her. The place was too noisy to hear anything anyway, which was lucky for me.

But I'd be glad when Bill got back. After all, he was my nearest neighbor. The community's older cemetery separated our properties, which lay along a parish road south of Bon Temps. I was out there all by myself, without Bill.

'Peru, I hear,' my brother Jason, said. He had his arm around his girl of the evening, a short, thin, dark twenty-one-year-old from somewhere way out in the sticks. (I'd carded her.) I gave her a close look. Jason didn't know it, but she was a shape-shifter of some kind. They're easy to spot. She was an attractive girl, but she changed into something with feathers or fur when the moon was full. I noticed Sam give her a hard glare when Jason's back was turned, to remind her to behave herself in his territory. She returned the glare, with interest. I had the feeling she didn't become a kitten, or a squirrel.

I thought of latching on to her brain and trying to read it, but shifter heads aren't easy. Shifter thoughts are kind of snarly and red, though every now and then you can get a good picture of emotions. Same with Weres.

Sam himself turns into a collie when the moon is bright and round. Sometimes he trots all the way over to my house, and I feed him a bowl of scraps and let him nap on my back porch, if the weather's good, or in my living room, if the weather's poor. I don't let him in the bedroom anymore, because he wakes up naked – in which state he looks *very* nice, but I just don't need to be tempted by my boss.

The moon wasn't full tonight, so Jason would be safe. I decided not to say anything to him about his date. Everyone's got a secret or two. Her secret was just a little more colorful.

Besides my brother's date, and Sam of course, there were two other supernatural creatures in Merlotte's Bar that New Year's Eve. One was a magnificent woman at least six feet tall, with long rippling dark hair. Dressed to kill in a skintight, long-sleeved orange dress, she'd come in by herself, and she was in the process of meeting every guy in the bar. I didn't know what she was, but I knew from her brain pattern that she was not human. The other creature was a vampire, who'd come in with a group of young people, most in their early twenties. I didn't know any of them. Only a sideways glance by a few other revelers marked the presence of a vampire. It just went to show the change in attitude in the few years since the Great Revelation.

Almost three years ago, on the night of the Great Revelation, the vampires had gone on TV in every nation to announce their existence. It had been a night in which many of the world's assumptions had been knocked sideways and rearranged for good.

This coming-out party had been prompted by the Japanese development of a synthetic blood that can keep vamps satisfied nutritionally. Since the Great Revelation, the United States has undergone numerous political and social upheavals in the bumpy process of accommodating our newest citizens, who just happen to be dead. The vampires have a public face and a public explanation for their condition – they claim an allergy to sunlight and garlic causes severe metabolic changes – but I've seen the other side of the vampire world. My eyes now see a lot of things most human beings don't ever see. Ask me if this knowledge has made me happy.

No.

But I have to admit, the world is a more interesting place to me now. I'm by myself a lot (since I'm not exactly Norma Normal), so the extra food for thought has been welcome. The fear and danger haven't. I've seen the private face of vampires, and I've learned about Weres and shifters and other stuff. Weres and shifters prefer to stay in the shadows – for now – while they watch how going public works out for the vamps.

See, I had all this to mull over while collecting tray after tray of glasses and mugs, and unloading and loading the dishwasher to help Tack, the new cook. (His real name is Alphonse Petacki. Can you be surprised he likes 'Tack' better?) When our part of the cleanup was just about finished, and this long evening was finally over, I hugged

Arlene and wished her a happy New Year, and she hugged me back. Holly's boyfriend was waiting for her at the employees' entrance at the back of the building, and Holly waved to us as she pulled on her coat and hurried out.

'What're your hopes for the New Year, ladies?' Sam asked. By that time, Kenya was leaning against the bar, waiting for him, her face calm and alert. Kenya ate lunch here pretty regularly with her partner, Kevin, who was as pale and thin as she was dark and rounded. Sam was putting the chairs up on the tables so Terry Bellefleur, who came in very early in the morning, could mop the floor.

'Good health, and the right man,' Arlene said dramatically, her hands fluttering over her heart, and we laughed. Arlene has found many men – and she's been married four times – but she's still looking for Mr Right. I could 'hear' Arlene thinking that Tack might be the one. I was startled; I hadn't even known she'd looked at him.

The surprise showed on my face, and in an uncertain voice Arlene said, 'You think I should give up?'

'Hell, no,' I said promptly, chiding myself for not guarding my expression better. It was just that I was so tired. 'It'll be this year, for sure, Arlene.' I smiled at Bon Temp's only black female police officer. 'You have to have a wish for the New Year, Kenya. Or a resolution.'

'I always wish for peace between men and women,' Kenya said. 'Make my job a lot easier. And my resolution is to bench-press one-forty.'

'Wow,' said Arlene. Her dyed red hair contrasted violently with Sam's natural curly red-gold as she gave him a quick hug. He wasn't much taller than Arlene – though she's at least five foot eight, two inches taller than I. 'I'm going to lose ten pounds, that's my resolution.' We all laughed. That had been Arlene's resolution for the past four years. 'What about you, Sam? Wishes and resolutions?' she asked.

'I have everything I need,' he said, and I felt the blue wave of sincerity coming from him. 'I resolve to stay on this course. The bar is doing great, I like living in my double- wide, and the people here are as good as people anywhere.'

I turned to conceal my smile. That had been a pretty ambiguous statement. The people of Bon Temps were, indeed, as good as people anywhere.

'And you, Sookie?' he asked. Arlene, Kenya, and Sam were all looking at me. I hugged Arlene again, because I like to. I'm ten years younger – maybe more, since though Arlene says she's thirty-six, I have my doubts – but we've been friends ever since we started working at Merlotte's together after Sam bought the bar, maybe five years now.

'Come on,' Arlene said, coaxing me. Sam put his arm around me. Kenya smiled, but drifted away into the kitchen to have a few words with Tack.

Acting on impulse, I shared my wish. 'I just hope to not be beaten up,' I said, my weariness and the hour combining in an ill-timed burst of honesty. 'I don't want to go to the hospital. I don't want to see a doctor.' I didn't want to have to ingest any vampire blood, either, which would cure you in a hurry but had various side effects. 'So my resolution is to stay out of trouble,' I said firmly.

Arlene looked pretty startled, and Sam looked – well, I couldn't tell about Sam. But since I'd hugged Arlene, I gave him a big hug, too, and felt the strength and warmth in his body. You think Sam's slight until you see him shirtless unloading boxes of supplies. He is really strong and built really smooth, and he has a high natural body temperature. I felt him kiss my hair, and then we were all saying good night to each other and walking out the back door. Sam's truck was parked in front of his trailer, which is set up behind Merlotte's Bar but at a right angle to it, but he climbed in Kenya's patrol car to ride to the bank. She'd bring him home, and then Sam could collapse. He'd been on his feet for hours, as had we all.

As Arlene and I unlocked our cars, I noticed Tack was waiting in his old pickup; I was willing to bet he was going to follow Arlene home.

With a last 'Good night!' called through the chilly silence of the Louisiana night, we separated to begin our new years.

I turned off onto Hummingbird Road to go out to my place, which is about three miles southeast of the bar. The relief of finally being alone was immense, and I began to relax mentally. My headlights flashed past the close-packed trunks of the pines that formed the backbone of the lumber industry hereabouts.

The night was extremely dark and cold. There are no streetlights way out on the parish roads, of course. Creatures were not stirring, not by any means. Though I kept telling myself to be alert for deer crossing the road, I was driving on autopilot. My simple thoughts were filled with the plan of scrubbing my face and pulling on my warmest nightgown and climbing into my bed.

Something white appeared in the headlights of my old car.

I gasped, jolted out of my drowsy anticipation of warmth and silence.

A running man: At three in the morning on January first, he was running down the parish road, apparently running for his life.

I slowed down, trying to figure out a course of action. I was a lone unarmed woman. If something awful was pursuing him, it might get me, too. On the other hand, I couldn't let someone suffer if I could help. I had a moment to notice that the man was tall, blond, and clad only in blue jeans, before I pulled up by him. I put the car into park and leaned over to roll down the window on the passenger's side.

'Can I help you?' I called. He gave me a panicked glance and kept on running.

But in that moment I realized who he was. I leaped out of the car and took off after him.

'Eric!' I yelled. 'It's me!'

He wheeled around then, hissing, his fangs fully out. I stopped so abruptly I swayed where I stood, my hands out in front of me in a gesture of peace. Of course, if Eric decided to attack, I was a dead woman. So much for being a good Samaritan.

Why didn't Eric recognize me? I'd known him for many months. He was Bill's boss, in the complicated vampire hierarchy that I was beginning to learn. Eric was the sheriff of Area Five, and he was a vampire on the rise. He was also gorgeous and could kiss like a house afire, but that was not the most pertinent side of him right at the moment. Fangs and strong hands curved into claws were what I was seeing. Eric was in full alarm mode, but he seemed just as scared of me as I was of him. He didn't leap to attack.

'Stay back, woman,' he warned me. His voice sounded like his throat was sore, raspy and raw.

'What are you doing out here?'

'Who are you?'

'You known darn good and well who I am. What's up with you? Why are you out here without your car?' Eric drove a sleek Corvette, which was simply Eric.

'You know me? Who am I?'

Well, that knocked me for a loop. He sure didn't sound like he was joking. I said cautiously, 'Of course I know you, Eric. Unless you have an identical twin. You don't, right?'

'I don't know.' His arms dropped, his fangs seemed to be retracting, and he straightened from his crouch, so I felt there'd been a definite improvement in the atmosphere of our encounter.

'You don't know if you have a brother?' I was pretty much at sea.

'No. I don't know. Eric is my name?' In the glare of my headlights, he looked just plain pitiful.

'Wow.' I couldn't think of anything more helpful to say. 'Eric Northman is the name you go by these days. Why are you out here?'

'I don't know that, either.'

I was sensing a theme here. 'For real? You don't remember anything?' I tried to get past being sure that at any second he'd grin down at me and explain everything and laugh, embroiling me in some trouble that would end in me . . . getting beaten up.

'For real.' He took a step closer, and his bare white chest made me shiver with sympathetic goose bumps. I also realized (now that I wasn't terrified) how forlorn he looked. It was an expression I'd never seen on the confident Eric's face before, and it made me feel unaccountably sad.

'You know you're a vampire, right?'

'Yes.' He seemed surprised that I asked. 'And you are not.'

'No, I'm real human, and I have to know you won't hurt me. Though you could have by now. But believe me, even if you don't remember it, we're sort of friends.'

'I won't hurt you.'

I reminded myself that probably hundreds and thousands of people had heard those very words before Eric ripped their throats out. But the fact is, vampires don't have to kill once they're past their first year.

A sip here, a sip there, that's the norm. When he looked so lost, it was hard to remember he could dismember me with his bare hands.

I'd told Bill one time that the smart thing for aliens to do (when they invaded Earth) would be to arrive in the guise of lop-eared bunnies.

'Come get in my car before you freeze,' I said. I was having that I'm-getting-sucked-in feeling again, but I didn't know what else to do.

'I do know you?' he said, as though he were hesitant about getting in a car with someone as formidable as a woman ten inches shorter, many pounds lighter, and a few centuries younger.

'Yes,' I said, not able to restrain an edge of impatience. I wasn't too happy with myself, because I still half suspected I was being tricked for some unfathomable reason. 'Now come on, Eric. I'm freezing, and so are you.' Not that vampires seemed to feel temperature extremes, as a rule; but even Eric's skin looked goosey. The dead can freeze, of course. They'll survive it – they survive almost everything – but I understand it's pretty painful. 'Oh my God, Eric, you're barefoot.' I'd just noticed.

I took his hand; he let me get close enough for that. He let me lead him back to the car and stow him in the passenger seat. I told him to roll up the window as I went around to my side, and after a long minute of studying the mechanism, he did.

I reached in the backseat for an old afghan I keep there in the winter (for football games, etc.) and wrapped it around him. He wasn't shivering, of course, because he was a vampire, but I just couldn't stand to look at all that bare flesh in this temperature. I turned the heater on full blast (which, in my old car, isn't saying much).

Eric's exposed skin had never made me feel cold before – when I'd seen this much of Eric before, I'd felt anything *but*. I was giddy enough by now to laugh out loud before I could censor my own thoughts.

He was startled, and looked at me sideways.

'You're the last person I expected to see,' I said. 'Were you coming out this way to see Bill? Because he's gone.'

'Bill?'

'The vampire who lives out here? My ex-boyfriend?'

He shook his head. He was back to being absolutely terrified.

'You don't know how you came to be here?'

He shook his head again.

I was making a big effort to think hard; but it was just that, an effort. I was worn out. Though I'd had a rush of adrenaline when I'd spotted the figure running down the dark road, that rush was wearing off fast. I reached the turnoff to my house and turned left, winding through the black and silent woods on my nice, level driveway – that, in fact, Eric had had re-graveled for me.

And that was why Eric was sitting in my car right now, instead of running through the night like a giant white rabbit. He'd had the intelligence to give me what I really wanted. (Of course, he'd also wanted me to go to bed with him for months. But he'd given me the driveway because I needed it.)

'Here we are,' I said, pulling around to the back of my old house. I switched off the car. I'd remembered to leave the outside lights on when I'd left for work that afternoon, thank goodness, so we weren't sitting there in total darkness.

'This is where you live?' He was glancing around the clearing where the old house stood, seemingly nervous about going from the car to the back door.

'Yes,' I said, exasperated.

He just gave me a look that showed white all around the blue of his eyes.

'Oh, come on,' I said, with no grace at all. I got out of the car and went up the steps to the back porch, which I don't keep locked because, hey, why lock a screened-in back porch? I do lock the inner door, and after a second's fumbling, I had it open so the light I leave on in the kitchen could spill out. 'You can come in,' I said, so he could cross the threshold. He scuttled in after me, the afghan still clutched around him.

Under the overhead light in the kitchen, Eric looked pretty pitiful. His bare feet were bleeding, which I hadn't noticed before. 'Oh, Eric,' I said sadly, and got a pan out from the cabinet, and started the hot water to running in the sink. He'd heal real quick, like vampires do, but I couldn't help but wash him clean. The blue jeans were filthy around the hem. 'Pull 'em off,' I said, knowing they'd just get wet if I soaked his feet while he was dressed.

With not a hint of a leer or any other indication that he was enjoying this development, Eric shimmied out of the jeans. I tossed them onto the back porch to wash in the morning, trying not to gape at my guest, who was now clad in underwear that was definitely over-the-top, a bright red bikini style whose stretchy quality was definitely being tested. Okay, another big surprise. I'd seen Eric's underwear only once before – which was once more than I ought to have – and he'd been a silk boxers guy. Did men change styles like that?

Without preening, and without comment, the vampire rewrapped his white body in the afghan. Hmmm. I was now convinced he wasn't himself, as no other evidence could have convinced me. Eric was way over six feet of pure magnificence (if a marble white magnificence), and he well knew it.

I pointed to one of the straight-back chairs at the kitchen table. Obediently, he pulled it out and sat. I crouched to put the pan on the floor, and I gently guided his big feet into the water. Eric groaned as the warmth touched his skin. I guess that even a vampire could feel the contrast. I got a clean rag from under the sink and some liquid soap, and I washed his feet. I took my time, because I was trying to think what to do next.

'You were out in the night,' he observed, in a tentative sort of way.

'I was coming home from work, as you can see from my clothes.' I was wearing our winter uniform, a long-sleeved white boat-neck T-shirt with 'Merlotte's Bar' embroidered over the left breast and worn tucked into black slacks.

''Women shouldn't be out alone this late at night,' he said disapprovingly.

'Tell me about it.'

'Well, women are more liable to be overwhelmed by an attack than men, so they should be more protected—'

'No, I didn't mean literally. I meant, I agree. You're preaching to the choir. I didn't want to be working this late at night.'

'Then why were you out?'

'I need the money,' I said, wiping my hand and pulling the roll of bills out of my pocket and dropping it on the table while I was thinking about it. 'I got this house to maintain, my car is old, and I have taxes and insurance to pay. Like everyone else,' I added, in case he thought I was complaining unduly. I hated to poor-mouth, but he'd asked.

'Is there no man in your family?'

Every now and then, their ages do show. 'I have a brother. I can't remember if you've ever met Jason.' A cut on his left foot looked especially bad. I put some more hot water into the basin to warm the remainder. Then I tried to get all the dirt out. He winced as I gently rubbed the washcloth over the margins of the wound. The smaller cuts and bruises seemed to be fading even as I watched. The hot water heater came on behind me, the familiar sound somehow reassuring.

'Your brother permits you to do this working?'

I tried to imagine Jason's face when I told him that I expected him to support me for the rest of my life because I was a woman and shouldn't work outside the home. 'Oh, for goodness sake, Eric.' I looked up at him, scowling. 'Jason's got his own problems.' Like being chronically selfish and a true tomcat.

I eased the pan of water to the side and patted Eric dry with a dishtowel. This vampire now had clean feet. Rather stiffly, I stood. My back hurt. My feet hurt. 'Listen, I think what I better do is call Pam. She'll probably know what's going on with you.'

'Pam?'

It was like being around a particularly irritating two-year-old.

'Your second-in-command.'

He was going to ask another question, I could just tell. I held up a hand. 'Just hold on. Let me call her and find out what's happening.'

'But what if she has turned against me?'

'Then we need to know that, too. The sooner the better.'

I put my hand on the old phone that hung on the kitchen wall right by the end of the counter. A high stool sat below it. My grandmother had always sat on the stool to conduct her lengthy phone conversations, with a pad and pencil handy. I missed her every day. But at the moment I had no room in my emotional palette for grief, or even nostalgia. I looked in my little address book for the number of Fangtasia, the vampire bar in Shreveport that provided Eric's principal income and served as the base of his operations, which I understood were far wider in scope. I didn't know how wide or what these other moneymaking projects were, and I didn't especially want to know.

I'd seen in the Shreveport paper that Fangtasia, too, had planned a big bash for the evening – 'Begin Your New Year with a Bite' – so I knew someone would be there. While the phone was ringing, I swung open the refrigerator and got out a bottle of blood for Eric. I popped it in the microwave and set the timer. He followed my every move with anxious eyes.

'Fangtasia,' said an accented male voice.

'Chow?'

'Yes, how may I serve you?' He'd remembered his phone persona of sexy vampire just in the nick of time.

'It's Sookie.'

'Oh,' he said in a much more natural voice. 'Listen, Happy New Year, Sook, but we're kind of busy here.'

'Looking for someone?'

There was a long, charged silence.

'Wait a minute,' he said, and then I heard nothing.

'Pam,' said Pam. She'd picked up the receiver so silently that I jumped when I heard her voice.

'Do you still have a master?' I didn't know how much I could say over the phone. I wanted to know if she'd been the one who'd put Eric in this state, or if she still owed him loyalty.

'I do,' she said steadily, understanding what I wanted to know. 'We are under . . . we have some problems.'

I mulled that over until I was sure I'd read between the lines. Pam was telling me that she still owed Eric her allegiance, and that Eric's group of followers was under some kind of attack or in some kind of crisis.

I said, 'He's here.' Pam appreciated brevity.

'Is he alive?'

'Yep.'

'Damaged?'

'Mentally.'

A *long* pause, this time.

'Will he be a danger to you?'

Not that Pam cared a whole hell of a lot if Eric decided to drain me dry, but I guess she wondered if I would shelter Eric. 'I don't think so at the moment,' I said. 'It seems to be a matter of memory.'

'I hate witches. Humans had the right idea, burning them at the stake.'

Since the very humans who had burned witches would have been delighted to sink that same stake into vampire hearts, I found that a little amusing – but not very, considering the hour. I immediately forgot what she'd been talking about. I yawned.

'Tomorrow night, we'll come,' she said finally. 'Can you keep him this day? Dawn's in less than four hours. Do you have a safe place?'

'Yes. But you get over here at nightfall, you hear me? I don't want to get tangled up in your vampire shit again.' Normally, I don't speak so bluntly; but like I say, it was the tail end of a long night.

'We'll be there.'

We hung up simultaneously. Eric was watching me with unblinking blue eyes. His hair was a snarly tangled mess of blond waves. His hair is the exact same color as mine, and I have blue eyes, too, but that's the end of the similarities.

I thought of taking a brush to his hair, but I was just too weary.

'Okay, here's the deal,' I told him. 'You stay here the rest of the night and tomorrow, and then Pam and them'll come get you tomorrow night and let you know what's happening.'

'You won't let anyone get in?' he asked. I noticed he'd finished the blood, and he wasn't quite as drawn as he'd been, which was a relief.

'Eric, I'll do my best to keep you safe,' I said, quite gently. I rubbed my face with my hands. I was going to fall asleep on my feet. 'Come on,' I said, taking his hand. Clutching the afghan with the other hand, he trailed down the hall after me, a snow white giant in tiny red underwear.

My old house has been added onto over the years, but it hasn't ever been more than a humble farmhouse. A second storey was added around the turn of the century, and two more bedrooms and a walk-in attic are upstairs, but I seldom go up there anymore. I keep it shut off, to save money on electricity. There are two bedrooms downstairs, the smaller one I'd used until my grandmother died and her large one across the hall from it. I'd moved into the large one after her death. But the hidey-hole Bill had built was in the smaller bedroom. I led Eric in there, switched on the light, and made sure the blinds were closed and the curtains drawn across them. Then I opened the door of the closet, removed its few contents, and pulled back the flap of carpet that covered the closet floor, exposing the trapdoor. Underneath was a light-tight space that Bill had built a few months before, so that he could stay over during the day or use it as a hiding place if his own home was unsafe. Bill liked having a bolt-hole, and I was sure he had some that I didn't know about. If I'd been a vampire (God forbid), I would have, myself.

I had to wipe thoughts of Bill out of my head as I showed my reluctant guest how to close the trapdoor on top of him and that the flap of carpet would fall back into place. 'When I get up, I'll put the stuff back in the closet so it'll look natural,' I reassured him, and smiled encouragingly.

'Do I have to get in now?' he asked.

Eric, making a request of me: The world was really turned upside-down. 'No,' I said, trying to sound like I was concerned. All I could think of was my bed. 'You don't have to. Just get in before sunrise. There's no way you could miss that, right? I mean, you couldn't fall asleep and wake up in the sun?'

He thought for a moment and shook his head. 'No,' he said. 'I know that can't happen. Can I stay in the room with you?'

Oh, God, *puppy dog eyes*. From a six-foot-five ancient Viking vampire. It was just too much. I didn't have enough energy to laugh, so I just gave a sad little snigger. 'Come on,' I said, my voice as limp as my legs. I turned off the light in that room, crossed the hall, and flipped on the one in my own room, yellow and white and clean and warm, and folded down the bedspread and blanket and sheet. While Eric sat forlornly in a slipper chair on the other side of the bed, I pulled off my shoes and socks, got a nightgown out of a drawer, and retreated into the bathroom. I was out in ten minutes, with clean teeth and face and swathed in a very old, very soft flannel nightgown that was cream-colored with blue flowers scattered around. Its ribbons were raveled and the ruffle around the bottom was pretty sad, but it suited me just fine. After I'd switched off the lights, I remembered my hair was still up in its usual ponytail, so I pulled out the band that held it and I shook my head to make it fall loose. Even my scalp seemed to relax, and I sighed with bliss.

As I climbed up into the high old bed, the large fly in my personal ointment did the same. Had I actually told him he could get in bed with me? Well, I decided, as I wriggled down under the soft old sheets and the blanket and the comforter, if Eric had designs on me, I was just too tired to care.

'Woman?'

'Hmmm?'

'What's your name?'

'Sookie. Sookie Stackhouse.'

'Thank you, Sookie.'

'Welcome, Eric.'

Because he sounded so lost – the Eric I knew had never been one to do anything other than assume others should serve him – I patted around under the covers for his hand. When I found it, I slid my own over it. His palm was turned up to meet my palm, and his fingers clasped mine.

And though I would not have thought it was possible to go to sleep holding hands with a vampire, that's exactly what I did.

Chapter 2

I woke up slowly. As I lay snuggled under the covers, now and then stretching an arm or a leg, I gradually remembered the surrealistic happenings of the night before.

Well, Eric wasn't in bed with me now, so I had to assume he was safely ensconced in the hidey-hole. I went across the hall. As I'd promised, I put the contents back in the closet to make it look normal. The clock told me it was noon, and outside the sun was bright, though the air was cold. For Christmas, Jason had given me a thermometer that read the outside temperature and showed it to me on a digital readout inside. He'd installed it for me, too. Now I knew two things: it was noon, and it was thirty-four degrees outside.

In the kitchen, the pan of water I'd washed Eric's feet with was still sitting on the floor. As I dumped it into the sink, I saw that at some point he'd rinsed out the bottle that had held the synthetic blood. I'd have to get some more to have around when he rose, since you didn't want a hungry vampire in your house, and it would be only polite to have extra to offer Pam and whoever else drove over from Shreveport. They'd explain things to me – or not. They'd take Eric away and work on whatever problems were facing the Shreveport vampire community, and I would be left in peace. Or not.

Merlotte's was closed on New Year's Day until four o'clock. On New Year's Day, and the day after, Charlsie and Danielle and the new girl were on the schedule, since the rest of us had worked New Year's

Eve. So I had two whole days off . . . and at least one of them I got to spend alone in a house with a mentally ill vampire. Life just didn't get any better.

I had two cups of coffee, put Eric's jeans in the washer, read a romance for a while, and studied my brand-new Word of the Day calendar, a Christmas gift from Arlene. My first word for the New Year was 'exsanguinate'. This was probably not a good omen.

Jason came by a little after four, flying down my drive in his black pickup with pink and aqua flames on the side. I'd showered and dressed by then, but my hair was still wet. I'd sprayed it with detangler and I was brushing through it slowly, sitting in front of the fireplace. I'd turned on the TV to a football game to have something to watch while I brushed, but I kept the sound way down. I was pondering Eric's predicament while I luxuriated in the feel of the fire's warmth on my back.

We hadn't used the fireplace much in the past couple of years because buying a load of wood was so expensive, but Jason had cut up a lot of trees that had fallen last year after an ice storm. I was well stocked, and I was enjoying the flames.

My brother stomped up the front steps and knocked perfunctorily before coming in. Like me, he had mostly grown up in this house. We'd come to live with Gran when my parents died, and she'd rented out their house until Jason said he was ready to live on his own, when he'd been twenty. Now Jason was twenty-eight and the boss of a parish road crew. This was a rapid rise for a local boy without a lot of education, and I'd thought it was enough for him until the past month or two, when he'd begun acting restless.

'Good,' he said, when he saw the fire. He stood squarely in front of it to warm his hands, incidentally blocking the warmth from me. 'What time did you get home last night?' he said over his shoulder.

'I guess I got to bed about three.'

'What did you think of that girl I was with?'

'I think you better not date her anymore.'

That wasn't what he'd expected to hear. His eyes slid sideways to meet mine. 'What did you get off her?' he asked in a subdued voice. My brother knows I am telepathic, but he would never discuss it with me, or anyone else. I've seen him get into fights with some man who accused me of being abnormal, but he knows I'm different. Everyone else does, too. They just choose not to believe it, or they believe I couldn't possibly read *their* thoughts – just someone else's. God knows, I try to act and talk like I'm not receiving an unwanted spate of ideas and emotions and regrets and accusations, but sometimes it just seeps through.

'She's not your kind,' I said, looking into the fire.

'She surely ain't a vamp,' he protested.

'No, not a vamp.'

'Well, then.' He glared at me belligerently.

'Jason, when the vampires came out – when we found out they were real after all those decades of thinking they were just a scary legend – didn't you ever wonder if there were other tall tales that were real?'

My brother struggled with that concept for a minute. I knew (because I could 'hear' him) that Jason wanted to deny any such idea absolutely and call me a crazy woman – but he just couldn't. 'You know for a fact,' he said. It wasn't quite a question.

I made sure he was looking me in the eyes, and I nodded emphatically.

'Well, shit,' he said, disgusted. 'I really liked that girl, and she was a tiger in the sack.'

'Really?' I asked, absolutely stunned that she had changed in front of him when it wasn't the full moon. 'Are you okay?' The next second, I was chastising myself for my stupidity. Of course she hadn't.

He gaped at me for a second, before bursting out laughing. 'Sookie, you are one weird woman! You looked just like you thought she really could—' And his face froze. I could feel the idea bore a hole through the protective bubble most people inflate around their brain, the bubble that repels sights and ideas that don't jibe with their expectation of the everyday. Jason sat down heavily in Gran's recliner. 'I wish I didn't know that,' he said in a small voice.

'That may not be specifically what happens to her – the tiger thing – but believe me, something happens.'

It took a minute for his face to settle back into more familiar lines, but it did. Typical Jason behavior: There was nothing he could do about his new knowledge, so he pushed it to the back of his mind. 'Listen, did you see Hoyt's date last night? After they left the bar, Hoyt got stuck in a ditch over to Arcadia, and they had to walk two miles to get to a phone because he'd let his cell run down.'

'He did not!' I exclaimed, in a comforting and gossipy way. 'And her in those heels.' Jason's equilibrium was restored. He told me the town gossip for a few minutes, he accepted my offer of a Coke, and he asked me if I needed anything from town.

'Yes, I do.' I'd been thinking while he was talking. Most of his news I'd heard from other brains the night before, in unguarded moments.

'Ah-oh; he said, looking mock-frightened. 'What am I in for now?'

'I need ten bottles of synthetic blood and clothes for a big man,' I said, and I'd startled him again. Poor Jason, he deserved a silly vixen of a sister who bore nieces and nephews who called him Uncle Jase and held on to his legs. Instead, he got me.

'How big is the man, and where is he?'

'He's about six foot four or five, and he's asleep,' I said. 'I'd guess a thirty-four waist, and he's got long legs and broad shoulders.' I reminded myself to check the size label on Eric's jeans, which were still in the dryer out on the back porch.

'What kind of clothes?'

'Work clothes.'

'Anybody I know?'

'Me,' said a much deeper voice.

Jason whipped around as if he was expecting an attack, which shows his instincts aren't so bad, after all. But Eric looked as unthreatening as a vampire his size can look. And he'd obligingly put on the brown velour bathrobe that I'd left in the second bedroom. It was one I'd kept here for Bill, and it gave me a pang to see it on someone else. But I had to be practical; Eric couldn't wander around in red bikini underwear – at least, not with Jason in the house.

Jason goggled at Eric and cast a shocked glance at me. 'This is your newest man, Sookie? You didn't let any grass grow under your feet.' He didn't know whether to sound admiring or indignant. Jason still didn't realize Eric was dead. It's amazing to me that lots of people can't tell for a few minutes. 'And I need to get him clothes?'

'Yes. His shirt got torn last night, and his blue jeans are still dirty.'

'You going to introduce me?'

I took a deep breath. It would have been so much better if Jason hadn't seen Eric. 'Better not,' I said.

They both took that badly. Jason looked wounded, and the vampire looked offended.

'Eric,' he said, and stuck out a hand to Jason.

'Jason Stackhouse, this rude lady's brother,' Jason said.

They shook, and I felt like wringing both their necks.

'I'm assuming there's a reason why you two can't go out to buy him more clothes,' Jason said.

'There's a good reason,' I said. 'And there's about twenty good reasons you should forget you ever saw this guy.'

'Are you in danger?' Jason asked me directly.

'Not yet,' I said.

'If you do something that gets my sister hurt, you'll be in a world of trouble,' Jason told Eric the vampire.

'I would expect nothing less,' Eric said. 'But since you are being blunt with me, I'll be blunt with you. I think you should support her and take her into your household, so she would be better protected.'

Jason's mouth fell open again, and I had to cover my own so I wouldn't laugh out loud. This was even better than I'd imagined.

'Ten bottles of blood and a change of clothes?' Jason asked me, and I knew by the change in his voice that he'd finally cottoned on to Eric's state.

'Right. Liquor store'll have the blood. You can get the clothes at Wal-Mart.' Eric had mostly been a jeans and T-shirt kind of guy, which was all I could afford, anyway. 'Oh, he needs some shoes, too.'

Jason went to stand by Eric and put his foot parallel to the vampire's. He whistled, which made Eric jump.

'Big feet,' Jason commented, and flashed me a look. 'Is the old saying true?'

I smiled at him. He was trying to lighten the atmosphere. 'You may not believe me, but I don't know.'

'Kind of hard to swallow . . . no joke intended. Well, I'm gone,' Jason said, nodding to Eric. In a few seconds, I heard his truck speeding around the curves in the driveway, through the dark woods. Night had fallen completely.

'I'm sorry I came out while he was here,' Eric said tentatively. 'You didn't want me to meet him, I think.' He came over to the fire and seemed to be enjoying the warmth as I had been doing.

'It's not that I'm embarrassed to have you here,' I said. 'It's that I have a feeling you're in a heap of trouble, and I don't want my brother drawn in.'

'He is your only brother?'

'Yes. And my parents are gone, my grandmother, too. He's all I have, except for a cousin who's been on drugs for years. She's lost, I guess.'

'Don't be so sad,' he said, as if he couldn't help himself.

'I'm fine.' I made my voice brisk and matter-of-fact.

'You've had my blood,' he said.

Ah-oh. I stood absolutely still.

'I wouldn't be able to tell how you feel if you hadn't had my blood,' he said. 'Are we – have we been – lovers?'

That was certainly a nice way to put it. Eric was usually pretty Anglo-Saxon about sex.

'No,' I said promptly, and I was telling the truth, though only by a narrow margin. We'd been interrupted in time, thank God. I'm not married. I have weak moments. He is gorgeous. What can I say?

But he was looking at me with intense eyes, and I felt color flooding my face.

'This is not your brother's bathrobe.'

Oh, boy. I stared into the fire as if it were going to spell out an answer for me.

'Whose, then?'

'Bill's,' I said. That was easy.

'He is your lover?'

I nodded. 'Was,' I said honestly.

'He is my friend?'

I thought that over. 'Well, not exactly. He lives in the area you're the sheriff of? Area Five?' I resumed brushing my hair and discovered it was dry. It crackled with electricity and followed the brush. I smiled at the effect in my reflection in the mirror over the mantel. I could see Eric in the reflection, too. I have no idea why the story went around that vampires can't be seen in mirrors. There was certainly plenty of Eric to see, because he was so tall and he hadn't wrapped the robe very tightly . . . I closed my eyes.

'Do you need something?' Eric asked anxiously.

More self-control.

'I'm just fine,' I said, trying not to grind my teeth. 'Your friends will be here soon. Your jeans are in the dryer, and I'm hoping Jason will be back any minute with some clothes.'

'My friends?'

'Well, the vampires who work for you. I guess Pam counts as a friend. I don't know about Chow.'

'Sookie, where do I work? Who is Pam?'

This was really an uphill conversation. I tried to explain to Eric about his position, his ownership of Fangtasia, his other business interests, but truthfully, I wasn't knowledgeable enough to brief him completely.

'You don't know much about what I do,' he observed accurately.

'Well, I only go to Fangtasia when Bill takes me, and he takes me when you make me do something.' I hit myself in the forehead with my brush. Stupid, stupid!

'How could I make you do anything? May I borrow the brush?' Eric asked. I stole a glance at him. He was looking all broody and thoughtful.

'Sure,' I said, deciding to ignore his first question. I handed over the brush. He began to use it on his own hair, making all the muscles in his chest dance around. *Oh, boy. Maybe I should get back in the shower and turn the water on cold?* I stomped into the bedroom and got an elastic band and pulled my hair back in the tightest ponytail I could manage, up at the crown of my head. I used my second-best brush to get it very smooth, and checked to make sure I'd gotten it centered by turning my head from side to side.

'You are tense,' Eric said from the doorway, and I yipped.

'Sorry, sorry!' he said hastily.

I glared at him, full of suspicion, but he seemed sincerely contrite.

When he was himself, Eric would have laughed. But darn if I didn't miss Real Eric. You knew where you were with him.

I heard a knock on the front door.

'You stay in here,' I said. He seemed pretty worried, and he sat on the chair in the corner of the room, like a good little fella. I was glad I'd picked up my discarded clothes the night before, so my room didn't seem so personal. I went through the living room to the front door, hoping for no more surprises.

'Who is it?' I asked, putting my ear to the door.

'We are here,' said Pam.

I began to turn the knob, stopped, then remembered they couldn't come in anyway, and opened the door.

Pam has pale straight hair and is as white as a magnolia petal. Other than that, she looks like a young suburban housewife who has a part-time job at a preschool.

Though I don't think you'd really ever want Pam to take care of your toddlers, I've never seen her do anything extraordinarily cruel or vicious. But she's definitely convinced that vampires are better than humans, and she's very direct and doesn't mince words. I'm sure if Pam saw that some dire action was necessary for her well-being, she'd do it without missing any sleep. She seems to be an excellent second-in-command, and not overly ambitious. If she wants to have her own bailiwick, she keeps that desire very well concealed.

Chow is a whole different kettle of fish. I don't want to know Chow any better than I already do. I don't trust him, and I've never felt comfortable around him. Chow is Asian, a small-built but powerful vampire with longish black hair. He is no more than five foot seven, but every inch of visible skin (except his face) is covered with those intricate tattoos that are true art dyed into human skin. Pam says they are yakuza tattoos. Chow acts as Fangtasia's bartender some evenings, and on other nights he just sits around to let patrons approach him. (That's the whole purpose of vampire bars, to let regular humans feel they're walking on the wild side by being in the same room with the in-the-flesh undead. It's very lucrative, Bill told me.)

Pam was wearing a fluffy cream sweater and golden- brown knit pants, and Chow was in his usual vest and slacks. He seldom wore a shirt, so the Fangtasia patrons could get the full benefit of his body art.

I called Eric, and he came into the room slowly. He was visibly wary.

'Eric,' Pam said, when she saw him. Her voice was full of relief. 'You're well?' Her eyes were fixed on Eric anxiously. She didn't bow, but she sort of gave a deep nod.

'Master,' Chow said, and bowed.

I tried not to overinterpret what I was seeing and hearing, but I assumed that the different greetings signified the relationships among the three.

Eric looked uncertain. 'I know you,' he said, trying to make it sound more statement than question.

The two other vampires exchanged a glance. 'We work for you,' Pam said. 'We owe you fealty.'

I began to ease out of the room, because they'd want to talk about secret vampire stuff, I was sure. And if there was anything I didn't want to know, it was more secrets.

'Please don't go,' Eric said to me. His voice was frightened. I froze and looked behind me. Pam and Chow were staring over Eric's shoulders at me, and they had quite different expressions. Pam looked almost amused. Chow looked openly disapproving.

I tried not to look in Eric's eyes, so I could leave him with a clear conscience, but it just didn't work. He didn't want to be left alone with his two sidekicks. I blew lots of air out, puffing up my cheeks. Well, *dammit*. I trudged back to Eric's side, glaring at Pam the whole way.

There was another knock at the door, and Pam and Chow reacted in a dramatic way. They were both ready to fight in an instant, and vampires in that readiness are very, very scary. Their fangs run out, their hands arch like claws, and their bodies are on full alert. The air seems to crackle around them.

'Yes?' I said from right inside the door. I *had* to get a peephole installed.

'It's your brother,' Jason said brusquely. He didn't know how lucky he was that he hadn't just walked in.

Something had put Jason into a foul mood, and I wondered if there was anyone with him. I almost opened the door. But I hesitated.

Finally, feeling like a traitor, I turned to Pam. I silently pointed down the hall to the back door, making an opening-and-closing gesture so she could not mistake what I meant. I made a circle in the air with my finger – *Come around the house, Pam* – and pointed at the front door.

Pam nodded and ran down the hall to the back of the house. I couldn't hear her feet on the floor. Amazing.

Eric moved away from the door. Chow got in front of him. I approved. This was exactly what an underling was supposed to do.

In less than a minute, I heard Jason bellow from maybe six inches away. I jumped away from the door, startled.

Pam said, 'Open up!'

I swung the door wide to see Jason locked in Pam's arms. She was holding him off the ground with no effort, though he was flailing wildly and making it as hard as he could, God bless him.

'You're by yourself,' I said, relief being my big emotion.

'Of course, dammit! Why'd you set her on me? Let me down!'

'It's my brother, Pam,' I said. 'Please put him down.'

Pam set Jason down, and he spun around to look at her. 'Listen, woman! You don't just sneak up on a man like that! You're lucky I didn't slap you upside the head!'

Pam looked amused all over again, and even Jason looked embarrassed. He had the grace to smile. 'I guess that might be pretty hard,' he admitted, picking up the bags he'd dropped. Pam helped him. 'It's lucky I got the blood in the big plastic bottles,' he said. 'Otherwise, this lovely lady would have to go hungry.'

He smiled at Pam engagingly. Jason loves women. With Pam, Jason was in way over his head, but didn't have the sense to know it.

'Thanks. You need to go now,' I said abruptly. I took the plastic bags from his hands. He and Pam were still in an eye-lock. She was putting the whammy on him. 'Pam,' I said sharply. 'Pam, this is my brother.'

'I know,' she said calmly. 'Jason, did you have something to tell us?'

I'd forgotten that Jason had sounded like he was barely containing himself when he'd come to the door.

'Yes,' he said, hardly able to tear his eyes away from the vampire. But when he glanced at me, he caught sight of Chow, and his eyes widened. He had enough sense to fear Chow, at least. 'Sookie?' he said. 'Are you all right?' He took a step into the room, and I could see the adrenaline left over from the fright Pam had given begin to pump through his system again.

'Yes. Everything's all right. These are just friends of Eric's who came to check on him.'

'Well, they better go take those wanted posters down.'

That got everyone's full attention. Jason enjoyed that.

'There's posters up at Wal-Mart, and Grabbit Kwik, and the Bottle Barn, and just about everywhere else in town,' he said. 'They all say, "Have you seen this man?" and they go on to tell about him being kidnapped and his friends being so anxious, and the reward for a confirmed sighting is fifty thousand dollars.'

I didn't process this too well. I was mostly thinking, *Huh?*, when Pam got the point.

'They're hoping to sight him and catch him,' she said to Chow. 'It will work.'

'We should take care of it,' he said, nodding toward Jason.

'Don't you lay one hand on my brother,' I said. I moved between Jason and Chow, and my hands itched for a stake or hammer or anything at all that would keep this vamp from touching Jason.

Pam and Chow focused on me with that unswerving attention. I didn't find it flattering, as Jason had. I found it deadly. Jason opened his mouth to speak – I could feel the anger building in him, and the impulse to confront – but my hand clamped down on his wrist, and he grunted, and I said, 'Don't say a word.' For a miracle, he didn't. He seemed to sense that events were moving forward too rapidly and in a grave direction.

'You'll have to kill me, too,' I said.

Chow shrugged. 'Big threat.'

Pam didn't say anything. If it came to a choice between upholding vamp interests and being my buddy . . . well, I guessed we were just going to have to cancel our sleepover, and here I'd been planning on French-braiding her hair.

'What is this about?' Eric asked. His voice was considerably stronger. 'Explain . . . Pam.'

A minute went by while things hung in the balance. Then Pam

turned to Eric, and she may have been slightly relieved that she didn't have to kill me right at the moment. 'Sookie and this man, her brother, have seen you,' she explained. 'They're human. They need the money. They will turn you in to the witches.'

'What witches?' Jason and I said simultaneously.

'Thank you, Eric, for getting us into this shit,' Jason muttered unfairly. 'And could you let go of my wrist, Sook? You're stronger than you look.'

I was stronger than I should be because I'd had vampire blood – most recently, Eric's. The effects would last around three more weeks, maybe longer. I knew this from past experience.

Unfortunately, I'd needed that extra strength at a low point in my life. The very vampire who was now draped in my former boyfriend's bathrobe had donated that blood when I was grievously wounded but had to keep going.

'Jason,' I said in a level voice – as though the vampires couldn't hear me – 'please watch yourself.' That was as close as I could come to telling Jason to be smart for once in his life. He was way too fond of walking on the wild side.

Very slowly and cautiously, as if an uncaged lion were in the room, Jason and I went to sit on the old couch to one side of the fireplace. That notched the situation down a couple of degrees. After a brief hesitation, Eric sat on the floor and pressed himself into my legs. Pam settled on the edge of the recliner, closest to the fireplace, but Chow chose to remain standing (within what I calculated was lunging distance) near Jason. The atmosphere became less tense, though not by any means relaxed – but still, this was an improvement over the moments before.

'Your brother must stay and hear this,' Pam said. 'No matter how much you don't want him to know. He needs to learn why he mustn't try to earn that money.'

Jason and I gave quick nods. I was hardly in a position to throw them out. Wait, I could! I could tell them all that their invitation to come in was rescinded, and whoosh, out the door they'd go, walking backward. I found myself smiling. Rescinding an invitation was extremely satisfying. I'd done it once before; I'd sent both Bill and Eric zooming out of my living room, and it had felt so good I'd rescinded the entrance invite of every vampire I knew. I could feel my smile fading as I thought more carefully.

If I gave way to this impulse, I'd have to stay in my house every night for the rest of my life, because they'd return at dusk the next day and the day after that and so on, until they got me, because I had their boss. I glowered at Chow. I was willing to blame this whole thing on him.

'Several night ago, we heard – at Fangtasia,' Pam explained for Jason's benefit, 'that a group of witches had arrived in Shreveport. A human told us, one who wants Chow. She didn't know why we were so interested in that information.'

That didn't sound too threatening to me. Jason shrugged. 'So?' he said. 'Geez, you all are vampires. What can a bunch of girls in black do to you?'

'Real witches can do plenty to vampires,' Pam said, with remarkable restraint. 'The "girls in black" you're thinking of are only poseurs. Real witches can be women or men of any age. They are very formidable, very powerful. They control magical forces, and our existence itself is rooted in magic. This group seems to have some extra . . .' She paused, casting around for a word.

Juice?' Jason suggested helpfully.

'Juice,' she agreed. 'We haven't discovered what makes them so strong.'

'What was their purpose in coming to Shreveport?' I asked.

'A good question,' Chow said approvingly. 'A much better question.'

I frowned at him. I didn't need his damn approval.

'They wanted – they want – to take over Eric's businesses,' Pam said. 'Witches want money as much as anyone, and they figure they can either take over the businesses, or make Eric pay them to leave him alone.'

'Protection money.' This was a familiar concept to a television viewer. 'But how could they force you into anything? You guys are so powerful.'

'You have no idea how many problems a business can develop if witches want a piece of it. When we met with them for the first time, their leaders – a sister and brother team – spelled it out. Hallow made it clear she could curse our labor, turn our alcoholic drinks bad, and cause patrons to trip on the dance floor and sue us, to say nothing of plumbing problems.' Pam threw up her hands in disgust. 'It would make every night a bad dream, and our revenues would plummet, maybe to the point that Fangtasia would become worthless.'

Jason and I gave each other cautious glances. Naturally, vampires were heavily into the bar business, since it was most lucrative at night, and they were up then. They'd dabbled in all-night dry cleaners, all-night restaurants, all-night movie theaters . . . but the bar business paid best. If Fangtasia closed, Eric's financial base would suffer a blow.

'So they want protection money,' Jason, said. He'd watched the *Godfather* trilogy maybe fifty times. I thought about asking him if he wanted to sleep with the fishes, but Chow was looking antsy, so I refrained. We were both of us just a snick and a snee away from an unpleasant death, and I knew it was no time for humor, especially humor that so nearly wasn't.

'So how did Eric end up running down the road at night without a shirt or shoes?' I asked, thinking it was time to get down to brass tacks.

Much exchanging of glances between the two subordinates. I looked down at Eric, pressed up against my legs. He seemed to be as interested in the answer as we were. His hand firmly circled my ankle. I felt like a large security blanket.

Chow decided to take a narrative turn. 'We told them we would discuss their threat. But last night, when we went to work, one of the lesser witches was waiting at Fangtasia with an alternative proposal.' He looked a little uncomfortable. 'During our initial meeting, the head of the coven, Hallow, decided she, uh, lusted after Eric. Such a coupling is very frowned upon among witches, you understand, since we are dead and witchcraft is supposed to be so . . . organic.' Chow spat the word out like it was something stuck to his shoe. 'Of course, most witches would never do what this coven was attempting. These are all people drawn to the power itself, rather than to the religion behind it.'

This was interesting, but I wanted to hear the rest of the story. So did Jason, who made a 'hurry along' gesture with his hand. With a little shake to himself, as if to rouse himself from his thoughts, Chow went on. 'This head witch, this Hallow, told Eric, through her subordinate, that if he would entertain her for seven nights, she would only demand a fifth of his business, rather than a half.'

'You must have some kind of reputation,' my brother said to Eric, his voice full of honest awe. Eric was not entirely successful at hiding his pleased expression. He was glad to hear he was such a Romeo. There was a slight difference in the way he looked up at me in the next moment, and I had a feeling of horrid inevitability – like when you see your car begin to roll downhill (though you're sure you left it in park), and you know there's no way you can catch up to it and put on the brakes, no matter how much you want to. That car is gonna crash.

'Though some of us thought he might be wise to agree, our master balked,' Chow said, shooting 'our master' a less than loving glance. And our master saw fit to refuse in such insulting terms that Hallow cursed him.'

Eric looked embarrassed.

'Why on earth would you turn down a deal like that?' Jason asked, honestly puzzled.

'I don't remember,' Eric said, moving fractionally closer to my legs. Fractionally was all the closer he could get. He looked relaxed, but I knew he wasn't. I could feel the tension in his body. 'I didn't know my name until this woman, Sookie, told me it.'

And how did you come to be out in the country?'

'I don't know that either.'

'He just vanished from where he was,' Pam said. 'We were sitting in the office with the young witch, and Chow and I were arguing with Eric about his refusal. And then we weren't.'

'Ring any bells, Eric?' I asked. I'd caught myself reaching out to stroke his hair, like I would a dog that was huddling close to me.

The vampire looked puzzled. Though Eric's English was excellent, every now and then an idiom would faze him.

'Do you recall anything about this?' I said, more plainly. 'Have any memories of it?'

'I was born the moment I was running down the road in the dark and the cold,' he said. 'Until you took me in, I was a void.'

Put that way, it sounded terrifying.

'This just doesn't track,' I said. 'This wouldn't just happen out of the blue, with no warning.'

Pam didn't look offended, but Chow tried to make the effort.

'You two did something, didn't you? You messed up. What did you do?' Both Eric's arms wrapped around my legs, so I was pinned in place. I suppressed a little ripple of panic. He was just insecure.

'Chow lost his temper with the witch,' Pam said, after a significant pause.

I closed my eyes. Even Jason seemed to grasp what Pam was saying, because his eyes got bigger. Eric turned his face to rub his cheek along my thigh. I wondered what he was making of this.

'And the minute she was attacked, Eric vanished?' I asked.

Pam nodded.

'So she was booby-trapped with a spell.'

'Apparently,' Chow said. 'Though I had never heard of such a thing, and I can't be held responsible.' His glare dared me to say anything.

I turned to Jason and rolled my eyes. Dealing with Chow's blunder was not my responsibility. I was pretty sure that if the whole story was told to the queen of Louisiana, Eric's overlord, she might have a few things to say to Chow about the incident.

There was a little silence, during which Jason got up to put another log on the fire. 'You've been in Merlotte's before, haven't you?' he asked the vampires. 'Where Sookie works?'

Eric shrugged; he didn't remember. Pam said, 'I have, but not Eric.' She looked at me to confirm, and after some thought, I nodded.

'So no one's going to instantly associate Eric with Sookie.' Jason dropped that observation casually, but he was looking very pleased and almost smug.

'No,' Pam said slowly. 'Maybe not.'

There was definitely something I ought to be worrying about right now, but I couldn't quite see the shape of it.

'So you're clear as far as Bon Temps goes,' Jason continued. 'I doubt if anyone saw him out last night, except Sookie, and I'm damned if I know why he ended up on that particular road.'

My brother had made a second excellent point. He was really operating on all his batteries tonight.

'But lots of people from here do drive to Shreveport to go to that
bar, Fangtasia. I've been myself,' Jason said. This was news to me, and
I gave him a narrow-eyed glare. He shrugged and looked just a tad
embarrassed. 'So what's gonna happen when someone tries to claim
the reward? When they call the number on the poster?'

Chow decided to contribute more to the conversation. 'Of course,
the "close friend" who answers will come right away to talk to the
informant firsthand. If the caller can convince the "close friend" that
he saw Eric after the whore witch worked her spell on him, the
witches will begin looking in a specific area. They're sure to find
him. They'll try to contact the local witches, too, get them working
on it.'

'No witches in Bon Temps,' Jason said, looking amazed that Chow
would even suggest the idea. There my brother went again, making
assumptions.

'Oh, I'll bet there are,' I said. 'Why not? Remember what I told you?'
Though I'd been thinking of Weres and shifters when I'd warned him
there were things in the world he wouldn't want to see.

My poor brother was getting overloaded with information this
evening. 'Why not?' he repeated weakly. 'Who would they be?'

'Some women, some men,' Pam said, dusting her hands together
as if she were talking about some infectious pest. 'They are like everyone else who has a secret life – most of them are quite pleasant, fairly
harmless.' Though Pam didn't sound too positive when she said that.
'But the bad ones tend to contaminate the good.'

'However,' Chow said, staring thoughtfully at Pam, 'this is such a
backwater that there may well be very few witches in the area. Not all
of them are in covens, and getting an unattached witch to cooperate
will be very difficult for Hallow and her followers.'

'Why can't the Shreveport witches just cast a spell to find Eric?'
I asked.

'They can't find anything of his to use to cast such a spell,' Pam said,
and she sounded as if she knew what she was talking about. 'They
can't get into his daytime resting place to find a hair or clothes that

bear his scent. And there's no one around who's got Eric's blood in her.'

Ah-oh. Eric and I looked at each other very briefly. There was me; and I was hoping devoutly that no one knew that but Eric.

'Besides,' Chow said, shifting from foot to foot, 'in my opinion, since we are dead, such things would not work to cast a spell.'

Pam's eyes latched on to Chow's. They were exchanging ideas again, and I didn't like it. Eric, the cause of all this message swapping, was looking back and forth between his two fellow vamps. Even to me he looked clueless.

Pam turned to me. 'Eric should stay here, where he is. Moving him will expose him to more danger. With him out of the way and in safety, we can take countermeasures against the witches.'

'Going to the mattresses,' Jason muttered in my ear, still stuck on the *Godfather* terminology.

Now that Pam had said it out loud, I could see clearly why I should have become concerned when Jason began emphasizing how impossible it was that anyone should associate Eric with me. No one would believe that a vampire of Eric's power and importance would be parked with a human barmaid.

My amnesiac guest looked bewildered. I leaned forward, gave in briefly to my impulse to stroke his hair, and then I held my hands over his ears. He permitted this, even putting his own hands on top of mine. I was going to pretend he couldn't hear what I was going to say.

'Listen, Chow, Pam. This is the worst idea of all time. I'll tell you why.' I could hardly get the words out fast enough, emphatically enough. 'How am I supposed to protect him? You know how this will end! I'll get beaten up. Or maybe even killed.'

Pam and Chow looked at me with twin blank expressions. They might as well have said, 'Your point being?'

'If my sister does this,' Jason said, disregarding me completely, 'she deserves to get paid for it.'

There was what you call a pregnant silence. I gaped at him.

Simultaneously, Pam and Chow nodded.

'At least as much as an informer would get if he called the phone number on the poster,' Jason said, his bright blue eyes going from one pale face to another. 'Fifty thousand.'

'Jason!' I finally found my voice, and I clamped my hands down even tighter over Eric's ears. I was embarrassed and humiliated, without being able to figure out exactly why. For one thing, my brother was arranging my business as though it were his.

'Ten,' Chow said.

'Forty-five,' Jason countered.

'Twenty.'

'Thirty-five.'

'Done.'

'Sookie, I'll bring you my shotgun,' Jason said.

Chapter 3

'How did this happen?' I asked the fire, when they were all gone.

All except for the big Viking vampire I was supposed to preserve and protect.

I was sitting on the rug in front of the fire. I'd just thrown in another piece of wood, and the flames were really lovely. I needed to think about something pleasant and comforting.

I saw a big bare foot out of the corner of my eye. Eric sank down to join me on the hearth rug. 'I think this happened because you have a greedy brother, and because you are the kind of woman who would stop for me even though she was afraid,' Eric said accurately.

'How are you feeling about all this?' I never would have asked the compos mentis Eric this question, but he still seemed so different, maybe not the completely terrified mess he'd been the night before, but still very un-Eric. 'I mean – it's like you're a package that they put in a storage locker, me being the locker.'

'I am glad they are afraid enough of me to take good care of me.'

'Huh,' I said intelligently. Not the answer I'd expected.

'I must be a frightening person, when I am myself. Or do I inspire so much loyalty through my good works and kind ways?'

I sniggered.

'I thought not.'

'You're okay,' I said reassuringly, though come to think of it, Eric didn't look like he needed much reassurance. However, now I was responsible for him. 'Aren't your feet cold?'

'No,' he said. But now I was in the business of taking care of Eric, who *so* didn't need taking care of. And I was being paid a staggering amount of money to do just that, I reminded myself sternly. I got the old quilt from the back of the couch and covered his legs and feet in green, blue, and yellow squares. I collapsed back onto the rug beside him.

'That's truly hideous,' Eric said.

'That's what Bill said.' I rolled over on my stomach and caught myself smiling.

'Where is this Bill?'

'He's in Peru.'

'Did he tell you he was going?'

'Yes.'

'Am I to assume that your relationship with him has waned?'

That was a pretty nice way to put it. 'We've been on the outs. It's beginning to look permanent,' I said, my voice even.

He was on his stomach beside me now, propped up on his elbows so we could talk. He was a little closer than I was comfortable with, but I didn't want to make a big issue out of scooting over. He half turned to toss the quilt over both of us.

'Tell me about him,' Eric said unexpectedly. He and Pam and Chow had all had a glass of TrueBlood before the other vampires left, and he was looking pinker.

'You know Bill,' I told him. 'He's worked for you for quite a while. I guess you can't remember, but Bill's – well, he's kind of cool and calm, and he's really protective, and he can't seem to get some things through his head.' I never thought I'd be rehashing my relationship with Bill with Eric, of all people.

'He loves you?'

I sighed, and my eyes watered, as they so often did when I thought of Bill – Weeping Willa, that was me. 'Well, he said he did,' I muttered dismally. 'But then when this vampire ho contacted him somehow, he went a-running.' For all I knew, she'd emailed him. 'He'd had an affair with her before, and she turned out to be his, I don't know what you call 'em, the one who turned him into a vampire. Brought him over, he said. So Bill took back up with her. He says he had to. And then he found out' – I looked sideways at Eric with a significant raise of the eyebrows, and Eric looked fascinated – 'that she was just trying to lure him over to the even-darker side.'

'Pardon?'

'She was trying to get him to come over to another vampire group in Mississippi and bring with him the really valuable computer data base he'd put together for your people, the Louisiana vamps,' I said, simplifying a little bit for the sake of brevity.

'What happened?'

This was as much fun as talking to Arlene. Maybe even more, because I'd never been able to tell her the whole story. 'Well, Lorena, that's her name, she *tortured* him,' I said, and Eric's eyes widened. 'Can you believe that? She could torture someone she'd made love with? Someone she'd lived with for years?' Eric shook his head disbelievingly. 'Anyway, you told me to go to Jackson and find him, and I sort of picked up clues at this nightclub for Supes only.' Eric nodded. Evidently, I didn't have to explain that Supes meant supernatural-beings. 'Its real name is Josephine's, but the Weres call it Club Dead. You told me to go there with this really nice Were who owed you a big favor, and I stayed at his place.' Alcide Herveaux still figured in my daydreams. 'But I ended up getting hurt pretty bad,' I concluded. Hurt pretty bad, as always.

'How?'

'I got staked, believe it or not.'

Eric looked properly impressed. 'Is there a scar?'

'Yeah, even though—' And here I stopped dead.

He gave every indication he was hanging on my words. 'What?'

'You got one of the Jackson vampires to work on the wound, so I'd survive for sure . . . and then you gave me blood to heal me quick, so I could look for Bill at daylight.' Remembering how Eric had given me blood made my cheeks turn red, and I could only hope Eric would attribute my flush to the heat of the fire.

'And you saved Bill?' he said, moving beyond that touchy part.

'Yes, I did,' I said proudly. 'I saved his ass.' I rolled onto my back and looked up at him. Gee, it was nice to have someone to talk to. I pulled up my T-shirt and inclined partially on my side to show Eric the scar, and he looked impressed. He touched the shiny area with a fingertip and shook his head. I rearranged myself.

'And what happened to the vampire ho?' he asked

I eyed him suspiciously, but he didn't seem to be making fun of me. 'Well,' I said, 'um, actually, I kind of . . . She came in while I was getting Bill untied, and she attacked me, and I kind of . . . killed her.'

Eric looked at me intently. I couldn't read his expression. 'Had you ever killed anyone before?' he asked.

'Of course not!' I said indignantly. 'Well, I did hurt a guy who was trying to kill me, but he didn't die. No, I'm a *human*. I don't have to kill anyone to live.'

'But humans kill other humans all the time. And they don't even need to eat them or drink their blood.'

'Not *all* humans.'

'True enough,' he said. 'We vampires are all murderers.'

'But in a way, you're like lions.'

Eric looked astonished. 'Lions?' he said weakly.

'Lions all kill stuff.' At the moment, this idea seemed like an inspiration. So you're predators, like lions and raptors. But you use what you kill. You have to kill to eat.'

'The catch in that comforting theory being that we look almost exactly like you. And we used to be you. And we can love you, as well as feed off you. You could hardly say the lion wanted to caress the antelope.'

Suddenly there was something in the air that hadn't been there the moment before. I felt a little like an antelope – that was being stalked – by a lion that was a deviant.

I'd felt more comfortable when I was taking care of a terrified victim.

'Eric,' I said, very cautiously, 'you know you're my guest here. And you know if I tell you to leave, which I will if you're not straight with me, you'll be standing out in the middle of a field somewhere in a bathrobe that's too short for you.'

'Have I said something to make you uncomfortable?' He was (apparently) completely contrite, blue eyes blazing with sincerity. 'I'm sorry. I was just trying to continue your train of thought. Do you have some more TrueBlood? What clothes did Jason get for me? Your brother is a very clever man.' He didn't sound a hundred percent admiring when he told me this. I didn't blame him. Jason's cleverness might cost him thirty-five thousand dollars. I got up to fetch the Wal-Mart bag, hoping that Eric liked his new Louisiana Tech sweatshirt and cheap jeans.

I turned in about midnight, leaving Eric absorbed in my tapes of the first season of *Buffy the Vampire Slayer*. (Though welcome, these were actually a *gag* gift from Tara.) Eric thought the show was a hoot, especially the way the vampires' foreheads bulged out when they got blood-lusty. From time to time, I could hear Eric laughing all the way back in my room. But the sound didn't bother me. I found it reassuring to hear someone else in the house.

It took me a little longer than usual to fall asleep, because I was thinking over the things that had happened that day. Eric was in the witness protection program, in a way, and I was providing the safe house. No one in the world – well, except for Jason, Pam, and Chow – knew where the sheriff of Area Five actually was at this moment.

Which was, sliding into my bed.

I didn't want to open my eyes and quarrel with him. I was just at that cusp between waking and dreaming. When he'd climbed in the night before, Eric had been so afraid that I'd felt quite maternal, comfortable in holding his hand to reassure him. Tonight it didn't seem so, well, neutral, having him in the bed with me.

'Cold?' I murmured, as he huddled close.

'Um-hum,' he whispered. I was on my back, so comfortable I could not contemplate moving. He was on his side facing me, and he put an arm across my waist. But he didn't move another inch, and he relaxed completely. After a moment's tension, I did, too, and then I was dead to the world.

The next thing I knew, it was morning and the phone was ringing. Of course, I was by myself in bed, and through my open doorway I could see across the hall into the smaller bedroom. The closet door was open, as he'd had to leave it when dawn came and he'd lowered himself into the light-tight hole.

It was bright and warmer today, up in the forties and heading for the fifties. I felt much more cheerful than I'd felt upon waking the day before. I knew what was happening now; or, at least I knew more or less what I was supposed to do, how the next few days would go. Or I thought I did. When I answered the phone, I discovered that I was way off.

'Where's your brother?' yelled Jason's boss, Shirley Hennessey. You thought a man named Shirley was funny only until you were face-to-face with the real deal, at which point you decided it would really be better to keep your amusement to yourself.

'How would I know?' I said reasonably. 'Probably slept over at some woman's place.' Shirley, who was universally known as Catfish, had never, ever called here before to track Jason down. In fact, I'd be surprised if he'd ever had to call anywhere. One thing Jason was good about was showing up at work on time and at least going through the motions until that time was up. In fact, Jason was pretty good at his job, which I'd never fully understood. It seemed to involve parking his fancy truck at the parish road department, getting into another truck with the Renard parish logo on the door, and driving around telling various road crews what to do. It also seemed to demand that he get out of the truck to stand with other men as they all stared into big holes in or near the road.

Catfish was knocked off balance by my frankness. 'Sookie, you shouldn't say that kind of thing,' he said, quite shocked at a single woman admitting she knew her brother wasn't a virgin.

'Are you telling me that Jason hasn't shown up at work? And you've called his house?'

'Yes and yes,' said Catfish, who in most respects was no fool. 'I even sent Dago out to his place.' Dago (road crew members had to have nicknames) was Antonio Guglielmi, who had never been farther from Louisiana than Mississippi. I was pretty sure the same could be said for his parents, and possibly his grandparents, though there was rumor they'd once been to Branson to take in the shows.

'Was his truck out there?' I was beginning to have that cold creeping feeling.

'Yes,' Catfish said. 'It was parked in front of his house, keys inside. Door hanging open.'

'The truck door or the house door?'

'What?'

'Hanging open. Which door?'

'Oh, the truck.'

'This is bad, Catfish,' I said. I was tingling all over with alarm.

'When you seen him last?'

'Just last night. He was over here visiting with me, and he left about . . . oh, let's see . . . it must have been nine-thirty or ten.'

'He have anybody with him?'

'No.' He hadn't brought anybody with him, so that was pretty much the truth.

'You think I oughta call the sheriff?' Catfish asked.

I ran a hand over my face. I wasn't ready for that yet, no matter how off the situation seemed. 'Let's give it another hour,' I suggested. 'If he hasn't dragged into work in an hour, you let me know. If he does come in, you make him call me. I guess it's me ought to tell the sheriff, if it comes to that.'

I hung up after Catfish had repeated everything he'd said several times, just because he hated to hang up and go back to worrying. No, I can't read minds over the telephone line, but I could read it in his voice. I've known Catfish Hennessey for many years. He was a buddy of my father's.

I carried the cordless phone into the bathroom with me while I took a shower to wake up. I didn't wash my hair, just in case I had to go outside right away. I got dressed, made some coffee, and braided my hair in one long braid. All the time while I performed these tasks, I was thinking, which is something that's hard for me to do when I'm sitting still.

I came up with these scenarios.

One. (This was my favorite.) Somewhere between my house and his house, my brother had met up with a woman and fallen in love so instantly and completely that he had abandoned his habit of years and forgotten all about work. At this moment, they were in a bed somewhere, having great sex.

Two. The witches, or whatever the hell they were, had somehow found out that Jason knew where Eric was, and they'd abducted him to force the information from him. (I made a mental note to learn more about witches.) How long could Jason keep the secret of Eric's location? My brother had lots of attitude, but he actually is a brave man – or maybe stubborn is a little more accurate. He wouldn't talk easily. Maybe a witch could spell him into talking? If the witches had him, he might be dead already, since they'd had him for hours. And if he'd talked, I was in danger and Eric was doomed. They could be coming at any minute, since witches are not bound by darkness. Eric was dead for the day, defenseless. This was definitely the worst-case scenario.

Three. Jason had returned to Shreveport with Pam and Chow. Maybe they'd decided to pay him some up-front money, or maybe Jason just wanted to visit Fangtasia because it was a popular nightspot. Once there, he could have been seduced by some vamp girl and stayed up all night with her, since Jason was like Eric in that women really, really took a shine to him. If she'd taken a little too much blood, Jason could be sleeping it off. I guess number three was really a variation on number one.

If Pam and Chow knew where Jason was but hadn't phoned before they died for the day, I was real mad. My gut instinct was to go get the hatchet and start chopping some stakes.

Then I remembered what I was trying so hard to forget: how it had felt when the stake pushed into Lorena's body, the expression on her face when she'd realized her long, long life was over. I shoved that thought away as hard as I could. You didn't kill someone (even an evil vampire) without it affecting you sooner or later: at least not unless you were a complete sociopath, which I wasn't.

Lorena would have killed me without blinking. In fact, she would have positively enjoyed it. But then, she was a vampire, and Bill never tired of telling me that vampires were different; that though they retained their human appearance (more or less), their internal functions and their personalities underwent a radical change. I believed him and took his warnings to heart, for the most part. It was just that they looked so human; it was so very easy to attribute normal human reactions and feelings to them.

The frustrating thing was, Chow and Pam wouldn't be up until dark, and I didn't know who – or what – I'd raise if I called Fangtasia during the day. I didn't think the two lived at the club. I'd gotten the impression that Pam and Chow shared a house . . . or a mausoleum . . . somewhere in Shreveport.

I was fairly sure that human employees came into the club during the day to clean, but of course a human wouldn't (couldn't) tell me anything about vampire affairs. Humans who worked for vampires learned pretty quick to keep their mouths shut, as I could attest.

On the other hand, if I went to the club I'd have a chance to talk to *someone* face-to-face. I'd have a chance to read a human mind. I couldn't read vampire minds, which had led to my initial attraction to Bill. Imagine the relief of silence after a lifetime of elevator music. (Now, why couldn't I hear vampire thoughts? Here's my big theory about that. I'm about as scientific as a Saltine, but I have read about neurons, which fire in your brain, right? When you're thinking? Since it's magic that animates vampires, not normal life force, their brains don't fire. So, nothing for me to pick up – except about once every three months, I'd get a flash from a vampire. And I took great care to conceal that, because that was a sure way to court instant death.)

Oddly enough, the only vampire I'd ever 'heard' twice was – you guessed it – Eric.

I'd been enjoying Eric's recent company so much for the same reason I'd enjoyed Bill's, quite apart from the romantic component I'd had with Bill. Even Arlene had a tendency to stop listening to me when I was talking, if she thought of something more interesting, like her children's grades or cute things they'd said. But with Eric, he could be thinking about his car needing new windshield wipers while I was pouring my heart out, and I was none the wiser.

The hour I'd asked Catfish to give me was almost up, and all my constructive thought had dwindled into the same murky maundering I'd gone through several times. Blah blah blah. This is what happens when you talk to yourself a lot.

Okay, action time.

The phone rang right at the hour, and Catfish admitted he had no news. No one had heard from Jason or seen him; but on the other hand, Dago hadn't seen anything suspicious at Jason's place except the truck's open door.

I was still reluctant to call the sheriff, but I didn't see that I had much choice. At this point, it would seem peculiar to skip calling him.

I expected a lot of hubbub and alarm, but what I got was even worse: I got benevolent indifference. Sheriff Bud Dearborn actually laughed.

'You callin' me because your tomcat of a brother is missing a day of work? Sookie Stackhouse, I'm surprised at you.' Bud Dearborn had a slow voice and the mashed-in face of a Pekinese, and it was all too easy to picture him snuffling into the phone.

'He never misses work, and his truck is at his house. The door was open,' I said.

He did grasp that significance, because Bud Dearborn is a man who knows how to appreciate a fine pickup.

'That does sound a little funny, but still, Jason is way over twenty-one and he has a reputation for . . .' (*Drilling anything that stands still*, I thought.) ' . . . being real popular with the ladies,' Bud concluded carefully. 'I bet he's all shacked up with someone new, and he'll be real sorry to have caused you any worry. You call me back if you haven't heard from him by tomorrow afternoon, you hear?'

'Right,' I said in my most frozen voice.

'Now, Sookie, don't you go getting all mad at me, I'm just telling you what any lawman would tell you,' he said.

I thought, *Any lawman with lead in his butt*, But I didn't say it out loud. Bud was what I had to work with, and I had to stay on his good side, as much as possible.

I muttered something that was vaguely polite and got off the phone. After reporting back to Catfish, I decided my only course of action was to go to Shreveport. I started to call Arlene, but I remembered she'd have the kids at home since it was still the school holiday. I thought of calling Sam, but I figured he might feel like he ought to do something, and I couldn't figure out what that would be. I just wanted to share my worries with someone. I knew that wasn't right.

No one could help me, but me. Having made up my mind to be brave and independent, I almost phoned Alcide Herveaux, who is a well-to-do and hardworking guy based in Shreveport. Alcide's dad runs a surveying firm that contracts for jobs in three states, and Alcide travels a lot among the various offices. I'd mentioned him the night before to Eric; Eric had sent Alcide to Jackson with me. But Alcide and I had some man-woman issues that were still unresolved, and it would be cheating to call him when I only wanted help he couldn't give. At least, that was how I felt.

I was scared to leave the house in case there might be news of Jason, but since the sheriff wasn't looking for him, I hardly thought there would be any word soon.

Before I left, I made sure I'd arranged the closet in the smaller bedroom so that it looked natural. It would be a little harder for Eric to get out when the sun went down, but it wouldn't be extremely difficult. Leaving him a note would be a dead giveaway if someone broke in, and he was too smart to answer the phone if I called just after dark had fallen. But he was so discombobulated by his amnesia, he might be scared to wake all by himself with no explanation of my absence, I thought.

I had a brainwave. Grabbing a little square piece of paper from last year's Word of the Day calendar ('enthrallment'), *I wrote: Jason, if you should happen to drop by, call me! I am very worried about you. No one knows where you area I'll be back this afternoon or evening. I'm going to drop by your house, and then I'll check to see if you went to Shreveport. Then, back here. Love, Sookie.* I got some tape and stuck the note to the refrigerator, just where a sister might expect her brother to head if he stopped by.

There. Eric was plenty smart enough to read between the lines. And yet every word of it was feasible, so if anyone did break in to search the house, they'd think I was taking a smart precaution.

But still, I was frightened of leaving the sleeping Eric so vulnerable. What if the witches came looking?

But why should they?

If they could have tracked Eric, they'd have been here by now, right? At least, that was the way I was reasoning. I thought of calling someone like Terry Bellefleur, who was plenty tough, to come sit in my house –

I could use waiting on a call about Jason as my pretext – but it wasn't right to endanger anyone else in Eric's defense.

I called all the hospitals in the area, feeling all the while that the sheriff should be doing this little job for me. The hospitals knew the name of everyone admitted, and none of them was Jason. I called the highway patrol to ask about accidents the night before and found there had been none in the vicinity. I called a few women Jason had dated, and I received a lot of negative responses, some of them obscene.

I thought I'd covered all the bases. I was ready to go to Jason's house, and I remember I was feeling pretty proud of myself as I drove north on Hummingbird Road and then took a left onto the highway. As I headed west to the house where I'd spent my first seven years, I drove past Merlotte's to my right and then past the main turnoff into Bon Temps. I negotiated the left turn and I could see our old home, sure enough with Jason's pickup parked in front of it. There was another pickup, equally shiny, parked about twenty feet away from Jason's.

When I got out of my car, a very black man was examining the ground around the truck. I was surprised to discover that the second pickup belonged to Alcee Beck, the only African-American detective on the parish force. Alcee's presence was both reassuring and disturbing.

'Miss Stackhouse,' he said gravely. Alcee Beck was wearing a jacket and slacks and heavy scuffed boots. The boots didn't go with the rest of his clothes, and I was willing to bet he kept them in his truck for when he had to go tromping around out in the country where the ground was less than dry. Alcee (whose name was pronounced Al-SAY) was also a strong broadcaster, and I could receive his thoughts clearly when I let down my shields to listen.

I learned in short order that Alcee Beck wasn't happy to see me, didn't like me, and did think something hinky had happened to Jason. Detective Beck didn't care for Jason, but he was actually scared of me. He thought I was a deeply creepy person, and he avoided me as much as possible.

Which was okay by me, frankly.

I knew more about Alcee Beck than I was comfortable knowing, and what I knew about Alcee was really unpleasant. He was brutal to uncooperative prisoners, though he adored his wife and daughter. He was lining his own pockets whenever he got a chance, and he made sure the chances came along pretty frequently. Alcee Beck confined this practice to the African-American community, operating on the theory that they'd never report him to the other white law enforcement personnel, and so far he'd been right.

See what I mean about not wanting to know things I heard? This was a lot different from finding out that Arlene really didn't think Charlsie's husband was good enough for Charlsie, or that Hoyt Fortenberry had dented a car in the parking lot and hadn't told the owner.

And before you ask me what I do about stuff like that, I'll tell you. I don't do squat. I've found out the hard way that it almost never works out if I try to intervene. What happens is no one is happier, and my little freakishness is brought to everyone's attention, and no one is comfortable around me for a month. I've got more secrets than Fort Knox has money. And those secrets are staying locked up just as tight.

I'll admit that most of those little facts I accumulated didn't make much difference in the grand scheme of things, whereas Alcee's misbehavior actually led to human misery. But so far I hadn't seen a single way to stop Alcee. He was very clever about keeping his activities under control and hidden from anyone with the power to intervene. And I wasn't too awful sure that Bud Dearborn *didn't* know.

'Detective Beck,' I said. 'Are you looking for Jason?'

'The sheriff asked me to come by and see if I could find anything out of order.'

'And have you found anything?'

'No, ma'am, I haven't.'

'Jason's boss told you the door to his truck was open?'

'I closed it so the battery wouldn't run down. I was careful not to touch anything, of course. But I'm sure your brother will show back up any time now, and he'll be unhappy if we mess with his stuff for no reason.'

'I have a key to his house, and I'm going to ask you to go in there with me.'

'Do you suspect anything happened to your brother in his house?' Alcee Beck was being so careful to spell everything out that I wondered if he had a tape recorder rolling away in his pocket.

'Could be. He doesn't normally miss work. In fact, he never misses work. And I always know where he is. He's real good about letting me know.'

'He'd tell you if he was running off with a woman? Most brothers wouldn't do that, Miss Stackhouse.'

'He'd tell me, or he'd tell Catfish.'

Alcee Beck did his best to keep his skeptical look on his dark face, but it didn't sit there easily.

The house was still locked. I picked out the right key from the ones on my ring, and we went inside. I didn't have the feeling of homecoming when I entered, the feeling I used to have as a kid. I'd lived in Gran's house so much longer than this little place. The minute Jason had turned twenty, he'd moved over here full-time, and though I'd dropped in, I'd probably spent less than twenty-four hours total in this house in the last eight years.

Glancing around me, I realized that my brother really hadn't changed the house much in all that time. It was a small ranch-style house with small rooms, but of course it was a lot younger than Gran's house – my house – and a lot more heating- and cooling-efficient. My father had done most of the work on it, and he was a good builder.

The small living room was still filled with the maple furniture my mother had picked out at the discount furniture store, and its upholstery (cream with green and blue flowers that had never been seen in nature) was still bright, more's the pity. It had taken me a few years to realize that my mother, while a clever woman in some respects, had had no taste whatsoever. Jason had never come to that realization. He'd replaced the curtains when they frayed and faded, and he'd gotten a new rug to cover the most worn spots on the ancient blue carpet. The appliances were all new, and he'd worked hard on updating the bathroom. But my parents, if they could have entered their home, would have felt quite comfortable.

It was a shock to realize they'd been dead for nearly twenty years.

While I stood close to the doorway, praying I wouldn't see bloodstains, Alcee Beck prowled through the house, which certainly seemed orderly. After a second's indecision, I decided to follow him. There wasn't much to see; like I say, it's a small house. Three bedrooms (two of them quite cramped), the living room, a kitchen, one bathroom, a fair-sized family room, and a small dining room: a house that could be duplicated any number of times in any town in America.

The house was quite tidy. Jason had never lived like a pig, though sometimes he acted like one. Even the king-size bed that almost filled the biggest bedroom was more-or-less pulled straight, though I could see the sheets were black and shiny. They were supposed to look like silk, but I was sure they were some artificial blend. Too slithery for me; I liked percale.

'No evidence of any struggle,' the detective pointed out.

'While I'm here, I'm just going to get something,' I told him, going over to the gun cabinet that had been my dad's. It was locked, so I checked my key ring again. Yes, I had a key for that, too, and I remembered some long story Jason had told me about why I needed one – in case he was out hunting and he needed another rifle, or something. As if I'd drop everything and run to fetch another rifle for him!

Well, I might, if I wasn't due at work, or something.

All Jason's rifles, and my father's, were in the gun cabinet – all the requisite ammunition, too.

'All present?' The detective was shifting around impatiently in the doorway to the dining room.

'Yes. I'm just going to take one of them home with me.'

'You expecting trouble at your place?' Beck looked interested for the first time.

'If Jason is gone, who knows what it means?' I said, hoping that was ambiguous enough. Beck had a very low opinion of my intelligence, anyway, despite the fact that he feared me. Jason had said he would bring me the shotgun, and I knew I would feel the better for having it. So I got out the Benelli and found its shells. Jason had very carefully taught me how to load and fire the shotgun, which was his pride and joy. There were two different boxes of shells.

'Which?' I asked Detective Beck.

'Wow, a Benelli.' He took time out to be impressed with the gun. 'Twelve-gauge, huh? Me, I'd take the turkey loads,' he advised. 'Those target loads don't have as much stopping power.'

I popped the box he indicated into my pocket.

I carried the shotgun out to my car, Beck trailing on my heels.

'You have to lock the shotgun in your trunk and the shells in the car,' the detective informed me. I did exactly what he said, even putting the shells in the glove compartment, and then I turned to face him. He would be glad to be out of my sight, and I didn't think he would look for Jason with any enthusiasm.

'Did you check around back?' I asked.

'I had just gotten here when you pulled up.'

I jerked my head in the direction of the pond behind the house, and we circled around to the rear. My brother, aided by Hoyt Fortenberry, had put in a large deck outside the back door maybe two years ago. He'd arranged some nice outdoor furniture he'd gotten on end-of-season sale at Wal-Mart. Jason had even put an ashtray on the wrought-iron table for his friends who went outside to smoke. Someone had used it. Hoyt smoked, I recalled. There was nothing else interesting on the deck.

The ground sloped down from the deck to the pond. While Alcee Beck checked the back door, I looked down to the pier my father had built, and I thought I could see a smear on the wood. Something in me crumpled at the sight, and I must have made a noise. Alcee came to stand by me, and I said, 'Look at the pier.'

He went on point, just like a setter. He said, 'Stay where you are,' in an unmistakably official voice. He moved carefully, looking down at the ground around his feet before he took each step. I felt like an hour passed before Alcee finally reached the pier. He squatted down on the sun-bleached boards to take a close look. He focused a little to the right of the smear, evaluating something I couldn't see, something I couldn't even make out in his mind. But then he wondered what kind of work boots my brother wore; that came in clear.

'Caterpillars,' I called. The fear built up in me till I felt I was vibrating with the intensity of it. Jason was all I had.

And I realized I'd made a mistake I hadn't done in years: I'd answered a question before it had been asked out loud. I clapped a hand over my mouth and saw the whites of Beck's eyes. He wanted away from me. And he was thinking maybe Jason was in the pond, dead. He was speculating that Jason had fallen and knocked his head against the pier, and then slid into the water. But there was a puzzling print . . .

'When can you search the pond?' I called.

He turned to look at me, terror on his face. I hadn't had anyone look at me like that in years. I had him spooked, and I hadn't wanted to have that effect on him.

'The blood is on the dock,' I pointed out, trying to improve matters. Providing a reasonable explanation was second nature. 'I'm scared Jason went into the water.'

Beck seemed to settle down a little after that. He turned his eyes back to the water. My father had chosen the site for the house to include the pond. He'd told me when I was little that the pond was very deep and fed by a tiny stream. The area around two-thirds of the pond was mowed and maintained as yard; but the farthest edge of it was left thickly wooded, and Jason enjoyed sitting on the deck in the late evening with binoculars, watching critters come to drink.

There were fish in the pond. He kept it stocked. My stomach lurched.

Finally, the detective walked up the slope to the deck. 'I have to call around, see who can dive,' Alcee Beck said. 'It may take a while to find someone who can do it. And the chief has to okay it.'

Of course, such a thing would cost money, and that money might not be in the parish budget. I took a deep breath. 'Are you talking hours, or days?'

'Maybe a day or two,' he said at last. 'No way anyone can do it who isn't trained. It's too cold, and Jason himself told me it was deep.'

'All right,' I said, trying to suppress my impatience and anger. Anxiety gnawed at me like another kind of hunger.

'Carla Rodriguez was in town last night,' Alcee Beck told me, and after a long moment, the significance of that sank into my brain.

Carla Rodriguez, tiny and dark and electric, had been the closest shave Jason had ever had with losing his heart. In fact, the little shifter Jason had had a date with on New Year's Eve had somewhat resembled Carla, who had moved to Houston three years ago, much to my relief. I'd been tired of the pyrotechnics surrounding her romance with my brother; their relationship had been punctuated by long and loud and public arguments, hung-up telephones, and slammed doors.

'Why? Who's she staying with?'

'Her cousin in Shreveport,' Beck said. 'You know, that Dovie.'

Dovie Rodriguez had visited Bon Temps a lot while Carla had lived here. Dovie had been the more sophisticated city cousin, down in the country to correct all our local yokel ways. Of course, we'd envied Dovie.

I thought that tackling Dovie was just what I wanted to do.

It looked like I'd be going to Shreveport after all.

Chapter 4

The detective hustled me off after that, telling me he was going to get the crime scene officer out to the house, and he'd be in touch. I got the idea, right out of his brain, that there was something he didn't want me to see, and that he'd thrown Carla Rodriguez at me to distract me.

And I thought he might take the shotgun away, since he seemed much more sure now he was dealing with a crime, and the shotgun might be part of some bit of evidence. But Alcee Beck didn't say anything, so I didn't remind him.

I was more shaken than I wanted to admit to myself. Inwardly, I'd been convinced that, though I needed to track my brother down, Jason was really okay – just misplaced. Or mislaid, more likely, ho ho ho. Possibly he was in some kind of not-too-serious trouble, I'd told myself. Now things were looking more serious.

I've never been able to squeeze my budget enough to afford a cell phone, so I began driving home. I was thinking of whom I should call, and I came up with the same answer as before. No one. There was no definite news to break. I felt as lonely as I ever have in my life. But I just didn't want to be Crisis Woman, showing up on friends' doorsteps with trouble on my shoulders.

Tears welled up in my eyes. I wanted my grandmother back. I pulled over to the side of the road and slapped myself on the cheek, hard. I called myself a few names.

Shreveport. I'd go to Shreveport and confront Dovie and Carla Rodriguez. While I was there, I'd find out if Chow and Pam knew anything about Jason's disappearance – though it was hours until they'd be up, and I'd just be kicking my heels in an empty club, assuming there'd be someone there to let me in. But I just couldn't sit at home, waiting. I could read the minds of the human employees and find out if they knew what was up.

On the one hand, if I went to Shreveport, I'd be out of touch with what was happening here. On the other hand, I'd be doing something.

While I was trying to decide if there were any more hands to consider, something else happened.

It was even odder than the preceding events of the day. There I was, parked in the middle of nowhere at the side of a parish road, when a sleek, black, brand-new Camaro pulled onto the shoulder behind me. Out of the passenger's side stepped a gorgeous woman, at least six feet tall. Of course, I remembered her; she'd been in Merlotte's on New Year's Eve. My friend Tara Thornton was in the driver's seat.

Okay, I thought blankly, staring into the rearview mirror, *this is weird*. I hadn't seen Tara in weeks, since we'd met by chance in a vampire club in Jackson, Mississippi. She'd been there with a vamp named Franklin Mott; he'd been very handsome in a senior-citizen sort of way, polished, dangerous, and sophisticated.

Tara always looks great. My high school friend has black hair, and dark eyes, and a smooth olive complexion, and she has a lot of intelligence that she uses running Tara's Togs, an upscale women's clothing store that rents space in a strip mall Bill owns. (Well, it's as upscale as Bon Temps has to offer.) Tara had become a friend of mine years before, because she came from an even sadder background than mine.

But the tall woman put even Tara in the shade. She was as dark-haired as Tara, though the new woman had reddish highlights that surprised the eye. She had dark eyes, too, but hers were huge and almond-shaped, almost abnormally large. Her skin was as pale as milk, and her legs were as long as a stepladder. She was quite gifted in the bosom department, and she was wearing fire-engine red from head to toe. Her lipstick matched.

'Sookie,' Tara called. 'What's the matter?' She walked carefully up to my old car, watching her feet because she was wearing glossy, brown leather, high-heeled boots she didn't want to scuff. They'd have lasted five minutes on my feet. I spend too much of my time standing up to worry about footwear that only looks good.

Tara looked successful, attractive, and secure, in her sage green sweater and taupe pants. 'I was putting on my makeup when I heard over the police scanner that something was up at Jason's house,' she said. She slid in the passenger's seat and leaned over to hug me. 'When I got to Jason's, I saw you pulling out. What's up?' The woman in red was standing with her back to the car, tactfully looking out into the woods.

I'd adored my father, and I'd always known (and my mother herself definitely believed) that no matter what Mother put me through, she was acting out of love. But Tara's parents had been evil, both alcoholics and abusers. Tara's older sisters and brothers had left home as fast as they could, leaving Tara, as the youngest, to foot the bill for their freedom.

Yet now that I was in trouble, here she was, ready to help.

'Well, Jason's gone missing,' I said, in a fairly level voice, but then I ruined the effect by giving one of those awful choking sobs. I turned my face so I'd be looking out my window. I was embarrassed to show such distress in front of the new woman.

Wisely ignoring my tears, Tara began asking me the logical questions: Had Jason called in to work? Had he called me the night before? Who had he been dating lately?

That reminded me of the shifter girl who'd been Jason's date New Year's Eve. I thought I could even talk about the girl's otherness, because Tara had been at Club Dead that night. Tara's tall companion was a Supe of some kind. Tara knew all about the secret world.

But she didn't, as it turned out.

Her memory had been erased. Or at least she pretended it had.

'What?' Tara asked, with almost exaggerated confusion. 'Were-wolves? At that nightclub? I remember seeing you there. Honey, didn't you drink a little too much and pass out, or something?'

Since I drink very sparingly, Tara's question made me quite angry, but it was also the most unremarkable explanation Franklin Mott could have planted in Tara's head. I was so disappointed at not getting to confide in her that I closed my eyes so I wouldn't have to see the blank look on her face. I felt tears leaving little paths down my cheeks. I should have just let it go, but I said, in a low, harsh voice, 'No, I didn't.'

'Omigosh, did your date put something in your drink?' In genuine horror, Tara squeezed my hand. 'That Rohypnol? But Alcide looked like such a nice guy!'

'Forget it,' I said, trying to sound gentler. 'It doesn't really have anything to do with Jason, after all.'

Her face still troubled, Tara pressed my hand again.

All of a sudden, I was certain I didn't believe her. Tara knew vampires could remove memory, and she was pretending Franklin Mott had erased hers. I thought Tara remembered quite well what had happened at Club Dead, but she was pretending she didn't to protect herself. If she had to do that to survive, that was okay. I took a deep breath.

'Are you still dating Franklin?' I asked, to start a different conversation.

'He got me this car.'

I was a little shocked and more than a little dismayed, but I hoped I was not the kind to point fingers.

'It's a wonderful car. You don't know any witches, do you?' I asked, trying to change the subject before Tara could read my misgivings. I was sure she would laugh at me for asking her such a question, but it was a good diversion. I wouldn't hurt her for the world.

Finding a witch would be a great help. I was sure Jason's abduction – and I swore to myself it was an abduction, it was not a murder – was linked to the witches' curse on Eric. It was just too much coincidence otherwise. On the other hand, I had certainly experienced the twists and turns of a bunch of coincidences in the past few months. There, I knew I'd find a third hand.

'Sure I do,' Tara said, smiling proudly. 'Now there I can help you. That is, if a Wiccan will do?'

I had so many expressions I wasn't sure my face could fit them all in. Shock, fear, grief, and worry were tumbling around in my brain. When the spinning stopped, we would see which one was at the top.

'You're a witch?' I said weakly.

'Oh, gosh, no, not me. I'm a Catholic. But I have some friends who are Wiccan. Some of them are witches.'

'Oh, really?' I didn't think I'd ever heard the word Wiccan before, though maybe I'd read it in a mystery or romance novel. 'I'm sorry, I don't know what that means,' I said, my voice humble.

'Holly can explain it better than I can,' Tara said.

'Holly. The Holly who works with me?'

'Sure. Or you could go to Danielle, though she's not going to be as willing to talk. Holly and Danielle are in the same coven.'

I was so shocked by now I might as well get even more stunned. 'Coven,' I repeated.

'You know, a group of pagans who worship together.'

'I thought a coven had to be witches?'

'I guess not – but they have to, you know, be non-Christian. I mean, Wicca is a religion.'

'Okay,' I said. 'Okay. Do you think Holly would talk to me about this?'

'I don't know why not.' Tara went back to her car to get her cell phone, and paced back and forth between our vehicles while she talked to Holly. I appreciated a little respite to allow me to get back on my mental feet, so to speak. To be polite I got out of my car and spoke to the woman in red, who'd been very patient.

'I'm sorry to meet you on such a bad day,' I said. 'I'm Sookie Stackhouse.'

'I'm Claudine,' she said, with a beautiful smile. Her teeth were Hollywood white. Her skin had an odd quality; it looked glossy and thin, reminding me of the skin of a plum; like if you bit her, sweet juice would gush out. 'I'm here because of all the activity.'

'Oh?' I said, taken aback.

'Sure. You have vampires, and Weres, and lots of other stuff all tangled up here in Bon Temps – to say nothing of several important and powerful crossroads. I was drawn to all the possibilities.'

'Uh-huh,' I said uncertainly. 'So, do you plan on just observing all this, or what?'

'Oh, no. Just observing is not my way.' She laughed. 'You're quite the wild card, aren't you?'

'Holly's up,' Tara said, snapping her phone shut and smiling because it was hard not to with Claudine around. I realized I was smiling from ear to ear, not my usual tense grin but an expression of sunny happiness. 'She says come on over.'

'Are you coming with me?' I didn't know what to think of Tara's companion.

'Sorry, Claudine's helping me today at the shop,' Tara said. 'We're having a New Year's sale on our old inventory, and people are doing some heavy shopping. Want me to put something aside for you? I've got a few really pretty party dresses left. Didn't the one you wore in Jackson get ruined?'

Yeah, because a fanatic had driven a stake through my side. The dress had definitely suffered. 'It got stained,' I said with great restraint. 'It's real nice of you to offer, but I don't think I'll have time to try anything on. With Jason and everything, I've got so much to think about.' And precious little extra money, I told myself.

'Sure,' said Tara. She hugged me again. 'You call me if you need me, Sookie. It's funny that I don't remember that evening in Jackson any better. Maybe I had too much to drink, too. Did we dance?'

'Oh, yes, you talked me into doing that routine we did at the high school talent show.'

'I did not!' She was begging me to deny it, with a half smile on her face.

''Fraid so.' I knew damn well she remembered it.

'I wish I'd been there,' said Claudine. 'I love to dance.'

'Believe me, that night in Club Dead is one I wish I'd missed,' I said.

'Well, remind me never to go back to Jackson, if I did that dance in public,' Tara said.

'I don't think either of us better go back to Jackson.' I'd left some very irate vampires in Jackson, but the Weres were even angrier. Not that there were a lot of them left, actually. But still.

Tara hesitated a minute, obviously trying to frame something she wanted to tell me. 'Since Bill owns the building Tara's Togs is in,' she said carefully, 'I do have a number to call, a number he said he'd check in with while he was out of the country. So if you need to let him know anything . . .?'

'Thanks,' I said, not sure if I felt thankful at all. 'He told me he left a number on a pad by the phone in his house.' There was a kind of finality to Bill's being out of the country, unreachable. I hadn't even thought of trying to get in touch with him about my predicament; out of all the people I'd considered calling, he hadn't even crossed my mind.

'It's just that he seemed pretty, you know, down.' Tara examined the toes of her boots. 'Melancholy,' she said, as if she enjoyed using a word that didn't pass her lips often. Claudine beamed with approval. What a strange gal. Her huge eyes were luminous with joy as she patted me on the shoulder.

I swallowed hard. 'Well, he's never exactly Mr Smiley,' I said. 'I do miss him. But . . .' I shook my head emphatically. 'It was just too hard. He just . . . upset me too much. I thank you for letting me know I can call him if I need to, and I really, really appreciate your telling me about Holly.'

Tara, flushed with the deserved pleasure of having done her good deed for the day, got back in her spanky-new Camaro. After folding her long self into the passenger seat, Claudine waved at me as Tara pulled away. I sat in my car for a moment longer, trying to remember where Holly Cleary lived. I thought I remembered her complaining about the closet size in her apartment, and that meant the Kingfisher Arms.

When I got to the U-shaped building on the southern approach to Bon Temps, I checked the mailboxes to discover Holly's apartment number. She was on the ground floor, in number 4. Holly had a five-year-old son, Cody. Holly and her best friend, Danielle Gray, had both gotten married right out of high school, and both had been divorced within five years. Danielle's mom was a great help to Danielle, but Holly was not so lucky. Her long-divorced parents had both moved away, and her grandmother had died in the Alzheimer's wing of the Renard Parish nursing home. Holly had dated Detective Andy Bellefleur for a few months, but nothing had come of it. Rumor had it that old Caroline Bellefleur, Andy's grandmother, had thought Holly wasn't 'good' enough for Andy. I had no opinion on that. Neither Holly nor Andy was on my shortlist of favorite people, though I definitely felt cooler toward Andy.

When Holly answered her door, I realized all of a sudden how much she'd changed over the past few weeks. For years, her hair had been dyed a dandelion yellow. Now it was matte black and spiked. Her ears had four piercings apiece. And I noticed her hipbones pushing at the thin denim of her aged jeans.

'Hey, Sookie,' she said, pleasantly enough. 'Tara asked me if I would talk to you, but I wasn't sure if you'd show up. Sorry about Jason. Come on in.'

The apartment was small, of course, and though it had been repainted recently, it showed evidence of years of heavy use. There was a living room-dining room-kitchen combo, with a breakfast bar separating the galley kitchen from the rest of the area. There were a few toys in a basket in the corner of the room, and there was a can of Pledge and a rag on the scarred coffee table. Holly had been cleaning.

'I'm sorry to interrupt,' I said.

'That's okay. Coke? Juice?'

'No, thanks. Where's Cody?'

'He went to stay with his dad,' she said, looking down at her hands. 'I drove him over the day after Christmas.'

'Where's his dad living?'

'David's living in Springhill. He just married this girl, Allie. She already had two kids. The little girl is Cody's age, and he just loves to play with her. It's always, "Shelley this", and "Shelley that".' Holly looked kind of bleak.

David Cleary was one of a large clan. His cousin Pharr had been in my grade all through school. For Cody's genes' sake, I hoped that David was more intelligent than Pharr, which would be real easy.

'I need to talk to you about something pretty personal, Holly.'

Holly looked surprised all over again. 'Well, we haven't exactly been on those terms, have we?' she said. 'You ask, and I'll decide whether to answer.'

I tried to frame what I was going to say – to keep secret what I needed to keep secret and ask of her what I needed without offending.

'You're a witch?' I said, embarrassed at using such a dramatic word.

'I'm more of a Wiccan.'

'Would you mind explaining the difference?' I met her eyes briefly, and then decided to focus on the dried flowers in the basket on top of the television. Holly thought I could read her mind only if I was looking into her eyes. (Like physical touching, eye contact does make the reading easier, but it certainly isn't necessary.)

'I guess not.' Her voice was slow, as if she were thinking as she spoke. 'You're not one to spread gossip.'

'Whatever you tell me, I won't share with anyone.' I met her eyes again, briefly.

'Okay,' she said. 'Well, if you're a witch, of course, you practice magic rituals.'

She was using 'you' in the general sense, I thought, because saying 'I' would mean too bold a confession.

'You draw from a power that most people never tap into. Being a witch isn't being wicked, or at least it isn't supposed to be. If you're a Wiccan, you follow a religion, a pagan religion. We follow the ways of the Mother, and we have our own calendar of holy days. You can be both a Wiccan and a witch; or more one, or more the other. It's very individualized. I practice a little witchcraft, but I'm more interested in the Wiccan life. We believe that your actions are okay if you don't hurt anyone else.'

Oddly, my first feeling was one of embarrassment, when I heard Holly tell me that she was a non-Christian. I'd never met anyone who didn't at least pretend to be a Christian or who didn't give lip-service to the basic Christian precepts. I was pretty sure there was a synagogue in Shreveport, but I'd never even met a Jew, to the best of my knowledge. I was certainly on a learning curve.

'I understand. Do you know lots of witches?'

'I know a few.' Holly nodded repeatedly, still avoiding my eyes.

I spotted an old computer on the rickety table in the corner. 'Do you have, like, a chat room online, or a bulletin board, or something?'

'Oh, sure.'

'Have you heard of a group of witches that's come into Shreveport lately?'

Holly's face became very serious. Her straight dark brows drew together in a frown. 'Tell me you're not involved with them,' she said.

'Not directly. But I know someone they've hurt, and I'm afraid they might've taken Jason.'

'Then he's in bad trouble,' she said bluntly. 'The woman who leads this group is out-and-out ruthless. Her brother is just as bad. That group, they're not like the rest of us. They're not trying to find a better way to live, or a path to get in touch with the natural world, or spells to increase their inner peace. They're Wiccans. They're evil.'

'Can you give me any clues about where I might track them down?' I was doing my best to keep my face in line. I could hear with my other sense that Holly was thinking that if the newly arrived coven had Jason, he'd be hurt badly, if not killed.

Holly, apparently in deep thought, looked out the front window of her apartment. She was afraid that they'd trace any information she gave me back to her, punish her – maybe through Cody. These weren't witches who believed in doing harm to no one else. These were witches whose lives were planned around the gathering of power of all kinds.

'They're all women?' I asked, because I could tell she was on the verge of resolving to tell me nothing.

'If you're thinking Jason would be able to charm them with his ways because he's such a looker, you can think again,' Holly told me, her face grim and somehow stripped down to basics. She wasn't trying for any effect; she wanted me to understand how dangerous these people were. 'There are some men, too. They're ... these aren't normal witches. I mean, they weren't even normal *people*.'

I was willing to believe that. I'd had to believe stranger things since the night Bill Compton had walked into Merlotte's Bar.

Holly spoke like she knew far more about this group of witches than I'd ever suspected ... more than the general background I'd hoped to glean from her. I prodded her a little. 'What makes them different?'

'They've had vampire blood.' Holly glanced to the side, as if she felt someone listening to her. The motion creeped me out. 'Witches – witches with a lot of power they're willing to use for evil – they're bad enough. Witches that strong who've also had vampire blood are ...

Sookie, you have no idea how dangerous they are. Some of them are Weres. Please, stay away from them.'

Werewolves? They were not only witches, but Weres? And they drank vampire blood? I was seriously scared. I didn't know how could you get any worse. 'Where are they?'

'Are you listening to me?'

'I am, but I have to know where they are!'

'They're in an old business not awful far from Pierre Bossier Mall,' she said, and I could see the picture of it in her head. She'd been there. She'd seen them. She had this all in her head, and I was getting a lot of it.

'Why were you there?' I asked, and she flinched.

'I was worried about talking to you,' Holly said, her voice angry. 'I shouldn't have even let you in. But I'd dated Jason . . . You're gonna get me killed, Sookie Stackhouse. Me and my boy.'

'No, I won't.'

'I was there because their leader sent out a call for all the witches in the area to have, like, a summit. It turned out that what she wanted to do was impose her will on all of us. Some of us were pretty impressed with her commitment and her power, but most of us smaller-town Wiccans, we didn't like her drug use – that's what drinking vampire blood amounts to – or her taste for the darker side of witchcraft. Now, that's all I want to say about it.'

'Thanks, Holly.' I tried to think of something I could tell her that would relieve her fear. But she wanted me to leave more than anything in the world, and I'd caused her enough upset. Holly's just letting me in the door had been a big concession, since she actually believed in my mind-reading ability. No matter what rumors they heard, people really wanted to believe that the contents of their heads were private, no matter what proof they had to the contrary.

I did myself.

I patted Holly on the shoulder as I left, but she didn't get up from the old couch. She stared at me with hopeless brown eyes, as if any moment someone was going to come in the door and cut off her head.

That look frightened me more than her words, more than her ideas, and I left the Kingfisher Arms as quickly as I could, trying to note the few people who saw me turn out of the parking lot. I didn't recognize any of them.

I wondered why the witches in Shreveport would want Jason, how they could have made a connection between the missing Eric and my brother. How could I approach them to find out? Would Pam and Chow help, or had they taken their own steps?

And whose blood had the witches been drinking?

Since vampires had made their presence known among us, nearly three years ago now, they'd become preyed upon in a new way. Instead of fearing getting staked through the heart by wanna-be Van Helsings, vampires dreaded modern entrepreneurs called Drainers. Drainers traveled in teams, singling out vampires by a variety of methods and binding them with silver chains (usually in a carefully planned ambush), then draining their blood into vials. Depending on the age of the vampire, a vial of blood could fetch from $200 to $400 on the black market. The effect of drinking this blood? Quite unpredictable, once the blood had left the vampire. I guess that was part of the attraction. Most commonly, for a few weeks, the drinker gained strength, visual acuity, a feeling of robust health, and enhanced attractiveness. It depended on the age of the drained vampire and the freshness of the blood.

Of course, those effects faded, unless you drank more blood.

A certain percentage of people who experienced drinking vampire blood could hardly wait to scratch up money for more. These blood junkies were extremely dangerous, of course. City police forces were glad to hire vampires to deal with them, since regular cops would simply get pulped.

Every now and then, a blood drinker simply went mad – sometimes in a quiet, gibbering kind of way, but sometimes spectacularly and murderously. There was no way to predict who would be stricken this way, and it could happen on the first drinking.

So there were men with glittering mad eyes in padded cells and there were electrifying movie stars who equally owed their condition to the Drainers. Draining was a hazardous job, of course. Sometimes the vampire got loose, with a very predictable result. A court in Florida had ruled this vampire retaliation justifiable homicide, in one celebrated case, because Drainers notoriously discarded their victims. They left a vampire, all but empty of blood, too weak to move, wherever the vamp happened to fall. The weakened vampire died when the sun came up, unless he had the good fortune to be discovered and helped to safety during the hours of darkness. It took years to recover from a draining, and that was years of help from other vamps. Bill had told me there were shelters for drained vamps, and that their location was kept very secret.

Witches with nearly the physical power of vampires – that seemed a very dangerous combination. I kept thinking of women when I thought of the coven that had moved into Shreveport, and I kept correcting myself. Men, Holly had said, were in the group.

I looked at the clock at the drive-through bank, and I saw it was just after noon. It would be full dark by a few minutes before six; Eric had gotten up a little earlier than that, at times. I could certainly go to Shreveport and come back by then. I couldn't think of another plan, and I just couldn't go home and sit and wait. Even wasting gas was better than going back to my house, though worry for Jason crawled up and down my spine. I could take the time to drop off the shotgun, but as long as it was unloaded and the shells were in a separate location, it should be legal enough to drive around with it.

For the first time in my life, I checked my rearview mirror to see if I was being followed. I am not up on spy techniques, but if someone was following me, I couldn't spot him. I stopped and got gas and an ICEE, just to see if anyone pulled into the gas station behind me, but no one did. That was real good, I decided, hoping that Holly was safe.

As I drove, I had time to review my conversation with Holly. I realized it was the first one I'd ever had with Holly in which Danielle's name had not come up once. Holly and Danielle had been joined at the hip since grade school. They probably had their periods at the same time. Danielle's parents, cradle members of the Free Will Church of God's Anointed, would have a fit if they knew, so it wasn't any wonder that Holly had been so discreet.

Our little town of Bon Temps had stretched its gates open wide enough to tolerate vampires, and gay people didn't have a very hard time of it anymore (kind of depending on how they expressed their sexual preference). However, I thought the gates might snap shut for Wiccans.

The peculiar and beautiful Claudine had told me that she was attracted to Bon Temps for its very strangeness. I wondered what else was out there, waiting to reveal itself.

Chapter 5

Carla Rodriguez my most promising lead came first. I'd looked up the old address I had for Dovie, with whom I'd exchanged the odd Christmas card. I found the house with a little difficulty. It was well away from the shopping areas that were my only normal stops in Shreveport. The houses were small and close together where Dovie lived, and some of them were in bad repair.

I felt a distinct thrill of triumph when Carla herself answered the door. She had a black eye, and she was hung-over, both signs that she'd had a big night the night before.

'Hey, Sookie,' she said, identifying me after a moment. 'What're you doing here? I was at Merlotte's last night, but I didn't see you there. You still working there?'

'I am. It was my night off.' Now that I was actually looking at Carla, I wasn't sure how to explain to her what I needed. I decided to be blunt. 'Listen, Jason's not at work this morning, and I kind of wondered if he might be here with you.'

'Honey, I got nothing against you, but Jason's the last man on earth I'd sleep with,' Carla said flatly. I stared at her, hearing that she was telling me the truth. 'I ain't gonna stick my hand in the fire twice, having gotten burnt the first time. I did look around the bar a little, thinking I might see him, but if I had, I'd have turned the other way.'

I nodded. That seemed all there was to say on the subject. We exchanged a few more polite sentences, and I chatted with Dovie, who had a toddler balanced on her hip, but then it was time for me to leave. My most promising lead had just evaporated in the length of two sentences.

Trying to suppress my desperation, I drove to a busy corner filling station and parked, to check my Shreveport map. It didn't take me long to figure out how to get from Dovie's suburb to the vampire bar.

Fangtasia was in a shopping center close to Toys 'R' Us. It opened at six P.M. year-round, but of course the vampires didn't show up until full dark, which depended on the season. The front of Fangtasia was painted flat gray, and the neon writing was all in red. 'Shreveport's Premier Vampire Bar,' read the newly added, smaller writing under the exotic script of the bar's name. I winced and looked away.

Two summers before, a small group of vamps from Oklahoma had tried to set up a rival bar in adjacent Bossier City. After one particularly hot, short August night, they'd never been seen again, and the building they'd been renovating had burned to the ground.

Tourists thought stories like this were actually amusing and colorful. It added to the thrill of ordering overpriced drinks (from human wait-resses dressed in trailing black 'vampire' outfits) while staring at real, honest-to-God, undead bloodsuckers. Eric made the Area Five vam-pires show up for this unappealing duty by giving them a set number of hours each week to present themselves at Fangtasia. Most of his underlings weren't enthusiastic about exhibiting themselves, but it did give them a chance to hook up with fang-bangers who actually yearned for the chance to be bitten. Such encounters didn't take place on the premises: Eric had rules about that. And so did the police department. The only legal biting that could take place between humans and vam-pires was between consenting adults, in private.

Automatically, I pulled around to the rear of the shopping center. Bill and I had almost always used the employee entrance. Back here, the door was just a gray door in a gray wall, with the name of the bar put on in stick-on letters from Wal-Mart. Right below that, a large, black, stenciled notice proclaimed STAFF ONLY. I lifted my hand to knock, and then I realized I could see that the inner dead bolt had not been employed.

The door was unlocked.

This was really, really bad.

Though it was broad daylight, the hair on the back of my neck stood up. Abruptly, I wished I had Bill at my back. I wasn't missing his tender love, either. It's probably a bad indicator of your lifestyle when you miss your ex-boyfriend because he's absolutely lethal.

Though the public face of the shopping center was fairly busy, the service side was deserted. The silence was crawling with possibilities, and none of them was pleasant. I leaned my forehead against the cold gray door. I decided to get back in my old car and get the hell out of there, which would have been amazingly smart.

And I would have gone, if I hadn't heard the moaning.

Even then, if I'd been able to spot a pay phone, I would've just called 911 and stayed outside until someone official showed up. But there wasn't one in sight, and I couldn't stand the possibility that someone needed my help real bad, and I'd withheld it because I was chicken.

There was a heavy garbage can right by the back door, and after I'd yanked the door open – standing aside for a second to avoid anything that might dart out – I maneuvered the can to hold the door ajar. I had goose bumps all over my arms as I stepped inside.

Windowless Fangtasia requires electric light, twenty-four/seven. Since none of these lights were on, the interior was just a dark pit. Winter daylight extended weakly down the hall that led to the bar proper. On the right were the doors to Eric's office and the book-keeper's room. On the left was the door to the large storeroom, which also contained the employee bathroom. This hall ended in a heavy door to discourage any fun lovers from penetrating to the back of the club. This door, too, was open, for the first time in my memory. Beyond it lay the black silent cavern of the bar. I wondered if anything was sitting at those tables or huddled in those booths.

I was holding my breath so I could detect the least little noise. After a few seconds, I heard a scraping movement and another sound of pain, coming from the storeroom. Its door was slightly ajar. I took four silent steps to that door. My heart was pounding all the way up in my throat as I reached into the darkness to flip the light switch.

The glare made me blink.

Belinda, the only half-intelligent fang-banger I'd ever met, was lying on the storeroom floor in a curiously contorted position. Her legs were bent double, her heels pressed against her hips. There was no blood – in fact, no visible mark – on her. Apparently, she was having a giant and perpetual leg cramp.

I knelt beside Belinda, my eyes darting glances in all directions. I saw no other movement in the room, though its corners were obscured with stacks of liquor cartons and a coffin that was used as a prop in a show the vampires sometimes put on for special parties. The employee bathroom door was shut.

'Belinda,' I whispered. 'Belinda, look at me.'

Belinda's eyes were red and swollen behind their glasses, and her cheeks were wet with tears. She blinked and focused on my face.

'Are they still here?' I asked, knowing she'd understand that I meant 'the people who did this to you'.

'Sookie,' she said hoarsely. Her voice was weak, and I wondered how long she'd lain there waiting for help. 'Oh, thank God. Tell Master Eric we tried to hold them off.' Still role-playing, you notice, even in her agony: 'Tell our chieftain we fought to the death' – you know the kind of thing.

'Who'd you try to hold off?' I asked sharply.

'The witches. They came in last night after we'd closed, after Pam and Chow had gone. Just Ginger and me . . .'

'What did they want?' I had time to notice that Belinda was still wearing her filmy black waitress outfit with the slit up the long skirt, and there were still puncture marks painted on her neck.

'They wanted to know where we'd put Master Eric. They seemed to think they'd done . . . something to him, and that we'd hidden him.' During her long pause, her face contorted, and I could tell she was in terrible pain, but I couldn't tell what was wrong with her. 'My legs,' she moaned. 'Oh . . .'

'But you didn't know, so you couldn't tell them.'

'I would never betray our master.'

And Belinda was the one with sense.

'Was anyone here besides Ginger, Belinda?' But she was so deep into a spasm of suffering that she couldn't answer. Her whole body was rigid with pain, that low moan tearing out of her throat again.

I called 911 from Eric's office, since I knew the location of the phone there. The room had been tossed, and some frisky witch had spray painted a big red pentagram on one of the walls. Eric was going to love that.

I returned to Belinda to tell her the ambulance was coming. 'What's wrong with your legs?' I asked, scared of the answer.

'They made the muscle in the back of my legs pull up, like it was half as long . . .' And she began moaning again. 'It's like one of those giant cramps you get when you're pregnant.'

It was news to me that Belinda had ever been pregnant.

'Where's Ginger?' I asked, when her pain seemed to have ebbed a little.

She was in the bathroom.'

Ginger, a pretty strawberry blonde, as dumb as a rock, was still there. I don't think they'd meant to kill her. But they'd put a spell on her legs like they'd done to Belinda's, it looked like; her legs were drawn up double in the same peculiar and painful way, even in death. Ginger had been standing in front of the sink when she'd crumpled, and her head had hit the lip of the sink on her way down. Her eyes were sightless and her hair was matted with some clotted blood that had oozed from the depression in her temple.

There was nothing to be done. I didn't even touch Ginger; she was so obviously dead. I didn't say anything about her to Belinda, who was in too much agony to understand, anyway. She had a couple more moments of lucidity before I took off. I asked her where to find Pam and Chow so I could warn them, and Belinda said they just showed up at the bar when it became dark.

She also said the woman who'd worked the spell was a witch named Hallow, and she was almost six feet tall, with short brown hair and a black design painted on her face.

That should make her easy to identify.

'She told me she was as strong as a vampire, too,' Belinda gasped. 'You see . . .' Belinda pointed beyond me. I whirled, expecting an attack. Nothing that alarming happened, but what I saw was almost as disturbing as what I'd imagined. It was the handle of the dolly the staff used to wheel cases of drinks around. The long metal handle had been twisted into a U.

'I know Master Eric will kill her when he returns,' Belinda said falteringly after a minute, the words coming out in jagged bursts because of the pain.

'Sure he will,' I said stoutly. I hesitated, feeling crummy beyond words. 'Belinda, I have to go because I don't want the police to keep me here for questioning. Please don't mention my name. Just say a passerby heard you, okay?'

'Where's Master Eric? Is he really missing?'

'I have no idea,' I said, forced to lie. 'I have to get out of here.'

'Go,' Belinda said, her voice ragged. 'We're lucky you came in at all.'

I had to get out of there. I knew nothing about what had happened at the bar, and being questioned for hours would cost me time I couldn't afford, with my brother missing.

Back in my car and on my way out of the shopping center, I passed the police cars and the ambulance as they headed in. I'd wiped the doorknob clean of my fingerprints. Other than that, I couldn't think of what I'd touched and what I hadn't, no matter how carefully I reviewed my actions. There'd be a million prints there, anyway; gosh, it was a bar.

After a minute, I realized I was just driving with no direction. I was overwhelmingly rattled. I pulled over into yet another filling station parking lot and looked at the pay phone longingly. I could call Alcide, ask him if he knew where Pam and Chow spent their daytime hours. Then I could go there and leave a message or something, warn them about what had happened.

I made myself take some deep breaths and think hard about what I was doing. It was extremely unlikely that the vamps would give a Were the address of their daytime resting place. This was not information that vampires passed out to anyone who asked. Alcide had no love for the vamps of Shreveport, who'd held his dad's gambling debt over Alcide's head until he complied with their wishes. I knew that if I called, he'd come, because he was just a nice guy. But his involvement could have serious consequences for his family and his business.

However, if this Hallow really *was* a triple threat – a Were witch who drank vampire blood – she was very dangerous, and the Weres of Shreveport should know about her. Relieved I'd finally made up my mind, I found a pay phone that worked, and I got Alcide's card out of its slot in my billfold.

Alcide was in his office, which was a miracle. I described my location, and he gave me directions on how to reach his office. He offered to come get me, but I didn't want him to think I was an utter idiot.

I used a calling card to phone Bud Dearborn's office, to hear there was no news about Jason.

Following Alcide's directions very carefully, I arrived at Herveaux and Son in about twenty minutes. It was not too far off I–30, on the eastern edge of Shreveport, actually on my way back to Bon Temps.

The Herveauxes owned the building, and their surveying company was its sole occupant. I parked in front of the low brick building. At the rear, I spotted Alcide's Dodge Ram pickup in the large parking lot for employees. The one in front, for visitors, was much smaller. It was clear to see that the Herveauxes mostly went to their clients, rather than the clients coming to them.

Feeling shy and more than a little nervous, I pushed open the front door and glanced around. There was a desk just inside the door, with a waiting area opposite. Beyond a half wall, I could see five or six workstations, three of them occupied. The woman behind the desk was in charge of routing phone calls, too. She had short dark brown hair that was carefully cut and styled, she was wearing a beautiful sweater, and she had wonderful makeup. She was probably in her forties, but it hadn't lessened her impressiveness.

'I'm here to see Alcide,' I said, feeling embarrassed and self-conscious.

'Your name?' She was smiling at me, but she looked a little crisp around the edges, as if she didn't quite approve of a young and obviously unfashionable woman showing up at Alcide's workplace. I was wearing a bright blue-and-yellow knit top with long sleeves under my old thigh-length blue cloth coat, and aged blue jeans, and Reeboks. I'd been worried about finding my brother when I dressed, not about standing inspection by the Fashion Police.

'Stackhouse,' I said.

'Ms Stackhouse here to see you,' Crispy said into an intercom.

'Oh, good!' Alcide sounded very happy, which was a relief.

Crispy was saying into the intercom, 'Shall I send her back?' when Alcide burst through the door behind and to the left of her desk.

'Sookie!' he said, and he beamed at me. He stopped for a second, as if he couldn't quite decide what he should do, and then he hugged me.

I felt like I was smiling all over. I hugged him back. I was so happy to see him! I thought he looked wonderful. Alcide is a tall man, with black hair that apparently can't be tamed with a brush and comb, and he has a broad face and green eyes.

We'd dumped a body together, and that creates a bond.

He pulled gently on my braid. 'Come on back,' he said in my ear, since Ms Crispy was looking on with an indulgent smile. I was sure the indulgent part was for Alcide's benefit. In fact, I knew it was, because she was thinking I didn't look chic enough or polished enough to date a Herveaux, and she didn't think Alcide's dad (with whom she'd been sleeping for two years) would appreciate Alcide taking up with a no-account girl like me. Oops, one of those things I didn't want to know. Obviously I wasn't shielding myself hard enough. Bill had made me practice, and now that I didn't see him anymore, I was getting sloppy. It wasn't entirely my fault; Ms Crispy was a clear broadcaster.

Alcide was not, since he's a werewolf.

Alcide ushered me down a hall, which was nicely carpeted and hung with neutral pictures – insipid landscapes and garden scenes – which I figured some decorator (or maybe Ms Crispy) had chosen. He showed me into his office, which had his name on the door. It was a big room, but not a grand or elegant one, because it was just chockfull of work stuff – plans and papers and hard hats and office equipment. Very utilitarian. A fax machine was humming, and set beside a stack of forms there was a calculator displaying figures.

'You're busy. I shouldn't have called,' I said, instantly cowed.

'Are you kidding? Your call is the best thing that's happened to me all day!' He sounded so sincere that I had to smile again. 'There's something I have to say to you, something I didn't tell you when

I dropped your stuff off after you got hurt.' After I'd been beaten up by hired thugs. 'I felt so bad about it that I've put off coming to Bon Temps to talk to you face-to-face.'

Omigod, he'd gotten back with his nasty rotten fiancée, Debbie Pelt. I was getting Debbie's name from his brain.

'Yes?' I said, trying to look calm and open. He reached down and took my hand between his own large palms.

'I owe you a huge apology.'

Okay, that was unexpected. 'How would that be?' I asked, looking up at him with narrowed eyes. I'd come here to spill my guts, but it was Alcide who was spilling his instead.

'That last night, at Club Dead,' he began, 'when you needed my help and protection the most, I . . .'

I knew what was coming now. Alcide had changed into a wolf rather than staying human and helping me out of the bar after I'd gotten staked. I put my free hand across his mouth. His skin was so warm. If you're used to touching vampires, you'll know just how roasty a regular human can feel, and a Were even more so, since they run a few degrees hotter.

I felt my pulse quicken, and I knew he could tell, too. Animals are good at sensing excitement. 'Alcide,' I said, 'never bring that up. You couldn't help it, and it all turned out okay, anyway.' Well, more or less – other than my heart breaking at Bill's perfidy.

'Thanks for being so understanding,' he said, after a pause during which he looked at me intently. 'I think I would have felt better if you'd been mad.' I believe he was wondering whether I was just putting a brave face on it or if I was truly sincere. I could tell he had an impulse to kiss me, but he wasn't sure if I'd welcome such a move or even allow it.

Well, I didn't know what I'd do, either, so I didn't give myself the chance to find out.

'Okay, I'm furious with you, but I'm concealing it real well,' I said. He relaxed all over when he saw me smile, though it might be the last smile we'd share all day. 'Listen, your office in the middle of day isn't a good time and place to tell you the things I need to tell you,' I said. I spoke very levelly, so he'd realize I wasn't coming on to him. Not only did I just plain old like Alcide, I thought he was one hell of a man – but until I was sure he was through with Debbie Pelt, he was off my list of guys I wanted to be around. The last I'd heard of Debbie, she'd been engaged to another shifter, though even that hadn't ended her emotional involvement with Alcide.

I was not going to get in the middle of that – not with the grief caused by Bill's infidelity still weighing heavily on my own heart.

'Let's go to the Applebee's down the road and have some coffee,' he suggested. Over the intercom, he told Crispy he was leaving. We went out through the back door.

It was about two o'clock by then, and the restaurant was almost empty. Alcide asked the young man who seated us to put us in a booth as far away from anyone else as we could get. I scooted down the bench on one side, expecting Alcide to take the other, but he slid in beside me. 'If you want to tell secrets, this is as close as we can get,' he said.

We both ordered coffee, and Alcide asked the server to bring a small pot. I inquired after his dad while the server was puttering around, and Alcide inquired after Jason. I didn't answer, because the mention of my brother's name was enough to make me feel close to crying. When our coffee had come and the young man had left, Alcide said, 'What's up?'

I took a deep breath, trying to decide where to begin. 'There's a bad witch coven in Shreveport,' I said flatly. 'They drink vampire blood, and at least a few of them are shifters.'

It was Alcide's turn to take a deep breath.

I help up a hand, indicating there was more to come. 'They're moving into Shreveport to take over the vampires' financial kingdom. They put a curse or a hex or something on Eric, and it took away his memory. They raided Fangtasia, trying to discover the day resting place of the vampires. They put some kind of spell on two of the waitresses, and one of them is in the hospital. The other one is dead.'

Alcide was already sliding his cell phone from his pocket.

'Pam and Chow have hidden Eric at my house, and I have to get back before dark to take care of him. And Jason is missing. I don't know who took him or where he is or if he's . . .' *Alive*. But I couldn't say the word.

Alcide's deep breath escaped in a whoosh, and he sat staring at me, the phone in his hand. He couldn't decide whom to call first. I didn't blame him.

'I don't like Eric being at your house,' he said. 'It puts you in danger.'

I was touched that his first thought was for my safety. 'Jason asked for a lot of money for doing it, and Pam and Chow agreed,' I said, embarrassed.

'But Jason isn't there to take the heat, and you are.'

Unanswerably true. But to give Jason credit, he certainly hadn't planned it that way. I told Alcide about the blood on the dock. 'Might be a red herring,' he said. 'If the type matches Jason's, then you can worry.' He took a sip of his coffee, his eyes focused inward. 'I've got to make some calls,' he said.

'Alcide, are you the packmaster for Shreveport?'

'No, no, I'm nowhere near important enough.'

That didn't seem possible to me, and I said as much. He took my hand.

'Packmasters are usually older than me,' he said. 'And you have to be really tough. Really, really tough.'

'Do you have to fight to get to be packmaster?'

'No, you get elected, but the candidates have to be very strong and clever. There's a sort of – well, you have a test you have to take.'

'Written? Oral?' Alcide looked relieved when he saw I was smiling. 'More like an endurance test?' I said.

He nodded. 'More like.'

'Don't you think your packmaster should know about this?'

'Yes. What else?'

'Why would they be doing this? Why pick on Shreveport? If they have that much going for them, the vampire blood and the will to do really bad things, why not set up shop in a more prosperous city?'

'That's a real good question.' Alcide was thinking hard. His green eyes squinted when he thought. 'I've never heard of a witch having this much power. I never heard of a witch being a shifter. I tend to think it's the first time this has ever happened.'

'The first time?'

'That a witch has ever tried to take control of a city, tried to take away the assets of the city's supernatural community,' he said.

'How do witches stand in the supernatural pecking order?'

'Well, they're humans who stay human.' He shrugged. 'Usually, the Supes feel like witches are just wanna-bes. The kind you have to keep an eye on, since they practice magic and we're magical creatures, but still . . .'

'Not a big threat?'

'Right. Looks like we might have to rethink that. Their leader takes vampire blood. Does she drain them herself?' He punched in a number and held the phone to his ear.

'I don't know.'

'And what does she shift into?' Shape-shifters had a choice, but there was one animal each shifter had an affinity for, her habitual animal. A shape-shifter could call herself a 'were-lynx' or a 'were-bat,' if she was out of hearing range of a werewolf. Werewolves objected very strenuously to any other two-natured creatures who termed themselves 'Were.'

'Well, she's . . . like you,' I said. The Weres considered themselves the kings of the two-natured community. They only changed into one animal, and it was the best. The rest of the two-natured community responded by calling the wolves thugs.

'Oh, no.' Alcide was appalled. At that moment, his packmaster answered the phone.

'Hello, this is Alcide.' A silence. 'I'm sorry to bother you when you were busy in the yard. Something important's come up. I need to see you as soon as possible.' Another silence. 'Yes, sir. With your permission, I'll bring someone with me.' After a second or two, Alcide pressed a button to end the conversation. 'Surely Bill knows where Pam and Chow live?' he asked me.

'I'm sure he does, but he's not here to tell me about it.' If he would.

'And where is he?' Alcide's voice was deceptively calm.

'He's in Peru.'

I'd been looking down at my napkin, which I'd pleated into a fan.

I glanced up at the man next to me to see him staring down at me with an expression of incredulity.

'He's gone? He left you there alone?'

'Well, he didn't know anything was going to happen,' I said, trying not to sound defensive, and then I thought, *What am I saying?* 'Alcide, I haven't seen Bill since I came back from Jackson, except when he came over to tell me he was leaving the country.'

'But she told me you were back with Bill,' Alcide said in a very strange voice.

'Who told you that?'

'Debbie. Who else?'

I'm afraid my reaction was not very flattering. 'And you believed Debbie?'

'She said she'd stopped by Merlotte's on her way over to see me, and she'd seen you and Bill acting very, ah, friendly while she was there.'

'And you *believed* her?' Maybe if I kept shifting the emphasis, he'd tell me he was just joking.

Alcide was looking sheepish now, or as sheepish as a werewolf can look.

'Okay, that was dumb,' he admitted. 'I'll deal with her.'

'Right.' Pardon me if I didn't sound very convinced. I'd heard that before.

'Bill's really in Peru?'

'As far as I know.'

'And you're alone in the house with Eric?'

'Eric doesn't know he's Eric.'

'He doesn't remember his identity?'

'Nope. He doesn't remember his character, either, apparently.'

'That's a good thing,' Alcide said darkly. He had never viewed Eric with any sense of humor, as I did. I'd always been leery of Eric, but I'd appreciated his mischief, his single-mindedness, and his flair. If you could say a vampire had joie de vivre, Eric had it in spades.

'Let's go see the packmaster now,' Alcide said, obviously in a much grimmer mood. We slid out of the booth after he'd paid for the coffee, and without phoning in to work ('No point being the boss if I can't vanish from time to time'), he helped me up into his truck and we took off back into Shreveport. I was sure Ms Crispy would assume we'd checked into a motel or gone to Alcide's apartment, but that was better than Ms Crispy finding out her boss was a werewolf.

As we drove, Alcide told me that the packmaster was a retired Air Force colonel, formerly stationed at Barksdale Air Force Base in Bossier City, which flowed into Shreveport. Colonel Flood's only child, a daughter, had married a local, and Colonel Flood had settled in the city to be close to his grandchildren.

'His wife is a Were, too?' I asked. If Mrs Flood was also a Were, their daughter would be, too. If Weres can get through the first few months, they live a good long while, barring accidents.

'She was; she passed away a few months ago.'

Alcide's packmaster lived in a modest neighborhood of ranch-style homes on smallish lots. Colonel Flood was picking up pinecones in his front yard. It seemed a very domestic and peaceable thing for a prominent werewolf to be doing. I'd pictured him in my head in an Air Force uniform, but of course he was wearing regular civilian outdoor clothes. His thick hair was white and cut very short, and he had a mustache that must have been trimmed with a ruler, it was so exact.

The colonel must have been curious after Alcide's phone call, but he asked us to come inside in a calm sort of way. He patted Alcide on the back a lot; he was very polite to me.

The house was as neat as his mustache. It could have passed inspection.

'Can I get you a drink? Coffee? Hot chocolate? Soda?' The colonel gestured toward his kitchen as if there were a servant standing there alert for our orders.

'No, thank you,' I said, since I was awash with Applebee's coffee. Colonel Flood insisted we sit in the company living room, which was an awkwardly narrow rectangle with a formal dining area at one end. Mrs Flood had liked porcelain birds. She had liked them a lot. I wondered how the grandchildren fared in this room, and I kept my hands tucked in my lap for fear I'd jostle something.

'So, what can I do for you?' Colonel Flood asked Alcide. 'Are you seeking permission to marry?'

'Not today,' Alcide said with a smile. I looked down at the floor to keep my expression to myself. 'My friend Sookie has some information that she shared with me. It's very important.' His smile died on the vine. 'She needs to relate what she knows to you.'

'And why do I need to listen?'

I understood that he was asking Alcide who I was – that if he was obliged to listen to me, he needed to know my bona fides. But Alcide was offended on my behalf.

'I wouldn't have brought her if it wasn't important. I wouldn't have introduced her to you if I wouldn't give my blood for her.'

I wasn't real certain what that meant, but I was interpreting it to assume Alcide was vouching for my truthfulness and offering to pay in some way if I proved false. Nothing was simple in the supernatural world.

'Let's hear your story, young woman,' said the colonel briskly.

I related all I'd told Alcide, trying to leave out the personal bits.

'Where is this coven staying?' he asked me, when I was through. I told him what I'd seen through Holly's mind.

'Not enough information,' Flood said crisply. 'Alcide, we need the trackers.'

'Yes, sir.' Alcide's eyes were gleaming at the thought of action.

'I'll call them. Everything I've heard is making me rethink something odd that happened last night. Adabelle didn't come to the planning committee meeting.'

Alcide looked startled. 'That's not good.'

They were trying to be cryptic in front of me, but I could read what was passing between the two shifters without too much difficulty. Flood and Alcide were wondering if their – hmmm, vice president? – Adabelle had missed the meeting for some innocent reason, or if the new coven had somehow inveigled her into joining them against her own pack.

'Arabelle has been chafing against the pack leadership for some time,' Colonel Flood told Alcide, with the ghost of a smile on his thin lips. 'I had hoped, when she got elected my second, that she'd consider that concession enough.'

From the bits of information I could glean from the packmaster's mind, the Shreveport pack seemed to be heavily on the patriarchal side. To Adabelle, a modern woman, Colonel Flood's leadership was stifling.

'A new regime might appeal to her,' Colonel Flood said, after a perceptible pause. 'If the invaders learned anything about our pack, it's Adabelle they'd approach.'

'I don't think Adabelle would ever betray the pack, no matter how unhappy she is with the status quo,' Alcide said. He sounded very sure. 'But if she didn't come to the meeting last night, and you can't raise her by phone this morning, I'm concerned.'

'I wish you'd go check on Adabelle while I alert the pack to action,' Colonel Flood suggested. 'If your friend wouldn't mind.'

Maybe his friend would like to get her butt back to Bon Temps and see to her paying guest. Maybe his friend would like to be searching for her brother. Though truly, I could not think of a single thing to do that would further the search for Jason, and it would be at least two hours before Eric rose.

Alcide said, 'Colonel, Sookie is not a pack member and she shouldn't have to shoulder pack responsibilities. She has her own troubles, and she's gone out of her way to let us know about a big problem we didn't even realize we had. We should have known. Someone in our pack hasn't been honest with us.'

Colonel Flood's face drew in on itself as if he'd swallowed a live eel. 'You're right about that,' he said. 'Thank you, Miss Stackhouse, for taking the time to come to Shreveport and to tell Alcide about our problem . . . which we should have known.'

I nodded to him in acknowledgment.

'And I think you're right, Alcide. One of us must have known about the presence of another pack in the city.'

'I'll call you about Adabelle,' Alcide said.

The colonel picked up the phone and consulted a red leather book before he dialed. He glanced sideways at Alcide. 'No answer at her shop.' He had as much warmth radiating from him as a little space heater. Since Colonel Flood kept his house about as cold as the great outdoors, the heat was quite welcome.

'Sookie should be named a friend of the pack.'

I could tell that was more than a recommendation. Alcide was saying something quite significant, but he sure wasn't going to explain. I was getting a little tired of the elliptical conversations going on around me.

'Excuse me, Alcide, Colonel,' I said as politely as I could. 'Maybe Alcide could run me back to my car? Since you all seem to have plans to carry out.'

'Of course,' the colonel said, and I could read that he was glad to be getting me out of the way. 'Alcide, I'll see you back here in, what? Forty minutes or so? We'll talk about it then.'

Alcide glanced at his watch and reluctantly agreed. 'I might stop by Adabelle's house while I'm taking Sookie to her car,' he said, and the colonel nodded, as if that were only pro forma.

'I don't know why Adabelle isn't answering the phone at work, and I don't believe she'd go over to the coven,' Alcide explained when we were back in his truck. 'Adabelle lives with her mother, and they don't get along too well. But we'll check there first. Adabelle's Flood's second in command, and she's also our best tracker.'

'What can the trackers do?'

'They'll go to Fangtasia and try to follow the scent trail the witches left there. That'll take them to the witches' lair. If they lose the scent, maybe we can call in help from the Shreveport covens. They have to be as worried as we are.'

'At Fangtasia, I'm afraid any scent might be obscured by all the emergency people,' I said regretfully. That would have been something to watch, a Were tracking through the city. 'And just so you know, Hallow has contacted all the witches hereabouts already. I talked to a Wiccan in Bon Temps who'd been called in to Shreveport to meet with Hallow's bunch.'

'This is bigger than I thought, but I'm sure the pack can handle it.' Alcide sounded quite confident.

Alcide backed the truck out of the colonel's driveway, and we began making our way through Shreveport once again. I was seeing more of the city this day than I'd seen in my whole life.

'Whose idea was it for Bill to go to Peru?' Alcide asked me suddenly.

'I don't know.' I was startled and puzzled. 'I think it was his queen's.'

'But he didn't tell you that directly.'

'No.'

'He might have been ordered to go.'

'I suppose.'

'Who had the power to do that?' Alcide asked, as if the answer would enlighten me.

'Eric, of course.' Since Eric was sheriff of Area Five. 'And then the queen.' That would be Eric's boss, the queen of Louisiana. Yeah, I know. It's dumb. But the vampires thought they were a marvel of modern organization.

'And now Bill's gone, and Eric's staying at your house.' Alcide's voice was coaxing me to reach an obvious conclusion.

'You think that Eric staged this whole thing? You think he ordered Bill out of the country, had witches invade Shreveport, had them curse him, began running half-naked out in the freezing cold when he supposed I might be near, and then just hoped I'd take him in and that Pam and Chow and my brother would talk to each other to arrange Eric's staying with me?'

Alcide looked properly flattened. 'You mean you'd thought of this?'

'Alcide, I'm not educated, but I'm not dumb.' Try getting educated when you can read the minds of all your classmates, not to mention your teacher. But I read a lot, and I've read lots of good stuff. Of course, now I read mostly mysteries and romances. So I've learned many curious odds and ends, and I have a great vocabulary. 'But the fact is, Eric would hardly go to this much trouble to get me to go to bed with him. Is that what you're thinking?' Of course, I knew it was. Were or not, I could see that much.

'Put that way ...' But Alcide still didn't look satisfied. Of course, this was the man who had believed Debbie Pelt when she said that I was definitely back with Bill.

I wondered if I could get some witch to cast a truth spell on Debbie Pelt, whom I despised because she had been cruel to Alcide, insulted me grievously, burned a hole in my favorite wrap and – oh – tried to kill me by proxy. Also, she had stupid hair.

Alcide wouldn't know an honest Debbie if she came up and bit him in the ass, though backbiting was a specialty of the real Debbie.

If Alcide had known Bill and I had parted, would he have come by? Would one thing have led to another?

Well, *sure* it would have. And there I'd be, stuck with a guy who'd take the word of Debbie Pelt.

I glanced over at Alcide and sighed. This man was just about perfect in many respects. I liked the way he looked, I understood the way he thought, and he treated me with great consideration and respect. Sure, he was a werewolf, but I could give up a couple of nights of month. True, according to Alcide it would be difficult for me to carry his baby to term, but it was at least possible. Pregnancy wasn't part of the picture with a vampire.

Whoa. Alcide hadn't offered to father my babies, and he was still seeing Debbie. What had happened to her engagement to the Clausen guy?

With the less noble side of my character – assuming my character had a noble side – I hoped that someday soon Alcide would see Debbie for the bitch she truly was, and that he'd finally take the knowledge to heart. Whether, consequently, Alcide turned to me or not, he deserved better than Debbie Pelt.

Adabelle Yancy and her mother lived in a cul-de-sac in an upper-middle-class neighborhood that wasn't too far from Fangtasia. The house was on a rolling lawn that raised it higher than the street, so the driveway mounted and went to the rear of the property. I thought Alcide might park on the street and we'd go up the brick walkway to the front door, but he seemed to want to get the truck out of sight. I scanned the cul-de-sac, but I didn't see anyone at all, much less anyone watching the house for visitors.

Attached to the rear of the house at a right angle, the three-car garage was neat as a pin. You would think cars were never parked there, that the gleaming Subaru had just strayed into the area. We climbed out of the truck.

'That's Adabelle's mother's car.' Alcide was frowning. 'She started a bridal shop. I bet you've heard of it – Verena Rose. Verena's retired from working there full-time. She drops in just often enough to make Adabelle crazy.'

I'd never been to the shop, but brides of any claim to prominence in the area made a point of shopping there. It must be a real profitable store. The brick home was in excellent shape, and no more than twenty years old. The yard was edged, raked, and landscaped.

When Alcide knocked at the back door, it flew open. The woman who stood revealed in the opening was as put-together and neat as the house and yard. Her steel-colored hair was in a neat roll on the back of her head, and she was in a dull olive suit and low-heeled brown pumps. She looked from Alcide to me and didn't find what she was seeking. She pushed open the glass storm door.

'Alcide, how nice to see you,' she lied desperately. This was a woman in deep turmoil.

Alcide gave her a long look. 'We have trouble, Verena.'

If her daughter was a member of the pack, Verena herself was a werewolf. I looked at the woman curiously, and she seemed like one of the more fortunate friends of my grandmother's. Verena Rose Yancy was an attractive woman in her late sixties, blessed with a secure income and her own home. I could not imagine this woman down on all fours loping across a field.

And it was obvious that Verena didn't give a damn what trouble Alcide had. 'Have you seen my daughter?' she asked, and she waited for his answer with terror in her eyes. 'She can't have betrayed the pack.'

'No,' Alcide said. 'But the packmaster sent us to find her. She missed a pack officers' meeting last night.'

'She called me from the shop last night. She said she had an unexpected appointment with a stranger who'd called the shop right at closing time.' The woman literally wrung her hands. 'I thought maybe she was meeting that witch.'

'Have you heard from her since?' I said, in the gentlest voice I could manage.

'I went to bed last night mad at her,' Verena said, looking directly at me for the first time. 'I thought she'd decided to spend the night with one of her friends. One of her *girl* friends,' she explained, looking at me with eyebrows arched, so I'd get her drift. I nodded. 'She never would tell me ahead of time, she'd just say, "Expect me when you see me", or "I'll meet you at the shop tomorrow morning", or something.' A shudder rippled through Verena's slim body. 'But she hasn't come home and I can't get an answer at the shop.'

'Was she supposed to open the shop today?' Alcide asked.

'No, Wednesday's our closed day, but she always goes in to work on the books and get paperwork out of the way. She always does,' Verena repeated.

'Why don't Alcide and I drive over there and check the shop for you?' I said gently. 'Maybe she left a note.' This was not a woman you patted on the arm, so I didn't make that natural gesture, but I did push the glass door shut so she'd understand she had to stay there and she shouldn't come with us. She understood all too clearly.

Verena Rose's Bridal and Formal Shop was located in an old home on a block of similarly converted two-story houses. The building had been renovated and maintained as beautifully as the Yancys' residence, and I wasn't surprised it had such cachet. The white-painted brick, the dark green shutters, the glossy black ironwork of the railings on the steps, and the brass details on the door all spoke of elegance and attention to detail. I could see that if you had aspirations to class, this is where you'd come to get your wedding gear.

Set a little back from the street, with parking behind the store, the building featured one large bay window in front. In this window stood a faceless mannequin wearing a shining brown wig. Her arms were gracefully bent to hold a stunning bouquet. Even from the truck, I could see that the bridal dress, with its long embroidered train, was absolutely spectacular.

We parked in the driveway without pulling around back, and I jumped out of the pickup. Together we took the brick sidewalk that led from the drive to the front door, and as we got closer, Alcide cursed. For a moment, I imagined some kind of bug infestation had gotten into the store window and landed on the snowy dress. But after that moment, I knew the dark flecks were surely spatters of blood.

The blood had sprayed onto the white brocade and dried there. It

was as if the mannequin had been wounded, and for a crazy second
I wondered. I'd seen a lot of impossible things in the past few months.

'Adabelle,' Alcide said, as if he was praying.

We were standing at the bottom of the steps leading up to the front
porch, staring into the bay window. The CLOSED sign was hanging in
the middle of the glass oval inset in the door, and venetian blinds were
closed behind it There were no live brainwaves emanating from that
house. I had taken the time to check. I'd discovered, the hard way, that
checking was a good idea.

'Dead things,' Alcide said, his face raised to the cold breeze, his eyes
shut to help him concentrate. 'Dead things inside and out.'

I took hold of the curved ironwork handrail with my left hand and
went up one step. I glanced around. My eyes came to rest on something
in the flowerbed under the bay window, something pale that stood out
against the pine bark mulch. I nudged Alcide, and I pointed silently
with my free right hand.

Lying by a pruned-back azalea, there was another hand – an
unattached extra. I felt a shudder run through Alcide's body as he
comprehended what he saw. There was that moment when you tried
to recognize it as anything but what it was.

'Wait here,' Alcide said, his voice thick and hoarse.

That was just fine with me.

But when he opened the unlocked front door to enter the shop,
I saw what lay on the floor just beyond. I had to swallow a scream.

It was lucky Alcide had his cell phone. He called Colonel Flood, told
him what had happened, and asked him to go over to Mrs Yancy's
house. Then he called the police. There was just no way around it.
This was a busy area, and there was a good chance someone had
noticed us going to the front door.

It was surely a day for finding bodies – for me, and for the Shreveport
police department. I knew there were some vampire cops on the force,
but of course the vamps had to work the night shift, so we spoke to
regular old human cops. There wasn't a Were or a shifter among 'em,
not even a telepathic human. All these police officers were regular
people who thought we were borderline suspicious.

'Why did you stop by here, buddy?' asked Detective Coughlin, who had brown hair, a weathered face, and a beer belly one of the Clydesdales would've been proud of.

Alcide looked surprised. He hadn't thought this far, which wasn't too amazing. I hadn't known Adabelle when she was alive, and I hadn't stepped inside the bridal shop as he had. I hadn't sustained the worst shock. It was up to me to pick up the reins.

'It was my idea, Detective,' I said instantly. 'My grandmother, who died last year? She always told me, "If you need a wedding dress, Sookie, you go to Verena Rose's for it". I didn't think to call ahead and check to see if they were open today.'

'So, you and Mr Herveaux are going to be married?'

'Yes,' said Alcide, pulling me against him and wrapping his arms around me. 'We're headed for the altar.'

I smiled, but in an appropriately subdued way.

'Well, congratulations.' Detective Coughlin eyed us thoughtfully. 'So, Miss Stackhouse, you hadn't ever met Adabelle Yancy face-to-face?'

'I may have met the older Mrs Yancy when I was a little girl,' I said cautiously. 'But I don't remember her. Alcide's family knows the Yancys, of course. He's lived here all his life.' Of course, they're also werewolves.

Coughlin was still focused on me. 'And you didn't go in the shop none? Just Mr Herveaux here?'

'Alcide just stepped in while I waited out here.' I tried to look delicate, which is not easy for me. I am healthy and muscular, and while I am not Emme, I'm not Kate Moss either. 'I'd seen the – the hand, so I stayed out.'

'That was a good idea,' Detective Coughlin said. 'What's in there isn't fit for people to see.' He looked about twenty years older as he said that. I felt sorry that his job was so tough. He was thinking that the savaged bodies in the house were a waste of two good lives and the work of someone he'd love to arrest. 'Would either of you have any idea why anyone would want to rip up two ladies like this?'

'Two,' Alcide said slowly, stunned.

'Two?' I said, less guardedly.

'Why, yes,' the detective said heavily. He had aimed to get our reactions and now he had them; what he thought of them, I would find out.

'Poor things,' I said, and I wasn't faking the tears that filled my eyes. It was kind of nice to have Alcide's chest to lean against, and as if he were reading my mind he unzipped his leather jacket so I'd be closer to him, wrapping the open sides around me to keep me warmer. 'But if one of them is Adabelle Yancy, who is the other?'

'There's not much left of the other,' Coughlin said, before he told himself to shut his mouth.

'They were kind of jumbled up,' Alcide said quietly, close to my ear. He was sickened. 'I didn't know . . . I guess if I'd analyzed what I was seeing . . .'

Though I couldn't read Alcide's thoughts clearly, I could understand that he was thinking that Adabelle had managed to take down one of her attackers. And when the rest of the group was getting away, they hadn't taken all the appropriate bits with them.

'And you're from Bon Temps, Miss Stackhouse,' the detective said, almost idly.

'Yes, sir,' I said, with a gasp. I was trying not to picture Adabelle Yancy's last moments.

'Where you work there?'

'Merlotte's Bar and Grill,' I said. 'I wait tables.'

While he registered the difference in social status between me and Alcide, I closed my eyes and laid my head against Alcide's warm chest. Detective Coughlin was wondering if I was pregnant; if Alcide's dad, a well-known and well-to-do figure in Shreveport, would approve of such a marriage. He could see why I'd want an expensive wedding dress, if I were marrying a Herveaux.

'You don't have an engagement ring, Miss Stackhouse?'

'We don't plan on a long engagement,' Alcide said. I could hear his voice rumbling in his chest. 'She'll get her diamond the day we marry.'

'You're so bad,' I said fondly, punching him in the ribs as hard as I could without being obvious.

'Ouch,' he said in protest.

Somehow this bit of byplay convinced Detective Coughlin that we were really engaged. He took down our phone numbers and addresses, then told us we could leave. Alcide was as relieved as I was.

We drove to the nearest place where we could pull over in privacy –
a little park that was largely deserted in the cold weather – and Alcide
called Colonel Flood again. I waited in the truck while Alcide, pacing
in the dead grass, gesticulated and raised his voice, venting some of
his horror and anger. I'd been able to feel it building up in him. Alcide
had trouble articulating emotions, like lots of guys. It made him seem
more familiar and dear.

Dear? I'd better stop thinking like that. The engagement had been
drummed up strictly for Detective Coughlin's benefit. If Alcide was
anyone's 'dear', it was the perfidious Debbie's.

When Alcide climbed back into the pickup, he was scowling.

'I guess I better go back to the office and take you to your car,' he
said. 'I'm sorry about all this.'

'I guess I should be saying that.'

'This is a situation neither of us created,' he said firmly. 'Neither of
us would be involved if we could help it.'

'That's the God's truth.' After a minute of thinking of the complicated supernatural world, I asked Alcide what Colonel Flood's plan
was.

'We'll take care of it,' Alcide said. 'I'm sorry, Sook, I can't tell you
what we're going to do.'

'Are you going to be in danger?' I asked, because I just couldn't help
it.

We'd gotten to the Herveaux building by then, and Alcide parked
his truck by my old car. He turned a little to face me, and he reached
over to take my hand. 'I'm gonna be fine. Don't worry,' he said gently.
'I'll call you.'

'Don't forget to do that,' I said. 'And I have to tell you what the
witches did about trying to find Eric.' I hadn't told Alcide about the
posted pictures, the reward. He frowned even harder when he thought
about the cleverness of this ploy.

'Debbie was supposed to drive over this afternoon, get here about
six,' he said. He looked at his watch. 'Too late to stop her coming.'

'If you're planning a big raid, she could help,' I said.

He gave me a sharp look. Like a pointed stick he wanted to poke in my eye. 'She's a shifter, not a Were,' he reminded me defensively.

Maybe she turned into a weasel or a rat.

'Of course,' I said seriously. I literally bit my tongue so I wouldn't make any of the remarks that waited just inside my mouth, dying to be spoken. 'Alcide, do you think the other body was Adabelle's girlfriend? Someone who just got caught at the shop with Adabelle when the witches came calling?'

'Since a lot of the second body was missing, I hope that the body was one of the witches. I hope Adabelle went down fighting.'

'I hope so, too.' I nodded, putting an end to that train of thought. 'I'd better get back to Bon Temps. Eric will be waking up soon. Don't forget to tell your dad that we're engaged.'

His expression provided the only fun I'd had all day.

Chapter 6

I thought all the way home about my day in Shreveport. I'd asked Alcide to call the cops in Bon Temps from his cell phone, and he'd gotten another negative message. No, they hadn't heard any more on Jason, and no one had called to say they'd seen him. So I didn't stop by the police station on my way home, but I did have to go to the grocery to buy some margarine and bread, and I did have to go in the liquor store to pick up some blood.

The first thing I saw when I pushed open the door of Super Save-A-Bunch was a little display of bottled blood, which saved me a stop at the liquor store. The second thing I saw was the poster with the headshot of Eric. I assumed it was the photo Eric had had made when he opened Fangtasia, because it was a very nonthreatening picture. He was projecting winsome worldliness; any person in this universe would know that he'd never, ever bite. It was headed, 'HAVE YOU SEEN THIS VAMPIRE?'

I read the text carefully. Everything Jason had said about it was true. Fifty thousand dollars is a lot of money. That Hallow must be really nuts about Eric to pay that much, if all she wanted was a hump. It was hard to believe gaining control of Fangtasia (and having the bed services of Eric) would afford her a profit after paying out a reward that large. I was increasingly doubtful that I knew the whole story, and I was increasingly sure I was sticking my neck out and might get it bitten off.

Hoyt Fortenberry, Jason's big buddy, was loading pizzas into his buggy in the frozen food aisle. 'Hey, Sookie, where you think ole Jason got to?' he called as soon as he saw me. Hoyt, big and beefy and no rocket scientist, looked genuinely concerned.

'I wish I knew,' I said, coming closer so we could talk without everyone in the store recording every word. 'I'm pretty worried.'

'You don't think he's just gone off with some girl he met? That girl he was with New Year's Eve was pretty cute.'

'What was her name?'

'Crystal. Crystal Norris.'

'Where's she from?'

'From round Hotshot, out thataway.' He nodded south.

Hotshot was even smaller than Bon Temps. It was about ten miles away and had a reputation for being a strange little community. The Hotshot kids who attended the Bon Temps school always stuck together, and they were all a smidge . . . different. It didn't surprise me at all that Crystal lived in Hotshot.

'So,' Hoyt said, persisting in making his point, 'Crystal might have asked him to come stay with her.' But his brain was saying he didn't believe it, he was only trying to comfort me and himself. We both knew that Jason would have phoned by now, no matter how good a time he was having with any woman.

But I decided I'd give Crystal a call when I had a clear ten minutes, which might not be any time tonight. I asked Hoyt to pass on Crystal's name to the sheriff's department, and he said he would. He didn't seem too happy about the idea. I could tell that if the missing man had been anyone but Jason, Hoyt would have refused. But Jason had always been Hoyt's source of recreation and general amusement, since Jason was far more clever and inventive than the slow-moving, slow-thinking Hoyt: If Jason never reappeared, Hoyt would have a dull life.

We parted in the Super Save-A-Bunch parking lot, and I felt relieved that Hoyt hadn't asked me about the TrueBlood I'd purchased. Neither had the cashier, though she'd handled the bottles with distaste. As I'd paid for it, I'd thought about how much I was in the hole from hosting Eric already. Clothes and blood mounted up.

It was just dark when I got to my house and pulled the plastic grocery bags out of the car. I unlocked my back door and went in, calling to Eric as I switched on the kitchen light. I didn't hear an answer, so I put the groceries away, leaving a bottle of TrueBlood out of the refrigerator so he could have it to hand when he got hungry. I got the shotgun out of my trunk and loaded it, sticking it in the shadow of the water heater. I took a minute to call the sheriff's department again. No news of Jason, said the dispatcher.

I slumped against the kitchen wall for a long moment, feeling dejected. It wasn't a good thing to just sit around, being depressed. Maybe I'd go out to the living room and pop a movie into the VCR, as entertainment for Eric. He'd gone through all my *Buffy* tapes, and I didn't have *Angel*. I wondered if he'd like *Gone with the Wind*. (For all I knew, he'd been around when they were filming it. On the other hand, he had amnesia. Anything should be new to him.)

But as I went down the hall, I heard some small movement. I pushed open the door of my old room gently, not wanting to make a big noise if my guest wasn't yet up. Oh, but he was. Eric was pulling on his jeans, with his back to me. He hadn't bothered with underwear, not even the itty-bitty red ones. My breath stuck in my throat. I made a sound like 'Guck,' and made myself close my eyes tight. I clenched my fists.

If there were an international butt competition, Eric would win, hands down – or cheeks up. He would get a large, large trophy. I had never realized a woman could have to struggle to keep her hands off a man, but here I was, digging my nails into my palms, staring at the inside of my eyelids as though I could maybe see through them if I peered hard enough.

It was somehow degrading, craving someone so . . . so *voraciously* – another good calendar word – just because he was physically beautiful. I hadn't thought that was something women did, either.

'Sookie, are you all right?' Eric asked. I floundered my way back to sanity through a swamp of lust. He was standing right in front of me, his hands resting on my shoulders. I looked up into his blue eyes, now focused on me and apparently full of nothing but concern. I was right on a level with his hard nipples. They were the size of pencil erasers. I bit the inside of my lip. I would *not* lean over those few inches.

'Excuse me,' I said, speaking very softly. I was scared to speak loudly, or move at all. If I did, I might knock him down. 'I didn't mean to walk in on you. I should have knocked.'

'You have seen all of me before.'

Not the rear view, bare. 'Yes, but intruding wasn't polite.'

'I don't mind. You look upset.'

You think? 'Well, I have had a very bad day,' I said, through clenched teeth. 'My brother is missing, and the Were witches in Shreveport killed the – the vice president of the Were pack there, and her hand was in the flowerbed. Well, someone's was. Belinda's in the hospital. Ginger is dead. I think I'll take a shower.' I turned on my heel and marched into my room. I went in the bathroom and shucked my clothes, tossing them into the hamper. I bit my lip until I could smile at my own streak of wildness, and then I climbed into the spray of hot water.

I know cold showers are more traditional, but I was enjoying the warmth and relaxation the heat brought. I got my hair wet and groped for the soap.

'I'll do that for you,' Eric said, pulling back the curtain to step into the shower with me.

I gasped, just short of a shriek. He had discarded the jeans. He was also in the mood, the same mood I was in. You could really tell, with Eric. His fangs were out some, too. I was embarrassed, horrified, and absolutely ready to jump him. While I stood stock-still, paralyzed by conflicting waves of emotion, Eric took the soap out of my hands and lathered up his own, set the soap back in its little niche, and began to wash my arms, raising each in turn to stroke my armpit, down my side, never touching my breasts, which were practically quivering like puppies who wanted to be petted.

'Have we ever made love?' he asked.

I shook my head, still unable to speak.

'Then I was a fool,' he said, moving one hand in a circular motion over my stomach. 'Turn around, lover.'

I turned my back to him, and he began to work on that. His fingers were very strong and very clever, and I had the most relaxed and cleanest set of shoulder blades in Louisiana by the time Eric got through.

My shoulder blades were the only thing at ease. My libido was hopping up and down. Was I really going to do this? It seemed more and more likely that I was, I thought nervously. If the man in my shower had been the real Eric, I would have had the strength to back off. I would have ordered him out the minute he stepped in. The real Eric came with a whole package of power and politics, something of which I had limited understanding and interest. This was a different Eric – without the personality that I'd grown fond of in a perverse way – but it was beautiful Eric, who desired me, who was hungry for me, in a world that often let me know it could do very well without me. My mind was about to switch off and my body was about to take over. I could feel part of Eric pressed against my back, and he wasn't standing that close. Yikes. Yahoo. Yum.

He shampooed my hair next.

'Are you trembling because you are frightened of me?' he asked.

I considered that. Yes, and no. But I wasn't about to have a long discussion over the pros and cons. The inner debate had been tough enough. Oh, yeah, I know, there wouldn't be a better time to have a long yada-yada with Eric about the moral aspects of mating with someone you didn't love. And maybe there would never be another time to lay ground rules about being careful to be gentle with me physically. Not that I thought Eric would beat me up, but his manhood (as my romance novels called it – in this case the popular adjectives 'burgeoning' or 'throbbing' might also be applied) was a daunting prospect to a relatively inexperienced woman like me. I felt like a car that had only been operated by one driver . . . a car its new prospective buyer was determined to take to the Daytona 500.

Oh, to hell with thinking.

I took the soap from the niche and lathered up my fingers. As I stepped very close to him, I kind of folded Mr Happy up against Eric's stomach, so I could reach around him and get my fingers on that absolutely gorgeous butt. I couldn't look him in the face, but he let me know he was delighted that I was responding. He spread his legs obligingly and I washed him very thoroughly, very meticulously. He began to make little noises, to rock forward. I began to work on his chest. I closed my lips around his right nipple and sucked. He liked that a lot. His hands pressed against the back of my head. 'Bite, a little,' he whispered, and I used my teeth. His hands began to move restlessly over whatever bit of my skin they could find, stroking and teasing. When he pulled away, he had decided to reciprocate, and he bent down. While his mouth closed over my breast, his hand glided between my legs. I gave a deep sigh, and did a little moving of my own. He had long fingers.

The next thing I knew, the water was off and he was drying me with a fluffy white towel, and I was rubbing him with another one. Then we just kissed for while, over and over.

'The bed,' he said, a little raggedly, and I nodded. He scooped me up and then we got into a kind of tangle with me trying to pull the bedspread down while he just wanted to dump me on the bed and proceed, but I had my way because it was just too cold for the top of the bed. Once we were arranged, I turned to him and we picked back up where we'd left off, but with an escalating tempo. His fingers and his mouth were busy learning my topography, and he pressed heavily against my thigh.

I was so on fire for him I was surprised that flames didn't flicker out of my fingertips. I curled my fingers around him and stroked.

Suddenly Eric was on top of me, about to enter. I was exhilarated and very ready. I reached between us to put him at just the right spot, rubbing the tip of him over my nub as I did so.

'My lover,' he said hoarsely, and pushed.

Though I'd been sure I was prepared, and I ached with wanting him, I cried out with the shock of it.

After a moment, he said, 'Don't close your eyes. Look at me, lover.' The way he said 'lover' was like a caress, like he was calling me by a name no other man had ever used before or ever would after. His fangs were completely extended and I stretched up to run my tongue over them. I expected he would bite my neck, as Bill nearly always did.

'Watch me,' he said in my ear, and pulled out. I tried to yank him back, but he began kissing his way down my body, making strategic stops, and I was hovering on the golden edge when he got all the way down. His mouth was talented, and his fingers took the place of his penis, and then all of a sudden he looked up the length of my body to make sure I was watching – I was – and he turned his face to my inner thigh, nuzzling it, his fingers moving steadily now, faster and faster, and then he bit.

I may have made a noise, I am sure I did, but in the next second I was floating on the most powerful wave of pleasure I'd ever felt. And the minute the shining wave subsided, Eric was kissing my mouth again, and I could taste my own fluids on him, and then he was back inside me, and it happened all over again. His moment came right after, as I was still experiencing aftershocks. He shouted something in a language I'd never heard, and he closed his own eyes, and then he collapsed on top of me. After a couple of minutes, he raised his head to look down. I wished he would pretend to breathe, as Bill always had during sex. (I'd never asked him, he'd just done it, and it had been reassuring.) I pushed the thought away. I'd never had sex with anyone but Bill, and I guess it was natural to think of that, but the truth was it hurt to remember my previous one-man status, now gone for good.

I yanked myself back into The Moment, which was fine enough. I stroked Eric's hair, tucking some behind his ear. His eyes on mine were intent, and I knew he was waiting for me to speak. 'I wish,' I said, 'I could save orgasms in a jar for when I need them, because I think I had a few extra.'

Eric's eyes widened, and all of a sudden he roared with laughter. That sounded good, that sounded like the real Eric. I felt comfortable with this gorgeous but unknown stranger, after I heard that laugh. He rolled onto his back and swung me over easily until I was straddling his waist.

'If I had known you would be this gorgeous with your clothes off, I would have tried to do this sooner,' he said.

'You did try to do this sooner, about twenty times,' I said, smiling down at him.

'Then I have good taste.' He hesitated for a long minute, some of the pleasure leaving his face. 'Tell me about us. How long have I known you?'

The light from the bathroom spilled onto the right side of his face. His hair spread over my pillow, shining and golden.

'I'm cold,' I said gently, and he let me lie beside him, pulling the covers up over us. I propped myself up on one elbow and he lay on his side, so we were facing each other. 'Let me think. I met you last year at Fangtasia, the vampire bar you own in Shreveport. And by the way, the bar got attacked today. Last night. I'm sorry, I should have told you that first, but I've been so worried about my brother.'

'I want to hear about today, but give me our background first. I find myself mightily interested.'

Another little shock: The real Eric cared about his own position first, relationships down about – oh, I don't know, tenth. This was definitely odd. I told him, 'You are the sheriff of Area Five, and my former boyfriend Bill is your subordinate. He's gone, out of the country. I think I told you about Bill.'

'Your unfaithful former boyfriend? Whose maker was the vampire Lorena?'

'That's the one,' I said briefly. 'Anyway, when I met you at Fangtasia . . .'

It all took longer than I thought, and by the time I had finished with the tale, Eric's hands were busy again. He latched onto one breast with his fangs extended, drawing a little blood and a sharp gasp from me, and he sucked powerfully. It was a strange sensation, because he was getting the blood and my nipple. Painful and very exciting – I felt like he was drawing the fluid from much lower. I gasped and jerked in arousal, and suddenly he raised my leg so he could enter me.

It wasn't such a shock this time, and it was slower. Eric wanted me to be looking into his eyes; that obviously flicked his Bic.

I was exhausted when it was over, though I'd enjoyed myself immensely. I'd heard a lot about men who didn't care if the woman had her pleasure, or perhaps such men assumed that if they were happy, their partner was, too. But neither of the men I'd been with had been like that. I didn't know if that was because they were vampires, or because I'd been lucky, or both.

Eric had paid me many compliments, and I realized I hadn't said anything to him that indicated my admiration. That hardly seemed fair. He was holding me, and my head was on his shoulder. I murmured into his neck, 'You are so beautiful.'

'What?' He was clearly startled.

'You've told me you thought my body was nice.' Of course that wasn't the adjective he'd used, but I was embarrassed to repeat his actual words. 'I just wanted you to know I think the same about you.'

I could feel his chest move as he laughed, just a little. 'What part do you like best?' he asked, his voice teasing. 'Oh, your butt,' I said instantly.

'My . . . bottom?'

'Yep.'

'I would have thought of another part.'

'Well, that's certainly . . . adequate,' I told him, burying my face in his chest. I knew immediately I'd picked the wrong word.

'*Adequate?*' He took my hand, placed it on the part in question. It immediately began to stir. He moved my hand on it, and I obligingly circled it with my fingers. 'This is *adequate?*'

'Maybe I should have said it's a gracious plenty?'

'A gracious plenty. I like that,' he said.

He was ready again, and honestly, I didn't know if I could. I was worn out to the point of wondering if I'd be walking funny the next day.

I indicated I would be pleased with an alternative by sliding down in the bed, and he seemed delighted to reciprocate. After another sublime release, I thought every muscle in my body had turned to Jell-O. I didn't talk anymore about the worry I felt about my brother, about the terrible things that had happened in Shreveport, about anything unpleasant. We whispered some heartfelt (on my part) mutual compliments, and I was just out of it. I don't know what Eric did for the rest of the night, because I fell asleep.

I had many worries waiting for me the next day; but thanks to Eric, for a few precious hours I just didn't care.

Chapter 7

The next morning the sun was shining outside when I woke. I lay in bed in a mindless pool of contentment. I was sore, but pleasantly so. I had a little bruise or two nothing that would show. And the fang marks that were a dead giveaway (har-de-har) were not on my neck, where they'd been in the past. No casual observer was going to be able to tell I'd enjoyed a vampire's company, and I didn't have an appointment with a gynecologist – the only other person who'd have a reason to check that area.

Another shower was definitely called for, so I eased out of bed and wobbled across the floor to the bathroom. We'd left it in something of a mess, with towels tossed everywhere and the shower curtain half-ripped from its plastic hoops (when had *that* happened?), but I didn't mind picking it up. I rehung the curtain with a smile on my face and a song in my heart.

As the water pounded on my back, I reflected that I must be pretty simple. It didn't take much to make me happy. A long night with a dead guy had done the trick. It wasn't just the dynamic sex that had given me so much pleasure (though that had contained moments I'd remember till the day I died); it was the companionship. Actually, the intimacy.

Call me stereotypical. I'd spent the night with a man who'd told me I was beautiful, a man who'd enjoyed me and who'd given me intense pleasure. He had touched me and held me and laughed with me.

We weren't in danger of making a baby with our pleasures, because vampires just can't do that. I wasn't being disloyal to anyone (though I'll admit I'd had a few pangs when I thought of Bill), and neither was Eric. I couldn't see the harm.

As I brushed my teeth and put on some makeup, I had to admit to myself that I was sure that the Reverend Fullenwilder wouldn't agree with my viewpoint.

Well, I hadn't been going to tell him about it, anyway. It would just be between God and me. I figured God had made me with the disability of telepathy, and he could cut me a little slack on the sex thing.

I had regrets, of course. I would love to get married and have babies. I'd be faithful as can be. I'd be a good mom, too. But I couldn't marry a regular guy, because I would always know when he lied to me, when he was angry with me, every little thought he had about me. Even dating a regular guy was more than I'd been able to manage. Vampires can't marry, not yet, not legally; not that a vampire had asked me, I reminded myself, tossing a washcloth into the hamper a little force-fully. Perhaps I could stand a long association with a Were or a shifter, since their thoughts weren't clear. But there again, where was the willing Were?

I had better enjoy what I had at this moment – something I've become quite good at doing. What I had was a handsome vampire who'd temporarily lost his memory and, along with it, a lot of his personality: a vampire who needed reassurance just as much as I did.

In fact, as I put in my earrings, I figured out that Eric had been so delighted with me for more than one reason. I could see that after days of being completely without memories of his possessions or underlings, days lacking any sense of self, last night he had gained something of his own – me. His lover.

Though I was standing in front of a mirror, I wasn't really seeing my reflection. I was seeing, very clearly, that – at the moment – I was all in the world that Eric could think of as his own.

I had better not fail him.

I was rapidly bringing myself down from 'relaxed happiness' to 'guilty grim resolution', so I was relieved when the phone rang. It had a built-in caller ID, and I noticed Sam was calling from the bar, instead of his trailer.

'Sookie?'

'Hey, Sam.'

'I'm sorry about Jason. Any news?'

'No. I called down to the sheriff's department when I woke up, and I talked to the dispatcher. She said Alcee Beck would let me know if anything new came up. That's what she's said the last twenty times I've called.'

'Want me to get someone to take your shift?'

'No. It would be better for me to be busy, than to sit here at home. They know where to reach me if they've got anything to tell me.'

'You sure?'

'Yes. Thanks for asking, though.'

'If I can do anything to help, you let me know.'

'There is something, come to think of it.'

'Name it.'

You remember the little shifter Jason was in the bar with New Year's Eve?'

Sam gave it thought. 'Yes,' he said hesitantly. 'One of the Norris girls? They live out in Hotshot.'

'That's what Hoyt said.'

'You have to watch out for people from out there, Sookie. That's an old settlement. An inbred settlement.'

I wasn't sure what Sam was trying to tell me. 'Could you spell that out? I'm not up to unraveling subtle hints today.'

'I can't right now.'

'Oh, not alone?'

'No. The snack delivery guy is here. Just be careful. They're really, really different.'

'Okay,' I said slowly, still in the dark. 'I'll be careful. See you at four-thirty,' I told him, and hung up, vaguely unhappy and quite puzzled.

I had plenty of time to go out to Hotshot and get back before I had to go to work. I pulled on some jeans, sneakers, a bright red long-sleeved T-shirt, and my old blue coat. I looked up Crystal Norris's address in the phone book and had to get out my chamber of commerce map to track it down. I've lived in Renard Parish my whole life, and I thought I knew it pretty well, but the Hotshot area was a black hole in my otherwise thorough knowledge.

I drove north, and when I came to the T-junction, I turned right. I passed the lumber processing plant that was Bon Temps's main employer, and I passed a reupholstering place, and I flew past the water department. There was a liquor store or two, and then a country store at a crossroads that had a prominent COLD BEER AND BAIT sign left over from the summer and propped up facing the road. I turned right again, to go south.

The deeper I went into the countryside, the worse the road seemed to grow. The mowing and maintenance crews hadn't been out here since the end of summer. Either the residents of the Hotshot community had no pull whatsoever in the parish government, or they just didn't want visitors. From time to time, the road dipped in some low-lying areas as it ran between bayous. In heavy rains, the low spots would be flooded. I wouldn't be surprised at all to hear folks out here encountered the occasional gator.

Finally I came to another crossroads, compared to which the one with the bait shop seemed like a mall. There were a few houses scattered around, maybe eight or nine. These were small houses, none of them brick. Most of them had several cars in the front yard. Some of them sported a rusty swing set or a basketball hoop, and in a couple of yards I spotted a satellite dish. Oddly, all the houses seemed pulled away from the actual crossroads; the area directly around the road intersection was bare. It was like someone had tied a rope to a stake sunk in the middle of the crossing and drawn a circle. Within it, there was nothing. Outside it, the houses crouched.

In my experience, in a little settlement like this, you had the same kind of people you had anywhere. Some of them were poor and proud and good. Some of them were poor and mean and worthless. But all of them knew each other thoroughly, and no action went unobserved.

On this chilly day, I didn't see a soul outdoors to let me know if this was a black community or a white community. It was unlikely to be both. I wondered if I was at the right crossroads, but my doubts were washed away when I saw an imitation green road sign, the kind you can order from a novelty company, mounted on a pole in front of one of the homes. It read, HOTSHOT.

I was in the right place. Now, to find Crystal Norris's house.

With some difficulty, I spotted a number on one rusty mailbox, and then I saw another. By process of elimination, I figured the next house must be the one where Crystal Norris lived. The Norris house was little different from any of the others; it had a small front porch with an old armchair and two lawn chairs on it, and two cars parked in front, one a Ford Fiesta and the other an ancient Buick.

When I parked and got out, I realized what was so unusual about Hotshot.

No dogs.

Any other hamlet that looked like this would have at least twelve dogs milling around, and I'd be wondering if I could safely get out of the car. Here, not a single yip broke the winter silence.

I crossed over the hard, packed dirt of the yard, feeling as though eyes were on every step I took. I opened the torn screen door to knock on the heavier wooden door. Inset in it was a pattern of three glass panes. Dark eyes surveyed me through the lowest one.

The door opened, just when the pause was beginning to make me anxious.

Jason's date from New Year's Eve was less festive today, in black jeans and a cream-colored T-shirt. Her boots had come from Payless, and her short curly hair was a sort of dusty black. She was thin, intense, and though I'd carded her, she just didn't look twenty-one.

'Crystal Norris?'

'Yeah?' She didn't sound particularly unfriendly, but she did sound preoccupied.

'I'm Jason Stackhouse's sister, Sookie.'

'Oh, yeah? Come in.' She stood back, and I stepped into the tiny living room. It was crowded with furniture intended for a much larger space: two recliners and a three-cushion couch of dark brown Naugahyde, the big buttons separating the vinyl into little hillocks. You'd stick to it in the summer and slide around on it in the winter. Crumbs would collect in the depression around the buttons.

There was a stained rug in dark red and yellows and browns, and there were toys strewn in an almost solid layer over it. A picture of the Last Supper hung above the television set, and the whole house smelled pleasantly of red beans and rice and cornbread.

A toddler was experimenting with Duplos in the doorway to the kitchen. I thought it was a boy, but it was hard to be sure. Overalls and a green turtleneck weren't exactly a clue, and the baby's wispy brown hair was neither cut short nor decorated with a bow.

'Your child?' I asked, trying to make my voice pleasant and conversational.

'No, my sister's,' Crystal said. She gestured toward one of the recliners.

'Crystal, the reason I'm here ... Did you know that Jason is missing?'

She was perched on the edge of the couch, and she'd been staring down at her thin hands. When I spoke, she looked into my eyes intently. This was not fresh news to her.

'Since when?' she asked. Her voice had a pleasantly hoarse sound to it; you'd listen to what this girl had to say, especially if you were a man.

'Since the night of January first. He left my house, and then the next morning he didn't show up for work. There was some blood on that little pier out behind the house. His pickup was still in his front yard. The door to it was hanging open.'

'I don't know nothing about it,' she said instantly.

She was lying.

'Who told you I had anything to do with this?' she asked, working up to being bitchy. 'I got rights. I don't have to talk to you.'

Sure, that was Amendment 29 to the Constitution: Shifters don't have to talk to Sookie Stackhouse.

'Yes, you do.' Suddenly, I abandoned the nice approach. She'd hit the wrong button on me. 'I'm not like you. I don't have a sister or a nephew,' and I nodded at the toddler, figuring I had a fifty-fifty chance of being right. 'I don't have a mom or a dad or anything, *anything*, except my brother.' I took a deep breath. 'I want to know where Jason is. And if you know anything, you better tell me.'

'Or you'll do what?' Her thin face was twisted into a snarl. But she genuinely wanted to know what kind of pull I had; I could read that much.

'Yeah, what?' asked a calmer voice.

I looked at the doorway to see a man who was probably on the upside of forty. He had a trimmed beard salted with gray, and his hair was cut close to his head. He was a small man, perhaps five foot seven or so, with a lithe build and muscular arms.

'Anything I have to,' I said. I looked him straight in the eyes. They were a strange golden green. He didn't seem inimical, exactly. He seemed curious.

'Why are you here?' he asked, again in that neutral voice.

'Who are you?' I had to know who this guy was. I wasn't going to waste my time repeating my story to someone who just had some time to fill. Given his air of authority, and the fact that he wasn't opting for mindless belligerence, I was willing to bet this man was worth talking to.

'I'm Calvin Norris. I'm Crystal's uncle.' From his brain pattern, he was also a shifter of some kind. Given the absence of dogs in this settlement, I assumed they were Weres.

'Mr Norris, I'm Sookie Stackhouse.' I wasn't imagining the increased interest in his expression. 'Your niece here went to the New Year's Eve party at Merlotte's Bar with my brother, Jason. Sometime the next night, my brother went missing. I want to know if Crystal can tell me anything that might help me find him.'

Calvin Norris bent to pat the toddler on the head, and then walked over to the couch where Crystal glowered. He sat beside her, his elbows resting on his knees, his hands dangling, relaxed, between them. His head inclined as he looked into Crystal's sullen face.

'This is reasonable, Crystal. Girl wants to know where her brother is. Tell her, if you know anything about it.'

Crystal snapped at him, 'Why should I tell her anything? She comes out here, tries to threaten me.'

'Because it's just common courtesy to help someone in trouble. You didn't exactly go to her to volunteer help, did you?'

'I didn't think he was just missing. I thought he—' And her voice cut short as she realized her tongue had led her into trouble.

Calvin's whole body tensed. He hadn't expected that Crystal actually knew anything about Jason's disappearance. He had just wanted her to be polite to me. I could read that, but not much else. I could not decipher their relationship. He had power over the girl, I could tell that easily enough, but what kind? It was more than the authority of an uncle; it felt more like he was her ruler. He might be wearing old work clothes and safety boots, he might look like any blue-collar man in the area, but Calvin Norris was a lot more.

Packmaster, I thought. But who would be in a pack, this far out in the boondocks? Just Crystal? Then I remembered Sam's veiled warning about the unusual nature of Hotshot, and I had a revelation. *Everyone* in Hotshot was two-natured.

Was that possible? I wasn't completely certain Calvin Norris was a Were – but I knew he didn't change into any bunny. I had to struggle with an almost irresistible impulse to lean over and put my hand on his forearm, touch skin to skin to read his mind as clearly as possible.

I was completely certain about one thing: I wouldn't want to be anywhere around Hotshot on the three nights of the full moon.

'You're the barmaid at Merlotte's,' he said, looking into my eyes as intently as he'd looked into Crystal's.

'I'm *a* barmaid at Merlotte's.'

'You're a friend of Sam's.'

'Yes,' I said carefully. 'I am. I'm a friend of Alcide Herveaux's, too. And I know Colonel Flood.'

These names meant something to Calvin Norris. I wasn't surprised that Norris would know the names of some prominent Shreveport Weres – and he'd know Sam, of course. It had taken my boss time to connect with the local two-natured community, but he'd been working on it.

Crystal had been listening with wide dark eyes, in no better mood than she had been before. A girl wearing overalls appeared from the back of the house, and she lifted the toddler from his nest of Duplos. Though her face was rounder and less distinctive and her figure was fuller, she was clearly Crystal's younger sister. She was also just as apparently pregnant again.

'You need anything, Uncle Calvin?' she asked, staring at me over the toddler's shoulder.

'No, Dawn. Take care of Matthew.' She disappeared into the back of the house with her burden. I had guessed right on the sex of the kid.

'Crystal,' said Calvin Norris, in a quiet and terrifying voice, 'you tell us now what you done.'

Crystal had believed she'd gotten away with something, and she was shocked at being ordered to confess.

But she'd obey. After a little fidgeting, she did.

'I was out with Jason on New Year's Eve,' she said. 'I'd met him at Wal-Mart in Bon Temps, when I went in to get me a purse.'

I sighed. Jason could find potential bedmates anywhere. He was going to end up with some unpleasant disease (if he hadn't already) or slapped with a paternity suit, and there was nothing I could do about it except watch it happen.

'He asked me if I'd spend New Year's Eve with him. I had the feeling the woman he'd had a date with had changed her mind, 'cause he's not the kind of guy to go without lining up a date for something big like that.'

I shrugged. Jason could have made and broken dates with five women for New Year's Eve, for all I knew. And it wasn't infrequent for women to get so exasperated by his earnest pursuit of anything with a vagina that they broke off plans with him.

'He's a cute guy, and I like to get out of Hotshot, so I said yeah. He asked me if he could come pick me up, but I knew some of my neighbors wouldn't like that, so I said I'd just meet him at the Fina station, and then we'd go in his truck. So that's what we did. And I had a real good time with him, went home with him, had a good night.' Her eyes gleamed at me. 'You want to know how he is in bed?'

There was a blur of movement, and then there was blood at the corner of her mouth. Calvin's hand was back dangling between his legs before I even realized he'd moved. 'You be polite. Don't show your worst face to this woman,' he said, and his voice was so serious I made up my mind I'd be extra polite, too, just to be safe.

'Okay. That wasn't nice, I guess,' she admitted, in a softer and chastened voice. 'Well, I wanted to see him the night after, too, and he wanted to see me again. So I snuck out and went over to his place. He had to leave to see his sister – you? You're the only sister he's got?'

I nodded.

'And he said to stay there, he'd be back in a bit. I wanted to go with him, and he said if his sister didn't have company, that woulda been fine, but she had vamp company, and he didn't want me to mix with them.'

I think Jason knew what my opinion of Crystal Norris would be, and he wanted to dodge hearing it, so he left her at his house.

'Did he come back home?' Calvin said, nudging her out of her reverie.

'Yes,' she said, and I tensed.

'What happened then?' Calvin asked, when she stopped again.

'I'm not real sure,' she said. 'I was in the house, waiting for him, and I heard his truck pull up, and I'm thinking, "Oh, good, he's here, we can party," and then I didn't hear him come up the front steps, and I'm wondering what's happening, you know? Of course all the outside lights are on, but I didn't go to the window, 'cause I knew it was him.' Of course a Were would know his step, maybe catch his smell. 'I'm listening real good,' she went on, 'and I hear him going around the outside of the house, so I'm thinking he's going to come in the back door, for some reason – muddy boots, or something.'

I took a deep breath. She'd get to the point in just a minute. I just knew she would.

'And then, to the back of the house, and farther 'way, yards away from the porch, I hear a lot of noise, and some shouting and stuff, and then nothing.'

If she hadn't been a shifter, she wouldn't have heard so much. There, I knew I'd think of a bright side if I searched hard enough.

'Did you go out and look?' Calvin asked Crystal. His worn hand stroked her black curls, as if he were petting a favorite dog.

'No sir, I didn't look.'

'Smell?'

'I didn't get close enough,' she admitted, just on the good side of sullen. The wind was blowing the other way. I caught a little of Jason, and blood. Maybe a couple of other things.'

'Like what?'

Crystal looked at her own hands. 'Shifter, maybe. Some of us can change when it's not the full moon, but I can't. Otherwise, I'd have had a better chance at the scent,' she said to me in near-apology.

'Vampire?' Calvin asked.

'I never smelled a vampire before,' she said simply. 'I don't know.'

'Witch?' I asked.

'Do they smell any different from regular people?' she asked doubtfully.

I shrugged. I didn't know.

Calvin said, 'What did you do after that?'

'I knew something had carried Jason off into the woods. I just . . . I lost it. I'm not brave.' She shrugged. 'I came home after that. Nothing more I could do.'

I was trying not to cry, but tears just rolled down my cheeks. For the first time, I admitted to myself that I wasn't sure I'd ever see my brother again. But if the attacker's intention was to kill Jason, why not just leave his body in the backyard? As Crystal had pointed out, the night of New Year's Day there hadn't been a full moon. There were things that didn't have to wait for the full moon . . .

The bad thing about learning about all the creatures that existed in the world besides us is that I could imagine that there were things that might swallow Jason in one gulp. Or a few bites.

But I just couldn't let myself think about that. Though I was still weeping, I made an effort to smile. 'Thank you so much,' I said politely. 'It was real nice of you to take the time to see me. I know you have things you need to do.'

Crystal looked suspicious, but her uncle Calvin reached over and patted my hand, which seemed to surprise everyone, himself included.

He walked me out to my car. The sky was clouding over, which made it feel colder, and the wind began to toss the bare branches of the large bushes planted around the yard. I recognized yellow bells (which the nursery calls forsythia), and spirea, and even a tulip tree. Around them would be planted jonquil bulbs, and iris – the same flowers that are in my grandmother's yard, the same bushes that have grown in southern yards for generations. Right now everything looked bleak and sordid. In the spring, it would seem almost charming, picturesque; the decay of poverty gilded by Mother Nature.

Two or three houses down the road, a man emerged from a shed behind his house, glanced our way, and did a double take. After a long moment, he loped back into his house. It was too far away to make out more of his features than thick pale hair, but his grace was phenomenal. The people out here more than disliked strangers; they seemed to be allergic to them.

'That's my house over there,' Calvin offered, pointing to a much more substantial home, small but foursquare, painted white quite recently. Everything was in good repair at Calvin Norris's house. The driveway and parking area were clearly defined; the matching white toolshed stood rust-free on a neat concrete slab.

I nodded. 'It looks real nice,' I said in a voice that wasn't too wobbly.

'I want to make you an offer,' Calvin Norris said.

I tried to look interested. I half turned to face him.

'You're a woman without protection now,' he said. 'Your brother's gone. I hope he comes back, but you don't have no one to stand up for you while he's missing.'

There were a lot of things wrong with this speech, but I wasn't in any mood to debate the shifter. He'd done me a large favor, getting Crystal to talk. I stood there in the cold wind and tried to look politely receptive.

'If you need some place to hide, if you need someone to watch your back or defend you, I'll be your man,' he said. His green and golden eyes met mine directly.

I'll tell you why I didn't dismiss this with a snort: He wasn't being superior about it. According to his mores, he was being as nice as he could be, extending a shield to me if I should need it. Of course he expected to 'be my man' in every way, along with protecting me; but he wasn't being lascivious in his manner, or offensively explicit. Calvin Norris was offering to incur injury for my sake. He meant it. That's not something to get all snitty about.

'Thanks,' I said. 'I'll remember you said that.'

'I heard about you,' he said. 'Shifters and Weres, they talk to each other. I hear you're different.'

'I am.' Regular men might have found my outer package attractive, but my inner package repelled them. If I ever began to get a swelled head, after the attention paid me by Eric, or Bill, or even Alcide, all I had to do was listen to the brains of some bar patrons to have my ego deflated. I clutched my old blue coat more closely around me. Like most of the two-natured, Calvin had a system that didn't feel cold as intensely as my completely human metabolism did. 'But my difference doesn't lie in being two-natured, though I appreciate your, ah, kindness.' This was as close as I could come to asking him why he was so interested.

'I know that.' He nodded in acknowledgment of my delicacy. 'Actually, that makes you more ... The thing is, here in Hotshot, we've inbred too much. You heard Crystal. She can only change at the moon, and frankly, even then she's not full-powered.' He pointed at his own face. 'My eyes can hardly pass for human. We need an infusion of new blood, new genes. You're not two-natured, but you're not exactly an ordinary woman. Ordinary women don't last long here.'

Well, that was an ominous and ambiguous way to put it. But I was sympathetic, and I tried to look understanding. Actually, I did understand, and I could appreciate his concern. Calvin Norris was clearly the leader of this unusual settlement, and its future was his responsibility.

He was frowning as he looked down the road at the house where I'd seen the man. But he turned to me to finish telling me what he wanted me to know. 'I think you would like the people here, and you would be a good breeder. I can tell by looking.'

That was a real unusual compliment. I couldn't quite think how to acknowledge it in an appropriate manner.

'I'm flattered that you think so, and I appreciate your offer. I'll remember what you said.' I paused to gather my thoughts. 'You know, the police will find out that Crystal was with Jason, if they haven't already. They'll come out here, too.'

'They won't find nothing,' Calvin Norris said. His golden green eyes met mine with faint amusement. 'They've been out here at other times; they'll be out here again. They never learn a thing. I hope you find your brother. You need help, you let me know. I got a job at Norcross. I'm a steady man.'

'Thank you,' I said, and got into my car with a feeling of relief. I gave Calvin a serious nod as I backed out of Crystal's driveway. So he worked at Norcross, the lumber processing plant. Norcross had good benefits, and they promoted from within. I'd had worse offers; that was for sure.

As I drove to work, I wondered if Crystal had been trying to get pregnant during her nights with Jason. It hadn't seemed to bother Calvin at all to hear that his niece had had sex with a strange man. Alcide had told me that Were had to breed with Were to produce a baby that had the same trait, so the inhabitants of this little community were trying to diversify, apparently. Maybe these lesser Weres were trying to breed out; that is, have children by regular humans. That would be better than having a generation of Weres whose powers were so weak they couldn't function successfully in their second nature, but who also couldn't be content as regular people.

Getting to Merlotte's was like driving from one century into another. I wondered how long the people of Hotshot had been clustered around the crossroads, what significance it had originally held for them. Though I couldn't help but be a little curious, I found it was a real relief to discard these wonderings and return to the world as I knew it.

That afternoon, the little world of Merlotte's Bar was very quiet. I changed, tied on my black apron, smoothed my hair, and washed my hands. Sam was behind the bar with his arms crossed over his chest, staring into space. Holly was carrying a pitcher of beer to a table where a lone stranger sat.

'How was Hotshot?' Sam asked, since we were alone at the bar.

'Very strange.'

He patted me on the shoulder. 'Did you find out anything useful?'

'Actually, I did. I'm just not sure what it means.' Sam needed a haircut, I noticed; his curly red-gold hair formed an arc around his face in a kind of Renaissance-angel effect.

'Did you meet Calvin Norris?'

'I did. He got Crystal to talk to me, and he made me a most unusual offer.'

'What's that?'

'I'll tell you some other time.' For the life of me, I couldn't figure out how to phrase it. I looked down at my hands, which were busy rinsing out a beer mug, and I could feel my cheeks burning.

'Calvin's an okay guy, as far as I know,' Sam said slowly. 'He works at Norcross, and he's a crew leader. Good insurance, retirement package, everything. Some of the other guys from Hotshot own a welding shop. I hear they do good work. But I don't know what goes on in Hotshot after they go home at night, and I don't think anyone else does, either. Did you know Sheriff Dowdy, John Dowdy? He was sheriff before I moved here, I think.'

'Yeah, I remember him. He hauled Jason in one time for vandalism. Gran had to go get him out of jail. Sheriff Dowdy read Jason a lecture that had him scared straight, at least for a while.'

'Sid Matt told me a story one night. It seems that one spring, John Dowdy went out to Hotshot to arrest Calvin Norris's oldest brother, Carlton.'

'For what?' Sid Matt Lancaster was an old and well-known lawyer.

'Statutory rape. The girl was willing, and she was even experienced, but she was underage. She had a new stepdad, and he decided Carlton had disrespected him.'

No politically correct stance could cover all those circumstances. 'So what happened?'

'No one knows. Late that night, John Dowdy's patrol car was found halfway back into town from Hotshot. No one in it. No blood, no fingerprints. He hasn't ever been seen since. No one in Hotshot remembered seeing him that day, they said.'

'Like Jason,' I said bleakly. 'He just vanished.'

'But Jason was at his own house, and according to you, Crystal didn't seem to be involved.'

I threw off the grip of the strange little story. 'You're right. Did anyone ever find out what happened to Sheriff Dowdy?'

'No. But no one ever saw Carlton Norris again, either.'

Now, that was the interesting part. 'And the moral of this story is?'

'That the people of Hotshot take care of their own justice.'

'Then you want them on your side.' I extracted my own moral from the story.

'Yes,' Sam said. 'You definitely want them on your side. You don't remember this? It was around fifteen years ago.'

'I was coping with my own troubles then,' I explained. I'd been an orphaned nine-year-old, coping with my growing telepathic powers.

Shortly after that, people began to stop by the bar on their way home from work. Sam and I didn't get a chance to talk the rest of the evening, which was fine with me. I was very fond of Sam, who'd often had a starring role in some of my most private fantasies, but at this point, I had so much to worry about I just couldn't take on any more.

That night, I discovered that some people thought Jason's disappearance improved Bon Temps society. Among these were Andy Bellefleur and his sister, Portia, who stopped by Merlotte's for supper, since their grandmother Caroline was having a dinner party and they were staying out of the way. Andy was a police detective and Portia was a lawyer, and they were both not on my list of favorite people. For one thing (a kind of sour-grapey thing), when Bill had found out they were his descendants, he'd made an elaborate plan to give the Bellefleurs money anonymously, and they'd really enjoyed their mysterious legacy to the hilt. But they couldn't stand Bill himself, and it made me constantly irritated to see their new cars and expensive clothes and the new roof on the Bellefleur mansion, when they dissed Bill all the time – and me, too, for being Bill's girlfriend.

Andy had been pretty nice to me before I started dating Bill. At least he'd been civil and left a decent, tip. I'd just been invisible to Portia, who had her own share of personal woes. She'd come up with a suitor, I'd heard, and I wondered maliciously if that might not be due to the sudden upsurge in the Bellefleur family fortunes. I also wondered, at times, if Andy and Portia got happy in direct proportion to my misery. They were in fine fettle this winter evening, both tucking into their hamburgers with great zest.

'Sorry about your brother, Sookie,' Andy said, as I refilled his tea glass.

I looked down at him, my face expressionless. *Liar*, I thought. After a second, Andy's eyes darted uneasily away from mine to light on the saltshaker, which seemed to have become peculiarly fascinating.

'Have you seen Bill lately?' Portia asked, patting her mouth with a napkin. She was trying to break the uneasy silence with a pleasant query, but I just got angrier.

'No,' I said. 'Can I get you all anything else?'

'No, thanks, we're just fine,' she said quickly. I spun on my heel and walked away. Then my mouth puckered in a smile. Just as I was thinking, *Bitch*, Portia was thinking, *What a bitch*.

Her ass is hot, Andy chimed in. Gosh, telepathy. What a blast. I wouldn't wish it on my worst enemy. I envied people who only heard with their ears.

Kevin and Kenya came in, too, very carefully not drinking. Theirs was a partnership that had given the people of Bon Temps much hilarity. Lily white Kevin was thin and reedy, a long-distance runner; all the equipment he had to wear on his uniform belt seemed almost too much for him to carry. His partner, Kenya, was two inches taller, pounds heavier, and fifteen shades darker. The men at the bar had been putting bets down for two years on whether or not they'd become lovers – of course, the guys at the bar didn't put it as nicely as that.

I was unwillingly aware that Kenya (and her handcuffs and nightstick) featured in all too many patrons' daydreams, and I also knew that the men who teased and derided Kevin the most mercilessly were the ones who had the most lurid fantasies. As I carried hamburger baskets over to Kevin and Kenya's table, I could tell that Kenya was wondering whether she should suggest to Bud Dearborn that he call in the tracking dogs from a neighboring parish in the search for Jason, while Kevin was worried about his mother's heart, which had been acting up more than usual lately.

'Sookie,' Kevin said, after I'd brought them a bottle of ketchup, 'I meant to tell you, some people came by the police department today putting out posters about a vampire.'

'I saw one at the grocery,' I said.

'I realize that just because you were dating a vampire, you aren't an expert,' Kevin said carefully, because Kevin always did his best to be nice to me, 'but I wondered if you'd seen this vamp. Before he disappeared, I mean.'

Kenya was looking up at me, too, her dark eyes examining me with great interest. Kenya was thinking I always seemed to be on the fringes of bad things that happened in Bon Temps, without being bad myself (thanks, Kenya). She was hoping for my sake that Jason was alive. Kevin was thinking I'd always been nice to him and Kenya; and he was thinking he wouldn't touch me with a ten-foot pole. I sighed, I hoped imperceptibly. They were waiting for an answer. I hesitated, wondering what my best choice was. The truth is always easiest to remember.

'Sure, I've seen him before. Eric owns the vampire bar in Shreveport,' I said. 'I saw him when I went there with Bill.'

'You haven't seen him recently?'

'I sure didn't abduct him from Fangtasia,' I said, with quite a lot of sarcasm in my voice.

Kenya gave me a sour look, and I didn't blame her. 'No one said you did,' she told me, in a 'Don't give me any trouble' kind of voice. I shrugged and drifted away.

I had plenty to do, since some people were still eating supper (and some were drinking it), and some regulars were drifting in after eating at home. Holly was equally busy, and when one of the men who worked for the phone company spilled his beer on the floor, she had to go get the mop and bucket. She was running behind on her tables when the door opened. I saw her putting Sid Matt Lancaster's order in front of him, with her back to the door. So she missed the next entrance, but I didn't. The young man Sam had hired to bus the tables during our busy hour was occupied with clearing two tables pulled together that had held a large party of parish workers, and so I was clearing off the Bellefleurs' table. Andy was chatting with Sam while he waited for Portia, who'd visited the ladies' room. I'd just pocketed my tip, which was fifteen percent of the bill to the penny. The Bellefleur tipping habits had improved – slightly – with the Bellefleur fortunes. I glanced up when the door was held open long enough for a cold gust of air to chill me.

The woman coming in was tall and so slim and broad-shouldered that I checked her chest, just to be sure I'd registered her gender correctly. Her hair was short and thick and brown, and she was wearing absolutely no makeup. There was a man with her, but I didn't see him until she stepped to one side. He was no slouch in the size department himself, and his tight T-shirt revealed arms more developed than any I'd ever seen. Hours in the gym; no, years in the gym. His chestnut hair trailed down to his shoulders in tight curls, and his beard and mustache were perceptibly redder. Neither of the two wore coats, though it was definitely coat weather. The newcomers walked over to me.

'Where's the owner?' the woman asked.

'Sam. He's behind the bar,' I said, looking down as soon as I could and wiping the table all over again. The man had looked at me curiously; that was normal. As they brushed past me, I saw that he carried some posters under his arm and a staple gun. He'd stuck his hand through a roll of masking tape, so it bounced on his left wrist.

I glanced over at Holly. She'd frozen, the cup of coffee in her hand halfway down on its way to Sid Matt Lancaster's placemat. The old lawyer looked up at her, followed her stare to the couple making their way between the tables to the bar. Merlotte's, which had been on the quiet and peaceful side, was suddenly awash in tension. Holly set down the cup without burning Mr Lancaster and spun on her heel, going through the swinging door to the kitchen at warp speed.

I didn't need any more confirmation on the identity of the woman.

The two reached Sam and began a low-voiced conversation with him, with Andy listening in just because he was in the vicinity. I passed by on my way to take the dirty dishes to the hatch, and I heard the woman say (in a deep, alto voice) '. . . put up these posters in town, just in case anyone spots him.'

This was Hallow, the witch whose pursuit of Eric had caused such an upset. She, or a member of her coven, was probably the murderer of Adabelle Yancy. This was the woman who might have taken my brother, Jason. My head began pounding as if there were a little demon inside trying to break out with a hammer.

No wonder Holly was in such a state and didn't want Hallow to glimpse her. She'd been to Hallow's little meeting in Shreveport, and her coven had rejected Hallow's invitation.

'Of course,' Sam said. 'Put up one on this wall.' He indicated a blank spot by the door that led back to the bathrooms and his office.

Holly stuck her head out the kitchen door, glimpsed Hallow, ducked back in. Hallow's eyes flicked over to the door, but not in time to glimpse Holly, I hoped.

I thought of jumping Hallow, beating on her until she told me what I wanted to know about my brother. That was what the pounding in my head was urging me to do – initiate action, any action. But I had a streak of common sense, and luckily for me it came to the fore. Hallow was big, and she had a sidekick who could crush me – plus, Kevin and Kenya would make me stop before I could get her to talk.

It was horribly frustrating to have her right in front of me and at the same time be unable to discover what she knew. I dropped all my shields, and I listened in as hard as I could.

But she suspected something when I touched inside her head.

She looked vaguely puzzled and glanced around. That was enough warning for me. I scrambled back into my own head as quickly as I could. I continued back behind the bar, passing within a couple of feet of the witch as she tried to figure out who'd brushed at her brain.

This had never happened to me before. No one, *no one*, had ever suspected I was listening in. I squatted behind the bar to get the big container of Morton Salt, straightened, and carefully refilled the shaker I'd snatched from Kevin and Kenya's table. I concentrated on this as hard as anyone can focus on performing such a nothing little task, and when I was through, the poster had been mounted with the staple gun. Hallow was lingering, prolonging her talk with Sam so she could figure out who had touched the inside of her head, and Mr Muscles was eyeing me – but only like a man looks at a woman – as I returned the shaker to its table. Holly hadn't reappeared.

'Sookie,' Sam called.

Oh, for goodness sake. I had to respond. He was my boss.

I went over to the three of them, dread in my heart and a smile on my face.

'Hey,' I said, by way of greeting, giving the tall witch and her stalwart sidekick a neutral smile. I raised my eyebrows at Sam to ask him what he'd wanted.

Marnie Stonebrook, Mark Stonebrook,' he said.

I nodded to each of them. *Hallow, indeed*, I thought, half-amused. 'Hallow' was just a tad more spiritual than 'Marnie.'

'They're looking for this guy,' Sam said, indicating the poster. 'You know him?'

Of course Sam knew that I knew Eric. I was glad I'd had years of concealing my feelings and thoughts from the eyes of others. I looked the poster over deliberately.

'Sure, I've seen him,' I said. 'When I went to that bar in Shreveport? He's kind of unforgettable, isn't he?' I gave Hallow – Marnie – a smile. We were just gals together, Marnie and Sookie, sharing a gal moment.

'Handsome guy,' she agreed in her throaty voice. 'He's missing now, and we're offering a reward for anyone who can give us information.'

'I see that from the poster,' I said, letting a tiny hint of irritation show in my voice. 'Is there any particular reason you think he might be around here? I can't imagine what a Shreveport vampire would be doing in Bon Temps.' I looked at her questioningly. Surely I wasn't out of line in asking that?

'Good question, Sookie,' Sam said. 'Not that I mind having the poster up, but how come you two are searching this area for the guy? Why would he be here? Nothing happens in Bon Temps.'

'This town has a vampire in residence, doesn't it?' Mark Stonebrook said suddenly. His voice was almost a twin of his sister's. He was so buff you expected to hear a bass, and even an alto as deep as Marnie's sounded strange coming from his throat. Actually, from Mark Stonebrook's appearance, you'd think he'd just grunt and growl to communicate.

'Yeah, Bill Compton lives here,' Sam said. 'But he's out of town.'

'Gone to Peru, I heard,' I said.

'Oh, yes, I'd heard of Bill Compton. Where does he live?' Hallow asked, trying to keep the excitement out of her voice.

'Well, he lives out across the cemetery from my place,' I said, because I had no choice. If the two asked someone else and got a different answer than the one I gave them, they'd know I had something (or in this case, someone) to conceal. 'Out off Hummingbird

Road.' I gave them directions, not very clear directions, and hoped they got lost out in somewhere like Hotshot.

'Well, we might drop by Compton's house, just in case Eric went to visit him,' Hallow said. Her eyes cut to her brother Mark, and they nodded at us and left the bar. They didn't care whether this made sense or not.

'They're sending witches to visit all the vamps,' Sam said softly. Of course. The Stonebrooks were going to the residences of all vampires who owed allegiance to Eric – the vamps of Area Five. They suspected that one of these vamps might be hiding Eric. Since Eric hadn't turned up, he was being hidden. Hallow had to be confident that her spell had worked, but she might not know exactly how it had worked.

I let the smile fade off my face, and I leaned against the bar on my elbows, trying to think real hard.

Sam said, 'This is big trouble, right?' His face was serious.

'Yes, this is big trouble.'

'Do you need to leave? There's not too much happening here. Holly can come out of the kitchen now that they're gone, and I can always see to the tables myself, if you need to get home . . .' Sam wasn't sure where Eric was, but he suspected, and he'd noticed Holly's abrupt bolt into the kitchen.

Sam had earned my loyalty and respect a hundred times over.

'I'll give them five minutes to get out of the parking lot.'

'Do you think they might have something to do with Jason's disappearance?'

'Sam, I just don't know.' I automatically dialed the sheriff's department and got the same answer I'd gotten all day – 'No news, we'll call you when we know something.' But after she said that, the dispatcher told me that the pond was going to be searched the next day; the police had managed to get hold of two search-and-rescue divers. I didn't know how to feel about this information. Mostly, I was relieved that Jason's disappearance was being taken seriously.

When I hung up the phone, I told Sam the news. After a second, I said, 'It seems too much to believe that two men could disappear in the Bon Temps area at the same time. At least, the Stonebrooks seem to think Eric's around here. I have to think that there's a connection.'

'Those Stonebrooks are Weres,' Sam muttered.

'*And* witches. You be careful, Sam. She's a killer. The Weres of Shreveport are out after her, and the vamps, too. Watch your step.'

'Why is she so scary? Why would the Shreveport pack have any trouble handling her?'

'She's drinking vampire blood,' I said, as close to his ear as I could get without kissing him. I glanced around the room, to see that Kevin was watching our exchange with a lot of interest.

'What does she want with Eric?'

'His business. All his businesses. And him.'

Sam's eyes widened. 'So it's business, and personal.'

'Yep.'

'Do you know where Eric is?' He'd avoided asking me directly until now.

I smiled at him. 'Why would I know that? But I confess, I'm worried about those two being right down the road from my house. I have a feeling they're going to break into Bill's place. They might figure Eric's hiding with Bill, or in Bill's house. I'm sure he's got a safe hole for Eric to sleep in and blood on hand.' That was pretty much all a vampire required, blood and a dark place.

'So you're going over to guard Bill's property? Not a good idea, Sookie. Let Bill's homeowners insurance take care of whatever damage they do searching. I think he told me he went with State Farm. Bill wouldn't want you hurt in defense of plants and bricks.'

'I don't plan on doing anything that dangerous,' I said, and truly, I didn't plan it. 'But I do think I'll run home. Just in case. When I see their car lights leaving Bill's house, I'll go over and check it out.'

'You need me to come with you?'

'Nah, I'm just going to do damage assessment, that's all. Holly'll be enough help here?' She'd popped out of the kitchen the minute the Stonebrooks had left.

'Sure.'

'Okay, I'm gone. Thanks so much.' My conscience didn't twinge as much when I noticed that the place wasn't nearly as busy as it'd been an hour ago. You got nights like that, when people just cleared out all of a sudden.

I had an itchy feeling between my shoulder blades, and maybe all our patrons had, too. It was that feeling that something was prowling that shouldn't be: that Halloween feeling, I call it, when you kind of picture something bad is easing around the corner of your house, to peer into your windows.

By the time I grabbed my purse, unlocked my car, and drove back to my house, I was almost twitching from uneasiness. Everything was going to hell in a handbasket, seemed to me. Jason was missing, the witch was here instead of Shreveport, and now she was within a half mile of Eric.

As I turned from the parish road onto my long, meandering driveway and braked for the deer crossing it from the woods on the south side to the woods on the north – moving away from Bill's house, I noticed – I had worked myself into a state. Pulling around to the back door, I leaped from the car and bounded up the back steps.

I was caught in midbound by a pair of arms like steel bands. Lifted and whirled, I was wrapped around Eric's waist before I knew it.

'Eric,' I said, 'you shouldn't be out—'

My words were cut off by his mouth over mine.

For a minute, going along with this program seemed like a viable alternative. I'd just forget all the badness and screw his brains out on my back porch, cold as it was. But sanity seeped back in past my overloaded emotional state, and I pulled a little away. He was wearing the jeans and Louisiana Tech Bulldogs sweatshirt Jason had bought for him at Wal-Mart. Eric's big hands supported my bottom, and my legs circled him as if they were used to it.

'Listen, Eric,' I said, when his mouth moved down to my neck.

'Ssshh,' he whispered.

'No, you have to let me speak. We have to hide.'

That got his attention. 'From whom?' he said into my ear, and I shivered. The shiver was unrelated to the temperature.

'The bad witch, the one that's after you,' I scrambled to explain. 'She came into the bar with her brother and they put up that poster.'

'So?' His voice was careless.

'They asked what other vampires lived locally, and of course we had to say Bill did. So they asked for directions to Bill's house, and I guess they're over there looking for you.'

'And?'

'That's right across the cemetery from here! What if they come over here?'

'You advise me to hide? To get back in that black hole below your house?' He sounded uncertain, but it was clear to me his pride was piqued.

'Oh, yes. Just for a little while! You're my responsibility; I have to keep you safe.' But I had a sinking feeling I'd expressed my fears in the wrong way. This tentative stranger, however uninterested he seemed in vampire concerns, however little he seemed to remember of his power and possessions, still had the vein of pride and curiosity Eric had always shown at the oddest moments. I'd tapped right into it. I wondered if maybe I could talk him into at least getting into my house, rather than standing out on the porch, exposed.

But it was too late. You just never could tell Eric anything.

Chapter 8

'Come on, lover, let's have a look,' Eric said, giving me a quick kiss. He jumped off the back porch with me still attached to him – like a large barnacle – and he landed silently, which seemed amazing. I was the noisy one, with my breathing and little sounds of surprise. With a dexterity that argued long practice, Eric slung me around so that I was riding his back. I hadn't done this since I was a child and my father had carried me piggyback, so I was considerably startled.

Oh, I was doing one great job of hiding Eric. Here we were, bounding through the cemetery, going *toward* the Wicked Witch of the West, instead of hiding in a dark hole where she couldn't find us. This was *so* smart.

At the same time, I had to admit that I was kind of having fun, despite the difficulties of keeping a grip on Eric in this gently rolling country. The graveyard was somewhat downhill from my house. Bill's house, the Compton house, was quite a bit more uphill from Sweet Home Cemetery. The journey downhill, mild as the slope was, was exhilarating, though I glimpsed two or three parked cars on the narrow blacktop that wound through the graves. That startled me. Teenagers sometimes chose the cemetery for privacy, but not in groups. But before I could think it through, we had passed them, swiftly and silently. Eric managed the uphill portion more slowly, but with no evidence of exhaustion.

We were next to a tree when Eric stopped. It was a huge oak, and when I touched it I became more or less oriented. There was an oak this size maybe twenty yards to the north of Bill's house.

Eric loosened my hands so I'd slide down his back, and then he put me between him and the tree trunk. I didn't know if he was trying to trap me or protect me. I gripped both his wrists in a fairly futile attempt to keep him beside me. I froze when I heard a voice drifting over from Bill's house.

'This car hasn't moved in a while,' a woman said. Hallow. She was in Bill's carport, which was on this side of the house. She was close. I could feel Eric's body stiffen. Did the sound of her voice evoke an echo in his memory?

'The house is locked up tight,' called Mark Stonebrook, from farther away.

'Well, we can take care of that.' From the sound of her voice, she was on the move to the front door. She sounded amused.

They were going to break into Bill's house! Surely I should prevent that? I must have made some sudden move, because Eric's body flattened mine against the trunk of the tree. My coat was worked up around my waist, and the bark bit into my butt through the thin material of my black pants.

I could hear Hallow. She was chanting, her voice low and somehow ominous. She was actually casting a spell. That should have been exciting and I should have been curious: a real magic spell, cast by a real witch. But I felt scared, anxious to get away. The darkness seemed to thicken.

'I smell someone,' Mark Stonebrook said.

Fee, fie, foe, fum.

'What? Here and now?' Hallow stopped her chant, sounding a little breathless.

I began to tremble.

'Yeah.' His voice came out deeper, almost a growl.

'Change,' she ordered, just like that. I heard a sound I knew I'd heard before, though I couldn't trace the memory. It was a sort of gloppy sound. Sticky. Like stirring a stiff spoon through some thick liquid that had hard things in it, maybe peanuts or toffee bits. Or bone chips.

Then I heard a real howl. It wasn't human at all. Mark had changed, and it wasn't the full moon. This was real power. The night suddenly seemed full of life. Snuffling. Yipping. Tiny movements all around us.

I was some great guardian for Eric, huh? I'd let him sweep me over here. We were about to be discovered by a vampire-blood drinking Were witch, and who knows what all else, and I didn't even have Jason's shotgun. I put my arms around Eric and hugged him in apology.

'Sorry,' I whispered, as tiny as a bee would whisper. But then I felt something brush against us, something large and furry, while I was hearing Mark's wolfy sounds from a few feet away on the other side of the tree. I bit my lip hard to keep from giving a yip myself.

Listening intently, I became sure there were more than two animals. I would have given almost anything for a floodlight. From maybe ten yards away came a short, sharp bark. Another wolf? A plain old dog, in the wrong place at the wrong time?

Suddenly, Eric left me. One minute, he was pressing me against the tree in the pitch-black dark, and the next minute, cold air hit me from top to bottom (so much for my holding on to his wrists). I flung my arms out, trying to discover where he was, and touched only air. Had he just stepped away so he could investigate what was happening? Had he decided to join in?

Though my hands didn't encounter any vampires, something big and warm pressed against my legs. I used my fingers to better purpose by reaching down to explore the animal. I touched lots of fur: a pair of upright ears, a long muzzle, a warm tongue. I tried to move, to step away from the oak, but the dog (wolf?) wouldn't let me. Though it was smaller than I and weighed less, it leaned against me with such pressure that there was no way I could move. When I listened to what was going on in the darkness – a lot of growling and snarling – I decided I was actually pretty glad about that. I sank to my knees and put one arm across the canine's back. It licked my face.

I heard a chorus of howls, which rose eerily into the cold night. The hair on my neck stood up, and I buried my face in the neck fur of my companion and prayed. Suddenly, over all the lesser noises, there was a howl of pain and a series of yips.

I heard a car start up, and headlights cut cones into the night. My side of the tree was away from the light, but I could see that I was huddled by a dog, not a wolf. Then the lights moved and gravel sprayed from Bill's driveway as the car reversed. There was a moment's pause, I presumed while the driver shifted into drive, and then the car screeched and I heard it going at high speed down the hill to the turnoff onto Hummingbird Road. There was a terrible thud and a high shrieking sound that made my heart hammer even harder. It was the sound of pain a dog makes when it's been hit by a car.

'Oh, Jesus,' I said miserably, and clutched my furry friend. I thought of something I could do to help, now that it seemed the witches had left.

I got up and ran for the front door of Bill's house before the dog could stop me. I pulled my keys out of my pocket as I ran. They'd been in my hand when Eric had seized me at my back door, and I'd stuffed them into my coat, where a handkerchief had kept them from jingling. I felt around for the lock, counted my keys until I arrived at Bill's – the third on the ring – and opened his front door. I reached in and flipped the outside light switch, and abruptly the yard was illuminated.

It was full of wolves.

I didn't know how scared I should be. Pretty scared, I guessed. I was just assuming both of the Were witches had been in the car. What if one of them was among the wolves present? And where was my vampire?

That question got answered almost immediately. There was a sort of *whump* as Eric landed in the yard.

'I followed them to the road, but they went too fast for me there,' he said, grinning at me as if we'd been playing a game.

A dog – a collie – went up to Eric, looked up at his face and growled.

'Shoo,' Eric said, making an imperious gesture with his hand.

My boss trotted over to me and sat against my legs again. Even in the darkness, I had suspected that my guardian was Sam. The first time I'd encountered him in this transformation, I'd thought he was a stray, and I'd named him Dean, after a man I knew with the same eye color. Now it was a habit to call him Dean when he went on four legs. I sat on Bill's front steps and the collie cuddled against me. I said, 'You are one great dog.' He wagged his tail. The wolves were sniffing Eric, who was standing stock-still.

A big wolf trotted over to me, the biggest wolf I'd ever seen. Weres turn into large wolves, I guess; I haven't seen that many. Living in Louisiana, I've never seen a standard wolf at all. This Were was almost pure black, which I thought was unusual. The rest of the wolves were more silvery, except for one that was smaller and reddish.

The wolf gripped my coat sleeve with its long white teeth and tugged. I rose immediately and went over to the spot where most of the other wolves were milling. We were at the outer edge of the light, so I hadn't noticed the cluster right away. There was blood on the ground, and in the middle of the spreading pool lay a young dark-haired woman. She was naked.

She was obviously and terribly injured.

Her legs were broken, and maybe one arm.

'Go get my car,' I told Eric, in the kind of voice that has to be obeyed.

I tossed him my keys, and he took to the air again. In one available corner of my brain, I hoped that he remembered how to drive. I'd noted that though he'd forgotten his personal history, his modern skills were apparently intact.

I was trying not to think about the poor injured girl right in front of me. The wolves circled and paced, whining. Then the big black one raised his head to the dark sky and howled again. This was a signal to all the others, who did the same thing. I glanced back to be sure that Dean was keeping away, since he was the outsider. I wasn't sure how much human personality was left after these two-natured people trans-formed, and I didn't want anything to happen to him. He was sitting on the small porch, out of the way, his eyes fixed on me.

I was the only creature with opposable thumbs on the scene, and I was suddenly aware that that gave me a lot of responsibility.

First thing to check? Breathing. Yes, she was! She had a pulse. I was no paramedic, but it didn't seem like a normal pulse to me – which would be no wonder. Her skin felt hot, maybe from the changeover back to human. I didn't see a terrifying amount of fresh blood, so I hoped that no major arteries had been ruptured.

I slid a hand beneath the girl's head, very carefully, and touched the dusty dark hair, trying to see if her scalp was lacerated. No.

Sometime during the process of this examination, I began shaking all over. Her injuries were really frightening. Everything I could see of her looked beaten, battered, broken. Her eyes opened. She shuddered. Blankets – she'd need to be kept warm. I glanced around. All the wolves were still wolves.

'It would be great if one or two of you could change back,' I told them. 'I have to get her to a hospital in my car, and she needs blankets from inside this house.'

One of the wolves, a silvery gray, rolled onto its side – okay, male wolf – and I heard the same gloppy noise again. A haze wrapped around the writhing figure, and when it dispersed, Colonel Flood was curled up in place of the wolf. Of course, he was naked, too, but I chose to rise above my natural embarrassment. He had to lie still for at least a minute or two, and it was obviously a great effort for him to sit up.

He crawled over to the injured girl. 'Maria-Star,' he said hoarsely. He bent to smell her, which looked very weird when he was in human form. He whined in distress.

He turned his head to look at me. He said, 'Where?' and I understood he meant the blankets.

'Go in the house, go up the stairs. There's a bedroom at the head of the stairs. There's a blanket chest at the foot of the bed. Get two blankets out of there'

He staggered to his feet, apparently having to deal with some disorientation from his rapid change, before he began striding toward the house.

The girl – Maria-Star – followed him with her eyes.

'Can you talk?' I asked.

'Yes,' she said, barely audibly.

'Where does it hurt worst?'

'I think my hips and legs are broken,' she said. 'The car hit me.'

'Did it throw you up in the air?'

'Yes.'

'The wheels didn't pass over you?'

She shuddered. 'No, it was the impact that hurt me.'

'What's your full name? Maria-Star what?' I'd need to know for the hospital. She might not be conscious by then. 'Cooper,' she whispered.

By then, I could hear a car coming up Bill's drive.

The colonel, moving more smoothly now, sped out of the house with the blankets, and all the wolves and the one human instantly arrayed themselves around me and their wounded pack member. The car was obviously a threat until they learned likewise. I admired the colonel. It took quite a man to face an approaching enemy stark naked.

The new arrival was Eric, in my old car. He pulled up to Maria-Star and me with considerable panache and squealing brakes. The wolves circled restlessly, their glowing yellow eyes fixed on the driver's door. Calvin Norris's eyes had looked quite different; fleetingly, I wondered why.

'It's my car; it's okay,' I said, when one of the Weres began growling. Several pairs of eyes turned to fix on me consideringly. Did I look suspicious, or tasty?

As I finished wrapping Maria-Star in the blankets, I wondered which one of the wolves was Alcide. I suspected he was the largest, darkest one, the one that just that moment turned to look me in the eyes. Yes, Alcide. This was the wolf I'd seen at Club Dead a few weeks ago, when Alcide had been my date on a night that had ended catastrophically – for me and a few other people.

I tried to smile at him, but my face was stiff with cold and shock.

Eric leaped out of the driver's seat, leaving the car running. He opened the back door. 'I'll put her in,' he called, and the wolves began barking. They didn't want their pack sister handled by a vampire, and they didn't want Eric to be anywhere close to Maria-Star.

Colonel Flood said, 'I'll lift her.' Eric looked at the older man's slight physique and lifted a doubtful eyebrow, but had the sense to stand aside. I'd wrapped the girl as well as I could without jarring her, but the colonel knew this was going to hurt her even worse. At the last minute, he hesitated.

'Maybe we should call the ambulance,' he muttered.

'And explain this how?' I asked. 'A bunch of wolves and a naked guy, and her being up here next to a private home where the owner's absent? I don't think so!'

'Of course.' He nodded, accepting the inevitable. Without even a hitch in his breathing, he stood with the bundle that was the girl and went to the car. Eric did run to the other side, open that door, and reach in to help pull her farther onto the backseat. The colonel permitted that. The girl shrieked once, and I scrambled behind the wheel as fast as I could. Eric got in the passenger side, and I said, 'You can't go.'

'Why not?' He sounded amazed and affronted.

'I'll have twice the explaining to do if I have a vampire with me!' It took most people a few minutes to decide Eric was dead, but of course they would figure it out eventually. Eric stubbornly stayed put. 'And everyone's seeing your face on the damn posters,' I said, working to keep my voice reasonable but urgent. 'I live among pretty good people, but there's no one in this parish who couldn't use that much money.'

He got out, not happily, and I yelled, 'Turn off the lights and relock the house, okay?'

'Meet us at the bar when you have word about Maria-Star!' Colonel Flood yelled back. 'We've got to get our cars and clothes out of the cemetery.' Okay, that explained the glimpse I'd caught on the way over.

As I steered slowly down the driveway, the wolves watched me go, Alcide standing apart from the rest, his black furry face turning to follow my progress. I wondered what wolfy thoughts he was thinking.

The closest hospital was not in Bon Temps, which is way too small to have its own (we're lucky to have a Wal-Mart), but in nearby Clarice, the parish seat. Luckily, it's on the outskirts of the town, on the side nearest Bon Temps. The ride to the Renard Parish Hospital only seemed to take years; actually, I got there in about twenty minutes. My passenger moaned for the first ten minutes, and then fell ominously silent. I talked to her, begged her to talk to me, asked her to tell me how old she was, and turned on the radio in attempt to spark some response from Maria-Star.

I didn't want to take the time to pull over and check on her, and I wouldn't have known what to do if I had, so I drove like a bat out of hell. By the time I pulled up to the emergency entrance and called to the two nurses standing outside smoking, I was sure the poor Were was dead.

She wasn't, judging from the activity that surrounded her in the next couple of minutes. Our parish hospital is a little one, of course, and it doesn't have the facilities that a city hospital can boast. We counted ourselves lucky to have a hospital at all. That night, they saved the Were's life.

The doctor, a thin woman with graying spiked hair and huge black-rimmed glasses, asked me a few pointed questions that I couldn't answer, though I'd been working on my basic story all the way to the hospital. After finding me clueless, the doctor made it clear I was to get the hell out of the way and let her team work. So I sat in a chair in the hall and waited, and worked on my story some more.

There was no way I could be useful here, and the glaring fluorescent lights and the gleaming linoleum made a harsh, unfriendly environment. I tried to read a magazine, and tossed it on the table after a couple of minutes. For the seventh or eighth time, I thought of skipping out. But there was a woman stationed at the night reception desk, and she was keeping a close eye on me. After a few more minutes, I decided to visit the women's room to wash the blood off my hands. While I was in there, I took a few swipes at my coat with a wet paper towel, which was largely a wasted effort.

When I emerged from the women's room, there were two cops waiting for me. They were big men, both of them. They rustled with their synthetic padded jackets, and they creaked with the leather of their belts and equipment. I couldn't imagine them sneaking up on anyone.

The taller man was the older. His steel gray hair was clipped close to his scalp. His face was carved with a few deep wrinkles, like ravines. His gut overhung his belt. His partner was a younger man, maybe thirty, with light brown hair and light brown eyes and light brown skin – a curiously monochromatic guy. I gave them a quick but comprehensive scan with all my senses.

I could tell the two were both prepared to find out I'd had a hand in the injuries of the girl I'd brought in, or that I at least knew more than I was saying.

Of course, they were partially right.

'Miss Stackhouse? You brought in the young woman Dr Skinner is treating?' the younger man said gently. 'Maria-Star,' I said. 'Cooper.'

'Tell us how you came to do that,' the older cop said.

It was definitely an order, though his tone was moderate. Neither man knew me or knew of me, I 'heard'. Good.

I took a deep breath and dove into the waters of mendacity. 'I was driving home from work,' I said. 'I work at Merlotte's Bar – you know where that is?'

They both nodded. Of course, police would know the location of every bar in the parish.

'I saw a body lying by the side of the road, on the gravel of the shoulder,' I said carefully, thinking ahead so I wouldn't say something I couldn't take back. 'So I stopped. There wasn't anyone else in sight. When I found out she was still alive, I knew I had to get to help. It took me a long time to get her into the car by myself.' I was trying to account for the passage of time since I'd left work and the gravel from Bill's driveway that I knew would be in her skin. I couldn't gauge how much care I needed to take in putting my story together, but more care was better than less.

'Did you notice any skid marks on the road?' The light brown policeman couldn't go long without asking a question.

'No, I didn't notice. They may have been there. I was just – after I saw her, all I thought about was her.'

'So?' the older man prompted.

'I could tell she was hurt real bad, so I got her here as fast as I could.' I shrugged. End of my story.

'You didn't think about calling an ambulance?'

'I don't have a cell phone.'

'Woman who comes home from work that late, by herself, really ought to have a cell phone, ma'am.'

I opened my mouth to tell him that if he felt like paying the bill, I'd be glad to have one, when I restrained myself. Yes, it *would* be handy to have a cell phone, but I could barely afford my regular phone. My only extravagance was cable TV, and I justified that by telling myself it was my only recreational spending. 'I hear you,' I said briefly.

'And your full name is?' This from the younger man. I looked up, met his eyes.

'Sookie Stackhouse,' I said. He'd been thinking I seemed kind of shy and sweet.

'You the sister of the man who's missing?' The gray-haired man bent down to look in my face.

'Yes, sir.' I looked down at my toes again.

'You're sure having a streak of bad luck, Miss Stackhouse.'

'Tell me about it,' I said, my voice shaking with sincerity.

'Have you ever seen this woman, the woman you brought in, before tonight?' The older officer was scribbling in a little notepad he'd produced from a pocket. His name was Curlew, the little pin on his pocket said.

I shook my head.

'You think your brother might have known her?'

I looked up, startled. I met the eyes of the brown man again. His name was Stans. 'How the heck would I know?' I asked. I knew in the next second that he'd just wanted me to look up again. He didn't know what to make of me. The monochromatic Stans thought I was pretty and seemed like a good little Samaritan. On the other hand, my job was one educated nice girls didn't often take, and my brother was well known as a brawler, though many of the patrol officers liked him.

'How is she doing?' I asked.

They both glanced at the door behind which the struggle to save the young woman went on.

'She's still alive,' Stans said.

'Poor thing,' I said. Tears rolled down my cheeks, and I began fumbling in my pockets for a tissue.

'Did she say anything to you, Miss Stackhouse?'

I had to think about that. 'Yes,' I said. 'She did.' The truth was safe, in this instance.

They both brightened at the news.

'She told me her name. She said her legs hurt worst, when I asked her,' I said. 'And she said that the car had hit her, but not run her over.'

The two men looked at each other.

'Did she describe the car?' Stans asked.

It was incredibly tempting to describe the witches' car. But I mistrusted the glee that bubbled up inside me at the idea. And I was glad I had, the next second, when I realized that the trace evidence they'd get off the car would be wolf fur. Good thinking, Sook.

'No, she didn't,' I said, trying to look as though I'd been groping through my memory. 'She didn't really talk much after that, just moaning. It was awful.' And the upholstery on my backseat was probably ruined, too. I immediately wished I hadn't thought of something so selfish.

'And you didn't see any other cars, trucks, any other vehicles on your way to your house from the bar, or even when you were coming back to town?'

That was a slightly different question. 'Not on my road,' I said hesitantly. 'I probably saw a few cars when I got closer to Bon Temps and went through town. And of course I saw more between Bon Temps and Clarice. But I don't recall any in particular.'

'Can you take us to the spot where you picked her up? The exact place?'

'I doubt it. There wasn't anything to mark it besides her,' I said. My coherence level was falling by the minute. 'No big tree, or road, or mile marker. Maybe tomorrow? In the daytime?'

Stans patted me on the shoulder. 'I know you're shook up, miss,' he said consolingly. 'You done the best you could for this girl. Now we gotta leave it up to the doctors and the Lord.'

I nodded emphatically, because I certainly agreed. The older Curlew still looked at me a little skeptically, but he thanked me as a matter of form, and they strode out of the hospital into the blackness. I stepped back a little, though I remained looking out into the parking lot. In a second or two, they reached my car and shone their big flashlights through the windows, checking out the interior. I keep the inside of my car spanky-clean, so they wouldn't see a thing but bloodstains in the backseat. I noticed that they checked out the front grille, too, and I didn't blame them one little bit.

They examined my car over and over, and finally they stood under one of the big lights, making notes on clipboards.

Not too long after that, the doctor came out to find me. She pulled her mask down and rubbed the back of her neck with a long, thin hand. 'Miss Cooper is doing better. She's stable,' she said.

I nodded, and then I closed my eyes for a moment with sheer relief. 'Thank you,' I croaked.

'We're going to airlift her to Schumpert in Shreveport. The helicopter'll be here any second.'

I blinked, trying to decide if that were a good thing or a bad thing. No matter what my opinion was, the Were had to go to the best and closest hospital. When she became able to talk, she'd have to tell them something. How could I ensure that her story jibed with mine?

'Is she conscious?' I asked.

'Just barely,' the doctor said, almost angrily, as if such injuries were an insult to her personally. 'You can speak to her briefly, but I can't guarantee she'll remember, or understand. I have to go talk to the cops.' The two officers were striding back into the hospital, I saw from my place at the window.

'Thank you,' I said, and followed her gesture to her left. I pushed open the door into the grim glaring room where they'd been working on the girl.

It was a mess. There were a couple of nurses in there even now, chatting about this or that and packing away some of the unused packages of bandages and tubes. A man with a bucket and mop stood waiting in a corner. He would clean the room when the Were – the girl – had been wheeled out to the helicopter. I went to the side of the narrow bed and took her hand.

I bent down close.

'Maria-Star, you know my voice?' I asked quietly. Her face was swollen from its impact with the ground, and it was covered with scratches and scrapes. These were the smallest of her injuries, but they looked very painful to me.

'Yes,' she breathed.

'I'm the one that found you by the *side of the road*,' I said. 'On the way to my house, south of Bon Temps. You were lying by the parish road.'

'Understand,' she murmured.

'I guess,' I continued carefully, 'that someone made you get out of his car, and that someone then hit you with the car. But you know how it is after a trauma, sometimes people don't remember *anything.*' One of the nurses turned to me, her face curious. She'd caught the last part of my sentence. 'So don't worry if you don't remember.'

'I'll try,' she said ambiguously, still in that hushed, faraway voice.

There was nothing more I could do here, and a lot more that could go wrong, so I whispered 'Good-bye,' told the nurses I appreciated them, and went out to my car. Thanks to the blankets (which I supposed I'd have to replace for Bill), my backseat wasn't messed up too bad.

I was glad to find something to be pleased about.

I wondered about the blankets. Did the police have them? Would the hospital call me about them? Or had they been pitched in the garbage? I shrugged. There was no point worrying about two rectangles of material anymore, when I had so much else crammed on my worry list. For one thing, I didn't like the Weres congregating at Merlotte's. That pulled Sam way too far into Were concerns. He was a shifter, after all, and shifters were much more loosely involved with the supernatural world. Shifters tended to be more 'every shifter for himself,' while the Weres were always organized. Now they were using Merlotte's for a meeting place, after hours.

And then there was Eric. Oh, Lord, Eric would be waiting for me at the house.

I found myself wondering what time it was in Peru. Bill had to be having more fun than I was. It seemed like I'd gotten worn out on New Year's Eve and never caught up; I'd never felt this exhausted.

I was just past the intersection where I'd turned left, the road that eventually passed Merlotte's. The headlights illuminated flashes of trees and bushes. At least there were no more vampires running down the side . . .

'Wake up,' said the woman sitting by me on the front seat.

'What?' My eyelids popped open. The car swerved violently.

'You were falling asleep.'

By this time, I wouldn't have been surprised if a beached whale had lain across the road.

'You're who?' I asked, when I felt my voice might be under my control.

'Claudine.'

It was hard to recognize her in the dashboard light, but sure enough, it seemed to be the tall and beautiful woman who'd been in Merlotte's New Year's Eve, who'd been with Tara the previous morning. 'How did you get in my car? Why are you here?'

'Because there's been an unusual amount of supernatural activity in this area in the past week or two. I'm the go-between.'

'Go between what?'

'Between the two worlds. Or, more accurately, between the three worlds.'

Sometimes life just hands you more than you can take. Then you just accept.

'So, you're like an angel? That's how come you woke me up when I was falling asleep at the wheel?'

'No, I haven't gotten that far yet. You're too tired to take this in. You have to ignore the mythology and just accept me for what I am.'

I felt a funny jolt in my chest.

'Look,' Claudine pointed out. 'That man's waving to you.'

Sure enough, in Merlotte's parking lot there stood a semaphoring vampire. It was Chow.

'Oh, just great,' I said, in the grumpiest voice I could manage. 'Well, I hope you don't mind us stopping, Claudine. I need to go in.'

'Sure, I wouldn't miss it.'

Chow waved me to the rear of the bar, and I was astonished to find the employee parking area jam-packed with cars that had been invisible from the road.

'Oh, boy!' Claudine said. 'A party!' She got out of my car as if she could hardly restrain her glee, and I had the satisfaction of seeing that Chow was absolutely stupefied when he took in all six feet of her. It's hard to surprise a vampire.

'Let's go in,' Claudine said gaily, and took my hand.

Chapter 9

Every Supe I'd ever met was in Merlotte's. Or maybe it just seemed like that, since I was dead tired and wanted to be by myself. The Were pack was there, all in human form and all more or less dressed, to my relief.

Alcide was in khakis and an unbuttoned shirt in green and blue plaid. It was hard to believe he could run on four legs. The Weres were drinking coffee or soft drinks, and Eric (looking happy and healthy) was having some TrueBlood. Pam was sitting on a barstool, wearing an ash green tracksuit, which she managed to make prim-but-sexy. She had a bow in her hair and beaded sneakers on her feet. She'd brought Gerald with her, a vampire I'd met once or twice at Fangtasia. Gerald looked about thirty, but I'd heard him refer to Prohibition once as if he'd lived through it. What little I knew of Gerald didn't predispose me to getting closer to him.

Even in such a company, my entrance with Claudine was nothing short of sensational. In the improved lighting of the bar, I could see that Claudine's strategically rounded body was packed into an orange knit dress, and her long legs ended in the highest of high heels. She looked like a scrumptious slut, super-sized.

Nope, she couldn't be an angel – at least, as I understood angels.

Looking from Claudine to Pam, I decided it was massively unfair that they looked so clean and appealing. Like I needed to feel unattractive, in addition to being worn out and scared and confused! Doesn't every gal want to walk into a room side by side with a gorgeous woman who practically has 'I want to fuck' tattooed on her forehead? If I hadn't caught a glimpse of Sam, whom I'd dragged into this whole thing, I would've turned around and walked right out.

'Claudine,' said Colonel Flood. 'What brings you here?'

Pam and Gerald were both staring at the woman in orange intently, as if they expected her to take off her clothes any second.

'My girl, here' – and Claudine inclined her head toward me – 'fell asleep at the wheel. How come you aren't watching out for her better?'

The colonel, as dignified in his civvies as he had been in his skin, looked a little startled, as if it was news to him that he was supposed to provide protection for me. 'Ah,' he said. 'Uh . . .'

'Should have sent someone to the hospital with her,' Claudine said, shaking her waterfall of black hair.

'I offered to go with her,' Eric said indignantly. She said it would be too suspicious if she went to the hospital with a vampire.'

'Well, hel-lo, tall, blond, and *dead*,' Claudine said. She looked Eric up and down, admiring what she saw. 'You in the habit of doing what human women ask of you?'

Thanks a lot, Claudine, I told her silently. I was supposed to be guarding Eric, and now he wouldn't even shut the door if I told him to. Gerald was still ogling her in the same stunned way. I wondered if anyone would notice if I stretched out on one of the tables and went to sleep. Suddenly, just as Pam's and Gerald's had done, Eric's gaze sharpened and he seemed fixed on Claudine. I had time to think it was like watching cats that'd suddenly spotted something skittering along the baseboards before big hands spun me around and Alcide gathered me to him. He'd maneuvered through the crowd in the bar until he'd reached me. Since his shirt wasn't buttoned, I found my face pressed against his warm chest, and I was glad to be there. The curly black hair did smell faintly of dog, true, but otherwise I was comforted at being hugged and cherished. It felt delightful.

'Who are you?' Alcide asked Claudine. I had my ear against his chest and I could hear him from inside and outside, a strange sensation.

'I'm Claudine, the fairy,' the huge woman said. 'See?'

I had to turn to see what she was doing. She'd lifted her long hair to show her ears, which were delicately pointed.

'Fairy,' Alcide repeated. He sounded as astonished as I felt.

'Sweet,' said one of the younger Weres, a spiky-haired male who might be nineteen. He looked intrigued with the turn of events, and he glanced around at the other Weres seated at his table as if inviting them to share his pleasure. 'For real?'

'For a while,' Claudine said. 'Sooner or later, I'll go one way or another.' No one understood that, with the possible exception of the colonel.

'You are one mouthwatering woman,' said the young Were. To back up the fashion statement of the spiked hair, he wore jeans and a ragged Fallen Angel T-shirt; he was barefoot, though Merlotte's was cool, since the thermostat was turned down for the rest of the night. He was wearing toe rings.

'Thanks!' Claudine smiled down at him. She snapped her fingers, and there was the same kind of haze around her that enveloped the Weres when they shifted. It was the haze of thick magic. When the air cleared, Claudine was wearing a spangled white evening gown.

'Sweet,' the boy repeated in a dazed way, and Claudine basked in his admiration. I noticed she was keeping a certain distance from the vampires.

'Claudine, now that you've shown off, could we please talk about something besides you?' Colonel Flood sounded as tired as I felt.

'Of course,' Claudine said in an appropriately chastened voice. 'Just ask away.'

'First things first. Miss Stackhouse, how is Maria-Star?'

'She survived the ride to the hospital in Clarice. They're airlifting her to Shreveport, to Schumpert hospital. She may already be on her way. The doctor sounded pretty positive about her chances.'

The Weres all looked at one another, and most of them let out gusty noises of relief. One woman, about thirty years old, actually did a little happy dance. The vampires, by now almost totally fixated on the fairy, didn't react at all.

'What did you tell the emergency room doctor?' Colonel Flood asked. 'I have to let her parents know what the official line is.' Maria-

Star would be their first-born, and their only Were child.

'I told the police that I found her by the side of the road, that I didn't see any signs of a car braking or anything. I told them she was lying on the gravel, so we won't have to worry about grass that isn't pressed down when it ought to be … . I hope she got it. She was pretty doped up when I talked to her.'

'Very good thinking,' Colonel Flood said. 'Thanks, Miss Stackhouse. Our pack is indebted to you.'

I waved my hand to disclaim any debt. 'How did you come to show up at Bill's house at the right time?'

'Emilio and Sid tracked the witches to the right area.' Emilio must be the small, dark man with huge brown eyes. There was a growing immigrant Mexican population in our area, and Emilio was apparently a part of that community. The spike-haired boy gave me a little wave, and I assumed he must be Sid. 'Anyway, after dark, we started keeping an eye on the building whcrc Hallow and her coven are holed up. It's hard to do; it's a residential neighborhood that's mostly black.' African-American twins, both girls, grinned at each other. They were young enough to find this exciting, like Sid. 'When Hallow and her brother left for Bon Temps, we followed them in our cars. We called Sam, too, to warn him.'

I looked at Sam reproachfully. He hadn't warned me, hadn't mentioned the Weres were heading our way, too.

Colonel Flood went on, 'Sam called me on my cell to tell me where he figured they were heading when they walked out of his bar. I decided an isolated place like the Compton house would be a good place to get them. We were able to park our cars in the cemetery and change, so we got there just in time. But they caught our scent early.' The colonel glared at Sid. Apparently, the younger Were had jumped the gun.

'So they got away,' I said, trying to sound neutral. 'And now they know you're on to them.'

'Yes, they got away. The murderers of Adabelle Yancy. The leaders of a group trying to take over not only the vamps' territory, but ours.' Colonel Flood had been sweeping the assembled Weres with a cold gaze, and they wilted under his stare, even Alcide. 'And now the witches'll be on their guard, since they know we're after them.'

Their attention momentarily pulled from the radiant fairy Claudine, Pam and Gerald seemed discreetly amused by the colonel's speech. Eric, as always these days, looked as confused as if the colonel were speaking in Sanskrit.

'The Stonebrooks went back to Shreveport when they left Bill's?' I asked.

'We assume so. We had to change back very quickly – no easy matter – and then get to our cars. A few of us went one way, a few another, but we caught no glimpse of them.'

'And now we're here. Why?' Alcide's voice was harsh.

'We're here for several reasons,' the packmaster said. 'First, we wanted to know about Maria-Star. Also, we wanted to recover for a bit before we drive back to Shreveport ourselves.'

The Weres, who seemed to have pulled their clothes on pretty hastily, did look a little ragged. The dark-moon transformation and the rapid change back to two-legged form had taken a toll on all of them.

'And why are you here?' I asked Pam.

'We have something to report, too,' she said. 'Evidently, we have the same goals as the Weres – on this matter, anyway.' She tore her gaze away from Claudine with an effort. She and Gerald exchanged glances, and as one, they turned to Eric, who looked back at them blankly. Pam sighed, and Gerald looked down at his booted feet.

'Our nest mate Clancy didn't return to us last night,' Pam said. Hard on this startling announcement, she focused once again on the fairy. Claudine seemed to have some overwhelming allure for the vampires.

Most of the Weres looked like they were thinking that one less vampire was a step in the right direction. But Alcide said, 'What do you think has happened?'

'We got a note,' Gerald said, one of the few times I'd ever heard him speak out loud. He had a faint English accent. 'The note said that the witches plan to drain one of our vampires for each day they have to search for Eric.'

All eyes went to Eric, who looked stunned. 'But why?' he asked. 'I can't understand what makes me such a prize.'

One of the Were girls, a tan blonde in her late twenties, took silent issue with that. She rolled her eyes toward me, and I could only grin back. But no matter how good Eric looked, and what ideas interested parties might have about the fun to be had with him in bed (and on top of that, the control he had over various vampire enterprises in Shreveport), this single-minded pursuit of Eric rang the 'Excessive' alarm. Even if Hallow had sex with Eric, and then drained him dry and consumed all his blood – Wait, there was an idea.

'How much blood can be got from one of you?' I asked Pam.

She stared at me, as close to surprised as I'd ever seen her. 'Let me see,' she said. She stared into space, and her fingers wiggled. It looked like Pam was translating from one unit of measurement to another. Six quarts,' she said at last.

'And how much blood do they sell in those little vials?'

'That's . . .' She did some more figuring. 'Well, that would be less than a fourth of a cup.' She anticipated where I was heading. 'So Eric contains over ninety-six saleable units of blood.'

'How much you reckon they could charge for that?'

'Well, on the street, the price has reached $225 for regular vampire blood,' Pam said, her eyes as cold as winter frost. 'For Eric's blood . . . He is so old . . .'

'Maybe $425 a vial?'

'Conservatively.'

'So, on the hoof, Eric's worth . . .'

'Over forty thousand dollars.'

The whole crowd stared at Eric with heightened interest – except for Pam and Gerald, who along with Eric had resumed their contemplation of Claudine. They appeared to have inched closer to the fairy.

'So, do you think that's enough motivation?' I asked. 'Eric spurned her. She wants him, she wants his stuff, and she wants to sell his blood.'

'That's a lot of motivation,' agreed a Were woman, a pretty brunette in her late forties.

'Plus, Hallow's nuts,' Claudine said cheerfully.

I didn't think the fairy had stopped smiling since she'd appeared in my car. 'How do you know that, Claudine?' I asked.

'I've been to her headquarters,' she said.

We all regarded her in silence for a long moment, but not as raptly as the three vampires did.

'Claudine, have you gone over?' Colonel Flood asked. He sounded more tired than anything else.

'James,' Claudine said. 'Shame on you! She thought I was an area witch.'

Maybe I wasn't the only one who was thinking that such overflowing cheer was a little weird. Most of the fifteen or so Weres in the bar didn't seem too comfortable around the fairy. 'It would have saved us a lot of trouble if you'd told us that earlier than tonight, Claudine,' the colonel said, his tone frosty.

'A real fairy,' Gerald said. 'I've only had one before.'

'They're hard to catch,' Pam said, her voice dreamy. She edged a little closer.

Even Eric had lost his blank and frustrated mien and took a step toward Claudine. The three vamps looked like chocaholics at the Hershey factory.

'Now, now,' Claudine said, a little anxiously. 'Anything with fangs, take a step back!'

Pam looked a bit embarrassed, and she tried to relax. Gerald subsided unwillingly. Eric kept creeping forward.

Neither of the vampires nor any of the Weres looked willing to take Eric on. I mentally girded my loins. After all, Claudine had awakened me before I could crash my car.

'Eric,' I said, taking three quick steps to stand between Eric and the fairy. 'Snap out of it!'

'What?' Eric paid no more attention to me than he would to a fly buzzing around his head.

'She's off limits, Eric,' I said, and Eric's eyes did flicker down to my face.

'Hi, remember me?' I put my hand on his chest to slow him down. 'I don't know why you're in such a lather, fella, but you need to hold your horses.'

'I want her,' Eric said, his blue eyes blazing down into mine.

'Well, she's gorgeous,' I said, striving for reasonable, though actually

I was a little hurt. 'But she's not available. Right, Claudine?' I aimed my voice back over my shoulder.

'Not available to a vampire,' the fairy said. 'My blood is intoxicating to a vampire. You don't want to know what they'd be like after they had me.' But she still sounded cheerful.

So I hadn't been too far wrong with the chocolate metaphor. Probably this was why I hadn't encountered any fairies before; I was too much in the company of the undead.

When you have thoughts like that, you know you're in trouble.

'Claudine, I guess we need you to step outside now,' I said a little desperately. Eric was pushing against me, not testing me seriously yet (or I'd be flat on my back), but I'd had to retreat a step already. I wanted to hear what Claudine had to tell the Weres, but I realized separating the vamps from the fairy was top priority.

'Just like a big petit four,' Pam sighed, watching Claudine twitch her white-spangled butt all the way out the front door with Colonel Flood close behind her. Eric seemed to snap to once Claudine was out of sight, and I breathed a sigh of relief.

'Vamps really like fairies, huh?' I said nervously. 'Oh, yeah,' they said simultaneously.

'You know, she saved my life, and she's apparently helping us out on this witch thing,' I reminded them.

They looked sulky.

'Claudine was actually quite helpful,' Colonel Flood said as he reentered, sounding surprised. The door swung shut behind him.

Eric's arm went around me, and I could feel one kind of hunger being morphed into another.

'Why was she in their coven headquarters?' Alcide asked, more angrily than was warranted.

'You know fairies. They love to flirt with disaster, they love to role-play.' The packmaster sighed heavily. 'Even Claudine, and she's one of the good ones. Definitely on her way up. What she tells me is this: This Hallow has a coven of about twenty witches. All of them are Weres or the larger shifters. They are all vampire blood users, maybe addicts.'

'Will the Wiccans help us fight them?' asked a middle- aged woman with dyed red hair and a couple of chins.

'They haven't committed to it yet.' A young man with a military haircut – I wondered if he was stationed at Barksdale Air Force Base – seemed to know the story on the Wiccans. 'Acting on our packmaster's orders, I called or otherwise contacted every Wiccan coven or individual Wiccan in the area, and they are all doing their best to hide from these creatures. But I saw signs that most of them were heading for a meeting tonight, though I don't know where. I think they are going to discuss the situation on their own. If they could mount an attack as well, it would help us.'

'Good work, Portugal,' said Colonel Flood, and the young man looked gratified.

Since we had our backs to the wall, Eric had felt free to let his hand roam over my bottom. I didn't object to the sensation, which was very pleasant, but I did object to the venue, which was too darn public.

'Claudine didn't say anything about prisoners who might have been there?' I asked, taking a step away from Eric.

'No, I'm sorry, Miss Stackhouse. She didn't see anyone answering your brother's description, and she didn't see the vampire Clancy.'

I wasn't exactly surprised, but I was very disappointed. Sam said, 'I'm sorry, Sookie. If Hallow doesn't have him, where can he be?'

'Of course, just because she didn't see him, doesn't mean he's not there for sure,' the colonel said. 'We're sure she took Clancy, and Claudine didn't catch sight of him.'

'Back to the Wiccans,' suggested the red-haired Were. 'What should we do about them?'

'Tomorrow, Portugal, call all your Wiccan contacts again,' Colonel Flood said. 'Get Culpepper to help you.'

Culpepper was a young woman with a strong, handsome face and a no-nonsense haircut. She looked pleased to be included in something Portugal was doing. He looked pleased, too, but he tried to mask it under a brusque manner. 'Yes, sir,' he said snappily. Culpepper thought that was cute as hell; I was lifting that directly from her brain. Were she might be, but you couldn't disguise an admiration that intense. 'Uh, why am I calling them again?' Portugal asked after a long moment.

'We need to know what they plan to do, if they'll share that with us,' Colonel Flood said. 'If they're not with us, they can at least stay out of the way.'

'So, we're going to war?' This was from an older man, who seemed to be a pair with the red-haired woman.

'It was the vampires that started it,' the redheaded woman said.

'That is *so* untrue,' I said indignantly.

'Vamp humper,' she said.

I'd had worse things said about me, but not to my face, and not from people who intended me to hear them.

Eric had left the floor before I could decide if I was more hurt or more enraged. He had instantly opted for enraged, and it made him very effective. She was on the ground on her back and he was on top of her with fangs extended before anyone could even be alarmed. It was lucky for the red-haired woman that Pam and Gerald were equally swift, though it took both of them to lift Eric off the redheaded Were. She was bleeding only a little, but she was yelping nonstop.

For a long second, I thought the whole room was going to erupt into battle, but Colonel Flood roared, 'SILENCE!' and you didn't disobey that voice.

'Amanda,' he said to the red-haired woman, who was whimpering as though Eric had removed a limb, and whose companion was busy checking out her injuries in a wholly unnecessary panic, 'you will be polite to our allies, and you will keep your damn opinions to yourself. Your offense cancels out the blood he spilled. No retaliation, Parnell!' The male Were snarled at the colonel, but finally gave a grudging nod.

'Miss Stackhouse, I apologize for the poor manners of the pack,' Colonel Flood said to me. Though I was still upset, I made myself nod. I couldn't help but notice that Alcide was looking from me to Eric, and he looked – well, he looked appalled. Sam had the sense to be quite expressionless. My back stiffened, and I ran a quick hand over my eyes to dash away the tears.

Eric was calming down, but it was with an effort. Pam was murmuring in his ear, and Gerald was keeping a good grip on his arm.

To make my evening perfect, the back door to Merlotte's opened once again, and Debbie Pelt walked in.

'Y'all are having a party without me.' She looked at the odd assemblage and raised her eyebrows. 'Hey, baby,' she said directly to Alcide, and ran a possessive hand down his arm, twining her fingers with his. Alcide had an odd expression on his face. It was as though he was simultaneously happy and miserable.

Debbie was a striking woman, tall and lean, with a long face. She had black hair, but it wasn't curly and disheveled like Alcide's. It was cut in asymmetrical tiny clumps, and it was straight and swung with her movement. It was the dumbest haircut I'd ever seen, and it had undoubtedly cost an arm and a leg. Somehow, men didn't seem to be interested in her haircut.

It would have been hypocritical of me to greet her. Debbie and I were beyond that. She'd tried to kill me, a fact that Alcide knew; and yet she still seemed to exercise some fascination for him, though he'd thrown her out when he first learned of it. For a smart and practical and hardworking man, he had a great big blind spot, and here it was, in tight Cruel Girl jeans and a thin orange sweater that hugged every inch of skin. What was she doing here, so far from her own stomping grounds?

I felt a sudden impulse to turn to Eric and tell him that Debbie had made a serious attempt on my life, just to see what would happen. But I restrained myself yet again. All this restraint was plain painful. My fingers were curled under, transforming my hands into tight fists.

'We'll call you if anything more happens in this meeting,' Gerald said. It took me a minute to understand I was being dismissed, and that it was because I had to take Eric back to my house lest he erupt again. From the look on his face, it wouldn't take much. His eyes were glowing blue, and his fangs were at least half extended. I was more than ever tempted to . . . no, I was *not*. I would leave.

'Bye, bitch,' Debbie said, as I went out the door. I caught a glimpse of Alcide turning to her, his expression appalled, but Pam grabbed me by the arm and hustled me out into the parking lot. Gerald had a hold of Eric, which was a good thing, too.

As the two vampires handed us out to Chow, I was seething.

Chow thrust Eric into the passenger's seat, so it appeared I was the designated driver. The Asian vamp said, 'We'll call you later, go home,' and I was about to snap back at him. But I glanced over at my passenger and decided to be smart instead and get out of there quickly. Eric's belligerence was dissolving into a muddle. He looked confused and lost, as unlike the hair-trigger avenger he'd been only a few minutes before as you can imagine.

We were halfway home before Eric said anything. 'Why are vampires so hated by Weres?' he asked.

'I don't know,' I answered, slowing down because two deer bounded across the road. You see the first one, you always wait: There'll be another one, most often. 'Vamps feel the same about Weres and shifters. The supernatural community seems to band together against humans, but other than that, you guys squabble a lot, at least as far as I can tell.' I took a deep breath and considered phraseology. 'Um, Eric, I appreciate your taking my part, when that Amanda called me a name. But I'm pretty used to speaking up for myself when I think it's called for. If I were a vampire, you wouldn't feel you had to hit people on my behalf, right?'

'But you're not as strong as a vampire, not even as strong as a Were,' Eric objected.

'No argument there, honey. But I also wouldn't have even thought of hitting her, because that would give her a reason to hit me back.'

'You're saying I made it come to blows when I didn't need to.'

'That's exactly what I'm saying.'

'I embarrassed you.'

'No,' I said instantly. Then I wondered if that wasn't exactly the case. 'No,' I repeated with more conviction, 'you didn't embarrass me. Actually, it made me feel good, that you felt, ah, fond enough of me to be angry when Amanda acted like I was something stuck to her shoe. But I'm used to that treatment, and I can handle it. Though Debbie's taking it to a whole different level.'

The new, thoughtful Eric gave that a mental chewing over.

'Why are you used to that?' he asked.

It wasn't the reaction I'd expected. By that time we were at the house, and I checked out the surrounding clearing before I got out of the car to unlock the back door. When we were safely inside with the dead bolt shot, I said, 'Because I'm used to people not thinking much of barmaids. Uneducated barmaids. Uneducated telepathic barmaids. I'm used to people thinking I'm crazy, or at least off mentally. I'm not trying to sound like I think I'm Poor Pitiful Pearl, but I don't have a lot of fans, and I'm used to that.'

'That confirms my bad opinion of humans in general,' Eric said. He pulled my coat off my shoulders, looked at it with distaste, hung it on the back of one of the chairs pushed in under the kitchen table. 'You are beautiful.'

No one had ever looked me in the eyes and said that. I found I had to lower my head. 'You are smart, and you are loyal,' he said relentlessly, though I waved a hand to ask him to quit. 'You have a sense of fun and adventure.'

'Cut it out,' I said.

'Make me,' he said. 'You have the most beautiful breasts I've ever seen. You're brave.' I put my fingers across his mouth, and his tongue darted out to give them a quick lick. I relaxed against him, feeling the tingle down to my toes. 'You're responsible and hardworking,' he continued. Before he could tell me that I was good about replacing the garbage can liner when I took the garbage out, I replaced my fingers with my lips.

'There,' he said softly, after a long moment. 'You're creative, too.'

For the next hour, he showed me that he, too, was creative.

It was the only hour in an extremely long day that I hadn't been consumed with fear: for the fate of my brother, about Hallow's malevolence, about the horrible death of Adabelle Yancy. There were probably a few more things that made me fearful, but in such a long day it was impossible to pick any one thing that was more awful than the other.

As I lay wrapped up in Eric's arms, humming a little wordless tune as I traced the line of his shoulder with an idle finger, I was bone-deep grateful for the pleasure he'd given me. A piece of happiness should never be taken as due.

'Thank you,' I said, my face pressed to his silent chest.

He put a finger under my chin so I would raise my eyes to his. 'No,' he said quietly. 'You took me in off the road and kept me safe. You're ready to fight for me. I can tell this about you. I can't believe my luck. When this witch is defeated, I would bring you to my side. I will share everything I have with you. Every vampire who owes me fealty will honor you.'

Was this medieval, or what? Bless Eric's heart, none of that was going to happen. At least I was smart enough, and realistic enough, not to deceive myself for a minute, though it was a wonderful fantasy. He was thinking like a chieftain with thralls at his disposal, not like a ruthless head vampire who owned a tourist bar in Shreveport.

'You've made me very happy,' I said, which was certainly the truth.

Chapter 10

The pond behind Jason's house had already been searched by the time I got up the next morning. Alcee Beck pounded on my door about ten o'clock, and since it sounded exactly like a lawman knocking, I pulled on my jeans and a sweatshirt before I went to the door.

'He's not in the pond,' Beck said, without preamble.

I sagged against the doorway. 'Oh, thank God.' I closed my eyes for a minute to do just that. 'Please come in.' Alcee Beck stepped over the threshold like a vampire, looking around him silently and with a certain wariness.

'Would you like some coffee?' I asked politely, when he was seated on the old couch.

'No, thank you,' he said stiffly, as uncomfortable with me as I was with him. I spotted Eric's shirt hanging on the doorknob of my bedroom, not quite visible from where Detective Beck was sitting. Lots of women wear men's shirts, and I told myself not to be paranoid about its presence. Though I tried not to listen to the detective's mind, I could tell that he was uneasy being alone in the house of a white woman, and he was wishing that Andy Bellefleur would get there.

'Excuse me for a minute,' I said, before I yielded to temptation and asked him why Andy was due to arrive. That would shake Alcee Beck to the core. I grabbed the shirt as I went into my room, folded it, and tucked it in a drawer before I brushed my teeth and washed my face. By the time I returned to the living room, Andy had made his appearance. Jason's boss, Catfish Hennessey, was with him. I could feel the blood leaving my head and I sat down very heavily on the ottoman sitting by the couch.

'What?' I said. I couldn't have uttered another word.

'The blood on the dock is probably feline blood, and there's a print in it, besides Jason's boot print,' said Andy. 'We've kept this quiet, because we didn't want those woods crawling with idiots.' I could feel myself swaying in an invisible wind. I would have laughed, if I hadn't had the 'gift' of telepathy. He wasn't thinking tabby or calico when he said feline; he was thinking panther.

Panthers were what we called mountain lions. Sure, there aren't mountains around here, but panthers – the oldest men hereabouts called them 'painters' – live in low bottomland, too. To the best of my knowledge, the only place panthers could be found in the wild was in Florida, and their numbers were dwindling to the brink of extinction. No solid evidence had been produced to prove that any live native panthers had been living in Louisiana in the past fifty years, give or take a decade.

But of course, there were stories. And our woods and streams could produce no end of alligators, nutria, possums, coons, and even the occasional black bear or wildcat. Coyotes, too. But there were no pictures, or scat, or print casts, to prove the presence of panthers . . . until now.

Andy Bellefleur's eyes were hot with longing, but not for me. Any red-blooded male who'd ever gone hunting, or even any P.C. guy who photographed nature, would give almost anything to see a real wild panther. Despite the fact that these large predators were deeply anxious to avoid humans, humans would not return the favor.

'What are you thinking?' I asked, though I knew damn good and well what they were thinking. But to keep them on an even keel, I had to pretend not to; they'd feel better, and they might let something slip. Catfish was just thinking that Jason was most likely dead. The two lawmen kept fixing me in their gaze, but Catfish, who knew me better than they did, was sitting forward on the edge of Gran's old recliner, his big red hands clasped to each other so hard the knuckles were white.

'Maybe Jason spotted the panther when he came home that night,' Andy said carefully. 'You know he'd run and get his rifle and try to track it.'

'They're endangered,' I said. 'You think Jason doesn't know that panthers are endangered?' Of course, they thought Jason was so impulsive and brainless that he just wouldn't care.

'Are you sure that would be at the top of his list?' Alcee Beck asked, with an attempt at gentleness.

'So you think Jason shot the panther,' I said, having a little difficulty getting the words out of my mouth.

'It's a possibility.'

'And then what?' I crossed my arms over my chest.

All three men exchanged a glance. 'Maybe Jason followed the panther into the woods,' Andy said. 'Maybe the panther wasn't so badly wounded after all, and it got him.'

'You think my brother would trail a wounded and dangerous animal into the woods – at night, by himself.' Sure they did. I could read it loud and clear. They thought that would be absolutely typical Jason Stackhouse behavior. What they didn't get was that (reckless and wild as my brother was) Jason's favorite person in the entire universe was Jason Stackhouse, and he would not endanger that person in such an obvious way.

Andy Bellefleur had some misgivings about this theory, but Alcee Beck sure didn't. He thought I'd outlined Jason's procedure that night exactly. What the two lawmen didn't know, and what I couldn't tell them, was that if Jason had seen a panther at his house that night, the chances were good the panther was actually a shape-shifting human. Hadn't Claudine said that the witches had gathered some of the larger shifters into their fold? A panther would be a valuable animal to have at your side if you were contemplating a hostile takeover.

'Jay Stans, from Clarice, called me this morning,' Andy said. His round face turned toward me and his brown eyes locked on me. 'He was telling me about this gal you found by the side of the road last night.'

I nodded, not seeing the connection, and too preoccupied with speculation about the panther to guess what was coming.

'This girl have any connection to Jason?'

'What?' I was stunned. 'What are you talking about?'

'You find this girl, this Maria-Star Cooper, by the side of the road. They searched, but they didn't find any trace of an accident.'

I shrugged. 'I told them I wasn't sure I could pin the spot down, and they didn't ask me to go looking, after I offered. I'm not real surprised they couldn't find any evidence, not knowing the exact spot. I tried to pin it down, but it was at night, and I was pretty scared. Or she could have just been dumped where I found her.' I don't watch the Discovery Channel for nothing.

'See, what we were thinking,' Alcee Beck rumbled, 'is that this girl was one of Jason's discards, and maybe he was keeping her somewhere secret? But you let her go when Jason disappeared.'

'Huh?' It was like they were speaking Urdu or something. I couldn't make any sense out of it.

'With Jason getting arrested under suspicion of those murders last year and all, we wondered if there wasn't some fire under all that smoke.'

'You know who did those killings. He's in jail, unless something's happened that I don't know about. And he confessed.' Catfish met my eyes, and his were very uneasy. This line of questioning had my brother's boss all twitchy. Granted, my brother was a little kinky in the sex department (though none of the women he'd kinked with seemed to mind), but the idea of him keeping a sex slave that I had to deal with when he vanished? Oh, come on!

'He did confess, and he's still in jail,' Andy said. Since Andy had taken the confession, I should hope so. 'But what if Jason was his accomplice?'

'Wait a damn minute now,' I said. My pot was beginning to boil over. 'You can't have it both ways. If my brother is dead out in the woods after chasing a mythical wounded panther, how could he have been holding, what's her name, Maria-Star Cooper, hostage somewhere? You're thinking I've been in on my brother's supposed bondage activities, too? You think I hit her with my car? And then I loaded her in and drove her to the emergency room?'

We all glared at each other for a long moment. The men were

tossing out waves of tension and confusion like they were necklaces at Mardi Gras.

Then Catfish launched himself off the couch like a bottle rocket. 'No,' he bellowed. 'You guys asked me to come along to break this bad news about the panther to Sookie. No one said anything about this stuff about some girl that got hit by a car! This here is a nice girl.' Catfish pointed at me. 'No one's going to call her different! Not only did Jason Stackhouse never have to do more than crook his little finger at a girl for her to come running, much less take one hostage and do weird stuff to her, but if you're saying Sookie let this Cooper girl free when Jason didn't come home, and then tried to run over her, well, all I got to say is, you can go straight to hell!'

God bless Catfish Hennessey is all I had to say.

Alcee and Andy left soon after, and Catfish and I had a disjointed talk consisting mostly of him cursing the lawmen. When he ran down, he glanced at his watch.

'Come on, Sookie. You and me got to get to Jason's.'

'Why?' I was willing but bewildered.

'We got us a search party together, and I know you'll want to be there.'

I stared at him with my mouth open, while Catfish fumed about Alcee and Andy's allegations. I tried real hard to think of some way to cancel a search party. I hated to think of those men and women putting on all their winter gear to plow through the underbrush, now bare and brown, that made the woods so difficult to navigate. But there was no way to stop them, when they meant so well; and there was every reason to join them.

There was the remote chance that Jason *was* out there in the woods somewhere. Catfish told me he'd gotten together as many men as he could, and Kevin Pryor had agreed to be the coordinator, though off-duty. Maxine Fortenberry and her churchwomen were bringing out coffee and doughnuts from the Bon Temps Bakery. I began crying, because this was just overwhelming, and Catfish turned even redder. Weeping women were way high on Catfish's long list of things that made him uncomfortable.

I eased his situation by telling him I had to get ready. I threw the bed together, washed my face clean of tears, and yanked my hair back into a ponytail. I found a pair of earmuffs that I used maybe once a year, and pulled on my old coat and stuck my yard work gloves in my pocket, along with a wad of Kleenex in case I got weepy again.

The search party was the popular activity for the day in Bon Temps. Not only do people like to help in our small town – but also rumors had inevitably begun circulating about the mysterious wild animal footprint. As far as I could tell, the word 'panther' was not yet currency; if it had been, the crowd would have been even larger. Most of the men had come armed – well, actually, most of the men were always armed. Hunting is a way of life around here, the NRA provides most of the bumper stickers, and deer season is like a holy holiday. There are special times for hunting deer with a bow and arrow, with a muzzleloader, or with a rifle. (There may be a spear season, for all I know.) There must have been fifty people at Jason's house, quite a party on a workday for such a small community.

Sam was there, and I was so glad to see him I almost began crying again. Sam was the best boss I'd ever had, and a friend, and he always came when I was in trouble. His red-gold hair was covered with a bright orange knit cap, and he wore bright orange gloves, too. His heavy brown jacket looked somber in contrast, and like all of the men, he was wearing work boots. You didn't go out in the woods, even in winter, with ankles unprotected. Snakes were slow and sluggish, but they were there, and they'd retaliate if you stepped on them.

Somehow the presence of all these people made Jason's disappearance seem that much more terrifying. If all these people believed Jason might be out in the woods, dead or badly wounded, he might be. Despite every sensible thing I could tell myself, I grew more and more afraid. I had a few minutes of blanking out on the scene entirely while I imagined all the things that could have happened to Jason, for maybe the hundredth go-round.

Sam was standing beside me, when I could hear and see again. He'd pulled off a glove, and his hand found mine and clasped it. His felt warm and hard, and I was glad to be holding on to him. Sam, though a shifter, knew how to aim his thoughts at me, though he couldn't 'hear' mine in return. *Do you really believe he's out there?* he asked me.

I shook my head. Our eyes met and held.

Do you think he's still alive?

That was a lot harder. Finally, I just shrugged. He kept hold of my hand, and I was glad of it.

Arlene and Tack scrambled out of Arlene's car and came toward us. Arlene's hair was as bright red as ever, but quite a bit more snarled than she usually wore it, and the short-order cook needed to shave. So he hadn't started keeping a razor at Arlene's yet, was the way I read it.

'Did you see Tara?' Arlene asked.

'No.'

'Look.' She pointed, as surreptitiously as you can, and I saw Tara in jeans and rubber boots that came up to her knees. She looked as unlike the meticulously groomed clothing-store proprietor as I could imagine, though she was wearing an adorable fake-fur hat of white and brown that made you want to go up and stroke her head. Her coat matched the hat. So did her gloves. But from the waist down, Tara was ready for the woods. Jason's friend Dago was staring at Tara with the stunned look of the newly smitten. Holly and Danielle had come, too, and since Danielle's boyfriend wasn't around, the search party was turning out to have an unexpected social side.

Maxine Fortenberry and two other women from her church had let down the tailgate of Maxine's husband's old pickup, and there were several thermoses containing coffee set up there, along with disposable cups, plastic spoons, and packages of sugar. Six dozen doughnuts steamed up the long boxes they'd been packed in. A large plastic trash can, already lined with a black bag, stood ready. These ladies knew how to throw a search party.

I couldn't believe all this had been organized in the space of a few hours. I had to take my hand from Sam's to fish out a tissue and mop my face with it. I would have expected Arlene to come, but the presence of Holly and Danielle was just about stunning, and Tara's attendance was even more surprising. She wasn't a search-the-woods kind of woman. Kevin Pryor didn't have much use for Jason, but here he was, with a map and pad and pencil, organizing away.

I caught Holly's eye, and she gave me a sad sort of smile, the kind of little smile you gave someone at a funeral.

Just then Kevin banged the plastic trash can lid against the tailgate of the truck, and when everyone's attention was on him, he began to give directions for the search. I hadn't realized Kevin could be so authoritative; on most occasions, he was overshadowed by his clingy mother, Jeneen, or his oversized partner, Kenya. You wouldn't catch Kenya out in the woods looking for Jason, I reflected, and just then I spotted her and had to swallow my own thoughts. In sensible gear, she was leaning against the Fortenberrys' pickup, her brown face absolutely expressionless. Her stance suggested that she was Kevin's enforcer – that she'd move or speak only if he were challenged in some way. Kenya knew how to project silent menace; I'll give her that. She would throw a bucket of water on Jason if he were on fire, but her feelings for my brother were certainly not overwhelmingly positive. She'd come because Kevin was volunteering. As Kevin divided people up into teams, her dark eyes left him only to scan the faces of the searchers, including mine. She gave me a slight nod, and I gave her the same.

'Each group of five has to have a rifleman,' Kevin called. 'That can't be just anybody. It has to be someone who's spent time out in the woods hunting.' The excitement level rose to the boiling point with this directive. But after that, I didn't listen to the rest of Kevin's instructions. I was still tired from the day before, for one thing; what an exceptionally full day it had been. And the whole time, in the background, my fear for my brother had been nagging and eating at me. I'd been woken early this morning after a long night, and here I was standing in the cold outside my childhood home, waiting to participate in a touching wild-goose chase – or at least I hoped it was a wild-goose chase. I was too dazed to judge any more. A chill wind began to gust through the clearing around the house, making the tears on my cheeks unbearably cold.

Sam put his arms around me, though in our coats it was quite awkward. It seemed to me I could feel the warmth of him even through all the material.

'You know we won't find him out there,' he whispered to me.

'I'm pretty sure we won't,' I said, sounding anything but certain.

Sam said, 'I'll smell him if he's out there.'

That was so practical.

I looked up at him. I didn't have to look far, because Sam's not a real tall man. Right now, his face was very serious. Sam has more fun with his shifter self than most of the two-natured, but I could tell he was intent on easing my fear. When he was in his second nature, he had the dog's keen sense of smell; when he was in his human form, that sense was still superior to that of a one-natured man. Sam would be able to smell a fairly recent corpse.

'You're going out in the woods,' I said.

'Sure. I'll do my best. If he's there, I think I'll know.'

Kevin had told me the sheriff had tried to hire the tracking dogs trained by a Shreveport police officer, but the officer had said they were booked for the day. I wondered if that were true, or if the man just hadn't wanted to risk his dogs in the woods with a panther. Truthfully, I couldn't blame him. And here was a better offer, right in front of me.

'Sam,' I said, my eyes filling with tears. I tried to thank him, but the words wouldn't come. I was lucky to have a friend like Sam, and well I knew it.

'Hush, Sookie,' he said. 'Don't cry. We'll find out what happened to Jason, and we'll find a way to restore Eric to his mind.' He rubbed the tears off my cheeks with his thumb.

No one was close enough to hear, but I couldn't help glancing around to make sure.

'Then,' Sam said, a distinctly grim edge to his voice, 'we can get him out of your house and back to Shreveport where he belongs.'

I decided no reply was the best policy.

'What was your word for the day?' he asked, standing back.

I gave him a watery smile. Sam always asked about the daily offering of my Word a Day calendar. 'I didn't check this morning. Yesterday was "farrago",' I said.

He raised his brows inquiringly.

'A confused mess,' I said.

'Sookie, we'll find a way out of this.'

When the searchers divided up into groups, I discovered that Sam was not the only two-natured creature out in Jason's yard that day.

I was astonished to see a contingent from Hotshot. Calvin Norris, his niece Crystal, and a second man who seemed vaguely familiar were standing by themselves. After a moment of stirring the sludge of my memory, I realized that the second man was the one I'd seen emerging from the shed behind the house down from Crystal's. His thick pale hair triggered the memory, and I was sure of it when I saw the graceful way he moved. Kevin assigned the Reverend Jimmy Fullenwilder to the trio as their armed man. The combination of the three Weres with the reverend would have made me laugh under other circumstances.

Since they lacked a fifth, I joined them.

The three Weres from Hotshot gave me sober nods, Calvin's golden green eyes fixed on me thoughtfully. 'This here's Felton Norris,' he said, by way of introduction.

I nodded back to Felton, and Jimmy Fullenwilder, a gray-haired man of about sixty, shook hands. 'Of course I know Miss Sookie, but the rest of you I'm not sure of. I'm Jimmy Fullenwilder, pastor of Greater Love Baptist,' he said, smiling all around. Calvin absorbed this information with a polite smile, Crystal sneered, and Felton Norris (had they run out of last names in Hotshot?) grew colder. Felton was an odd one, even for an inbred werewolf. His eyes were remarkably dark, set under straight thick brown brows, which contrasted sharply with his pale hair. His face was broad at the eyes, narrowing a little too abruptly to a thin-lipped mouth. Though he was a bulky man, he moved lightly and quietly, and as we began to move out into the woods, I realized that all the Hotshot residents had that in common. In comparison with the Norrises, Jimmy Fullenwilder and I were blundering elephants.

At least the minister carried his 30–30 like he knew how to use it.

Following our instructions, we stood in a row, stretching out our arms at shoulder height so we were fingertip to fingertip. Crystal was on my right, and Calvin was on my left. The other groups did the same. We began the search in the fanlike shape determined by the curve of the pond.

'Remember who's in your group,' Kevin bellowed. 'We don't want to leave people out here! Now, start.'

We began scanning the ground ahead of us, moving at a steady pace. Jimmy Fullenwilder was a couple of steps ahead, since he was armed. It was apparent right away that there were woodcraft disparities between the Hotshot folks, the reverend, and me. Crystal seemed to flow through the undergrowth, without having to wade through it or push it aside, though I could hear her progress. Jimmy Fullenwilder, an avid hunter, was at home in the woods and an experienced outdoorsman, and I could tell he was getting much more information from his surroundings than I was, but he wasn't able to move like Calvin and Felton. They glided through the woods like ghosts, making about as much noise.

Once, when I ran into a particularly dense thicket of thorny vines, I felt two hands clamp on either side of my waist, and I was just lifted over it before I had a chance to react. Calvin Norris put me down very gently and went right back to his position. I don't think anyone else noticed. Jimmy Fullenwilder, the only one who would have been startled, had gotten a little ahead.

Our team found nothing: not a shred of cloth or flesh, not a boot print or panther print, not a smell or a trace or a drop of blood. One of the other teams yelled over that they'd found a chewed-up possum corpse, but there was no immediate way to tell what had caused its death.

The going got tougher. My brother had hunted in these woods, allowed some friends of his to hunt there, but otherwise had not interfered with nature in the twenty acres around the house. That meant he hadn't cleared away fallen branches or pulled up seedlings, which compounded the difficulty of our movement.

My team happened to be the one that found his deer stand, which he and Hoyt had built together about five years ago.

Though the stand faced a natural clearing running roughly north-south, the woods were so thick around it that we were temporarily out of sight of the other searchers, which I would not have thought possible in winter, with the branches bare. Every now and then a human voice, raised in a distant call, would make its way through the pines and the bushes and the branches of the oaks and gum trees, but the sense of isolation was overwhelming.

Felton Norris swarmed up the deer stand ladder in such an unhuman

way that I had to distract Reverend Fullenwilder by asking him if he'd
mind praying in church for my brother's return. Of course, he told me
he already had, and furthermore, he notified me he'd be glad to see
me in his church on Sunday to add my voice to those lifted in prayer.
Though I missed a lot of churchgoing because of my job, and when
I did go I attended the Methodist church (which Jimmy Fullenwilder
well knew), I pretty much had to say yes. Just then Felton called down
that the stand was empty. 'Come down careful, this ladder's not too
steady,' Calvin called back, and I realized Calvin was warning Felton
to look human when he descended. As the shifter descended slowly
and clumsily, I met Calvin's eyes, and he looked amused.

Bored by the wait at the foot of the deer stand, Crystal had flitted
ahead of our point man, the Reverend Fullenwilder, something Kevin
had warned us not to do. Just as I was thinking, *I can't see her*, I heard
her scream.

In the space of a couple of seconds, Calvin and Felton had bounded
over the clearing toward the sound of Crystal's voice, and the Reverend
Jimmy and I were left to run behind. I hoped the agitation of the
moment would obscure his perception of the way Calvin and Felton
were moving. Up ahead of us, we heard an indescribable noise, a loud
chorus of squeals and frenetic movement coming from the undergrowth. Then a hoarse shout and another shrill scream came to us
muffled by the cold thickness of the woods.

We heard yelling from all directions as the other searchers
responded, hurrying toward the alarming sounds.

My heel caught in a snarl of vines and I went down, ass over
teacup. Though I rolled to my feet and began running again, Jimmy
Fullenwilder had gotten ahead of me, and as I plunged through a stand
of low pines, each no bigger around than a mailing tube, I heard the
boom of the rifle.

Oh, my God, I thought. *Oh, my God*.

The little clearing was filled with blood and tumult. A huge animal
was thrashing in the dead leaves, spraying scarlet drops on everything
in its vicinity. But it was no panther. For the second time in my life,
I was seeing a razorback hog, that ferocious feral pig that grows to a
huge size.

In the time it took me to realize what was in front of me, the sow collapsed and died. She reeked of pig and blood. A crashing and squealing in the undergrowth around us indicated she hadn't been alone when Crystal stumbled upon her.

But not all the blood was the sow's.

Crystal Norris was swearing a blue streak as she sat with her back against an old oak, her hands clamped over her gored thigh. Her jeans were wet with her own blood, and her uncle and her – well, I didn't know what relationship Felton bore to Crystal, but I was sure there was one – kinsman were bending over her. Jimmy Fullenwilder was standing with his rifle still pointed at the beast, and he had an expression on his face that I can only describe as shell-shocked.

'How is she?' I asked the two men, and only Calvin looked up. His eyes had gone very peculiar, and I realized they'd gotten more yellow, rounder. He cast an unmistakable look at the huge carcass, a look of sheer desire. There was blood around his mouth. There was a patch of fur on the back of his hand, kind of buff-colored. He must make a strange-looking wolf. I pointed silently at this evidence of his nature, and he shivered with longing as he nodded acknowledgment. I yanked a handkerchief out of my coat pocket, spat on it, and wiped his face with it before Jimmy Fullenwilder could fall out of his fascination with his kill and observe his strange companions. When Calvin's mouth wasn't stained anymore, I knotted the handkerchief around his hand to conceal the fur.

Felton seemed to be normal, until I observed what was at the end of his arms. They weren't really hands anymore . . . but not really wolf paws, either. They were something very odd, something big and flat and clawed.

I couldn't read the men's thoughts, but I could feel their desires, and most of those desires had to do with raw red pig meat, and lots of it. Felton actually rocked back and forth once or twice with the force of his desire. Their silent struggle was painful to endure, even second-hand. I felt the change when the two men began to force their brains into human patterns. In a few seconds, Calvin managed to speak.

'She's losing blood fast, but if we get her to the hospital she'll be all right.' His voice was thick, and he spoke with an effort. Felton, his eyes still downcast, began tearing clumsily at his flannel shirt. With his hands misshapen, he couldn't manage the job, and I took it over. When Crystal's wound was bound as tightly as the makeshift bandage could compress it, the two men lifted the now white and silent Crystal and began to carry her rapidly out of the woods. The position of Felton's hands hid them from sight, thank God.

This all occurred so quickly that the other searchers converging on the clearing were just beginning to absorb what had happened, and react.

'I shot a hog,' Jimmy Fullenwilder was saying, shaking his head from side to side, as Kevin and Kenya burst into the clearing from the east. 'I can't believe it. It just threw her over and the other sows and little ones scattered and then the two men were on it, and then they got out of the way and I shot it in the throat.' He didn't know if he was a hero or if he was in big trouble with the Department of Wildlife. He'd had more to fear than he would ever realize. Felton and Calvin had almost gone into full Were mode at the threat to Crystal and the arousal of their own hunting instincts, and the fact that they'd thrown themselves away from the pig rather than change utterly proved they were very strong, indeed. But the fact that they'd begun to change, hadn't been able to stop it, seemed to argue the opposite. The line between the two natures of some of the denizens of Hotshot seemed be growing very blurred.

In fact, there were bite marks on the hog. I was so overwhelmed with anxiety that I couldn't keep up my guard, and all the excitement of all the searchers poured into my head – all the revulsion/fear/panic at the sight of the blood, the knowledge that a searcher had been seriously injured, the envy of other hunters at Jimmy Fullenwilder's coup. It was all too much, and I wanted to get away more than I've ever wanted anything.

'Let's go. This'll be the end of the search, at least for today,' Sam said at my elbow. We walked out of the woods together, very slowly. I told Maxine what had happened, and after I'd thanked her for her wonderful contribution and accepted a box of doughnuts, I drove home. Sam followed me. I was a little more myself by the time we got there.

As I unlocked the back door, it felt quite strange knowing that there was actually someone else already in the house. Was Eric conscious on some level of my footsteps on the floor above his head – or was he as dead as an ordinary dead person? But the wondering ran through my head and out the other side, because I was just too overloaded to consider it.

Sam began to make coffee. He was somewhat at home in the kitchen, as he'd dropped in a time or two when my Gran was alive, and he'd visited on other occasions.

As I hung up our coats, I said, 'That was a disaster.'

Sam didn't disagree.

'Not only did we not find Jason, which I truly never expected we would, but the guys from Hotshot almost got outed, and Crystal got hurt. I don't know why they thought they should be there anyway, frankly.' I know it wasn't nice of me to say that, but I was with Sam, who'd seen enough of my bad side to be under no illusions.

'I talked to them before you got there. Calvin wanted to show he was willing to court you, in a Hotshot kind of way,' Sam said, his voice quiet and even. 'Felton is their best tracker, so he made Felton come, and Crystal just wanted to find Jason.'

Instantly I felt ashamed of myself. 'I'm sorry,' I said, holding my head in my hands and dropping into a chair. 'I'm sorry.'

Sam knelt in front of me and put his hands on my knees. 'You're entitled to be cranky,' he said.

I bent over him and kissed the top of his head. 'I don't know what I'd do without you,' I said, without any thought at all.

He looked up at me, and there was a long, odd moment, when the light in the room seemed to dance and shiver. 'You'd call Arlene,' he said with a smile. 'She'd come over with the kids, and she'd try to spike your coffee, and she'd tell you about Tack's angled dick, and she'd get you to laughing, and you'd feel better.'

I blessed him for letting the moment pass. 'You know, that kind of makes me curious, that bit about Tack, but it probably falls into the category of "too much information",' I said.

'I thought so, too, but that didn't prevent me from hearing it when she was telling Charlsie Tooten.'

I poured us each a cup of coffee and put the half-empty sugar bowl within Sam's reach, along with a spoon. I glanced over at the kitchen counter to see how full the clear sugar canister was, and I noticed that the message light on the answering machine was blinking. I only had to get up and take a step to press the button. The message had been recorded at 5:01 A.M. Oh. I'd turned the phone ringer off when I'd gone to bed exhausted. Almost invariably my messages were real mundane – Arlene asking me if I'd heard a piece of gossip, Tara passing the time of day during a slow hour at the store – but this one was a real doozy.

Pam's clear voice said, 'Tonight we attack the witch and her coven. The Weres have persuaded the local Wiccans to join us. We need you to bring Eric. He can fight, even if he doesn't know who he is. He will be useless to us if we can't break the spell, anyway.' That Pam, ever practical. She was willing to use Eric for cannon fodder, since we might not be able to restore him to full Eric leadership mode. After a little pause, she continued, 'The Weres of Shreveport are allying with vampires in battle. You can watch history being made, my telepathic friend.'

The sound of the phone being put back in the cradle. The click that heralded the next message, which came in two minutes after the first.

'Thinking of that,' Pam said, as if she'd never hung up, 'there is the idea that your unusual ability can help us in our fight, and we want to explore that. Isn't that the right buzzword now? Explore? So get here as close to first dark as possible.' She hung up again.

Click. '"Here" is 714 Parchman Avenue,' Pam said. Hung up.

'How can I do that, with Jason still missing?' I asked, when it became clear Pam hadn't called again.

'You're going to sleep now,' Sam said. 'Come on.' He pulled me to my feet, led me to my room. 'You're going to take off your boots and jeans, crawl back in the bed, and take a long nap. When you get up, you'll feel better. You leave Pam's number so I can reach you. Tell the cops to call the bar if they learn anything, and I'll phone you if I hear from Bud Dearborn.'

'So you think I should do this?' I was bewildered.

'No, I'd give anything if you wouldn't. But I think you have to. It's not my fight; I wasn't invited.' Sam gave me a kiss on the forehead and left to go back to Merlotte's.

His attitude was kind of interesting, after all the vampire insistence (both Bill's and Eric's) that I was a possession to be guarded. I felt pretty empowered and gung-ho for about thirty seconds, until I remembered my New Year's resolution: *no getting beaten up*. If I went to Shreveport with Eric, then I was sure to see things I didn't want to see, learn things I didn't want to know, and get my ass whipped, too.

On the other hand, my brother Jason had made a deal with the vampires, and I had to uphold it. Sometimes I felt that my whole life had been spent stuck between a rock and a hard place. But then, lots of people had complicated lives.

I thought of Eric, a powerful vampire whose mind had been stripped clean of his identity. I thought of the carnage I'd seen in the bridal shop, the white lace and brocade speckled with dried blood and matter. I thought of poor Maria-Star, in the hospital in Shreveport. These witches were bad, and bad should be stopped; bad should be overcome. That's the American model.

It seemed kind of strange to think that I was on the side of vampires and werewolves, and that was the good side. That made me laugh a little, all to myself. Oh, yes, we good guys would save the day.

Chapter 11

Amazingly, I did sleep. I woke with Eric on the bed beside me. He was smelling me.

'Sookie, what is this?' he asked in a very quiet voice. He knew, of course, when I woke. 'You smell of the woods, and you smell of shifter. And something even wilder.'

I supposed the shifter he smelled was Sam. 'And Were,' I prompted, not wanting him to miss out on anything.

'No, not Were,' he said.

I was puzzled. Calvin had lifted me over the brambles, and his scent should still have been on me.

'More than one kind of shifter,' Eric said in the near-dark of my room. 'What have you been doing, my lover?'

He didn't exactly sound angry, but he didn't sound happy, either. Vampires. They wrote the book on possessive.

'I was in the search party for my brother, in the woods behind his home,' I said.

Eric was still for a minute. Then he wrapped his arms around me and hauled me up against him. 'I'm sorry,' he said. 'I know you are worried.'

'Let me ask you something,' I said, willing to test a theory of mine.

'Of course.'

'Look inside yourself, Eric. Are you really, really sorry? Worried about Jason?' Because the real Eric, in his right mind, would not have cared one little bit.

'Of course,' he protested. Then, after a long moment – I wished I could see his face – he said, 'Not really.' He sounded surprised. 'I know I should be. I should be concerned about your brother, because I love having sex with you, and I should want you to think well of me so you'll want sex, too.'

You just had to like the honesty. This was the closest to the real Eric I'd seen in days.

'But you'll listen, right? If I need to talk? For the same reason?'

'Of course, my lover.'

'Because you want to have sex with me.'

'That, of course. But also because I find I really do . . .' He paused, as if he were about to say something outrageous. 'I find I have feelings for you.'

'Oh,' I said into his chest, sounding as astonished as Eric had. His chest was bare, as I suspected the rest of him was. I felt the light sprinkling of curly blond hair against my cheek.

'Eric,' I said, after a long pause, 'I almost hate to say this, but I have feelings for you, too.' There was a lot I needed to tell Eric, and we should be in the car on our way to Shreveport already. But I was taking this moment to savor this little bit of happiness.

'Not love, exactly,' he said. His fingers were busy trying to find out how best to get my clothes off.

'No, but something close.' I helped him. 'We don't have much time, Eric,' I said, reaching down, touching him, making him gasp. 'Let's make it good.'

'Kiss me,' he said, and he wasn't talking about his mouth. 'Turn this way,' he whispered. 'I want to kiss you, too.'

It didn't take long, after all, for us to be holding each other, sated and happy.

'What's happened?' he asked. 'I can tell something is frightening you.'

'We have to go to Shreveport now,' I said. 'We're already past the time Pam said on the phone. Tonight's the night we face off against Hallow and her witches.'

'Then you must stay here,' he said immediately.

'No,' I said gently, putting my hand on his cheek. 'No, baby, I have to go with you.' I didn't tell him Pam thought using me in the battle would be a good idea. I didn't tell him he was going to be used as a fighting machine. I didn't tell him I was sure someone was going to die tonight; maybe quite a few someones, human and Were and vampire. It was probably the last time I would use an endearment when I addressed Eric. It was perhaps the last time Eric would wake up in my house. One of us might not survive this night, and if we did, there was no way to know how we'd be changed.

The drive to Shreveport was silent. We'd washed up and dressed without talking much, either. At least seven times, I thought of heading back to Bon Temps, with or without Eric.

But I didn't.

Eric's skills did not include map reading, so I had to pull over to check my Shreveport map to plot our course to Parchman, something I hadn't foreseen before we got to the city. (I'd somehow expected Eric to remember the directions, but of course, he didn't.)

'Your word of the day was "annihilate",' he told me cheerfully.

'Oh. Thanks for checking.' I probably didn't sound very thankful. 'You're sounding pretty excited about all this.'

'Sookie, there's nothing like a good fight,' he said defensively.

'That depends on who wins, I would think.'

That kept him quiet for a few minutes, which was fine. I was having trouble negotiating the strange streets in the darkness, with so much on my mind. But we finally got to the right street, and the right house on that street. I had always pictured Pam and Chow living in a mansion, but the vampires had a large ranch-style house in an upper-middle-class suburb. It was a trimmed-lawn, bike-riding, lawn-sprinkling street, from what I could tell.

The light by the driveway was on at 714, and the three-car garage around at the rear was full. I drove up the slope to the concrete apron that was placed for overflow parking. I recognized Alcide's truck and the compact car that had been parked in Colonel Flood's carport.

Before we got out of my old car, Eric leaned over to kiss me. We looked at each other, his eyes wide and blue, the whites so white you could hardly look away, his golden hair neatly brushed. He'd tied it back with one of my elastic bands, a bright blue one. He was wearing a pair of jeans and a new flannel shirt.

'We could go back,' he said. In the dome light of the car, his face looked hard as stone. 'We could go back to your house. I can stay with you always. We can know each other's bodies in every way, night after night. I could love you.' His nostrils flared, and he looked suddenly proud. 'I could work. You would not be poor. I would help you.'

'Sounds like a marriage,' I said, trying to lighten the atmosphere. But my voice was too shaky.

'Yes,' he said.

And he would never be himself again. He would be a false version of Eric, an Eric cheated out of his true life. Providing our relationship (such as it was) lasted, he would stay the same; but I wouldn't.

Enough with the negative thinking, Sookie, I told myself. I would be a total idiot to pass up living with this gorgeous creature for however long. We actually had a good time together, and I enjoyed Eric's sense of humor and his company, to say nothing of his lovemaking. Now that he'd lost his memory, he was lots of uncomplicated fun.

And that was the fly in the ointment. We would have a counterfeit relationship, because this was the counterfeit Eric. I'd come full loop.

I slid out of the car with a sigh. 'I'm a total idiot,' I said as he came around the back of the car to walk with me to the house.

Eric didn't say anything. I guess he agreed with me.

'Hello,' I called, pushing open the door after my knock brought no response. The garage door led into the laundry room and from there into the kitchen.

As you would expect in a vampire home, the kitchen was absolutely clean, because it wasn't used. This kitchen was small for a house the size of this one. I guess the real estate agent had thought it was her lucky day – her lucky night – when she'd shown it to vampires, since a real family who cooked at home would have trouble dealing with a kitchen the size of a king bed. The house had an open floor plan, so you could see over the breakfast bar into the 'family' room – in this case, the main room for a mighty odd family. There were three open doorways that probably led into the formal living room, the dining room, and the bedroom area.

Right at the moment, this family room was crammed with people. I got the impression, from the glimpses of feet and arms, that more people were standing in the open doorways into the other rooms.

The vampires were there: Pam, Chow, Gerald, and at least two more I recognized from Fangtasia. The two-natured were represented by Colonel Flood, red-haired Amanda (my big fan), the teenage boy with spiked brown hair (Sid), Alcide, Culpepper, and (to my disgust) Debbie Pelt. Debbie was dressed in the height of fashion – at least her version of fashion – which seemed a little out of place for a meeting of this kind. Maybe she wanted to remind me that she had a very good job working at an advertising agency.

Oh, good. Debbie's presence made the night just about perfect.

The group I didn't recognize had to be the local witches, by the process of elimination. I assumed that the dignified woman sitting on the couch was their leader. I didn't know what her correct title would be – coven master? Mistress? She was in her sixties, and she had iron-gray hair. An African American with skin the color of coffee, she had brown eyes that looked infinitely wise and also skeptical. She'd brought a pale young man with glasses, who wore pressed khakis with a striped shirt and polished loafers. He might work in Office Depot or Super One Foods in some kind of managerial position, and his kids would think that he was out bowling or attending some church meeting on this cold January night. Instead, he and the young female witch beside him were about to embark on a fight to the death.

The remaining two empty chairs were clearly intended for Eric and me.

'We expected you earlier,' Pam said crisply.

'Hi, good to see you, too, thanks for coming on such short notice,' I muttered. For one long moment, everyone in the room looked at Eric, waiting for him to take charge of the action, as he had for years. And Eric looked back at them blankly. The long pause began to be awkward.

'Well, let's lay this out,' Pam said. All the assembled Supes turned their faces to her. Pam seemed to have taken the leadership bit between her teeth, and she was ready to run with it.

'Thanks to the Were trackers, we know the location of the building Hallow is using for her headquarters,' Pam told me. She seemed to be ignoring Eric, but I sensed it was because she didn't know what else to do. Sid grinned at me; I remembered he and Emilio had tracked the killers from the bridal shop to the house. Then I realized he was showing me he'd filed his teeth to points. Ick.

I could understand the presence of the vamps, the witches, and the Weres, but why was Debbie Pelt at this meeting? She was a shifter, not a Were. The Weres had always been so snobby about the shifters, and here was one; furthermore, one out of her own territory. I loathed and distrusted her. She must have insisted on being here, and that made me trust her even less, if that was possible.

If she was so determined to join in, put Debbie in the first line of fire, would be my advice. You wouldn't have to worry about what she was doing behind your back.

My grandmother would certainly have been ashamed of my vindictiveness; but then (like Alcide) she would have found it almost impossible to believe that Debbie had really tried to kill me.

'We'll infiltrate the neighborhood slowly,' Pam said. I wondered if she'd been reading a commando manual. 'The witches have already broadcast a lot of magic in the area, so there aren't too many people out on the streets. Some of the Weres are already in place. We won't be so obvious. Sookie will go in first.'

The assembled Supes turned their eyes to me at the same moment. That was pretty disconcerting: like being in a ring of pickup trucks at night, when they all turn on their headlights to illuminate the center.

'Why?' Alcide asked. His big hands gripped his knees. Debbie, who'd slumped down to sit on the floor beside the couch, smiled at me, knowing Alcide couldn't see her.

'Because Sookie is human,' Pam pointed out. 'And she's more of a natural phenomenon than a true Supe. They won't detect her.'

Eric had taken my hand. He was gripping it so hard that I thought I could hear my bones grinding together. Prior to his enchantment, he would have nipped Pam's plan in the bud, or maybe he would've enthusiastically endorsed it. Now he was too cowed to comment, which he clearly wanted to do.

'What am I supposed to do when I get there?' I was proud of myself for sounding so calm and practical. I'd rather be taking a complicated drink order from a table of drunken tree-trimmers than be first in the line of battle.

'Read the minds of the witches inside while we get into position. If they detect us approaching, we lose the surprise of it, and we stand a greater chance of sustaining serious injury.' When she got excited, Pam had a slight accent, though I'd never been able to figure out what it was. I thought it might just be English as it had been spoken three hundred years ago. Or whatever. 'Can you count them? Is that possible?'

I thought for a second. 'Yes, I can do that.'

'That would be a big help, too.'

'What do we do when we get in the building?' asked Sid. Jittery with the thrill of it all, he was grinning, his pointed teeth showing.

Pam looked mildly astonished. 'We kill them all,' she said.

Sid's grin faded. I flinched. I wasn't the only one.

Pam seemed to realize she'd said something unpalatable. 'What else would we do?' she asked, genuinely amazed.

That was a stumper.

'They'll do their best to kill *us*,' Chow pointed out. 'They only made one attempt at negotiation, and it cost Eric his memory and Clancy his life. They delivered Clancy's clothes to Fangtasia this morning.' People glanced away from Eric, embarrassed. He looked stricken, and I patted his hand with my free one. His grip on my right hand relaxed a little. My circulation resumed in that hand, and it tingled. That was a relief.

'Someone needs to go with Sookie,' Alcide said. He glowered at Pam. 'She can't go close to that house by herself.'

'I'll go with her,' said a familiar voice from the corner of the room, and I leaned forward, searching the faces.

'Bubba!' I said, pleased to see the vampire. Eric stared in wonder at the famous face. The glistening black hair was combed back in a pompadour, and the pouty lower lip was stretched in the trademark smile. His current keeper must have dressed him for the evening, because instead of a jumpsuit decked with rhinestones, or jeans and a T-shirt, Bubba was wearing camo.

'Pleased to see ya, Miss Sookie,' Bubba said. 'I'm wearing my Army duds.'

'I see that. Looking good, Bubba.'

'Thank you, ma'am.'

Pam considered. 'That might be a good idea,' she said. 'His, ah – the mental broadcast, the signature, you all get what I'm telling you? – is so, ah, atypical that they won't discover a vampire is near.' Pam was being very tactful.

Bubba made a terrible vampire. Though stealthy and obedient, he couldn't reason very clearly, and he liked cat blood better than human blood.

'Where's Bill, Miss Sookie?' he asked, as I could have predicted he would. Bubba had always been very fond of Bill.

'He's in Peru, Bubba. That's way down in South-America.'

'No, I'm not,' said a cool voice, and my heart flip-flopped. 'I'm back.' Out of an open doorway stepped my former flame.

This was just an evening for surprises. I hoped some of them would be pleasant.

Seeing Bill so unexpectedly gave me a heavier jolt than I'd figured. I'd never had an ex-boyfriend before, my life having been pretty devoid of boyfriends altogether, so I didn't have much experience in handling my emotions about being in his presence, especially with Eric gripping my hand like I was Mary Poppins and he was my charge.

Bill looked good in his khakis. He was wearing a Calvin Klein dress shirt I'd picked out for him, a muted plaid in shades of brown and gold. Not that I noticed.

'Good, we need you tonight,' Pam said. Ms Businesslike. 'You'll have to tell me how the ruins were, the ones everyone talks about. You know the rest of the people here?'

Bill glanced around. 'Colonel Flood,' he said, nodding. 'Alcide.' His nod to Alcide had less cordiality. 'I haven't met these new allies,' he said, indicating the witches. Bill waited until the introductions were complete to ask, 'What is Debbie Pelt doing here?'

I tried not to gape at having my innermost thoughts spoken aloud. My question exactly! And how did Bill know Debbie? I tried to remember if their paths had crossed in Jackson, if they'd actually met face-to-face; and I couldn't recall such a meeting, though of course Bill knew what she'd done.

'She's Alcide's woman,' Pam said, in a cautious, puzzled sort of way.

I raised my eyebrows, looking at Alcide, and he turned a dusky red.

'She's here for a visit, and she decided to come along with him,' Pam went on. 'You object to her presence?'

'She joined in while I was being tortured in the king of Mississippi's compound,' Bill said. 'She enjoyed my pain.'

Alcide stood, looking as shocked as I'd ever seen him. 'Debbie, is this true?'

Debbie Pelt tried not to flinch, now that every eye was on her, and every eye was unfriendly. 'I just happened to be visiting a Were friend who lived there, one of the guards,' she said. Her voice didn't sound calm enough to match the words. 'Obviously, there was nothing I could do to free you. I would have been ripped to shreds. I can't believe you remember me being there very clearly. You were certainly out of it.' There was a hint of contempt in her words.

'You joined in the torture,' Bill said, his voice still impersonal and all the more convincing for it. 'You liked the pincers best.'

'You didn't tell anyone he was there?' Alcide asked Debbie. His voice was not impersonal at all. It held grief, and anger, and betrayal. 'You knew someone from another kingdom was being tortured at Russell's, and you didn't do anything?'

'He's a *vamp*, for God's sake,' Debbie said, sounding no more than irritated. 'When I found out later that you'd been taking Sookie around to hunt for him so you could get your dad out of hock with the vamps, I felt terrible. But at the time, it was just vamp business. Why should I interfere?'

'But why would any decent person join in torture?' Alcide's voice was strained.

There was a long silence.

'And of course, she tried to kill Sookie,' Bill said. He still managed to sound quite dispassionate.

'I didn't know you were in the trunk of the car when I pushed her in! I didn't know I was closing her in with a hungry vampire!' Debbie protested.

I don't know about anyone else, but I wasn't convinced for a second.

Alcide bent his rough black head to look down into his hands as if they held an oracle. He raised his face to look at Debbie. He was a man unable to dodge the bullet of truth any longer. I felt sorrier for him than I'd felt for anyone in a long, long time.

'I abjure you,' Alcide said. Colonel Flood winced, and young Sid, Amanda, and Culpepper looked both astonished and impressed, as if this were a ceremony they'd never thought to witness. 'I see you no longer. I hunt with you no longer. I share flesh with you no longer.'

This was obviously a ritual of great significance among the two-natured. Debbie stared at Alcide, aghast at his pronouncement. The witches murmured to one another, but otherwise the room remained silent. Even Bubba was wide-eyed, and most things went right over his shiny head.

'No,' Debbie said in a strangled voice, waving a hand in front of her, as if she could erase what had passed. 'No, Alcide!'

But he stared right through her. He saw her no longer.

Even though I loathed Debbie, her face was painful to see. Like most of the others present, as soon as I could, I looked anywhere else but at the shifter. Facing Hallow's coven seemed like a snap compared to witnessing this episode.

Pam seemed to agree. 'All right then,' she said briskly. 'Bubba will lead the way with Sookie. She will do her best to do whatever it is that she does – and she'll signal us.' Pam pondered for a moment. 'Sookie, a recap: We need to know the number of people in the house, whether or not they are all witches, and any other tidbit you can glean. Send Bubba back to us with whatever information you find and stand guard in case the situation changes while we move up. Once we're in position, you can retire to the cars, where you'll be safer.'

I had no problem with that whatsoever. In a crowd of witches, vampires, and Weres, I was no kind of combatant.

'This sounds okay, if I have to be involved at all,' I said. A tug on my hand drew my eyes to Eric's. He looked pleased at the prospect of fighting, but there was still uncertainty in his face and posture. 'But what will happen to Eric?'

'What do you mean?'

'If you go in and kill everyone, who'll un-curse him?' I turned slightly to face the experts, the Wiccan contingent. 'If Hallow's coven dies, do their spells die with them? Or will Eric still be without a memory?'

'The spell must be removed,' said the oldest witch, the calm African-American woman. 'If it is removed by the one who laid it in the first place, that's best. It can be lifted by someone else, but it will take more time, more effort, since we don't know what went into the making of the spell.'

I was trying to avoid looking at Alcide, because he was still shaking with the violence of the emotions that had led him to cast out Debbie. Though I hadn't known such an action was possible, my first reaction was to feel a little bitter about his *not* casting her out right after I'd told him a month ago she'd tried to kill me. However, he could have told himself I'd been mistaken, that it hadn't been Debbie I'd sensed near me before she'd pushed me into the Cadillac's trunk.

As far as I knew, this was the first time Debbie had admitted she had done it. And she'd protested she hadn't known Bill was in the trunk, unconscious. But shoving a person into a car trunk and shutting the lid was no kind of amusing prank, right?

Maybe Debbie had been lying to herself some, too.

I needed to listen to what was happening now. I'd have lots of time to think about the human ego's capacity to deceive itself, if I survived the night.

Pam was saying, 'So you're thinking we need to save Hallow? To take the spell off Eric?' She didn't sound happy at the prospect. I swallowed my painful feelings and made myself listen. This was no time to start brooding.

'No,' the witch said instantly. 'Her brother, Mark. There is too much danger in leaving Hallow alive. She must die as quickly as we can reach her.'

'What will you be doing?' Pam asked. 'How will you help us in this attack?'

'We will be outside, but within two blocks,' the man said. 'We'll be winding spells around the building to make the witches weak and indecisive. And we have a few tricks up our sleeves.' He and the young woman, who had on a huge amount of black eye makeup, looked pretty pleased at a chance to use those tricks.

Pam nodded as if winding spells was sufficient aid. I thought waiting outside with a flamethrower would have been better.

All this time, Debbie Pelt had been standing as if she'd been paralyzed. Now she began to pick her way through to the back door. Bubba leaped up to grab her arm. She hissed at him, but he didn't falter, though I would have.

None of the Weres reacted to this occurrence. It really was as though she were invisible to them.

'Let me leave. I'm not wanted,' she said to Bubba, fury and misery fighting for control of her face.

Bubba shrugged. He just held on to her, waiting for Pam's judgment.

'If we let you go, you might run to the witches and let them know we are coming,' Pam said. 'That would be of a piece with your character, apparently.'

Debbie had the gall to look outraged. Alcide looked as if he were watching the Weather Channel.

'Bill, you take charge of her,' Chow suggested. 'If she turns on us, kill her.'

'That sounds wonderful,' Bill said, smiling in a fangy way.

After a few more arrangements about transportation, and some more quiet consultation among the witches, who were facing a completely different kind of fight, Pam said, 'All right, let's go.' Pam, who looked more than ever like Alice in Wonderland in her pale pink sweater and darker pink slacks, stood up and checked her lipstick in the mirror on the wall close to where I'd been sitting. She gave her reflection an experimental smile, as I've seen women do a thousand times.

'Sookie, my friend,' she said, turning to aim the smile at me. 'Tonight is a great night.'

'It is?'

'Yes.' Pam put her arm around my shoulders. 'We defend what is ours! We fight for the restoration of our leader!' She grinned past me at Eric. 'Tomorrow, Sheriff, you will be back at your desk at Fangtasia. You'll be able to go to your own house, your own bedroom. We've kept it clean for you.'

I checked Eric's reaction. I'd never heard Pam address Eric by his title before. Though the head vampire for each section was called a sheriff, and I should have been used to that by now, I couldn't help but picture Eric in a cowboy outfit with a star pinned to his chest, or (my favorite) in black tights as the villainous sheriff of Nottingham. I found it interesting, too, that he didn't live here with Pam and Chow.

Eric gave Pam such a serious look that the grin faded right off her face. 'If I die tonight,' he said, 'pay this woman the money that was promised her.' He gripped my shoulder. I was just draped in vampires.

'I swear,' Pam said. 'Chow and Gerald will know, too.'

Eric said, 'Do you know where her brother is?'

Startled, I stepped away from Pam.

Pam looked equally taken aback. 'No, Sheriff.'

'It occurred to me that you might have taken him hostage to ensure she didn't betray me.'

The idea had never crossed my mind, but it should have. Obviously, I had a lot to learn about being devious.

'I wish I'd thought of that,' Pam said admiringly, echoing my thoughts with her own twist. 'I wouldn't have minded spending some time with Jason as my hostage.' I couldn't understand it: Jason's allure just seemed universal. 'But I didn't take him,' Pam said. 'If we get through this, Sookie, I'll look for him myself. Could it be Hallow's witches have him?'

'It's possible,' I said. 'Claudine said she didn't see any hostages, but she also said there were rooms she didn't look into. Though I don't know why they would have taken Jason, unless Hallow knows I have Eric? Then they might have used him to make me talk, just the way you would have used him to make me keep silent. But they haven't approached me. You can't use blackmail on someone who doesn't know anything about the hold you have on them.'

'Nonetheless, I'll remind all those who are going to enter the building to watch out for him,' Pam said.

'How is Belinda?' I asked. 'Have you made arrangements to pay her hospital bills?'

She looked at me blankly.

'The waitress who was hurt defending Fangtasia,' I reminded her, a little dryly. 'You remember? The friend of Ginger, who *died*?'

'Of course,' said Chow, from his place against the wall. 'She is recovering. We sent her flowers and candy,' he told Pam. Then he focused on me. 'Plus, we have a group insurance policy.' He was proud as a new father about that.

Pam looked pleased with Chow's report. 'Good,' she said. 'You have to keep them happy. Are we ready to go?'

I shrugged. 'I guess so. No point in waiting.'

Bill stepped in front of me as Chow and Pam consulted about which vehicle to take. Gerald had gone out to make sure everyone was on the same page as far as the plan of battle.

'How was Peru?' I asked Bill. I was very conscious of Eric, a huge blond shadow at my elbow.

'I made a lot of notes for my book,' Bill said. 'South America hasn't been good to vampires as a whole, but Peru is not as hostile as the other countries, and I was able to talk to a few vampires I hadn't heard of before.' For months, Bill had been compiling a vampire directory at the behest of the queen of Louisiana, who thought having such an item would be very handy. Her opinion was certainly not the universal opinion of the vampire community, some of whom had very strong objections to being outed, even among their own kind. I guess secrecy could be almost impossible to give up, if you'd clung to it for centuries.

There were vampires who still lived in graveyards, hunting every night, refusing to recognize the change in their status; it was like the stories about the Japanese soldiers who'd held out on Pacific islands long after World War II was over.

'Did you get to see those ruins you talked about?'

'Machu Picchu? Yes, I climbed up to them by myself. It was a great experience.'

I tried to picture Bill going up a mountain at night, seeing the ruins of an ancient civilization in the moonlight. I couldn't even imagine what that must have been like. I'd never been out of the country. I hadn't often been out of the state, for that matter.

'This is Bill, your former mate?' Eric's voice sounded a little ... strained.

'Ah, this is – well, yes, sort of,' I said unhappily. The 'former' was correct; the 'mate' was a little off.

Eric placed both his hands on my shoulders and moved in close to me. I had no doubt he was staring over the top of my head at Bill, who was staring right back. Eric might as well have stuck a SHE'S MINE sign on top of my head. Arlene had told me that she loved moments like this, when her ex saw plainly that someone else valued her even if he didn't. All I can say is, my taste in satisfaction runs completely different. I hated it. I felt awkward and ridiculous.

'You really don't remember me,' Bill said to Eric, as if he'd doubted it up until this moment. My suspicion was confirmed when he told me, as if Eric wasn't standing there, 'Truly, I thought this was an elaborate scheme on Eric's part to stay in your house so he could talk his way into your bed.'

Since the same thought had occurred to me, though I'd discarded it pretty quickly, I couldn't protest; but I could feel myself turning red.

'We need to get in the car,' I told Eric, turning to catch a glimpse of his face. It was rock hard and expressionless, which usually signaled he was in a dangerous state of mind. But he came with me when I moved toward the door, and the whole house slowly emptied its inhabitants into the narrow suburban street. I wondered what the neighbors thought. Of course, they knew the house was inhabited by vampires – no one around during the day, all the yard work done by human hirelings, the people who came and went at night being so very pale. This sudden activity had to invite neighborhood attention.

I drove in silence, Eric beside me on the front seat. Every now and then he reached over to touch me. I don't know who Bill had caught a ride with, but I was glad it wasn't me. The testosterone level would have been too high in the car, and I might have been smothered.

Bubba was sitting in the backseat, humming to himself. It sounded like 'Love Me Tender.'

'This is a crappy car,' Eric said, out of the blue, as far as I was concerned.

'Yes,' I agreed.

'Are you afraid?'

'I am.'

'If this whole thing works, will you still see me?'

'Sure,' I said, to make him happy. I was convinced that after this confrontation, nothing would be the same. But without the true Eric's conviction of his own prowess and intelligence and ruthlessness, this Eric was pretty shaky. He'd be up for the actual battle, but right now he needed a boost.

Pam had plotted out where everyone should park, to prevent Hallow's coven from becoming alarmed by the sudden appearance of a lot of cars. We had a map with our spot marked on it. That turned out to be an E-Z Mart on the corner of a couple of larger roads in a down-sliding area that was changing over from residential to commercial. We parked in the most out-of-the-way corner the E-Z Mart afforded. Without further discussion, we set out to our appointed locations.

About half the houses on the quiet street had real-estate signs in the front lawn, and the ones that remained in private hands were not well maintained. Cars were as battered as mine, and big bare patches indicated that the grass wasn't fertilized or watered in the summer. Every lighted window seemed to show the flickering of a television screen.

I was glad it was winter so the people who lived here were all inside. Two white vampires and a blond woman would excite comment, if not aggression, in this neighborhood. Plus, one of the vampires was pretty recognizable, despite the rigors of his changeover – which was why Bubba was almost always kept out of sight.

Soon we were at the corner where Eric was supposed to part from us so he could rendezvous with the other vampires. I would have continued on to my appointed post without a word; by now I was keyed up to such a pitch of tension I felt I could vibrate if you tapped me with a finger. But Eric wasn't content with a silent separation. He gripped my arms and kissed me for all he was worth, and believe me, that was plenty.

Bubba made a sound of disapproval. 'You're not supposed to be kissing on anybody else, Miss Sookie,' he said. 'Bill said it was okay, but I don't like it.'

After one more second, Eric released me. 'I'm sorry if we offended you,' he said coldly. He looked back down at me. 'I'll see you later, my lover,' he said very quietly.

I laid my hand against his cheek. 'Later,' I said, and I turned and walked away with Bubba at my heels.

'You ain't mad at me, are you, Miss Sookie?' he asked anxiously.

'No,' I said. I made myself smile at him, since I knew he could see me far more clearly than I could see him. It was a cold night, and though I was wearing my coat, it didn't seem to be as warm as it used to be. My bare hands were quivering with cold, and my nose felt numb. I could just detect a whiff of wood smoke from a fireplace, and automobile exhaust, and gasoline, and oil, and all the other car odors that combine to make City Smell.

But there was another smell permeating the neighborhood, an aroma that indicated this neighborhood was contaminated by more than urban blight. I sniffed, and the odor curled through the air in almost visible flourishes. After a moment's thought, I realized this must be the smell of magic, thick and stomach-clenching. Magic smells like I imagine a bazaar in some exotic foreign country might. It reeks of the strange, the different. The scent of a lot of magic can be quite overwhelming. Why weren't the residents complaining to the police about it? Couldn't everyone pick up on that odor?

'Bubba, do you smell something unusual?' I asked in a very low voice. A dog or two barked as we walked past in the black night, but they quickly quieted when they caught the scent of vampire. (To them, I guess, Bubba was the something unusual.) Dogs are almost always frightened of vampires, though their reaction to Weres and shifters is more unpredictable.

I found myself convinced I wanted nothing more than to go back to the car and leave. It was a conscious effort to make my feet move in the correct direction.

'Yeah, I sure do,' he whispered back. 'Someone's been laying some spells. Stay-away magic.' I didn't know if the Wiccans on our side, or the witches on Hallow's, had been responsible for this pervasive piece of craft, but it was effective.

The night seemed almost unnaturally silent. Maybe three cars passed us as we walked the maze of suburban streets. Bubba and I saw no other pedestrians, and the sense of ominous isolation grew. The stay-away intensified as we came closer to what we were supposed to stay away from.

The darkness between the pools of light below the street-lamps seemed darker, and the light didn't seem to reach as far. When Bubba took my hand, I didn't pull away. My feet seemed to drag at each step.

I'd caught a whiff of this smell before, at Fangtasia. Maybe the Were tracker had had an easier job than I'd thought.

'We're there, Miss Sookie,' Bubba said, his voice just a quiet thread in the night. We'd come around a corner. Since I knew there was a spell, and I knew I could keep walking, I did; but if I'd been a resident of the area, I would have found an alternative route, and I wouldn't have thought twice about it. The impulse to avoid this spot was so strong that I wondered if the people who lived on this block had been able to come home from their jobs. Maybe they were eating out, going to movies, drinking in bars – anything to avoid returning to their homes. Every house on the street looked suspiciously dark and untenanted.

Across the road, and at the opposite end of the block, was the center of the magic.

Hallow's coven had found a good place to hole up: a business up for lease, a large building that had held a combination florist shop-bakery. Minnie's Flowers and Cakes stood in a lonely position, the largest store in a strip of three that had, one by one, faded and gone out like flames on a candelabra. The building had apparently been empty for years. The big plate-glass windows were plastered with posters for events long past and political candidates long since defeated. Plywood nailed over the glass doors was proof that vandals had broken in more than once.

Even in the winter chill, weeds pushed up through cracks in the parking area. A big Dumpster stood to the right side of the parking lot. I viewed it from across the street, getting as much of a picture of the outside as I could before closing my eyes to concentrate on my other senses. I took a moment to be rueful.

If you'd asked me, I would've had a hard time tracing the steps that had led me to this dangerous place at this dangerous time. I was on the edges of a battle in which both sides were pretty dubious. If I'd fallen in with Hallow's witches first, I would probably have been convinced that the Weres and the vampires deserved to be eradicated.

At this time a year ago, no one in the world really understood what I was, or cared. I was just Crazy Sookie, the one with the wild brother, a woman others pitied and avoided, to varying degrees. Now here I was, on a freezing street in Shreveport, gripping the hand of a vampire whose face was legendary and whose brain was mush. Was this betterment?

And I was here not for amusement, or improvement, but to reconnoiter for a bunch of supernatural creatures, gathering information on a group of homicidal, blood-drinking, shape-changing witches.

I sighed, I hoped inaudibly. Oh, well. At least no one had hit me.

My eyes closed, and I dropped my shields and reached out with my mind to the building across the street.

Brains, busy busy busy. I was startled at the bundle of impressions I was receiving. Maybe the absence of other humans in the vicinity, or the overwhelming pervasion of magic, was responsible; but some factor had sharpened my other sense to the point of pain. Almost stunned by the flow of information, I realized I had to sort through it and organize it. First, I counted brains. Not literally ('One temporal lobe, two temporal lobes . . . '), but as a thought cluster. I came up with fifteen. Five were in the front room, which had been the showroom of the store, of course. One was in the smallest space, which was most likely the bathroom, and the rest were in the third and largest room, which lay to the rear. I figured it had been the work area.

Everyone in the building was awake. A sleeping brain still gives me a low mumble of a thought or two, in dreaming, but it's not the same as a waking brain. It's like the difference between a dog twitching in its sleep and an alert puppy.

To get as much information as possible, I had to get closer. I had never attempted to pick through a group to get details as specific as guilt or innocence, and I wasn't even sure that was possible. But if any of the people in the building were not evil witches, I didn't want them to be in the thick of what was to come.

'Closer,' I breathed to Bubba. 'But under cover.'

'Yes'm,' he whispered back. 'You gonna keep your eyes closed?'

I nodded, and he led me very carefully across the street and into the shadow of the Dumpster that stood about five yards south of the building. I was glad it was cold, because that kept the garbage smell at an acceptable level. The ghosts of the scents of doughnuts and blossoms lay on top of the funk of spoiled things and old diapers that passersby had tossed into the handy receptacle. It didn't blend happily with the magic smell.

I adjusted, blocked out the assault on my nose, and began listening. Though I'd gotten better at this, it was still like trying to hear twelve phone conversations at once. Some of them were Weres, too, which complicated matters. I could only get bits and pieces.

. . . hope that's not a vaginal infection I feel coming on . . .

She won't listen to me, she doesn't think men can do the job.

If I turned her into a toad, who could tell the difference?

. . . wish we'd gotten some diet Coke . . .

I'll find that damn vamp and kill him . . .

Mother of the Earth, listen to my pleas.

I'm in too deep . . .

I better get a new nail file.

This was not decisive, but no one had been thinking, 'Oh, these demonic witches have trapped me, won't somebody help?' or 'I hear the vampires approaching!' or anything dramatic like that. This sounded like a band of people who knew each other, were at least relaxed in each other's company, and therefore held the same goals. Even the one who was praying was not in any state of urgency or need. I hoped Hallow wouldn't sense the crush of my mind, but everyone I'd touched had seemed preoccupied.

'Bubba,' I said, just a little louder than a thought, 'you go tell Pam there are fifteen people in there, and as far as I can tell, they're all witches.'

'Yes'm.'

'You remember how to get to Pam?'

'Yes'm.'

'So you can let go my hand, okay?'

'Oh. Okay.'

'Be silent and careful,' I whispered.

And he was gone. I crouched in the shadow that was darker than the night, beside the smells and cold metal, listening to the witches. Three brains were male, the rest female. Hallow was in there, because one of the women was looking at her and thinking of her . . . dreading her, which kind of made me uneasy. I wondered where they'd parked their cars – unless they flew around on broomsticks, ha ha. Then I wondered about something that should already have crossed my mind.

If they were so darn wary and dangerous, where were their sentries?

At that moment, I was seized from behind.

Chapter 12

'Who are you?' asked a thin voice.

Since she had one hand clapped over my mouth and the other was holding a knife to my neck, I couldn't answer. She seemed to grasp that after a second, because she told me, 'We're going in,' and began to push me toward the back of the building.

I couldn't have that. If she'd been one of the witches in the building, one of the blood-drinking witches, I couldn't have gotten away with this, but she was a plain old witch, and she hadn't watched Sam break up as many bar fights as I had. With both hands, I reached up and grabbed her knife wrist, and I twisted it as hard as I could while I hit her hard with my lower body. Over she went, onto the filthy cold pavement, and I landed right on top of her, pounding her hand against the ground until she released the knife. She was sobbing, the will seeping out of her.

'You're a lousy lookout,' I said to Holly, keeping my voice low.

'Sookie?' Holly's big eyes peered out from under a knit watch cap. She'd dressed for utility tonight, but she still had on bright pink lipstick.

'What the hell are you doing here?'

'They told me they'd get my boy if I didn't help them.'

I felt sick. 'How long have you been helping them? Before I came to your apartment, asking for help? How long?' I shook her as hard as I could.

'When she came to the bar with her brother, she knew there was another witch there. And she knew it wasn't you or Sam, after she'd talked to you. Hallow can do anything. She knows everything. Late that night, she and Mark came to my apartment. They'd been in a fight; they were all messed up, and they were mad. Mark held me down while Hallow punched me. She liked that. She saw my picture of my son; she took it and said she could curse him long distance, all the way from Shreveport – make him run out in the traffic or load his daddy's gun . . .' Holly was crying by now. I didn't blame her. It made me sick to think of it, and he wasn't even my child. 'I had to say I'd help her,' Holly whimpered.

'Are there others like you in there?'

'Forced to do this? A few of them.'

That made some thoughts I'd heard more understandable.

'And Jason? He in there?' Though I'd looked at all three of the male brains in the building, I still had to ask.

'Jason is a Wiccan? For real?' She pulled off the watch cap and ran her fingers through her hair.

'No, no, no. Is she holding him hostage?'

'I haven't seen him. Why on earth would Hallow have Jason?'

I'd been fooling myself all along. A hunter would find my brother's remains someday: it's always hunters, or people walking their dogs, isn't it? I felt a falling away beneath my feet, as if the ground had literally dropped out from under me, but I called myself back to the here and now, away from emotions I couldn't afford to feel until I was in a safer place.

'You have to get out of here,' I said in the lowest voice I could manage. 'You have to get out of this area now.'

'She'll get my son!'

'I guarantee she won't.'

Holly seemed to read something in the dim view she had of my face. 'I hope you kill them all,' she said as passionately as you can in a whisper. The only ones worth saving are Parton and Chelsea and Jane. They got blackmailed into this just like I did. Normally, they're just Wiccans who like to live real quiet, like me. We don't want to do no one no harm.'

'What do they look like?'

'Parton's a guy about twenty-five, brown hair, short, birthmark on his cheek. Chelsea is about seventeen, her hair's dyed that bright red. Jane, um, well – Jane's just an old woman, you know? White hair, pants, blouse with flowers on it. Glasses.' My grandmother would have reamed Holly for lumping all old women together, but God bless her, she wasn't around anymore, and I didn't have the time.

'Why didn't Hallow put one of her toughest people out here on guard duty?' I asked, out of sheer curiosity.

'They got a big ritual spell thing set up for tonight. I can't believe the stay-away spell didn't work on you. You must be resistant.' Then Holly whispered, with a little rill of laughter in her voice, 'Plus, none of 'em wanted to get cold.'

'Go on, get out of here,' I said almost inaudibly, and helped her up. 'It doesn't matter where you parked your car, go north out of here.' In case she didn't know which direction was north, I pointed.

Holly took off, her Nikes making almost no sound on the cracked sidewalk. Her dull dyed black hair seemed to soak up the light from the streetlamp as she passed beneath it. The smell around the house, the smell of magic, seemed to intensify. I wondered what to do now. Somehow I had to make sure that the three local Wiccans within the dilapidated building, the ones who'd been forced to serve Hallow, wouldn't be harmed. I couldn't think of a way in hell to do that. Could I even save one of them?

I had a whole collection of half thoughts and abortive impulses in the next sixty seconds. They all led to a dead end.

If I ran inside and yelled, 'Parton, Chelsea, Jane – out!' that would alert the coven to the impending attack. Some of my friends – or at least my allies – would die.

If I hung around and tried to tell the vampires that three of the people in the building were innocent, they would (most likely) ignore me. Or, if a bolt of mercy struck them, they'd have to save all the witches and then cull the innocent ones out, which would give the coven witches time to counterattack. Witches didn't need physical weapons.

Too late, I realized I should have kept a hold of Holly and used her as my entree into the building. But endangering a frightened mother was not a good option, either.

Something large and warm pressed against my side. Eyes and teeth gleamed in the city's night light. I almost screamed until I recognized the wolf as Alcide. He was very large. The silver fur around his eyes made the rest of his coat seem even darker.

I put an arm across his back. 'There are three in there who mustn't die,' I said. 'I don't know what to do.'

Since he was a wolf, Alcide didn't know what to do, either. He looked into my face. He whined, just a little. I was supposed to be back at the cars by now; but here I was, smack in the danger zone. I could feel movement in the dark all around me. Alcide slunk away to his appointed position at the rear door of the building.

'What are you doing here?' Bill said furiously, though it sounded strange coming out in a tiny thread of a whisper. Pam told you to leave once you'd counted.'

'Three in there are innocent,' I whispered back. 'They're locals. They were forced.'

Bill said something under his breath, and it wasn't a happy something.

I passed along the sketchy descriptions Holly had given me.

I could feel the tension in Bill's body, and then Debbie joined us in our foxhole. What was she thinking, to pack herself in so closely with the vampire and the human who hated her most?

'I told you to stay back,' Bill said, and his voice was frightening.

'Alcide abjured me,' she told me, just as if I hadn't been there when it happened.

'What did you expect?' I was exasperated at her timing and her wounded attitude. Hadn't she ever heard of consequences?

'I have to do something to earn back his trust.'

She'd come to the wrong shop, if she wanted to buy some self-respect.

'Then help me save the three in there who are innocent.' I recounted my problem again. 'Why haven't you changed into your animal?'

'Oh, I can't,' she said bitterly. 'I've been abjured. I can't change with Alcide's pack anymore. They have license to kill me, if I do.'

'What did you shift into, anyway?'

'Lynx.'

That was appropriate.

'Come on,' I said. I began to wriggle toward the building. I loathed this woman, but if she could be of use to me, I had to ally with her.

'Wait, I'm supposed to go to the back door with the Were,' Bill hissed. 'Eric's already back there.'

'So go!'

I sensed that someone else was at my back and risked a quick glance to see that it was Pam. She smiled at me, and her fangs were out, so that was a little unnerving.

Maybe if the witches inside hadn't been involved in a ritual, and hadn't been relying on their less-than-dedicated sentry and their magic, we wouldn't have made it to the door undetected. But fortune favored us for those few minutes. We got to the front door of the building, Pam and Debbie and I, and there met up with the young Were, Sid. I could recognize him even in his wolf body. Bubba was with him.

I was struck with a sudden inspiration. I moved a few feet away with Bubba.

'Can you run back to the Wiccans, the ones on our side? You know where they are?' I whispered.

Bubba nodded his head vigorously.

'You tell them there are three local Wiccans inside who're being forced into this. Ask if they can make up some spell to get the three innocent ones to stand out.'

'I'll tell them, Miss Sookie. They're real sweet to me.'

'Good fella. Be quick, be quiet.'

He nodded, and was gone into the darkness.

The smell around the building was intensifying to such a degree that I was having trouble breathing. The air was so permeated with scent, I was reminded of passing a candle shop in a mall.

Pam said, 'Where have you sent Bubba?'

'Back to our Wiccans. They need to make three innocent people stand out somehow so we won't kill 'em.'

'But he has to come back now. He has to break down the door for me!'

'But . . .' I was disconcerted at Pam's reaction. 'He can't go in without an invitation, like you.'

'Bubba is brain damaged, degraded. He's not altogether a true vampire. He can enter without an express invitation.'

I gaped at Pam. 'Why didn't you tell me?' She just raised her eyebrows. When I thought back, it was true that I could remember at least twice that Bubba had entered dwellings without an invitation. I'd never put two and two together.

'So I'll have to be the first through the door,' I said, more matter-of-factly than I was really feeling. 'Then I invite you all in?'

'Yes. Your invitation will be enough. The building doesn't belong to them.'

'Should we do this now?'

Pam gave an almost inaudible snort. She was smiling in the glow of the streetlight, suddenly exhilarated. 'You waiting for an engraved invite?'

Lord save me from sarcastic vampires. 'You think Bubba's had enough time to get to the Wiccans?'

'Sure. Let's nail some witch butt,' she said happily. I could tell the fate of the local Wiccans was very low on her list of priorities. Everyone seemed to be looking forward to this but me. Even the young Were was showing a lot of fang.

'I kick, you go in,' Pam said. She gave me a quick peck on the cheek, utterly surprising me.

I thought, *I* so *don't want to be here.*

Then I got up from my crouch, stood behind Pam, and watched in awe while she cocked a leg and kicked with the force of four or five mules. The lock shattered, the door sprang inward while the old wood nailed over it splintered and cracked, and I leaped inside and screamed 'Come in!' to the vampire behind me and the ones at the back door. For an odd moment, I was in the lair of the witches by myself, and they'd all turned to look at me in utter astonishment.

The room was full of candles and people sitting on cushions on the floor; during the time we'd waited outside, all the others in the building seemed to have come into this front room, and they were sitting cross-legged in a circle, each with a candle burning before her, and a bowl, and a knife.

Of the three I'd try to save, 'old woman' was easiest to recognize. There was only one white-haired woman in the circle. She was wearing bright pink lipstick, a little skewed and smeared, and there was dried blood on her cheek. I grabbed her arm and pushed her into a corner, while all about me was chaos. There were only three human men in the room. Hallow's brother, Mark, now being attacked by a pack of wolves, was one of them. The second male was a middle-aged man with concave cheeks and suspicious black hair, and he not only was muttering some kind of spell but pulling a switchblade from the jacket lying on the floor to his right. He was too far away for me to do anything about it; I had to rely on the others to protect themselves. Then I spotted the third man, birthmark on cheek – must be Parton. He was cowering with his hands over his head. I knew how he felt.

I grabbed his arm and pulled up, and he came up punching, of course. But I wasn't having any of that, no one was going to hit me, so I aimed my fist through his ineffectually flailing arms and got him right on the nose. He shrieked, adding another layer of noise to the already cacophonous room, and I yanked him over to the same corner where I'd stashed Jane. Then I saw that the older woman and the young man were both shining. Okay, the Wiccans had come through with a spell and it was working, though just a tad late. Now I had to find a shining young woman with dyed red hair, the third local.

But my luck ran out then; hers already had. She was shining, but she was dead. Her throat had been torn out by one of the wolves: one of ours, or one of theirs, it didn't really matter.

I scrambled though the melee back to the corner and seized both of the surviving Wiccans by the arm. Debbie Pelt came rushing up. 'Get out of here,' I said to them. 'Find the other Wiccans out there, or go home now. Walk, get a cab, whatever.'

'It's a bad neighborhood out there,' quavered Jane.

I stared at her. 'And this isn't?' The last I saw of the two, Debbie was pointing and giving them instructions. She had stepped out the doorway with them. I was about to take off after them, since I wasn't supposed to be here anyway, when one of the Were witches snapped at my leg. Its teeth missed flesh but snagged my pants leg, and that was enough to yank me back. I stumbled and nearly fell to the floor, but managed to grasp the doorjamb in time to regain my feet. At that moment, the second wave of Weres and vamps came through from the back room, and the wolf darted off to meet the new assault from the rear.

The room was full of flying bodies and spraying blood and screams.

The witches were fighting for all they were worth, and the ones who could shift had done so. Hallow had changed, and she was a snarling mass of snapping teeth. Her brother was trying to work some kind of magic, which required him to be in his human form, and he was trying to hold off the Weres and the vampires long enough to complete the spell.

He was chanting something, he and the concave-cheeked man, even as Mark Stonebrook drove a fist into Eric's stomach.

A heavy mist began to crawl through the room. The witches, who were fighting with knives or wolf teeth, got the idea, and those who could speak began to add to whatever Mark was saying. The cloud of mist in the room began to get thicker and thicker, until it was impossible to tell friend from foe.

I leaped for the door to escape from the suffocating cloud. This stuff made breathing a real effort. It was like trying to inhale and exhale cotton balls. I extended my hand, but the bit of wall I touched didn't include a door. It had been right there! I felt a curl of panic in my stomach as I patted frantically, trying to trace the outline of the exit.

Not only did I fail to find the doorjamb, I lost touch with the wall altogether on my next sideways step. I stumbled over a wolf's body. I couldn't see a wound, so I got hold of its shoulders and dragged, trying to rescue it from the thick smoke.

The wolf began to writhe and change under my hands, which was pretty disconcerting. Even worse, it changed into a naked Hallow. I didn't know anyone could change that fast. Terrified, I let go of her immediately and backed away into the cloud. I'd been trying to be a good Samaritan with the wrong victim. A nameless woman, one of the witches, grabbed me from behind with superhuman strength. She tried to grip my neck with one hand while holding my arm with the other, but her hand kept slipping, and I bit her as hard as I could. She might be a witch, and she might be a Were, and she might have drunk a gallon of vamp blood, but she was no warrior. She screamed and released me.

By now I was completely disoriented. Which way was out? I was coughing and my eyes were streaming. The only sense I was sure of was gravity. Sight, hearing, touch: all were affected by the thick white billows, which were getting ever denser. The vampires had an advantage in this situation; they didn't need to breathe. All the rest of us did. Compared to the thickening atmosphere in the old bakery, the polluted city air outside had been pure and delicious.

Gasping and weeping, I flung my arms out in front of me and tried to find a wall or a doorway, any sort of landmark. A room that had not seemed so large now seemed cavernous. I felt I'd stumbled through yards of nothingness, but that wasn't possible unless the witches had changed the dimensions of the room, and my prosaic mind just couldn't accept the possibility. From around me I heard screams and sounds that were muffled in the cloud, but no less frightening. A spray of blood suddenly appeared down the front of my coat. I felt the spatter hit my face. I made a noise of distress that I couldn't form into words. I knew it wasn't my blood, and I knew I hadn't been hurt, but somehow that was hard for me to believe.

Then something fell past me, and as it was on its way to the floor I glimpsed a face. It was the face of Mark Stonebrook, and he was in the process of dying. The smoke closed in around him, and he might as well have been in another city.

Maybe I should crouch, too? The air might be better close to the floor. But Mark's body was down there, and other things. So much for Mark removing the spell on Eric, I thought wildly. Now we'll need Hallow. 'The best-laid plans of mice and men . . .' Where'd my grandmother gotten that quote? Gerald knocked me sideways as he pushed past in pursuit of something I couldn't see.

I told myself I was brave and resourceful, but the words rang hollow. I blundered ahead, trying not trip over the debris on the floor. The witches' paraphernalia, bowls and knives and bits of bone and vegetation that I couldn't identify, had been scattered in the scuffle. A clear spot opened up unexpectedly, and I could see an overturned bowl and one of the knives on the floor at my feet. I scooped up the knife just before the cloud rolled back over it. I was sure the knife was supposed to be used for some ritual – but I wasn't a witch, and I needed it to defend myself. I felt better when I had the knife, which was real pretty and felt very sharp.

I wondered what our Wiccans were doing. Could they be responsible for the cloud? I wished I'd gotten to vote.

Our witches, as it turned out, were getting a live feed from the scene of the fight from one of their coven sisters, who was a scryer. (Though she was physically with them, she could see what was happening on the surface of a bowl of water, I learned later.) She could make out more using that method than we could, though why she didn't see just a bunch of white smoke billowing on the surface of that water, I don't know.

Anyway, our witches made it rain . . . in the building. Somehow the rain slowly cut back on the cloud cover, and though I felt damp and extremely cold, I also discovered I was close to the inner door, the one leading into the second, large room. Gradually, I became aware that I could see; the room had started to glow with light, and I could discern shapes. One bounded toward me on legs that seemed not-quite-human, and Debbie Pelt's face snarled at me. What was she doing here? She'd stepped out the door to show the Wiccans which way to find safety, and now she was back in the room.

I don't know if she could help it or not, or if she'd just gotten swept up in the madness of battle, but Debbie had partially changed. Her face was sprouting fur, and her teeth had begun to lengthen and sharpen. She snapped at my throat, but a convulsion caused by the change made her teeth fall short. I tried to step back, but I stumbled over something on the floor and took a precious second or two to regain my footing. She began to lunge again, her intent unmistakable, and I recalled that I had a knife in my hand. I slashed at her, and she hesitated, snarling.

She was going to use the confusion to settle our score. I wasn't strong enough to fight a shape-shifter. I'd have to use the knife, though something inside me cringed at the thought.

Then from the tags and tatters of the mist came a big hand stained with blood, and that big hand grabbed Debbie Pelt's throat and squeezed. And squeezed. Before I could track the hand up the arm to the face of its owner, a wolf leaped from the floor to knock me down.

And sniff my face.

Okay, that was . . . then the wolf on top of me was knocked off and rolling on the floor, snarling and snapping at another wolf. I couldn't help, because the two were moving so quickly I couldn't be sure I'd help the right party.

The mist was dispersing at a good rate now, and I could see the room as a whole, though there were still patches of opaque fog. Though I'd been desperate for this moment, I was almost sorry now that it'd arrived. Bodies, both dead and wounded, littered the floor among the paraphernalia of the coven, and blood spattered the walls. Portugal, the handsome young Were from the air force base, lay sprawled in front of me. He was dead. Culpepper crouched beside him, keening. This was a small piece of war, and I hated it.

Hallow was still standing and completely in her human form, bare and smeared with blood. She picked up a wolf and slung it at the wall as I watched. She was magnificent and horrible. Pam was creeping up behind her, and Pam was disheveled and dirty. I'd never seen the vampire so much as ruffled, and I almost didn't recognize her. Pam launched herself, catching Hallow at the hips and knocking her to the floor. It was as good a tackle as I'd ever seen in years of Friday night football, and if Pam had caught Hallow a little higher up and could have gotten a grip on her, it would have been all over. But Hallow was slippery with the misty rain and with blood, and her arms were free. She twisted in Pam's grasp and seized Pam's long straight hair in both hands and pulled, and clumps of the hair came off, attached to a good bit of scalp.

Pam shrieked like a giant teakettle. I'd never heard a noise that loud come out of a throat – in this case not a human throat, but a throat nonetheless. Since. Pam was definitely of the 'get even' school, she pinned Hallow to the floor by gripping both her upper arms and pressing, pressing, until Hallow was flattened. Since the witch was so strong, it was a terrible struggle, and Pam was hampered by the blood streaming down her face. But Hallow was human, and Pam was not. Pam was winning until one of the witches, the hollow-cheeked man, crawled over to the two woman and bit into Pam's neck. Both her arms were occupied, and she couldn't stop him. He didn't just bite, he drank, and as he drank, his strength increased, as if his battery was getting charged. He was draining right from the source. No one seemed to be watching but me. I scrambled across the limp, furry body of a wolf and one of the vampires to pummel on the hollow-cheeked man, who simply ignored me.

I would have to use the knife. I'd never done something like this; when I'd struck back at someone, it had always been a life-or-death situation, and the life and the death had been mine. This was different. I hesitated, but I had to do something quick. Pam was weakening before my eyes, and she would not be able to restrain Hallow much longer. I took the black-bladed knife with its black handle, and I held it to his throat; I jabbed him, a little.

'Let go of her,' I said. He ignored me.

I jabbed harder, and a stream of scarlet ran down the skin of his neck. He let go of Pam then. His mouth was all covered in her blood. But before I could rejoice that he'd freed her, he spun over while he was still underneath me and came after me, his eyes absolutely insane and his mouth open to drink from me, too. I could feel the yearning in his brain, the *want, want, want*. I put the knife to his neck again, and just as I was steeling myself, he lunged forward and pushed the blade into his own neck.

His eyes went dull almost instantly.

He'd killed himself by way of me. I don't think he'd ever realized the knife was there.

This was a close killing, a right-in-my-face killing, and I'd been the instrument of death, however inadvertently.

When I could look up, Pam was sitting on Hallow's chest, her knees pinning Hallow's arms, and she was smiling. This was so bizarre that I looked around the room to find the reason, and I saw that the battle appeared to be over. I couldn't imagine how long it had lasted, that loud but invisible struggle in the thick mist, but now I could see the results all too clearly.

Vampires don't kill neat, they kill messy. Wolves, too, are not known for their table manners. Witches seemed to manage to splash a little less blood, but the end result was really horrible, like a very bad movie, the kind you were ashamed you'd paid to see.

We appeared to have won.

At the moment, I hardly cared. I was really tired, mentally and physically, and that meant all the thoughts of the humans, and some of the thoughts of the Weres, rolled around in my brain like clothes in a dryer. There was nothing I could do about it, so I let the tag ends drift around in my head while, using the last of my strength, I pushed off of the corpse. I lay on my back and stared up at the ceiling. Since I had no thoughts, I filled up with everyone else's. Almost everyone was thinking the same kind of thing I was: how tired they were, how bloody the room was, how hard it was to believe they'd gone through a fight like this and survived. The spiky-haired boy had reverted to his human form, and he was thinking how much more he'd enjoyed it than he thought he should. In fact, his unclothed body was showing visible evidence of how much he'd enjoyed it, and he was trying to feel embarrassed about that. Mostly, he wanted to track down that cute young Wiccan and find a quiet corner. Hallow was hating Pam, she was hating me, she was hating Eric, she was hating everyone. She began to try to mumble a spell to make us all sick, but Pam gave her an elbow in the neck, and that shut her right up.

Debbie Pelt got up from the floor in the door and surveyed the scene. She looked amazingly pristine and energetic, as if she'd never had a furry face and wouldn't even begin to know how to kill someone. She picked her way through the bodies strewn on the floor, some living and some not, until she found Alcide, still in his wolf form. She squatted down to check him over for wounds, and he growled at her in clear warning. Maybe she didn't believe he would attack, or maybe she just fooled herself into believing it, but she laid her hand on his shoulder, and he bit her savagely enough to draw blood. She shrieked and scrambled back. For a few seconds, she crouched there, cradling her bleeding hand and crying. Her eyes met mine and almost glowed with hatred. She would never forgive me. She would blame me the rest of her life for Alcide's discovery of her dark nature. She'd toyed with him for two years, pulling him to her, pushing him back, concealing from him the elements of her nature he would never accept, but wanting him with her nonetheless. Now it was all over.

And this was my fault?

But I wasn't thinking in Debbie terms, I was thinking like a rational human being, and of course Debbie Pelt was not. I wished the hand that had caught her neck during the struggle in the cloud had choked her to death. I watched her back as she pushed open the door and strode into the night, and at that moment I knew Debbie Pelt would be out to get me for the rest of her life. Maybe Alcide's bite would get infected and she'd get blood poisoning?

In reflex action, I chastised myself: That was an evil thought; God didn't want us to wish ill on anyone. I just hoped He was listening in to Debbie, too, the way you hope the highway patrolman who stopped you for a ticket is also going to stop the guy behind you who was trying to pass you on the double yellow line.

The redheaded Were, Amanda, came over to me. She was bitten here and there, and she had a swollen lump on her forehead, but she was quietly beaming. 'While I'm in a good mood, I want to apologize for insulting you,' she said directly. 'You came through in this fight. Even if you can tolerate vamps, I won't hold that against you anymore. Maybe you'll see the light.' I nodded, and she strolled away to check on her packmates.

Pam had tied up Hallow, and Pam, Eric, and Gerald had gone to kneel beside someone on the other side of the room. I wondered vaguely what was happening over there, but Alcide was shimmering back into human form, and when he'd oriented himself, he crawled over to me. I was too exhausted to care that he was naked, but I had a floating idea that I should try to remember the sight, since I'd want to recall it at my leisure later.

He had some grazes and bloody spots, and one deep laceration, but overall he looked pretty good.

'There's blood on your face,' he said, with an effort.

'Not mine.'

'Thank God,' he said, and he lay on the floor beside me. 'How bad are you hurt?'

'I'm not hurt, not really,' I said. 'I mean, I got shoved around a lot, and choked a little maybe, and snapped at, but no one hit me!' By golly, I was going to make my New Year's resolution come true, after all.

'I'm sorry we didn't find Jason here,' he said.

'Eric asked Pam and Gerald if the vampires were holding him, and they said no,' I remarked. 'He'd thought of a real good reason for the vamps to have him. But they didn't.'

'Chow is dead.'

'How?' I asked, sounding as calm as if it hardly mattered. Truthfully, I had never been very partial to the bartender, but I would have shown a decent concern if I hadn't been so tired.

'One of Hallow's group had a wooden knife.'

'I never saw one before,' I said after a moment, and that was all I could think to say about the death of Chow.

'Me, neither.'

After a long moment, I said, 'I'm sorry about Debbie.' What I meant was, I was sorry Debbie had hurt him so badly, had proved to be such a dreadful person that he'd had to take a drastic step to get her out of his life.

'Debbie who?' he asked, and rolled to his feet and padded away across the filthy floor strewn with blood, bodies, and supernatural debris.

Chapter 13

The aftermath of a battle is melancholy and nasty. I guess you could call what we'd had a battle ... maybe more like a supernatural skirmish? The wounded have to be tended, the blood has to be cleaned up, the bodies have to be buried. Or, in this case, disposed of – Pam decided to burn the store down, leaving the bodies of Hallow's coven inside.

They hadn't all died. Hallow, of course, was still alive. One other witch survived, though she was badly hurt and very low on blood. Of the Weres, Colonel Flood was gravely wounded; Portugal had been killed by Mark Stonebrook. The others were more or less okay. Only Chow had died, out of the vampire contingent. The others had wounds, some very horrible, but vampires will heal.

It surprised me that the witches hadn't made a better showing.

'They were probably good witches, but they weren't good fighters,' Pam said. 'They were picked for their magical ability and their willingness to follow Hallow, not for their battle skills. She shouldn't have tried to take over Shreveport with such a following.'

'Why Shreveport?' I asked Pam.

'I'm going to find out,' Pam said, smiling.

I shuddered. I didn't want to consider Pam's methods. 'How are you going to keep her from doing a spell on you while you question her?'

Pam said, 'I'll think of something.' She was still smiling.

'Sorry about Chow,' I said, a little hesitantly.

The job of bartender at Fangtasia doesn't seem to be a good-luck job,' she admitted. 'I don't know if I'll be able to find someone to replace Chow. After all, he and Long Shadow both perished within a year of starting work.'

'What are you going to do about un-hexing Eric?'

Pam seemed glad enough to talk to me, even if I was only a human, since she'd lost her sidekick. 'We'll make Hallow do it, sooner or later. And she'll tell us why she did it.'

'If Hallow just gives up the general outline of the spell, will that be enough? Or will she have to perform it herself?' I tried to rephrase that in my head so it was clearer, but Pam seemed to understand me.

'I don't know. We'll have to ask our friendly Wiccans. The ones you saved should be grateful enough to give us any help we need,' Pam said, while she tossed some more gasoline around the room. She'd already checked the building to remove the few things she might want from it, and the local coven had gathered up the magical paraphernalia, in case one of the cops who came to investigate this fire could recognize the remnants.

I glanced at my watch. I hoped that Holly had made it safely home by now. I would tell her that her son was safe.

I kept my eyes averted from the job the youngest witch was doing on Colonel Flood's left leg. He'd sustained an ugly gash in the quad-riceps. It was a serious wound. He made light of it, and after Alcide fetched their clothes, the colonel limped around with a smile on his face. But when blood seeped through the bandage, the packmaster had to allow his Weres to take him to a doctor who happened to be two-natured and willing to help off the books, since no one could think of a good story that would explain such a wound. Before he left, Colonel Flood shook hands ceremoniously with the head witch and with Pam, though I could see the sweat beading on his forehead even in the frigid air of the old building.

I asked Eric if he felt any different, but he was still oblivious to his past. He looked upset and on the verge of terror. Mark Stonebrook's death hadn't made a bit of difference, so Hallow was in for a few

dreadful hours, courtesy of Pam. I just accepted that. I didn't want to
think about it closely. Or at all.

As for me, I was feeling completely at a loss. Should I go home to
Bon Temps, taking Eric with me? (Was I in charge of him anymore?)
Should I try to find a place to spend the remaining hours of the night
here in the city? Shreveport was home for everyone but Bill and me,
and Bill was planning on using Chow's empty bed (or whatever it was)
for the coming day, at Pam's suggestion.

I dithered around indecisively for a few minutes, trying to make up
my mind. But no one seemed to need me for anything specific, and
no one sought me out for conversation. So when Pam got involved in
giving the other vampires directions about Hallow's transportation,
I just walked out. The night was quite as still as it had been, but a few
dogs did bark as I walked down the street. The smell of magic had
lessened. The night was just as dark, and even colder, and I was at a
low ebb. I didn't know what I'd say if a policeman stopped me; I was
blood-spattered and tattered, and I had no explanation. At the moment,
I found it hard to care.

I'd gotten maybe a block when Eric caught up with me. He was
very anxious – almost fearful. 'You weren't there. I just looked around
and you weren't there,' he said accusingly. 'Where are you going? Why
didn't you tell me?'

'Please,' I said, and held up a hand to beg him to be silent. 'Please.'
I was too tired to be strong for him, and I had to fight an overwhelming
depression, though I couldn't have told you exactly why; after all, no
one had hit me. I should be happy, right? The goals of the evening had
been met. Hallow was conquered and in captivity; though Eric hadn't
been restored to himself, he soon would be, because Pam was sure to
bring Hallow around to the vampire way of thinking, in a painful and
terminal way.

Undoubtedly, Pam would also discover why Hallow had begun this
whole course of action. And Fangtasia would acquire a new bartender,
some fangy hunk who would bring in the tourist bucks. She and Eric
would open the strip club they'd been considering, or the all-night dry-
cleaners, or the bodyguard service.

My brother would still be missing.

'Let me go home with you. I don't know them,' Eric said, his voice low and almost pleading. I hurt inside when Eric said something that was so contrary to his normal personality. Or was I seeing Eric's true nature? Was his flash and assurance something he'd assumed, like another skin, over the years?

'Sure, come on,' I said, as desperate as Eric was, but in my own way. I just wanted him to be quiet, and strong.

I'd settle for quiet.

He loaned me his physical strength, at least. He picked me up and carried me back to the car. I was surprised to find that my cheeks were wet with tears.

'You have blood all over you,' he said into my ear.

'Yes, but don't get excited about it,' I warned. 'It doesn't do a thing for me. I just want to shower.' I was at the hiccupping-sob stage of crying, almost done.

'You'll have to get rid of this coat now,' he said, with some satisfaction.

'I'll get it cleaned.' I was too tired to respond to disparaging comments about my coat.

Getting away from the weight and smell of the magic was almost as good as a big cup of coffee and a hit of oxygen. By the time I got close to Bon Temps, I wasn't feeling so ragged, and I was calm as I let us in the back door. Eric came in behind me and took a step to my right to go around the kitchen table, as I leaned left to flick on the light switch.

When I turned on the light, Debbie Pelt was smiling at me.

She had been sitting in the dark at my kitchen table, and she had a gun in her hand.

Without saying a word, she fired at me.

But she'd reckoned without Eric, who was so fast, faster than any human. He took the bullet meant for me, and he took it right in the chest. He went down in front of me.

She hadn't had time to search the house, which was lucky. From behind the water heater, I yanked the shotgun I'd taken from Jason's house. I pumped it – one of the scariest sounds in the world – and I shot Debbie Pelt while she was still staring, shocked, at Eric, who was on his knees and coughing up blood. I racked another shell, but I didn't need to shoot her again. Her fingers relaxed and her gun fell to the floor.

I sat on the floor myself, because I couldn't stay upright anymore.

Eric was now full length on the floor, gasping and twitching in a pool of blood.

There wasn't much left of Debbie's upper chest and neck.

My kitchen looked like I'd been dismembering pigs, pigs that'd put up a good fight.

I started to reach up to scrabble for the telephone at the end of the counter. My hand dropped back to the floor when I wondered whom I was going to call.

The law? Ha.

Sam? And mire him down further in my troubles? I didn't think so.

Pam? Let her see how close I'd come to letting my charge get killed? Uh-uh.

Alcide? Sure, he'd love seeing what I'd done with his fiancée, abjure or no abjure.

Arlene? She had her living to make, and two little kids. She didn't need to be around something illegal.

Tara? Too queasy.

This is when I would have called my brother, if I'd known where he was. When you have to clean the blood out of the kitchen, it's family you want.

I'd have to do this by myself.

Eric came first. I scrambled over to him, reclined by him with one elbow to prop me up.

'Eric,' I said loudly. His blue eyes opened. They were bright with pain.

The hole in his chest bubbled blood. I hated to think what the exit wound looked like. Maybe it had been a twenty-two? Maybe the bullet was still inside? I looked at the wall behind where he'd been standing, and I couldn't see a spray of blood or a bullet hole. Actually, I realized, if the bullet had gone through him, it would have struck me. I looked down at myself, fumbled the coat off. No, no fresh blood.

As I watched Eric, he began to look a little better. 'Drink,' he said, and I almost put my wrist to his lips, when I reconsidered. I managed to get some TrueBlood out of the refrigerator and heat it up, though the front of the microwave was less than pristine.

I knelt to give it to him. 'Why not you?' he asked painfully.

'I'm sorry,' I apologized. 'I know you earned it, sweetie. But I have to have all my energy. I've got more work ahead.'

Eric downed the drink in a few big gulps. I'd unbuttoned his coat and his flannel shirt, and as I looked at his chest to mark the progression of his bleeding, I saw an amazing thing. The bullet that had hit him popped out of the wound. In another three minutes, or perhaps less, the hole had closed. The blood was still drying on his chest hair, and the bullet wound was gone.

'Another drink?' Eric asked.

'Sure. How do you feel?' I was numb myself.

His smile was crooked. 'Weak.'

I got him more blood and he drank this bottle more slowly. Wincing, he pulled himself to a full sitting position. He looked at the mess on the other side of the table.

Then he looked at me.

'I know, I know, I did terrible!' I said. 'I'm so sorry!' I could feel tears – again – trailing down my cheeks. I could hardly feel more miserable. I'd done a dreadful thing. I'd failed in my job. I had a massive cleanup ahead of me. And I looked awful.

Eric looked mildly surprised at my outburst. 'You might have died of the bullet, and I knew I wouldn't,' he pointed out. 'I kept the bullet from you in the most expedient way, and then you defended me effectively.'

That was certainly a skewed way to look at it, but oddly enough, I did feel less horrible.

'I killed another human,' I said. That made two in one night; but in my opinion, the hollow-cheeked witch had killed himself by pushing down on the knife.

I'd definitely fired the shotgun all by myself.

I shuddered and turned away from the ragged shell of bone and flesh that had once held Debbie Pelt.

'You didn't,' he said sharply. 'You killed a shifter who was a treacherous, murderous bitch, a shifter who had tried to kill you twice already.' So it had been Eric's hand that had squeezed her throat and made her let go of me. 'I should have finished the job when I had her earlier,' he said, by way of confirmation. 'It would have saved us both some heartache; in my case, literally.'

I had a feeling this was not what the Reverend Fullenwilder would be saying. I muttered something to that effect.

'I was never a Christian,' Eric said. Now, that didn't surprise me. 'But I can't imagine a belief system that would tell you to sit still and get slaughtered.'

I blinked, wondering if that wasn't exactly what Christianity taught. But I am no theologian or Bible scholar, and I would have to leave the judgment on my action to God, who was also no theologian.

Somehow I felt better, and I was in fact grateful to be alive.

'Thank you, Eric,' I said. I kissed him on the cheek. Now you go clean up in the bathroom while I start in here.'

But he was not having any of that. God bless him, he helped me with great zeal. Since he could handle the most disgusting things with no apparent qualms, I was delighted to let him.

You don't want to know how awful it was, or all the details. But we got Debbie together and bagged up, and Eric took her way out into the woods and buried her and concealed the grave, he swore, while I cleaned. I had to take down the curtains over the sink and soak them in the washing machine in cold water, and I stuck my coat in with them, though without much hope of its being wearable again. I pulled on rubber gloves and used bleach-soaked wipes to go over and over the chair and table and floor, and I sprayed the front of the cabinets with wood soap and wiped and wiped.

You just wouldn't believe where specks of blood had landed.

I realized that attention to these tiny details was helping me keep my mind off of the main event, and that the longer I avoided looking at it squarely – the longer I let Eric's practical words sink into my awareness – the better off I'd be. There was nothing I could undo. There was no way I could mend what I had done. I'd had a limited number of choices, and I had to live with the choice I'd made. My

Gran had always told me that a woman – any woman worth her salt – could do whatever she had to. If you'd called Gran a liberated woman, she would have denied it vigorously, but she'd been the strongest woman I'd ever known, and if she believed I could complete this grisly task just because I had to, I would do it.

When I was through, the kitchen reeked of cleaning products, and to the naked eye it was literally spotless. I was sure a crime scene expert would be able to find trace evidence (a tip of the hat to the Learning Channel), but I didn't intend that a crime scene expert would ever have reason to come into my kitchen.

She'd broken in the front door. It had never occurred to me to check it before I came in the back. So much for my career as a bodyguard. I wedged a chair under the doorknob to keep it blocked for the remainder of the night.

Eric, returned from his burial detail, seemed to be high on excitement, so I asked him to go scouting for Debbie's car. She had a Mazda Miata, and she'd hidden it on a four-wheeler trail right across the parish road from the turnoff to my place. Eric had had the foresight to retain her keys, and he volunteered to drive her car somewhere else. I should have followed him, to bring him back to my house, but he insisted he could do the job by himself, and I was too exhausted to boss him around. I stood under a stream of water and scrubbed myself clean while he was gone. I was glad to be alone, and I washed myself over and over. When I was as clean as I could get on the outside, I pulled on a pink nylon nightgown and crawled in the bed. It was close to dawn, and I hoped Eric would be back soon. I had opened the closet and the hole for him, and put an extra pillow in it.

I heard him come in just as I was falling asleep, and he kissed me on the cheek. 'All done,' he said, and I mumbled, 'Thanks, baby.'

'Anything for you,' he said, his voice gentle. 'Good night, my lover.'

It occurred to me that I was lethal for exes. I'd dusted Bill's big love (and his mom); now I'd killed Alcide's off-and-on-again sweetie. I knew hundreds of men. I'd never gone homicidal on their exes. But creatures I cared about, well, that seemed to be different. I wondered if Eric had any old girlfriends around. Probably about a hundred or so. Well, they'd better beware of me.

After that, whether I willed it or not, I was sucked down into a black hole of exhaustion.

Chapter 14

I guess Pam worked on Hallow right up until dawn was peeking over the horizon. I myself was so heavily asleep, so in need of both physical and mental healing, I didn't wake until four in the afternoon. It was a gloomy winter day, the kind that makes you switch on the radio to see if an ice storm is coming. I checked to make sure I had three or four days' worth of firewood moved up onto the back porch.

Eric would be up early today.

I dressed and ate at the speed of a snail, trying to get a handle on my state of being.

Physically, I was fine. A bruise here or there, a little muscle soreness – that was nothing. It was the second week of January and I was sticking to my New Year's resolution just great.

On the other hand – and there's always another hand – mentally, or maybe emotionally, I was less than rock-steady. No matter how practical you are, no matter how strong-stomached you are, you can't do something like I'd done without suffering some consequences.

That's the way it should be.

When I thought of Eric getting up, I thought of maybe doing some snuggling before I had to go to work. And I thought of the pleasure of being with someone who thought I was so important.

I hadn't anticipated that the spell would have been broken.

Eric got up at five-thirty. When I heard movement in the guest bedroom, I tapped on the door and opened it. He whirled, his fangs running out and his hands clawing in front of him.

I'd almost said, 'Hi, honey,' but caution kept me mute.

'Sookie,' he said slowly. 'Am I in your house?'

I was glad I'd gotten dressed. 'Yes,' I said, regrouping like crazy. 'You've been here for safekeeping. Do you know what happened?'

'I went to a meeting with some new people,' he said, doubt in his voice. 'Didn't I?' He looked down at his Wal-Mart clothes with some surprise. 'When did I buy these?'

'I had to get those for you,' I said.

'Did you dress me, too?' he asked, running his hands down his chest and lower. He gave me a very Eric smile.

He didn't remember. Anything.

'No,' I said. I flashed on Eric in the shower with me. The kitchen table. The bed.

'Where is Pam?' he asked.

'You should call her,' I said. 'Do you recall anything about yesterday?'

'Yesterday I had the meeting with the witches,' he said, as if that was indisputable.

I shook my head. 'That was days ago,' I told him, unable to add the number of them up in my head. My heart sank even lower.

'You don't remember last night, after we came back from Shreveport,' I pressed him, suddenly seeing a gleam of light in all this.

'Did we make love?' he asked hopefully. 'Did you finally yield to me, Sookie? It's only a matter of time, of course.' He grinned at me.

No, last night we cleaned up a body, I thought.

I was the only one who knew. And even I didn't know where Debbie's remains were buried, or what had happened to her car.

I sat down on the edge of my old narrow bed. Eric looked at me closely. 'Something's wrong, Sookie? What happened while I was – Why don't I remember what happened?'

Least said, soonest mended.

All's well that ends well.

Out of sight, out of mind. (Oh, I wished that were true.)

'I bet Pam will be here any minute,' I said. 'I think I'll let her tell you all about it.'

'And Chow?'

'No, he won't be here. He died last night. Fangtasia seems to have a bad effect on bartenders.'

'Who killed him? I'll have vengeance.'

'You've already had it.'

'Something more is wrong with you,' Eric said. He'd always been astute.

'Yes, lots of stuff is wrong with me.' I would've enjoyed hugging him right then, but it would just complicate everything. 'And I think it's going to snow.'

'Snow, here?' Eric was as delighted as a child. 'I love snow!'

Why was I not surprised?

'Maybe we will get snowed in together,' he said suggestively, waggling his blond eyebrows.

I laughed. I just couldn't help it. And it was a hell of a lot better than crying, which I'd done quite enough of lately. 'As if you'd ever let the weather stop you from doing what you wanted to do,' I said, and stood. 'Come on, I'll heat you up some blood.'

Even a few nights of intimacy had softened me enough that I had to watch my actions. Once I almost stroked his hair as I passed him; and once I bent to give him a kiss, and had to pretend I'd dropped something on the floor.

When Pam knocked on my front door thirty minutes later, I was ready for work, and Eric was antsy as hell.

Pam was no sooner seated opposite him than he began bombarding her with questions. I told them quietly that I was leaving, and I don't think they even noticed when I went out the kitchen door.

Merlotte's wasn't too busy that night, after we dealt with a rather large supper crowd. A few flakes of snow had convinced most of the regulars that going home sober might be a very good idea. There were enough customers left to keep Arlene and me moderately busy. Sam caught me as I was loading my tray with seven mugs of beer and wanted to be filled in on the night before.

'I'll tell you later,' I promised, thinking I'd have to edit my narrative pretty carefully.

'Any trace of Jason?' he asked.

'No,' I said, and felt sadder than ever. The dispatcher at the law enforcement complex had sounded almost snappish when I'd called to ask if there was any news.

Kevin and Kenya came in that night after they'd gotten off duty. When I took their drinks to the table (a bourbon and Coke and a gin and tonic), Kenya said, 'We've been looking for your brother, Sookie. I'm sorry.'

'I know you all have been trying,' I said. 'I appreciate you all organizing the search party so much! I just wish . . .' And then I couldn't think of anything else to say. Thanks to my disability, I knew something about each of them that the other didn't know. They loved each other. But Kevin knew his mother would stick her head in the oven before she'd see him married to a black woman, and Kenya knew her brothers would rather ram Kevin through a wall than see him walk down the aisle with her.

And I knew this, despite the fact that neither of them did; and I hated having this personal knowledge, this intimate knowledge, that I just couldn't help knowing.

Worse than knowing, even, was the temptation to interfere. I told myself very sternly that I had enough problems of my own without causing problems for other people. Luckily, I was busy enough the rest of the night to erase the temptation from my mind. Though I couldn't reveal those kinds of secrets, I reminded myself that I owed the two officers, big-time. If I heard of something I could let them know, I would.

When the bar closed, I helped Sam put the chairs up on the tables so Terry Bellefleur could come in and mop and clean the toilets early in the morning. Arlene and Tack had left, singing 'Let It Snow' while they went out the back door. Sure enough, the flakes were drifting down outside, though I didn't think they'd stick past morning. I thought of the creatures out in the woods tonight, trying to keep warm and dry. I knew that in some spot in the forest, Debbie Pelt lay in a hole, cold forever.

I wondered how long I'd think of her like that, and I hoped very much I could remember just as clearly what an awful person she'd been, how vindictive and murderous.

In fact, I'd stood staring out the window for a couple of minutes when Sam came up behind me.

'What's on your mind?' he asked. He gripped my elbow, and I could feel the strength in his fingers.

I sighed, not for the first time. 'Just wondering about Jason,' I said. That was close enough to the truth.

He patted me in a consoling way. 'Tell me about last night,' he said, and for one second I thought he was asking me about Debbie. Then, of course, I knew he referred to the battle with the witches, and I was able to give him an account.

'So Pam showed up tonight at your place.' Sam sounded pleased about that. She must have cracked Hallow, made her undo the spell. Eric was himself again?'

'As far as I could tell.'

'What did he have to say about the experience?'

'He didn't remember anything about it,' I said slowly. 'He didn't seem to have a clue.'

Sam looked away from me when he said, 'How are you, with that?'

'I think it's for the best,' I told him. 'Definitely.' But I would be going home to an empty house again. The knowledge skittered at the edges of my awareness, but I wouldn't look at it directly.

'Too bad you weren't working the afternoon shift,' he said, somehow following a similar train of thought. 'Calvin Norris was in here.'

'And?'

'I think he came in hopes of seeing you.'

I looked at Sam skeptically. 'Right.'

'I think he's serious, Sookie.'

'Sam,' I said, feeling unaccountably wounded, 'I'm on my own, and sometimes that's no fun, but I don't have to take up with a werewolf just because he offers.'

Sam looked mildly puzzled. 'You wouldn't have to. The people in Hotshot aren't Weres.'

'He said they were.'

'No, not Weres with a capital W. They're too proud to call themselves shifters, but that's what they are. They're were-panthers.'

'What?' I swear I saw dots floating in the air around my eyes.

'Sookie? What's wrong?'

'Panthers? Didn't you know that the print on Jason's dock was the print of a panther?'

'No, no one told me about any print! Are you sure?'

I gave him an exasperated look. 'Of course, I'm sure. And he vanished the night Crystal Norris was waiting for him in his house. You're the only bartender in the world who doesn't know all the town gossip.'

'Crystal – *she's* the Hotshot girl he was with New Year's Eve? The skinny black-headed girl at the search?'

I nodded.

'The one Felton loves so much?'

'He what?'

'Felton, you know, the one who came along on the search. She's been his big love his whole life.'

'And you know this how?' Since I, the mind reader, didn't, I was distinctly piqued.

'He told me one night when he'd had too much to drink. These guys from Hotshot, they don't come in much, but when they do, they drink serious.'

'So why would he join in the search?'

'I think maybe we'd better go ask a few questions.'

'This late?'

'You got something better to do?'

He had a point, and I sure wanted to know if they had my brother or could tell me what had happened to him. But in a way, I was scared of finding out.

'That jacket's too light for this weather, Sookie,' Sam said, as we bundled up.

'My coat is at the cleaner's,' I said. Actually, I hadn't had a chance to put it in the dryer, or even to check to make sure all the blood had come out. And it had holes in it.

'Hmmm' was all Sam said, before he loaned me a green pullover sweater to wear under my jacket. We got in Sam's pickup because the snow was really coming down, and like all men, Sam was convinced he could drive in the snow, though he'd almost never done so.

The drive out to Hotshot seemed even longer in the dark night, with the snow swirling down in the headlights.

'I thank you for taking me out here, but I'm beginning to think we're crazy,' I said, when we were halfway there.

'Is your seat belt on?' Sam asked.

'Sure.'

'Good,' he said, and we kept on our way.

Finally we reached the little community. There weren't any street-lights out here, of course, but a couple of the residents had paid to have security lights put up on the electric poles. Windows were glowing in some of the houses.

'Where do you think we should go?'

'Calvin's. He's the one with the power,' Sam said, sounding certain.

I remembered how proud Calvin had been of his house, and I was a little curious to see the inside. His lights were on, and his pickup was parked in front of the house. Stepping out of the warm truck into the snowy night was like walking through a chilly wet curtain to reach the front door. I knocked, and after a long pause, the door came open. Calvin looked pleased until he saw Sam behind me.

'Come in,' he said, not too warmly, and stood aside. We stamped our feet politely before we entered.

The house was plain and clean, decorated with inexpensive but carefully arranged furniture and pictures. None of the pictures had people in them, which I thought interesting. Landscapes. Wildlife.

'This is a bad night to be out driving around,' Calvin observed.

I knew I'd have to tread carefully, as much as I wanted to grab the front of his flannel shirt and scream in his face. This man was a ruler. The size of the kingdom didn't really matter.

'Calvin,' I said, as calmly as I could, 'did you know that the police found a panther print on the dock, by Jason's bootprint?'

'No,' he said, after a long moment. I could see the anger building behind his eyes. 'We don't hear a lot of town gossip out here. I wondered why the search party had men with guns, but we make other people kind of nervous, and no one was talking to us much. Panther print. Huh.'

'I didn't know that was your, um, other identity, until tonight.'

He looked at me steadily. 'You think that one of us made off with your brother.'

I stood silent, not shifting my eyes from his. Sam was equally still beside me.

'You think Crystal got mad at your brother and did him harm?'

'No,' I said. His golden eyes were getting wider and rounder as I spoke to him.

'Are you afraid of me?' he asked suddenly.

'No,' I said. 'I'm not.'

'Felton,' he said.

I nodded.

'Let's go see,' he said.

Back out into the snow and darkness. I could feel the sting of the flakes on my cheeks, and I was glad my jacket had a hood. Sam's gloved hand took mine as I stumbled over some discarded tool or toy in the yard of the house next to Felton's. As we trailed up to the concrete slab that formed Felton's front porch, Calvin was already knocking at the door.

'Who is it?' Felton demanded.

'Open,' said Calvin.

Recognizing his voice, Felton opened the door immediately. He didn't have the same cleanliness bug as Calvin, and his furniture was not so much arranged as shoved up against whatever wall was handiest. The way he moved was not human, and tonight that seemed even more pronounced than it had at the search. Felton, I thought, was closer to reverting to his animal nature. Inbreeding had definitely left its mark on him.

'Where is the man?' Calvin asked without preamble.

Felton's eyes flared wide, and he twitched, as if he was thinking about running. He didn't speak.

'Where?' Calvin demanded again, and then his hand changed into a paw and he swiped it across Felton's face. 'Does he live?'

I clapped my hands across my mouth so I wouldn't scream. Felton sank to his knees, his face crossed with parallel slashes filling with blood.

'In the shed in back,' he said indistinctly.

I went back out the front door so quickly that Sam barely caught up with me. Around the corner of the house I flew, and I fell full-length over a woodpile. Though I knew it would hurt later, I jumped up and found myself supported by Calvin Norris, who, as he had in the woods, lifted me over the pile before I knew what he intended. He vaulted it himself with easy grace, and then we were at the door of the shed, which was one of those you order from Sears or Penney's. You have your neighbors come help put it up, when the concrete truck comes to pour your slab.

The door was padlocked, but these sheds aren't meant to repel determined intruders, and Calvin was very strong. He broke the lock, and pushed back the door, and turned on the light. It was amazing to me that there was electricity out here, because that's certainly not the norm.

At first I wasn't sure I was looking at my brother, because this creature looked nothing like Jason. He was blond, sure, but he was so filthy and smelly that I flinched, even in the freezing air. And he was blue with the cold, since he had only pants on. He was lying on a single blanket on the concrete floor.

I was on my knees beside him, gathering him up as best I could in my arms, and his eyelids fluttered open. 'Sookie?' he said, and I could hear the disbelief in his voice. 'Sookie? Am I saved?'

'Yes,' I said, though I was by no means so sure. I remembered what had happened to the sheriff who'd come out here and found something amiss. 'We're going to take you home.'

He'd been bitten.

He'd been bitten a lot.

'Oh, no,' I said softly, the significance of the bites sinking in.

'I didn't kill him,' Felton said defensively, from outside.

'You bit him,' I said, and my voice sounded like another person's. 'You wanted him to be like you.'

'So Crystal wouldn't like him better. She knows we need to breed outside, but she really likes me best,' Felton said.

'So you grabbed him, and you kept him, and you bit him.'

Jason was too weak to stand.

'Please carry him to the truck,' I said stiffly, unable to meet the eyes of anyone around me. I could feel the fury rising in me like a black wave, and I knew I had to restrain it until we were out of here. I had just enough control to do this. I knew I did.

Jason cried out when Calvin and Sam lifted him. They got the blanket, too, and sort of tucked it around him. I stumbled after them as they made their way back to Calvin's and the truck.

I had my brother back. There was a chance he was going to turn into a panther from time to time, but I had him back. I didn't know if the rules for all shifters were the same, but Alcide had told me that Weres who were bitten, not born – created Weres, rather than genetic Weres – changed into the half-man, half-beast creatures who populated horror movies. I forced myself to get off that track, to think of the joy of having my brother back, alive.

Calvin got Jason into the truck and slid him over, and Sam climbed into the driver's seat. Jason would be between us after I climbed into the truck. But Calvin had to tell me something first.

'Felton will be punished,' he said. 'Right now.'

Punishing Felton hadn't been at the top of my list of things to think about, but I nodded, because I wanted to get the hell out of there.

'If we're taking care of Felton, are you going to go to the police?' he asked. He was standing stiffly, as if he was trying to be casual about the question. But this was a dangerous moment. I knew what happened to people who drew attention to the Hotshot community.

'No,' I said. 'It was just Felton.' Though, of course, Crystal had to have known, at least on some level. She'd told me she'd smelled an animal that night at Jason's. How could she have mistaken the smell of panther, when she was one? And she had probably known all along that that panther had been Felton. His smell would be familiar to her. But it just wasn't the time to go into that; Calvin would know that as well as I, when he'd had a moment to think. 'And my brother may be one of you now. He'll need you,' I added, in the most even voice I could manage. It wasn't very even, at that.

'I'll come get Jason, next full moon.'

I nodded again. 'Thank you,' I told him, because I knew we would never have found Jason if he'd stonewalled us. 'I have to get my brother home now.' I knew Calvin wanted me to touch him, wanted me to connect with him somehow, but I just couldn't do it.

'Sure,' he said, after a long moment. The shape-shifter stepped back while I scrambled up into the cab. He seemed to know I wouldn't want any help from him right now.

I'd thought I'd gotten unusual brain patterns from the Hotshot people because they were inbred. It had never occurred to me they were something other than wolves. I'd assumed. I know what my high school volleyball coach always said about 'assume'. Of course, he'd also told us that we had to leave everything out on the court so it would be there when we came back, which I had yet to figure out.

But he'd been right about assumptions.

Sam had already gotten the heater in the truck going, but not at full blast. Too much heat too soon would be bad for Jason, I was sure. As it was, the second Jason began to warm up, his smell was pretty evident, and I nearly apologized to Sam, but sparing Jason any further humiliation was more important.

'Aside from the bites, and being so cold, are you okay?' I asked, when I thought Jason had stopped shivering and could speak.

'Yes,' he said. 'Yes. Every night, every damn night, he'd come in the shed, and he'd change in front of me, and I'd think, Tonight he's going to kill me and eat me. And every night, he'd bite me. And then he'd just change back and leave. I could tell it was hard for him, after he'd smelled the blood . . . but he never did more than bite.'

'They'll kill him tonight,' I said. 'In return for us not going to the police.'

'Good deal,' said Jason, and he meant it.

Chapter 15

Jason was able to stand on his own long enough to take a shower, which he said was the best one he'd taken in his life. When he was clean and smelled like every scented thing in my bathroom, and he was modestly draped with a big towel, I went all over him with Neosporin. I used up a whole tube on the bites. They seemed to be healing clean already, but I could not stop myself from trying to think of things to do for him. He'd had hot chocolate, and he'd eaten some hot oatmeal (which I thought was an odd choice, but he said all Felton had brought him to eat had been barely cooked meat), and he'd put on the sleeping pants I'd bought for Eric (too big, but the drawstring waist helped), and he'd put on a baggy old T-shirt I'd gotten when I'd done the Walk for Life two years before. He kept touching the material as if he was delighted to be dressed.

He seemed to want to be warm and to sleep, more than anything. I put him in my old room. With a sad glance at the closet, which Eric had left all askew, I told my brother good night. He asked me to turn the hall light on and leave the door cracked a little. It cost Jason to ask that, so I didn't say a word. I just did as he'd requested.

Sam was sitting in the kitchen, drinking a cup of hot tea. He looked up from watching the steam of it and smiled at me. 'How is he?'

I sank down into my usual spot. 'He's better than I thought he would be,' I said. 'Considering he spent the whole time in the shed with no heat and being bitten every day.'

'I wonder how long Felton would have kept him?'

'Until the full moon, I guess. Then Felton would've found out if he'd succeeded or not.' I felt a little sick.

'I checked your calendar. He's got a couple of weeks.'

'Good. Give Jason time to get his strength back before he has something else to face.' I rested my head in my hands for a minute. 'I have to call the police.'

'To let them know to stop searching?'

'Yep.'

'Have you made up your mind what to say? Did Jason mention any ideas?'

'Maybe that the male relatives of some girl had kidnapped him?' Actually, that was sort of true.

'The cops would want to know where he'd been held. If he'd gotten away on his own, they'd want to know how, and they'd be sure he'd have more information for them.'

I wondered if I had enough brainpower left to think. I stared blankly at the table: the familiar napkin holder that my grandmother had bought at a craft fair, and the sugar bowl, and the salt- and pepper-shakers shaped like a rooster and a hen. I noticed something had been tucked under the saltshaker.

It was a check for $50,000, signed by Eric Northman. Eric had not only paid me, he had given me the biggest tip of my career.

'Oh,' I said, very gently. 'Oh, boy.' I looked at it for a minute more, to make sure I was reading it correctly. I passed it across the table to Sam.

'Wow. Payment for keeping Eric?' Sam looked up at me, and I nodded. 'What will you do with it?'

'Put it through the bank, first thing tomorrow morning.'

He smiled. 'I guess I was thinking longer term than that.'

'Just relax. It'll just relax me to have it. To know that ...' To my embarrassment, here came tears. Again. *Damn.* 'So I won't have to *worry* all the time.'

'Things have been tight recently, I take it.' I nodded, and Sam's mouth compressed. 'You ...' he began, and then couldn't finish his sentence.

'Thanks, but I can't do that to people,' I said firmly. 'Gran always said that was the surest way to end a friendship.'

'You could sell this land, buy a house in town, have neighbors,' Sam suggested, as if he'd been dying to say that for months.

'Move out of this house?' Some member of my family had lived in this house continuously for over a hundred and fifty years. Of course, that didn't make it sacred or anything, and the house had been added to and modernized many times. I thought of living in a small modern house with level floors and up-to-date bathrooms and a convenient kitchen with lots of plugs. No exposed water heater. Lots of blown-in insulation in the attic. A carport!

Dazzled at the vision, I swallowed. 'I'll consider it,' I said, feeling greatly daring to even entertain the idea. 'But I can't think of anything much right now. Just getting through tomorrow will be hard enough.'

I thought of the police man-hours that had been put into searching for Jason. Suddenly I was so tired, I just couldn't make an attempt to fashion a story for the law.

'You need to go to bed,' Sam said astutely.

I could only nod. 'Thank you, Sam. Thank you so much.' We stood and I gave him a hug. It turned into a longer hug than I'd planned, because hugging him was unexpectedly restful and comfortable. 'Good night,' I said. 'Please drive careful going back.' I thought briefly of offering him one of the beds upstairs, but I kept that floor shut off and it would be awfully cold up there; and I'd have to go up and make the bed. He'd be more comfortable making the short drive home, even in the snow.

'I will,' he said, and released me. 'Call me in the morning.

'Thanks again.'

'Enough thank-yous,' he said. Eric had put a couple of nails in the front door to hold it shut, until I could get a dead bolt put on. I locked the back door behind Sam, and I barely managed to brush my teeth and change into a nightgown before I crawled in my bed.

The first thing I did the next morning was check on my brother. Jason was still deeply asleep, and in the light of day, I could clearly see the effects of his imprisonment. His face had a coating of stubble. Even in his sleep, he looked older. There were bruises here and there, and that was just on his face and arms. His eyes opened as I sat by the bed, looking at him. Without moving, he rolled his eyes around, taking in the room. They stopped when they came to my face.

'I didn't dream it,' he said. His voice was hoarse. 'You and Sam came and got me. They let me go. The panther let me go.'

'Yes.'

'So what's been happening while I was gone?' he asked next. 'Wait, can I go to the bathroom and get a cup of coffee before you tell me?'

I liked his asking instead of telling (a Jason trait, telling), and I was glad to tell him yes and even volunteer to get the coffee. Jason seemed happy enough to crawl back in bed with the mug of coffee and sugar, and prop himself up on the pillows while we talked.

I told him about Catfish's phone call, our to-and-fro with the police, the search of the yard and my conscription of his Benelli shotgun, which he immediately demanded to see.

'You fired it!' he said indignantly, after checking it over.

I just stared at him.

He flinched first. 'I guess it worked like a shotgun is 'spose to,' he said slowly. 'Since you're sitting here looking pretty much okay.'

'Thanks, and don't ask me again,' I said.

He nodded.

'Now we have to think of a story for the police.'

'I guess we can't just tell them the truth.'

'Sure, Jason, let's tell them that the village of Hotshot is full of were-panthers, and that since you slept with one, her boyfriend wanted to make you a were-panther, too, so she wouldn't prefer you over him. That's why he changed into a panther and bit you every day.'

There was a long pause.

'I can just see Andy Bellefleur's face,' Jason said in a subdued kind of way. 'He still can't get over me being innocent of murdering those girls last year. He'd love to get me committed as being delusional. Catfish would have to fire me, and I don't think I'd like it at the mental hospital.'

'Well, your dating opportunities would sure be limited.'

'Crystal – God, that girl! You warned me. But I was so bowled over by her. And she turns out to be a . . . you know.'

'Oh, for goodness sake, Jason, she's a shape-shifter. Don't go on like she's the creature from the Black Lagoon, or Freddy Krueger, or something.'

'Sook, you know a lot of stuff we don't know, don't you? I'm getting that picture.'

'Yes, I guess so.'

'Besides vampires.'

'Right.'

'There's lots else.'

'I tried to tell you.'

'I believed what you said, but I just didn't get it. Some people I know – I mean besides Crystal – they're not always people, huh?'

'That's right.'

'Like how many?'

I counted up the two-natured I'd seen in the bar: Sam, Alcide, that little were-fox who'd been standing Jason and Hoyt drinks a couple of weeks ago . . . 'At least three,' I said.

'How do you know all this?' ·

I just stared at him.

'Right,' he said, after a long moment. 'I don't want to know.'

'And now, you,' I said gently.

'Are you sure?'

'No, and we won't be sure for a couple of weeks,' I said. 'But Calvin'll help you if you need it.'

'I won't take help from them!' Jason's eyes were blazing, and he looked positively feverish.

'You don't have a choice,' I said, trying not to snap. 'And Calvin didn't know you were there. He's an okay guy. But it's not even time to talk about it yet. We have to figure out what to tell the police right now.'

For at least an hour we went over and over our stories, trying to find threads of truth to help us stitch together a fabrication.

Finally, I called the police station. The day-shift dispatcher was tired of hearing my voice, but she was still trying to be nice. 'Sookie, like I told you yesterday, hon, we'll call you when we find out something about Jason,' she said, trying to suppress the note of exasperation beneath her soothing tone.

'I've got him,' I said.

'You – WHAT?' The shriek came over loud and clear. Even Jason winced.

'I've got him.'

'I'll send someone right over.'

'Good,' I said, though I didn't mean it.

I had the foresight to get the nails out of the front door before the police got there. I didn't want them asking what had happened to it. Jason had looked at me oddly when I got out the hammer, but he didn't say a word.

'Where's your car?' Andy Bellefleur asked first thing.

'It's at Merlotte's.'

'Why?'

'Can I just tell you and Alcee, together, one time?' Alcee Beck was coming up the front steps. He and Andy came in the house together, and at the sight of Jason lying wrapped up on my couch, they both stopped dead in their tracks. I knew then that they'd never expected to see Jason alive again.

'Glad to see you safe and sound, man,' Andy said, and shook Jason's hand. Alcee Beck followed on his heels. They sat down, Andy in Gran's recliner and Alcee in the armchair I usually took, and I perched on the couch beside Jason's feet. 'We're glad you're in the land of the living, Jason, but we need to know where you've been and what happened to you.'

'I have no idea,' Jason said.

And he stuck to it for hours.

There had been no believable story Jason could tell that could account for everything: his absence, his poor physical condition, the bite marks, his sudden reappearance. The only possible line he could take was to say the last thing he remembered, he'd heard a funny noise outside while he was entertaining Crystal, and when he'd gone to investigate, he'd been hit on the head. He didn't remember anything until somehow he'd felt himself pushed from a vehicle to land in my yard the night before. I'd found him there when Sam brought me home from work. I'd ridden home with Sam because I was scared to drive in the snow.

Of course, we'd cleared this with Sam ahead of time, and he'd agreed, reluctantly, that it was the best we could come up with. I knew Sam didn't like to lie, and I didn't either, but we had to keep that particular can of worms closed.

The beauty of this story was its simplicity. As long as Jason could resist the temptation to embroider, he'd be safe. I'd known that would be hard for Jason; he loved to talk, and he loved to talk big. But as long as I was sitting there, reminding him of the consequences, my brother managed to restrain himself. I had to get up to get him another cup of coffee – the lawmen didn't want any more – and as I was coming back in the living room, Jason was saying he thought he remembered a cold dark room. I gave him a very plain look, and he said, 'But you know, my head is so confused, that may just be something I dreamed.'

Andy looked from Jason to me, clearly getting angrier and angrier. 'I just can't understand you two,' he said. His voice was almost a growl. 'Sookie, I know you worried about him. I'm not making that up, am I?'

'No, I am so glad to have him back.' I patted my brother's foot under the blanket.

'And you, you didn't want to be wherever you were, right? You missed work, you cost the parish thousands of dollars from our budget to search for you, and you disrupted the lives of hundreds of people. And you're sitting here lying to us!' Andy's voice was almost a shout as he finished. 'Now, the same night you show up, this missing vampire on all the posters called the police in Shreveport to say he's recovering from memory loss, too! And there's a strange fire in Shreveport with all kinds of bodies recovered! And you're trying to tell me there's no connection!'

Jason and I gaped at each other. Actually, there *was* no connection between Jason and Eric. It just hadn't occurred to me how strange that would look.

'What vampire?' Jason asked. It was so good, I almost believed him myself.

'Let's leave, Alcee,' Andy said. He slapped his notebook shut. He put his pen back in his shirt pocket with such an emphatic thrust that I was surprised he had a pocket left. 'This bastard won't even tell us the truth.'

'Don't you think I'd tell you if I could?' Jason said. 'Don't you think I'd like to lay hands on whoever did this to me?' He sounded absolutely, one hundred percent sincere, because he was. The two detectives were shaken in their disbelief, especially Alcee Beck. But they still left unhappy with the two of us. I felt sorry for it, but there was nothing I could do.

Later that day, Arlene picked me up so I could fetch my car from Merlotte's. She was happy to see Jason, and she gave him a big hug. 'You had your sister some kind of worried, you rascal,' she said, with mock ferocity. 'Don't you ever scare Sookie like that again.'

'I'll do my best,' Jason said, with a good approximation of his old roguish smile. 'She's been a good sister to me.'

'Now, that's God's truth,' I said, a little sourly. 'When I bring my car back, I think I might just run you home, big brother.'

Jason looked scared for a minute. Being alone had never been his favorite thing, and after hours by himself in the cold of the shed, it might be even harder.

'I bet girls all over Bon Temps are making food to bring to your place now that they heard you're back,' Arlene said, and Jason brightened perceptibly. ''Specially since I've been telling everyone what an invalid you are.'

'Thanks, Arlene,' Jason said, looking much more like himself.

I echoed that on the way into town. 'I really appreciate you cheering him up. I don't know what all he went through, but he's going to have a rough time getting over it, I think.'

'Honey, you don't need to worry about Jason. He's the original survivor. I don't know why he didn't try out for the show.'

We laughed all the way into town at the idea of staging a *Survivor* episode in Bon Temps.

'What with the razorbacks in the woods, and that panther print, they might have an exciting time of it if we had *Survivor: Bon Temps,*' Arlene said. 'Tack and me would just sit back and laugh at them.'

That gave me a nice opening to tease her about Tack, which she enjoyed, and altogether she cheered up me just as much as Jason. Arlene was good about stuff like that. I had a brief conversation with Sam in the storeroom of Merlotte's, and he told me Andy and Alcee had already been by to see if his story meshed with mine.

He hushed me before I could thank him again.

I took Jason home, though he hinted broadly he'd like to stay with me one more night. I took the Benelli with us, and I told him to clean it that evening. He promised he would, and when he looked at me, I could tell he wanted to ask me again why I'd had to use it. But he didn't. Jason had learned some things in the past few days, himself.

I was working the late shift again, so I would have a little time on my hands when I got home before I had to go in to work. The prospect felt good. I didn't see any running men on my way back to my house, and no one phoned or popped in with a crisis for a whole two hours. I was able to change the sheets on both beds, wash them, and sweep the kitchen and straighten up the closet concealing the hidey-hole, before the knock came at the front door.

I knew who it would be. It was full dark outside, and sure enough, Eric stood on my front porch.

He looked down at me with no very happy face. 'I find myself troubled,' he said without preamble.

'Then I've got to drop everything so I can help you out,' I said, going instantly on the offensive.

He cocked an eyebrow. 'I'll be polite and ask if I can come in.' I hadn't rescinded his invitation, but he didn't want to just stroll into my house. Tactful.

'Yes, you can.' I stepped back.

'Hallow is dead, having been forced to counter the curse on me, obviously.'

'Pam did a good job.'

He nodded. 'It was Hallow or me,' he said. 'I like me better.'

'Why'd she pick Shreveport?'

'Her parents were jailed in Shreveport. They were witches, too, but they also ran confidence games of some kind, using their craft to make their victims more convinced of their sincerity. In Shreveport, their luck ran out. The supernatural community refused to make any effort to get the older Stonebrooks out of jail. The woman ran afoul of a voodoo priestess while she was incarcerated, and the man ran afoul of a knife in some bathroom brawl.'

'Pretty good reason to have it in for the supernaturals of Shreveport.'

'They say I was here for several nights.' Eric had decided to change the subject.

'Yes,' I said. I tried to look agreeably interested in what he had to say.

'And in that time, we never . . .?'

I didn't pretend to misunderstand him.

'Eric, does that seem likely?' I asked.

He hadn't sat down, and he moved closer to me, as if looking at me hard would reveal the truth. It would have been easy to take a step, be even closer.

'I just don't know,' he said. 'And it's making me a little aggravated.'

I smiled. 'Are you enjoying being back at work?'

'Yes. But Pam ran everything well during my absence. I'm sending lots of flowers to the hospital. Belinda, and a wolf named Maria-Comet or something.'

'Maria-Star Cooper. You didn't send any to me,' I pointed out tartly.

'No, but I left you something more meaningful under the saltshaker,' he said, with much the same edge. 'You'll have to pay taxes on it. If I know you, you'll give your brother some of it. I hear you got him back.'

'I did,' I said briefly. I knew I was getting closer to bursting out with something, and I knew he should leave soon. I'd given Jason such good advice about being quiet, but it was hard to follow it myself. 'And your point is?'

'It won't last for long.'

I don't think Eric realized how much money fifty thousand dollars was, by my standards. 'What's your point? I can tell you have one, but I don't have an idea what it might be.'

'Was there a reason I found brain tissue on my coat sleeve?'

I felt all the blood drain from my face, the way it does when you're on the edge of passing out. The next thing I knew, I was on the couch and Eric was beside me.

'I think there are some things you're not telling me, Sookie, my dear,' he said. His voice was gentler, though.

The temptation was almost overwhelming.

But I thought of the power Eric would have over me, even more power than he had now; he would know I had slept with him, and he would know that I had killed a woman and he was the only one who'd witnessed it. He would know that not only did he owe me his life (most likely), I certainly owed him mine.

'I liked you a lot better when you didn't remember who you were,' I said, and with that truth forefront in my mind, I knew I had to keep quiet.

'Harsh words,' he said, and I almost believed he was really hurt.

Luckily for me, someone else came to my door. The knock was loud and peremptory, and I felt a jolt of alarm.

The caller was Amanda, the insulting redheaded female Were from Shreveport. 'I'm on official business today,' she said, 'so I'll be polite.'

That would be a nice change.

She nodded to Eric and said, 'Glad to have you back in your right mind, vampire,' in a completely unconcerned tone. I could see that the Weres and vampires of Shreveport had reverted to their old relationship.

'And good to see you, too, Amanda,' I said.

'Sure,' she said, but hardly as if she cared. 'Miss Stackhouse, we're making inquiries for the shifters of Jackson.'

Oh, no. 'Really? Won't you please sit down? Eric was just leaving.'

'No, I'd love to stay and hear Amanda's questions,' Eric said, beaming.

Amanda looked at me, eyebrows raised.

There wasn't a hell of a lot I could do about it.

'Oh, by all means, stay,' I said. 'Please sit down, both of you. I'm sorry, but I don't have a lot of time before I'm due at work.'

'Then I'll get right to the point,' Amanda said. 'Two nights ago, the woman that Alcide abjured – the shifter from Jackson, the one with the weird haircut?'

I nodded, to show I was on the same page. Eric looked pleasantly blank. He wouldn't in a minute.

'Debbie,' the Were recalled. 'Debbie Pelt.'

Eric's eyes widened. Now, that name he did know. He began to smile.

'Alcide abjured her?' he said.

'You were sitting right there,' snapped Amanda. 'Oh, wait, I forgot. That was while you were *under a curse*.'

She enjoyed the hell out of saying that.

'Anyway, Debbie didn't make it back to Jackson. Her family is worried about her, especially since they heard that Alcide abjured her, and they're afraid something might have happened to her.'

'Why do you think she would have said anything to me?'

Amanda made a face. 'Well, actually, I think she would rather have eaten glass than talked to you again. But we're obliged to check with everyone who was there.'

So this was just routine. I wasn't being singled out. I could feel myself relax. Unfortunately, so could Eric. I'd had his blood; he could tell things about me. He got up and wandered back to the kitchen. I wondered what he was doing.

'I haven't seen her since that night,' I said, which was true, since I didn't specify what time. 'I have no idea where she is now.' That was even truer.

Amanda told me, 'No one admits to having seen Debbie after she left the area of the battle. She drove off in her own car.'

Eric strolled back into the living room. I glanced at him, worried about what he was up to.

'Has her car been seen?' Eric asked.

He didn't know he'd been the one who'd hidden it.

'No, neither hide nor hair,' Amanda said, which was a strange image to use for a car. 'I'm sure she just ran off somewhere to get over her rage and humiliation. Being abjured; that's pretty awful. It's been years since I've heard the words said.'

'Her family doesn't think that's the case? That's she's gone some-where to, ah, think things over?'

'They're afraid she's done something to herself.' Amanda snorted. We exchanged glances, showing we agreed perfectly about the like-lihood of Debbie committing suicide. 'She wouldn't do anything that convenient,' Amanda said, since she had the nerve to say it out loud and I didn't.

'How's Alcide taking this?' I asked anxiously.

'He can hardly join in the search,' she pointed out, 'since he's the one who abjured her. He acts like he doesn't care, but I notice the colonel calls him to let him know what's happening. Which, so far, is nothing.' Amanda heaved herself to her feet, and I got up to walk her to the door. 'This sure has been a bad season for people going missing,' she said. 'But I hear through the grapevine that you got your brother back, and Eric's returned to his normal self, looks like.' She cast him a glance to make sure he knew how little she liked that normal self. 'Now Debbie has gone missing, but maybe she'll turn up, too. Sorry I had to bother you.'

'That's all right. Good luck,' I said, which was meaningless under the circumstances. The door closed behind her, and I wished desperately that I could just walk out and get in my car and drive to work.

I made myself turn around. Eric was standing.

'You're going?' I said, unable to keep from sounding startled and relieved.

'Yes, you said you had to get to work,' he said blandly.

'I do.'

'I suggest you wear that jacket, the one that's too light for the weather,' he said. 'Since your coat is still in bad shape.'

I'd run it through the washer on cold water wash, but I guess I hadn't checked it well enough to be sure everything had come off. That's where he'd been, searching for my coat. He'd found it on its hanger on the back porch, and examined it.

'In fact,' Eric said, as he went to the front door, 'I'd throw it away entirely. Maybe burn it.'

He left, closing the door behind him very quietly.

I knew, as sure as I knew my name, that tomorrow he would send me another coat, in a big fancy box, with a big bow on it. It would be the right size, it would be a top brand, and it would be warm.

It was cranberry red, with a removable liner, a detachable hood, and tortoiseshell buttons.

Dead As A Doornail

This book is dedicated to a wonderful woman I don't get to see often enough. Janet Hutchings (then an editor at Walker, now editor of Ellery Queen Mystery Magazine) *was brave enough to take me on many years after I'd taken a long sabbatical from writing. God bless her.*

Chapter 1

I knew my brother would turn into a panther before he did. As I drove to the remote crossroads community of Hotshot, my brother watched the sunset in silence. Jason was dressed in old clothes, and he had a plastic Wal-Mart bag containing a few things he might need – toothbrush, clean underwear. He hunched inside his bulky camo jacket, looking straight ahead. His face was tense with the need to control his fear and his excitement.

'You got your cell phone in your pocket?' I asked, knowing I'd already asked him as soon as the words left my mouth. But Jason just nodded instead of snapping at me. It was still afternoon, but at the end of January the dark comes early.

Tonight would be the first full moon of the New Year. When I stopped the car, Jason turned to look at me, and even in the dim light I saw the change in his eyes. They weren't blue like mine anymore. They were yellowish. The shape of them had changed.

'My face feels funny,' he said. But he still hadn't put two and two together.

Tiny Hotshot was silent and still in the waning light. A cold wind was blowing across the bare fields, and the pines and oaks were shivering in the gusts of frigid air. Only one man was visible. He was standing outside one of the little houses, the one that was freshly painted. This man's eyes were closed, and his bearded face was raised to the darkening sky. Calvin Norris waited until Jason was climbing out the passenger's door of my old Nova before he walked over and bent to my window. I rolled it down.

His golden-green eyes were as startling as I'd remembered, and the rest of him was just as unremarkable. Stocky, graying, sturdy, he looked like a hundred other men I'd seen in Merlotte's Bar, except for those eyes.

'I'll take good care of him,' Calvin Norris said. Behind him, Jason stood with his back to me. The air around my brother had a peculiar quality; it seemed to be vibrating.

None of this was Calvin Norris's fault. He hadn't been the one who'd bitten my brother and changed him forever. Calvin, a werepanther, had been born what he was; it was his nature. I made myself say, 'Thank you.'

'I'll bring him home in the morning.'

'To my house, please. His truck is at my place.'

'All right, then. Have a good night.' He raised his face to the wind again, and I felt the whole community was waiting, behind their windows and doors, for me to leave.

So I did.

Jason knocked on my door at seven the next morning. He still had his little Wal-Mart bag, but he hadn't used anything in it. His face was bruised, and his hands were covered with scratches. He didn't say a word. He just stared at me when I asked him how he was, and walked past me through the living room and down the hall. He closed the door to the hall bathroom with a decisive click. I heard the water running after a second, and I heaved a weary sigh all to myself. Though I'd gone to work and come home tired at about two a.m., I hadn't gotten much sleep.

By the time Jason emerged, I'd fixed him some bacon and eggs. He sat down at the old kitchen table with an air of pleasure: a man doing a familiar and pleasant thing. But after a second of staring down at the plate, he leaped to his feet and ran back into the bathroom, kicking the door shut behind him. I listened to him throw up, over and over.

I stood outside the door helplessly, knowing he wouldn't want me to come in. After a moment, I went back to the kitchen to dump the food into the trash can, ashamed of the waste but utterly unable to force myself to eat.

When Jason returned, he said only, 'Coffee?' He looked green around the gills, and he walked like he was sore.

'Are you okay?' I asked, not sure if he would be able to answer or not. I poured the coffee into a mug.

'Yes,' he said after a moment, as though he'd had to think about it. 'That was the most incredible experience of my life.'

For a second, I thought he meant throwing up in my bathroom, but that was sure no new experience for Jason. He'd been quite a drinker in his teens, until he'd figured out that there was nothing glamorous or attractive about hanging over a toilet bowl, heaving your guts out.

'Shifting,' I said tentatively.

He nodded, cradling his coffee mug in his hands. He held his face over the steam rising from the hot, strong blackness. He met my eyes. His own were once again their ordinary blue. 'It's the most incredible rush,' he said. 'Since I was bitten, not born, I don't get to be a true panther like the others.'

I could hear envy in his voice.

'But even what I become is amazing. You feel the magic inside you, and you feel your bones moving around and adapting, and your vision changes. Then you're lower to the ground and you walk in a whole different way, and as for running, damn, you can *run*. You can chase. . . .' And his voice died away.

I would just as soon not know that part, anyway.

'So it's not so bad?' I asked, my hands clasped together. Jason was all the family I had, except for a cousin who'd drifted away into the underworld of drugs years before.

'It's not so bad,' Jason agreed, scraping up a smile to give me. 'It's great while you're actually the animal. Everything's so simple. It's when you're back to being human that you start to worry about stuff.'

He wasn't suicidal. He wasn't even despondent. I wasn't aware I'd been holding my breath until I let it out. Jason was going to be able to live with the hand he'd been dealt. He was going to be okay.

The relief was incredible, like I'd removed something jammed painfully between my teeth or shaken a sharp rock out of my shoe. For days, weeks even, I'd been worried, and now that anxiety was gone. That didn't mean Jason's life as a shape-shifter would be worry-free, at least from my point of view. If he married a regular human woman, their kids would be normal. But if he married into the shifter community at Hotshot, I'd have nieces or nephews who turned into animals once a month. At least, they would after puberty; that would give them, and their auntie Sook, some preparation time.

Luckily for Jason, he had plenty of vacation days, so he wasn't due at the parish road department. But I had to work tonight. As soon as Jason left in his flashy pickup truck, I crawled back into bed, jeans and all, and in about five minutes I was fast asleep. The relief acted as a kind of sedative.

When I woke up, it was nearly three o'clock and time for me to get ready for my shift at Merlotte's. The sun outside was bright and clear, and the temperature was fifty-two, said my indoor-outdoor thermometer. This isn't too unusual in north Louisiana in January. The temperature would drop after the sun went down, and Jason would shift. But he'd have some fur – not a full coat, since he turned into half-man, half-cat – and he'd be with other panthers. They'd go hunting. The woods around Hotshot, which lay in a remote corner of Renard Parish, would be dangerous again tonight.

As I went about eating, showering, folding laundry, I thought of a dozen things I'd like to know. I wondered if the shifters would kill a human being if they came upon one in the woods. I wondered how much of their human consciousness they retained in their animal form. If they mated in panther form, would they have a kitten or a baby? What happened when a pregnant werepanther saw the full moon? I wondered if Jason knew the answer to all these questions yet, if Calvin had given him some kind of briefing.

But I was glad I hadn't questioned Jason this morning while everything was still so new to him. I'd have plenty of chances to ask him later.

For the first time since New Year's Day, I was thinking about the future. The full moon symbol on my calendar no longer seemed to be a period marking the end of something, but just another way of counting time. As I pulled on my waitress outfit (black pants and a white boat-neck T-shirt and black Reeboks), I felt almost giddy with cheer. For once, I left my hair down instead of pulling it back and up into a ponytail. I put in some bright red dot earrings and matched my lipstick to the color. A little eye makeup and some blush, and I was good to go.

I'd parked at the rear of the house last night, and I checked the back porch carefully to make sure there weren't any lurking vampires before I shut and locked the back door behind me. I'd been surprised before, and it wasn't a pleasant feeling. Though it was barely dark, there might be some early risers around. Probably the last thing the Japanese had expected when they'd developed synthetic blood was that its availability would bring vampires out of the realm of legend and into the light of fact. The Japanese had just been trying to make a few bucks hawking the blood substitute to ambulance companies and hospital emergency rooms. Instead, the way we looked at the world had changed forever.

Speaking of vampires (if only to myself), I wondered if Bill Compton was home. Vampire Bill had been my first love, and he lived right across the cemetery from me. Our houses lay on a parish road outside the little town of Bon Temps and south of the bar where I worked. Lately, Bill had been traveling a lot. I only found out he was home if he happened to come into Merlotte's, which he did every now and then to mix with the natives and have some warm O-positive. He preferred TrueBlood, the most expensive Japanese synthetic. He'd told me it almost completely satisfied his cravings for blood fresh from the source. Since I'd witnessed Bill going into a bloodlust fit, I could only thank God for TrueBlood. Sometimes I missed Bill an awful lot.

I gave myself a mental shake. Snapping out of a slump, that was what today was all about. No more worry! No more fear! Free and twenty-six! Working! House paid for! Money in the bank! These were all good, positive things.

The parking lot was full when I got to the bar. I could see I'd be busy tonight. I drove around back to the employees' entrance. Sam Merlotte, the owner and my boss, lived back there in a very nice double-wide that even had a little yard surrounded by a hedge, Sam's equivalent of a white picket fence. I locked my car and went in the

employees' back door, which opened into the hallway off of which lay
the men's and the ladies', a large stock room, and Sam's office. I stowed
my purse and coat in an empty desk drawer, pulled up my red socks,
shook my head to make my hair hang right, and went through the
doorway (this door was almost always propped open) that led to
the big room of the bar/restaurant. Not that the kitchen produced
anything but the most basic stuff: hamburgers, chicken strips, fries and
onion rings, salads in the summer and chili in the winter.

Sam was the bartender, the bouncer, and on occasion the cook, but
lately we'd been lucky in getting our positions filled: Sam's seasonal
allergies had hit hard, making him less than ideal as a food handler.
The new cook had shown up in answer to Sam's ad just the week
before. Cooks didn't seem to stay long at Merlotte's, but I was hoping
that Sweetie Des Arts would stick around a while. She showed up on
time, did her job well, and never gave the rest of the staff any trouble.
Really, that was all you could ask for. Our last cook, a guy, had given
my friend Arlene a big rush of hope that he was The One – in this
case, he'd have been her fourth or fifth One – before he'd decamped
overnight with her plates and forks and a CD player. Her kids had
been devastated; not because they'd loved the guy, but because they
missed their CD player.

I walked into a wall of noise and cigarette smoke that made it seem
like I was passing into another universe. Smokers all sit on the west
side of the room, but the smoke doesn't seem to know it should stay
there. I put a smile on my face and stepped behind the bar to give Sam
a pat on the arm. After he expertly filled a glass with beer and slid it
to a patron, he put another glass under the tap and began the process
all over again.

'How are things?' Sam asked carefully. He knew all about Jason's
problems, since he'd been with me the night I'd found Jason being
held prisoner in a toolshed in Hotshot. But we had to be roundabout
in our speech; vampires had gone public, but shape-shifters and Weres
were still cloaked in secrecy. The underground world of supernatural
beings was waiting to see how vampires fared before they followed
the vampire example by going public.

'Better than I expected.' I smiled up at him, though not too far up, since Sam's not a big man. He's built lean, but he's much stronger than he looks. Sam is in his thirties – at least, I think he is – and he has reddish gold hair that halos his head. He's a good man, and a great boss. He's also a shape-shifter, so he can change into any animal. Most often, Sam turns into a very cute collie with a gorgeous coat. Sometimes he comes over to my place and I let him sleep on the rug in the living room. 'He's gonna be fine.'

'I'm glad,' he said. I can't read shifter minds as easily as I read human minds, but I can tell if a mood is true or not. Sam was happy because I was happy.

'When are you taking off?' I asked. He had that faraway look in his eyes, the look that said he was mentally running through the woods, tracking possums.

'As soon as Terry gets here.' He smiled at me again, but this time the smile was a bit strained. Sam was getting antsy.

The door to the kitchen was just outside the bar area at the west end, and I stuck my head in the door to say hi to Sweetie. Sweetie was bony and brunette and fortyish, and she wore a lot of makeup for someone who was going to be out of sight in the kitchen all evening. She also seemed a little sharper, perhaps better educated, than any of Merlotte's previous short-order cooks.

'You doing okay, Sookie?' she called, flipping a hamburger as she spoke. Sweetie was in constant motion in the kitchen, and she didn't like anyone getting in her way. The teenager who assisted her and bussed tables was terrified of Sweetie, and he took care to dodge her as she moved from griddle to fryer. This teenage boy got the plates ready, made the salads, and went to the window to tell the barmaids which order was up. Out on the floor, Holly Cleary and her best friend, Danielle, were working hard. They'd both looked relieved when they'd seen me come in. Danielle worked the smoking section to the west, Holly usually worked the middle area in front of the bar, and I worked the east when three of us were on duty.

'It looks like I better get moving,' I told Sweetie.

She gave me a quick smile and turned back to the griddle. The cowed teenager, whose name I had yet to catch, gave me a ducked-head nod and went back to loading the dishwasher.

I wished Sam had called me before things had gotten so busy; I wouldn't have minded coming in a little earlier. Of course, he wasn't exactly himself tonight. I began checking the tables in my section, getting fresh drinks and clearing off food baskets, collecting money and bringing change.

'Barmaid! Bring me a Red Stuff!' The voice was unfamiliar, and the order was unusual. Red Stuff was the cheapest artificial blood, and only the newest vampires would be caught dead asking for it. I got a bottle from the clear-fronted refrigerator and stuck it in the microwave. While it warmed, I scanned the crowd for the vamp. He was sitting with my friend Tara Thornton. I'd never seen him before, which was worrisome. Tara'd been dating an older vampire (much older: Franklin Mott had been older than Tara in human years before he died, and he'd been a vampire for over three hundred years), and he'd been giving her lavish gifts – like a Camaro. What was she doing with this new guy? At least Franklin had nice manners.

I put the warm bottle on a tray and carried it over to the couple. The lighting in Merlotte's at night isn't particularly bright, which is how patrons like it, and it wasn't until I'd gotten quite near that I could appreciate Tara's companion. He was slim and narrow shouldered with slicked-back hair. He had long fingernails and a sharp face. I supposed that, in a way, he was attractive – if you like a liberal dose of danger with your sex.

I put the bottle down in front of him and glanced uncertainly at Tara. She looked great, as usual. Tara is tall, slim, and dark haired, and she has a wardrobe of wonderful clothes. She'd overcome a truly horrible childhood to own her own business and actually join the chamber of commerce. Then she started dating the wealthy vampire, Franklin Mott, and she quit sharing her life with me.

'Sookie,' she said, 'I want you to meet Franklin's friend Mickey.' She didn't sound like she wanted us to meet. She sounded like she wished I'd never come over with Mickey's drink. Her own glass was almost empty, but she said, 'No,' when I asked her if she was ready for another.

I exchanged a nod with the vampire; they don't shake hands, not normally. He was watching me as he took a gulp from the bottled blood, his eyes as cold and hostile as a snake's. If he was a friend of the ultra-urbane Franklin, I was a silk purse. Hired hand, more like. Maybe a bodyguard? Why would Franklin give Tara a bodyguard?

She obviously wasn't going to talk openly in front of this slimeball, so I said, 'Catch you later,' and took Mickey's money to the till.

I was busy all night, but in the spare moments I had, I thought about my brother. For a second night, he was out frolicking under the moon with the other beasties. Sam had taken off like a shot the moment Terry Bellefleur arrived, though his office wastebasket was full of crumpled tissues. His face had been tense with anticipation.

It was one of those nights that made me wonder how the humans around me could be so oblivious to the other world operating right beside ours. Only willful ignorance could ignore the charge of magic in the air. Only a group lack of imagination could account for people not wondering what went on in the dark around them.

But not too long ago, I reminded myself, I'd been as willfully blind as any of the crowd in Merlotte's. Even when the vampires had made their carefully coordinated worldwide announcement that their existence was fact, few authorities or citizens seemed to take the next mental step: *If vampires exist, what else could be lurking just outside the edge of the light?*

Out of curiosity, I began to dip into the brains around me, testing to see their fears. Most of the people in the bar were thinking about Mickey. The women, and some of the men, were wondering what it would be like to be with him. Even stick-in-the-mud lawyer Portia Bellefleur was peeking around her conservative beau to study Mickey. I could only wonder at these speculations. Mickey was terrifying. That negated any physical attraction I might have felt toward him. But I had lots of evidence that the other humans in the bar didn't feel the same way.

I've been able to read minds all my life. The ability is no great gift. Most peoples' minds don't bear reading. Their thoughts are boring, disgusting, disillusioning, but very seldom amusing. At least Bill had helped me learn how to cut out some of the buzz. Before he'd given me some clues, it had been like tuning in to a hundred radio stations simultaneously. Some of them had come in crystal clear, some had been remote, and some, like the thoughts of shape-shifters, had been full of static and obscurity. But they'd all added up to cacophony. No wonder lots of people had treated me as a half-wit.

Vampires were silent. That was the great thing about vamps, at least from my point of view: They were dead. Their minds were dead, too. Only once in a coon's age did I get any kind of flash from a vampire mind.

Shirley Hunter, my brother's boss at his parish roadwork job, asked me where Jason was when I brought a pitcher of beer to his table. Shirley was universally known as 'Catfish'.

'Your guess is as good as mine,' I said mendaciously, and he winked at me. The first guess as to where Jason was always involved a woman, and the second guess usually included another woman. The tableful of men, still in their working clothes, laughed more than the answer warranted, but then they'd had a lot of beer.

I raced back to the bar to get three bourbon-and-Cokes from Terry Bellefleur, Portia's cousin, who was working under pressure. Terry, a Vietnam vet with a lot of physical and emotional scars, appeared to be holding up well on this busy night. He liked simple jobs that required concentration. His graying auburn hair was pulled back in a ponytail and his face was intent as he plied the bottles. The drinks were ready in no time, and Terry smiled at me as I put them on my tray. A smile from Terry was a rare thing, and it warmed me.

Just as I was turning with my tray resting on my right hand, trouble erupted. A Louisiana Tech student from Ruston got into a one-on-one class war with Jeff LaBeff, a redneck who had many children and made a kind of living driving a garbage truck. Maybe it was just a case of two stubborn guys colliding and really didn't have much to do with town vs. gown (not that we were that close to Ruston). Whatever the reason for the original quarrel, it took me a few seconds to realize the fight was going to be more than a shouting match.

In those few seconds, Terry tried to intervene. Moving quickly, he got between Jeff and the student and caught firm hold of both their wrists. I thought for a minute it would work, but Terry wasn't as young or as active as he had been, and all hell broke loose.

'You could stop this,' I said furiously to Mickey as I hurried past his and Tara's table on my way to try to make peace.

He sat back in his chair and sipped his drink. 'Not my job,' he said calmly.

I got that, but it didn't endear the vampire to me, especially when the student whirled and took a swing at me as I approached him from behind. He missed, and I hit him over the head with my tray. He staggered to one side, maybe bleeding a little, and Terry was able to subdue Jeff LaBeff, who was looking for an excuse to quit.

Incidents like this had been happening with more frequency, especially when Sam was gone. It was evident to me that we needed a bouncer, at least on weekend nights . . . and full-moon nights.

The student threatened to sue.

'What's your name?' I asked.

'Mark Duffy,' the young man said, clutching his head.

'Mark, where you from?'

'Minden.'

I did a quick evaluation of his clothes, his demeanor, and the contents of his head. 'I'm gonna enjoy calling your mama and telling her you took a swing at a woman,' I said. He blanched and said no more about suing, and he and his buds left soon after. It always helps to know the most effective threat.

We made Jeff leave, too.

Terry resumed his place behind the bar and began dispensing drinks, but he was limping slightly and had a strained look in his face, which worried me. Terry's war experiences hadn't left him real stable. I'd had enough trouble for one night.

But of course the night wasn't over yet.

About an hour after the fight, a woman came into Merlotte's. She was plain and plainly dressed in old jeans and a camo coat. She had on boots that had been wonderful when they'd been new, but that had been a long time ago. She didn't carry a purse, and she had her hands thrust into her pockets.

There were several indicators that made my mental antennae twitch. First of all, this gal didn't look right. A local woman might dress like that if she were going hunting or doing farm work, but not to come to Merlotte's. For an evening out at the bar, most women fixed themselves up. So this woman was in a working mode; but she wasn't a whore by the same reasoning.

That meant drugs.

To protect the bar in Sam's absence, I tuned in to her thoughts. People don't think in complete sentences, of course, and I'm smoothing it out, but what was running through her head was along the order of: *Three vials left getting old losing power gotta sell it tonight so I can get back to Baton Rouge and buy some more. Vampire in the bar if he catches me with vamp blood I'm dead. This town is a dump. Back to the city first chance I get.*

She was a Drainer, or maybe she was just a distributor. Vampire blood was the most intoxicating drug on the market, but of course vamps didn't give it up willingly. Draining a vampire was a hazardous occupation, boosting prices of the tiny vials of blood to amazing sums.

What did the drug user get for parting with a lot of money? Depending on the age of the blood – that is, the time since it'd been removed from its owner – and the age of the vampire from whom the blood had been removed, and the individual chemistry of the drug user, it could be quite a lot. There was the feeling of omnipotence, the increased strength, acute vision, and hearing. And most important of all for Americans, an enhanced physical appearance.

Still, only an idiot would drink black-market vampire blood. For one thing, the results were notoriously unpredictable. Not only did the effects vary, but those effects could last anywhere from two weeks to two months. For another thing, some people simply went mad when the blood hit their system – sometimes homicidally mad. I'd heard of dealers who sold gullible users pig's blood or contaminated human blood. But the most important reason to avoid the black market in vamp blood was this: Vampires hated Drainers, and they hated the users of the drained blood (commonly known as bloodheads). You just don't want a vampire pissed off at you.

There weren't any off-duty police officers in Merlotte's that night. Sam was out wagging his tail somewhere. I hated to tip off Terry, because I didn't know how he'd react. I had to do something about this woman.

Truly, I try not to intervene in events when my only connection comes through my telepathy. If I stuck my oar in every time I learned something that would affect the lives around me (like knowing the parish clerk was embezzling, or that one of the local detectives took bribes), I wouldn't be able to live in Bon Temps, and it was my home. But I couldn't permit this scraggy woman to sell her poison in Sam's bar.

She perched on an empty barstool and ordered a beer from Terry. His gaze lingered on her. Terry, too, realized something was wrong about the stranger.

I came to pick up my next order and stood by her. She needed a bath, and she'd been in a house heated by a wood fireplace. I made myself touch her, which always improved my reception. Where was the blood? It was in her coat pocket. Good.

Without further ado, I dumped a glass of wine down her front.

'Dammit!' she said, jumping off the stool and patting ineffectually at her chest. 'You are the clumsiest-ass woman I ever saw!'

''Scuse me,' I said abjectly, putting my tray on the bar and meeting Terry's eyes briefly. 'Let me put some soda on that.' Without waiting for her permission, I pulled her coat down her arms. By the time she understood what I was doing and began to struggle, I had taken charge of the coat. I tossed it over the bar to Terry. 'Put some soda on that, please,' I said. 'Make sure the stuff in her pockets didn't get wet, too.' I'd used this ploy before. I was lucky it was cold weather and she'd had the stuff in her coat, not in her jeans pocket. That would have taxed my inventiveness.

Under the coat, the woman was wearing a very old Dallas Cowboys T-shirt. She began shivering, and I wondered if she'd been sampling more conventional drugs. Terry made a show of patting soda on the wine stain. Following my hint, he delved into the pockets. He looked down at his hand with disgust, and I heard a clink as he threw the vials in the trash can behind the bar. He returned everything else to her pockets.

She'd opened her mouth to shriek at Terry when she realized she really couldn't. Terry stared directly at her, daring her to mention the blood. The people around us watched with interest. They knew something was up, but not what, because the whole thing had gone down very quickly. When Terry was sure she wasn't going to start yelling, he handed me the coat. As I held it so she could slide her arms in, Terry told her, 'Don't you come back here no more.'

If we kept throwing people out at this rate, we wouldn't have many customers.

'You redneck son of a bitch,' she said. The crowd around us drew in a collective breath. (Terry was almost as unpredictable as a bloodhead.)

'Doesn't matter to me what you call me,' he said. 'I guess an insult from you is no insult at all. You just stay away.' I expelled a long breath of relief.

She shoved her way through the crowd. Everyone in the room marked her progress toward the door, even Mickey the vampire. In fact, he was doing something with a device in his hands. It looked like one of those cell phones that can take a picture. I wondered to whom he was sending it. I wondered if she'd make it home.

Terry pointedly didn't ask how I'd known the scruffy woman had something illegal in her pockets. That was another weird thing about the people of Bon Temps. The rumors about me had been floating around as long as I could remember, from when I was little and my folks put me through the mental health battery. And yet, despite the evidence at their disposal, almost everyone I knew would much rather regard me as a dim and peculiar young woman than acknowledge my strange ability. Of course, I was careful not to stick it in their faces. And I kept my mouth shut.

Anyway, Terry had his own demons to fight. Terry subsisted on some kind of government pension, and he cleaned Merlotte's early in the morning, along with a couple of other businesses. He stood in for Sam three or four times a month. The rest of his time was his own, and no one seemed to know what he did with it. Dealing with people exhausted Terry, and nights like tonight were simply not good for him.

It was lucky he wasn't in Merlotte's the next night, when all hell broke loose.

Chapter 2

At first, I thought everything had returned to normal. The bar seemed a little calmer the next night. Sam was back in place, relaxed and cheerful. Nothing seemed to rile him, and when I told him what had happened with the dealer the night before, he complimented me on my finesse.

Tara didn't come in, so I couldn't ask her about Mickey. But was it really any of my business? Probably not my business – but my concern, definitely.

Jeff LaBeff was back and sheepish about getting riled by the college kid the night before. Sam had learned about the incident through a phone call from Terry, and he gave Jeff a word of warning.

Andy Bellefleur, a detective on the Renard parish force and Portia's brother, came in with the young woman he was dating, Halleigh Robinson. Andy was older than me, and I'm twenty-six. Halleigh was twenty-one – just old enough to be in Merlotte's. Halleigh taught at the elementary school, she was right out of college, and she was real attractive, with short earlobe-length brown hair and huge brown eyes and a nicely rounded figure. Andy had been dating Halleigh for about two months, and from the little I saw of the couple, they seemed to be progressing in their relationship at a predictable rate.

Andy's true thoughts were that he liked Halleigh very much (though she was a tad boring), and he was really ready for her to give it up. Halleigh thought Andy was sexy and a real man of the world, and she really loved the newly restored Bellefleur family mansion, but she didn't believe he'd hang around long after she slept with him. I hate knowing more about relationships than the people in them know – but no matter how battened down I am, I pick up a trickle of stuff.

Claudine came in the bar that night, toward closing time. Claudine is six feet tall, with black hair that ripples down her back and bruised-looking white skin that looks thin and glossy like a plum's. Claudine dresses for attention. Tonight she was wearing a terracotta pants suit, cut very snug on her Amazonian body. She works in the complaint department of a big store at the mall in Ruston during the day. I wished she'd brought her brother, Claude, with her. He doesn't swing in my direction, but he's a treat for the eyes.

He's a fairy. I mean, literally. So's Claudine, of course.

She waved at me across the heads of the crowd. I waved back smiling. Everyone's happy around Claudine, who is always cheerful when there are no vampires in her vicinity. Claudine is unpredictable and a lot of fun, though like all fairies, she's as dangerous as a tiger when she's angry. Fortunately, that doesn't happen often.

Fairies occupy a special place in the hierarchy of magical creatures. I haven't figured out exactly what it is yet, but sooner or later I'll piece it together.

Every man in the bar was drooling over Claudine, and she was eating it up. She gave Andy Bellefleur a long, big-eyed look, and Halleigh Robinson glared, mad enough to spit, until she remembered she was a sweet southern girl. But Claudine abandoned all interest in Andy when she saw he was drinking ice tea with lemon. Fairies are even more violently allergic to lemon than vampires are to garlic.

Claudine worked her way over to me, and she gave me a big hug, to the envy of every male in the bar. She took my hand to pull me into Sam's office. I went with her out of sheer curiosity.

'Dear friend,' Claudine said, 'I have bad news for you.'

'What?' I'd gone from bemused to scared in a heartbeat.

'There was a shooting early this morning. One of the werepanthers was hit.'

'Oh, no! Jason!' But surely one of his friends would've called if he hadn't gone into work today?

'No, your brother is fine, Sookie. But Calvin Norris was shot.'

I was stunned. Jason hadn't called to tell me this? I had to find out from someone else?

'Shot dead?' I asked, hearing my voice shake. Not that Calvin and I were close – far from it – but I was shocked. Heather Kinman, a teenager, had been fatally shot the week before. What was happening in Bon Temps?

'Shot in the chest. He's alive, but he's bad hurt.'

'Is he in the hospital?'

'Yes, his nieces took him to Grainger Memorial.'

Grainger was a town farther southeast than Hotshot, and a shorter drive from there than the parish hospital in Clarice.

'Who did it?'

'No one knows. Someone shot him early this morning, when Calvin was on his way to work. He'd come home from his, um, time of the month, changed, and started into town for his shift.' Calvin worked at Norcross.

'How'd you come to know all this?'

'One of his cousins came into the store to buy some pajamas, since Calvin didn't have any. Guess he sleeps in the buff,' Claudette said. 'I don't know how they think they're going to get a pajama top on over the bandages. Maybe they just needed the pants? Calvin wouldn't like to be shuffling around the hospital with only one of those nasty gowns between him and the world.'

Claudine often took long side trails in her conversation.

'Thanks for telling me,' I said. I wondered how the cousin had known Claudine, but I wasn't going to ask.

'That's okay. I knew you'd want to know. Heather Kinman was a shape-shifter, too. Bet you didn't know that. Think about it.'

Claudine gave me a kiss on the forehead – fairies are very touchy-feely – and we went back into the bar area. She'd stunned me into silence. Claudine herself was back to business as usual. The fairy ordered a 7-and-7 and was surrounded by suitors in about two minutes flat. She never left with anyone, but the men seemed to enjoy trying. I'd decided that Claudine fed off this admiration and attention.

Even Sam was beaming at her, and she didn't tip.

By the time we were closing the bar, Claudine had left to go back to Monroe, and I'd passed along her news to Sam. He was as appalled by the story as I was. Though Calvin Norris was the leader of the small shifter community of Hotshot, the rest of the world knew him as a steady, quiet bachelor who owned his own home and had a good job as crew foreman at the local lumber mill. It was hard to imagine either of his personas leading to an assassination attempt. Sam decided to send some flowers from the bar's staff.

I pulled on my coat and went out the bar's back door just ahead of Sam. I heard him locking the door behind me. Suddenly I remembered that we were getting low on bottled blood, and I turned to tell Sam this. He caught my movement and stopped, waiting for me to speak, his face expectant. In the length of time it takes to blink, his expression changed from expectant to shocked, dark red began to spread on his left leg, and I heard the sound of a shot.

Then blood was everywhere, Sam crumpled to the ground, and I began to scream.

Chapter 3

I'd never had to pay the cover charge at Fangtasia before. The few times I'd come through the public entrance, I'd been with a vampire. But now I was by myself and feeling mighty conspicuous. I was exhausted from an especially long night. I'd been at the hospital until six in the morning, and I'd had only a few hours' fitful sleep after I'd gotten home.

Pam was taking the cover charge and showing the customers to tables. She was wearing the long filmy black outfit she usually wore when she was on door duty. Pam never looked happy when she was dressed like a fictional vampire. She was the real thing and proud of it. Her personal taste leaned more toward slack sets in pastel colors and penny loafers. She looked as surprised as a vampire can look when she saw me.

'Sookie,' she said, 'do you have an appointment with Eric?' She took my money without a blink.

I was actually happy to see her: pathetic, huh? I don't have a lot of friends, and I value the ones I have, even if I suspect they dream about catching me in a dark alley and having their bloody way with me. 'No, but I do need to talk to him. Business,' I added hastily. I didn't want anyone thinking I was courting the romantic attention of the undead head honcho of Shreveport, a position called 'sheriff' by the vamps. I shrugged off my new cranberry-colored coat and folded it carefully over my arm. WDED, the Baton Rouge-based all-vampire radio station, was being piped over the sound system. The smooth voice of the early night deejay, Connie the Corpse, said, 'And here's a song for all you lowlifes who were outside howling earlier this week ... "Bad Moon Rising", an old hit from Creedence Clearwater Revival.' Connie the Corpse was giving a private tip of the hat to the shape-shifters.

'Wait at the bar while I tell him you're here,' Pam said. 'You'll enjoy the new bartender.'

Bartenders at Fangtasia didn't tend to last long. Eric and Pam always tried to hire someone colorful – an exotic bartender drew in the human tourists who came by the busloads to take a walk on the wild side – and in this they were successful. But somehow the job had acquired a high attrition rate.

The new man gave me a white-toothed smile when I perched on one of the high stools. He was quite an eyeful. He had a head full of long, intensely curly hair, chestnut brown in color. It clustered thickly on his shoulders. He also sported a mustache and a Vandyke. Covering his left eye was a black eye patch. Since his face was narrow and the features on it sizable, his face was crowded. He was about my height, five foot six, and he was wearing a black poet shirt and black pants and high black boots. All he needed was a bandanna tied around his head and a pistol.

'Maybe a parrot on your shoulder?' I said.

'Aaargh, dear lady, you are not the first to suggest such a thing.' He had a wonderful rich baritone voice. 'But I understand there are health department regulations against having an uncaged bird in an establishment serving drinks.' He bowed to me as deeply as the narrow area behind the bar permitted. 'May I get you a drink and have the honor of your name?'

I had to smile. 'Certainly, sir. I'm Sookie Stackhouse.' He'd caught the whiff of otherness about me. Vampires almost always pick up on it. The undead usually note me; humans don't. It's kind of ironic that my mind reading doesn't work on the very creatures who believe it distinguishes me from the rest of the human race, while humans would rather believe I was mentally ill than credit me with an unusual ability.

The woman on the barstool next to me (credit cards maxed out, son with ADD) half turned to listen in. She was jealous, having been trying to entice the bartender into showing her some attention for the past thirty minutes. She eyed me, trying to figure out what had caused the vamp to choose to open a conversation with me. She wasn't impressed at all with what she saw.

'I am delighted to meet you, fair maiden,' the new vampire said smoothly, and I grinned. Well, at least I was fair – in the blond-and-blue-eyed sense. His eyes took me in; of course, if you're a woman who works in a bar, you're used to that. At least he didn't look at me offensively; and believe me, if you're a woman who works in a bar, you can tell the difference between an evaluation and an eye fuck.

'I bet good money she's no maiden,' said the woman next to me.

She was right, but that was beside the point.

'You must be polite to other guests,' the vampire told her, with an altered version of his smile. Not only were his fangs slightly extended, but I also noticed he had crooked (though beautifully white) teeth. American standards of tooth straightness are very modern.

'No one tells me how to act,' the woman said combatively. She was sullen because the evening wasn't going as she'd planned. She'd thought it would be easy to attract a vampire, that any vamp would think he was lucky to have her. She'd planned to let one bite her neck, if he'd just settle her credit card bills.

She was overestimating herself and underestimating vampires.

'I beg your pardon, madam, but while you are in Fangtasia, most definitely I shall tell you how to act,' the bartender said.

She subsided after he fixed her with his quelling gaze, and I wondered if he hadn't given her a dose of glamour.

'My name,' he said, returning his attention to me, 'is Charles Twining.'

'Pleased to meet you,' I said.

'And the drink?'

'Yes, please. A ginger ale.' I had to drive back to Bon Temps after I'd seen Eric.

He raised his arched brows but poured me the drink and placed it on a napkin in front of me. I paid him and deposited a good tip in the jar. The little white napkin had some fangs outlined in black, with a single, drop of red falling from the right fang – custom-made napkins for the vampire bar. 'Fangtasia' was printed in jazzy red script on the opposite corner of the napkin, duplicating the sign outside. Cute. There were T-shirts for sale in a case over in a corner, too, along with glasses decorated with the same logo. The legend underneath read, 'Fangtasia – The Bar with a Bite.' Eric's merchandising expertise had made great strides in the past few months.

As I waited my turn for Eric's attention, I watched Charles Twining work. He was polite to everyone, served the drinks swiftly, and never got rattled. I liked his technique much better than that of Chow, the previous bartender, who'd always made patrons feel like he was doing them a favor by bringing them drinks at all. Long Shadow, the bartender before Chow, had had too much of an eye for the female customers. That'll cause a lot of strife in a bar.

Lost in my own thoughts, I didn't realize Charles Twining was right across the bar from me until he said, 'Miss Stackhouse, may I tell you how lovely you look tonight?'

'Thank you, Mr Twining,' I said, entering into the spirit of the encounter. The look in Charles Twining's one visible brown eye let me know that he was a first-class rogue, and I didn't trust him any farther than I could throw him, which was maybe two feet. (The effects of my last infusion of vampire blood had worn off, and I was my regular human self. Hey, I'm no junkie; it had been an emergency situation calling for extra strength.)

Not only was I back at average stamina for a fit woman in her twenties, my looks were back to normal; no vampire-blood enhancement. I hadn't dressed up, since I didn't want Eric to think I was dressing up for him, but I hadn't wanted to look like a slob, either. So I was wearing low-riding blue jeans and a fuzzy white long-sleeved sweater with a boat- neck. It stopped just at my waist, so some tummy showed when I walked. That tummy wasn't fish-belly white, either, thanks to the tanning bed at the video rental place.

'Please, dear lady, call me Charles,' the bartender said, pressing his hand to his heart.

I laughed out loud, despite my weariness. The gesture's theatricality wasn't diminished by the fact that Charles's heart wasn't beating.

'Of course,' I said agreeably. 'If you'll call me Sookie.'

He rolled his eyes up as if the excitement was too much for him, and I laughed again. Pam tapped me on the shoulder.

'If you can tear yourself away from your new buddy, Eric's free.'

I nodded to Charles and eased off the stool to follow Pam. To my surprise, she didn't lead me back to Eric's office, but to one of the booths. Evidently, tonight Eric was on bar duty. All the Shreveport-area vampires had to agree to show themselves at Fangtasia for a certain number of hours each week so the tourists would keep coming; a vampire bar without any actual vampires is a money-losing establishment. Eric set a good example for his underlings by sitting out in the bar at regular intervals.

Usually the sheriff of Area Five sat in the center of the room, but tonight he was in the corner booth. He watched me approach. I knew he was taking in my jeans, which were on the tight side, and my tummy, which was on the flat side, and my soft fuzzy white sweater, which was filled with natural bounty. I should have worn my frumpiest clothes. (Believe me, I have plenty in my closet.) I shouldn't have carried the cranberry coat, which Eric had given me. I should have done *anything* but look good for Eric – and I had to admit to myself that that had been my goal. I'd blindsided myself.

Eric slid out of the booth and rose to his considerable height – around six foot four. His mane of blond hair rippled down his back, and his blue eyes sparkled from his white, white face. Eric has bold features, high cheekbones, and a square jaw. He looks like a lawless Viking, the kind that could pillage a village in no time at all; and that's exactly what he had been.

Vampires don't shake hands except under extraordinary circumstances, so I didn't expect any salutation from Eric. But he bent to give me a kiss on the cheek, and he gave it lingeringly, as if he wanted me to know he'd like to seduce me.

He didn't realize he'd already kissed just about every inch of Sookie Stackhouse. We'd been as up close and personal as a man and a woman could be.

Eric just couldn't remember anything about it. I wanted it to stay that way. Well, not exactly *wanted;* but I knew it was better all the way around if Eric didn't recall our little fling.

'What pretty nail polish,' Eric said, smiling. He had a slight accent. English was not his second language, of course; it was maybe his twenty-fifth.

I tried not to smile back, but I was pleased at his compliment. Trust Eric to pick out the one thing that was new and different about me. I'd never had long nails until recently, and they were painted a wonderful deep red – cranberry, in fact, to match the coat.

'Thank you,' I murmured. 'How you been doing?'

'Just fine.' He raised a blond eyebrow. Vampires didn't have variable health. He waved a hand at the empty side of the booth, and I slid into it.

'Had any trouble picking up the reins?' I asked, to clarify.

A few weeks previously, a witch had given Eric amnesia, and it had taken several days to restore his sense of identity. During that time, Pam had parked him with me to keep him concealed from the witch who'd cursed him. Lust had taken its course. Many times.

'Like riding a bicycle,' Eric said, and I told myself to focus. (Though I wondered when bicycles had been invented, and if Eric had had anything to do with it.) 'I did receive a call from Long Shadow's sire, an American Indian whose name seems to be Hot Rain. I'm sure you remember Long Shadow.'

'I was just thinking of him,' I said.

Long Shadow had been the first bartender of Fangtasia. He'd been embezzling from Eric, who had coerced me into interrogating the barmaids and other human employees until I discovered the culprit. About two seconds before Long Shadow would have ripped out my throat, Eric had executed the bartender with the traditional wooden stake. Killing another vampire is a very serious thing, I gathered, and Eric had had to pay a stiff fine – to whom, I hadn't known, though now I was sure the money had gone to Hot Rain. If Eric had killed Long Shadow without any justification, other penalties would have come into play. I was content to let those remain a mystery.

'What did Hot Rain want?' I said.

'To let me know that though I had paid him the price set by the arbitrator, he didn't consider himself satisfied.'

'Did he want more money?'

'I don't think so. He seemed to think financial recompense was not all he required.' Eric shrugged. 'As far as I'm concerned, the matter is settled.' Eric took a swallow of synthetic blood, leaned back in his chair, and looked at me with unreadable blue eyes. 'And so is my little amnesia episode. The crisis is over, the witches are dead, and order is restored in my little piece of Louisiana. How have things been for you?'

'Well, I'm here on business,' I said, and I put my business face on.

'What can I do for you, my Sookie?' he asked.

'Sam wants to ask you for something,' I said.

'And he sends you to ask for it. Is he very clever or very stupid?' Eric asked himself out loud.

'Neither,' I said, trying not to sound snippy. 'He's very leg-broken. That is to say, he got his leg broken last night. He got shot.'

'How did this come about?' Eric's attention sharpened.

I explained. I shivered a little when I told him Sam and I had been alone, how silent the night had been.

'Arlene was just out of the parking lot. She went on home without knowing a thing. The new cook, Sweetie – she'd just left, too. Someone shot him from the trees north of the parking lot.' I shivered again, this time with fear.

'How close were you?'

'Oh,' I said, and my voice shook. 'I was real close. I'd just turned to ... then he was ... There was blood all over.'

Eric's face looked hard as marble. 'What did you do?'

'Sam had his cell phone in his pocket, thank God, and I held one hand over the hole in his leg and I dialed nine-one-one with the other.'

'How is he?'

'Well.' I took a deep breath and tried to make myself still. 'He's pretty good, all things considered.' I'd put that quite calmly. I was proud. 'But of course, he's down for a while, and so much ... so many odd things have been happening at the bar lately. ... Our substitute bartender, he just can't handle it for more than a couple of nights. Terry's kind of damaged.'

'So what's Sam's request?'

'Sam wants to borrow a bartender from you until his leg heals.'

'Why's he making this request of me, instead of the pack-master of

Shreveport?' Shifters seldom got organized, but the city werewolves had. Eric was right: It would have been far more logical for Sam to make the request of Colonel Flood.

I looked down at my hands wrapped around the ginger ale glass. 'Someone's gunning for the shifters and Weres in Bon Temps,' I said. I kept my voice very low. I knew he would hear me through the music and the talk of the bar.

Just then a man lurched up to the booth, a young serviceman from Barksdale Air Force Base, which is a part of the Shreveport area. (I pigeonholed him instantly from his haircut, fitness, and his running buddies, who were more or less clones.) He rocked on his heels for a long moment, looking from me to Eric.

'Hey, you,' the young man said to me, poking my shoulder. I looked up at him, resigned to the inevitable. Some people court their own disaster, especially when they drink. This young man, with his buzz haircut and sturdy build, was far from home and determined to prove himself.

There's not much I dislike more than being addressed as 'Hey, you' and being poked with a finger. But I tried to present a pleasant face to the young man. He had a round face and round dark eyes, a small mouth and thick brown brows. He was wearing a clean knit shirt and pressed khakis. He was also primed for a confrontation.

'I don't believe I know you,' I said gently, trying to defuse the situation.

'You shouldn't be sitting with a vamp,' he said. 'Human girls shouldn't go with dead guys.'

How often had I heard that? I'd gotten an earful of this kind of crap when I'd been dating Bill Compton.

'You should go back over there to your friends, Dave. You don't want your mama to get a phone call about you being killed in a bar fight in Louisiana. Especially not in a vampire bar, right?'

'How'd you know my name?' he asked slowly.

'Doesn't make any difference, does it?'

From the corner of my eye, I could see that Eric was shaking his head. Mild deflection was not his way of dealing with intrusion.

Abruptly, Dave began to simmer down.

'How'd you know about me?' he asked in a calmer voice.

'I have x-ray vision,' I said solemnly. 'I can read your driver's license in your pants.'

He began to smile. 'Hey, can you see other stuff through my pants?'

I smiled back at him. 'You're a lucky man, Dave,' I said ambiguously. 'Now, I'm actually here to talk business with this guy, so if you'd excuse us . . .'

'Okay. Sorry, I . . .'

'No problem at all,' I assured him. He went back to his friends, walking cocky. I was sure he'd give them a highly embellished account of the conversation.

Though everyone in the bar had tried to pretend they weren't watching the incident, which had so much potential for some juicy violence, they had to scramble to look busy when Eric's eyes swept the surrounding tables.

'You were starting to tell me something when we were so rudely interrupted,' he said. Without my asking, a barmaid came up and deposited a fresh drink in front of me, whisking my old glass away. Anyone sitting with Eric got the deluxe treatment.

'Yes. Sam isn't the only shape-shifter who's been shot in Bon Temps lately. Calvin Norris was shot in the chest a few days ago. He's a werepanther. And Heather Kinman was shot before that. Heather was just nineteen, a werefox.'

Eric said, 'I still don't see why this is interesting.'

'Eric, she was killed.'

He still looked inquiring.

I clenched my teeth together so I wouldn't try to tell him what a nice girl Heather Kinman had been: She'd just graduated from high school and she was working at her first job as a clerk at Bon Temps Office Supplies. She'd been drinking a milkshake at the Sonic when she'd been shot. Today, the crime lab would be comparing the bullet that had shot Sam with the bullet that had killed Heather, and both of those with the bullet from Calvin's chest. I assumed the bullets would match.

'I'm trying to explain to you why Sam doesn't want to ask another shape-shifter or Were to step in to help,' I said through clenched teeth.

'He thinks that might be putting him or her in danger. And there's just not a local human who's got the qualifications for the job. So he asked me to come to you.'

'When I stayed at your house, Sookie . . .'

I groaned. 'Oh, Eric, give it a *rest*.'

It griped Eric's butt that he couldn't remember what had happened while he was cursed. 'Someday I'll remember,' he said almost sullenly.

When he remembered everything, he wouldn't just recall the sex.

He'd also recall the woman who'd been waiting in my kitchen with a gun. He'd remember that he'd saved my life by taking the bullet meant for me. He'd remember that I'd shot her. He'd remember disposing of the body.

He'd realize that he had power over me forever.

He might also recall that he'd humbled himself enough to offer to abandon all his businesses and come to live with me.

The sex, he'd enjoy remembering. The power, he'd enjoy remembering. But somehow I didn't think Eric would enjoy remembering that last bit.

'Yes,' I said quietly, looking down at my hands. 'Someday, I expect you will remember.' WDED was playing an old Bob Seger song, 'Night Moves'. I noticed Pam was twirling unselfconsciously in her own dance, her unnaturally strong and limber body bending and twisting in ways human bodies couldn't.

I'd like to see her dance to live vampire music. You ought to hear a vampire band. You'll never forget that. They mostly play New Orleans and San Francisco, sometimes Savannah or Miami. But when I'd been dating Bill, he'd taken me to hear a group playing in Fangtasia for one night while making their way south to New Orleans. The lead singer of the vampire band – Renfield's Masters, they'd called themselves – had wept tears of blood as he sang a ballad.

'Sam was clever to send you to ask me,' Eric said after a long pause. I had nothing to say to that. 'I'll spare someone.' I could feel my shoulders relax with relief. I focused on my hands and took a deep breath. When I glanced over at him, Eric was looking around the bar, considering the vampires present.

I'd met most of them in passing. Thalia had long black ringlets down her back and a profile that could best be described as classical. She had a heavy accent – Greek, I thought – and she also had a hasty temper. Indira was a tiny Indian vamp, complete with doe eyes and tikal; no one would take her seriously until things got out of hand. Maxwell Lee was an African-American investment banker. Though strong as any vampire, Maxwell tended to enjoy more cerebral pastimes than acting as a bouncer.

'What if I send Charles?' Eric sounded casual, but I knew him well enough to suspect he wasn't.

'Or Pam,' I said. 'Or anyone else who can keep their temper.' I watched Thalia crush a metal mug with her fingers to impress a human male who was trying to put the moves on her. He blanched and scurried back to his table. Some vampires enjoy human company, but Thalia was not one of them.

'Charles is the least temperamental vampire I've ever met, though I confess I don't know him well. He's been working here only two weeks.'

'You seem to be keeping him busy here.'

'I can spare him.' Eric gave me a haughty look that said quite clearly it was up to him to decide how busy he wanted to keep his employee.

'Um . . . okeydokey.' The patrons of Merlotte's would like the pirate just fine, and Sam's revenue would jump in consequence.

'Here are the terms,' Eric said, fixing me with his gaze. 'Sam supplies unlimited blood for Charles and a secure place to stay. You might want to keep him in your house, as you did me.'

'And I might not,' I said indignantly. 'I'm not running any hostel for traveling vampires.' Frank Sinatra began to croon 'Strangers in the Night' in the background.

'Oh, of course, I forgot. But you were generously paid for my board.'

He'd touched on a sore spot. In fact, he'd poked it with a sharp stick. I flinched. 'That was my brother's idea,' I said. I saw Eric's eyes flash, and I flushed all over. I'd just confirmed a suspicion he'd had. 'But he was absolutely right,' I said with conviction. 'Why should I have put a vampire up in my house without getting paid? After all, I needed the money.'

'Is the fifty thousand already gone?' Eric said very quietly. 'Did Jason ask for a share of it?'

'None of your business,' I said, my voice exactly as sharp and indignant as I'd intended it to be. I'd given Jason only a fifth of it. He hadn't exactly asked, either, though I had to admit to myself he'd clearly expected me to give him some. Since I needed it a lot worse, I'd kept more of it than I'd initially planned.

I had no health insurance. Jason, of course, was covered through the parish plan. I'd begun thinking, *What if I was disabled? What if I broke my arm or had to have my appendix out?* Not only would I not put in my hours at work, but I'd have hospital bills. And any stay in a hospital, in this day and age, is an expensive one. I'd incurred a few medical bills during the past year, and it had taken me a long, painful time to pay them off.

Now I was profoundly glad I'd had that twinge of caution. In the normal course of things, I don't look real far ahead, because I'm used to living day to day. But Sam's injury had opened my eyes. I'd been thinking of how badly I needed a new car – well, a newer secondhand one. I'd been thinking of how dingy the living room drapes were, how pleasant it would be to order new ones from JCPenney. It had even crossed my mind that it would be a lot of fun to buy a dress that wasn't on sale. But I'd been shocked out of such frivolity when Sam had his leg broken.

As Connie the Corpse introduced the next song ('One of These Nights'), Eric examined my face. 'I wish that I could read your mind as you can read the minds of others,' he said. 'I wish very much that I could know what was going on in your head. I wish I knew why I cared what's going on in that head.'

I gave him a lopsided smile. 'I agree to the terms: free blood and lodging, though the lodging won't necessarily be with me. What about the money?'

Eric smiled. 'I'll take my payment in kind. I like Sam owing me a favor.'

I called Sam with the cell phone he'd lent me. I explained.

Sam sounded resigned. 'There's a place in the bar the vamp can sleep. All right. Room and board, and a favor. When can he come?'

I relayed the question to Eric.

'Right now.' Eric beckoned to a human waitress, who was wearing the low-cut long black dress all the female human employees wore. (I'll tell you something about vampires: They don't like to wait tables. And they're pretty poor at it, too. You won't catch a vamp bussing tables, either. The vamps almost always hire humans to do the grubbier work at their establishments.) Eric told her to fetch Charles from behind the bar. She bowed, fist to her opposite shoulder, and said, 'Yes, Master.'

Honestly, it just about made you sick.

Anyway, Charles leapt over the bar theatrically, and while patrons applauded, he made his way to Eric's booth.

Bowing to me, he turned to Eric with an air of attentiveness that should have seemed subservient but instead seemed simply matter-of-fact.

'This woman will tell you what to do. As long as she needs you, she is your master.' I just couldn't decipher Charles Twining's expression as he heard Eric's directive. Lots of vampires simply wouldn't agree to being at a human's beck and call, no matter what their head honcho said.

'No, Eric!' I was shocked. 'If you make him answerable to anyone, it should be Sam.'

'Sam sent you. I'm entrusting Charles's direction to you.' Eric's face closed down. I knew from experience that once Eric got that expression, there was no arguing with him.

I couldn't see where this was going, but I knew it wasn't good.

'Let me get my coat, and I'll be ready anytime it pleases you to leave,' Charles Twining said, bowing in a courtly and gracious way that made me feel like an idiot. I made a strangled noise in acknowledgment, and though he was still in the down position, his patch-free eye rolled up to give me a wink. I smiled involuntarily and felt much better.

Over the music system, Connie the Corpse said, 'Hey, you night listeners. Continuing ten in a row for us genuine deadheads, here's a favorite.' Connie began playing 'Here Comes the Night', and Eric said, 'Will you dance?'

I looked over at the little dance floor. It was empty. However, Eric had arranged for a bartender and bouncer for Sam as Sam had asked. I should be gracious. 'Thank you,' I said politely, and slid out of the booth. Eric offered me his hand, I took it, and he put his other hand on my waist.

Despite the difference in our heights, we managed quite well. I pretended I didn't know everyone in the bar was looking at us, and we glided along as if we knew what we were doing. I focused on Eric's throat so I wouldn't be looking up into his eyes.

When the dance was over, he said, 'Holding you seems very familiar, Sookie.'

With a tremendous effort, I kept my eyes fixed on his Adam's apple. I had a dreadful impulse to say, 'You told me you loved me and would stay with me forever.'

'You wish,' I said briskly instead. I let go of his hand as quickly as I could and stepped away from his embrace. 'By the way, have you ever run across a kind of mean-looking vampire named Mickey?'

Eric grabbed my hand again and squeezed it. I said, 'Ow!' and he eased up.

'He was in here last week. Where have you seen Mickey?' he demanded.

'In Merlotte's.' I was astonished at the effect my last-minute question had had on Eric. 'What's the deal?'

'What was he doing?'

'Drinking Red Stuff and sitting at a table with my friend Tara. You know, you saw her? At Club Dead, in Jackson?'

'When I saw her she was under the protection of Franklin Mott.'

'Well, they were dating. I can't understand why he'd let her go out with Mickey. I hoped maybe Mickey was just there as her bodyguard or something.' I retrieved my coat from the booth. 'So, what's the bottom line on this guy?' I asked.

'Stay away from him. Don't talk to him, don't cross him, and don't try to help your friend Tara. When he was here, Mickey talked mostly to Charles. Charles tells me he is a rogue. He's capable of . . . things that are barbarous. Don't go around Tara.'

I opened my hands, asking Eric to explain.

'He'll do things the rest of us won't,' Eric said.

I stared up at Eric, shocked and deeply worried. 'I can't just ignore her situation. I don't have so many friends that I can afford to let one go down the drain.'

'If she's involved with Mickey, she's just meat on the hoof,' Eric said with a brutal simplicity. He took my coat from me and held it while I slid into it. His hands massaged my shoulders after I'd buttoned it.

'It fits well,' he said. It didn't take a mind reader to guess that he didn't want to say any more about Mickey.

'You got my thank-you note?'

'Of course. Very, ah, seemly.'

I nodded, hoping to indicate this was the end of the subject. But, of course, it wasn't.

'I still wonder why your old coat had bloodstains on it,' Eric murmured, and my eyes flashed up to his. I cursed my carelessness once again. When he'd come back to thank me for keeping him, he'd roamed the house while I was busy until he'd come across the coat. 'What did we do, Sookie? And to whom?'

'It was chicken blood. I killed a chicken and cooked it,' I lied. I'd seen my grandmother do that when I was little, many a time, but I'd never done it myself.

'Sookie, Sookie. My bullshit meter is reading that as a 'false,' ' Eric said, shaking his head in a chiding way.

I was so startled I laughed. It was a good note on which to leave. I could see Charles Twining standing by the front door, thoroughly modern padded jacket at the ready. 'Good-bye, Eric, and thanks for the bartender,' I said, as if Eric had loaned me some AA batteries or a cup of rice. He bent and brushed my cheek with his cool lips.

'Drive safely,' he said. 'And stay away from Mickey. I need to find out why he's in my territory. Call me if you have any problems with Charles.' (If the batteries are defective, or if the rice is full of worms.) Beyond him I could see the same woman was still sitting at the bar, the one who'd remarked that I was no maiden. She was obviously wondering what I had done to secure the attention of a vampire as ancient and attractive as Eric.

I often wondered the same thing.

Chapter 4

The drive back to Bon Temps was pleasant. Vampires don't smell like humans or act like humans, but they're sure relaxing to my brain. Being with a vampire is almost as tension-free as being alone, except, of course, for the blood-sucking possibilities.

Charles Twining asked a few questions about the work for which he'd been hired and about the bar. My driving seemed to make him a little uneasy – though possibly his unease was due to simply being in a car. Some of the pre-Industrial Revolution vamps loathe modern transportation. His eye patch was on his left eye, on my side, which gave me the curious feeling I was invisible.

I'd run him by the vampire hostel where he'd been living so he could gather a few things. He had a sports bag with him, one large enough to hold maybe three days' worth of clothes. He'd just moved into Shreveport, he told me, and hadn't had time to decide where he would settle.

After we'd been on our way for about forty minutes, the vampire said, 'And you, Miss Sookie? Do you live with your father and mother?'

'No, they've been gone since I was seven,' I said. Out of the corner of my eye, I caught a hand gesture inviting me to continue. 'There was a whole lot of rain in a real short time one night that spring, and my dad tried to cross a little bridge that had water already over it. They got swept away.'

I glanced to my right to see that he was nodding. People died, sometimes suddenly and unexpectedly, and sometimes for very little reason. A vampire knew that better than anyone. 'My brother and I grew up with my grandmother,' I said. 'She died last year. My brother has my parents' old house, and I have my grandmother's.'

'Lucky to have a place to live,' he commented.

In profile, his hooked nose was an elegant miniature. I wondered if he cared that the human race had gotten larger, while he had stayed the same.

'Oh, yes,' I agreed. 'I'm major lucky. I've got a job, I've got my brother, I've got a house, I've got friends. And I'm healthy.'

He turned to look at me full-face, I think, but I was passing a battered Ford pickup, so I couldn't return his gaze. 'That's interesting. Forgive me, but I was under the impression from Pam that you have some kind of disability.'

'Oh, well, yeah.'

'And that would be . . .? You look very, ah, robust.'

'I'm a telepath.'

He mulled that over. 'And that would mean?'

'I can read other humans' minds.'

'But not vampires.'

'No, not vampires.'

'Very good.'

'Yes, I think so.' If I could read vampire minds, I'd have been dead long ago. Vampires value their privacy.

'Did you know Chow?' he asked.

'Yes.' It was my turn to be terse.

'And Long Shadow?'

'Yes.'

'As the newest bartender at Fangtasia, I have a definite interest in their deaths.'

Understandable, but I had no idea how to respond. 'Okay,' I said cautiously.

'Were you there when Chow died again?' This was the way some vamps referred to the final death.

'Um . . . yes.'

'And Long Shadow?'

'Well . . . yes.'

'I would be interested in hearing what you had to say.'

'Chow died in what they're calling the Witch War. Long Shadow was trying to kill me when Eric staked him because he'd been embezzling.'

'You're sure that's why Eric staked him? For embezzling?'

'I was there. I oughta know. End of subject.'

'I suppose your life has been complicated,' Charles said after a pause.

'Yes.'

'Where will I be spending the sunlight hours?'

'My boss has a place for you.'

'There is a lot of trouble at this bar?'

'Not until recently.' I hesitated.

'Your regular bouncer can't handle shifters?'

'Our regular bouncer is the owner, Sam Merlotte. He is a shifter. Right now, he's a shifter with a broken leg. He got shot. And he's not the only one.'

This didn't seem to astonish the vampire. 'How many?'

'Three that I know of. A werepanther named Calvin Norris, who wasn't mortally wounded, and then a shifter girl named Heather Kinman, who's dead. She was shot at the Sonic. Do you know what Sonic is?' Vampires didn't always pay attention to fast-food restaurants, because they didn't eat. (Hey, how many blood banks can you locate off the top of your head?)

Charles nodded, his curly chestnut hair bouncing on his shoulders. 'That's the one where you eat in your car?'

'Yes, right,' I said. 'Heather had been in a friend's car, talking, and she got out to walk back to her car a few slots down. The shot came from across the street. She had a milkshake in her hand.' The melting chocolate ice cream had blended with blood on the pavement. I'd seen it in Andy Bellefleur's mind. 'It was late at night, and all the businesses on the other side of the street had been closed for hours. So the shooter got away.'

'All three shootings were at night?'

'Yes.'

'I wonder if that's significant.'

'Could be; but maybe it's just that there's better concealment at night.'

Charles nodded.

'Since Sam got hurt, there's been a lot of anxiety among the shifters because it's hard to believe three shootings could be a coincidence. And regular humans are worried because in their view three people have been shot at random, people with nothing in common and few enemies. Since everyone's tense, there are more fights in the bar.'

'I've never been a bouncer before,' Charles said conversationally. 'I was the youngest son of a minor baronet, so I've had to make my own way, and I've done many things. I've worked as a bartender before, and many years ago I was shill for a whorehouse. Stood outside, trumpeted the wares of the strumpets – that's a neat phrase, isn't it? – threw out men who got too rough with the whores. I suppose that's the same as being a bouncer.'

I was speechless at this unexpected confidence.

'Of course, that was after I lost my eye, but before I became a vampire,' the vampire said.

'Of course,' I echoed weakly.

'Which was while I was a pirate,' he continued. He was smiling. I checked with a sideways glance.

'What did you, um, pirate?' I didn't know if that was a verb or not, but he got my meaning clearly.

'Oh, we'd try to catch almost anyone unawares,' he said blithely. 'Off and on I lived on the coast of America, down close to New Orleans, where we'd take small cargo ships and the like. I sailed aboard a small hoy, so we couldn't take on too large or well defended a ship. But when we caught up with some bark, then there was fighting!' He sighed – recalling the happiness of whacking at people with a sword, I guess.

'And what happened to you?' I asked politely, meaning how did he come to depart his wonderful warm-blooded life of rapine and slaughter for the vampire edition of the same thing.

'One evening, we boarded a galleon that had no living crew,' he said. I noticed that his hands had curled into fists. His voice chilled. 'We had sailed to the Tortugas. It was dusk. I was the first man to go down into the hold. What was in the hold got me first.'

After that little tale, we fell silent by mutual consent.

Sam was on the couch in the living room of his trailer. Sam had had the double-wide anchored so it was at a right angle to the back of the bar. That way, at least he opened his front door to a view of the parking lot, which was better than looking at the back of the bar, with its large garbage bin between the kitchen door and the employees' entrance.

'Well, there you are,' Sam said, and his tone was grumpy. Sam was never one for sitting still. Now that his leg was in a cast, he was fretting from the inactivity. What would he do during the next full moon? Would the leg be healed enough by then for him to change? If he changed, what would happen to the cast? I'd known other injured shape-shifters before, but I hadn't been around for their recuperation, so this was new territory for me. 'I was beginning to think you'd gotten lost on the way back.' Sam's voice returned me to the here and now. It had a distinct edge.

'"Gee, thanks, Sookie, I see you returned with a bouncer",' I said. '"I'm so sorry you had to go through the humiliating experience of asking Eric for a favor on my behalf".' At that moment, I didn't care if he was my boss or not.

Sam looked embarrassed.

'Eric agreed, then,' he said. He nodded at the pirate.

'Charles Twining, at your service,' said the vampire.

Sam's eyes widened. 'Okay. I'm Sam Merlotte, owner of the bar. I appreciate your coming to help us out here.'

'I was ordered to do so,' the vampire said coolly.

'So the deal you struck was room, board, and favor,' Sam said to me. 'I owe Eric a favor.' This was said in a tone that a kind person would describe as grudging.

'Yes.' I was mad now. 'You sent me to make a deal. I checked the terms with you! That's the deal I made. You asked Eric for a favor; now he gets a favor in return. No matter what you told yourself, that's what it boils down to.'

Sam nodded, though he didn't look happy. 'Also, I changed my mind. I think Mr Twining, here, should stay with you.'

'And why would you think that?'

'The closet looked a little cramped. You have a light-tight place for vampires, right?'

'You didn't ask me if that was okay.'

'You're refusing to do it?'

'Yes! I'm not the vampire hotel keeper!'

'But you work for me, and he works for me . . .'

'Uh-huh. And would you ask Arlene or Holly to put him up?'

Sam looked even more amazed. 'Well, no, but that's because—' He stopped then.

'Can't think of how to finish the sentence, can you?' I snarled. 'Okay, buddy, I'm out of here. I spent a whole evening putting myself in an embarrassing situation for you. And what do I get? *No effing thanks!'*

I stomped out of the double-wide. I didn't slam the door because I didn't want to be childish. Door slamming just isn't adult. Neither is whining. Okay, maybe stomping out isn't, either. But it was a choice between making an emphatic verbal exit or slapping Sam. Normally Sam was one of my favorite people in the world, but tonight . . . not.

I was working the early shift for the next three days – not that I was sure I had a job anymore. When I got into Merlotte's at eleven the next morning, dashing to the employees' door through the pouring rain in my ugly but useful rain slicker, I was nearly sure that Sam would tell me to collect my last paycheck and hit the door. But he wasn't there. I had a moment of what I recognized as disappointment. Maybe I'd been spoiling for another fight, which was odd.

Terry Bellefleur was standing in for Sam again, and Terry was having a bad day. It wasn't a good idea to ask him questions or even to talk to him beyond the necessary relay of orders.

Terry particularly hated rainy weather, I'd noticed, and he also didn't like Sheriff Bud Dearborn. I didn't know the reason for either prejudice. Today, gray sheets of rain battered at the walls and roof, and Bud Dearborn was pontificating to five of his cronies over on the smoking side. Arlene caught my eye and widened her eyes to give me a warning.

Though Terry was pale, and perspiring, he'd zipped up the light jacket he often wore over his Merlotte's T-shirt. I noticed his hands shaking as he pulled a draft beer. I wondered if he could last until dark.

At least there weren't many customers, if something did go wrong. Arlene drifted over to catch up with a married couple who'd come in, friends of hers. My section was almost empty, with the exception of my brother, Jason, and his friend Hoyt.

Hoyt was Jason's sidekick. If they weren't both definitely heterosexual, I would have recommended they marry, they complemented each other so well. Hoyt enjoyed jokes, and Jason enjoyed telling them. Hoyt was at a loss to fill his free time, and Jason was always up to something. Hoyt's mother was a little overwhelming, and Jason was parent-free. Hoyt was firmly anchored in the here and now, and had an iron sense of what the community would tolerate and what it would not. Jason didn't.

I thought of what a huge secret Jason now had, and I wondered if he was tempted to share it with Hoyt.

'How you doing, Sis?' Jason asked. He held up his glass, indicating he'd like a refill on his Dr Pepper. Jason didn't drink until after his workday was over, a large point in his favor.

'Fine, Brother. You want some more, Hoyt?' I asked.

'Please, Sookie. Ice tea,' Hoyt said.

In a second I was back with their drinks. Terry glared at me when I went behind the bar, but he didn't speak. I can ignore a glare.

'Sook, you want to go with me to the hospital in Grainger this afternoon after you get off?' Jason asked.

'Oh,' I said. 'Yeah, sure.' Calvin had always been good to me.

Hoyt said, 'Sure is crazy, Sam and Calvin and Heather getting shot. What do you make of it, Sookie?' Hoyt has decided I am an oracle.

'Hoyt, you know as much about it as I do,' I told him. 'I think we all should be careful.' I hoped the significance of this wasn't lost on my brother. He shrugged.

When I looked up, I saw a stranger waiting to be seated and hurried over to him. His dark hair, turned black by the rain, was pulled back in a ponytail. His face was scarred with one long thin white line that ran along one cheek. When he pulled off his jacket, I could see that he was a bodybuilder.

'Smoking or non?' I asked, with a menu already in my hand.

'Non,' he said, and followed me to a table. He carefully hung his wet jacket on the back of a chair and took the menu after he was seated. 'My wife will be along in a few minutes,' he said. 'She's meeting me here.'

I put another menu at the adjacent place. 'Do you want to order now or wait for her?'

'I'd like some hot tea,' he asked. 'I'll wait until she comes to order food. Kind of a limited menu here, huh?' He glanced over at Arlene and then back at me. I began to feel uneasy. I knew he wasn't here because this place was convenient for lunch.

'That's all we can handle,' I said, taking care to sound relaxed. 'What we've got, it's good.'

When I assembled the hot water and a tea bag, I put a saucer with a couple of lemon slices on the tray, too. No fairies around to offend.

'Are you Sookie Stackhouse?' he asked when I returned with his tea.

'Yes, I am.' I put the saucer gently on the table, right beside the cup. 'Why do you want to know?' I already knew why, but with regular people, you had to ask.

'I'm Jack Leeds, a private investigator,' he said. He laid a business card on the table, turned so I could read it. He waited for a beat, as if he usually got a dramatic reaction to that statement. 'I've been hired by a family in Jackson, Mississippi – the Pelt family,' he continued, when he saw I wasn't going to speak.

My heart sank to my shoes before it began pounding at an accelerated rate. This man believed that Debbie was dead. And he thought there was a good chance I might know something about it.

He was absolutely right.

I'd shot Debbie Pelt dead a few weeks before, in self-defense. Hers was the body Eric had hidden. Hers was the bullet Eric had taken for me.

Debbie's disappearance after leaving a 'party' in Shreveport, Louisiana (in fact a life-and-death brawl between witches, vamps, and Weres), had been a nine days' wonder. I'd hoped I'd heard the end of it.

'So the Pelts aren't satisfied with the police investigation?' I asked. It was a stupid question, one I picked out of the air at random. I had to say something to break up the gathering silence.

'There really wasn't an investigation,' Jack Leeds said. 'The police in Jackson decided she probably vanished voluntarily.' He didn't believe that, though.

His face changed then; it was like someone had switched on a light behind his eyes. I turned to look where he was looking, and I saw a blond woman of medium height shaking her umbrella out at the door. She had short hair and pale skin, and when she turned, I saw that she was very pretty; at least, she would have been if she had been more animated.

But that wasn't a factor to Jack Leeds. He was looking at the woman he loved, and when she saw him, the same light switched on behind her eyes, too. She came across the floor to his table as smoothly as if she were dancing, and when she shed her own wet jacket, I saw her arms were as muscular as his. They didn't kiss, but his hand slid over hers and squeezed just briefly. After she'd taken her chair and asked for some diet Coke, her eyes went to the menu. She was thinking that all the food Merlotte's offered was unhealthy. She was right.

'Salad?' Jack Leeds asked.

'I have to have something hot,' she said. 'Chili?'

'Okay. Two chilis,' he told me. 'Lily, this is Sookie Stackhouse. Ms Stackhouse, this is Lily Bard Leeds.'

'Hello,' she said. 'I've just been out to your house.'

Her eyes were light blue, and she had a stare like a laser. 'You saw Debbie Pelt the night she disappeared.' Her mind added, *You're the one she hated so much.*

They didn't know Debbie Pelt's true nature, and I was relieved that the Pelts hadn't been able to find a Were investigator. They wouldn't out their daughter to regular detectives. The longer the two-natured could keep the fact of their existence a secret, the better, as far as they were concerned.

'Yes,' I said. 'I saw her that night.'

'Can we come talk to you about that? After you get off work?'

'I have to go see a friend in the hospital after work,' I said.

'Sick?' Jack Leeds asked.

'Shot,' I said.

Their interest quickened. 'By someone local?' the blond woman asked.

Then I saw how it might all work. 'By a sniper,' I said. 'Someone's been shooting people at random in this area.'

'Have any of them vanished?' Jack Leeds asked.

'No,' I admitted. 'They've all been left lying. Of course, there were witnesses to all of the shootings. Maybe that's why.' I hadn't heard of anyone actually seeing Calvin get shot, but someone had come along right afterward and called 911.

Lily Leeds asked me if they could talk to me the next day before I went to work. I gave them directions to my house and told them to come at ten. I didn't think talking to them was a very good idea, but I didn't think I had much of a choice, either. I would become more of an object of suspicion if I refused to talk about Debbie.

I found myself wishing I could call Eric tonight and tell him about Jack and Lily Leeds; worries shared are worries halved. But Eric didn't remember any of it. I wished that I could forget Debbie's death, too. It was awful to know something so heavy and terrible, to be unable to share it with a soul.

I knew so many secrets, but almost none of them were my own. This secret of mine was a dark and bloody burden.

Charles Twining was due to relieve Terry at full dark. Arlene was working late, since Danielle was attending her daughter's dance recital, and I was able to lighten my mood a little by briefing Arlene on the new bartender/bouncer. She was intrigued. We'd never had an Englishman visit the bar, much less an Englishman with an eye patch.

'Tell Charles I said hi,' I called as I began to put on my rain gear. After a couple of hours of sprinkling, the drops were beginning to come faster again.

I splashed out to my car, the hood pulled well forward over my face. Just as I unlocked the driver's door and pulled it open, I heard a voice call my name. Sam was standing on crutches in the door of his trailer. He'd added a roofed porch a couple of years before, so he wasn't getting wet, but he didn't need to be standing there, either. Slamming the car door shut, I leaped over puddles and across the stepping stones.

In a second or two, I was standing on his porch and dripping all over it.

'I'm sorry,' he said.

I stared at him. 'You should be,' I said gruffly.

'Well, I am.'

'Okay. Good.' I resolutely didn't ask him what he'd done with the vampire.

'Anything happen over at the bar today?'

I hesitated. 'Well, the crowd was thin, to put it mildly. But ...' I started to tell him about the private detectives, but then I knew he'd ask questions. And I might end up telling him the whole sorry story just for the relief of confessing to someone. 'I have to go, Sam. Jason's taking me to visit Calvin Norris in the hospital in Grainger.'

He looked at me. His eyes narrowed. The lashes were the same red-gold as his hair, so they showed up only when you were close to him. And I had no business at all thinking about Sam's eyelashes, or any other part of him, for that matter.

'I was a shit yesterday,' he said. 'I don't have to tell you why.'

'Well, I guess you do,' I said, bewildered. 'Because I sure don't understand.'

'The point is, you know you can count on me.'

To get mad at me for no reason? To apologize afterward? 'You've really confused me a lot lately,' I said. 'But you've been my friend for years, and I have a very high opinion of you.' That sounded way too stilted, so I tried smiling. He smiled back, and a drop of rain fell off my hood and splashed on my nose, and the moment was over. I said, 'When do you think you'll get back to the bar?'

'I'll try to come in tomorrow for a while,' he said. 'At least I can sit in the office and work on the books, get some filing done.'

'See you.'

'Sure.'

And I dashed back to my car, feeling that my heart was much lighter than it had been before. Being at odds with Sam had felt wrong. I didn't realize how that wrongness had colored my thoughts until I was right with him again.

Chapter 5

The rain pelted down as we pulled in to the parking lot of the Grainger hospital. It was as small as the one in Clarice, the one most Renard Parish people were carried to. But the Grainger hospital was newer and had more of the diagnostic machines modern hospitals seemed to require.

I'd changed into jeans and a sweater, but I'd resumed wearing my lined slicker. As Jason and I hurried to the sliding glass doors, I was patting myself on the back for wearing boots. Weather-wise, the evening was proving as nasty as the morning had been.

The hospital was roiling with shifters. I could feel their anger as soon as I was inside. Two of the werepanthers from Hotshot were in the lobby; I figured they were acting as guards. Jason went to them and took their hands firmly. Maybe he exchanged some kind of secret shake or something; I don't know. At least they didn't rub against one another's legs. They didn't seem quite as happy to see Jason as he was to see them, and I noticed that Jason stepped back from them with a little frown between his eyes. The two looked at me intently. The man was of medium height and stocky, and he had thick brownish-blond hair. His eyes were full of curiosity.

'Sook, this is Dixon Mayhew,' Jason said. 'And this is Dixie Mayhew, his twin sister.' Dixie wore her hair, the same color as her brother's, almost as short as Dixon's, but she had dark, almost black, eyes. The twins were certainly not identical.

'Has it been quiet here?' I asked carefully.

'No problems so far,' Dixie said, keeping her voice low. Dixon's gaze was fixed on Jason. 'How's your boss?'

'He's in a cast, but he'll heal.'

'Calvin was shot bad.' Dixie eyed me for a minute. 'He's up in 214.'

Having been given the seal of approval, Jason and I went to the stairs. The twins watched us all the way. We passed the hospital auxiliary 'pink lady' on duty at the visitors' desk. I felt kind of worried about her: white-haired, heavy glasses, sweet face with a full complement of wrinkles. I hoped nothing would happen during her watch to upset her worldview.

It was easy to pick which room was Calvin's. A slab of muscle was leaning against the wall outside, a barrel-shaped man I'd never seen. He was a werewolf. Werewolves make good bodyguards, according to the common wisdom of the two-natured, because they are ruthless and tenacious. From what I've seen, that's just the bad-boy image Weres have. But it's true that as a rule, they're the roughest element of the two-natured community. You won't find too many Were doctors, for example, but you will find a lot of Weres in construction work. Jobs relating to motorcycles are heavily dominated by Weres, too. Some of those gangs do more than drink beer on the full-moon nights.

Seeing a Were disturbed me. I was surprised the panthers of Hotshot had brought in an outsider. Jason murmured, 'That's Dawson. He owns the small engine repair shop between Hotshot and Grainger.'

Dawson was on the alert as we came down the hall.

'Jason Stackhouse,' he said, identifying my brother after a minute. Dawson was wearing a denim shirt and jeans, but his biceps were about to burst through the material. His black leather boots were battle scarred.

'We've come to see how Calvin is doing,' Jason said. 'This here's my sister, Sookie.'

'Ma'am,' Dawson rumbled. He eyeballed me slowly, and there wasn't anything lascivious about it. I was glad I'd left my purse in the locked truck. He would've gone through it, I was sure. 'You want to take off that coat and turn around for me?'

I didn't take offense; Dawson was doing his job. I didn't want Calvin to get hurt again, either. I took off my slicker, handed it to Jason, and rotated. A nurse who'd been entering something in a chart watched this procedure with open curiosity. I held Jason's jacket as he took his turn. Satisfied, Dawson knocked on the door. Though I didn't hear a response, he must have, because he opened the door and said, 'The Stackhouses.'

Just a whisper of a voice came from the room. Dawson nodded.

'Miss Stackhouse, you can go in,' he said. Jason started to follow me, but Dawson put a massive arm in front of him. 'Only your sister,' he said.

Jason and I began to protest at the same moment, but then Jason shrugged. 'Go ahead, Sook,' he said. There was obviously no budging Dawson, and there was no point to upsetting a wounded man, for that matter. I pushed the heavy door wide open.

Calvin was by himself, though there was another bed in the room. The panther leader looked awful. He was pale and drawn. His hair was dirty, though his cheeks above his trim beard had been shaved. He was wearing a hospital gown, and he was hooked up to lots of things.

'I'm so sorry,' I blurted. I was horrified. Though many brains had indicated as much, I could see that if Calvin hadn't been two-natured, the wound would have killed him instantly. Whoever had shot him had wanted his death.

Calvin turned his head to me, slowly and with effort. 'It's not as bad as it looks,' he said dryly, his voice a thread. 'They're going to take me off some of this stuff tomorrow.'

'Where were you hit?' I asked.

Calvin moved one hand to touch his upper left chest. His golden brown eyes captured mine. I went closer to him and covered his hand with mine. 'I'm so sorry,' I said again. His fingers curled under mine until he was holding my hand.

'There've been others,' he said in a whisper of a voice.

'Yes.'

'Your boss.'

I nodded.

'That poor girl.'

I nodded again.

'Whoever's doing this, they've got to be stopped.'

'Yes.'

'It's got to be someone who hates shifters. The police will never find out who's doing this. We can't tell them what to look for.'

Well, that was part of the problem of keeping your condition a secret. 'It'll be harder for them to find the person,' I conceded. 'But maybe they will.'

'Some of my people wonder if the shooter is someone who's a shifter,' Calvin said. His fingers tightened around mine. 'Someone who didn't want to become a shifter in the first place. Someone who was bitten.'

It took a second for the light to click on in my head. I am such an idiot.

'Oh, no, Calvin, no, no,' I said, my words stumbling over each other in my haste. 'Oh, Calvin, please don't let them go after Jason. Please, he's all I've got.' Tears began to run down my cheeks as if someone had turned on a faucet in my head. 'He was telling me how much he enjoyed being one of you, even if he couldn't be exactly like a born panther. He's so new, he hasn't had time to figure out who all else is two-natured. I don't think he even realized Sam and Heather were. . . .'

'No one's gonna take him out until we know the truth,' Calvin said. 'Though I might be in this bed, I'm still the leader.' But I could tell he'd had to argue against it, and I also knew (from hearing it right out of Calvin's brain) that some of the panthers were still in favor of executing Jason. Calvin couldn't prevent that. He might be angry afterward, but if Jason were dead, that wouldn't make one little bit of difference. Calvin's fingers released mine, and his hand rose with an effort to wipe the tears off my cheek.

'You're a sweet woman,' he said. 'I wish you could love me.'

'I wish I could, too,' I said. So many of my problems would be solved if I loved Calvin Norris. I'd move out to Hotshot, become a member of the secretive little community. Two or three nights a month, I'd have to be sure to stay inside, but other than that, I'd be safe. Not only would Calvin defend me to the death, but so would the other members of the Hotshot clan.

But the thought of it just made me shudder. The windswept open fields, the powerful and ancient crossroads around which the little houses clustered . . . I didn't think I could handle the perpetual isolation from the rest of the world. My Gran would have urged me to accept Calvin's offer. He was a steady man, was a shift leader at Norcross, a job that came with good benefits. You might think that's laughable, but wait until you have to pay for your insurance all by yourself; then laugh.

It occurred to me (as it should have right away) that Calvin was in a perfect position to force my compliance – Jason's life for my companionship – and he hadn't taken advantage of it.

I leaned over and gave Calvin a kiss on the cheek. 'I'll pray for your recovery,' I said. 'Thank you for giving Jason a chance.' Maybe Calvin's nobility was partly due to the fact that he was in no shape to take advantage of me, but it was nobility, and I noted and appreciated it. 'You're a good man,' I said, and touched his face. The hair of his neat beard felt soft.

His eyes were steady as he said good-bye. 'Watch out for that brother of yours, Sookie,' he said. 'Oh, and tell Dawson I don't want no more company tonight.'

'He won't take my word for it,' I said.

Calvin managed to smile. 'Wouldn't be much of a bodyguard if he did, I guess.'

I relayed the message to the Were. But sure enough, as Jason and I walked back to the stairs, Dawson was going into the room to check with Calvin.

I debated for a couple of minutes before I decided it would be better if Jason knew what he was up against. In the truck, as he drove home, I relayed my conversation with Calvin to my brother.

He was horrified that his new buddies in the werepanther world could believe such a thing of him. 'If I'd thought of that before I changed for the first time, I can't say it wouldn't have been tempting,' Jason said as we drove back to Bon Temps through the rain. 'I was mad. Not just mad, furious. But now that I've changed, I see it different.' He went on and on while my thoughts ran around inside my head in a circle, trying to think of a way out of this mess.

The sniping case had to be solved by the next full moon. If it wasn't, the others might tear Jason up when they changed. Maybe he could just roam the woods around his house when he turned into his panther-man form, or maybe he could hunt the woods around my place – but he wouldn't be safe out at Hotshot. And they might come looking for him. I couldn't defend him against them all.

By the next full moon, the shooter had to be in custody.

Until I was washing my few dishes that night, it didn't strike me as odd that though Jason was being accused by the werepanther community of being an assassin, I was the one who'd actually shot a shifter. I'd been thinking of the private detectives' appointment to meet me here the next morning. And, as I found myself doing out of habit, I'd been scanning the kitchen for signs of the death of Debbie Pelt. From watching the Discovery Channel and the Learning Channel, I knew that there was no way I could completely eradicate the traces of blood and tissue that had spattered my kitchen, but I'd scrubbed and cleaned over and over. I was certain that no casual glance – in fact, no careful inspection by the naked eye – could reveal anything amiss in this room.

I had done the only thing I could, short of standing there to be murdered. Was that what Jesus had meant by turning the other cheek? I hoped not, because every instinct in me had urged me to defend myself, and the means at hand had been a shotgun.

Of course, I should immediately have reported it. But by then, Eric's wound had healed, the one made when Debbie'd hit him while trying to shoot me. Aside from the testimony of a vampire and myself, there was no proof that she'd fired first, and Debbie's body would have been a powerful statement of our guilt. My first instinct had been to cover up her visit to my house. Eric hadn't given me any other advice, which also might have changed things.

No, I wasn't blaming my predicament on Eric. He hadn't even been in his right mind at the time. It was my own fault that I hadn't sat down to think things through. There would have been gunshot residue on Debbie's hand. Her gun had been fired. Some of Eric's dried blood would have been on the floor. She'd broken in through my front door, and the door had shown clear signs of her trespass. Her car was hidden across the road, and only her fingerprints would've been in it.

I'd panicked, and blown it.

I just had to live with that.

But I was very sorry about the uncertainty her family was suffering. I owed them certainty – which I couldn't deliver.

I wrung out the washcloth and hung it neatly over the sink divider. I dried off my hands and folded the dish towel. Okay, now I'd gotten my guilt straight. That was so much better! *Not*. Angry with myself, I stomped out to the living room and turned on the television: another mistake. There was a story about Heather's funeral; a news crew from Shreveport had come to cover the modest service this afternoon. Just think of the sensation it would cause if the media realized how the sniper was selecting his victims. The news anchor, a solemn African-American man, was saying that police in Renard Parish had discovered other clusters of apparently random shootings in small towns in Tennessee and Mississippi. I was startled. A serial shooter, here?

The phone rang. 'Hello,' I said, not expecting anything good.

'Sookie, hi, it's Alcide.'

I found myself smiling. Alcide Herveaux, who worked in his father's surveying business in Shreveport, was one of my favorite people. He was a Were, he was both sexy and hardworking, and I liked him very much. He'd also been Debbie Pelt's fiancé. But Alcide had abjured her before she vanished, in a rite that made her invisible and inaudible to him – not literally, but in effect.

'Sookie, I'm at Merlotte's. I'd thought you might be working tonight, so I drove over. Can I come to the house? I need to talk to you.'

'You know you're in danger, coming to Bon Temps.'

'No, why?'

'Because of the sniper.' I could hear the bar sounds in the background. There was no mistaking Arlene's laugh. I was betting the new bartender was charming one and all.

'Why would I worry about that?' Alcide hadn't been thinking about the news too hard, I decided.

'All the people who got shot? They were two-natured,' I said. 'Now

they're saying on the news there've been a lot more across the south.
Random shootings in small towns. Bullets that match the one recovered from Heather Kinman here. And I'm betting all the other victims
were shape-shifters, too.'

There was a thoughtful silence on the end of the line, if silence can
be characterized.

'I hadn't realized,' Alcide said. His deep, rumbly voice was even
more deliberate than normal.

'Oh, and have you talked to the private detectives?'

'What? What are you talking about?'

'If they see us talking together, it'll look very suspicious to Debbie's
family.'

'Debbie's family has hired private eyes to look for her?'

'That's what I'm saying.'

'Listen, I'm coming to your house.' He hung up the phone.

I didn't know why on earth the detectives would be watching my
house, or where they'd watch it from, but if they saw Debbie's former
fiancé tootling down my driveway, it would be easy to connect the
dots and come up with a totally erroneous picture. They'd think Alcide
killed Debbie to clear the way for me, and nothing could be more
wrong. I hoped like hell that Jack Leeds and Lily Bard Leeds were
sound asleep rather than staked out in the woods somewhere with a
pair of binoculars.

Alcide hugged me. He always did. And once again I was overwhelmed by the size of him, the masculinity, the familiar smell. Despite
the warning bell ringing in my head, I hugged him back.

We sat on the couch and half turned to face each other. Alcide was
wearing work clothes, which in this weather consisted of a flannel
shirt worn open over a T-shirt, heavy jeans, and thick socks under his
work boots. His tangle of black hair had a crease in it from his hard
hat, and he was beginning to look a little bristly.

'Tell me about the detectives,' he said, and I described the couple
and told him what they'd said.

'Debbie's family didn't say anything to me about it,' Alcide said. He
turned it over in his head for a minute. I could follow his thinking.
'I think that means they're sure I made her vanish.'

'Maybe not. Maybe they just think you're so grieved they don't want to bring it up.'

'Grieved.' Alcide mulled that over for a minute. 'No. I spent all the . . .' He paused, grappling for words. 'I used up all the energy I had to spare for her,' he said finally. 'I was so blind, I almost think she used some kind of magic on me. Her mother's a spellcaster and half shifter. Her dad's a full-blooded shifter.'

'You think that's possible? Magic?' I wasn't questioning that magic existed, but that Debbie had used it.

'Why else would I stick with her for so long? Ever since she's gone missing, it's been like someone took a pair of dark glasses off my eyes. I was willing to forgive her so much, like when she pushed you into the trunk.'

Debbie had taken an opportunity to push me in a car trunk with my vampire boyfriend, Bill, who'd been starved for blood for days. And she'd walked off and left me in the trunk with Bill, who was about to awake.

I looked down at my feet, pushing away the recollection of the desperation, the pain.

'She let you get raped,' Alcide said harshly.

Him saying it like that, flat out, shocked me. 'Hey, Bill didn't know it was me,' I said. 'He hadn't had anything to eat for days and days, and the impulses are so closely related. I mean, he stopped, you know? He stopped, when he knew it was me.' I couldn't put it like that to myself; I couldn't say that word. I knew beyond a doubt that Bill would rather have chewed off his own hand than done that to me if he'd been in his right mind. At that time, he'd been the only sex partner I'd ever had. My feelings about the incident were so confused that I couldn't even bear to try to pick through them. When I'd thought of rape before, when other girls had told me what had happened to them or I'd read it in their brains, I hadn't had the ambiguity I felt over my own short, awful time in the trunk.

'He did something you didn't want him to do,' Alcide said simply.

'He wasn't himself,' I said.

'But he did it.'

'Yes, he did, and I was awful scared.' My voice began to shake. 'But he came to his senses, and he *stopped*, and I was okay, and he was really, really sorry. He's never laid a finger on me since then, never asked me if we could have sex, never . . .' My voice trailed off. I stared down at my hands. 'Yes, Debbie was responsible for that.' Somehow, saying that out loud made me feel better. 'She knew what would happen, or at least she didn't care what would happen.'

'And even then,' Alcide said, returning to his main point, 'she kept coming back and I kept trying to rationalize her behavior. I can't believe I would do that if I wasn't under some kind of magical influence.'

I wasn't about to try to make Alcide feel guiltier. I had my own load of guilt to carry. 'Hey, it's over.'

'You sound sure.'

I looked Alcide directly in the eyes. His were narrow and green. 'Do you think there's the slightest chance that Debbie's alive?' I asked.

'Her family . . .' Alcide stopped. 'No, I don't.'

I couldn't get rid of Debbie Pelt, dead or alive.

'Why'd you need to talk to me in the first place?' I asked. 'You said over the phone you needed to tell me something.'

'Colonel Flood died yesterday.'

'Oh, I'm so sorry! What happened?'

'He was driving to the store when another driver hit him broadside.'

'That's awful. Was anyone in the car with him?'

'No, he was by himself. His kids are coming back to Shreveport for the funeral, of course. I wondered if you'd come to the funeral with me.'

'Of course. It's not private?'

'No. He knew so many people still stationed at the Air Force base, and he was head of his Neighborhood Watch group and the treasurer of his church, and of course he was the packmaster.'

'He had a big life,' I said. 'Lots of responsibility.'

'It's tomorrow at one. What's your work schedule?'

'If I can swap shifts with someone, I'd need to be back here at four thirty to change and go to work.'

'That shouldn't be a problem.'

'Who'll be packmaster now?'

'I don't know,' Alcide said, but his voice wasn't as neutral as I'd expected.

'Do you want the job?'

'No.' He seemed a little hesitant, I thought, and I felt the conflict in his head. 'But my father does.' He wasn't finished. I waited.

'Were funerals are pretty ceremonial,' he said, and I realized he was trying to tell me something. I just wasn't sure what it was.

'Spit it out.' Straightforward is always good, as far as I'm concerned.

'If you think you can overdress for this, you can't,' he said. 'I know the rest of the shifter world thinks Weres only go for leather and chains, but that's not true. For funerals, we go all out.' He wanted to give me even more fashion tips, but he stopped there. I could see the thoughts crowding right behind his eyes, wanting to be let out.

'Every woman wants to know what's appropriate to wear,' I said. 'Thanks. I won't wear pants.'

He shook his head. 'I know you can do that, but I'm always taken by surprise.' I could hear that he was disconcerted. 'I'll pick you up at eleven thirty,' he said.

'Let me see about swapping shifts.'

I called Holly and found it suited her to switch shifts with me. 'I can just drive over there and meet you,' I offered. 'No,' he said. 'I'll come get you and bring you back.'

Okay, if he wanted to go to the trouble of fetching me, I could live with it. I'd save mileage on my car, I figured. My old Nova was none too reliable.

'All right. I'll be ready.'

'I better go,' he said. The silence drew out. I knew Alcide was thinking of kissing me. He leaned over and kissed me lightly on the lips. We regarded each other from a few inches apart.

'Well, I have some things I need to be doing, and you should be going back to Shreveport. I'll be ready at eleven thirty tomorrow.'

After Alcide left, I got my library book, Carolyn Haines's latest, and tried to forget my worries. But for once, a book just couldn't do the trick. I tried a hot soak in the bathtub, and I shaved my legs until they were perfectly smooth. I painted my toenails and fingernails a deep pink and then I plucked my eyebrows. Finally, I felt relaxed, and when I crawled into my bed I had achieved peace through pampering. Sleep came upon me in such a rush that I didn't finish my prayers.

Chapter 6

You have to figure out what to wear to a funeral, just like any other social occasion, even if it seems your clothes should be the last thing on your mind. I had liked and admired Colonel Flood during our brief acquaintance, so I wanted to look appropriate at his burial service, especially after Alcide's comments.

I just couldn't find anything in my closet that seemed right. About eight the next morning, I phoned Tara, who told me where her emergency key was. 'Get whatever you need out of my closet,' Tara said. 'Just be sure you don't go into any other rooms, okay? Go straight from the back door to my room and back out again.'

'That's what I'd be doing anyway,' I said, trying not to sound offended. Did Tara think I'd rummage around her house just to pry?

'Of course you would, but I just feel responsible.'

Suddenly, I understood that Tara was telling me that there was a vampire sleeping in her house. Maybe it was the bodyguard Mickey, maybe Franklin Mott. After Eric's warning, I wanted to stay far away from Mickey. Only the very oldest vampires could rise before dark, but coming across a sleeping vampire would give me a nasty start in and of itself.

'Okay, I get you,' I said hastily. The idea of being alone with Mickey made me shiver, and not with happy anticipation. 'Straight in, straight out.' Since I didn't have any time to waste, I jumped in my car and drove into town to Tara's little house. It was a modest place in a modest part of town, but Tara's owning her own home was a miracle, when I recalled the place where she'd grown up.

Some people should never breed; if their children have the misfortune to be born, those children should be taken away immediately. That's not allowed in our country, or any country that I know of, and I'm sure in my brainier moments that's a good thing. But the Thorntons, both alcoholics, had been vicious people who should have died years earlier than they did. (I forget my religion when I think of them.) I remember Myrna Thornton tearing my grandmother's house up looking for Tara, ignoring my grandmother's protests, until Gran had to call the sheriff's department to come drag Myrna out. Tara had run out our back door to hide in the woods behind our house when she had seen the set of her mother's shoulders as Mrs Thornton staggered to our door, thank God. Tara and I had been thirteen at the time.

I can still see the look on my grandmother's face while she talked to the deputy who'd just put Myrna Thornton in the back of the patrol car, handcuffed and screaming.

'Too bad I can't drop her off in the bayou on the way back to town,' the deputy had said. I couldn't recall his name, but his words had impressed me. It had taken me a minute to be sure what he meant, but once I was, I realized that other people knew what Tara and her siblings were going through. These other people were all-powerful adults. If they knew, why didn't they solve the problem?

I sort of understood now that it hadn't been so simple; but I still thought the Thornton kids could have been spared a few years of their misery.

At least Tara had this neat little house with all-new appliances, and a closet full of clothes, and a rich boyfriend. I had an uneasy feeling that I didn't know everything that was happening in Tara's life, but on the surface of it, she was still way ahead of the predictions.

As she'd directed, I went through the spanky-clean kitchen, turned right, and crossed a corner of the living room to pass through the doorway to Tara's bedroom. Tara hadn't had a chance to make her bed that morning. I pulled the sheets straight in a flash and made it look nice. (I couldn't help it.) I couldn't decide if that was a favor to her or not, since now she'd know I minded it not being made, but for the life of me I couldn't mess it up again.

I opened her walk-in closet. I spotted exactly what I needed right away. Hanging in the middle of the rear rack was a knit suit. The jacket was black with creamy pink facings on the lapels, meant to be worn over the matching pink shell on the hanger beneath it. The black skirt was pleated. Tara had had it hemmed up; the alteration tag was still on the plastic bag covering the garment. I held the skirt up to me and looked in Tara's full-length mirror. Tara was two or three inches taller than I, so the skirt fell just an inch above my knees, a fine length for a funeral. The sleeves of the jacket were a little long, but that wasn't so obvious. I had some black pumps and a purse, and even some black gloves that I'd tried to save for nice.

Mission accomplished, in record time.

I slid the jacket and shell into the plastic bag with the skirt and walked straight out of the house. I'd been in Tara's place less than ten minutes. In a hurry, because of my ten o'clock appointment, I began getting ready. I French braided my hair and rolled the remaining tail under, securing everything with some antique hairpins my grand-mother had stashed away; they'd been her grandmother's. I had some black hose, fortunately, and a black slip, and the pink of my fingernails at least coordinated with the pink of the jacket and shell. When I heard a knock on the front door at ten, I was ready except for my shoes. I stepped into my pumps on the way to the door.

Jack Leeds looked openly astonished at my transformation, while Lily's eyebrows twitched.

'Please come in,' I said. 'I'm dressed for a funeral.'

'I hope you're not burying a friend,' Jack Leeds said. His com-panion's face might have been sculpted from marble. Had the woman never heard of a tanning bed?

'Not a close one. Won't you sit down? Can I get you anything? Coffee?'

'No, thank you,' he said, his smile transforming his face.

The detectives sat on the couch while I perched on the edge of the La-Z-Boy. Somehow, my unaccustomed finery made me feel braver.

'About the evening Ms Pelt vanished,' Leeds began. 'You saw her in Shreveport?'

'Yes, I was invited to the same party she was. At Pam's place.' All of us who'd lived through the Witch War – Pam, Eric, Clancy, the three Wiccans, and the Weres who had survived – had agreed on our story: Instead of telling the police that Debbie had left from the dilapidated and abandoned store where the witches had established their hideout, we'd said that we'd stayed the whole evening at Pam's house, and Debbie had left in her car from that address. The neighbors might have testified that everyone had left earlier en masse if the Wiccans hadn't done a little magic to haze their memories of the evening.

'Colonel Flood was there,' I said. 'Actually, it's his funeral I'm going to.'

Lily looked inquiring, which was probably the equivalent of someone else exclaiming, 'Oh, you've got to be kidding!'

'Colonel Flood died in a car accident two days ago,' I told them.

They glanced at each other. 'So, were there quite a few people at this party?' Jack Leeds said. I was sure he had a complete list of the people who'd been sitting in Pam's living room for what had been essentially a war council.

'Oh, yes. Quite a few. I didn't know them all. Shreveport people.' I'd met the three Wiccans that evening for the first time. I'd known the werewolves slightly. The vampires, I'd known.

'But you'd met Debbie Pelt before?'

'Yes.'

'When you were dating Alcide Herveaux?'

Well. They'd certainly done their homework.

'Yes,' I said. 'When I was dating Alcide.' My face was as smooth and impassive as Lily's. I'd had lots of practice in keeping secrets.

'You stayed with him once at the Herveaux apartment in Jackson?'

I started to blurt out that we'd stayed in separate bedrooms, but it really wasn't their business. 'Yes,' I said with a certain edge to my voice.

'You two ran into Ms Pelt one night in Jackson at a club called Josephine's?'

'Yes, she was celebrating her engagement to some guy named Clausen,' I said.

'Did something happen between you that night?'

'Yes.' I wondered whom they'd been talking to; someone had given the detectives a lot of information that they shouldn't have. 'She came over to the table, made a few remarks to us.'

'And you also went to see Alcide at the Herveaux office a few weeks ago? You two were at a crime scene that afternoon?'

They'd done *way* too much homework. 'Yes,' I said.

'And you told the officers at that crime scene that you and Alcide Herveaux were engaged?'

Lies will come back to bite you in the butt. 'I think it was Alcide who said that,' I said, trying to look thoughtful.

'And was his statement true?'

Jack Leeds was thinking that I was the most erratic woman he'd ever met, and he couldn't understand how someone who could get engaged and unengaged so adeptly could be the sensible hardworking waitress he'd seen the day before.

She was thinking my house was very clean. (Strange, huh?) She also thought I was quite capable of killing Debbie Pelt, because she'd found people were capable of the most horrible things. She and I shared more than she'd ever know. I had the same sad knowledge, since I'd heard it directly from their brains.

'Yes,' I said. 'At the time, it was true. We were engaged for, like, ten minutes. Just call me Britney.' I hated lying. I almost always knew when someone else was lying, so I felt I had LIAR printed in big letters on my forehead.

Jack Leeds's mouth quirked, but my reference to the pop singer's fifty-five-hour marriage didn't make a dent in Lily Bard Leeds.

'Ms Pelt object to your seeing Alcide?'

'Oh, yes.' I was glad I'd had years of practice of hiding my feelings. 'But Alcide didn't want to marry her.'

'Was she angry with you?'

'Yes,' I said, since undoubtedly they knew the truth of that. 'Yes, you could say that. She called me some names. You've probably heard that Debbie didn't believe in hiding her emotions.'

'So when did you last see her?'

'I last saw her . . .' *(with half her head gone, sprawled on my kitchen floor, her legs tangled up in the legs of a chair)* 'Let me think. . . . As she left the party that night. She walked off into the dark by herself.' Not from Pam's, but from another location altogether; one full of dead bodies, with blood splashed on the walls. 'I just assumed she was starting back to Jackson.' I shrugged.

'She didn't come by Bon Temps? It's right off the interstate on her return route.'

'I can't imagine why she would. She didn't knock on my door.' She'd broken in.

'You didn't see her after the party?'

'I have not seen her since that night.' Now, *that* was the absolute truth.

'You've seen Mr Herveaux?'

'Yes, I have.'

'Are you engaged now?'

I smiled. 'Not that I know of,' I said.

I wasn't surprised when the woman asked if she could use my bathroom. I'd let down my guard to find out how suspicious the detectives were, so I knew she wanted to have a more extensive look at my house. I showed her to the bathroom in the hall, not the one in my bedroom; not that she'd find anything suspicious in either of them.

'What about her car?' Jack Leeds asked me suddenly. I'd been trying to steal a glimpse of the clock on the mantel over the fireplace, because I wanted to be sure the duo were gone before Alcide picked me up for the funeral.

'Hmm?' I'd lost track of the conversation.

'Debbie Pelt's car.'

'What about it?'

'Do you have any idea where it is?'

'Not an idea in the world,' I said with complete honesty.

As Lily came back into the living room, he asked, 'Ms Stackhouse, just out of curiosity, what do you think happened to Debbie Pelt?'

I thought, *I think she got what was coming to her.* I was a little shocked at myself. Sometimes I'm not a very nice person, and I don't seem to be getting any nicer. 'I don't know, Mr Leeds,' I said. 'I guess I have to tell you that except for her family's worry, I don't really care. We didn't like each other. She burned a hole in my shawl, she called me a whore, and she was awful to Alcide; though since he's a grown-up, that's his problem. She liked to jerk people around. She liked to make them dance to her tune.' Jack Leeds was looking a little dazed at this flow of information. 'So,' I concluded, 'that's the way I feel.'

'Thanks for your honesty,' he said, while his wife fixed me with her pale blue eyes. If I'd had any doubt, I understood clearly now that she was the more formidable of the two. Considering the depth of the investigation Jack Leeds had performed, that was saying something.

'Your collar is crooked,' she said quietly. 'Let me fix it.' I held still while her deft fingers reached behind me and twitched the jacket until the collar lay down correctly.

They left after that. After I watched their car go down the driveway, I took my jacket off and examined it very carefully. Though I hadn't picked up any such intention from her brain, maybe she'd put a bug on me? The Leeds might be more suspicious than they'd sounded. No, I discovered: she really was the neat freak she'd seemed, and she really had been unable to withstand my turned-up collar. As long as I was being suspicious, I inspected the hall bathroom. I hadn't been in it since the last time I'd cleaned it a week ago, so it looked quite straight and as fresh and as sparkly as a very old bathroom in a very old house can look. The sink was damp, and the towel had been used and refolded, but that was all. Nothing extra was there, and nothing was missing, and if the detective had opened the bathroom cabinet to check its contents, I just didn't care.

My heel caught on a hole where the flooring had worn through. For about the hundredth time, I wondered if I could teach myself how to lay linoleum, because the floor could sure use a new layer. I also wondered how I could conceal the fact that I'd killed a woman in one minute, and worry about the cracked linoleum in the bathroom the next.

'She was bad,' I said out loud. 'She was mean and bad, and she wanted me to die for no very good reason at all.'

That was how I could do it. I'd been living in a shell of guilt, but it had just cracked and fallen apart. I was tired of being all angst-y over someone who would have killed me in a New York minute, someone who'd tried her best to cause my death. I would never have lain in wait to ambush Debbie, but I hadn't been prepared to let her kill me just because it suited her to have me dead.

To hell with the whole subject. They'd find her, or they wouldn't. No point in worrying about it either way.

Suddenly, I felt a lot better.

I heard a vehicle coming through the woods. Alcide was right on time. I expected to see his Dodge Ram, but to my surprise he was in a dark blue Lincoln. His hair was as smooth as it could be, which wasn't very, and he was wearing a sober charcoal gray suit and a burgundy tie. I gaped at him through the window as he came up the stepping-stones to the front porch. He looked good enough to eat, and I tried not to *giggle* like an idiot at the mental image.

When I opened the door, he seemed equally stunned. 'You look wonderful,' he said after a long stare.

'You, too,' I said, feeling almost shy.

'I guess we need to get going.'

'Sure, if we want to be there on time.'

'We need to be there ten minutes early,' he said.

'Why that, exactly?' I picked up my black clutch purse, glanced in the mirror to make sure my lipstick was still fresh, and locked the front door behind me. Fortunately, the day was just warm enough for me to leave my coat at home. I didn't want to cover up my outfit.

'This is a Were funeral,' he said in a tone of significance.

'That's different from a regular funeral how?'

'It's a packmaster's funeral, and that makes it more . . . formal.'

Okay, he'd told me that the day before. 'How do you keep regular people from realizing?'

'You'll see.'

I felt misgivings about the whole thing. 'Are you sure I should be going to this?'

'He made you a friend of the pack.'

I remembered that, though at the time I hadn't realized it was a title, the way Alcide made it sound now: Friend of the Pack.

I had an uneasy feeling that there was a lot more to know about Colonel Flood's funeral ceremony. Usually I had more information than I could handle about any given subject, since I could read minds; but there weren't any Weres in Bon Temps, and the other shifters weren't organized like the wolves were. Though Alcide's mind was hard to read, I could tell he was preoccupied with what was going to happen in the church, and I could tell he was worried about a Were named Patrick.

The service was being held at Grace Episcopal, a church in an older, affluent suburb of Shreveport. The church edifice was very traditional, built of gray stone, and topped with a steeple. There wasn't an Episcopal church in Bon Temps, but I knew that the services were similar to those of the Catholic church. Alcide had told me that his father was attending the funeral, too, and that we'd come over from Bon Temps in his father's car. 'My truck didn't look dignified enough for the day, my father thought,' Alcide said. I could tell that his father was foremost in Alcide's thoughts.

'Then how's your dad getting here?' I asked.

'His other car,' Alcide said absently, as if he weren't really listening to what I was saying. I was a little shocked at the idea of one man owning two cars: In my experience, men might have a family car and a pickup, or a pickup and a four-wheeler. My little shocks for the day were just beginning. By the time we had reached I-20 and turned west, Alcide's mood had filled up the car. I wasn't sure what it was, but it involved silence.

'Sookie,' Alcide said abruptly, his hands tightening on the wheel until his knuckles were white.

'Yes?' The fact that bad stuff was coming into the conversation might as well have been written in blinking letters above Alcide's head. Mr Inner Conflict.

'I need to talk to you about something.'

'What? Is there something suspicious about Colonel Flood's death?' *I should have wondered!* I chided myself. But the other shifters had been shot. A traffic accident was such a contrast.

'No,' Alcide said, looking surprised. 'As far as I know, the accident was just an accident. The other guy ran a red light.'

I settled back into the leather seat. 'So what's the deal?'

'Is there anything you want to tell me?'

I froze. 'Tell you? About what?'

'About that night. The night of the Witch War.'

Years of controlling my face came to my rescue. 'Not a thing,' I said calmly enough, though I may have been clenching my hands as I said it.

Alcide said nothing more. He parked the car and came around to help me out, which was unnecessary but nice. I'd decided I wouldn't need to take my purse inside, so I stuck it under the seat and Alcide locked the car. We started toward the front of the church. Alcide took my hand, somewhat to my surprise. I might be a friend of the pack, but I was apparently supposed to be friendlier with one member of the pack than the others.

'There's Dad,' Alcide said as we approached a knot of mourners. Alcide's father was a little shorter than Alcide, but he was a husky man like his son. Jackson Herveaux had iron-gray hair instead of black, and a bolder nose. He had the same olive skin as Alcide. Jackson looked all the darker because he was standing by a pale, delicate woman with gleaming white hair.

'Father,' Alcide said formally, 'this is Sookie Stackhouse.'

'A pleasure to meet you, Sookie,' Jackson Herveaux said. 'This is Christine Larrabee.' Christine, who might have been anything from fifty-seven to sixty-seven, looked like a painting done in pastels. Her eyes were a washed-out blue, her smooth skin was magnolia pale with the faintest tinge of pink, her white hair was immaculately groomed. She was wearing a light blue suit, which I personally wouldn't have worn until the winter was completely over, but she looked great in it, for sure.

'Nice to meet you,' I said, wondering if I should curtsy. I'd shaken hands with Alcide's father, but Christine didn't extend hers. She gave me a nod and a sweet smile. Probably didn't want to bruise me with her diamond rings, I decided after a squint at her fingers. Of course, they matched her earrings. I was outclassed, no doubt about it. *Eff it*, I thought. It seemed to be my day for shrugging off unpleasant things.

'Such a sad occasion,' Christine said.

If she wanted to do polite chitchat, I was up to it. 'Yes, Colonel Flood was a wonderful man,' I said.

'Oh, you knew him, dear?'

'Yes,' I said. As a matter of fact, I'd seen him naked, but in decidedly unerotic circumstances.

My brief answer didn't leave her much of anywhere to go. I saw genuine amusement lurking in her pale eyes. Alcide and his dad were exchanging low-voiced comments, which we were obviously supposed to be ignoring. 'You and I are strictly decorations today,' Christine said.

'Then you know more than I do.'

'I expect so. You're not one of the two-natured?'

'No.' Christine was, of course. She was a full-blooded Were, like Jackson and Alcide. I couldn't picture this elegant woman changing into a wolf, especially with the down-and-dirty reputation the Weres had in the shifter community, but the impressions I got from her mind were unmistakable.

'The funeral of the packmaster marks the opening of the campaign to replace him,' Christine said. Since that was more solid information than I'd gotten in two hours from Alcide, immediately I felt kindly disposed toward the older woman.

'You must be something extraordinary, for Alcide to choose you as his companion today,' Christine continued.

'I don't know about extraordinary. In the literal sense, I guess I am. I have extras that aren't ordinary.'

'Witch?' Christine guessed. 'Fairy? Part goblin?'

Gosh. I shook my head. 'None of the above. So what's going to happen in there?'

'There are more roped-off pews than usual. The whole pack will sit at the front of the church, the mated ones with their mates, of course, and their children. The candidates for packmaster will come in last.'

'How are they chosen?'

'They announce themselves,' she said. 'But they'll be put to the test, and then the membership votes.'

'Why is Alcide's dad bringing you, or is that a real personal question?'

'I'm the widow of the packmaster prior to Colonel Flood,' Christine

Larrabee said quietly. 'That gives me a certain influence.'

I nodded. 'Is the packmaster always a man?'

'No. But since strength is part of the test, males usually win.'

'How many candidates are there?'

'Two. Jackson, of course, and Patrick Furnan.' She inclined her patrician head slightly to her right, and I gave a closer look at the couple that had been on the periphery of my attention.

Patrick Furnan was in his mid-forties, somewhere between Alcide and his father. He was a thick-bodied man with a light brown crew cut and a very short beard shaved into a fancy shape. His suit was brown, too, and he'd had trouble buttoning the jacket. His companion was a pretty woman who believed in a lot of lipstick and jewelry. She had short brown hair, too, but it was highlighted with blond streaks and elaborately styled. Her heels were at least three inches high. I eyed the shoes with awe. I would break my neck if I tried to walk in them. But this woman maintained a smile and offered a good word to everyone who approached. Patrick Furnan was colder. His narrow eyes measured and assessed every Were in the gathering crowd.

'Tammy Faye, there, is his wife?' I asked Christine in a discreetly low tone.

Christine made a sound that I would have called snigger if it had issued from someone less patrician. 'She does wear a lot of makeup,' Christine said. 'Her name is Libby, actually. Yes, she's his wife and a full-blooded Were, and they have two children. So he's added to the pack.'

Only the oldest child would become a Were at puberty.

'What does he do for a living?' I asked.

'He owns a Harley-Davidson dealership,' Christine said.

'That's a natural.' Weres tended to like motorcycles a lot.

Christine smiled, probably as close as she came to laughing out loud.

'Who's the front-runner?' I'd been dumped into the middle of a game, and I needed to learn the rules. Later, I was going to let Alcide have it right between the eyes; but right now, I was going to get through the funeral, since that's what I'd come for.

'Hard to say,' Christine murmured. 'I wouldn't have thrown in with either one, given a choice, but Jackson called on our old friendship, and I had to come down on his side.'

'That's not nice.'

'No, but it's practical,' she said, amused. 'He needs all the support he can get. Did Alcide ask you to endorse his father?'

'No. I'd be completely ignorant of the situation if you hadn't been kind enough to fill me in.' I gave her a nod of thanks.

'Since you're not a Were – excuse me, honey, but I'm just trying to figure this out – what can you do for Alcide, I wonder? Why'd he drag you into this?'

'He'll have to tell me that real soon,' I said, and if my voice was cold and ominous, I just didn't care.

'His last girlfriend disappeared,' Christine said thoughtfully. 'They were pretty on-again, off-again, Jackson tells me. If his enemies had something to do with it, you might watch your step.'

'I don't think I'm in danger,' I said.

'Oh?'

But I'd said enough.

'Hmmmm,' Christine said after a long, thoughtful look at my face. 'Well, she was too much of a diva for someone who isn't even a Were.' Christine's voice expressed the contempt the Weres feel for the other shifters. ('Why bother to change, if you can't change into a wolf?' I'd heard a Were say once.)

My attention was caught by the dull gleam of a shaved head, and I stepped a bit to my left to have a better view. I'd never seen this man before. I would certainly have remembered him; he was very tall, taller than Alcide or even Eric, I thought. He had big shoulders and arms roped with muscle. His head and arms were the brown of a Caucasian with a real tan. I could tell, because he was wearing a sleeveless black silk tee tucked into black pants and shiny dress shoes. It was a nippy day at the end of January, but the cold didn't seem to affect him at all. There was a definite space between him and the people around him.

As I looked at him, wondering, he turned and looked at me, as if he could feel my attention. He had a proud nose, and his face was as smooth as his shaved head. At this distance, his eyes looked black.

'Who is that?' I asked Christine, my voice a thread in the wind that had sprung up, tossing the leaves of the holly bushes planted around the church.

Christine darted a look at the man, and she must have known whom I meant, but she didn't answer.

Regular people had gradually been filtering through the Weres, going up the steps and into the church. Now two men in black suits appeared at the doors. They crossed their hands in front of them, and the one on the right nodded at Jackson Herveaux and Patrick Furnan.

The two men, with their female companions, came to stand facing each other at the bottom of the steps. The assembled Weres passed between them to enter the church. Some nodded at one, some at the other, some at both. Fence-sitters. Even after their ranks had been reduced by the recent war with the witches, I counted twenty-five full-blooded adult Weres in Shreveport, a very large pack for such a small city. Its size was attributable to the Air Force base, I figured.

Everyone who walked between the two candidates was a full Were. I saw only two children. Of course, some parents might have left their kids in school rather than bring them to the funeral. But I was pretty sure I was seeing the truth of what Alcide had told me: Infertility and a high infant mortality rate plagued the Weres.

Alcides younger sister, Janice, had married a human. She herself would never change shape, since she was not the firstborn child. Her son's recessive Were traits, Alcide had told me, might show as increased vigor and a great healing ability. Many professional athletes came from couples whose genetic pool contained a percentage of Were blood.

'We go in a second,' Alcide murmured. He was standing beside me, scanning the faces as they went by.

'I'm going to kill you later,' I told him, keeping my face calm for the Weres passing by. 'Why didn't you explain this?'

The tall man walked up the steps, his arms swinging as he walked, his large body moving with purpose and grace. His head swung toward me as he went by, and I met his eyes. They were very dark, but still I couldn't distinguish the color. He smiled at me.

Alcide touched my hand, as if he knew my attention had wandered. He leaned over to whisper in my ear, 'I need your help. I need you to find a chance after the funeral to read Patrick's mind. He's going to do something to sabotage my father.'

'Why didn't you just ask me?' I was confused, and mostly I was hurt.

'I thought you might feel like you owed me anyway!'

'How do you figure that?'

'I know you killed Debbie.'

If he'd slapped me, it couldn't have shocked me more. I have no idea what my face looked like. After the impact of the shock and the reflexive guilt wore off, I said, 'You'd abjured her. What's it to you?'

'Nothing,' he said. 'Nothing. She was already dead to me.' I didn't believe that for a minute. 'But you thought it would be a big deal to me, and you concealed it. I figure you'd guess you owed me.'

If I'd had a gun in my purse, I would've been tempted to pull it out then. 'I don't owe you squat,' I said. 'I think you came to get me in your dad's car because you knew I'd drive away once you said that.'

'No,' he said. We were still keeping our voices down, but I could see from the sideways glances we were getting that our intense colloquy was attracting attention. 'Well, maybe. Please, forget what I said about you owing me. The fact is, my dad's in trouble and I'd do just about anything to help him out. And you can help.'

'Next time you need help, just *ask*. Don't trying blackmailing me into it or maneuvering me into it. I like to help people. But I hate to be pushed and tricked.' He'd lowered his eyes, so I grabbed his chin and made him look into mine. '*I hate it.*'

I glanced up at the top of the steps to gauge how much interest our quarrel was attracting. The tall man had reappeared. He was looking down at us without perceptible expression. But I knew we had his attention.

Alcide glanced up, too. His face reddened. 'We need to go in now. Will you go with me?'

'What is the meaning of me going in with you?'

'It means you're on my father's side in his bid for the pack.'

'What does that oblige me to do?'

'Nothing.'

'Then why is it important for me to do it?'

'Though choosing a packmaster is pack business, it may influence those who know how much you helped us during the Witch War.'

Witch Skirmish would have been more accurate, because though it had certainly been them vs. us, the total number of people involved had been fairly small – say, forty or fifty. But in the history of the Shreveport pack, it was an epic episode, I gathered.

I glared down at my black pumps. I struggled with my warring instincts. They seemed about equally strong. One said, 'You're at a funeral. Don't make a scene. Alcide has been good to you, and it wouldn't hurt you to do this for him.' The other said, 'Alcide helped you in Jackson because he was trying to get his dad out of trouble with the vampires. Now, again, he's willing to involve you in something dangerous to help his dad out.' The first voice chipped in, 'He knew Debbie was bad. He tried to pull away from her, and then he abjured her.' The second said, 'Why'd he love a bitch like Debbie in the first place? Why'd he even consider sticking with her when he had clear evidence she was evil? No one else has suggested she had spellcasting power. This 'spellcasting' thing is a cheap excuse.' I felt like Linda Blair in the *The Exorcist*, with her head whirling around on her neck.

Voice number one won out. I put my hand on Alcide's crooked elbow and we went up the stairs and into the church.

The pews were full of regular people. The front three rows on both sides had been saved for the pack. But the tall man, who would stand out anywhere, sat in the back row. I caught a glimpse of his big shoulders before I had to pay strict attention to the pack ceremony. The two Furnan children, cute as the dickens, went solemnly down to the front pew on the right of the church. Then Alcide and I entered, preceding the two candidates for packmaster. This seating ceremony was oddly like a wedding, with Alcide and me being the best man and maid of honor. Jackson and Christine and Patrick and Libby Furnan would enter like the parents of the bride and groom.

What the civilians made of this I don't know.

I knew they were all staring, but I'm used to that. If being a barmaid will get you used to anything, it's being looked over. I was dressed appropriately and I looked as good as I could make myself look, and

Alcide had done the same, so let them stare. Alcide and I sat on the front row on the left side of the church, and moved in. I saw Patrick Furnan and his wife, Libby, enter the pew across the aisle. Then I looked back to see Jackson and Christine coming in slowly, looking fittingly grave. There was a slight flutter of heads and hands, a tiny buzz of whispers, and then Christine sidled into the pew, Jackson beside her.

The coffin, draped with an elaborately embroidered cloth, was wheeled up the aisle as we all stood, and then the somber service began.

After going through the litany, which Alcide showed me in the Prayer Book, the priest asked if anyone would like to say a few words about Colonel Flood. One of his Air Force friends went first and spoke of the colonel's devotion to duty and his sense of pride in his command. One of his fellow church members took the next turn, praising the colonel's generosity and applauding the time he'd spent balancing the church's books.

Patrick Furnan left his pew and strode to the lectern. He didn't do a good stride; he was too stout for that. But his speech was certainly a change from the elegies the two previous men had given. 'John Flood was a remarkable man and a great leader,' Furnan began. He was a much better speaker than I'd expected. Though I didn't know who'd written his remarks, it was someone educated. 'In the fraternal order we shared, he was always the one who told us the direction we should take, the goal we should achieve. As he grew older, he remarked often that this was a job for the young.'

A right turn from eulogy to campaign speech. I wasn't the only one who'd noticed this; all around me there were little movements, whispered comments.

Though taken aback by the reaction he'd aroused, Patrick Furnan plowed ahead. 'I told John that he was the finest man for the job we'd ever had, and I still believe that. No matter who follows in his footsteps, John Flood will never be forgotten or replaced. The next leader can only hope to work as hard as John. I'll always be proud that John put his trust in me more than once, that he even called me his right hand.' With those sentences, the Harley dealer underscored his bid to take

Colonel's Flood's job as packmaster (or, as I referred to it internally, Leader of the Pack).

Alcide, to my right, was rigid with anger. If he hadn't been sitting in the front row of a funeral, he would have loved to address a few remarks to me on the subject of Patrick Furnan. On the other side of Alcide, I could just barely see Christine, whose face looked carved out of ivory. She was suppressing quite a few things herself.

Alcide's dad waited a moment to begin his trip to the lectern. Clearly, he wanted us to cleanse our mental palate before he gave his address.

Jackson Herveaux, wealthy surveyor and werewolf, gave us the chance to examine his maturely handsome face. He began, 'We will not soon see the likes of John Flood. A man whose wisdom had been tempered and tested by the years . . .' Oh, ouch. This wasn't going to be pointed or anything, no sirree.

I tuned out for the rest of the service to think my own thoughts. I had plenty of food for thought. We stood as John Flood, Air Force colonel and packmaster, exited this church for the last time. I remained silent during the ride to the cemetery, stood by Alcide's side during the graveside service, and got back in the car when it was over and all the post-funeral handshaking was done.

I looked for the tall man, but he wasn't at the cemetery.

On the drive back to Bon Temps, Alcide obviously wanted to keep our silence nice and clean, but it was time to answer some questions.

'How did you know?' I asked.

He didn't even try to pretend to misunderstand what I was talking about. 'When I came to your house yesterday, I could smell a very, very faint trace of her at your front door,' he said. 'It took me a while to think it through.'

I'd never considered the possibility.

'I don't think I would've picked up on it if I hadn't known her so well,' he offered. 'I certainly didn't pick up a whiff anywhere else in the house.'

So all my scrubbing had been to some avail. I was just lucky Jack and Lily Leeds weren't two-natured. 'Do you want to know what happened?'

'I don't think so,' he said after an appreciable pause. 'Knowing Debbie, I'm guessing you only did what you had to do. After all, it was her scent at your house. She had no business there.'

This was far from a ringing endorsement.

'And Eric was still at your house then, wasn't he? Maybe it was Eric?' Alcide sounded almost hopeful.

'No,' I said.

'Maybe I do want the whole story.'

'Maybe I've changed my mind about telling it to you. You either believe in me, or you don't. Either you think I'm the kind of person who'd kill a woman for no good reason, or you know I'm not.' Truly, I was hurt more than I thought I'd be. I was very careful not to slip into Alcide's head, because I was afraid I might pick up on something that would have been even more painful.

Alcide tried several times to open another conversation, but the drive couldn't end soon enough for me. When he pulled into the clearing and I knew I was yards away from being in my own house, the relief was overwhelming. I couldn't scramble out of that fancy car fast enough.

But Alcide was right behind me.

'I don't care,' he said in a voice that was almost a growl.

'What?' I'd gotten to my front door, and the key was in the lock.

'I don't care.'

'I don't believe that for one minute.'

'What?'

'You're harder to read than a plain human, Alcide, but I can see the pockets of reservation in your mind. Since you wanted me to help you out with your dad, I'll tell you: Patrick Whatsisname plans to bring up your dad's gambling problems to show he's unsuitable as packleader.' Nothing more underhanded and supernatural than the truth. 'I'd read his mind before you asked me to. I don't want to see you for a long, long, long time.'

'What?' Alcide said again. He looked like I'd hit him in the head with an iron.

'Seeing you … listening to your head … makes me feel bad.' Of course, there were several different reasons they did, but I didn't want to enumerate them. 'So, thanks for the ride to the funeral.' (I may have sounded a bit sarcastic.) 'I appreciate your thinking of me.' (Even a higher probability of sarcasm here.) I entered the house, shut the door on his startled face, and locked it just to be on the safe side. I marched across the living room so he could hear my steps, but then I stopped in the hall and waited to listen while he got back in the Lincoln. I listened to the big car rocket down the driveway, probably putting ruts in my beautiful gravel.

As I shed Tara's suit and bundled it up to drop at the dry cleaner's, I confess I was mopey. They say when one door shuts, another one opens. But they haven't been living at my house.

Most of the doors I open seem to have something scary crouched behind them, anyway.

Chapter 7

Sam was in the bar that night, seated at a corner table like a visiting king, his leg propped up on another chair cushioned with pillows. He was keeping one eye on Charles, one eye on the clientele's reaction to a vampire bartender.

People would stop by, drop down in the chair across from him, visit for a few minutes, and then vacate the chair. I knew Sam was in pain. I can always read the preoccupation of people who are hurting. But he was glad to be seeing other people, glad to be back in the bar, pleased with Charles's work.

All this I could tell, and yet when it came to the question of who had shot him, I didn't have a clue. Someone was gunning for the two-natured, someone who'd killed quite a few and wounded even more. Discovering the identity of the shooter was imperative. The police didn't suspect Jason, but his own people did. If Calvin Norris's people decided to take matters into their own hands, they could easily find a chance to take out Jason. They didn't know there were more victims than those in Bon Temps.

I probed into minds, I tried to catch people in unguarded moments, I even tried to think of the most promising candidates for the role of assassin so I wouldn't waste time listening to (for example) Liz Baldwin's worries about her oldest granddaughter.

I assumed the shooter was almost certainly a guy. I knew plenty of women who went hunting and plenty more with access to rifles. But weren't snipers always men? The police were baffled by this sniper's selection of targets, because they didn't know the true nature of all the victims. The two-natured were hampered in their search because they were looking only at local suspects.

'Sookie,' Sam said as I passed close to him. 'Kneel down here a minute.'

I sank to one knee right by his chair so he could speak in a low voice.

'Sookie, I hate to ask you again, but the closet in the storeroom isn't working out for Charles.' The cleaning supplies closet in the storeroom was not exactly built to be light tight, but it was inaccessible to daylight, which was good enough. After all, the closet had no windows, and it was inside a room with no windows.

It took me a minute to switch my train of thought to another track. 'You can't tell me he's not able to sleep,' I said incredulously. Vampires could sleep in the daytime under any circumstances. 'And I'm sure you put a lock on the inside of the door, too.'

'Yes, but he has to kind of huddle on the floor, and he says it smells like old mops.'

'Well, we did keep the cleaning stuff in there.'

'What I'm saying is, would it be so bad for him to stay at your place?'

'Why do you really want me to have him at the house?' I asked. 'There's got to be a reason more than a strange vampire's comfort during the day, when he's dead, anyway.'

'Haven't we been friends a long time, Sookie?'

I smelled something big and rotten.

'Yes,' I admitted, standing so that he would have to look up at me. 'And?'

'I hear through the grapevine that the Hotshot community has hired a Were bodyguard for Calvin's hospital room.'

'Yeah, I think that's kind of strange, too.' I acknowledged his unspoken concern. 'So I guess you heard what they suspect.'

Sam nodded. His bright blue eyes caught mine. 'You have to take this seriously, Sookie.'

'What makes you think I don't?'

'You refused Charles.'

'I don't see what telling him he couldn't sleep in my house has to do with worrying about Jason.'

'I think he'd help you protect Jason, if it came to that. I'm down with this leg, or I'd . . . I don't believe it was Jason who shot me.'

A knot of tension within me relaxed when Sam said that. I hadn't realized I'd been worried about what he thought, but I had.

My heart softened a little. 'Oh, all right,' I said with poor grace. 'He can come stay with me.' I stomped off grumpily, still not certain why I'd agreed.

Sam beckoned Charles over, conferred with him briefly. Later in the evening Charles borrowed my keys to stow his bag in the car. After a few minutes, he was back at the bar and signaled he'd returned my keys to my purse. I nodded, maybe a little curtly. I wasn't happy, but if I had to be saddled with a houseguest, at least he was a polite houseguest.

Mickey and Tara came into Merlotte's that night. As before, the dark intensity of the vampire made everyone in the bar a little excited, a little louder. Tara's eyes followed me with a kind of sad passivity. I was hoping to catch her alone, but I didn't see her leave the table for any reason. I found that was another cause for alarm. When she'd come into the bar with Franklin Mott, she'd always taken a minute to give me a hug, chat with me about family and work.

I caught a glimpse of Claudine the fairy across the room, and though I planned to work my way over to have a word with her, I was too preoccupied with Tara's situation. As usual, Claudine was surrounded by admirers.

Finally, I got so anxious that I took the vampire by the fangs and went over to Tara's table. The snakelike Mickey was staring at our flamboyant bartender, and he scarcely flicked a gaze at me as I approached. Tara looked both hopeful and frightened, and I stood by her and laid my hand on her shoulder to get a clearer picture of her head. Tara has done so well for herself I seldom worry over her one weakness: She picks the wrong men. I was remembering when she dated 'Eggs' Benedict, who'd apparently died in a fire the previous fall. Eggs had been a heavy drinker and a weak personality. Franklin Mott had at least treated Tara with respect and had showered her with presents, though the nature of the presents had said, 'I'm a mistress,' rather than 'I'm an honored girlfriend.' But how had it come to pass that she was in Mickey's company – Mickey, whose name made even Eric hesitate?

I felt like I'd been reading a book only to discover that someone had ripped a few pages from the middle.

'Tara,' I said quietly. She looked up at me, her big brown eyes dull and dead: past fear, past shame.

To the outer eye she looked almost normal. She was well groomed and made up, and her clothing was fashionable and attractive. But inside, Tara was in torment. What was wrong with my friend? Why hadn't I noticed before that something was eating her up from the inside out?

I wondered what to do next. Tara and I were just staring at each other, and though she knew what I was seeing inside her, she wasn't responding. 'Wake up,' I said, not even knowing where the words were coming from. 'Wake up, Tara!'

A white hand grabbed my arm and removed my hand from Tara's shoulder forcibly. 'I'm not paying you to touch my date,' Mickey said. He had the coldest eyes I'd ever seen – mud colored, reptilian. 'I'm paying you to bring our drinks.'

'Tara is my friend,' I said. He was still squeezing my arm, and if a vampire squeezes you, you know about it. 'You're doing something to her. Or you're letting someone else hurt her.'

'It's none of your concern.'

'It is my concern,' I said. I knew my eyes were tearing up from the pain, and I had a moment of sheer cowardice. Looking into his face, I knew he could kill me and be out of the bar before anyone there could stop him. He could take Tara with him, like a pet dog or his livestock. Before the fear could get a grip, I said, 'Let go of me.' I made each word clear and distinct, even though I knew he could hear a pin drop in a storm.

'You're shaking like a sick dog,' he said scornfully.

'Let go of me,' I repeated.

'Or you'll do – what?'

'You can't stay awake forever. If it's not me, it'll be someone else.'

Mickey seemed to be reconsidering. I don't think it was my threat, though I meant it from the tips of my toes to the roots of my hair.

He looked down at Tara, and she spoke, as though he'd pulled a string. 'Sookie, don't make such a big deal out of nothing. Mickey is my man now. Don't embarrass me in front of him.'

My hand dropped back to her shoulder and I risked taking my eyes off Mickey to look down at her. She definitely wanted me to back off; she was completely sincere about that. But her thinking about her motivation was curiously murky.

'Okay, Tara. Do you need another drink?' I asked slowly. I was feeling my way through her head, and I was meeting a wall of ice, slippery and nearly opaque.

'No, thank you,' Tara said politely. 'Mickey and I need to be going now.'

That surprised Mickey, I could tell. I felt a little better; Tara was in charge of herself, at least to some extent.

'I'll return your suit. I took it by the cleaner's, already,' I said.

'No hurry.'

'All right. I'll see you later.' Mickey had a firm grip on my friend's arm as the two made their way through the crowd.

I got the empty glasses off the table, swabbed it down, and turned back to the bar. Charles Twining and Sam were on alert. They'd been observing the whole small incident. I shrugged, and they relaxed.

When we closed the bar that night, the new bouncer was waiting at the back door for me when I pulled on my coat and got my keys out of my purse.

I unlocked my car doors and he climbed in.

'Thanks for agreeing to have me in your home,' he said. I made myself say the polite thing back. No point in being rude.

'Do you think Eric will mind my being here?' Charles asked as we drove down the narrow parish road.

'It's not his say-so,' I said curtly. It irked me that he automatically wondered about Eric.

'He doesn't come to see you often?' enquired Charles with unusual persistence.

I didn't answer until we'd parked behind my house. 'Listen,' I said,

'I don't know what you heard, but he's not . . . we're not . . . like that.' Charles looked at my face and wisely said nothing as I unlocked my back door.

'Feel free to explore,' I said after I'd invited him over the threshold. Vampires like to know entrances and exits. 'Then I'll show you your sleeping place.' While the bouncer looked curiously around the humble house where my family had lived for so many years, I hung up my coat and put my purse in my room. I made myself a sandwich after asking Charles if he wanted some blood. I keep some type O in the refrigerator, and he seemed glad to sit down and drink after he'd studied the house. Charles Twining was a peaceful sort of guy to be around, especially for a vampire. He didn't letch after me, and he didn't seem to want anything from me.

I showed him the lift-up floor panel in the guest bedroom closet. I told him how the television remote worked, showed him my little collection of movies, and pointed out the books on the shelves in the guest bedroom and living room.

'Is there anything else you can think of you might need?' I asked. My grandmother brought me up right, though I don't think she ever imagined I'd have to be hostess to a bunch of vampires.

'No, thank you, Miss Sookie,' Charles said politely. His long white fingers tapped his eye patch, an odd habit of his that gave me the cold gruesomes.

'Then, if you'll excuse me, I'll say good night.' I was tired, and it was exhausting work making conversation with a near stranger.

'Of course. Rest easy, Sookie. If I want to roam in the woods . . .?'

'Feel free,' I said immediately. I had an extra key to the back door, and I got it out of the drawer in the kitchen where I kept all the keys. This had been the odds and ends drawer for perhaps eighty years, since the kitchen had been added onto the house. There were at least a hundred keys in it. Some, those that were old when the kitchen was added, were mighty strange looking. I'd labeled the ones from my generation, and I'd put the back door key on a bright pink plastic key ring from my State Farm insurance agent. 'Once you're in for the night – well, for good – shoot the dead bolt, please.'

He nodded and took the key.

It was usually a mistake to feel sympathy for a vampire, but I couldn't help but think there was something sad about Charles. He struck me as lonely, and there's always something pathetic about loneliness. I'd experienced it myself. I would ferociously deny I was pathetic, but when I viewed loneliness in someone else, I could feel the tug of pity.

I scrubbed my face and pulled on some pink nylon pajamas. I was already half-asleep as I brushed my teeth and crawled into the high old bed my grandmother had slept in until she died. My great-grandmother had made the quilt I pulled over me, and my great-aunt Julia had embroidered the pattern on the edges of the bedspread. Though I might actually be alone in the world – with the exception of my brother, Jason – I went to sleep surrounded by my family.

My deepest sleep is around three a.m., and sometime during that period I was awakened by the grip of a hand on my shoulder.

I was shocked into total awareness, like a person being thrown into a cold pool. To fight off the shock that was close to paralyzing me, I swung my fist. It was caught in a chilly grip.

'No, no, no, ssshhh' came a piercing whisper out of the darkness. English accent. Charles. 'Someone's creeping around outside your house, Sookie.'

My breath was as wheezy as an accordion. I wondered if I was going to have a heart attack. I put a hand over my heart, as if I could hold it in when it seemed determined to pound its way out of my chest.

'Lie down!' he said right into my ear, and then I felt him crouch beside my bed in the shadows. I lay down and closed my eyes almost all the way. The headboard of the bed was situated between the two windows in the room, so whoever was creeping around my house couldn't really get a good look at my face. I made sure I was lying still and as relaxed as I could get. I tried to think, but I was just too scared. If the creeper was a vampire, he or she couldn't come in – unless it was Eric. Had I rescinded Eric's invitation to enter? I couldn't remember. *That's the kind of thing I need to keep track of* I babbled to myself.

'He's passed on,' Charles said in a voice so faint it was almost the ghost of a voice.

'What is it?' I asked in a voice I hoped was nearly as soundless.

'It's too dark outside to tell.' If a vampire couldn't see what was out there, it must be really dark. 'I'll slip outside and find out.'

'No,' I said urgently, but it was too late.

Jesus Christ, shepherd of Judea! What if the prowler was Mickey? He'd kill Charles – I just knew it.

'Sookie!' The last thing I expected – though frankly, I was way beyond consciously expecting anything – was for Charles to call to me. 'Come out here, if you please!'

I slid my feet into my pink fuzzy slippers and hurried down the hall to the back door; that was where the voice had been coming from, I thought.

'I'm turning on the outside light,' I yelled. Didn't want anyone to be blinded by the sudden electricity. 'You sure it's safe out there?'

'Yes,' said two voices almost simultaneously.

I flipped the switch with my eyes shut. After a second, I opened them and stepped to the door of the screened-in back porch, in my pink jammies and slippers. I crossed my arms over my chest. Though it wasn't cold tonight, it was cool.

I absorbed the scene in front of me. 'Okay,' I said slowly. Charles was in the graveled area where I parked, and he had an elbow around the neck of Bill Compton, my neighbor. Bill is a vampire, has been since right after the Civil War. We have a history. It's probably just a pebble of a history in Bill's long life, but in mine, it's a boulder.

'Sookie,' Bill said between clenched teeth. 'I don't want to cause this foreigner harm. Tell him to get his hands off me.'

I mulled that over at an accelerated rate. 'Charles, I think you can let him go,' I said, and as fast as I could snap my fingers, Charles was standing beside me.

'You know this man?' Charles's voice was steely.

Just as coldly, Bill said, 'She does know me, intimately.'

Oh, *gack*.

'Now, is that polite?' I may have had a little cold steel in my own voice. 'I don't go around telling everyone the details of our former relationship. I would expect the same of any gentleman.'

To my gratification, Charles glared at Bill, raising one eyebrow in a very superior and irritating way.

'So this one is sharing your bed now?' Bill jerked his head toward the smaller vampire.

If he'd said anything else, I could've held on to my temper. I don't lose it a lot, but when I do, it's well and truly lost. 'Is that any of your business?' I asked, biting off each word. 'If I sleep with a hundred men, or a hundred sheep, it's not any of your business! Why are you creeping around my house in the middle of the night? You scared me halfway to death.'

Bill didn't look remotely repentant. 'I'm sorry you wakened and were frightened,' he said insincerely. 'I was checking on your safety.'

'You were roaming around the woods and smelled another vampire,' I said. He'd always had an extremely acute sense of smell. 'So you came over here to see who it was.'

'I wanted to be sure you weren't being attacked,' Bill said. 'I thought I caught a sniff of human, too. Did you have a human visitor today?'

I didn't believe for a minute Bill was only concerned with my safety, but I didn't want to believe jealousy brought him to my window, or some kind of prurient curiosity. I just breathed in and out for a minute, calming down and considering.

'Charles is not attacking me,' I said, proud I was speaking so levelly.

Bill sneered. 'Charles,' he repeated in tones of great scorn.

'Charles Twining,' said my companion, bowing – if you could call a slight inclination of his curly brown head a bow.

'Where did you come up with this one?' Bill's voice had regained its calm.

'Actually, he works for Eric, like you do.'

'Eric's provided you with a bodyguard? You need a bodyguard?'

'Listen, bozo,' I said through clenched jaws, 'my life goes on while you're gone. So does the town. People are getting shot around here, among them Sam. We needed a substitute bartender, and Charles was volunteered to help us out.' That may not have been entirely accurate, but I was not in the accuracy business at the moment. I was in the Make My Point business.

At least Bill was appropriately taken aback by the information.

'Sam. Who else?'

I was shivering, since it wasn't nylon pajama weather. But I didn't want Bill in the house. 'Calvin Norris and Heather Kinman.'

'Shot dead?'

'Heather was. Calvin was pretty badly wounded.'

'Have the police arrested anyone?'

'No.'

'Do you know who did it?'

'No.'

'You're worried about your brother.'

'Yes.'

'He turned at the full moon.'

'Yes.'

Bill looked at me with what might have been pity. 'I'm sorry, Sookie,' he said, and he meant it.

'No point telling me about it,' I snapped. 'Tell Jason – it's him who turns fuzzy.'

Bill's face went cold and stiff. 'Excuse my intrusion,' he said. 'I'll go.' He melted into the woods.

I don't know how Charles reacted to the episode, because I turned and stalked back into the house, turning off the outside light as I went. I threw myself back in bed and lay there, fuming and fussing silently. I pulled the covers up over my head so the vampire would take the hint that I didn't want to discuss the incident. He moved so quietly, I couldn't be sure where he was in the house; I think he paused in the doorway for a second, and then moved on.

I lay awake for at least forty-five minutes, and then I found myself settling back into sleep.

Then someone shook me by the shoulder. I smelled sweet perfume, and I smelled something else, something awful. I was terribly groggy.

'Sookie, your house is on fire,' a voice said.

'Couldn't be,' I said. 'I didn't leave anything on.'

'You have to get out now,' the voice insisted. A persistent shriek reminded me of fire drills at the elementary school.

'Okay,' I said, my head thick with sleep and (I saw when I opened my eyes) smoke. The shriek in the background, I slowly realized, was my smoke detector. Thick gray plumes were drifting through my yellow and white bedroom like evil genies. I wasn't moving fast enough for Claudine, who yanked me out of bed and carried me out the front door. A woman had never lifted me, but, of course, Claudine was no ordinary woman. She set me on my feet in the chilly grass of the front yard. The cold feel of it suddenly woke me up. This was not a nightmare.

'My house caught on fire?' I was still struggling to be alert.

'The vampire says it was that human, there,' she said, pointing to the left of the house. But for a long minute my eyes were fixed on the terrible sight of flames, and the red glow of fire lighting the night. The back porch and part of the kitchen were blazing.

I made myself look at a huddled form on the ground, close to a forsythia in bud. Charles was kneeling by it. 'Have you called the fire department?' I asked them both as I picked my way around the house in my bare feet to have a look at the recumbent figure. I peered at the dead man's slack face in the poor light. He was white, clean-shaven, and probably in his thirties. Though conditions were hardly ideal, I didn't recognize him.

'Oh, no, I didn't think of it.' Charles looked up from the body. He came from a time before fire departments.

'And I forgot my cell phone,' said Claudine, who was thoroughly modern.

'Then I have to go back in and do it, if the phones still work,' I said, turning on my heel. Charles rose to his inconsiderable height and stared at me.

'You will not go back in there.' This was definitely an order from Claudine. 'New man, you run fast enough to do that.'

'Fire,' Charles said, 'is very quickly fatal to vampires.'

It was true; they went up like a torch once they caught. Selfishly, for a second I almost insisted; I wanted my coat and my slippers and my purse.

'Go call from Bill's phone,' I said, pointing in the right direction, and off he took like a jackrabbit. The minute he was out of sight and before Claudine could stop me, I dashed back in the front door and made my way to my room. The smoke was much thicker, and I could see the flames a few feet down the hall in the kitchen. As soon as I saw the flames I knew I'd made a huge mistake by reentering the house, and it was hard not to panic. My purse was right where I'd left it, and my coat was tossed over the slipper chair in a corner of my room. I couldn't find my slippers, and I knew I couldn't stay. I fumbled in a drawer for a pair of socks, since I knew for sure they were there, and then I ran out of my room, coughing and choking. Acting through sheer instinct, I turned briefly to my left to shut the door to the kitchen, and then whirled to hurry out the front door. I fell over a chair in the living room.

'That was stupid,' said Claudine the fairy, and I shrieked. She grabbed me around the waist and ran out of the house again, with me under her arm like a rolled-up carpet.

The combination of shrieking and coughing tied my respiratory system in knots for a minute or two, during which time Claudine moved me farther away from my house. She sat me down on the grass and put the socks on my feet. Then she helped me stand up and get my arms into the coat. I buttoned it around me gratefully.

This was the second time Claudine had appeared out of nowhere when I was about to get into serious trouble. The first time, I'd fallen asleep at the wheel after a very long day.

'You're making it awfully hard on me,' she said. She still sounded cheerful, but maybe not quite as sweet.

Something changed about the house, and I realized the night-light in the hall had gone out. Either the electricity was out, or the line had been shut down in town by the fire department.

'I'm sorry,' I said, feeling that was appropriate, though I had no idea why Claudine felt put upon when it was my house that was burning. I wanted to hurry to the backyard to get a better view, but Claudine caught hold of my arm.

'No closer,' she said simply, and I could not break her hold. 'Listen, the trucks are coming.'

Now I could hear the fire engines, and I blessed every person who was coming to help. I knew the pagers had gone off all over the area, and the volunteers had rushed to the firehouse straight from their beds.

Catfish Hunter, my brother's boss, pulled up in his car. He leaped out and ran right to me. 'Anyone left inside?' he asked urgently. The town's fire truck pulled in after him, scattering my new gravel all to hell.

'No,' I said.

'Is there a propane tank?'

'Yes.'

'Where?'

'Backyard.'

'Where's your car, Sookie?'

'In the back,' I said, and my voice was starting to shake. 'Propane tank in the back!' Catfish bellowed over his shoulder.

There was an answering yell, followed by a lot of purposeful activity. I recognized Hoyt Fortenberry and Ralph Tooten, plus four or five other men and a couple of women.

Catfish, after a quick conversation with Hoyt and Ralph, called over a smallish woman who seemed swamped by her gear. He pointed to the still figure in the grass, and she threw off her helmet and knelt beside him. After some peering and touching, she shook her head. I barely recognized her as Dr Robert Meredith's nurse, Jan something.

'Who's the dead man?' asked Catfish. He didn't seem too upset by the corpse.

'I have no idea,' I said. I only discovered how shocked I was by the way my voice came out – quavery, small. Claudine put her arm around me.

A police car pulled in to the side of the fire truck, and Sheriff Bud Dearborn got out of the driver's seat. Andy Bellefleur was his passenger.

Claudine said, 'Ah-oh.'

'Yeah,' I said.

Then Charles was with me again, and Bill was right on his heels. The vampires took in the frantic but purposeful activity. They noticed Claudine.

The small woman, who'd stood to resume her gear, called, 'Sheriff, do me a favor and call an ambulance to take this body away.'

Bud Dearborn glanced at Andy, who turned away to speak into the car radio.

'Having one dead beau ain't enough, Sookie?' Bud Dearborn asked me.

Bill snarled, the firefighters broke out the window by my great-great-grandmother's dining table, and a visible rush of heat and sparks gushed into the night. The pumper truck made a lot of noise, and the tin roof that covered the kitchen and porch separated from the house.

My home was going up in flames and smoke.

Chapter 8

Claudine was on my left. Bill came to stand to my right and took my hand. Together, we watched the fire-fighters aim the hose through the broken window. A sound of shattering glass from the other side of the house indicated they were breaking the window over the sink, too. While the firefighters concentrated on the fire, the police concentrated on the body. Charles stepped up to bat right away.

'I killed him,' he said calmly. 'I caught him setting fire to the house. He was armed, and he attacked me.'

Sheriff Bud Dearborn looked more like a Pekinese than any human should look. His face was practically concave. His eyes were round and bright, and at the moment extremely curious. His brown hair, liberally streaked with gray, was combed back from his face all around, and I expected him to snuffle when he spoke. 'And you would be?' he asked the vampire.

'Charles Twining,' Charles answered gracefully. 'At your service.'

I wasn't imagining the snort the sheriff gave or Andy Bellefleur's eye roll.

'And you'd be on the spot because . . .?'

'He's staying with me,' Bill said smoothly, 'while he works at Merlotte's.'

Presumably the sheriff had already heard about the new bartender, because he just nodded. I was relieved at not having to confess that

Charles was supposed to be sleeping in my closet, and I blessed Bill for having lied about that. Our eyes met for a moment.

'So you admit you killed this man?' Andy asked Charles. Charles nodded curtly.

Andy beckoned to the woman in hospital scrubs who'd been waiting by her car – which made maybe five cars in my front yard, plus the fire truck. This new arrival glanced at me curiously as she walked past to the huddled form in the bushes. Pulling a stethoscope from a pocket, she knelt by the man and listened to various parts of his body. 'Yep, dead as a doornail,' she called.

Andy had gotten a Polaroid out of the police car to take pictures of the body. Since the only light was the flash of the camera and the flicker of flame from my burning house, I didn't think the pictures would turn out too well. I was numb with shock, and I watched Andy as if this were an important activity.

'What a pity. It would have been a good thing to find out why he torched Sookie's house,' Bill said as he watched Andy work. His voice rivaled a refrigerator for coldness.

'In my fear for Sookie's safety, I suppose I struck too hard.' Charles tried to look regretful.

'Since his neck seems to be broken, I suppose you did,' said the doctor, studying Charles's white face with the same careful attention she'd given mine. The doctor was in her thirties, I thought; a woman slim to the point of skinny, with very short red hair. She was about five foot three, and she had elfin features, or at least the kind I'd always thought of as elfin: a short, turned-up nose, wide eyes, large mouth. Her words were both dry and bold, and she didn't seem at all disconcerted by or excited at being called out in the middle of the night for something like this. She must be the parish coroner, so I must have voted for her, but I couldn't recall her name.

'Who are you?' Claudine asked in her sweetest voice.

The doctor blinked at the vision of Claudine. Claudine, at this ungodly hour of the morning, was in full makeup and a fuchsia knit top with black knit leggings. Her shoes were fuchsia and black striped, and her jacket was, too. Claudine's black rippling hair was held off her face with fuchsia combs.

'I'm Dr Tonnesen. Linda. Who are you?'

'Claudine Crane,' the fairy said. I'd never known the last name Claudine used.

'And why were you here on the spot, Ms Crane?' Andy Bellefleur asked.

'I'm Sookie's fairy godmother,' Claudine said, laughing. Though the scene was grim, everyone else laughed, too. It was like we just couldn't stop being cheerful around Claudine. But I wondered very much about Claudine's explanation.

'No, really,' Bud Dearborn said. 'Why are you here, Ms Crane?'

Claudine smiled impishly. 'I was spending the night with Sookie,' she said, winking.

In a second, we were the objects of fascinated scrutiny from every male within hearing, and I had to lock down my head as if it were a maximum-security prison to block the mental images the guys were broadcasting.

Andy shook himself, closed his mouth, and squatted by the dead man. 'Bud, I'm going to roll him,' he said a little hoarsely, and turned the corpse so he could feel inside the dead man's pockets. The man's wallet proved to be in his jacket, which seemed a little unusual to me. Andy straightened and stepped away from the body to examine the billfold's contents.

'You want to have a look, see if you recognize him?' Sheriff Dearborn asked me. Of course I didn't, but I also saw that I really didn't have a choice. Nervously, I inched a little closer and looked again at the face of the dead man. He still looked ordinary. He still looked dead. He might be in his thirties. 'I don't know him,' I said, my voice small in the din of the firefighters and the water pouring onto the house.

'What?' Bud Dearborn was having trouble hearing me. His round brown eyes were locked onto my face.

'Don't know him!' I said, almost yelling. 'I've never seen him, that I remember. Claudine?'

I don't know why I asked Claudine.

'Oh, yes, I've seen him,' she said cheerfully.

That attracted the undivided attention of the two vampires, the two lawmen, the doctor, and me.

'Where?'

Claudine threw her arm around my shoulders. 'Why, he was in Merlotte's tonight. You were too worried about your friend to notice, I guess. He was over in the side of the room where I was sitting.' Arlene had been working that side.

It wasn't too amazing that I'd missed one male face in a crowded bar. But it did bother me that I'd been listening in to people's thoughts and I'd missed out on thoughts that must have been relevant to me. After all, he was in the bar with me, and a few hours later he'd set fire to my house. He must have been mulling me over, right?

'This driver's license says he's from Little Rock, Arkansas,' Andy said.

'That wasn't what he told me,' Claudine said. 'He said he was from Georgia.' She looked just as radiant when she realized he'd lied to her, but she wasn't smiling. 'He said his name was Marlon.'

'Did he tell you why he was in town, Ms Crane?'

'He said he was just passing through, had a motel room up on the interstate.'

'Did he explain any further?'

'Nope.'

'Did you go to his motel, Ms Crane?' Bud Dearborn asked in his best nonjudgmental voice.

Dr Tonnesen was looking from speaker to speaker as if she was at a verbal tennis match.

'Gosh, no, I don't do things like that.' Claudine smiled all around.

Bill looked as if someone had just waved a bottle of blood in front of his face. His fangs extended, and his eyes fixed on Claudine. Vampires can only hold out so long when fairies are around. Charles had stepped closer to Claudine, too.

She had to leave before the lawmen observed how the vampires were reacting. Linda Tonnesen had already noticed; she herself was pretty interested in Claudine. I hoped she'd just attribute the vamps' fascination to Claudine's excellent looks, rather than the overwhelming allure fairies held for vamps.

'Fellowship of the Sun,' Andy said. 'He has an honest-to-God membership card in here. There's no name written on the card; that's strange. His license is issued to Jeff Marriot.' He looked at me questioningly.

I shook my head. The name meant nothing to me.

It was just like a Fellowship member to think that he could do something as nasty as torching my house – with me in it – and no one would question him. It wasn't the first time the Fellowship of the Sun, an anti-vampire hate group, had tried to burn me alive.

'He must have known you've had, ah, an association with vampires,' Andy said into the silence.

'I'm losing my home, and I could have died, because I know vampires?'

Even Bud Dearborn looked a little embarrassed.

'Someone must have heard you used to date Mr Compton, here,' Bud muttered. 'I'm sorry, Sookie.'

I said, 'Claudine needs to leave.'

The abrupt change of subject startled both Andy and Bud, as well as Claudine. She looked at the two vampires, who were perceptibly closer to her, and hastily said, 'Yes, I'm sorry, I have to get back home. I have to work tomorrow.'

'Where's your car, Ms Crane?' Bud Dearborn looked around elaborately. 'I didn't see any car but Sookie's, and it's parked in the back.'

'I'm parked over at Bill's,' Claudine lied smoothly, having had years of practice. Without waiting for further discussion, she disappeared into the woods, and only my hands gripping their arms prevented Charles and Bill from gliding into the darkness after her. They were staring into the blackness of the trees when I pinched them, hard.

'What?' asked Bill, almost dreamily.

'Snap out of it,' I muttered, hoping Bud and Andy and the new doctor wouldn't overhear. They didn't need to know that Claudine was supernatural.

'That's quite a woman,' Dr Tonnesen said, almost as dazed as the vampires. She shook herself. 'The ambulance will come get, uh, Jeff Marriot. I'm just here because I had my scanner turned on as I was driving back from my shift at the Clarice hospital. I need to get home and get some sleep. Sorry about your fire, Ms Stackhouse, but at least you didn't end up like this guy here.' She nodded down at the corpse.

As she got into her Ranger, the fire chief trudged up to us. I'd known Catfish Hunter for years – he'd been a friend of my dad's – but I'd never seen him in his capacity as volunteer fire chief. Catfish was sweating despite the cold, and his face was smudged with smoke.

'Sookie, we done got it out,' he said wearily. 'It's not as bad as you might think.'

'It's not?' I asked in a small voice.

'No, honey. You lost your back porch and your kitchen and your car, I'm afraid. He splashed some gas in that, too. But most of the house should be okay.'

The kitchen . . . where the only traces of the death I'd caused could have been found. Now not even the technicians featured on the Discovery Channel could find any blood traces in the scorched room. Without meaning to, I began to laugh. 'The kitchen,' I said between giggles. 'The kitchen's all gone?'

'Yes,' said Catfish uneasily. 'I hope you got you some homeowners insurance.'

'Oh,' I said, trying hard not to giggle any more. 'I do. It was hard for me to keep up the payments, but I kept the policy Grandmother had on the house.' Thank God my grandmother had been a great believer in insurance. She'd seen too many people drop policy payments to cut their monthly expenses and then suffer losses they were unable to recoup.

'Who's it with? I'll call right now.' Catfish was so anxious to stop me laughing, he was ready to make clown faces and bark if I asked him to.

'Greg Aubert,' I said.

The whole night suddenly rose up and whalloped me one. My house had burned, at least partially. I'd had more than one prowler. I had a vampire in residence for whom daytime cover had to be provided. My car was gone. There was a dead man named Jeff Marriot in my yard, and he'd set fire to my house and car out of sheer prejudice. I was overwhelmed.

'Jason isn't at home,' Catfish said from a distance. 'I tried him. He'd want her to come over to his house.'

'She and Charles – that is, Charles and I will take her over to my house,' Bill said. He seemed to be equally far away.

'I don't know about that,' Bud Dearborn said doubtfully. 'Sookie, is that okay with you?'

I could barely make my mind shuffle through a few options. I couldn't call Tara because Mickey was there. Arlene's trailer was as crowded as it needed to be already.

'Yes, that would be all right,' I said, and my voice sounded remote and empty, even to my own ears.

'All right, long's we know where to reach you.'

'I called Greg, Sookie, and left a message on his office answering machine. You better call him yourself in the morning,' Catfish said.

'Fine,' I said.

And all the firefighters shuffled by, and they all told me how sorry they were. I knew every one of them: friends of my father's, friends of Jason's, regulars at the bar, high school acquaintances.

'You all did the best you could,' I said over and over. 'Thanks for saving most of it.'

And the ambulance came to cart away the arsonist.

By then, Andy had found a gasoline can in the bushes, and the corpse's hands reeked of gasoline, Dr Tonnesen said.

I could hardly believe that a stranger had decided I should lose my home and my life because of my dating preference. Thinking at that moment of how close I'd come to death, I didn't feel it was unjust that he'd lost his own life in the process. I admitted to myself that I thought Charles had done a good thing. I might owe my life to Sam's insistence that the vampire be billeted at my house. If Sam had been there at the moment, I would have given him a very enthusiastic thank-you.

Finally Bill and Charles and I started over to Bill's house. Catfish had advised me not to go back into my house until the morning, and then only after the insurance agent and the arson investigator had checked it over. Dr Tonnesen had told me that if I felt wheezy, to come in to her office in the morning. She'd said some other stuff, but I hadn't quite absorbed it.

It was dark in the woods, of course, and by then it was maybe five in the morning. After a few paces into the trees, Bill picked me up and carried me. I didn't protest, because I was so tired I'd been wondering how I was going to manage stumbling through the cemetery.

He put me down when we reached his house. 'Can you make it up the stairs?' he asked.

'I'll take you,' offered Charles.

'No, I can do it,' I said, and started up before they could say anything more. To tell the truth, I was not so sure I could, but slowly I made my way up to the bedroom I'd used when Bill had been my boyfriend. He had a snug light-tight place somewhere on the ground floor of the house, but I'd never asked him exactly where. (I had a pretty good idea it was in the space the builders had lopped off the kitchen to create the hot tub/plant room.) Though the water table is too high in Louisiana for houses to have basements, I was almost as sure there was another dark hole concealed somewhere. He had room for Charles without them bunking together, anyway – not that that was too high on my list of concerns. One of my nightgowns still lay in the drawer in the old-fashioned bedroom, and there was still a toothbrush of mine in the hall bathroom. Bill hadn't put my things in the trash; he'd left them, like he'd expected me to return.

Or maybe he just hadn't had much reason to go upstairs since we'd broken up.

Promising myself a long shower in the morning, I took off my smelly, stained pajamas and ruined socks. I washed my face and pulled on the clean nightgown before I crawled in the high bed, using the antique stool still positioned where I'd left it. As the incidents of the day and night buzzed in my head like bees, I thanked God for the fact that my life had been spared, and that was all I had time to say to Him before sleep swallowed me up.

I slept only three hours. Then worry woke me up. I was up in plenty of time to meet Greg Aubert, the insurance agent. I dressed in a pair of Bill's jeans and a shirt of his. They'd been left outside my door, along with heavy socks. His shoes were out of the question, but to my delight I found an old pair of rubber-soled slippers I'd left at the very back of the closet. Bill still had some coffee and a coffeemaker in his kitchen from our courtship, and I was grateful to have a mug to carry with me as I made my way carefully across the cemetery and through the belt of woods surrounding what was left of my house.

Greg was pulling into the front yard as I stepped from the trees. He got out of his truck, scanned my oddly fitting ensemble, and politely ignored it. He and I stood side by side, regarding the old house. Greg had sandy hair and rimless glasses, and he was an elder in the Presbyterian Church. I'd always liked him, at least in part because whenever I'd taken my grandmother by to pay her premiums, he'd come out of his office to shake her hand and make her feel like a valued client. His business acumen was matched only by his luck. People had said for years that his personal good fortune extended to his policyholders, though of course they said this in a joking kind of way.

'If only I could have foreseen this,' Greg said. 'Sookie, I am so sorry this happened.'

'What do you mean, Greg?'

'Oh, I'm just . . . I wish I'd thought of you needing more coverage,' he said absently. He began walking around to the back of the house, and I trailed behind him. Curious, I began to listen in to his head, and I was startled out of my gloom by what I heard there.

'So casting spells to back up your insurance really works?' I asked.

He yelped. There's no other word for it. 'It's true about you,' he gasped. 'I – I don't – it's just . . .' He stood outside my blackened kitchen and gaped at me.

'It's okay,' I said reassuringly. 'You can pretend I don't know if it'll help you feel better.'

'My wife would just die if she knew,' he said soberly. 'And the kids, too. I just want them kept separate from this part of my life. My mother was . . . she was . . .'

'A witch?' I supplied helpfully.

'Well, yes.' Greg's glasses glinted in the early morning sun as he looked at what was left of my kitchen. 'But my dad always pretended he didn't know, and though she kept training me to take her place, I wanted to be a normal man more than anything in the world.' Greg nodded, as if to say he'd achieved his goal.

I looked down into my mug of coffee, glad I had something to hold in my hands. Greg was lying to himself in a major way, but it wasn't up to me to point that out to him. It was something he'd have to square with his God and his conscience. I wasn't saying Greg's method was a bad one, but it sure wasn't a normal man's choice. Insuring your livelihood (literally) by the use of magic had to be against some kind of rule.

'I mean, I'm a good agent,' he said, defending himself, though I hadn't said a word. 'I'm careful about what I insure. I'm careful about checking things out. It's not all the magic.'

'Oh, no,' I said, because he would just explode with anxiety if I didn't. 'People have accidents anyway, right?'

'Regardless of what spells I use,' he agreed gloomily. 'They drive drunk. And sometimes metal parts give way, no matter what.'

The idea of conventional Greg Aubert going around Bon Temps putting spells on cars was almost enough to distract me from the ruin of my house . . . but not quite.

In the clear chilly daylight, I could see the damage in full. Though I kept telling myself it could have been much worse – and that I was very lucky that the kitchen had extended off the back of the house, since it had been built at a later date – it had also been the room that had held big-ticket items. I'd have to replace the stove, the refrigerator, the hot water heater, and the microwave, and the back porch had been home to my washer and drier.

After the loss of those major appliances, there came the dishes and the pots and the pans and the silverware, some of it very old indeed. One of my greats had come from a family with a little money, and she'd brought a set of fine china and a silver tea service that had been a pain to polish. I'd never have to polish it again, I realized, but there was no joy in the thought. My Nova was old, and I'd needed to replace it for a long time, but I hadn't planned on that being now.

Well, I had insurance, and I had money in the bank, thanks to the vampires who'd paid me for keeping Eric when he'd lost his memory.

'And you had smoke detectors?' Greg was asking.

'Yes, I did,' I said, remembering the high-pitched pulsing that had started up right after Claudine had woken me. 'If the ceiling in the hall is still there, you'll be able to see one.'

There were no more back steps to get us up onto the porch, and the porch floorboards looked very unsteady. In fact, the washer had half fallen through and was tilted at an odd angle. It made me sick, seeing my everyday things, things I'd touched and used hundreds of times, exposed to the world and ruined.

'We'll go through from the front door,' Greg suggested, and I was glad to agree.

It was still unlocked, and I felt a flutter of alarm before I realized how ludicrous that was. I stepped in. The first thing I noticed was the smell. Everything reeked of smoke. I opened the windows, and the cool breeze that blew through began to clear the smell out until it was just tolerable.

This end of the house was better than I'd expected. The furniture would need cleaning, of course. But the floor was solid and undamaged. I didn't even go up the stairs; I seldom used the rooms up there, so whatever had happened up there could wait.

My arms were crossed under my breasts. I looked from side to side, moving slowly across the room toward the hall. I felt the floor vibrate as someone else came in. I knew without looking around that Jason was behind me. He and Greg said something to each other, but after a second Jason fell silent, as shocked as I was.

We passed into the hall. The door to my bedroom and the door to the bedroom across the hall were both open. My bedding was still thrown back. My slippers were beside the night table. All the windows were smudged with smoke and moisture, and the dreadful odor grew even stronger. There was the smoke detector on the hall ceiling. I pointed to it silently. I opened the door to the linen closet and found that everything in it felt damp. Well, these things could be washed. I went into my room and opened my closet door. My closet shared a wall with the kitchen. At first glance my clothes looked intact, until I noticed that each garment hanging on a wire hanger had a line across the shoulders where the heated hanger had singed the cloth. My shoes had baked. Maybe three pairs were usable

I gulped.

Though I felt shakier by the second, I joined my brother and the insurance agent as they carefully continued down the hall to the kitchen.

The floor closest to the old part of the house seemed okay. The kitchen had been a large room, since it had also served as the family dining room. The table was partially burned, as were two of the chairs. The linoleum on the floor was all broken up, and some of it was charred. The hot water heater had gone through the floor, and the curtains that had covered the window over the sink were hanging in strips. I remembered Gran making those curtains; she hadn't enjoyed sewing, but the ones from JCPenney that she'd liked were just too much. So she'd gotten out her mother's old sewing machine and bought some cheap but pretty flowered material at Hancock's, and she'd measured, and cursed under her breath, and worked and worked until finally she'd gotten them done. Jason and I had admired them extravagantly to make her feel it had been worth the effort, and she'd been so pleased.

I opened one drawer, the one that had held all the keys. They were melted together. I pressed my lips together, hard. Jason stood beside me, looked down.

'Shit,' he said, his voice low and vicious. That helped me push the tears back.

I held on to his arm for just a minute. He patted me awkwardly. Seeing items so familiar, items made dear by use, irrevocably altered by fire was a terrible shock, no matter how many times I reminded myself that the whole house could have been consumed by the flames; that I could have died, too. Even if the smoke detector had wakened me in time, there was every likelihood I would have run outside to be confronted by the arsonist, Jeff Marriot.

Almost everything on the east side of the kitchen was ruined. The floor was unstable. The kitchen roof was gone.

'It's lucky the rooms upstairs don't extend over the kitchen,' Greg said when he came down from examining the two bedrooms and the attic. 'You'll have to get a builder to let you know, but I think the second story is essentially sound.'

I talked to Greg about money after that. When would it come? How much would it be? What deductible would I have to pay?

Jason wandered around the yard while Greg and I stood by his car. I could interpret my brother's posture and movements. Jason was very angry: at my near-death escape, at what had happened to the house. After Greg drove off, leaving me with an exhausting list of things to do and phone calls to make (from where?) and work to get ready for (wearing what?), Jason meandered over to me and said, 'If I'd been here, I coulda killed him.'

'In your new body?' I asked.

'Yeah. It would've given that sumbitch the scare of his life before he left it.'

'I think Charles probably was pretty scary, but I appreciate the thought.'

'They put the vamp in jail?'

'No, Bud Dearborn just told him not to leave town. After all, the Bon Temps jail doesn't have a vampire cell. And regular cells don't hold 'em, plus they have windows.'

'That's where the guy was from – Fellowship of the Sun? Just a stranger who came to town to do you in?'

'That's what it looks like.'

'What they got against you? Other than you dating Bill and associating with some of the other vamps?'

Actually, the Fellowship had quite a bit against me. I'd been responsible for their huge Dallas church being raided and one of their main leaders going underground. The papers had been full of what the police had found in the Fellowship building in Texas. Arriving to find the members dashing in turmoil around their building, claiming vampires had attacked them, the police entered the building to search it and found a basement torture chamber, illegal arms adapted to shoot wooden stakes into vampires, and a corpse. The police failed to see a single vampire. Steve and Sarah Newlin, the leaders of the Fellowship church in Dallas, had been missing since that night.

I'd seen Steve Newlin since then. He'd been at Club Dead in Jackson. He and one of his cronies had been preparing to stake a vampire in the club when I'd prevented them. Newlin had escaped; his buddy hadn't.

It appeared that the Newlins' followers had tracked me down. I hadn't foreseen such a thing, but then, I'd never foreseen anything that had happened to me in the past year. When Bill had been learning how to use his computer, he'd told me that with a little knowledge and money, anyone could be found through a computer.

Maybe the Fellowship had hired private detectives, like the couple who had been in my house yesterday. Maybe Jack and Lily Leeds had just been pretending to be hired by the Pelt family? Maybe the Newlins were their real employers? They hadn't struck me as politicized people, but the power of the color green is universal.

'I guess dating a vampire was enough for them to hate me,' I told Jason. We were sitting on the tailgate of his truck, staring dismally at the house. 'Who do you think I should call about rebuilding the kitchen?'

I didn't think I needed an architect: I just wanted to replace what was missing. The house was raised up off the ground, so slab size wasn't a factor. Since the floor was burned through in the kitchen and would have to be completely replaced, it wouldn't cost much more to make the kitchen a little bigger and enclose the back porch completely. The washer and dryer wouldn't be so awful to use in bad weather, I thought longingly. I had more than enough money to satisfy the deductible, and I was sure the insurance would pay for most of the rest.

After a while, we heard another truck coming. Maxine Fortenberry, Hoyt's mother, got out with a couple of laundry baskets. 'Where's your clothes, girl?' she called. 'I'm gonna take them home and wash them, so you'll have something to wear that don't smell like smoke.'

After I protested and she insisted, we went into the chokingly unpleasant air of the house to get some clothes. Maxine also insisted on getting an armful of linens out of the linen closet to see if some of them could be resurrected.

Right after Maxine left, Tara drove her new car into the clearing, followed by her part-time help, a tall young woman called McKenna, who was driving Tara's old car.

After a hug and a few words of sympathy, Tara said, 'You drive this old Malibu while you're getting your insurance stuff straightened out. It's just sitting in my carport doing nothing, and I was just about to put it in the paper in the For Sale column. You can be using it.'

'Thank you,' I said in a daze. 'Tara, that's so nice of you.' She didn't look good, I noticed vaguely, but I was too sunk in my own troubles to really evaluate Tara's demeanor. When she and McKenna left, I gave them a limp wave good-bye.

After that, Terry Bellefleur arrived. He offered to demolish the burned part for a very nominal sum, and for a little bit more he'd haul all the resultant trash to the parish dump. He'd start as soon as the police gave him the go-ahead, he said, and to my astonishment he gave me a little hug.

Sam came after that, driven by Arlene. He stood and looked at the back of the house for a few minutes. His lips were tightly compressed. Almost any man would have said, 'Pretty lucky I sent the vampire home with you, huh?' But Sam didn't. 'What can I do?' he said instead.

'Keep me working,' I said, smiling. 'Forgive me coming to work in something besides my actual work clothes.' Arlene walked all around the house, and then hugged me wordlessly.

'That's easily done,' he said. He still wasn't smiling. 'I hear that the guy who started the fire was a Fellowship member, that this is some kind of payback for you dating Bill.'

'He had the card in his wallet, and he had a gas can.' I shrugged.

'But how'd he find you? I mean, no one around here . . .' Sam's voice trailed off as he considered the possibility more closely.

He was thinking, as I had, that though the arson could be just because I'd dated Bill, it seemed a drastic overreaction. A more typical retaliation was a Fellowship member throwing pig's blood on humans who dated, or had a work partnership with, a vampire. That had happened more than once, most notably to a designer from Dior who'd employed all vampire models for one spring show. Such incidents usually occurred in big cities, cities that hosted large Fellowship 'churches' and a bigger vampire population.

What if the man had been hired to set fire to my house by someone else? What if the Fellowship card in his wallet was planted there for misdirection?

Any of these things could be true; or all of them, or none of them. I couldn't decide what I believed. So, was I the target of an assassin, like the shape-shifters? Should I, too, fear the shot from the dark, now that the fire had failed?

That was such a frightening prospect that I flinched from pursuing it. Those were waters too deep for me.

The state police arson investigator appeared while Sam and Arlene were there. I was eating a lunch plate Arlene had brought me. That Arlene was not much of a food person is the nicest way to put it, so my sandwich was made of cheap bologna and plastic cheese, and my canned drink was off-brand sugared tea. But she'd thought of me and she'd brought them to me, and her kids had drawn a picture for me. I would have been happy if she'd brought me just a slice of bread under those conditions.

Automatically, Arlene made eyes at the arson investigator. He was a lean man in his late forties named Dennis Pettibone. Dennis had a camera, a notebook, and a grim outlook. It took Arlene maybe two minutes of conversation to coax a little smile from Mr Pettibone's lips, and his brown eyes were admiring her curves after two more minutes had passed. Before Arlene drove Sam home, she had a promise from the investigator that he'd drop by the bar that evening.

Also before she left, Arlene offered me the foldout couch in her trailer, which was sweet of her, but I knew it would crowd her and throw off her get-the-kids-to-school morning routine, so I told her I had a place to stay. I didn't think Bill would evict me. Jason had mentioned his house was open to me, and to my amazement, before he left, Sam said, 'You can stay with me, Sookie. No strings. I have two empty bedrooms in the double-wide. There's actually a bed in one of them.'

'That's so nice of you,' I said, putting all my sincerity into my voice. 'Every soul in Bon Temps would have us on the way to being married if I did that, but I sure do appreciate it.'

'You don't think they won't make assumptions if you stay with Bill?'

'I can't marry Bill. Not legal,' I replied, cutting off that argument. 'Besides, Charles is there, too.'

'Fuel to the fire,' Sam pointed out. 'That's even spicier.'

'That's kind of flattering, crediting me with enough pizzazz to take care of two vampires at a go.'

Sam grinned, which knocked about ten years off his age. He looked over my shoulder as we heard the sound of gravel crunching under yet another vehicle. 'Look who's coming,' he said.

A huge and ancient pickup lumbered to a stop. Out of it stepped Dawson, the huge Were who'd been acting as Calvin Norris's bodyguard.

'Sookie,' he rumbled, his voice so deep I expected the ground to vibrate.

'Hey, Dawson.' I wanted to ask, 'What are you doing here?' but I figured that would sound plain rude.

'Calvin heard about your fire,' Dawson said, not wasting time with preliminaries. 'He told me to come by here and see was you hurt, and to tell you that he is thinking about you and that if he were well, he would be here pounding nails already.'

I saw from the corner of my eye that Dennis Pettibone was eyeing Dawson with interest. Dawson might as well have been wearing a sign that said DANGEROUS DUDE on it.

'You tell him I'm real grateful for the thought. I wish he were well, too. How's he doing, Dawson?'

'He got a couple of things unhooked this morning, and he's been walking a little. It was a bad wound,' Dawson said. 'It'll take a bit.' He glanced over to see how far away the arson investigator was. 'Even for one of us,' he added.

'Of course,' I said. 'I appreciate your coming by.'

'Also, Calvin says his house is empty while he's in the hospital, if you need a place to stay. He'd be glad to give you the use of it.'

That, too, was kind, and I said so. But I would feel very awkward, being obliged to Calvin in such a significant way.

Dennis Pettibone called me over. 'See, Ms Stackhouse,' he said. 'You can see where he used the gasoline on your porch. See the way the fire ran out from the splash he made on the door?'

I gulped. 'Yes, I see.'

'You're lucky there wasn't any wind last night. And most of all, you're lucky that you had that door shut, the one between the kitchen and the rest of the house. The fire would have gone right down that hall if you hadn't shut the door. When the firefighters smashed that window on the north side, the fire ran that way looking for oxygen, instead of trying to make it into the rest of the house.'

I remembered the impulse that had pushed me back into the house against all common sense, the last-minute slam of that door.

'After a couple of days, I don't think the bulk of the house will even smell as bad,' the investigator told me. 'Open the windows now, pray it don't rain, and fairly soon I don't think you'll have much problem. Course, you got to call the power company and talk to them about the electricity. And the propane company needs to take a look at the tank. So the house ain't livable, from that point of view.'

The gist of what he was saying was, I could just sleep there to have a roof over my head. No electricity, no heat, no hot water, no cooking. I thanked Dennis Pettibone and excused myself to have a last word with Dawson, who'd been listening in.

'I'll try to come see Calvin in a day or two, once I get this straightened out,' I said, nodding toward the blackened back of my house.

'Oh, yeah,' the bodyguard said, one foot already in his pickup. 'Calvin said let him know who done this, if it was ordered by someone besides the sumbitch dead at the scene.'

I looked at what remained of my kitchen and could almost count the feet from the flames to my bedroom. 'I appreciate that most of all,' I said, before my Christian self could smother the thought. Dawson's brown eyes met mine in a moment of perfect accord.

Chapter 9

Thanks to Maxine, I had clean-smelling clothes to wear to work, but I had to go buy some footwear at Payless. Normally, I put a little money into my shoes since I have to stand up so much, but there was no time to go to Clarice to the one good shoe shop there or to drive over to Monroe to the mall. When I got to work, Sweetie Des Arts came out of the kitchen to hug me, her thin body wrapped in a white cook's apron. Even the boy who bussed the tables told me he was sorry. Holly and Danielle, who were switching off shifts, each gave me a pat on the shoulder and told me they hoped things got better for me.

Arlene asked me if I thought that handsome Dennis Pettibone would be coming by, and I told her I was sure he would.

'I guess he has to travel a lot,' she said thoughtfully. 'I wonder where he's based.'

'I got his business card. He's based in Shreveport. He told me he bought himself a small farm right outside of Shreveport, now that I think about it.'

Arlene's eyes narrowed. 'Sounds like you and Dennis had a nice talk.'

I started to protest that the arson investigator was a little long in the tooth for me, but since Arlene had stuck to saying she was thirty-six for the past three years, I figured that would be less than tactful. 'He was just passing the time of day,' I told her. 'He asked me how long I'd worked with you, and did you have any kids.'

'Oh. He did?' Arlene beamed. 'Well, well.' She went to check on her tables with a cheerful strut to her walk.

I set about my work, having to take longer than usual to do everything because of the constant interruptions. I knew some other town sensation would soon eclipse my house fire. Though I couldn't hope anyone else would experience a similar disaster, I would be glad when I wasn't the object of discussion of every single bar patron.

Terry hadn't been able to handle the light daytime bar duties today, so Arlene and I pitched in to cover it. Being busy helped me feel less self-conscious.

Though I was coasting on three hours of sleep, I managed okay until Sam called me from the hallway that led to his office and the public bathrooms.

Two people had come in earlier and gone up to his corner table to talk to him; I'd noted them only in passing. The woman was in her sixties, very round and short. She used a cane. The young man with her was brown haired, with a sharp nose and heavy brows to give his face some character. He reminded me of someone, but I couldn't make the reference pop to the top of my head. Sam had ushered them back into his office.

'Sookie,' Sam said unhappily, 'the people in my office want to talk to you.'

'Who are they?'

'She's Jeff Marriot's mother. The man is his twin.'

'Oh my God,' I said, realizing the man reminded me of the corpse. 'Why do they want to talk to me?'

'They don't think he ever had anything to do with the Fellowship. They don't understand anything about his death.'

To say I dreaded this encounter was putting it mildly. 'Why talk to me?' I said in a kind of subdued wail. I was nearly at the end of my emotional endurance.

'They just . . . want answers. They're grieving.'

'So am I,' I said. 'My home.'

'Their loved one.'

I stared at Sam. 'Why should I talk to them?' I asked. 'What is it you want from me?'

'You need to hear what they have to say,' Sam said with a note of finality in his voice. He wouldn't push any more, and he wouldn't explain any more. Now the decision was up to me.

Because I trusted Sam, I nodded. 'I'll talk to them when I get off work,' I said. I secretly hoped they'd leave by then. But when my shift was over, the two were still sitting in Sam's office. I took off my apron, tossed it in the big trash can labeled DIRTY LINEN (reflecting for the hundredth time that the trash can would probably implode if anyone put some actual linen in it), and plodded into the office.

I looked the Marriots over more carefully now that we were face-to-face. Mrs Marriot (I assumed) was in bad shape. Her skin was grayish, and her whole body seemed to sag. Her glasses were smeared because she'd been weeping so much, and she was clutching damp tissues in her hands. Her son was shocked expressionless. He'd lost his twin, and he was sending me so much misery I could hardly absorb it.

'Thanks for talking to us,' he said. He rose from his seat automatically and extended his hand. 'I'm Jay Marriot, and this is my mother, Justine.'

This was a family that found a letter of the alphabet it liked and stuck to it.

I didn't know what to say. Could I tell them I was sorry their loved one was dead, when he'd tried to kill me? There was no rule of etiquette for this; even my grandmother would have been stymied.

'Miss – Ms – Stackhouse, had you ever met my brother before?'

'No,' I said. Sam took my hand. Since the Marriots were seated in the only two chairs Sam's office could boast, he and I leaned against the front of his desk. I hoped his leg wasn't hurting.

'Why would he set fire to your house? He'd never been arrested before, for anything,' Justine spoke for the first time. Her voice was rough and choked with tears; it had an undertone of pleading. She was asking me to let this not be true, this allegation about her son Jeff.

'I sure don't know.'

'Could you tell us how this happened? His – death, I mean?'

I felt a flare of anger at being obliged to pity them – at the necessity for being delicate, for treating them specially. After all, who had almost died here? Who had lost part of her home? Who was facing a financial crunch that only chance had reduced from a disaster? Rage surged through me, and Sam let go of my hand and put his arm around me. He could feel the tension in my body. He was hoping I would control the impulse to lash out.

I held on to my better nature by my fingernails, but I held on.

'A friend woke me up,' I said. 'When we got outside, we found a vampire who is staying with my neighbor – also a vampire – standing by Mr Marriot's body. There was a gasoline can near to the . . . nearby. The doctor who came said there was gas on his hands.'

'What killed him?' The mother again.

'The vampire.'

'Bit him?'

'No, he . . . no. No biting.'

'How, then?' Jay was showing some of his own anger.

'Broke his neck, I think.'

'That was what we heard at the sheriff's office,' Jay said. 'But we just didn't know if they were telling the truth.'

Oh, for goodness's sake.

Sweetie Des Arts stuck her head in to ask Sam if she could borrow the storeroom keys because she needed a case of pickles. She apologized for interrupting. Arlene waved a hand at me as she went down the hall to the employees' door, and I wondered if Dennis Pettibone had come in the bar. I'd been so sunk in my own problems, I hadn't noticed. When the outside door clunked shut behind her, the silence seemed to gather in the little room.

'So why was the vampire in your yard?' Jay asked impatiently. 'In the middle of the night?'

I did not tell him it was none of his business. Sam's hand stroked my arm. 'That's when they're up. And he was staying at the only other house out by mine.' That's what we'd told the police. 'I guess he heard someone in my yard while he was close and came to investigate.'

'We don't know how Jeff got there,' Justine said. 'Where is his car?'

'I don't know.'

'And there was a card in his wallet?'

'Yes, a Fellowship of the Sun membership card,' I told her.

'But he had nothing particular against vampires,' Jay protested.

'We're twins. I would have known if he'd had some big grudge. This just doesn't make any sense.'

'He did give a woman in the bar a fake name and hometown,' I said, as gently as I could.

'Well, he was just passing through,' Jay said. 'I'm a married man, but Jeff's divorced. I don't like to say this in front of my mother, but it's not unknown for men to give a false name and history when they meet a woman in a bar.'

This was true. Though Merlotte's was primarily a neighborhood bar, I'd listened to many a tale from out-of-towners who'd dropped in; and I'd known for sure they were lying.

'Where was the wallet?' Justine asked. She looked up at me like an old beaten dog, and it made my heart sick.

'In his jacket pocket,' I said.

Jay stood up abruptly. He began to move, pacing in the small space he had at his disposal. 'There again,' he said, his voice more animated, 'that's just not like Jeff. He kept his billfold in his jeans, same as me. We never put our wallets in our jacket.'

'What are you saying?' Sam asked.

'I'm saying that I don't think Jeff did this,' his twin said. 'Even those people at the Fina station, they could be mistaken.'

'Someone at the Fina says he bought a can of gas there?' Sam asked.

Justine flinched again, the soft skin of her chin shaking.

I'd been wondering if there might be something to the Marriots' suspicions, but that idea was extinguished now. The phone rang, and all of us jumped. Sam picked it up and said, 'Merlotte's,' in a calm voice. He listened, said, 'Um-hum,' and 'That right?' and finally, 'I'll tell her.' He hung up.

'Your brother's car's been found,' he told Jay Marriot. 'It's on a little road almost directly across from Sookie's driveway.'

The light went out completely on the little family's ray of hope, and I could only feel sorry for them. Justine seemed ten years older than she had when she'd come into the bar, and Jay looked like he'd gone days without sleep or food. They left without another word to me, which was a mercy. From the few sentences they exchanged with each other, I gathered they were going to see Jeff's car and ask if they could remove any of his belongings from it. I thought they would meet another blank wall there.

Eric had told me that that little road, a dirt track leading back to a deer camp, was where Debbie Pelt had hidden her car when she'd come to kill me. Might as well put up a sign: PARKING FOR SOOKIE STACKHOUSE NIGHTTIME ATTACKS.

Sam came swinging back into the room. He'd been seeing the Marriots out. He stood by me propped against his desk and set his crutches aside. He put his arm around me. I turned to him and slid my arms around his waist. He held me to him, and I felt peaceful for a wonderful minute. The heat of his body warmed me, and the knowledge of his affection comforted me.

'Does your leg hurt?' I asked when he moved restlessly.

'Not my leg,' he said.

I looked up, puzzled, to meet his eyes. He looked rueful. Suddenly, I became aware of exactly what was hurting Sam, and I flushed red. But I didn't let go of him. I was reluctant to end the comfort of being close to someone – no, of being close to Sam. When I didn't move away, he slowly put his lips to mine, giving me every chance to step out of reach. His mouth brushed mine once, twice. Then he settled in to kissing me, and the heat of his tongue filled my mouth, stroking.

That felt incredibly good. With the visit of the Marriot family, I'd been browsing the Mystery section. Now I'd definitely wandered over to the Romances.

His height was close enough to mine that I didn't have to strain upward to meet his mouth. His kiss became more urgent. His lips strayed down my neck, to the vulnerable and sensitive place just at the base, and his teeth nipped very gently.

I gasped. I just couldn't help it. If I'd had the gift of teleportation, I would've had us somewhere more private in an instant. Remotely, I felt there was something kind of tacky at feeling this lustful in a messy office in a bar. But the heat surged as he kissed me again. We'd always had something between us, and the smoldering ember had just burst into flame.

I struggled to hold on to some sense. Was this survivor lust? What about his leg? Did he really need the buttons on his shirt?

'Not good enough for you here,' he said, doing a little gasping of his own. He pulled away and reached for his crutches, but then he hauled me back and kissed me again. 'Sookie, I'm going to—'

'What are you going to do?' asked a cold voice from the doorway.

If I was shocked senseless, Sam was enraged. In a split second I was pushed to one side, and he launched himself at the intruder, broken leg and all.

My heart was thumping like a scared rabbit's, and I put one hand over it to make sure it stayed in my chest. Sam's sudden attack had knocked Bill to the floor. Sam pulled back his fist to get in a punch, but Bill used his greater weight and strength to roll Sam until he was on the bottom. Bill's fangs were out and his eyes were glowing.

'Stop!' I yelled at a reduced volume, scared the patrons would come running. In a little fast action of my own, I gripped Bill's smooth dark hair with both hands and used it to yank his head back. In the excitement of the moment, Bill reached behind him to catch my wrists in his hands, and he began twisting. I choked with pain. Both my arms were about to break when Sam took the opportunity to sock Bill in the jaw with all his power. Shifters are not as powerful as Weres and vampires, but they can pack quite a punch, and Bill was rocked sideways. He also came to his senses. Releasing my arms, he rose and turned to me in one graceful movement.

My eyes welled full of tears from the pain, and I opened them wide, determined not to let the drops roll down my cheeks. But I'm sure I looked exactly like someone who was trying hard not to cry. I was holding my arms out in front of me, wondering when they'd stop hurting.

'Since your car was burned, I came to get you because it was time for you to get off work,' Bill said, his fingers gently evaluating the marks on my forearms. 'I swear I just intended to do you a favor. I swear I wasn't spying on you. I swear I never intended you any harm.'

That was a pretty good apology, and I was glad he'd spoken first. Not only was I in pain, I was totally embarrassed. Naturally, Bill had no way of knowing that Tara had loaned me a car. I should have left him a note or left a message on his answering machine, but I'd driven straight to work from the burned house, and it simply hadn't crossed my mind. Something else did occur to me, as it should have right away.

'Oh, Sam, did your leg get hurt worse?' I brushed past Bill to help Sam to his feet. I took as much of his weight as I could, knowing he'd rather lie on the floor forever than accept any assistance from Bill. Finally, with some difficulty, I maneuvered Sam upright, and I saw he was careful to keep his weight on his good leg. I couldn't even imagine how Sam must be feeling.

He was feeling pretty pissed off, I discovered directly. He glared past me at Bill. 'You come in without calling out, without knocking? I'm sure you don't expect me to say I'm sorry for jumping you.' I'd never seen Sam so angry. I could tell that he was embarrassed that he hadn't 'protected' me more effectively, that he was humiliated that Bill had gained the upper hand and furthermore had hurt me. Last but not least, Sam was coping with the backwash from all those hormones that had been exploding when we'd been interrupted.

'Oh, no. I don't expect that.' Bill's voice dropped in temperature when he spoke to Sam. I expected to see icicles form on the walls.

I wished I were a thousand miles away. I longed for the ability to walk out, get into my own car, and drive to my own home. Of course, I couldn't. At least I had the use of a car, and I explained that to Bill.

'Then I needn't have gone to the trouble of coming to get you, and you two could have continued uninterrupted,' he said in an absolutely lethal tone. 'Where are you going to spend the night, if I may ask? I was going to go to the store to buy food for you.'

Since Bill hated grocery shopping, that would have been a major effort, and he wanted to be sure I knew about it. (Of course, it was also possible that he was making this up on the spot to be sure I felt as guilty as possible.)

I reviewed my options. Though I never knew what I'd walk into over at my brother's, that seemed my safest choice. 'I'm going to run by my house to get some makeup out of the bathroom, and then I'm going to Jason's,' I said. 'Thank you for putting me up last night, Bill. I guess you brought Charles to work? Tell him if he wants to spend the night at my house, I guess the, ah, hole is okay.'

'Tell him yourself. He's right outside,' Bill said in a voice I can only characterize as grumpy. Bill's imagination had evidently spun a whole different scenario for the evening. The way events were unfolding was making him mighty unhappy.

Sam was in so much pain (I could see it hovering like a red glow around him) that the most merciful thing I could do was clear out of there before he gave into it. 'I'll see you tomorrow, Sam,' I said, and kissed him on the cheek.

He tried to smile at me. I didn't dare offer to help him over to his trailer while the vampires were there, because I knew Sam's pride would suffer. At the moment, that was more important to him than the state of his injured leg.

Charles was behind the bar and already busy. When Bill offered accommodations again for a second day, Charles accepted rather than opting for my untested hidey-hole. 'We have to check your hiding place, Sookie, for cracks that may have occurred during the fire,' Charles said seriously.

I could understand the necessity, and without saying a word to Bill, I got into the loaner car and drove to my house. We'd left the windows open all day, and the smell had largely dissipated. That was a welcome development. Thanks to the strategy of the firefighters and the inexpert way the fire had been set, the bulk of my house would be livable in short order. I'd called a contractor, Randall Shurtliff, that evening from the bar, and he'd agreed to stop by the next day at noon. Terry Bellefleur had promised to start removing the remains of the kitchen early the next day. I would have to be there to set aside anything I could salvage. I felt like I had two jobs now.

I was suddenly and completely exhausted, and my arms ached. I would have huge bruises the next day. It was almost too warm to justify long sleeves, but I'd have to wear them. Armed with a flashlight from the glove compartment of Tara's car, I got my makeup and some more clothes from my bedroom, throwing them all into a sport duffle I'd won at the Relay for Life. I tossed in a couple of paperbacks I hadn't read yet – books I'd traded for at the library swap rack. That prompted another line of thought. Did I have any movies that needed to go back to the rental place? No. Library books? Yes, had to return some, and I needed to air them out first. Anything else that belonged to another person? Thank goodness I'd dropped Tara's suit at the cleaner's.

There was no point in closing and locking the windows, which I'd left open to dissipate the odor, as the house was easily accessible through the burned kitchen. But when I went out my front door, I locked it behind me. I'd gotten to Hummingbird Road before I realized how silly that had been, and as I drove to Jason's, I found myself smiling for the first time in many, many hours.

Chapter 10

My melancholy brother was glad to see me. The fact that his new 'family' didn't trust him had been eating away at Jason all day. Even his panther girlfriend, Crystal, was nervous about seeing him while the cloud of suspicion hung around him. She'd sent him packing when he'd shown up on her front doorstep this evening. When I found out he'd actually driven out to Hotshot, I exploded. I told my brother in no uncertain terms that he apparently had a death wish and I was not responsible for whatever happened to him. He responded that I'd never been responsible for anything that he did, anyway, so why would I start now?

It went on like that for a while.

After he'd grudgingly agreed to stay away from his fellow shifters, I carried my bag down the short hall to the guest bedroom. This was where he kept his computer, his old high school trophies from the baseball team and the football team, and an ancient foldout couch on hand primarily for visitors who drank too much and couldn't drive home. I didn't even bother to unfold it but spread out an ancient quilt over the glossy Naugahyde. I pulled another one over me.

After I said my prayers, I reviewed my day. It had been so full of incident that I got tired trying to remember everything. In about three minutes, I was out like a light. I dreamed about growling animals that night: they were all around me in the fog, and I was scared. I could hear Jason screaming somewhere in the mist, though I couldn't find him to defend him.

Sometimes you don't need a psychiatrist to interpret a dream, right?

I woke up just a bit when Jason left for work in the morning, mostly because he slammed the door behind him. I dozed off again for another hour, but then I woke up decisively. Terry would be coming to my house to begin tearing down the ruined part, and I needed to see if any of my kitchen things could be saved.

Since this was liable to be a dirty job, I borrowed Jason's blue jumpsuit, the one he put on when he worked on his car. I looked in his closet and pulled out an old leather jacket Jason wore for rough work. I also appropriated a box of garbage bags. As I started Tara's car, I wondered how on earth I could repay her for its use. I reminded myself to pick up her suit. Since it was on my mind, I made a slight detour to retrieve it from the dry cleaner's.

Terry was in a stable mood today, to my relief. He was smiling as he smacked away at the charred boards of the back porch with a sledgehammer. Though the day was very cool, Terry wore only a sleeveless T-shirt tucked in his jeans. It covered most of the dreadful scars. After greeting him and registering that he didn't want to talk, I went in through the front door. I was drawn down the hall to the kitchen to look again at the damage.

The firefighters had said the floor was safe. It made me nervous to step out onto the scorched linoleum, but after a moment or two, I felt easier. I pulled on gloves and began to work, going through cabinets and cupboards and drawers. Some things had melted or twisted with the heat. A few things, like my plastic colander, were so warped it took me a second or two to identify what I was holding.

I tossed the ruined things directly out the south kitchen window, away from Terry.

I didn't trust any of the food that had been in the cabinets that were on the outer wall. The flour, the rice, the sugar – they'd all been in Tupperware containers, and though the seals had held, I just didn't want to use the contents. The same held true of the canned goods; for some reason, I felt uneasy about using food from cans that had gotten so hot.

Fortunately, my everyday stoneware and the good china that had belonged to my great-great-grandmother had survived, since they were in the cabinet farthest from the flames. Her sterling silver was in fine shape, too. My far more useful stainless tableware, much closer to the fire, was warped and twisted. Some of the pots and pans were usable.

I worked for two or three hours, consigning things to the growing pile outside the window or bagging them in Jason's garbage bags for future use in a new kitchen. Terry worked hard, too, taking a break every now and then to drink bottled water while he perched on the tailgate of his pickup. The temperature rose to the upper sixties. We might have a few more hard frosts, and there was always the chance of an ice storm, but it was possible to count on spring coming soon.

It wasn't a bad morning. I felt like I was taking a step toward regaining my home. Terry was an undemanding companion, since he didn't like to talk, and he was exorcising his demons with hard work. Terry was in his late fifties now. Some of the chest hair I could see above his T-shirt neck was gray. The hair on his head, once auburn, was fading as he aged. But he was a strong man, and he swung his sledgehammer with vigor and loaded boards onto the flatbed of his truck with no sign of strain.

Terry left to take a load to the parish dump. While he was gone, I went into my bedroom and made my bed – a strange and foolish thing to do, I know. I would have to take the sheets off and wash them; in fact, I'd have to wash almost every piece of fabric in the house to completely rid it of the smell of burning. I'd even have to wash the walls and repaint the hall, though the paint in the rest of the house seemed clean enough.

I was taking a break out in the yard when I heard a truck approaching a moment before it appeared, coming out of the trees that surrounded the driveway. To my astonishment, I recognized it as Alcide's truck, and I felt a pang of dismay. I'd told him to stay away.

He seemed miffed about something when he leaped out of the cab. I'd been sitting in the sunshine on one of my aluminum lawn chairs, wondering what time it was and wondering when the contractor would get here. After the all-round discomfort of my night at Jason's,

I was also planning on finding somewhere else to stay while the kitchen was being rebuilt. I couldn't imagine the rest of my house being habitable until the work was complete, and that might be months from now. Jason wouldn't want me around that long, I was sure. He'd have to put up with me if I wanted to stay – he was my brother, after all – but I didn't want to strain his fraternal spirit. There wasn't *anyone* I wanted to stay with for a couple of months, when I came to consider the matter.

'Why didn't you tell me?' Alcide bellowed as his feet touched the ground.

I sighed. Another angry man.

'We aren't big buddies right now,' I reminded him. 'But I would have gotten around to it. It's only been a couple of days.'

'You should have called me first thing,' he told me, striding around the house to survey the damage. He stopped right in front of me. 'You could have died,' he said, as if it was big news.

'Yes,' I said. 'I know that.'

'A vampire had to save you.' There was disgust in his voice. Vamps and Weres just didn't get along.

'Yes,' I agreed, though actually my savior had been Claudine. But Charles had killed the arsonist. 'Oh, would you rather I'd burned?'

'No, of course not!' He turned away, looked at the mostly dismantled porch. 'Someone's working on tearing down the damaged part already?'

'Yes.'

'I could have gotten a whole crew out here.'

'Terry volunteered.'

'I can get you a good rate on the reconstruction.'

'I've lined up a contractor.'

'I can loan you the money to do it.'

'I have the money, thank you very much.'

That startled him. 'You do? Where'd—' He stopped before saying something inexcusable. 'I didn't think your grandmother had had much to leave you,' he said, which was almost as bad.

'I earned the money,' I said.

'You earned the money from Eric?' he guessed accurately. Alcide's green eyes were hot with anger. I thought he was going to shake me.

'You just calm down, Alcide Herveaux,' I said sharply. 'How I earned it is none of your damn business. I'm glad to have it. If you'll get down off your high horse, I'll tell you that I'm glad you're concerned about me, and I'm grateful you're offering help. But don't treat me like I'm a slow fifth grader in the special class.'

Alcide stared down at me while my speech soaked in. 'I'm sorry. I thought you – I thought we were close enough for you to've called me that night. I thought . . . maybe you needed help.'

He was playing the 'you hurt my feelings' card.

'I don't mind asking for help when I need it. I'm not that proud,' I said. 'And I'm glad to see you.' (Not totally true.) 'But don't act like I can't do things for myself, because I can, and I am.'

'The vampires paid you for keeping Eric while the witches were in Shreveport?'

'Yes,' I said. 'My brother's idea. It embarrassed me. But now I'm grateful I've got the money. I won't have to borrow any to get the house put into shape.'

Terry Bellefleur returned with his pickup just then, and I introduced the two men. Terry didn't seem at all impressed by meeting Alcide. In fact, he went right back to work after he gave Alcide's hand a perfunctory shake. Alcide eyed Terry doubtfully.

'Where are you staying?' Alcide had decided not to ask questions about Terry's scars, thank goodness.

'I'm staying with Jason,' I said promptly, leaving out the fact that I hoped that would be temporary.

'How long is it gonna take to rebuild?'

'Here's the guy who can tell me,' I said gratefully. Randall Shurtliff was in a pickup, too, and he had his wife and partner with him. Delia Shurtliff was younger than Randall, pretty as a picture, and tough as nails. She was Randall's second wife. When he'd gotten divorced from his 'starter' wife, the one who'd had three children and cleaned his house for twelve years, Delia had already been working for Randall and had gradually begun to run his business for him far more efficiently than he'd ever done. He was able to give his first wife and sons more advantages with the money his second wife had helped him earn than he otherwise might have, had he married someone else. It was common knowledge (by which I mean I wasn't the only one who knew this) that Delia was very ready for Mary Helen to remarry and for the three Shurtliff boys to graduate from high school.

I shut out Delia's thoughts with a firm resolve to work on keeping my shields up. Randall was pleased to meet Alcide, whom he'd known by sight, and Randall was even more eager to take on rebuilding my kitchen when he knew I was a friend of Alcide's. The Herveaux family carried a lot of weight personally and financially in the building trade. To my irritation, Randall began addressing all his remarks to Alcide instead of to me. Alcide accepted this quite naturally.

I looked at Delia. Delia looked at me. We were very unlike, but we were of one mind at that moment.

'What do you think, Delia?' I asked her. 'How long?'

'He'll huff and he'll puff,' she said. Her hair was paler than mine, courtesy of the beauty salon, and she wore emphatic eye makeup, but she was dressed sensibly in khakis and a polo shirt with 'Shurtliff Construction' in script above her left breast. 'But he's got that house over on Robin Egg to finish. He can work on your kitchen before he begins a house in Clarice. So, say, three to four months from now, you'll have you a usable kitchen.'

'Thanks, Delia. Do I need to sign something?'

'We'll get an estimate ready for you. I'll bring it to the bar for you to check. We'll include the new appliances, because we can get a dealer discount. But I'll tell you right now, you're looking at this ballpark.'

She showed me the estimate on a kitchen renovation they had done a month before.

'I have it,' I said, though I gave one long shriek deep inside. Even with the insurance money, I'd be using up a big chunk of what I had in the bank.

I should be thankful, I reminded myself sternly, that Eric had paid me all that money, that I had it to spend. I wouldn't have to borrow from the bank or sell the land or take any other drastic step. I should think of that money as just passing through my account rather than living there. I hadn't actually owned it. I'd just had custody of it for a while.

'You and Alcide good friends?' Delia asked, our business concluded.

I gave it some thought. 'Some days,' I answered honestly.

She laughed, a harsh cackle that was somehow sexy. Both men looked around, Randall smiling, Alcide quizzical. They were too far away to hear what we were saying.

'I'll tell you something,' Delia Shurtliff said to me quietly. 'Just between you and me and the fencepost. Jackson Herveaux's secretary, Connie Babcock – you met her?'

I nodded. I'd at least seen her and talked to her when I'd dropped by Alcide's office in Shreveport.

'She got arrested this morning for stealing from Herveaux and Son.'

'What did she take?' I was all ears.

'This is what I don't understand. She was caught sneaking some papers out of Jackson Herveaux's office. Not business papers, but personal, the way I heard it. She said she'd been paid to do it.'

'By?'

'Some guy who owns a motorcycle dealership. Now, does that make sense?'

It did if you knew that Connie Babcock had been sleeping with Jackson Herveaux, as well as working in his office. It did if you suddenly realized that Jackson had taken Christine' Larrabee, a pure Were and influential, to the funeral of Colonel Flood, instead of taking the powerless human Connie Babcock.

While Delia elaborated on the story, I stood, lost in thought. Jackson Herveaux was without a doubt a clever businessman, but he was proving to be a stupid politician. Having Connie arrested was dumb. It drew attention to the Weres, had the potential to expose them. A people so secretive would not appreciate a leader who couldn't manage a problem with more finesse than that.

As a matter of fact, since Alcide and Randall were still discussing the rebuilding of my house with each other instead of with me, a lack of finesse appeared to run in the Herveaux family.

Then I frowned. It occurred to me that Patrick Furnan might be devious and clever enough to have engineered the whole thing – bribing the spurned Connie to steal Jackson's private papers, then ensuring she was caught – knowing that Jackson would react with a hot head. Patrick Furnan might be much smarter than he looked, and Jackson Herveaux much stupider, at least in the way that mattered if you wanted to be packmaster. I tried to shake off these disturbing speculations. Alcide hadn't said a word about Connie's arrest, so I had to conclude that he considered it none of my business. Okay, maybe he thought I had enough to worry about, and he was right. I turned my mind back to the moment.

'You think they'd notice if we left?' I asked Delia.

'Oh, yeah,' Delia said confidently. 'It might take Randall a minute, but he'd look around for me. He'd get lost if he couldn't find me.'

Here was a woman who knew her own worth. I sighed and thought about getting in my borrowed car and driving away. Alcide, catching sight of my face, broke off his discussion with my contractor and looked guilty. 'Sorry,' he called. 'Habit.'

Randall came back to where I was standing quite a bit faster than he'd wandered away. 'Sorry,' he apologized. 'We were talking shop. What did you have in mind, Sookie?'

'I want the same dimensions for the kitchen as before,' I said, having dropped visions of a larger room after seeing the estimate. 'But I want the new back porch to be just as wide as the kitchen, and I want to enclose it.'

Randall produced a tablet, and I sketched what I wanted.

'You want the sinks where they were? You want all the appliances where they were?'

After some discussion, I drew everything I wanted, and Randall said he'd call me when it was time to pick out the cabinets and the sinks and all the other incidentals.

'One thing I wish you'd do for me today or tomorrow is fix the door from the hall into the kitchen,' I said. 'I want to be able to lock the house.'

Randall rummaged around in the back of his pickup for a minute or two and came up with a brand-new doorknob with a lock, still in its package. 'This won't keep out anyone really determined,' he said, still in the apologetic vein, 'but it's better'n nothing.' He had it installed within fifteen minutes, and I was able to lock the sound part of the house away from the burned part. I felt much better, though I knew this lock wasn't worth much. I needed to put a dead bolt on the inside of the door; that would be even better. I wondered if I could do it myself, but I recalled that would entail cutting away some of the door frame, and I wasn't anything of a carpenter. Surely I could find someone who'd help me with that task.

Randall and Delia left with many assurances that I would be next on the list, and Terry resumed work. Alcide said, 'You're never alone,' in mildly exasperated tones.

'What did you want to talk about? Terry can't hear us over here.' I led the way over to where my aluminum chair was sitting under a tree. Its companion was leaning up against the rough bark of the oak, and Alcide unfolded it. It creaked a little under his weight as he settled into it. I assumed he was going to tell me about the arrest of Connie Babcock.

'I upset you the last time I talked to you,' he said directly.

I had to change mental gears at the unexpected opening. Okay, I liked a man who could apologize. 'Yes, you did.'

'You didn't want me to tell you I knew about Debbie?'

'I just hate that the whole thing happened. I hate that her family is taking it so hard. I hate that they don't know, that they're suffering. But I'm glad to be alive, and I'm not going to jail for defending myself.'

'If it'll make you feel any better, Debbie wasn't that close to her family. Her parents always preferred Debbie's little sister, though she didn't inherit any shifter characteristics. Sandra is the apple of their eye, and the only reason they're pursuing this with such vigor is that Sandra expected it.'

'You think they'll give up?'

'They think I did it,' Alcide said. 'The Pelts think that because Debbie got engaged to another man, I killed her. I got an e-mail from Sandra in response to mine about the private eyes.'

I could only gape at him. I had a horrible vista of the future in which I saw myself going down to the police station and confessing to save Alcide from a jail term. Even to be suspected of a murder he hadn't committed was an awful thing, and I couldn't permit it. It just hadn't occurred to me that someone else would be blamed for what I'd done.

'But,' Alcide continued, 'I can prove I didn't. Four pack members have sworn I was at Pam's house after Debbie left, and one female will swear I spent the night with her.'

He had been with the pack members, just somewhere else. I slumped with relief. I was not going to have a jealous spasm about the female. He wouldn't have called her that if he'd actually had sex with her.

'So the Pelts will just have to suspect someone else. That's not what I wanted to talk to you about, anyway.'

Alcide took my hand. His were big, and hard, and enclosed mine like he was holding something wild that would fly away if he relaxed his grip. 'I want you to think about seeing me on a steady basis,' Alcide said. 'As in, every day.'

Once again, the world seemed to rearrange itself around me. 'Huh?' I said.

'I like you very much,' he said. 'I think you like me, too. We want each other.' He leaned over to kiss me once on the cheek and then, when I didn't move, on the mouth. I was too surprised to get into it and unsure whether I wanted to anyway. It's not often a mind reader gets taken by surprise, but Alcide had achieved it.

He took a deep breath and continued. 'We enjoy each other's company. I want to see you in my bed so much it makes me ache. I wouldn't have spoken this soon, without us being together more, but you need a place to live right now. I have a condo in Shreveport. I want you to think about staying with me.'

If he'd whomped me upside the head with a two-by-four, I couldn't have been more stunned. Instead of trying so hard to stay out of people's heads, I should consider getting back into them. I started several sentences in my head, discarded them all. The warmth of him, the attraction of his big body, was something I had to fight as I struggled to sort my thoughts.

'Alcide,' I began at last, speaking over the background noise of Terry's sledgehammer knocking down the boards of my burned kitchen, 'you're right that I like you. In fact, I more than like you.' I couldn't even look at his face. I looked instead at his big hands, with their dusting of dark hair across the backs. If I looked down past his hands, I could see his muscular thighs and his ... Well, back to the hands. 'But the timing seems all wrong. I think you need more time to get over your relationship with Debbie, since you seemed so enslaved to her. You may feel that just saying the words 'I abjure you' got rid of all your feelings for Debbie, but I'm not convinced that's so.'

'It's a powerful ritual of my people,' Alcide said stiffly, and I risked a quick glance at his face.

'I could tell it was a powerful ritual,' I assured him, 'and it had a big effect on everyone there. But I can't believe that, quick as a flash, every single feeling you had for Debbie was uprooted when you said the words. That's just not how people work.'

'That's how werewolves work.' He looked stubborn. And determined.

I thought very hard about what I wanted to say.

'I'd love for someone to step in and solve all my problems,' I told him. 'But I don't want to accept your offer because I need a place to live and we're hot for each other. When my house is rebuilt, then we'll talk, if you still feel the same.'

'This is when you need me the most,' he protested, the words spilling out of his mouth in his haste to persuade me. 'You need me *now*. I need you *now*. We're right for each other. You know it.'

'No, I don't. I know that you're worried about a lot of things right now. You lost your lover, however it happened. I don't think it's sunk into you yet that you'll never see her again.'

He flinched.

'I shot her, Alcide. With a shotgun.'

His whole face clenched.

'See? Alcide, I've seen you rip into a person's flesh when you were being a wolf. And it didn't make me scared of you. Because *I'm on your side*. But you loved Debbie, at least for a time. We get into a relationship now, at some point you're going to look up and say, "Here's the one who ended her life".'

Alcide opened his mouth to protest, but I held up a hand. I wanted to finish.

'Plus, Alcide, your dad's in this succession struggle. He wants to win the election. Maybe you being in a settled relationship would help his ambitions. I don't know. But I don't want any part of Were politics.

I didn't appreciate you dragging me into it cold last week at the funeral. You should have let me decide.'

'I wanted them to get used to the sight of you by my side,' Alcide said, his face stiffening with offense. 'I meant it as an honor to you.'

'I might have appreciated that honor more if I'd known about it,' I snapped. It was a relief to hear another vehicle approaching, to see Andy Bellefleur get out of his Ford and watch his cousin knocking down my kitchen. For the first time in months, I was glad to see Andy.

I introduced Andy to Alcide, of course, and watched them size each other up. I like men in general, and some men in specific, but when I saw them practically circle each other as they sniffed each other's butts – excuse me, exchanged greetings – I just had to shake my head. Alcide was the taller by a good four inches, but Andy Bellefleur had been on his college wrestling team, and he was still a block of muscle. They were about the same age. I would put even money on them in a fight, providing that Alcide kept his human form.

'Sookie, you asked me to keep you posted on the man who died here,' Andy said.

Sure, but it had never occurred to me he'd actually do it. Andy did not have any very high opinion of me, though he'd always been a big fan of my rear end. It's wonderful being telepathic, huh?

'He has no prior record,' Andy said, looking down at the little notebook he'd produced. 'He has no known association with the Fellowship of the Sun.'

'But that doesn't make sense,' I said into the little silence that followed. 'Why would he set the fire otherwise?'

'I was hoping you could tell me that,' Andy said, his clear gray eyes meeting mine.

I'd had it with Andy, abruptly and finally. In our dealings over the years, he'd insulted me and wounded me, and now I'd encountered that last straw.

'Listen to me, Andy,' I said, and I looked right back into his eyes. 'I never did anything to you that I know of. I've never been arrested. I've never even jaywalked, or been late paying my taxes, or sold a drink to an underage teen. I've never even had a speeding ticket. Now someone tried to barbecue me inside my own home. Where do you get off, making me feel like I've done something wrong?' *Other than shoot Debbie Pelt*, a voice whispered in my head. It was the voice of my conscience.

'I don't think there's anything in this guy's past that would indicate he'd do this to you.'

'Fine! Then find out who did! Because someone burned my house, and it sure wasn't me!' I was yelling when I got to the last part, partly to drown the voice. My only recourse was to turn and walk away, striding around the house until I was out of Andy's sight. Terry gave me a sidelong look, but he didn't stop swinging his sledgehammer.

After a minute, I heard someone picking his way through the debris behind me. 'He's gone,' Alcide said, his deep voice just a tiny bit amused. 'I guess you're not interested in going any further with our conversation.'

'You're right,' I said briefly.

'Then I'll go back to Shreveport. Call me if you need me.'

'Sure.' I made myself be more polite. 'Thanks for your offer of help.'

'"Help"? I asked you to live with me!'

'Then thank you for asking me to live with you.' I couldn't help it if I didn't sound completely sincere. I said the right words. Then my grandmother's voice sounded in my head, telling me that I was acting like I was seven years old. I made myself turn around.

'I do appreciate your ... affection,' I said, looking up into Alcide's face. Even this early in the spring, he had a tan line from wearing a hard hat. His olive complexion would be shades darker in a few weeks. 'I do appreciate ...' I trailed off, not sure how to put it. I appreciated his willingness to consider me as an eligible woman to mate with, which so many men didn't, as well as his assumption that I would make a good mate and a good ally. This was as close as I could get to phrasing what I meant.

'But you're not having any.' The green eyes regarded me steadily.

'I'm not saying that.' I drew a breath. 'I'm saying now is not the time to work on a relationship with you.' *Though I wouldn't mind jumping your bones*, I added to myself wistfully.

But I wasn't going to do that on a whim, and certainly not with a man like Alcide. The new Sookie, the rebound Sookie, wasn't going to make the same mistake twice in a row. I was double rebounding. (If you rebound from the two men you've had so far, do you end up a virgin again? To what state are you rebounding?) Alcide gave me a hard hug and dropped a kiss on my cheek. He left while I was still mulling that over. Soon after Alcide left, Terry knocked off for the day. I changed from the jumpsuit into my work clothes. The afternoon had chilled, so I pulled on the jacket I'd borrowed from Jason's closet. It smelled faintly of Jason.

I detoured on the way to work to drop off the pink and black suit at Tara's house. Her car wasn't there, so I figured she was still at the shop. I let myself in and went back to her bedroom to put the plastic bag in her closet. The house was dusky and deep shadowed. It was almost dark outside. Suddenly my nerves thrummed with alarm. I shouldn't be here. I turned away from the closet and stared around the room. When my eyes got to the doorway, it was filled with a slim figure. I gasped before I could stop myself. Showing them you're scared is like waving a red flag in front of a bull.

I couldn't see Mickey's face to read his expression, if he had any.

'Where did that new bartender at Merlotte's come from?' he asked.

If I'd expected anything, it wasn't that.

'When Sam got shot, we needed another bartender in a hurry. We borrowed him from Shreveport,' I said. 'From the vampire bar.'

'Had he been there long?'

'No,' I said, managing to feel surprised even through my creeping fear. 'He hadn't been there long at all.'

Mickey nodded, as if that confirmed some conclusion he'd reached. 'Get out of here,' he said, his deep voice quite calm. 'You're a bad influence on Tara. She doesn't need anything but me, until I'm tired of her. Don't come back.'

The only way out of the room was through the door he was filling. I didn't trust myself to speak. I walked toward him as confidently as I could, and I wondered if he would move when I reached him. It felt like three hours later by the time I rounded Tara's bed and eased my way around her dressing table. When I showed no sign of slowing down, the vampire stepped aside. I couldn't stop myself from looking up at his face as I passed him, and he was showing fang. I shuddered.

I felt so sick for Tara that I couldn't stop myself. How had this happened to her?

When he saw my revulsion, he smiled.

I tucked the problem of Tara away in my heart to pull out later. Maybe I could think of something to do for her, but as long as she seemed willing to stay with this monstrous creature, I didn't see what I could do to help.

Sweetie Des Arts was outside smoking a cigarette when I parked my car at the back of Merlotte's. She looked pretty good, despite being wrapped in a stained white apron. The outside floodlights lit up every little crease in her skin, revealing that Sweetie was a little older than I'd thought, but she still looked very fit for someone who cooked most of the day. In fact, if it hadn't been for the white apron swathing her and the lingering perfume of cooking oil, Sweetie might have been a sexy woman. She certainly carried herself like a person who was used to being noticed.

We'd had such a succession of cooks that I hadn't made much effort to know her. I was sure she'd drift away sooner or later – probably sooner. But she raised a hand in greeting and seemed to want to talk to me, so I paused.

'I'm sorry about your house,' she said. Her eyes were shining in the artificial light. It didn't smell so great here by the Dumpster, but Sweetie was as relaxed as if she were on an Acapulco beach.

'Thanks,' I said. I just didn't want to talk about it. 'How are you today?'

'Fine, thanks.' She waved the hand with the cigarette around, indicating the parking lot. 'Enjoying the view. Hey, you got something on your jacket.' Holding her hand carefully to one side so she wouldn't get ash on me, she leaned forward, closer than my comfort zone permitted, and flicked something off my shoulder. She sniffed. Maybe the smoky smell of the burned wood clung to me, despite all my efforts.

'I need to go in. Time for my shift,' I said.

'Yeah, I gotta get back in myself. It's a busy night.' But Sweetie stayed where she was. 'You know, Sam's just nuts about you.'

'I've worked for him for a long time.'

'No, I think it goes a little beyond that.'

'Ah, I don't think so, Sweetie.' I couldn't think of any polite way to conclude a conversation that had gotten way too personal.

'You were with him when he got shot, right?'

'Yeah, he was heading for his trailer and I was heading for my car.' I wanted to make it clear we were going in different directions.

'You didn't notice anything?' Sweetie leaned against the wall and tilted her head back, her eyes closed as if she were sunbathing.

'No. I wish I had. I'd like the police to catch whoever's doing this.'

'Did you ever think there might be a reason those people were targeted?'

'No,' I lied stoutly. 'Heather and Sam and Calvin have nothing in common.'

Sweetie opened one brown eye and squinted up at me. 'If we were in a mystery, they'd all know the same secret, or they'd have witnessed the same accident, or something. Or the police would find out they all had the same dry cleaner.' Sweetie flicked the ashes off her cigarette.

I relaxed a little. 'I see what you're getting at,' I said. 'But I think real life doesn't have as many patterns as a serial killer book. I think they were all chosen at random.'

Sweetie shrugged. 'You're probably right.' I saw she'd been reading a Tami Hoag suspense novel, now tucked into an apron pocket. She tapped her book with one blunt fingernail. 'Fiction just makes it all more interesting. Truth is so boring.'

'Not in my world,' I said.

Chapter 11

Bill brought a date into Merlotte's that night. I assumed this was payback for my kissing Sam, or maybe I was just being proud. This possible payback was in the form of a woman from Clarice. I'd seen her in the bar before every once in a while. She was a slim brunette with shoulder-length hair, and Danielle could hardly wait to tell me she was Selah Pumphrey, a real estate saleswoman who'd gotten the million-dollar sales award the year before.

I hated her instantly, utterly, and passionately.

So I smiled as brightly as a thousand-watt bulb and brought them Bill's warm TrueBlood and her cold screwdriver quick as a wink. I didn't spit in the screwdriver, either. That was beneath me, I told myself. Also, I didn't have enough privacy.

Not only was the bar crowded, but Charles was eyeing me watchfully. The pirate was in fine form tonight, wearing a white shirt with billowing sleeves and navy blue Dockers, a bright scarf pulled through the belt loops for a dash of color. His eye patch matched the Dockers, and it was embroidered with a gold star. This was as exotic as Bon Temps could get.

Sam beckoned me over to his tiny table, which we'd wedged into a corner. He had his bad leg propped up on another chair. 'Are you all right, Sookie?' Sam murmured, turning away from the crowd at the bar so no one could even read his lips.

'Sure, Sam!' I gave him an amazed expression. 'Why not?' At that moment, I hated him for kissing me, and I hated me for responding.

He rolled his eyes and smiled for a fleeting second. 'I think I've solved your housing problem,' he said to distract me. 'I'll tell you later.' I hurried off to take an order. We were swamped that night. The warming weather and the attraction of a new bartender had combined to fill Merlotte's with the optimistic and the curious.

I'd left *Bill*, I reminded myself proudly. Though he'd cheated on me, he hadn't wanted us to break up. I had to keep telling myself that, so I wouldn't hate everyone present who was witnessing my humiliation. Of course, none of the people knew any of the circumstances, so they were free to imagine that Bill had dropped me for this brunette bitch. Which was *so* not the case.

I stiffened my back, broadened my smile, and hustled drinks. After the first ten minutes, I began to relax and see that I was behaving like a fool. Like millions of couples, Bill and I had broken up. Naturally, he'd begun dating someone else. If I'd had the normal run of boyfriends, starting when I was thirteen or fourteen, my relationship with Bill would just be another in a long line of relationships that hadn't panned out. I'd be able to take this in stride, or at least in perspective.

I had no perspective. Bill was my first love, in every sense.

The second time I brought drinks to their table, Selah Pumphrey looked at me uneasily when I beamed at her. 'Thanks,' she said uncertainly.

'Don't mention it,' I advised her through clenched teeth, and she blanched.

Bill turned away. I hoped he wasn't hiding a smile. I went back to the bar.

Charles said, 'Shall I give her a good scare, if she spends the night with him?'

I'd been standing behind the bar with him, staring into the glass-fronted refrigerator we kept back there. It held soft drinks, bottled blood, and sliced lemons and limes. I'd come to get a slice of lemon and a cherry to put on a Tom Collins, and I'd just stayed. He was entirely too perceptive.

'Yes, please,' I said gratefully. The vampire pirate was turning into an ally. He'd saved me from burning, he'd killed the man who'd set fire to my house, and now he was offering to scare Bill's date. You had to like that.

'Consider her terrified,' he said in a courtly way, bowing with a florid sweep of his arm, his other hand on his heart.

'Oh, you,' I said with a more natural smile, and got out the bowl of sliced lemons.

It took every ounce of self-control I had to stay out of Selah Pumphrey's head. I was proud of myself for making the effort.

To my horror, the next time the door opened, Eric came in. My heart rate picked up immediately, and I felt almost faint. I was going to have to stop reacting like this. I wished I could forget our 'time together' (as one of my favorite romance novels might term it) as thoroughly as Eric had. Maybe I should track down a witch, or a hypnotherapist, and give myself a dose of amnesia. I bit down on the inside of my cheek, hard, and carried two pitchers of beer over to a table of young couples who were celebrating the promotion of one of the men to supervisor – of someone, somewhere.

Eric was talking to Charles when I turned around, and though vampires can be pretty stone-faced when they're dealing with each other, it seemed apparent to me that Eric wasn't happy with his loaned-out bartender. Charles was nearly a foot shorter than his boss, and his head was tilted up as they talked. But his back was stiff, his fangs protruded a bit, and his eyes were glowing. Eric was pretty scary when he was mad, too. He was now definitely looking toothy. The humans around the bar were tending to find something to do somewhere else in the room, and any minute they'd start finding something to do at some other bar.

I saw Sam grabbing at a cane – an improvement over the crutches – so he could get up and go over to the pair, and I sped over to his table in the corner. 'You stay put,' I told him in a very firm low voice. 'Don't you think about intervening.'

I heel and toed it over to the bar. 'Hi, Eric! How you doing? Is there anything I can help you with?' I smiled up at him.

'Yes. I need to talk to you, too,' he growled.

'Then why don't you come with me? I was just going to step out back to take a break,' I offered.

I took hold of his arm and towed him through the door and down the hall to the employees' entrance. We were outside in the night-cold air before you could say Jack Robinson.

'You better not be about to tell me what to do,' I said instantly. 'I've had enough of that for one day, and Bill's in here with a woman, and I lost my kitchen. I'm in a bad mood.' I underlined this by squeezing Eric's arm, which was like gripping a small tree trunk.

'I care nothing about your mood,' he said instantly, and he was showing fang. 'I pay Charles Twining to watch you and keep you safe, and who hauls you out of the fire? A fairy. While Charles is out in the yard, killing the fire setter rather than saving his hostess's life. Stupid Englishman!'

'He's supposed to be here as a favor to Sam. He's supposed to be here helping Sam out.' I peered at Eric doubtfully.

'Like I give a damn about a shifter,' the vampire said impatiently.

I stared up at him.

'There's something about you,' Eric said. His voice was cold, but his eyes were not. 'There is something I am almost on the verge of knowing about you, and it's under my skin, this feeling that something happened while I was cursed, something I should know about. Did we have sex, Sookie? But I can't think that was it, or it alone. Something happened. Your coat was ruined with brain tissue. Did I kill someone, Sookie? Is that it? You're protecting me from what I did while I was cursed?' His eyes were glowing like lamps in the darkness.

I'd never thought he might be wondering whom he'd killed. But frankly, if it had occurred to me, I wouldn't have thought Eric would care; what difference would one human life make to a vampire as old as this one? But he seemed mighty upset. Now that I understood what he was worried about, I said, 'Eric, you did not kill anyone at my house that night.' I stopped short.

'You have to tell me what happened.' He bent a little to look into my face. 'I hate not knowing what I did. I've had a life longer than you can even imagine, and I remember every second of it, except for those days I spent with you.'

'I can't make you remember,' I said as calmly as I could. 'I can only tell you that you stayed with me for several days, and then Pam came to get you.'

Eric stared into my eyes a little longer. 'I wish I could get in your head and get the truth out of you,' he said, which alarmed me more than I wanted to show. 'You've had my blood. I can tell you're concealing things from me.' After a moment's silence, he said, 'I wish I knew who's trying to kill you. And I hear you had a visit from some private detectives. What did they want of you?'

'Who told you that?' Now I had something else to worry about. Someone was informing on me. I could feel my blood pressure rise. I wondered if Charles was reporting to Eric every night.

'Is this something to do with the woman who's missing, that bitch the Were loved so much? Are you protecting him? If I didn't kill her, did he? Did she die in front of us?'

Eric had gripped my shoulders, and the pressure was excruciating.

'Listen, you're hurting me! Let go.'

Eric's grip loosened, but he didn't remove his hands.

My breath began to come faster and shallower, and the air was full of the crackling of danger. I was sick to death of being threatened.

'Tell me now,' he demanded.

He would have power over me for the rest of my life if I told him he'd seen me kill someone. Eric already knew more about me than I wanted him to, because I'd had his blood, and he'd had mine. Now I rued our blood exchange more than ever. Eric was sure I was concealing something important.

'You were so sweet when you didn't know who you were,' I said, and whatever he'd been expecting me to say, it wasn't that. Astonishment played tag with outrage across his handsome face. Finally, he was amused.

'Sweet?' he said, one corner of his mouth turning up in a smile.

'Very,' I said, trying to smile back. 'We gossiped like old buddies.' My shoulders ached. Probably everyone in the bar needed a new drink. But I couldn't go back in just yet. 'You were scared and alone, and you liked to talk to me. It was fun having you around.'

'Fun,' he said thoughtfully. 'I'm not fun now?'

'No, Eric. You're too busy being . . . yourself.' Head boss vampire, political animal, budding tycoon.

He shrugged. 'Is myself so bad? Many women seem to think not.'

'I'm sure they do.' I was tired to the bone.

The back door opened. 'Sookie, are you all right?' Sam had hobbled to my rescue. His face was stiff with pain.

'Shifter, she doesn't need your assistance,' Eric said.

Sam didn't say anything. He just kept Eric's attention.

'I was rude,' Eric said, not exactly apologetically, but civilly enough. 'I'm on your premises. I'll be gone. Sookie,' he said to me, 'we haven't finished this conversation, but I see this isn't the time or place.'

'I'll see you,' I said, since I knew I had no choice.

Eric melted into the darkness, a neat trick that I'd love to master someday.

'What is he so upset about?' Sam asked. He hobbled out of the doorway and leaned against the wall.

'He doesn't remember what happened while he was cursed,' I said, speaking slowly out of sheer weariness. 'That makes him feel like he's lost control. Vampires are big on having control. I guess you noticed.'

Sam smiled – a small smile, but genuine. 'Yes, that had come to my attention,' he admitted. 'I'd also noticed they're pretty possessive.'

'You're referring to Bill's reaction when he walked in on us?' Sam nodded. 'Well, he seems to have gotten over it.'

'I think he's just repaying you in kind.'

I felt awkward. Last night, I'd been on the verge of going to bed with Sam. But I was far from feeling passionate at this moment, and Sam's leg had been hurt badly in his fall. He didn't look as if he could romance a rag doll, much less a robust woman like me. I knew it was wrong to think of indulging in some sex play with my boss, though Sam and I had been teetering on a fine edge for months. Coming down on the 'no' side was the safest, sanest thing to do. Tonight, particularly after the emotionally jangling events of the past hour, I wanted to be safe.

'He stopped us in time,' I said.

Sam raised a fine red-gold eyebrow. 'Did you want to be stopped?'

'Not at that moment,' I admitted. 'But I guess it was for the best.'

Sam just looked at me for a moment. 'What I was going to tell you, though I was going to wait until after the bar closed, is that one of my rental houses is empty right now. It's the one next to – well, you remember, the one where Dawn . . .'

'Died,' I finished.

'Right. I had that one redone, and it's rented out now. So you'd have a neighbor, and you're not used to that. But the empty side is furnished. You'd only have to bring a few linens, your clothes, and some pots and pans.' Sam smiled. 'You could get that in a car. By the way, where'd you get this?' He nodded at the Malibu.

I told him how generous Tara had been, and I also told him I was worried about her. I repeated the warning Eric had given me about Mickey.

When I saw how anxious Sam looked, I felt like a selfish creep for burdening him with all this. Sam had enough to worry about. I said, 'I'm sorry. You don't need to hear more troubles. Come on, let's go back inside.'

Sam stared at me. 'I do need to sit down,' he said after a moment.

'Thanks for the rental. Of course I'll pay you. I'm so glad to have a place to live where I can come and go without bothering anyone! How much is it? I think my insurance will pay for me renting a place to live while my house is being fixed.'

Sam gave me a hard look, and then named a price that I was sure was well below his usual rate. I slid my arm around him because his limp was so bad. He accepted the help without a struggle, which made me think even better of him. He hobbled down the hall with my help and settled in the rolling chair behind his desk with a sigh. I pushed over one of the visitor chairs so he could put his leg up on it if he wanted, and he used it immediately. Under the strong fluorescent light in his office, my boss looked haggard.

'Get back to work,' he said mock-threateningly. 'I'll bet they're mobbing Charles.'

The bar was just as chaotic as I'd feared, and I began tending to my tables immediately. Danielle shot me a dirty look, and even Charles looked less than happy. But gradually, moving as fast as I could, I served fresh drinks, took away empty glasses, dumped the occasional ashtray, wiped the sticky tables, and smiled at and spoke to as many people as I could. I could kiss my tips good-bye, but at least peace was restored.

Bit by bit, the pulse of the bar slowed and returned to normal. Bill and his date were deep in conversation, I noticed . . . though I made a great effort not to keep glancing their way. To my dismay, every single time I saw them as a couple, I felt a wave of rage that did not speak well for my character. For another thing, though my feelings were a matter of indifference to almost ninety percent of the bar's patrons, the other ten percent were watching like hawks to see if Bill's date was making me suffer. Some of them would be glad to see it, and some wouldn't – but it was no one's business, either way.

As I was cleaning off a table that had just been vacated, I felt a tap on my shoulder. I picked up a foreshadowing just as I turned, and that enabled me to keep my smile in place. Selah Pumphrey was waiting for my attention, her own smile bright and armor plated.

She was taller than I, and perhaps ten pounds lighter. Her makeup was expensive and expert, and she smelled like a million bucks. I reached out and touched her brain without even thinking twice.

Selah was thinking she had it all over me, unless I was fantastic in bed. Selah thought that lower-class women must always be better in bed, because they were less inhibited. She knew she was slimmer, was smarter, made more money, and was far more educated and better read than the waitress she was looking at. But Selah Pumphrey doubted her own sexual skill and had a terror of making herself vulnerable. I blinked. This was more than I wanted to know.

It was interesting to discover that (in Selah's mind) since I was poor and uneducated, I was more in touch with my nature as a sexual being. I'd have to tell all the other poor people in Bon Temps. Here we'd been having a wonderful time screwing one another, having much better sex than smart upper-class people, and we hadn't even appreciated it.

'Yes?' I asked.

'Where is the ladies' room?' she asked.

'Through that door there. The one with restrooms' on the sign above it.' I should be grateful I was clever enough to read signs.

'Oh! Sorry, I didn't notice.'

I just waited.

'So, um, you got any tips for me? About dating a vampire?' She waited, looking nervous and defiant all at once.

'Sure,' I said. 'Don't eat any garlic.' And I turned away from her to wipe down the table.

Once I was certain she was out of the room, I swung around to carry two empty beer mugs to the bar, and when I turned back, Bill was standing there. I gave a gasp of surprise. Bill has dark brown hair and of course the whitest skin you can imagine. His eyes are as dark as his hair. Right at the moment, those eyes were fixed on mine.

'Why did she talk to you?' he asked.

'Wanted to know the way to the bathroom.'

He cocked an eyebrow, glancing up at the sign.

'She just wanted to take my measure,' I said. 'At least, that's my guess.' I felt oddly comfortable with Bill at that moment, no matter what had passed between us.

'Did you scare her?'

'I didn't try to.'

'Did you scare her?' he asked again in a sterner voice. But he smiled at me.

'No,' I said. 'Did you want me to?'

He shook his head in mock disgust. 'Are you jealous?'

'Yes.' Honesty was always safest. 'I hate her skinny thighs and her elitist attitude. I hope she's a dreadful bitch who makes you so miserable that you howl when you remember me.'

'Good,' said Bill. 'That's good to hear.' He gave me a brush of lips on my cheek. At the touch of his cool flesh, I shivered, remembering. He did, too. I saw the heat flare in his eyes, the fangs begin to run out. Then Catfish Hunter yelled to me to stir my stumps and bring him another bourbon and Coke, and I walked away from my first lover.

It had been a long, long day, not only from a physical-energy-expended measurement, but also from an emotional-depths-plumbed point of view. When I let myself into my brother's house, there were giggles and squeakings coming from his bedroom, and I deduced Jason was consoling himself in the usual way. Jason might be upset that his new community suspected him of a foul crime, but he was not so upset that it affected his libido.

I spent as brief a time in the bathroom as I could and went into the guest room, shutting the door firmly behind me. Tonight the couch looked a lot more inviting than it had the evening before. As I curled up on my side and pulled the quilt over me, I realized that the woman spending the night with my brother was a shifter; I could feel it in the faint pulsing redness of her brain.

I hoped she was Crystal Norris. I hoped Jason had somehow persuaded the girl that he had nothing to do with the shootings. If Jason wanted to compound his troubles, the best way possible would be to cheat on Crystal, the woman he'd chosen from the werepanther community. And surely even Jason wasn't that stupid. Surely.

He wasn't. I met Crystal in the kitchen the next morning after ten o'clock. Jason was long gone, since he had to be at work by seven forty-five. I was drinking my first mug of coffee when Crystal stumbled in, wearing one of Jason's shirts, her face blurry with sleep.

Crystal was not my favorite person, and I was not hers, but she said, 'Morning' civilly enough. I agreed that it was morning, and I got out a mug for her. She grimaced and got out a glass, filling it with ice and then Coca-Cola. I shuddered.

'How's your uncle?' I asked, when she seemed conscious.

'He's doing better,' she said. 'You ought to go see him. He liked having you visit.'

'I guess you're sure Jason didn't shoot him.'

'I am,' she said briefly. 'I didn't want to talk to him at first, but once he got me on the phone, he just talked his way out of me suspecting him.'

I wanted to ask her if the other inhabitants of Hotshot were willing to give Jason the benefit of the doubt, but I hated to bring up a touchy subject.

I thought of what I had to do today: I had to go get enough clothes, some sheets and blankets, and some kitchen gear from the house, and get those things installed in Sam's duplex.

Moving into a small, furnished place was a perfect solution to my housing problem. I had forgotten Sam owned several small houses on Berry Street, three of them duplexes. He worked on them himself, though sometimes he hired JB du Rone, a high school friend of mine, to do simple repairs and maintenance chores. Simple was the best way to keep it, with JB.

After I retrieved my things, I might have time to go see Calvin. I showered and dressed, and Crystal was sitting in the living room watching TV when I left. I assumed that was okay with Jason.

Terry was hard at work when I pulled into the clearing. I walked around back to check his progress, and I was delighted to see he'd done more than I'd have thought possible. He smiled when I said so, and paused in loading broken boards into his truck. 'Tearing down is always easier than building up,' he said. This was no big philosophical statement, but a builder's summary. 'I should be done in two more days, if nothing happens to slow me down. There's no rain in the forecast.'

'Great. How much will I owe you?'

'Oh,' he muttered, shrugging and looking embarrassed. 'A hundred? Fifty?'

'No, not enough.' I ran a quick estimate of his hours in my head, multiplied. 'More like three.'

'Sookie, I'm not charging you that much.' Terry got his stubborn face on. 'I wouldn't charge you anything, but I got to get a new dog.'

Terry bought a very expensive Catahoula hunting dog about every four years. He wasn't turning in the old models for new ones. Something always seemed to happen to Terry's dogs, though he took great care of them. After he'd had the first hound about three years, a truck had hit him. Someone had fed poisoned meat to the second. The third one, the one he'd named Molly, had gotten snake-bit, and the bite had turned septic. For months now, Terry had been on the list for one in the next litter born at the kennel in Clarice that bred Catahoulas.

'You bring that puppy around for me to hug,' I suggested, and he smiled. Terry was at his best in the outdoors, I realized for the first time. He always seemed more comfortable mentally and physically when he was not under a roof, and when he was outside with a dog, he seemed quite normal.

I unlocked the house and went in to gather what I might need. It was a sunny day, so the absence of electric light wasn't a problem. I filled a big plastic laundry basket with two sets of sheets and an old chenille bedspread, some more clothes, and a few pots and pans. I would have to get a new coffeepot. My old one had melted.

And then, standing there looking out the window at the coffee-maker, which I'd pitched to the top of the trash heap, I understood how close I'd come to dying. The realization hit me broadside.

One minute I was standing at my bedroom window, looking out at the misshaped bit of plastic; the next I was sitting on the floor, staring at the painted boards and trying to breathe.

Why did it hit me now, after three days? I don't know. Maybe there was something about the way the Mr Coffee looked: cord charred, plastic warped with the heat. The plastic had literally bubbled. I looked at the skin of my hands and shuddered. I stayed on the floor, shivering and shaking, for an unmeasured bit of time. For the first minute or two after that, I had no thoughts at all. The closeness of my brush with death simply overwhelmed me.

Claudine had not only most probably saved my life; she had certainly saved me from pain so excruciating that I would have wanted to be dead. I owed her a debt I would never be able to repay.

Maybe she really was my fairy godmother.

I got up, shook myself. Grabbing up the plastic basket, I left to go move into my new home.

Chapter 12

I let myself in with the key I'd gotten from Sam. I was on the right side of a duplex, the mirror of the one next door presently occupied by Halleigh Robinson, the young schoolteacher dating Andy Bellefleur. I figured I was likely to have police protection at least part of the time, and Halleigh would be gone during most of the day, which was nice considering my late hours.

The living room was small and contained a flowered couch, a low coffee table, and an armchair. The next room was the kitchen, which was tiny, of course. But it had a stove, a refrigerator, and a microwave. No dishwasher, but I'd never had one. Two plastic chairs were tucked under a tiny table.

After I'd glanced at the kitchen I went through into the small hall that separated the larger (but still small) bedroom on the right from the smaller (tiny) bedroom and the bathroom on the left. At the end of the hall there was a door to the little back porch.

This was a very basic accommodation, but it was quite clean. There was central heating and cooling, and the floors were level. I ran a hand around the windows. They fit well. Nice. I reminded myself I'd have to keep the venetian blinds drawn down, since I had neighbors.

I made up the double bed in the larger bedroom. I put my clothes away in the freshly painted chest of drawers. I started a list of other things I needed: a mop, a broom, a bucket, some cleaning products . . . those had been on the back porch. I'd have to get my vacuum cleaner out of the house. It had been in the closet in the living room, so it should be fine. I'd brought one of my phones to plug in over here, so I would have to arrange with the phone company for them to route calls to this address. I'd loaded my television into my car, but I had to arrange for my cable to be hooked up here. I'd have to call from Merlotte's. Since the fire, all my time was being absorbed with the mechanics of living.

I sat on the hard couch, staring into space. I tried to think of something fun, something I could look forward to. Well, in two months, it'd be sunbathing time. That made me smile. I enjoyed lying in the sun in a little bikini, timing myself carefully so I didn't burn. I loved the smell of coconut oil. I took pleasure in shaving my legs and removing most of my other body hair so I'd look smooth as a baby's bottom. And I don't want to hear any lectures about how bad tanning is for you. That's my vice. Everybody gets one.

More immediately, it was time to go to the library and get another batch of books; I'd retrieved my last bagful while I was at the house, and I'd spread them out on my tiny porch here so they'd air out. So going to the library – that would be fun.

Before I went to work, I decided I'd cook myself something in my new kitchen. That necessitated a trip to the grocery store, which took longer than I'd planned because I kept seeing staples I was sure I'd need. Putting the groceries away in the duplex cabinets made me feel that I really lived there. I browned a couple of pork chops and put them in the oven, microwaved a potato, and heated some peas. When I had to work nights, I usually went to Merlotte's at about five, so my home meal on those days was a combination lunch and dinner.

After I'd eaten and cleaned up, I thought I just had time to drive down to visit Calvin in the Grainger hospital.

The twins had not arrived to take up their post in the lobby again, if they were still keeping vigil. Dawson was still stationed outside Calvin's room. He nodded to me, gestured to me to stop while I was several feet away, and stuck his head in Calvin's room. To my relief, Dawson swung the door wide open for me to enter and even patted my shoulder as I went in.

Calvin was sitting up in the padded chair. He clicked off the television as I came in. His color was better, his beard and hair were clean and trimmed, and he looked altogether more like himself. He was wearing pajamas of blue broadcloth. He still had a tube or two in, I saw. He actually tried to push himself up out of the chair.

'No, don't you dare get up!' I pulled over a straight chair and sat in front of him. 'Tell me how you are.'

'Glad to see you,' he said. Even his voice was stronger. 'Dawson said you wouldn't take any help. Tell me who set that fire.'

'That's the strange thing, Calvin. I don't know why this man set the fire. His family came to see me . . .' I hesitated, because Calvin was recuperating from his own brush with death, and he shouldn't have to worry about other stuff.

But he said, 'Tell me what you're thinking,' and he sounded so interested that I ended up relating everything to the wounded shifter: my doubts about the arsonist's motives, my relief that the damage could be repaired, my concern about the trouble between Eric and Charles Twining. And I told Calvin that the police here had learned of more clusters of sniper activity.

'That would clear Jason,' I pointed out, and he nodded. I didn't push it.

'At least no one else has been shot,' I said, trying to think of something positive to throw in with the dismal mix.

'That we know of,' Calvin said.

'What?'

'That we know of. Maybe someone else has been shot, and no one's found 'em yet.'

I was astonished at the thought, and yet it made sense. 'How'd you think of that?'

'I don't have nothing else to do,' he said with a small smile. 'I don't read, like you do. I'm not much one for television, except for sports.' Sure enough, the station he'd had on when I'd entered had been ESPN.

'What do you do in your spare time?' I asked out of sheer curiosity.

Calvin was pleased I'd asked him a personal question. 'I work pretty long hours at Norcross,' he said. 'I like to hunt, though I'd rather hunt at the full moon.' In his panther body. Well, I could understand that.

'I like to fish. I love mornings when I can just sit in my boat on the water and not worry about a thing.'

'Uh-huh,' I said encouragingly. 'What else?'

'I like to cook. We have shrimp boils sometimes, or we cook up a whole mess of catfish and we eat outside – catfish and hush puppies and slaw and watermelon. In the summer, of course.'

It made my mouth water just to think about it.

'In the winter, I work on the inside of my house. I go out and cut wood for the people in our community who can't cut their own. I've always got something to do, seems like.'

Now I knew twice as much about Calvin Norris as I had.

'Tell me how you're recovering,' I asked.

'I've still got the damn IV in,' he said, gesturing with his arm. 'Other than that, I'm a lot better. We heal pretty good, you know.'

'How are you explaining Dawson to the people from your work who come to visit?' There were flower arrangements and bowls of fruit and even a stuffed cat crowding the level surfaces in the room.

'Just tell 'em he's my cousin here to make sure I won't get too wore out with visitors.'

I was pretty sure no one would question Dawson directly.

'I have to get to work,' I said, catching a glimpse of the clock on the wall. I was oddly reluctant to leave. I'd enjoyed having a regular conversation with someone. Little moments like these were rare in my life.

'Are you still worried about your brother?' he asked.

'Yes.' But I'd made my mind up I wouldn't beg again. Calvin had heard me out the first time. There wasn't any need for a repeat.

'We're keeping an eye on him.'

I wondered if the watcher had reported to Calvin that Crystal was spending the night with Jason. Or maybe Crystal herself was the watcher? If so, she was certainly taking her job seriously. She was watching Jason about as close as he could be watched.

'That's good,' I said. 'That's the best way to find out he didn't do it.' I was relieved to hear Calvin's news, and the longer I pondered it, the more I realized I should have figured it out myself.

'Calvin, you take care.' I rose to leave, and he held up his cheek. Rather reluctantly, I touched my lips to it.

He was thinking that my lips were soft and that I smelled good. I couldn't help but smile as I left. Knowing someone simply finds you attractive is always a boost to the spirits.

I drove back to Bon Temps and stopped by the library before I went to work. The Renard Parish library is an old ugly brown-brick building erected in the thirties. It looks every minute of its age. The librarians had made many justified complaints about the heating and cooling, and the electrical wiring left a lot to be desired. The library's parking lot was in bad shape, and the old clinic next door, which had opened its doors in 1918, now had boarded-up windows – always a depressing sight. The long-closed clinic's overgrown lot looked more like a jungle than a part of downtown.

I had allotted myself ten minutes to exchange my books. I was in and out in eight. The library parking lot was almost empty, since it was just before five o'clock. People were shopping at Wal-Mart or already home cooking supper.

The winter light was fading. I was not thinking about anything in particular, and that saved my life. In the nick of time, I identified intense excitement pulsing from another brain, and reflexively I ducked, feeling a sharp shove in my shoulder as I did so, and then a hot lance of blinding pain, and then wetness and a big noise. This all happened so fast I could not definitely sequence it when I later tried to reconstruct the moment.

A scream came from behind me, and then another. Though I didn't know how it had happened, I found myself on my knees beside my car, and blood was spattered over the front of my white T-shirt.

Oddly, my first thought was *Thank God I didn't have my new coat on.*

The person who'd screamed was Portia Bellefleur. Portia was not her usual collected self as she skidded across the parking lot to crouch beside me. Her eyes went one way, then another, as she tried to spot danger coming from any direction.

'Hold still,' she said sharply, as though I'd proposed running a marathon. I was still on my knees, but keeling over appeared to be a pleasant option. Blood was trickling down my arm. 'Someone shot you, Sookie. Oh my God, oh my God.'

'Take the books,' I said. 'I don't want to get blood on the books. I'll have to pay for them.'

Portia ignored me. She was talking into her cell phone. People talked on their phones at the damnedest times! In the library, for goodness's sake, or at the optometrist. Or in the bar. Jabber, jabber, jabber. As if everything was so important it couldn't wait. So I put the books on the ground beside me all by myself.

Instead of kneeling, I found myself sitting, my back against my car. And then, as if someone had taken a slice out of my life, I discovered I was lying on the pavement of the library parking lot, staring at someone's big old oil stain. People should take better care of their cars. . . .

Out.

'Wake up,' a voice was saying. I wasn't in the parking lot, but in a bed. I thought my house was on fire again, and Claudine was trying to get me out. People were always trying to get me out of bed. Though this didn't sound like Claudine; this sounded more like . . .

'Jason?' I tried to open my eyes. I managed to peer through my barely parted lids to identify my brother. I was in a dimly lit blue room, and I hurt so bad I wanted to cry.

'You got shot,' he said. 'You got shot, and I was at Merlotte's, waiting for you to get there.'

'You sound . . . happy,' I said through lips that felt oddly thick and stiff. Hospital.

'I couldn't have done it! I was with people the whole time! I had Hoyt in the truck with me from work to Merlotte's, because his truck's in the shop. I am *covered*.'

'Oh, good. I'm glad I got shot, then. As long as you're okay.' It was such an effort to say it, I was glad when Jason picked up on the sarcasm.

'Yeah, hey, I'm sorry about that. At least it wasn't serious.'

'It isn't?'

'I forgot to tell you. Your shoulder got creased, and it's going to hurt for a while. Press this button if it hurts. You can give yourself pain medication. Cool, huh? Listen, Andy's outside.'

I pondered that, finally deduced Andy Bellefleur was there in his official capacity. 'Okay,' I said. 'He can come in.' I stretched out a finger and carefully pushed the button.

I blinked then, and it must have been a long blink, because when I pried my eyes open again, Jason was gone and Andy was in his place, a little notebook and a pen in his hands. There was something I had to tell him, and after a moment's reflection, I knew what it was.

'Tell Portia I said thank you,' I told him.

'I will,' he said seriously. 'She's pretty shook up. She's never been that close to violence before. She thought you were gonna die.'

I could think of nothing to say to that. I waited for him to ask me what he wanted to know. His mouth moved, and I guess I answered him.

'. . . said you ducked at the last second?'

'I heard something, I guess,' I whispered. That was the truth, too. I just hadn't heard something with my ears. . . . But Andy knew what I meant, and he was a believer. His eyes met mine and widened.

And out again. The ER doctor had certainly given me some excellent painkiller. I wondered which hospital I was in. The one in Clarice was a little closer to the library; the one in Grainger had a higher-rated ER. If I was in Grainger, I might as well have saved myself the time driving back to Bon Temps and going to the library. I could have been shot right in the hospital parking lot when I left from visiting Calvin, and that would have saved me the trip.

'Sookie,' said a quiet, familiar voice. It was cool and dark, like water running in a stream on a moonless night.

'Bill,' I said, feeling happy and safe. 'Don't go.'

'I'll be right here.'

And he was there, reading, in a chair by my bed when I woke up at three in the morning. I could feel the minds in the rooms around me all shut down in sleep. But the brain in the head of the man next to me was a blank. At that moment, I realized that the person who'd shot me had not been a vampire, though all the shootings had taken place at dusk or full dark. I'd heard the shooter's brain in the second before the shot, and that had saved my life.

Bill looked up the instant I moved. 'How are you feeling?' he asked.

I pushed the button to raise the head of the bed. 'Like hell warmed over,' I said frankly after evaluating my shoulder. 'My pain stuff has lapsed, and my shoulder aches like it's going to fall off. My mouth feels like an army has marched through it, and I need to go to the bathroom in the worst way.'

'I can help you take care of that,' he said, and before I could get embarrassed, he'd moved the IV pole around the bed and helped me up. I stood cautiously, gauging how steady my legs were. He said, 'I won't let you fall.'

'I know,' I said, and we started across the floor to the bathroom. When he got me settled on the toilet, he tactfully stepped out, but left the door cracked while he waited just outside. I managed everything awkwardly, but I became profoundly aware I was lucky I'd been shot in my left shoulder instead of my right. Of course, the shooter must have been aiming for my heart.

Bill got me back into the bed as deftly as if he'd been nursing people all his life. He'd already smoothed the bed and shaken the pillows, and I felt much more comfortable. But the shoulder continued to nag me, and I pressed the pain button. My mouth was dry, and I asked Bill if there was water in the plastic pitcher. Bill pressed the Nurse button. When her tinny voice came over the intercom, Bill said, 'Some water for Miss Stackhouse,' and the voice squawked back that she'd be right down. She was, too. Bill's presence might have had something to do with her speed. People might have accepted the reality of vampires, but that didn't meant they liked undead Americans. Lots of middle-class Americans just couldn't relax around vamps. Which was smart of them, I thought.

'Where are we?' I asked.

'Grainger,' he said. 'I get to sit with you in a different hospital this time.' Last time, I'd been in Renard Parish Hospital in Clarice.

'You can go down the hall and visit Calvin.'

'If I had any interest in doing so.'

He sat on the bed. Something about the deadness of the hour, the strangeness of the night, made me feel like being frank. Maybe it was just the drugs.

'I never was in a hospital till I knew you,' I said.

'Do you blame me?'

'Sometimes.' I watched his face glow. Other people didn't always know a vamp when they saw one; that was hard for me to understand.

'When I met you, that first night I came into Merlotte's, I didn't know what to think of you,' he said. 'You were so pretty, so full of vitality. And I could tell there was something different about you. You were interesting.'

'My curse,' I said.

'Or your blessing.' He put one of his cool hands on my cheek. 'No fever,' he said to himself. 'You'll heal.' Then he sat up straighter. 'You slept with Eric while he was staying with you.'

'Why are you asking, if you already know?' There was such a thing as too much honesty.

'I'm not asking. I knew when I saw you together. I smelled him all over you; I could tell how you felt about him. We've had each other's blood. It's hard to resist Eric,' Bill went on in a detached way. 'He's as vital as you are, and you share a zest for life. But I'm sure you know that . . .' He paused, seemed to be trying to think how to frame what he wanted to say.

'I know that you'd be happy if I never slept with anyone else in my life,' I said, putting his thoughts into words for him.

'And how do you feel about me?'

'The same. Oh, but wait, you already *did* sleep with someone else. Before we even broke up.' Bill looked away, the line of his jaw like granite. 'Okay, that's water under the bridge. No, I don't want to think about you with Selah, or with anyone. But my head knows that's unreasonable.'

'Is it unreasonable to hope that we'll be together again?'

I considered the circumstances that had turned me against Bill. I thought of his infidelity with Lorena; but she had been his maker, and he had had to obey her. Everything I'd heard from other vamps had confirmed what he'd told me about that relationship. I thought of his near-rape of me in the trunk of a car; but he'd been starved and tortured, and hadn't known what he was doing. The minute he'd come to his senses, he'd stopped.

I remembered how happy I'd been when I'd had what I thought was his love. I'd never felt more secure in my life. How false a feeling that had been: He'd become so absorbed in his work for the Queen of Louisiana that I'd begun to come in a distant second. Out of all the vampires who could have walked into Merlotte's Bar, I'd gotten the workaholic.

'I don't know if we can ever have the same relationship again,' I said. 'It might be possible, when I'm a little less raw from the pain of it. But I'm glad you're here tonight, and I wish you would lie down with me for a little while . . . if you want to.' I moved over on the narrow bed and turned on my right side, so the wounded shoulder was up. Bill lay down behind me and put his arm over me. No one could approach me without him knowing. I felt perfectly secure, absolutely safe, and cherished. 'I'm so glad you're here,' I mumbled as the medicine kicked in. As I was drifting off to sleep again, I remembered my New Year's Eve resolution: I wanted not to get beaten up. Note to self: I should have included 'shot'.

I was released the next morning. When I went to the business office, the clerk, whose name tag read MS. BEESON, said, 'It's already been taken care of.'

'By who?' I asked.

'The person wishes to remain anonymous,' the clerk said, her round brown face set in a way that implied I shouldn't look gift horses in the mouth.

This made me uneasy, very uneasy. I actually had the money in the bank to pay the whole bill, instead of sending a check each month. And nothing comes without a price. There were some people to whom I just didn't want to be beholden. When I absorbed the total at the bottom of the bill, I was shocked to find how very beholden I'd be.

Maybe I should have stayed in the office longer and argued with Ms Beeson more forcefully, but I just didn't feel up to it. I wanted to shower, or at least bathe – something more thorough than the high-spots scrub I'd given myself (very slowly and carefully) that morning. I wanted to eat my own food. I wanted some solitude and peace. So I got back in the wheelchair and let the aide wheel me out of the main entrance. I felt like the biggest idiot when it occurred to me that I didn't have a way home. My car was still in the library parking lot in Bon Temps – not that I was supposed to drive it for a couple of days.

Just as I was about to ask the aide to wheel me back inside so I could ride up to Calvin's room (maybe Dawson could give me a lift), a sleek red Impala came to a halt in front of me. Claudine's brother, Claude, leaned over to push open the passenger door. I sat gaping at him. He said irritably, 'Well, are you going to get in?'

'Wow,' muttered the aide. 'Wow.' I thought her blouse buttons were going to pop open, she was breathing so hard.

I'd met Claudine's brother Claude only once before. I'd forgotten what an impact he made. Claude was absolutely breathtaking, so lovely that his proximity made me tense as a high wire. Relaxing around Claude was like trying to be nonchalant with Brad Pitt.

Claude had been a stripper on ladies' night at Hooligans, a club in Monroe, but lately he'd not only moved into managing the club, he'd also branched into print and runway modeling. The opportunities for such work were few and far between in northern Louisiana, so Claude (according to Claudine) had decided to compete for Mr Romance at a romance readers' convention. He'd even had his ears surgically altered so they weren't pointed anymore. The big payoff was the chance to appear on a romance cover. I didn't know too much about the contest, but I knew what I saw when I looked at Claude. I felt pretty confident Claude would win by acclamation.

Claudine had mentioned that Claude had just broken up with his boyfriend, too, so he was unattached: all six feet of him, accessorized with rippling black hair and rippling muscles and a six-pack that could have been featured in *Abs Weekly*. Mentally add to that a pair of brown velour-soft eyes, a chiseled jaw, and a sensuous mouth with a pouty bottom lip, and you've got Claude. Not that I was noticing.

Without the help of the aide, who was still saying, 'Wow, wow, wow,' very quietly, I got out of the wheelchair and eased myself into the car. 'Thanks,' I said to Claude, trying not to sound as astonished as I felt.

'Claudine couldn't get off work, so she called me and woke me up so I'd be here to chauffeur you,' Claude said, sounding totally put out.

'I'm grateful for the ride,' I said, after considering several possible responses.

I noticed that Claude didn't have to ask me for directions to Bon Temps, though I'd never seen him in the area – and I think I've made the point that he was hard to miss.

'How is your shoulder?' he said abruptly, as if he'd remembered that was the polite question to ask.

'On the mend,' I said. 'And I have a prescription for some painkillers to fill.'

'So I guess you need to do that, too?'

'Um, well, that would be nice, since I'm not supposed to drive for another day or two.'

When we reached Bon Temps, I directed Claude to the pharmacy, where he found a parking slot right in front. I managed to get out of the car and take in the prescription, since Claude didn't offer. The pharmacist, of course, had heard what had happened already and wanted to know what this world was coming to. I couldn't tell him.

I passed the time while he was filling my prescription by speculating on the possibility that Claude was bisexual – even a little bit? Every woman who came into the pharmacy had a glazed look on her face. Of course, they hadn't had the privilege of having an actual conversation with Claude, so they hadn't had the benefit of his sparkling personality.

'Took you long enough,' Claude said as I got back in the car.

'Yes, Mr Social Skills,' I snapped. 'I'll try to hurry from now on. Why should getting shot slow me down? I apologize.'

Out of the corner of my eye, I noticed Claude's cheeks reddening.

'I'm sorry,' he said stiffly. 'I was abrupt. People tell me I'm rude.'

'No! Really?'

'Yes,' he admitted, and then realized I'd been a tad sarcastic. He gave me a look I would have called a glower from a less beautiful creature. 'Listen, I have a favor to ask you.'

'You're certainly off to a good start. You've softened me up now.'

'Would you stop that? I know I'm not . . . not . . .'

'Polite? Minimally courteous? Gallant? Going about this the right way?'

'Sookie!' he bellowed. 'Be quiet!'

I wanted one of my pain pills. 'Yes, Claude?' I said in a quiet, reasonable voice.

'The people running the pageant want a portfolio. I'll go to the studio in Ruston for some glamour shots, but I think it might be a good idea to do some posed pictures, too. Like the covers of the books Claudine is always reading. Claudine says I should have a blonde pose with me, since I'm dark. I thought of you.'

I guess if Claude had told me he wanted me to have his baby I could have been more surprised, but only just. Though Claude was the surliest man I'd ever encountered, Claudine had a habit of saving my life. For her sake, I wanted to oblige.

'Would I need, like, a costume?'

'Yes. But the photographer also does amateur dramatics and he rents out Halloween costumes, so he thought he might have some things that would do. What size do you wear?'

'An eight.' Sometimes more like a ten. But then again, once in a blue moon, a six, okay?

'So when can you do this?'

'My shoulder has to heal,' I said gently. 'The bandage wouldn't look good in the pictures.'

'Oh, right. So you'll call me?'

'Yes.'

'You won't forget?'

'No. I'm so looking forward to it.' Actually, at the moment what I wanted was my own space, free and clear of any other person, and a Diet Coke, and one of the pills I was clutching in my hand. Maybe I'd have a little nap before I took the shower that also featured on my list.

'I've met the cook at Merlotte's before,' Claude said, the floodgates evidently now wide open.

'Uh-huh. Sweetie.'

'That's what she's calling herself? She used to work at the Foxy Femmes.'

'She was a stripper?'

'Yeah, until the accident.'

'Sweetie was in an accident?' I was getting more worn out by the second.

'Yeah, so she got scarred and didn't want to strip anymore. It would've required too much makeup, she said. Besides, by then she was getting a little on the, ah, old side to be stripping.'

'Poor thing,' I said. I tried to picture Sweetie parading down a runway in high heels and feathers. Disturbing.

'I'd never let her hear you say that,' he advised.

We parked in front of the duplex. Someone had brought my car back from the library parking lot. The door to the other side of the duplex opened, and Halleigh Robinson stepped out, my keys in her hand. I was wearing the black pants I'd had on since I had been on my way to work, but my Merlotte's T-shirt had been ruined so the hospital had given me a white sweatshirt that someone had left there once upon a time. It was huge on me, but that wasn't why Halleigh was standing stock-still, catching flies with her mouth. Claude had actually gotten out to help me into the house, and the sight of him had paralyzed the young schoolteacher.

Claude eased his arm tenderly around my shoulders, bent his head to look adoringly into my face, and winked.

This was the first hint I'd had that Claude had a sense of humor. It pleased me to find he wasn't universally disagreeable.

'Thanks for bringing me my keys,' I called, and Halleigh suddenly remembered she could walk.

'Um,' she said. 'Um, sure.' She put the keys somewhere in the vicinity of my hand, and I snagged them.

'Halleigh, this is my friend Claude,' I said with what I hoped was a meaningful smile.

Claude moved his arm down to circle my waist and gave her a distracted smile of his own, hardly moving his eyes from mine. Oh, brother. 'Hello, Halleigh,' he said in his richest baritone.

'You're lucky to have someone to bring you home from the hospital,' Halleigh said. 'That's very nice of you, uh, Claude.'

'I would do anything for Sookie,' Claude said softly.

'Really?' Halleigh shook herself. 'Well, how nice. Andy drove your car back over here, Sookie, and he asked if I'd give you your keys. It's lucky you caught me. I just ran home to eat lunch. I, um, I have to go back to . . .' She gave Claude a final comprehensive stare before getting into her own little Mazda to drive back to the elementary school.

I unlocked my door clumsily and stepped into my little living room. 'This is where I'm staying while my house is being rebuilt,' I told Claude. I felt vaguely embarrassed at the small sterile room. 'I just moved in the day I got shot. Yesterday,' I said with some wonder.

Claude, his faux admiration having been dropped when Halleigh pulled away, eyed me with some disparagement. 'You have mighty bad luck,' he observed.

'In some ways,' I said. But I thought of all the help I'd already gotten, and of my friends. I remembered the simple pleasure of sleeping close to Bill the night before. 'My luck could definitely be worse,' I added, more or less to myself.

Claude was massively uninterested in my philosophy.

After I thanked him again and asked him to give Claudine a hug from me, I repeated my promise to call him when my wound had healed enough for the posing session.

My shoulder was beginning to ache now. When I locked the door behind him, I swallowed a pill. I'd called the phone company from the library the afternoon before, and to my surprise and pleasure I got a dial tone when I picked up my phone. I called Jason's cell to tell him I was out of the hospital, but he didn't answer so I left a message on his voice mail. Then I called the bar to tell Sam I'd be back at work the next day. I'd missed two days' worth of pay and tips, and I couldn't afford any more.

I stretched out on the bed and took a long nap.

When I woke up, the sky was darkening in a way that meant rain. In the front yard of the house across the street, a small maple was whipping around in an alarming way. I thought of the tin roof my Gran had loved and of the clatter the rain made when it hit the hard surface. Rain here in town was sure to be quieter.

I was looking out my bedroom window at the identical duplex next door, wondering who my neighbor was, when I heard a sharp knock. Arlene was breathless from running through the first drops of rain.

She had a bag from Wendy's in her hand, and the smell of the food made my stomach wake up with a growl.

'I didn't have time to cook you anything,' she said apologetically as I stood aside to let her in. 'But I remembered you liked to get the double hamburger with bacon when you were feeling low, and I figured you'd be feeling pretty low.'

'You figured right,' I said, though I was discovering I was much better than I'd been that morning. I went to the kitchen to get a plate, and Arlene followed, her eyes going to every corner.

'Hey, this is nice!' she said. Though it looked barren to me, my temporary home must have looked wonderfully uncluttered to her.

'What was it like?' Arlene asked. I tried not to hear that she was thinking that I got into more trouble than anyone she knew. 'You must have been so scared!'

'Yes.' I was serious, and my voice showed it. 'I was very scared.'

'The whole town is talking about it,' Arlene said artlessly. That was just what I wanted to hear: that I was the subject of many conversations. 'Hey, you remember that Dennis Pettibone?'

'The arson expert?' I said. 'Sure.'

'We've got a date tomorrow night.'

'Way to go, Arlene. What are you all gonna do?'

'We're taking the kids to the roller rink in Grainger. He's got a girl, Katy. She's thirteen.'

'Well, that sounds like fun.'

'He's on stakeout tonight,' Arlene said importantly. I blinked. 'What's he staking out?'

'They needed all the officers they could call in. They're staking out different parking lots around town to see if they can catch this sniper in the act.'

I could see a flaw in their plan. 'What if the sniper sees them first?'

'These are professionally trained men, Sookie. I think they know how to handle this.' Arlene looked, and sounded, quite huffy. All of a sudden, she was Ms Law Enforcement.

'Chill,' I said. 'I'm just concerned.' Besides, unless the lawmen were Weres, they weren't in danger. Of course, the big flaw in that theory was that I had been shot. And I was no Were, no shifter. I still hadn't figured out how to work that into my scenario.

'Where's the mirror?' Arlene asked, and I looked around.

'I guess the only big one's in the bathroom,' I said, and it felt strange to have to think about the location of an item in my own place. While Arlene fussed with her hair, I put my food on a plate, hoping I'd get to eat while it was still warm. I caught myself standing like a fool with the empty food bag in my hand, wondering where the garbage can was. Of course there wasn't a garbage can until I went out to buy one. I'd never lived anywhere but my Gran's house for the past nineteen years. I'd never had to start housekeeping from the ground up.

'Sam's still not driving, so he can't come to see you, but he's thinking about you,' Arlene called. 'You gonna be able to work tomorrow night?'

'I'm planning on it.'

'Good. I'm scheduled to be off, Charlsie's granddaughter's in the hospital with pneumonia, so she's gone, and Holly doesn't always show up when she's scheduled. Danielle's going to be out of town. That new girl, Jada – she's better than Danielle, anyway.'

'You think?'

'Yeah.' Arlene snorted. 'I don't know if you've noticed, but Danielle just doesn't seem to care anymore. People can be wanting drinks and calling to her, and it doesn't make a smidge of difference to her. She'll just stand there talking to her boyfriend while people holler at her.'

It was true that Danielle had been less than scrupulous about her work habits since she'd started steady-dating a guy from Arcadia. 'You think she's gonna quit?' I asked, and that opened up another conversational pit we mined for about five minutes, though Arlene had said she was in a hurry. She'd ordered me to eat while the food was good, so I chewed and swallowed while she talked. We didn't say anything startlingly new or original, but we had a good time. I could tell that Arlene (for once) was just enjoying sitting with me, being idle.

One of the many downsides to telepathy is the fact that you can tell the difference between when someone's really listening to you, and when you're talking to just a face instead of a mind.

Andy Bellefleur arrived as Arlene was getting into her car. I was glad I'd stuffed the bag from Wendy's in a cabinet just to get it out of the way.

'You're right next to Halleigh,' Andy said – an obvious opening gambit.

'Thanks for leaving my keys with her and getting my car over here,' I said. Andy had his moments.

'She says the guy that brought you home from the hospital was really, ah, interesting.' Andy was obviously fishing. I smiled at Andy. Whatever Halleigh had said had made him curious and maybe a little jealous.

'You could say that,' I agreed.

He waited to see if I'd expound. When I didn't, he became all business.

'The reason I'm here, I wanted to find out if you remembered any more about yesterday.'

'Andy, I didn't know anything then, much less now.'

'But you ducked.'

'Oh, Andy,' I said, exasperated, since he knew good and well about my condition, 'you don't have to ask why I ducked.'

He turned red, slowly and unbecomingly. Andy was a fireplug of a man and an intelligent police detective, but he had such ambiguity toward things he knew to be true, even if those things weren't completely conventional items of common knowledge.

'We're here all by ourselves,' I pointed out. 'And the walls are thick enough that I don't hear Halleigh moving around.'

'Is there more?' he asked suddenly, his eyes alight with curiosity. 'Sookie, is there more?'

I knew exactly what he meant. He would never spell it out, but he wanted to know if there was even more in this world than humans, and vampires, and telepaths. 'So much more,' I said, keeping my voice quiet and even. 'Another world.'

Andy's eyes met mine. His suspicions had been confirmed, and he was intrigued. He was right on the edge of asking me about the people who'd been shot – right on the verge of making the leap – but at the last instant, he drew back. 'You didn't see anything or hear anything that would help us? Was there anything different about the night Sam was shot?'

'No,' I said. 'Nothing. Why?'

He didn't answer, but I could read his mind like a book. The bullet from Sam's leg didn't match the other recovered bullets.

After he left, I tried to dissect that quick impression I'd gotten, the one that had prompted me to duck. If the parking lot hadn't been empty, I might not have caught it at all, since the brain that had made it had been at some distance. And what I'd felt had been a tangle of determination, anger, and above all, disgust. The person who'd been shooting had been sure I was loathsome and inhuman. Stupidly enough, my first reaction was hurt – after all, no one likes to be despised. Then I considered the strange fact that Sam's bullet didn't match any of the previous Were shootings. I couldn't understand that at all. I could think of many explanations, but all of them seemed far-fetched.

The rain began to pour down outside, hitting the north-facing windows with a hiss. I didn't have a reason to call anyone, but I felt like making one up. It wasn't a good night to be out of touch. As the pounding of the rain increased, I became more and more anxious. The sky was a leaden gray; soon it would be full dark.

I wondered why I was so twitchy. I was used to being by myself, and it seldom bothered me. Now I was physically closer to people than I'd ever been in my house on Hummingbird Road, but I felt more alone.

Though I wasn't supposed to drive, I needed things for the duplex. I would have made the errand a necessity and gone to Wal-Mart despite the rain – or because of the rain – if the nurse hadn't made such a big deal out of resting my shoulder. I went restlessly from room to room until the crunch of gravel told me that I was having yet more company. This was town living, for sure.

When I opened the door, Tara was standing there in a leopard-print raincoat with a hood. Of course I asked her in, and she tried her best to shake out the coat on the little front porch. I carried it into the kitchen to drip on the linoleum.

She hugged me very gently and said, 'Tell me how you are.'

After I went over the story once again, she said, 'I've been worried about you. I couldn't get away from the shop until now, but I just had to come see you. I saw the suit in my closet. Did you come to my house?'

'Yes,' I said. 'The day before yesterday. Didn't Mickey tell you?'

'He was in the house when you were there? I warned you,' she said, almost panic-stricken. 'He didn't hurt you, did he? He didn't have anything to do with you getting shot?'

'Not that I know of. But I did go into your house kind of late, and I know you told me not to. It was just dumb. He did, ah, try to scare me. I wouldn't let him know you've been to see me, if I were you. How were you able to come here tonight?'

A shutter dropped over Tara's face. Her big dark eyes hardened, and she pulled away from me. 'He's out somewhere,' she said.

'Tara, can you tell me how you came to be involved with him? What happened to Franklin?' I tried to ask these questions as gently as I could, because I knew I was treading on delicate ground.

Tara's eyes filled with tears. She was struggling to answer me, but she was ashamed. 'Sookie,' she began at last, almost whispering, 'I thought Franklin really cared about me, you know? I mean, I thought he respected me. As a person.'

I nodded, intent on her face. I was scared of disrupting the flow of her story now that she'd finally begun to talk to me.

'But he . . . he just passed me along when he was through with me.'

'Oh, no, Tara! He . . . surely he explained to you why you two were breaking up. Or did you have a big fight?' I didn't want to believe Tara had been passed from vamp to vamp like some fang-banger at a bloodsucker's party.

'He said, "Tara, you're a pretty girl and you've been good company, but I owe a debt to Mickey's master, and Mickey wants you now".'

I knew my mouth was hanging open, and I didn't care. I could scarcely believe what Tara was telling me. I could hear the humiliation rolling off of her in waves of self-loathing. 'You couldn't do anything about it?' I asked. I was trying to keep the incredulity out of my voice.

'Believe me, I tried,' Tara said bitterly. She wasn't blaming me for my question, which was a relief. 'I told him I wouldn't. I told him

I wasn't a whore, that I'd been dating him because I liked him.' Her shoulders collapsed. 'But you know, Sookie, I wasn't telling the whole truth, and he knew it. I took all the presents he gave me. They were expensive things. But they were freely given, and he didn't tell me there were strings attached! I never asked for anything!'

'So he was saying that because you'd accepted his gifts, you were bound to do as he said?'

'He said—' Tara began weeping, and her sobs made everything come out in little jerks. 'He said that I was acting like a mistress, and he'd paid for everything I had, and that I might as well be of more use to him. I said I wouldn't, that I'd give him back everything, and he said he didn't want it. He told me this vamp named Mickey had seen me out with him, that Franklin owed Mickey a big favor.'

'But this is America,' I protested. 'How can they do that?'

'Vampires are awful,' Tara said dismally. 'I don't know how you can stand hanging out with them. I thought I was so cool, having a vamp boyfriend. Okay, he was more like a sugar daddy, I guess.' Tara sighed at the admission. 'It was just so nice being, you know, treated so well. I'm not used to that. I really thought he liked me, too. I wasn't just being greedy.'

'Did he take blood from you?' I asked.

'Don't they always?' she asked, surprised. 'During sex?'

'As far as I know,' I said. 'Yeah. But you know, after he had your blood, he could tell how you felt about him.'

'He could?'

'After they've had your blood, they're tuned in to your feelings.' I was quite sure that Tara hadn't been as fond of Franklin Mott as she'd been saying, that she was much more interested in his lavish gifts and courteous treatment than in him. Of course, he'd known that. He might not have much cared if Tara liked him for himself or not, but that had surely made him more inclined to trade her off. 'So how'd it happen?'

'Well, it wasn't so abrupt as I've made it sound,' she said. She stared down at her hands. 'First Franklin said he couldn't go somewhere with me, so would it be okay if this other guy took me instead? I thought he was thinking of me, of how disappointed I'd be if I didn't get to go –

it was a concert – so I really didn't brood over it. Mickey was on his best behavior, and it wasn't a bad evening. He left me at the door, like a gentleman.'

I tried not to raise my eyebrows in disbelief. The snakelike Mickey, whose every pore breathed 'bad to the bone', had persuaded Tara he was a gentleman? 'Okay, so then what?'

'Then Franklin had to go out of town, so Mickey came by to see if I had everything I needed, and he brought me a present, which I thought was from Franklin.'

Tara was lying to me, and halfway lying to herself. She had surely known the present, a bracelet, was from Mickey. She had persuaded herself it was kind of a vassal's tribute to his lord's lady, but she had known it wasn't from Franklin.

'So I took it, and we went out, and then when we came back that night, he started making advances. And I broke that off.' She gave me a calm and regal face.

She may have repulsed his advances that night, but she hadn't done it instantly and decisively.

Even Tara forgot I could read her mind.

'So that time he left,' she said. She took a deep breath. 'The next time, he didn't.'

He'd given plenty of advance warning of his intentions. I looked at her. She flinched. 'I know,' she wailed. 'I know, I did wrong!'

'So, is he living at your place?'

'He's got a day place somewhere close,' she said, limp with misery. 'He shows up at dark, and we're together the whole night. He takes me to meetings, he takes me out, and he . . .'

'Okay, okay.' I patted her hand. That didn't seem like enough, and I hugged her closer. Tara was taller than I, so it wasn't a very maternal hug, but I just wanted my friend to know I was on her side.

'He's real rough,' Tara said very quietly. 'He's going to kill me some day.'

'Not if we kill him first.'

'Oh, we can't.'

'You think he's too strong?'

'I think I can't kill someone, even him.'

'Oh.' I had thought Tara had more grit to her, after what her parents had put her through. 'Then we have to think of a way to pry him off you.'

'What about your friend?'

'Which one?'

'Eric. Everyone says that Eric has a thing for you.'

'Everyone?'

'The vampires around here. Did Bill pass you to Eric?'

He'd told me once I should go to Eric if anything happened to him, but I hadn't taken that as meaning Eric should assume the same role that Bill had in my life. As it turned out, I had had a fling with Eric, but under entirely different circumstances.

'No, he didn't,' I said with absolute clarity. 'Let me think.' I mulled it over, feeling the terrible pressure of Tara's eyes. 'Who's Mickey's boss?' I asked. 'Or his sire?'

'I think it's a woman,' Tara said. 'At least, Mickey's taken me to a place in Baton Rouge a couple of times, a casino, where he's met with a female vamp. Her name is Salome.'

'Like in the Bible?'

'Yeah. Imagine naming your kid that.'

'So, is this Salome a sheriff?'

'What?'

'Is she a regional boss?'

'I don't know. Mickey and Franklin never talked about that stuff.'

I tried not to look as exasperated as I felt. 'What's the name of the casino?'

'Seven Veils.'

Hmmm. 'Okay, did he treat her with deference?' That was a good Word of the Day entry from my calendar, which I hadn't seen since the fire.

'Well, he kind of bowed to her.'

'Just his head, or from the waist?'

'From the waist. Well, more than the head. I mean, he bent over.'

'Okay. What did he call her?'

'Mistress.'

'Okay.' I hesitated, and then asked again, 'You're sure we can't kill him?'

'Maybe you can,' she said morosely. 'I stood over him with an ice pick for fifteen minutes one night when he went to sleep after, you know, sex. But I was too scared. If he finds out I've been here to see you, he'll get mad. He doesn't like you at all. He thinks you're a bad influence.'

'He got that right,' I said with a confidence I was far from feeling. 'Let me see what I can think of.'

Tara left after another hug. She even managed a little smile, but I didn't know how justified her flash of optimism might be.

There was only one thing I could do.

The next night I'd be working. It was full dark by now, and he'd be up.

I had to call Eric.

Chapter 13

'Fangtasia,' said a bored feminine voice. 'Where all your bloody dreams come true.'

'Pam, it's Sookie.'

'Oh, hello,' she said more cheerfully. 'I hear you're in even more trouble. Got your house burned. You won't live much longer if you keep that up.'

'No, maybe not,' I agreed. 'Listen, is Eric there?'

'Yes, he's in his office.'

'Can you transfer me to him?'

'I don't know how,' she said disdainfully.

'Could you take the phone to him, please, ma'am?'

'Of course. Something always happens around here after you call. It's quite the break in routine.' Pam was carrying the phone through the bar; I could tell by the change in the ambient noise. There was music in the background. KDED again: 'The Night Has a Thousand Eyes' this time. 'What's happening in Bon Temps, Sookie?' Pam asked, saying in a clear aside to some bar patron, 'Step aside, you son of a misbegotten whore!

'They like that kind of talk,' she said to me conversationally. 'Now, what's up?'

'I got shot.'

'Oh, too bad,' she said. 'Eric, do you know what Sookie is telling me? Someone shot her.'

'Don't get so emotional, Pam,' I said. 'Someone might think you care.'

She laughed. 'Here is the man,' she said.

Sounding just as matter-of-fact as Pam had, Eric said, 'It can't be critical or you wouldn't be talking to me.'

This was true, though I would have enjoyed a more horrified reaction. But this was no time to think of little issues. I took a deep breath. I knew, sure as shooting, what was coming, but I had to help Tara. 'Eric,' I said with a feeling of doom, 'I need a favor.'

'Really?' he said. Then, after a notable pause, 'Really?'

He began to laugh.

'Gotcha,' he said.

He arrived at the duplex an hour later and paused on the doorsill after I'd responded to his knock. 'New building,' he reminded me.

'You are welcome to come in,' I said insincerely, and he stepped in, his white face practically blazing with – triumph? Excitement? Eric's hair was wet with rain and straggled over his shoulders in rattails. He was wearing a golden brown silk T-shirt and brown pleated trousers with a magnificent belt that was just barbaric: lots of leather, and gold, and dangling tassels. You can take the man out of the Viking era, but you can't take the Viking out of the man.

'Can I get you a drink?' I said. 'I'm sorry, I don't have any TrueBlood, and I'm not supposed to drive, so I couldn't go get any.' I knew that was a big breach of hospitality, but there was nothing I could do about it. I hadn't been about to ask anyone to bring me blood for Eric.

'Not important,' he said smoothly, looking around the small room. 'Please sit down.'

Eric said onto the couch, his right ankle on the knee of his left leg. His big hands were restless. 'What's the favor you need, Sookie?' He was openly gleeful.

I sighed. At least I was pretty sure he'd help, since he could practically taste the leverage he'd have over me.

I perched on the edge of the lumpy armchair. I explained about Tara, about Franklin, about Mickey. Eric got serious in a hurry. 'She could leave during the day and she doesn't,' he pointed out.

'Why should she leave her business and her home? He's the one should leave,' I argued. (Though I have to confess, I'd wondered to myself why Tara didn't just take a vacation. Surely Mickey wouldn't stick around too long if his free ride was gone?) 'Tara would be looking over her shoulder for the rest of her life if she tried to shake him loose by running,' I said firmly.

'I've learned more about Franklin since I met him in Mississippi,' Eric said. I wondered if Eric had learned this from Bill's database. 'Franklin has an outdated mind-set.'

This was rich, coming from a Viking warrior whose happiest days had been spent pillaging and raping and laying waste.

'Vampires used to pass willing humans around,' Eric explained. 'When our existence was secret, it was convenient to have a human lover, to maintain that person . . . that is, not to take too much blood . . . and then, when there was no one left who wanted her – or him,' Eric added hastily, so my feminist side would not be offended, 'that person would be, ah, completely used.'

I was disgusted and showed it. 'You mean drained,' I said.

'Sookie, you have to understand that for hundreds, thousands, of years we have considered ourselves better than humans, separate from humans.' He thought for a second. 'Very much in the same relationship to humans as humans have to, say, cows. Edible like cows, but cute, too.'

I was knocked speechless. I had sensed this, of course, but to have it spelled out was just . . . nauseating. Food that walked and talked, that was us. McPeople.

'I'll just go to Bill. He knows Tara, and she rents her business premises from him, so I bet he'll feel obliged to help her,' I said furiously.

'Yes. He'd be obliged to try to kill Salome's underling. Bill doesn't rank any higher than Mickey, so he can't order him to leave. Who do you think would survive the fight?'

The idea paralyzed me for a minute. I shuddered. What if Mickey won?

'No, I'm afraid I'm your best hope here, Sookie.' Eric gave me a brilliant smile. 'I'll talk to Salome and ask her to call her dog off.

Franklin is not her child, but Mickey is. Since he's been poaching in my area, she'll be obliged to recall him.'

He raised a blond eyebrow. 'And since you're asking me to do this for you, of course, you owe me.'

'Gosh, I wonder what you want in return?' I asked, maybe a little on the dry and sarcastic side.

He grinned at me broadly, giving me a flash of fang. 'Tell me what happened while I was staying with you. Tell me completely, leaving out nothing. After that, I'll do what you want.' He put both feet on the floor and leaned forward, focused on me.

'All right.' Talk about being caught between a rock and a hard place. I looked down at my hands clasped in my lap.

'Did we have sex?' he asked directly.

For about two minutes, this might actually be fun. 'Eric,' I said, 'we had sex in every position I could imagine, and some I couldn't. We had sex in every room in my house, and we had sex outdoors. You told me it was the best you'd ever had.' (At the time he couldn't recall all the sex he'd ever had. But he'd paid me a compliment.) 'Too bad you can't remember it,' I concluded with a modest smile.

Eric looked like I'd hit him in the forehead with a mallet. For all of thirty seconds his reaction was completely gratifying. Then I began to be uneasy.

'Is there anything else I should know?' he said in a voice so level and even that it was simply scary.

'Um, yes.'

'Then perhaps you'll enlighten me.'

'You offered to give up your position as sheriff and come to live with me. And get a job.'

Okay, maybe this *wasn't* going so well. Eric couldn't get any whiter or stiller. 'Ah,' he said. 'Anything else?'

'Yes.' I ducked my head because I'd gotten to the absolutely un-fun part. 'When we came home that last night, the night we'd had the battle with the witches in Shreveport, we came in the back door, right, like I always do. And Debbie Pelt – you remember her. Alcide's – oh, whatever she was to him . . . Debbie was sitting at my kitchen table. And she had a gun and was gonna shoot me.' I risked a glance and found Eric's brows had drawn in together in an ominous frown. 'But you threw yourself in front of me.' I leaned forward very quickly and patted him on the knee. Then I retreated into my own space. 'And you took the bullet, which was really, really sweet of you. But she was *going* to shoot again, and I pulled out my brother's shotgun, and I killed her.' I hadn't cried at all that night, but I felt a tear run down my cheek now. 'I killed her,' I said, and gasped for breath.

Eric's mouth opened as though he was going to ask a question, but I held up a hand in a *wait* gesture. I had to finish. 'We gathered up the body and bagged it, and you took it and buried her somewhere while I cleaned the kitchen. And you found her car and you hid it. I don't know where. It took me hours to get the blood out of the kitchen. It was on everything.' I grabbed desperately at my self-possession. I rubbed my eyes with the back of my wrist. My shoulder ached, and I shifted in the chair, trying to ease it.

'And now someone else has shot at you and I wasn't there to take the bullet,' Eric said. 'You must be living wrong. Do you think the Pelt family is trying to get revenge?'

'No,' I said. I was pleased that Eric was taking all this so calmly. I don't know what I'd expected, but it wasn't this. He seemed, if anything, subdued. 'They hired private detectives, and as far as I know, the private detectives didn't find any reason to suspect me any more than anyone else. The only reason I was a suspect anyway was because when Alcide and I found that body in Shreveport at Verena Rose's, we told the police we were engaged. We had to explain why we went together to a bridal shop. Since he had such an on-and-off relationship with Debbie, him saying we were getting married naturally raised a red flag when the detectives checked it out. He had a good alibi for the time she died, as it turned out. But if they ever seriously suspect me, I'll be in trouble. I can't give you as an alibi, because of course you weren't even here, as far as anyone knows. You can't give me an alibi because you don't remember that night; and of course, I'm just plain old guilty. I killed her. I had to do it.' I'm sure Cain had said that when he'd killed Abel.

'You're talking too much,' Eric said.

I pressed my lips together. One minute he wanted me to tell him everything; the next minute he wanted me to stop talking.

For maybe five minutes, Eric just looked at me. I wasn't always sure he was seeing me. He was lost in some deep thoughts.

'I told you I would leave everything for you?' he said at the end of all this rumination.

I snorted. Trust Eric to select that as the pertinent idea.

'And how did you respond?'

Okay, that astonished me. 'You couldn't just stay with me, not remembering. That wouldn't be right.'

He narrowed his eyes. I got tired of being regarded through slits of blue. 'So,' I said, curiously deflated. Maybe I'd expected a more emotional scene than this. Maybe I'd expected Eric to grab me and kiss me silly and tell me he still felt the same. Maybe I was too fond of daydreams. 'I did your favor. Now you do mine.'

Not taking his eyes off me, Eric whipped a cell phone from his pocket and dialed a number from memory. 'Rose-Anne,' he said. 'Are you well? Yes, please, if she's free. Tell her I have information that will interest her.' I couldn't hear the response on the other end, but Eric nodded, as he would if the speaker had been present. 'Of course I'll hold. Briefly.' In a minute, he said, 'And hello to you, too, most beautiful princess. Yes, it keeps me busy. How's business at the casino? Right, right. There's one born every minute. I called to tell you something about your minion, that one named Mickey. He has some business connection with Franklin Mott?'

Then Eric's eyebrows rose, and he smiled slightly. 'Is that right? I don't blame you. Mott is trying to stick to the old ways, and this is America.' He listened again. 'Yes, I'm giving you this information for free. If you choose not to grant me a small favor in return, of course that's of no consequence. You know in what esteem I hold you.' Eric smiled charmingly at the telephone. 'I did think you should know about Mott's passing on a human woman to Mickey. Mickey's keeping her under his thumb by threatening her life and property. She's quite unwilling.'

After another silence, during which his smile widened, Eric said, 'The small favor is removing Mickey. Yes, that's all. Just make sure he knows he should never again approach this woman, Tara Thornton.

He should have nothing more to do with her, or her belongings and friends. The connection should be completely severed. Or I'll have to see about severing some part of Mickey. He's done this in my area, without the courtesy of coming to visit me. I really expected better manners of any child of yours. Have I covered all the bases?'

That Americanism sounded strange, coming from Eric Northman. I wondered if he'd ever played baseball.

'No, you don't need to thank me, Salome. I'm glad to be of service. And if you could let me know when the thing is accomplished? Thanks. Well, back to the grindstone.' Eric flipped the phone shut and began tossing it in the air and catching it, over and over.

'You knew Mickey and Franklin were doing something wrong to start with,' I said, shocked but oddly unsurprised. 'You know their boss would be glad to find out they were breaking the rules, since her vamp was violating your territory. So this won't affect you at all.'

'I only realized that when you told me what you wanted,' Eric pointed out, the very essence of reason. He grinned at me. 'How could I know that your heart's desire would be for me to help someone else?'

'What did you think I wanted?'

'I thought maybe you wanted me to pay for rebuilding your house, or you would ask me to help find out who's shooting the Weres. Someone who could have mistaken you for a Were,' Eric told me, as if I should have known that. 'Who had you been with before you were shot?'

'I'd been to visit Calvin Norris,' I said, and Eric looked displeased.

'So you had his smell on you.'

'Well, I gave him a hug good-bye, so yeah.'

Eric eyed me skeptically. 'Had Alcide Herveaux been there?'

'He came by the house site,' I said.

'Did he hug you, too?'

'I don't remember,' I said. 'It's no big deal.'

'It is for someone looking for shifters and Weres to shoot. And you are hugging too many people.'

'Maybe it was Claude's smell,' I said thoughtfully. 'Gosh, I didn't think of that. No, wait, Claude hugged me after the shooting. So I guess the fairy smell didn't matter.'

'A fairy,' Eric said, the pupils of his eyes actually dilating. 'Come here, Sookie.'

Ah-oh. I might have overplayed my hand out of sheer irritation.

'No,' I said. 'I told you what you wanted, you did what I asked, and now you can go back to Shreveport and let me get some sleep. Remember?' I pointed to my bandaged shoulder.

'Then I'll come to you,' Eric said, and knelt in front of me. He pressed against my legs and leaned over so his head was against my neck. He inhaled, held it, exhaled. I had to choke back a nervous laugh at the similarity the process held to smoking dope. 'You reek,' Eric said, and I stiffened. 'You smell of shifter and Were and fairy. A cocktail of other races.' I stayed completely immobile. His lips were about two millimeters from my ear. 'Should I just bite you, and end it all?' he whispered. 'I would never have to think about you again. Thinking about you is an annoying habit, and one I want to be rid of. Or should I start arousing you, and discover if sex with you was really the best I've ever had?'

I didn't think I was going to get a vote on this. I cleared my throat. 'Eric,' I said, a little hoarsely, 'we need to talk about something.'

'No. No. No,' he said. With each 'no' his lips brushed my skin.

I was looking past his shoulder at the window. 'Eric,' I breathed, 'someone's watching us.'

'Where?' His posture didn't change, but Eric had shifted from a mood that was definitely dangerous to me to one that was dangerous for someone else.

Since the eyes-at-the-window scenario was an eerie echo of the situation the night my house had burned, and that night the skulker had proved to be Bill, I hoped the watcher might be Bill again. Maybe he was jealous, or curious, or just checking up on me. If the trespasser was a human, I could have read his brain and found out who he was, or at least what he intended; but this was a vampire, as the blank hole where the brain pattern should be had informed me.

'It's a vampire,' I told Eric in the tiniest whisper I could manage, and he put his arms around me and pulled me into him.

'You're so much trouble,' Eric said, and yet he didn't sound exasperated. He sounded excited. Eric loved the action moments.

By then, I was sure that the lurker wasn't Bill, who would have made himself known. And Charles was presumably busy at Merlotte's, mixing daiquiris. That left one vampire in the area unaccounted for. 'Mickey,' I breathed, my fingers gripping Eric's shirt.

'Salome moved more quickly than I thought,' Eric said in a regular voice. 'He's too angry to obey her, I suppose. He's never been in here, correct?'

'Correct.' Thank God.

'Then he can't come inside.'

'But he can break the window,' I said as glass shattered to our left. Mickey had thrown a large rock as big as my fist, and to my dismay the rock hit Eric squarely in the head. He went down like a – well, like a rock. He lay without moving. Dark blood welled from a deep cut in his temple. I leaped to my feet, completely stunned at seeing the powerful Eric apparently out cold.

'Invite me in,' said Mickey, just outside the window. His face, white and angry, shone in the pelting rain. His black hair was plastered to his head.

'Of course not,' I said, kneeling beside Eric, who blinked, to my relief. Not that he could be dead, of course, but still, when you see someone take a blow like that, vampire or not, it's just plain terrifying. Eric had fallen in front of the armchair, which had its back to the window, so Mickey couldn't see him.

But now I could see what Mickey was holding by one hand: Tara. She was almost as pale as he was, and she'd been beaten to a pulp. Blood was running out of the corner of her mouth. The lean vampire had a merciless grip on her arm. 'I'll kill her if you don't let me in,' he said, and to prove his point, he put both hands around her neck and began to squeeze. A clap of thunder and a bolt of lightning lit up Tara's desperate face as she clawed weakly at his arms. He smiled, fangs completely exposed.

If I let him in, he'd kill all of us. If I left him out there, I would have to watch him kill Tara. I felt Eric's hands take hold of my arm. 'Do it,' I said, not moving my gaze from Mickey. Eric bit, and it hurt like hell. He wasn't finessing this at all. He was desperate to heal in a hurry.

I'd just have to swallow the pain. I tried hard to keep my face still, but then I realized I had a great reason to look upset. 'Let her go!' I yelled at Mickey, trying to buy a few seconds. I wondered if any of the neighbors were up, if they could hear the ruckus, and I prayed they wouldn't come searching to find out what was going on. I was even afraid for the police, if they came. We didn't have any vampire cops to handle vampire lawbreakers, like the cities did.

'I'll let her go when you let me in,' Mickey yelled. He looked like a demon out there in the rain. 'How's your tame vamp doing?'

'He's still out,' I lied. 'You hurt him bad.' It didn't take any effort at all to make my voice crack as if I were on the verge of tears. 'I can see his skull,' I wailed, looking down at Eric to see that he was still feeding as greedily as a hungry baby. His head was mending as I watched. I'd seen vamps heal before, but it was still amazing. 'He can't even open his eyes,' I added in a heartbroken way, and just then Eric's blue eyes blazed up at me. I didn't know if he was in fighting trim yet, but I could not watch Tara being choked. 'Not yet,' Eric said urgently, but I had already told Mickey to come in.

'Oops,' I said, and then Mickey slithered through the window in an oddly boneless movement. He knocked the broken glass out of the way carelessly, like it didn't hurt him to get cut. He dragged Tara through after him, though at least he'd switched his grip from her neck to her arm. Then he dropped her on the floor, and the rain coming in the window pelted down on her, though she couldn't be any wetter than she already was. I wasn't even sure she was conscious. Her eyes were closed in her bloody face, and her bruises were turning dark. I stood, swaying with the blood loss, but keeping my wrist concealed by resting it on the back of the armchair. I'd felt Eric lick it, but it would take a few minutes to heal.

'What do you want?' I asked Mickey. As if I didn't know.

'Your head, bitch,' he said, his narrow features twisted with hatred, his fangs completely out. They were white and glistening and sharp in the bright overhead light. 'Get down on your knees to your betters!' Before I could react in any way – in fact before I could blink – the vampire backhanded me, and I stumbled across the small room, landing half on the couch before I slid to the floor. The air went out of me in a big whoosh, and I simply couldn't move, couldn't even gasp for air, for an agonizingly long minute. In the meantime, Mickey was on top of me, his intentions completely clear when he reached down to unzip his pants. 'This is all you're good for!' he said, contempt making him even uglier. He tried to push his way into my head, too, forcing the fear of him into my brain to cow me.

And my lungs inflated. The relief of breathing was exquisite, even under the circumstances. With air came rage, as if I'd inhaled it along with oxygen. This was the trump card male bullies played, always. I was sick of it – sick of being scared of the bogeyman's dick.

'No!' I screamed up at him. '*No!*' And finally I could think again; finally the fear let loose of me. 'Your invitation is *rescinded*!' I yelled, and it was his turn to panic. He reared up off of me, looking ridiculous with his pants open, and he went backward out of the window, stepping on poor Tara as he went. He tried to bend, to grip her so he could yank her with him, but I lunged across the little room to grab her ankles, and her arms were too slick with rain to give him purchase, and the magic that had hold of him was too strong. In a second, he was outside looking in, screaming with rage. Then he looked east, as if he heard someone calling, and he vanished into the darkness.

Eric pushed himself to his feat, looking almost as startled as Mickey. 'That was clearer thinking than most humans can manage,' he said mildly into the sudden silence. 'How are you, Sookie?' He reached down a hand and pulled me to my feet. 'I myself am feeling much better. I've had your blood without having to talk you into it, and I didn't have to fight Mickey. You did all the work.'

'You got hit in the head with a rock,' I pointed out, content just to stand for a minute, though I knew I had to call an ambulance for Tara. I was feeling a little on the weak side myself.

'A small price to pay,' Eric told me. He brought out his cell phone, flipped it open, and pressed the REDIAL button. 'Salome,' Eric said, 'glad you answered the phone. He's trying to run. . . .'

I heard the gleeful laughter coming from the other end of the phone. It was chilling. I couldn't feel the least bit sorry for Mickey, but I was glad I wouldn't have to witness his punishment.

'Salome'll catch him?' I asked.

Eric nodded happily as he returned his phone to his pocket. 'And she can do things to him more painful than anything I could imagine,' he said. 'Though I can imagine plenty right now.'

'She's that, ah, creative?'

'He's hers. She's his sire. She can do with him what she wishes. He can't disobey her and go unpunished. He has to go to her when she calls him, and she's calling.'

'Not on the phone, I take it,' I ventured.

His eyes glinted down at me. 'No, she won't need a phone. He's trying to run away, but he'll go to her eventually. The longer he holds out, the more severe his torture will be. Of course,' he added, in case I missed the point, 'that's as it should be.'

'Pam is yours, right?' I asked, falling to my knees and putting my fingers to Tara's cold neck. I didn't want to look at her.

'Yes,' Eric said. 'She's free to leave when she wants, but she comes back when I let her know I need her help.'

I didn't know how I felt about that, but it didn't really make a hell of a lot of difference. Tara gasped and moaned. 'Wake up, girl,' I said. 'Tara! I'm gonna call an ambulance for you.'

'No,' she said sharply. 'No.' There was a lot of that word going around tonight.

'But you're bad hurt.'

'I can't go to the hospital. Everyone will know.'

'Everyone will know someone beat the shit out of you when you can't go to work for a couple of weeks, you idiot.'

'You can have some of my blood,' Eric offered. He was looking down at Tara without any obvious emotion.

'No,' she said. 'I'd rather die.'

'You might,' I said, looking her over. 'Oh, but you've had blood from Franklin or Mickey.' I was assuming some tit-for-tat in their lovemaking.

'Of course not,' she said, shocked. The horror in her voice took me aback. I'd had vampire blood when I'd needed it. The first time, I'd have died without it.

'Then you have to go to the hospital.' I was really concerned that Tara might have internal injuries. 'I'm scared for you to move,' I protested, when she tried to push herself to a seated position. Mr Super Strength didn't help, which irritated me, since he could have shifted her easily.

But at last Tara managed to sit with her back against the wall, the empty window allowing the chilly wind to gust in and blow the curtains to and fro. The rain had abated until only a drop or two was coming in. The linoleum in front of the window was wet with water and blood, and the glass lay in glittering sharp fragments, some stuck to Tara's damp clothes and skin.

'Tara, listen to me,' Eric said. She looked up at him. Since he was close to the fluorescent light, she had to squint. I thought she looked pitiful, but Eric didn't seem to see the same person I was seeing. 'Your greed and selfishness put my – my friend Sookie in danger. You say you're her friend, too, but you don't act like it.'

Hadn't Tara loaned me a suit when I needed one? Hadn't she loaned me her car when mine burned? Hadn't she helped me on other occasions when I needed it? 'Eric, this isn't any of your business,' I said.

'You called me and asked me for my help. That makes it my business. I called Salome and told her what her child was doing, and she's taken him away to punish him for it. Isn't that what you wanted?'

'Yes,' I said, and I'm ashamed to say I sounded sullen.

'Then I'm going to make my point with Tara.' He looked back down at her. 'Do you understand me?'

Tara nodded painfully. The bruises on her face and throat seemed to be darkening more every minute.

'I'm getting some ice for your throat,' I told her, and ran into the kitchen to dump ice from the plastic trays into a Ziploc bag. I didn't want to listen to Eric scold her; she seemed so pitiful.

When I came back less than a minute later, Eric had finished whatever he was going to say to Tara. She was touching her neck gingerly, and she took the bag from me and held it to her throat. While I was leaning over her, anxious and scared, Eric was back on his cell phone.

I twitched with worry. 'You need a doctor,' I urged her.

'No,' she said.

I looked up at Eric, who was just finishing his phone call. He was the injury expert.

'She'll heal without going to the hospital,' he said briefly. His indifference made a chill run down my spine. Just when I thought I was used to them, vampires would show me their true face, and I would have to remind myself all over again that they were a different race. Or maybe it was centuries of conditioning that made the difference; decades of disposing of people as they chose, taking what they wanted, enduring the dichotomy of being the most powerful beings on earth in the darkness, and yet completely helpless and vulnerable during the hours of light.

'But will she have some permanent damage? Something doctors could fix if she got to them quick?'

'I'm fairly certain that her throat is only badly bruised. She has some broken ribs from the beating, possibly some loose teeth. Mickey could have broken her jaw and her neck very easily, you know. He probably wanted her to be able to talk to you when he brought her here, so he held back a little. He counted on you panicking and letting him in. He didn't think you could gather your thoughts so quickly. If I'd been him, my first move would have been to damage your mouth or neck so you couldn't rescind my entrance.'

That possibility hadn't occurred to me, and I blanched.

'When he backhanded you, I think that was what he was aiming for,' Eric continued dispassionately.

I'd heard enough. I thrust a broom and dustpan into his hands. He looked at them as if they were ancient artifacts and he could not fathom their use.

'Sweep up,' I said, using a wet washcloth to clean the blood and dirt off my friend. I didn't know how much of this conversation Tara was absorbing, but her eyes were open and her mouth was shut, so maybe she was listening. Maybe she was just working through the pain.

Eric moved the broom experimentally and made an attempt to sweep the glass into the pan while it lay in the middle of the floor. Of course, the pan slid away. Eric scowled.

I'd finally found something Eric did poorly.

'Can you stand?' I asked Tara. She focused on my face and nodded very slightly. I squatted and took her hands. Slowly and painfully, she drew her knees up, and then she pushed as I pulled. Though the window had broken mostly in big pieces, a few bits of glass fell from her as she rose, and I flicked an eye at Eric to make sure he understood he should clean them up. He had a truculent set to his mouth.

I tried to put my arm around Tara to help her into my bedroom, but my wounded shoulder gave a throb of pain so unexpected that I flinched. Eric tossed down the dustpan. He picked up Tara in one smooth gesture and put her on the couch instead of my bed. I opened my mouth to protest and he looked at me. I shut my mouth. I went into the kitchen and fetched one of my pain pills, and I got Tara to swallow one, which took some coaxing. The medicine seemed to knock her out, or maybe she just didn't want to acknowledge Eric anymore. Anyway, she kept her eyes closed and her body slack, and gradually her breathing grew even and deep.

Eric handed me the broom with a triumphant smile. Since he'd lifted Tara, clearly I was stuck with his task. I was awkward because of my bad shoulder, but I finished sweeping up the glass and disposing of it in a garbage bag. Eric turned toward the door. I hadn't heard anyone arrive, but Eric opened the door to Bill before Bill even knocked. Eric's earlier phone conversation must have been with Bill. In a way, that made sense; Bill lived in Eric's fiefdom, or whatever they called it. Eric needed help, so Bill was obliged to supply it. My ex was burdened with a large piece of plywood, a hammer, and a box of nails.

'Come in,' I said when Bill halted in the doorway, and without speaking a word to each other, the two vampires nailed the wood across the window. To say I felt awkward would be an understatement, though thanks to the events of the evening I wasn't as sensitive as I would've been at another time. I was mostly preoccupied with the pain in my shoulder, and Tara's recovery, and the current whereabouts of Mickey. In the extra space I had left over after worrying about those items, I crammed in some anxiety about replacing Sam's window, and whether the neighbors had heard enough of this fracas to call the police. On the whole, I thought they hadn't; someone would be here by now.

After Bill and Eric finished their temporary repair, they both watched me mopping up the water and blood on the linoleum. The silence began to weigh heavily on all three of us: at least, on my third of the three of us. Bill's tenderness in caring for me the night before had touched me. But Eric's just acquired knowledge of our intimacy raised my self-consciousness to a whole new level. I was in the same room with two guys who both knew I'd slept with the other.

I wanted to dig a hole and lie down in it and pull the opening inside with me, like a character in a cartoon. I couldn't look either of them in the face.

If I rescinded both their invitations, they'd have to walk outside without a word; but in view of the fact that they'd both just helped me, such a procedure would be rude. I'd solved my problems with them before in exactly that way. Though I was tempted to repeat it to ease my personal embarrassment, I simply couldn't. So what did we do next?

Should I pick a fight? Yelling at one another might clear the air. Or maybe a frank acknowledgment of the situation . . . no.

I had a sudden mental picture of us all three climbing in the double bed in the little bedroom. Instead of *duking* out our conflicts, or *talking* out our problems, we could . . . no. I could feel my face flame red, as I was torn between semi-hysterical amusement and a big dash of shame at even thinking the thought. Jason and his buddy Hoyt had often discussed (in my hearing) that every male's fantasy was to be in bed with two women. And men who came into the bar echoed that idea, as I knew from checking Jason's theory by reading a random sample of male minds. Surely I was allowed to entertain the same kind of fantasy? I gave a hysterical kind of giggle, which definitely startled both vampires.

'This is amusing?' Bill asked. He gestured from the plywood, to the recumbent Tara, to the bandage on my shoulder. He omitted pointing from Eric to himself. I laughed out loud.

Eric cocked a blond eyebrow. '*We* are amusing?'

I nodded wordlessly. I thought, *Instead of a cook-off we could have a cock-off. Instead of a fishing derby, we could have a . . .*

At least in part because I was tired, and strained, and blood depleted, I went way into the silly zone. I laughed even harder when I looked at Eric's and Bill's faces. They wore almost identical expressions of exasperation.

Eric said, 'Sookie, we haven't finished our discussion.'

'Oh yes, we have,' I said, though I was still smiling. 'I asked you for a favor: releasing Tara from her bondage to Mickey. You asked me for payment for that favor: telling you what happened when you lost your memory. You performed your side of the bargain, and so did I. Bought and paid for. The end.'

Bill looked from Eric to me. Now he knew that Eric knew what I knew. . . . I giggled again. Then the giddiness just poofed out of me. I was a deflated balloon, for sure. 'Good night, both of you,' I said. 'Thanks, Eric, for taking that rock in the head, and for sticking to your phone throughout the evening. Thanks, Bill, for turning out so late with window-repair supplies. I appreciate it, even if you got volunteered by Eric.' Under ordinary circumstances – if there were such things as ordinary circumstances with vampires around – I would've given them each a hug, but that just seemed too weird. 'Shoo,' I said. 'I have to go to bed. I'm all worn out.'

'Shouldn't one of us stay here with you tonight?' Bill asked.

If I'd had to say yes to that, had to pick one of them to stay with me that night, it would have been Bill – if I could have counted on him to be as undemanding and gentle as he'd been the night before. When you're down and hurting, the most wonderful thing in the world is to feel cherished. But that was too big a bunch of if's for tonight.

'I think I'll be fine,' I said. 'Eric assures me that Salome will scoop up Mickey in no time, and I need sleep more than anything. I appreciate both of you coming out tonight.'

For a long moment I thought they might just say 'No' and try to outwait each other. But Eric kissed me on the forehead and left, and Bill, not to be outdone, brushed my lips with his and took his leave. When the two vampires had departed, I was delighted to be by myself.

Of course, I wasn't exactly alone. Tara was passed out on the couch. I made sure she was comfortable – took off her shoes, got the blanket off my bed to cover her – and then I fell into my own bed.

Chapter 14

I slept for hours.

When I woke up, Tara was gone.

I felt a stab of panic, until I realized she'd folded the blanket, washed her face in the bathroom (wet washcloth), and put her shoes on. She had left me a little note, too, on an old envelope that already held the beginnings of my shopping list. It said, 'I'll call you later. T' – a terse note, and not exactly redolent of sisterly love.

I felt a little sad. I figured I wouldn't be Tara's favorite person for a while. She'd had to look more closely at herself than she wanted to look.

There are times to think, and times to lie fallow. Today was a fallow day. My shoulder felt much better, and I decided I would drive to the Wal-Mart Supercenter in Clarice and get all my shopping over with in one trip. Also, there I wouldn't see as many people I knew, and I wouldn't have to discuss getting shot.

It was very peaceful, being anonymous in the big store. I moved slowly and read labels, and I even selected a shower curtain for the duplex bathroom. I took my time completing my list. When I transferred the bags from the buggy into the car, I tried to do all the lifting with my right arm. I was practically reeking with virtue when I got back to the house on Berry Street.

The Bon Temps Florist van was in the driveway. Every woman has a little lift in her heart when the florist's van pulls up, and I was no exception.

'I have a multiple delivery here,' said Bud Dearborn's wife, Greta. Greta was flat-faced like the sheriff and squatty like the sheriff, but her nature was happy and unsuspicious. 'You're one lucky girl, Sookie.'

'Yes, ma'am, I am,' I agreed, with only a tincture of irony. After Greta had helped me carry in my bags, she began carrying in flowers.

Tara had sent me a little vase of daisies and carnations. I am very fond of daisies, and the yellow and white looked pretty in my little kitchen. The card just read 'From Tara.'

Calvin had sent a very small gardenia bush wrapped up in tissue and a big bow. It was ready to pop out of the plastic tub and be planted as soon as the danger of a frost was over. I was impressed with the thoughtfulness of the gift, since the gardenia bush would perfume my yard for years. Because he'd had to call in the order, the card bore the conventional sentiment 'Thinking of you – Calvin.'

Pam had sent a mixed bouquet, and the card read, 'Don't get shot anymore. From the gang at Fangtasia.' That made me laugh a little. I automatically thought of writing thank-you notes, but of course I didn't have my stationery with me. I'd stop by the pharmacy and get some. The downtown pharmacy had a corner that was a card shop, and also it accepted packages for UPS pickup. You had to be diverse in Bon Temps.

I put away my purchases, awkwardly hung the shower curtain, and got cleaned up for work.

Sweetie Des Arts was the first person I saw when I came through the employees' entrance. She had an armful of kitchen towels, and she'd tied on her apron. 'You're a hard woman to kill,' she remarked. 'How you feeling?'

'I'm okay,' I said. I felt like Sweetie had been waiting for me, and I appreciated the gesture.

'I hear you ducked just in time,' she said. 'How come? Did you hear something?'

'Not exactly,' I said. Sam limped out of his office then, using his cane. He was scowling. I sure didn't want to explain my little quirk to

Sweetie on Sam's time. I said, 'I just had a feeling,' and shrugged, which was unexpetedly painful.

Sweetie shook her head at my close call and turned to go through the bar and back to the kitchen.

Sam jerked his head toward his office, and with a sinking heart I followed him in. He shut the door behind us. 'What were you doing when you got shot?' he asked. His eyes were bright with anger.

I wasn't going to get blamed for what had happened to me. I stood right up to Sam, got in his face. 'I was just checking out library books,' I said through my teeth.

'So why would he think you're a shifter?'

'I have no idea.'

'Who had you been around?'

'I'd been to see Calvin, and I'd . . .' My voice trailed off as I caught at the tail end of a thought.

'So, who can tell you smell like a shifter?' I asked slowly. 'No one but another shifter, right? Or someone with shifter blood. Or a vampire. Some supernatural thing.'

'But we haven't had any strange shifters around here lately.'

'Have you gone to where the shooter must have been, to smell?'

'No, the only time I was on the spot at a shooting, I was too busy screaming on the ground with blood running out of my leg.'

'But maybe now you could pick up something.'

Sam looked down at his leg doubtfully. 'It's rained, but I guess it's worth a try,' he conceded. 'I should have thought of it myself. Okay, tonight, after work.'

'It's a date,' I said flippantly as Sam sank down in his squeaky chair. I put my purse in the drawer Sam kept empty and went out to check my tables.

Charles was hard at work, and he gave me a nod and a smile before he concentrated on the level of beer in the pitcher he was holding to the tap. One of our consistent drunks, Jane Bodehouse, was seated at the bar with Charles fixed in her sights. It didn't seem to make the vampire uncomfortable. I saw that the rhythm of the bar was back to normal; the new bartender had been absorbed into the background.

After I'd worked about an hour, Jason came in. He had Crystal cuddled up in the curve of his arm. He was as happy as I'd ever seen him. He was excited by his new life and very pleased with Crystal's company. I wondered how long that would last. But Crystal herself seemed of much the same mind.

She told me that Calvin would be getting out of the hospital the next day and going home to Hotshot. I made sure to mention the flowers he'd sent and told her I'd be fixing Calvin some dish to mark his homecoming.

Crystal was pretty sure she was pregnant. Even through the tangle of shifter brain, I could read that thought as clear as a bell. It wasn't the first time I'd learned that some girl 'dating' Jason was sure he was going to be a dad, and I hoped that this time was as false as the last time. It wasn't that I had anything against Crystal . . . Well, that was a lie I was telling myself. I did have something against Crystal. Crystal was part of Hotshot, and she'd never leave it. I didn't want any niece or nephew of mine to be brought up in that strange little community, within the pulsing magic influence of the crossroads that formed its center.

Crystal was keeping her late period a secret from Jason right now, determined to stay quiet until she was sure what it meant. I approved. She nursed one beer while Jason downed two, and then they were off to the movies in Clarice. Jason gave me a hug on the way out while I was distributing drinks to a cluster of law enforcement people. Alcee Beck, Bud Dearborn, Andy Bellefleur, Kevin Pryor, and Kenya Jones, plus Arlene's new crush, arson investigator Dennis Pettibone, were all huddled around two tables pushed together in a corner. There were two strangers with them, but I picked up easily enough that the two men were cops, too, part of some task force.

Arlene might have liked to wait on them, but they were clearly in my territory, and they clearly were talking about something heap big. When I was taking drink orders, they all hushed up, and when I was walking away, they'd start their conversation back up. Of course, what they said with their mouths didn't make any difference to me, since I knew what each and every one of them was thinking.

And they all knew this good and well; and they all forgot it. Alcee Beck, in particular, was scared to death of me, but even he was quite oblivious to my ability, though I'd demonstrated it for him before. The same could be said of Andy Bellefleur.

'What's the law enforcement convention in the corner cooking up?' asked Charles. Jane had tottered off to the ladies', and he was temporarily by himself at the bar.

'Let me see,' I said, closing my eyes so I could concentrate better. 'Well, they're thinking of moving the stakeout for the shooter to another parking lot tonight, and they're convinced that the arson is connected to the shootings and that Jeff Marriot's death is tied in with everything, somehow. They're even wondering if the disappearance of Debbie Pelt is included in this clutch of crimes, since she was last seen getting gas on the interstate at the filling station closest to Bon Temps. And my brother, Jason, disappeared for a while a couple of weeks ago; maybe that's part of the picture, too.' I shook my head and opened my eyes to find that Charles was disconcertingly close. His one good eye, his right, stared hard into my left.

'You have very unusual gifts, young woman,' he said after a moment. 'My last employer collected the unusual.'

'Who'd you work for before you came into Eric's territory?' I asked. He turned away to get the Jack Daniel's.

'The King of Mississippi,' he said.

I felt as if someone had pulled the rug out from under my feet. 'Why'd you leave Mississippi and come here?' I asked, ignoring the hoots from the table five feet away.

The King of Mississippi, Russell Edgington, knew me as Alcide's girlfriend, but he didn't know me as a telepath occasionally employed by vampires. It was quite possible Edgington might have a grudge against me. Bill had been held in the former stables behind Edgington's mansion and tortured by Lorena, the creature who'd turned Bill into a vampire over a hundred and forty years before. Bill had escaped. Lorena had died. Russell Edgington didn't necessarily know I was the agent of these events. But then again, he might.

'I got tired of Russell's ways,' Sir Charles said. 'I'm not of his sexual persuasion, and being surrounded by perversity became tiresome.'

Edgington enjoyed the company of men, it was true. He had a house full of them, as well as a steady human companion, Talbot.

It was possible Charles had been there while I was visiting, though I hadn't noticed him. I'd been severely injured the night I was brought to the mansion. I hadn't seen all its inhabitants, and I didn't necessarily remember the ones I'd seen.

I became aware that the pirate and I were maintaining our eye contact. If they've survived for any length of time, vampires read human emotions very well, and I wondered what Charles Twining was gleaning from my face and demeanor. This was one of the few times I wished I could read a vampire's mind. I wondered, very much, if Eric was aware of Charles's background. Surely Eric wouldn't have taken him on without a background check? Eric was a cautious vampire. He'd seen history I couldn't imagine, and he'd lived through it because he was careful.

Finally I turned to answer the summons of the impatient roofers who'd been trying to get me to refill their beer pitchers for several minutes.

I avoided speaking to our new bartender for the rest of the evening. I wondered why he'd told me as much as he had. Either Charles wanted me to know he was watching me, or he really had no idea I'd been in Mississippi recently.

I had a lot to think about.

The working part of the night finally came to an end. We had to call Jane's son to come get his soused relative, but that was nothing new. The pirate bartender had been working at a good clip, never making mistakes, being sure to give every patron a good word as he filled the orders. His tip jar looked healthy.

Bill arrived to pick up his boarder as we were closing up for the night. I wanted to have a quiet word with him, but Charles was by Bill's side in a flash, so I didn't have an opportunity. Bill gave me an odd look, but they were gone without my making an opportunity to talk to him. I wasn't sure what I would say, anyway. I was reassured when I realized that of course Bill had seen the worst employees of Russell Edgington, because those employees had tortured him. If Charles Twining was unknown to Bill, he might be okay.

Sam was ready to go on our sniffing mission. It was cold and brilliant outside, the stars glittering in the night sky. Sam was bundled up, and

I pulled on my pretty red coat. I had a matching set of gloves and a hat, and I would need them now. Though spring was coming closer every day, winter hadn't finished with us yet.

No one was at the bar but us. The entire parking lot was empty, except for Jane's car. The glare of the security lights made the shadows deeper. I heard a dog bark way off in the distance. Sam was moving carefully on his crutches, trying to negotiate the uneven parking lot.

Sam said, 'I'm going to change.' He didn't mean his clothes.

'What'll happen to your leg if you do?'

'Let's find out.'

Sam was full-blood shifter on both sides. He could change when it wasn't the full moon, though the experiences were very different, he'd said. Sam could change into more than one animal, though dogs were his preference, and a collie was his choice among dogs.

Sam retired behind the hedge in front of his trailer to doff his clothes. Even in the night, I saw the air disturbance that signaled magic was working all around him. He fell to his knees and gasped, and then I couldn't see him anymore through the dense bushes. After a minute, a bloodhound trotted out, a red one, his ears swinging from side to side. I wasn't used to seeing Sam this way, and it took me a second to be sure it was him. When the dog looked up at me, I knew my boss was inside.

'Come on, Dean,' I said. I'd named Sam that in his animal guise before I'd realized the man and the dog were the same being. The bloodhound trotted ahead of me across the parking lot and into the woods where the shooter had waited for Sam to come out of the club. I watched the way the dog was moving. It was favoring its right rear leg, but not drastically.

In the cold night woods, the sky was partially blocked. I had a flashlight, and I turned it on, but somehow that just made the trees creepier. The bloodhound – Sam – had already reached the place the police had decided marked the shooter's vantage point. The dog, jowls jouncing, bent its head to the ground and moved around, sorting through all the scent information he was receiving. I stayed out of the way, feeling useless. Then Dean looked up at me and said, 'Rowf'. He began making his way back to the parking lot. I guessed he'd gathered all he could.

As we'd arranged, I loaded Dean in the Malibu to take him to another shooting site, the place behind some old buildings opposite the Sonic where the shooter had hidden on the night poor Heather Kinman had been killed. I turned into the service alley behind the old stores and parked behind Patsy's Cleaners, which had moved to a new and more convenient location fifteen years ago. Between the cleaners and the dilapidated and long-empty Louisiana Feed and Seed, a narrow gap afforded a great view of the Sonic. The drive-in restaurant was closed for the night but still bright with light. Since the Sonic was on the town's main drag, there were lights up and down the street, and I could actually see pretty well in the areas where the structures allowed light to go; unfortunately, that made the shadows impenetrable.

Again, the bloodhound worked the area, paying particular interest to the weedy strip of ground between the two old stores, a strip so narrow it was no more than a gap wide enough for one person. He seemed pretty excited at some particular scent he found. I was excited, too, hoping that he'd found something we could translate into evidence for the police.

Suddenly Dean let out a 'Whoof!' and raised his head to look past me. He was certainly focusing on something, or someone. Almost unwillingly, I turned to see. Andy Bellefleur stood at the point where the service alley crossed the gap between the buildings. Only his face and upper torso were in the light.

'Jesus Christ, Shepherd of Judea! Andy, you scared the hell out of me!' If I hadn't been watching the dog so intently, I would've sensed him coming. The stakeout, dammit. I should have remembered.

'What are you doing here, Sookie? Where'd you get the dog?'

I couldn't think of a single answer that would sound plausible. 'It seemed worth a try to see if a trained dog could pick up a single scent from the places where the shooter stood,' I said. Dean leaned against my legs, panting and slobbering.

'So when did you get on the parish payroll?' Andy asked conversationally. 'I didn't realize you'd been hired as an investigator.'

Okay, this wasn't going well.

'Andy, if you'll move out of the way, me and the dog'll just get back into my car, and we'll drive away, and you won't have to be mad at me anymore.' He was plenty mad, and he was determined to have it out with me, whatever that entailed. Andy wanted to get the world realigned, with facts he knew forming the tracks it should run on. I didn't fit in that world. I wouldn't run on those tracks. I could read his mind, and I didn't like what I was hearing.

I realized, too late, that Andy'd had one drink too many during the conference at the bar. He'd had enough to remove his usual constraints.

'You shouldn't be in our town, Sookie,' he said.

'I have as much right to be here as you, Andy Bellefleur.'

'You're a genetic fluke or something. Your grandmother was a real nice woman, and people tell me your dad and mom were good people. What happened to you and Jason?'

'I don't think there's much wrong with me and Jason, Andy,' I said calmly, but his words stung like fire ants. 'I think we're regular people, no better and no worse than you and Portia.'

Andy actually snorted.

Suddenly the bloodhound's side, pressed against my legs, began to vibrate. Dean was growling almost inaudibly. But he wasn't looking at Andy. The hound's heavy head was turned in another direction, toward the dark shadows of the other end of the alley. Another live mind: a human. Not a regular human, though.

'Andy,' I said. My whisper pierced his self-absorption. 'You armed?'

I didn't know whether I felt that much better when he drew his pistol.

'Drop it, Bellefleur,' said a no-nonsense voice, one that sounded familiar.

'Bullshit,' Andy sneered. 'Why should I?'

'Because I got a bigger gun,' said the voice, cool and sarcastic. Sweetie Des Arts stepped from the shadows, carrying a rifle. It was pointed at Andy, and I had no doubt she was ready to fire. I felt like my insides had turned to Jell-O.

'Why don't you just leave, Andy Bellefleur?' Sweetie asked. She was wearing a mechanic's coverall and a jacket, and her hands were gloved.

She didn't look anything like a short-order cook. 'I've got no quarrel with you. You're just a person.'

Andy was shaking his head, trying to clear it. I noticed he hadn't dropped his gun yet. 'You're the cook at the bar, right? Why are you doing this?'

'You should know, Bellefleur. I heard your little conversation with the shifter here. Maybe this dog is a human, someone you know.' She didn't wait for Andy to answer. 'And Heather Kinman was just as bad. She turned into a fox. And the guy that works at Norcross, Calvin Norris? He's a damn panther.'

'And you shot them all? You shot me, too?' I wanted to be sure Andy was registering this. 'There's just one thing wrong with your little vendetta, Sweetie. I'm not a shifter.'

'You smell like one,' Sweetie said, clearly sure she was right.

'Some of my friends are shifters, and that day I'd hugged a few of 'em. But me myself – not a shifter of any kind.'

'Guilty by association,' Sweetie said. 'I'll bet you got a dab of shifter from somewhere.'

'What about you?' I asked. I didn't want to get shot again. The evidence suggested that Sweetie was not a sharpshooter: Sam, Calvin, and I had lived. I knew aiming at night had to be difficult, but still, you would've thought she could have done better. 'Why are you on this vendetta?'

'I'm just a fraction of a shifter,' she said, snarling just as much as Dean. 'I got bit when I had a car wreck. This half-man half-wolf . . . thing . . . ran out of the woods near where I lay bleeding, and the damn thing bit me . . . and then another car came around the curve and it ran away. But the first full moon after that, my hands changed! My parents threw up.'

'What about your boyfriend? You had one?' I kept speaking, trying to distract her. Andy was moving as far away from me as he could get, so she couldn't shoot both of us quickly. She planned on shooting me first, I knew. I wanted the bloodhound to move away from me, but he stayed loyally pressed against my legs. She wasn't sure the dog was a shifter. And, oddly, she hadn't mentioned shooting Sam.

'I was a stripper then, living with a great guy,' she said, rage bubbling through her voice. 'He saw my hands and the extra hair and he loathed me. He left when the moon was full. He'd take business trips. He'd go golfing with his buddies. He'd be stuck at a late meeting.'

'So how long have you been shooting shifters?'

'Three years,' she said proudly. 'I've killed twenty-two and wounded forty-one.'

'That's awful,' I said.

'I'm proud of it,' she said. 'Cleaning the vermin off the face of the earth.'

'You always find work in bars?'

'Gives me a chance to see who's one of the brethren,' she said, smiling. 'I check out the churches and restaurants, too. The day care centers.'

'Oh, no.' I thought I was going to throw up.

My senses were hyperalert, as you can imagine, so I knew there was someone coming up the alley behind Sweetie. I could feel the anger roiling in a two-natured head. I didn't look, trying to keep Sweetie's attention for as long as I could. But there was a little noise, maybe the sound of a piece of paper trash rustling against the ground, and that was enough for Sweetie. She whirled around with the rifle up to her shoulder, and she fired. There was a shriek from the darkness at the south end of the alley, and then a high whining.

Andy took his moment and shot Sweetie Des Arts while her back was turned. I pressed myself against the uneven bricks of the old Feed and Seed, and as the rifle dropped from her hand, I saw the blood come out of her mouth, black in the starlight. Then she folded to the earth.

While Andy was standing over her, his gun dangling from his hand, I made my way past them to find out who had come to our aid. I switched on my flashlight to discover a werewolf, terribly wounded. Sweetie's bullet had hit him in the middle of the chest, as best I could tell through the thick fur, and I yelled at Andy, 'Use your cell phone! Call for help!' I was pressing down on the bubbling wound as hard as I could, hoping I was doing the right thing. The wound kept moving in a very disconcerting way, since the Were was in the process of changing back into a human. I glanced back to see that Andy was still lost in his own little vale of horror at what he'd done. 'Bite him,' I told Dean, and Dean padded over to the policeman and nipped his hand.

Andy cried out, of course, and raised his gun as if he were going to shoot the bloodhound. 'No!' I yelled, jumping up from the dying Were. 'Use your phone, you idiot. Call an ambulance.'

Then the gun swung around to point at me.

For a long, tense moment I thought for sure the end of my life had come. We'd all like to kill what we don't understand, what scares us, and I powerfully scared Andy Bellefleur.

But then the gun faltered and dropped back to Andy's side. His broad face stared at me with dawning comprehension. He fumbled in his pocket, withdrew a cell phone. To my profound relief, he holstered the gun after he punched in a number.

I turned back to the Were, now wholly human and naked, while Andy said, 'There's been a multiple shooting in the alley behind the old Feed and Seed and Patsy's Cleaners, across Magnolia Street from Sonic. Right. Two ambulances, two gunshot wounds. No, I'm fine.'

The wounded Were was Dawson. His eyes flickered open, and he tried to gasp. I couldn't even imagine the pain he must be suffering. 'Calvin,' he tried to say.

'Don't worry now. Help's on the way,' I told the big man. My flashlight was lying on the ground beside me, and by its oddly skewed light I could see his huge muscles and bare hairy chest. He looked cold, of course, and I wondered where his clothes were. I would have been glad to have his shirt to wad up over the wound, which was steadily leaking blood. My hands were covered in it.

'Told me to finish out my last day by watching over you,' Dawson said. He was shuddering all over. He tried to smile. 'I said, "Piece of cake".' And then he didn't say anything else, but lost consciousness.

Andy's heavy black shoes came to stand in my field of vision. I thought Dawson was going to die. I didn't even know his first name. I had no idea how we were going to explain a naked guy to the police. Wait . . . was that up to me? Surely Andy was the one who'd have the hard explaining to do?

As if he'd been reading my mind – for a change – Andy said, 'You know this guy, right?'

'Slightly.'

'Well, you're going to have to say you know him better than that, to explain his lack of clothes.'

I gulped. 'Okay,' I said, after a brief, grim pause.

'You two were back here looking for his dog. You,' Andy said to Dean. 'I don't know who you are, but you stay a dog, you hear me?' Andy stepped away nervously. 'And I came back here because I'd followed the woman – she was acting suspiciously.'

I nodded, listening to the air rattle in Dawson's throat. If I could only give him blood to heal him, like a vampire. If I only knew a medical procedure . . . But I could already hear the police cars and the ambulances coming closer. Nothing in Bon Temps was very far from anything else, and on this side of town, the south side, the Grainger hospital would be closest.

'I heard her confess,' I said. 'I heard her say she shot the others.'

'Tell me something, Sookie,' Andy said in a rush. 'Before they get here. There's nothing weird about Halleigh, right?'

I stared up at him, amazed he could think of such a thing at this moment. 'Nothing aside from the stupid way she spells her name.' Then I reminded myself who'd shot the bitch lying on the ground five feet away. 'No, not a thing,' I said. 'Halleigh is just plain old normal.'

'Thank God,' he said. 'Thank God.'

And then Alcee Beck dashed down the alley and stopped in his tracks, trying to make sense of the scene before him. Right behind him was Kevin Pryor, and Kevin's partner Kenya crept along hugging the wall with her gun out. The ambulance teams were hanging back until they were sure the scene was secure. I was up against the wall getting searched before I knew what was happening. Kenya kept saying, 'Sorry, Sookie' and 'I have to do this,' until I told her, 'Just get it done. Where's my dog?'

'He run off,' she said. 'I guess the lights spooked him. He's a bloodhound, huh? He'll come home.' When she'd done her usual thorough job, Kenya said, 'Sookie? How come this guy is naked?'

This was just the beginning. My story was extremely thin. I read disbelief written large on almost every face. It wasn't the temperature for outdoor loving, and I was completely dressed. But Andy backed me up every step of the way, and there was no one to say it hadn't happened the way I told it.

About two hours later, they let me get back in my car to return to the duplex. The first thing I did when I got inside was phone the hospital to find out how Dawson was. Somehow, Calvin got ahold of the phone. 'He's alive,' he said tersely.

'God bless you for sending him after me,' I said. My voice was as limp as a curtain on a still summer day. 'I'd be dead if it wasn't for him.'

'I hear the cop shot her.'

'Yes, he did.'

'I hear a lot of other stuff.'

'It was complicated.'

'I'll see you this week.'

'Yes, of course.'

'Go get some sleep.'

'Thanks again, Calvin.'

My debt to the werepanther was piling up at a rate that scared me. I knew I'd have to work it off later. I was tired and aching. I was filthy inside from Sweetie's sad story, and filthy outside from being on my knees in the alley, helping the bloody Were. I dropped my clothes on the floor of the bedroom, went into the bathroom, and stood under the shower, trying hard to keep my bandage dry with a shower cap, the way one of the nurses had shown me.

When the doorbell rang the next morning, I cursed town living. But as it turned out, this was no neighbor who wanted to borrow a cup of flour. Alcide Herveaux was standing outside, holding an envelope.

I glared at him through eyes that felt crusty with sleep. Without saying a word, I plodded back to my bedroom and crawled into the bed. This wasn't enough to deter Alcide, who strode in after me.

'You're now doubly a friend of the pack,' he said, as if he was sure that was the concern uppermost in my mind. I turned my back to him and snuggled under the covers. 'Dawson says you saved his life.'

'I'm glad Dawson's well enough to speak,' I muttered, closing my eyes tightly and wishing Alcide would go away. 'Since he got shot on my account, your pack doesn't owe me a damn thing.'

From the movement of the air, I could tell that Alcide was kneeling at the side of the bed. 'That's not for you to decide, but us,' he said chidingly. 'You're summoned to the contest for the packleader.'

'What? What do I have to do?'

'You just watch the proceedings and congratulate the winner, no matter who it is.'

Of course, to Alcide, this struggle for succession was the most important thing going. It was hard for him to get that I didn't have the same priorities. I was getting swamped by a wave of supernatural obligations.

The werewolf pack of Shreveport said they owed me. I owed Calvin. Andy Bellefleur owed me and Dawson and Sam for solving his case. I owed Andy for saving my life. Though I'd cleared Andy's mind about Halleigh's complete normality, so maybe that canceled my debt to him for shooting Sweetie.

Sweetie had owed payback to her assailant.

Eric and I were even, I figured.

I owed Bill slightly.

Sam and I were more or less caught up.

Alcide personally owed me, as far as I was concerned. I had showed up for this pack shit and tried to follow the rules to help him out.

In the world I lived in, the world of human people, there were ties and debts and consequences and good deeds. That was what bound people to society; maybe that was what constituted society. And I tried to live in my little niche in it the best way I could.

Joining in the secret clans of the two-natured and the undead made my life in human society much more difficult and complicated.

And interesting.

And sometimes . . . fun.

Alcide had been talking at least some of the time I'd been thinking, and I'd missed a lot of it. He was picking up on that. He said, 'I'm sorry if I'm boring you, Sookie,' in a stiff voice.

I rolled over to face him. His green eyes were full of hurt. 'Not bored. I just have a lot to think about. Leave the invitation, okay? I'll get back with you on that.' I wondered what you wore to a fighting-for-packmaster event. I wondered if the senior Mr Herveaux and the somewhat pudgy motorcycle dealership owner would actually roll on the ground and grapple.

Alcide's green eyes were full of puzzlement. 'You're acting so strange, Sookie. I felt so comfortable with you before. Now I feel like I don't know you.'

Valid had been one of my Words of the Day last week. 'That's a valid observation,' I said, trying to sound matter-of-fact. 'I felt just as comfortable with you when I first met you. Then I started to find out stuff. Like about Debbie, and shifter politics, and the servitude of some shifters to the vamps.'

'No society is perfect,' Alcide said defensively. 'As for Debbie, I don't ever want to hear her name again.'

'So be it,' I said. God knew I couldn't get any sicker of hearing her name.

Leaving the cream envelope on the bedside table, Alcide took my hand, bent over it, and laid a kiss on the back of it. It was a ceremonial gesture, and I wished I knew its significance. But the moment I would have asked, Alcide was gone.

'Lock the door behind you,' I called. 'Just turn the little button on the doorknob.' I guess he did, because I went right back to sleep, and no one woke me up until it was almost time for me to go to work. Except there was a note on my front door that said, 'Got Linda T. to stand in for you. Take the night off. Sam.' I went back inside and took off my waitress clothes and pulled on some jeans. I'd been ready to go to work, and now I felt oddly at a loss.

I was almost cheered to realize I had another obligation, and I went into the kitchen to start fulfilling it.

After an hour and a half of struggling to cook in an unfamiliar kitchen with about half the usual paraphernalia, I was on my way to Calvin's house in Hotshot with a dish of chicken breasts baked with rice in a sour-cream sauce, and some biscuits. I didn't call ahead. I planned to drop off the food and go. But when I reached the little community, I saw there were several cars parked on the road in front of Calvin's trim little house. 'Dang,' I said. I didn't want to get involved any further with Hotshot than I already was. My brother's new nature and Calvin's courting had already dragged me in too far.

Heart sinking, I parked and ran my arm through the handle of the basket full of biscuits. I took the hot dish of chicken and rice in oven-mitted hands, gritted my teeth against the ache in my shoulder, and marched my butt up to Calvin's front door. Stackhouses did the right thing.

Crystal answered the door. The surprise and pleasure on her face shamed me. 'I'm so glad you're here,' she said, doing her best to be offhand. 'Please come in.' She stood back, and now I could see that the small living room was full of people, including my brother. Most of them were werepanthers, of course. The werewolves of Shreveport had sent a representative; to my astonishment, it was Patrick Furnan, contender for the throne and Harley-Davidson salesman.

Crystal introduced me to the woman who appeared to be acting as hostess, Maryelizabeth Norris. Maryelizabeth moved as if she hadn't any bones. I was willing to bet Maryelizabeth didn't often leave Hotshot. The shifter introduced me around the room very carefully, making sure I understood the relationship Calvin bore to each individual. They all began to blur after a bit. But I could see that (with a few exceptions) the natives of Hotshot ran to two types: the small, dark-haired, quick ones like Crystal, and the fairer, stockier ones with beautiful green or golden-brown eyes, like Calvin. The surnames were mostly Norris or Hart.

Patrick Furnan was the last person Crystal reached. 'Why, of course I know you,' he said heartily, beaming at me as if we'd danced at a wedding together. 'This here's Alcide's girlfriend,' he said, making sure he was heard by everyone in the room. 'Alcide's the son of the other candidate for pack-master.'

There was long silence, which I would definitely characterize as 'charged.'

'You're mistaken,' I said in a normal conversational tone. 'Alcide and I are friends.' I smiled at him in such a way as to let him know he better not be alone with me in an alley anytime soon.

'My mistake,' he said, smooth as silk.

Calvin was receiving a hero's welcome home. There were balloons and banners and flowers and plants, and his house was meticulously clean. The kitchen had been full of food. Now Maryelizabeth stepped forward, turned her back to cut Patrick Furnan dead, and said, 'Come this way, honey. Calvin's ready to see you.' If she'd had a trumpet handy, she'd have blown a flourish on it. Maryelizabeth was not a subtle woman, though she had a deceptive air of mystery due to her wide-spaced golden eyes.

I guess I could have been more uncomfortable, if there'd been a bed of red-hot coals to walk on.

Maryelizabeth ushered me into Calvin's bedroom. His furniture was very nice, with spare, clean lines. It looked Scandinavian, though I know little about furniture – or style, for that matter. He had a high bed, a queen-size, and he was propped up in it against sheets with an African motif of hunting leopards. (Someone had a sense of humor, anyway.) Against the deep colors in the sheets and the deep orange of the bedspread, Calvin looked pale. He was wearing brown pajamas, and he looked exactly like a man who'd just been released from the hospital. But he was glad to see me. I found myself thinking there was something a bit sad about Calvin Norris, something that touched me despite myself.

'Come sit,' he said, indicating the bed. He moved over a little so I'd have room to perch. I guess he'd made some signal, because the man and the woman who'd been in the room – Dixie and Dixon – silently eased out through the door, shutting it behind them.

I perched, a little uneasily, on the bed beside him. He had one of those tables you most often see in hospitals, the kind that can be rolled across the bed. There was a glass of ice tea and a plate on it, steam rising from the food. I gestured that he should begin. He bowed his head and said a silent prayer while I sat quietly. I wondered to whom the prayer was addressed.

'Tell me about it,' Calvin said as he unfolded his napkin, and that made me a lot more comfortable. He ate while I told him what had happened in the alley. I noticed that the food on the tray was the chicken-and-rice casserole I'd brought, with a dab of mixed vegetable casserole and two of my biscuits. He wanted me to see that he was eating the food I'd prepared for him. I was touched, which sounded a warning bell at the back of my brain.

'So, without Dawson, there's no telling what would've happened,'

I concluded. 'I thank you for sending him. How is he?'

Calvin said, 'Hanging on. They airlifted him from Grainger to Baton Rouge. He would be dead, if he wasn't a Were. He's lasted this long; I think he'll make it.'

I felt terrible.

'Don't go blaming yourself for this,' Calvin said, his voice suddenly sounding deeper. 'This is Dawson's choice.'

'Huh?' would've sounded ignorant, so I said, 'How so?'

'His choice of professions. His choice of actions. Maybe he should have leaped for her a few seconds earlier. Why'd he wait? I don't know. How'd she know to aim low, given the poor light? I don't know. Choices lead to consequences.' Calvin was struggling to express something. He was not naturally an articulate man, and he was trying to convey a thought both important and abstract. 'There's no blame,' he said finally.

'It would be nice to believe that, and I hope some day I do,' I said. 'Maybe I'm on my way to believing it.' It was true that I was sick of self-blame and second-guessing.

'I suspect the Weres are going to invite you to their little packleader shindig,' Calvin said. He took my hand. His was warm and dry.

I nodded.

'I bet you'll go,' he said.

'I think I have to,' I said uneasily, wondering what his goal was.

'I'm not going to tell you what to do,' Calvin said. 'I have no authority over you.' He didn't sound too happy about that. 'But if you go, please watch your back. Not for my sake; that don't mean nothing to you, yet. But for yourself.'

'I can promise that,' I said after a careful pause. Calvin was not a guy to whom you blurted the first idea in your head. He was a serious man.

Calvin gave me one of his rare smiles. 'You're a damn fine cook,' he said. I smiled back.

'Thank you, sir,' I said, and got up. His hand tightened on mine and pulled. You don't fight a man who's just gotten out of the hospital, so I bent toward him and laid my cheek to his lips.

'No,' he said, and when I turned a little to find out what was wrong, he kissed me on the lips.

Frankly, I expected to feel nothing. But his lips were as warm and dry as his hands, and he smelled like my cooking, familiar and homey. It was surprising, and surprisingly comfortable, to be so close to Calvin Norris. I backed off a little, and I am sure my face showed the mild shock I felt. The werepanther smiled and released my hand.

'The good thing about being in the hospital was you coming to see me,' he said. 'Don't be a stranger now that I'm home.'

'Of course not,' I said, ready to be out of the room so I could regain my composure.

The outer room had emptied of most of its crowd while I talked to Calvin. Crystal and Jason had vanished, and Maryelizabeth was gathering up plates with the help of an adolescent werepanther. 'Terry,' Maryelizabeth said with a sideways inclination of her head. 'My daughter. We live next door.'

I nodded to the girl, who gave me a darting look before turning back to her task. She was not a fan of mine. She was from the fairer bloodstock, like Maryelizabeth and Calvin, and she was a thinker. 'Are you going to marry my dad?' she asked me.

'I'm not planning on marrying anyone,' I said cautiously. 'Who's your dad?'

Maryelizabeth gave Terry a sidelong look that promised Terry she'd be sorry later. 'Terry is Calvin's,' she said.

I was still puzzled for a second or two, but suddenly, the stance of both the younger and the older woman, their tasks, their air of comfort in this house, clicked into place.

I didn't say a word. My face must have shown something, for Maryelizabeth looked alarmed, and then angry.

'Don't presume to judge how we live our life,' she said. 'We are not like you.'

'That's true,' I said, swallowing my revulsion. I forced a smile to my lips. 'Thank you for introducing me around. I appreciate it. Is there anything I can help you with?'

'We can take care of it,' said Terry, giving me another look that was a strange combination of respect and hostility.

'We should never have sent you to school,' Maryelizabeth said to the girl. Her wide-spaced golden eyes were both loving and regretful.

'Good-bye,' I said, and after I recovered my coat, I left the house, trying not to hurry. To my dismay, Patrick Furnan was waiting for me beside my car. He was holding a motorcycle helmet under his arm, and I spotted the Harley a little farther down the road.

'You interested in hearing what I've got to say?' the bearded Were asked.

'No, actually not,' I told him.

'He's not going to keep on helping you out for nothing,' Furnan said, and my whole head snapped around so I could look at this man.

'What are you talking about?'

'A thank-you and a kiss ain't going to hold him. He's going to demand payment sooner or later. Won't be able to help it.'

'I don't recall asking you for advice,' I said. He stepped closer. 'And you keep your distance.' I let my gaze roam to the houses surrounding us. The watchful gaze of the community was full upon us; I could feel its weight.

'Sooner or later,' Furnan repeated. He grinned at me suddenly. 'I hope it's sooner. You can't two-time a Were, you know. Or a panther. You'll get ripped to shreds between 'em.'

'I'm not two-timing *anyone*,' I said, frustrated almost beyond bearing at his insistence that he knew my love life better than I did. 'I'm not dating either of them.'

'Then you have no protection,' he said triumphantly.

I just couldn't win.

'Go to hell,' I said, completely exasperated. I got in my car and drove away, letting my eyes glide over the Were as if he weren't there. (This 'abjure' concept could come in handy.) The last thing I saw in my rearview mirror was Patrick Furnan sliding his helmet on, still watching my retreating car.

If I hadn't really cared who won the King of the Mountain contest between Jackson Herveaux and Patrick Furnan, I did now.

Chapter 15

I was washing the dishes I'd used as I cooked for Calvin. My little duplex was peaceful. If Halleigh was home, she was being quiet as a mouse. I didn't mind washing dishes, to tell you the truth. It was a good time to let my mind drift around, and often I made good decisions while I was doing something completely mundane. Not too surprisingly, I was thinking of the night before. I was trying to remember exactly what Sweetie had said. Something about it had struck me wrong, but at the moment I hadn't exactly been in a position to raise my hand to ask a question. It had something to do with Sam.

I finally recalled that though she'd told Andy Bellefleur that the dog in the alley was a shapeshifter, she hadn't known it was Sam. There wasn't anything strange about that, since Sam had been in a bloodhound shape, not his usual collie form.

After I'd realized what had been bothering me, I thought my mind would be at peace. That didn't happen. There was something else – something else Sweetie had said. I thought and thought, but it just wouldn't pop to the top of my brain.

To my surprise, I found myself calling Andy Bellefleur at home. His sister Portia was just as surprised as I was when she answered, and she said rather coldly that she'd find Andy.

'Yes, Sookie?' Andy sounded neutral.

'Let me ask a question, Andy.'

'I'll listen.'

'When Sam was shot,' I said, and paused, trying to figure out what to say.

'Okay,' Andy said. 'What about it?'

'Is it true that the bullet didn't match the others?'

'We didn't retrieve a bullet in every case.' Not a direct answer, but probably as good as I was going to get.

'Hmmm. Okay,' I said, then thanked him and hung up, uncertain if I'd learned what I wanted or not. I had to push it out of my mind and do something else. If there was a question there, it would eventually work its way to the top of the heap of the issues that burdened my thoughts.

What remained of the evening was quiet, which was getting to be a rare pleasure. With so little house to clean, and so little yard to care for, there would be lots of free hours to come. I read for an hour, worked a crossword puzzle, and went to bed at about eleven.

Amazingly, no one woke me all night. No one died, there weren't any fires, and no one had to alert me to any emergency.

The next morning I rose feeling better than I had in a week. A glance at the clock told me I'd slept all the way through to ten o'clock. Well, that wasn't so surprising. My shoulder felt nearly healed; my conscience had settled itself. I didn't think I had many secrets to keep, and that was a tremendous relief. I was used to keeping other people's secrets, but not my own.

The phone rang as I swallowed the last of my morning coffee. I put my paperback facedown on the kitchen table to mark my place and got up to answer it. 'Hello,' I said cheerfully.

'It's today,' Alcide said, voice vibrating with excitement. 'You need to come.'

Thirty minutes my peace had lasted. Thirty minutes. 'I'm guessing you mean the contest for the position of packmaster.'

'Of course.'

'And I need to be there why?'

'You need to be there because the entire pack and all friends of the pack have to be there,' Alcide said, his voice brooking no dissent. 'Christine especially thought you should be a witness.'

I might have argued if he hadn't added the bit about Christine. The wife of the former packmaster had struck me as a very intelligent woman with a cool head.

'All right,' I said, trying not to sound grumpy. 'Where and when?'

'At noon, be at the empty building at 2005 Clairemont. It used to be David & Van Such, the printing company.'

I got a few directions and hung up. While I showered, I reasoned that this was a sporting event, so I dressed in my old denim skirt with a long-sleeved red tee. I pulled on some red tights (the skirt was quite short) and some black Mary Janes. They were a little scuffed, so I hoped that Christine would not look down at my shoes. I tucked my silver cross into my shirt; the religious significance wouldn't bother the Weres at all, but the silver might.

The defunct printing company of David & Van Such had been in a very modern building, in an equally modern industrial park, largely deserted this Saturday. All the businesses had been constructed to match: low gray stone and dark glass edifices, with crepe myrtle bushes all around, grass medians, and nice curbing. David & Van Such featured an ornamental bridge over an ornamental pond, and a red front door. In the spring, and after some restorative maintenance, it would be as pretty as a modern business building could get. Today, in the fading phase of winter, the dead weeds that had grown high during the previous summer waved in a chilly breeze. The skeletal crepe myrtles needed pruning back, and the water in the pond looked stagnant, with trash floating dismally here and there. The David & Van Such parking lot contained about thirty cars, including – ominously – an ambulance.

Though I wore a jacket, the day suddenly seemed colder as I went from the parking lot and across the bridge to the front door. I was sorry I'd left my heavier coat at home, but it hadn't seemed worth bringing for a brief run between enclosed spaces. The glass front of David & Van Such, broken only by the red door, reflected the clear pale blue sky and the dead grass.

It didn't seem right to knock at a business door, so I slipped inside. Two people were ahead of me, having crossed the now-empty reception area. They passed through plain gray double doors. I followed them, wondering what I was getting into.

We entered what had been the manufacturing area, I suppose; the huge presses were long gone. Or maybe this cavern of a room had been full of desks manned by clerks taking orders or doing accounting work. Skylights in the roof let in some illumination. There was a cluster of people close to the middle of the space.

Well, I hadn't gotten the clothes thing right. The women were mostly wearing nicer pants outfits, and I glimpsed a dress here and there. I shrugged. Who could have known?

There were a few people in the crowd I hadn't seen at the funeral. I nodded at a red-haired Were named Amanda (I knew her from the Witch War), and she nodded back. I was surprised to spot Claudine and Claude. The twins looked marvelous, as always. Claudine was wearing a deep green sweater and black pants, and Claude was wearing a black sweater and deep green pants. The effect was striking. Since the two fairies were the only obvious non-Weres in attendance, I went to stand with them.

Claudine bent and kissed me on the cheek, and so did Claude. Their kisses felt exactly the same.

'What's going to happen?' I whispered the question because the group was abnormally quiet. I could see things hanging from the ceiling, but in the poor light I couldn't imagine what they were.

'There will be several tests,' Claudine murmured. 'You're not much of a screamer, right?'

I never had been, but I wondered if I'd break new ground today.

A door opened on the far side of the room, and Jackson Herveaux and Patrick Furnan came in. They were naked. Having seen very few men naked, I didn't have much basis for comparison, but I have to say that these two Weres weren't my ideal. Jackson, though certainly fit, was an older man with skinny legs, and Patrick (though he, too, looked strong and muscular) was barrel-like in form.

After I'd adjusted to the nakedness of the men, I noticed that each was accompanied by another Were. Alcide followed his father, and a young blond man trailed Patrick. Alcide and the blond Were remained fully clothed. 'It would've been nice if *they'd* been naked, huh?' Claudine whispered, nodding at the younger men. 'They're the seconds.'

Like in a duel. I looked to see if they carried pistols or swords, but their hands were empty.

I noticed Christine only when she went to the front of the crowd. She reached above her head and clapped her hands one time. There hadn't been much chatter before this, but now the huge space fell completely silent. The delicate woman with her silver hair commanded all attention.

She consulted a booklet before she began. 'We meet to discern the next leader of the Shreveport pack, also called the Long Tooth pack. To be the leader of the pack, these Weres must compete in three tests.' Christine paused to look down at the book.

Three was a good mystical number. I would have expected three.

I hoped none of these tests involved blood. Fat chance.

'The first test is the test of agility.' Christine gestured behind her at a roped-off area. It looked like a giant playground in the dim light. 'Then the test of endurance.' She pointed at a carpeted area to her left. 'Then the test of might in battle.' She waved a hand at a structure behind her.

So much for no blood.

'Then the winner must mate with another Were, to ensure the survival of the pack.'

I sure hoped part four would be symbolic. After all, Patrick Furnan had a wife, who was standing apart with a group that was definitely pro-Patrick.

That seemed like four tests to me, not three, unless the mating part was kind of like the winner's trophy.

Claude and Claudine took my hands and gave them a simultaneous squeeze. 'This is gonna be bad,' I whispered, and they nodded in unison.

I saw two uniformed paramedics standing toward the back of the crowd. They were both shifters of some kind, their brain patterns told me. With them was a person – well, maybe a creature – I hadn't seen for months: Dr Ludwig. She caught my eye and bowed to me. Since she was around three feet tall, she didn't have far to lean. I bowed back. Dr Ludwig had a large nose, olive skin, and thick wavy brown hair. I was glad she was there. I had no idea what Dr Ludwig actually was, other than nonhuman, but she was a good doctor. My back would have been permanently scarred – assuming I'd lived – if Dr Ludwig hadn't treated me after a maenad attack. I'd escaped with a couple of bad days and a fine white tracery across my shoulder blades, thanks to the tiny doctor.

The contestants entered the 'ring' – actually a large square marked off by those velvet ropes and metal-topped posts that they use in hotels. I'd thought the enclosed area looked like a playground, but now, as the lights came up, I realized I was seeing something more like a jumping arena for horses crossed with a gymnastics arena – or a course for a dog agility competition for giant dogs.

Christine said, 'You will change.' Christine moved away to melt back into the crowd. Both candidates dropped to the ground, and the air around them began to shimmer and distort. Changing quickly at one's desire was a great source of pride among shifters. The two Weres achieved their change at nearly the same instant. Jackson Herveaux became a huge black wolf, like his son. Patrick Furnan was pale gray, broad in the chest, a bit shorter in length.

As the small crowd drew closer, hugging the velvet ropes, one of the biggest men I'd ever seen emerged from the darkest shadows to step into the arena. I recognized him as the man whom I'd last seen at Colonel Flood's funeral. At least six and half feet tall, today he was bare-chested and barefoot. He was impressively muscular, and his chest was as hairless as his head. He looked like a genie; he would have appeared quite natural with a sash and pantaloons. Instead, he was wearing aged blue jeans. His eyes were pits of pitch. Of course, he was a shape-shifter of some kind, but I could not imagine what he turned into.

'Whoa,' breathed Claude.

'Hooboy,' whispered Claudine.

'Wowzers,' I muttered.

Standing between the contenders, the tall man led them to the start of the course.

'Once the test begins, no pack member can interrupt,' he said, looking from one Were to the other.

'First contestant is Patrick, wolf of this pack,' the tall man said. His bass voice was as dramatic as the distant rumble of drums.

I understood, then; he was the referee. 'Patrick goes first, by coin flip,' the tall man said.

Before I could think it was pretty funny that all this ceremony included a coin toss, the pale wolf was off, moving so fast that I could hardly keep track of him. He flew up a ramp, leaped three barrels, hit the ground on the far side at a dash, went up another ramp and through a ring hanging from the ceiling (which rocked violently after he was through it), and dropped down on the ground, crawling on all fours through a clear tunnel that was very narrow and twisted at intervals. It was like the one sold in pet stores for ferrets or gerbils, just bigger. Once out of the tunnel, the wolf, mouth open in a pant, came to a level area covered with Astroturf. Here, he paused and considered before putting out a foot. Every step was like that, as the wolf worked its way across the twenty yards or so of this particular area. Suddenly a section of Astroturf leaped up as a trap snapped shut, narrowly missing the wolf's hind leg. The wolf yipped in consternation, frozen in place. It must have been agonizing, trying to restrain himself from dashing for the safety of the platform that was now only a few feet away.

I was shivering, though this contest had little to do with me. The tension was clearly showing among the Weres. They didn't seem to be moving quite as humans did anymore. Even the overly made-up Mrs Furnan had wide round eyes now, eyes that didn't look like a woman's even under all that makeup.

As the gray wolf took his final test, a leap from a dead stop that had to cover the length of perhaps two cars, a howl of triumph erupted from Patrick's mate's throat. The gray wolf stood safely on the platform. The referee checked a stopwatch in his hand.

'Second candidate,' said the big man, 'Jackson Herveaux, wolf of this pack.' A brain close to me supplied me with the big man's name.

'Quinn,' I whispered to Claudine. Her eyes opened wide. The name was significant to her in a way I could not guess.

Jackson Herveaux began the same test of skills that Patrick had already completed. He was more graceful going through the suspended hoop; it scarcely moved as he sailed through. He took a little longer, I thought, getting through the tunnel. He seemed to realize it, too, because he stepped into the trap field more hastily than I thought wise. He stopped dead, maybe coming to the same conclusion. He bent to use his nose more carefully. The information he got from this made him quiver all over. With exquisite care, the werewolf raised one black forepaw and moved it a fraction of an inch. We were holding our breath as he worked forward in a completely different style from his predecessor. Patrick Furnan had moved in big steps, with longish pauses in between for careful sniffing, a sort of hurry-up-and-wait style. Jackson Herveaux moved very steadily in small increments, his nose always busy, his movements cannily plotted. To my relief, Alcide's father made it across unharmed, without springing any of the traps.

The black wolf gathered himself for the final long leap and launched himself into the air with all his power. His landing was less than graceful, as his hind paws had to scrabble to cling to the edge of the landing site. But he made it, and a few congratulatory yips echoed through the empty space.

'Both candidates pass the agility test,' Quinn said. His eyes roamed the crowd. When they passed over our odd trio – two tall black-haired twin fairies and a much shorter blond human – his gaze may have lingered a moment, but it was hard to say.

Christine was trying to get my attention. When she saw I was looking at her, she gave a tiny, sharp nod of her head to a spot by the test-of-endurance pen. Puzzled but obedient, I eased through the crowd. I didn't know the twins had followed me until they resumed standing to either side of me. There was something about this that Christine wanted me to see, to ... Of course. She wanted me to use my talent here. She suspected ... skulduggery. As Alcide and his blond counterpart took their places in the pen, I noticed they were both gloved. Their attention was totally absorbed by this contest; leaving nothing for me to sieve from that focus. That left the two wolves. I'd never tried to look inside the mind of a shifted person.

With considerable anxiety, I concentrated on opening myself to their thoughts. As you might expect, the blend of human and dog thought patterns was quite challenging. At first scan I could only pick up the same kind of focus, but then I detected a difference.

As Alcide lifted an eighteen-inch-long silver rod, my stomach felt cold and shivery. Watching the blond Were next to him repeat the gesture, I felt my lips draw back in distaste. The gloves were not totally necessary, because in human form, a Were's skin would not be damaged by the silver. In wolf form, silver was terribly painful.

Furnan's blond second ran his covered hands over the silver, as if testing the bar for hidden faults.

I had no idea why silver weakened vampires and burned them, and why it could be fatal to Weres, while it had no effect on fairies – who, however, could not bear prolonged exposure to iron. But I knew these things were true, and I knew the upcoming test would be awful to watch.

However, I was there to witness it. Something was going to happen that needed my attention. I turned my mind back to the little difference I'd read in Patrick's thoughts. In his Were form, these were so primitive they hardly qualified as 'thoughts.'

Quinn stood between the two seconds, his smooth scalp picking up a gleam of light. He had a timing watch in his hands.

'The candidates will take the silver now,' he said, and with his gloved hands Alcide put the bar in his father's mouth. The black wolf clamped down and sat, just as the light gray wolf did with his silver bar. The two seconds drew back. A high whine of pain came from Jackson Herveaux, while Patrick Furnan showed no signs of stress other than heavy panting. As the delicate skin of his gums and lips began to smoke and smell a little, Jackson's whining became louder. Patrick's skin showed the same painful symptoms, but Patrick was silent.

'They're so brave,' whispered Claude, watching with fascinated horror at the torment the two wolves were enduring. It was becoming apparent that the older wolf would not win this contest. The visible signs of pain were increasing every second, and though Alcide stood there focusing solely on his father to add his support, at any moment it would be over. Except . . .

'He's cheating,' I said clearly, pointing at the gray wolf.

'No member of the pack may speak.' Quinn's deep voice was not angry, merely matter-of-fact.

'I'm not a pack member.'

'You challenge the contest?' Quinn was looking at me now. All the pack members who'd been standing close around me dropped back until I stood alone with the two fairies, who were looking down at me with some surprise and dismay.

'You bet your ass I do. Smell the gloves Patrick's second was wearing.'

The blond second looked completely blindsided. And guilty.

'Drop the bars,' Quinn commanded, and the two wolves complied, Jackson Herveaux with a whimper. Alcide dropped to his knees by his father, putting his arms around the older wolf.

Quinn, moving as smoothly as if his joints were oiled, knelt to retrieve the gloves that Patrick's second had tossed to the floor. Libby Furnan's hand darted over the velvet rope to snatch them up, but a deep snarl from Quinn told her to stop. It made my own spine tingle, and I was much farther away than Libby.

Quinn picked up the gloves and smelled them.

He looked down at Patrick Furnan with a contempt so heavy that I was surprised the wolf didn't crumple under its weight.

He turned to face the rest of the crowd. 'The woman is right.' Quinn's deep voice gave the words the gravity of stone. 'There's a drug on the gloves. It made Furnan's skin numb when the silver was placed in his mouth, so he could last longer. I declare him loser of this part of the contest. The pack will have to decide whether he should forfeit any right to continue, and whether his second should still be a pack member.' The fair-haired Were was cringing as if he expected someone to hit him. I didn't know why his punishment should be worse than Patrick's; maybe the lower your rank, the worse your punishment? Not exactly fair; but then, I wasn't a Were.

'The pack will vote,' Christine called. She met my eyes and I knew this was why she wanted me here. 'If the rest of you would step into the outer room?'

Quinn, Claude, Claudine, and three shape-shifters moved with me to the doors leading into the other room. There was more natural light there, which was a pleasure. Less of a pleasure was the curiosity that pooled around me. My shields were still down, and I felt the suspicion and conjecture flowing from the brains of my companions, except, of course, from the two fairies. To Claude and Claudine, my peculiarity was a rare gift, and I was a lucky woman.

'Come here,' Quinn rumbled, and I thought about telling him to take his commands and shove them where the sun don't shine. But that would be childish, and I had nothing to fear. (At least that's what I told myself about seven times in rapid succession.) I made my spine stiffen, and I strode up to him and looked up into his face.

'You don't have to stick your jaw out like that,' he said calmly. 'I'm not going to hit you.'

'I never thought you were,' I said with a snap in my voice that I was proud of. I found that his round eyes were the very dark, rich, purple-brown of pansies. Wow, they were pretty! I smiled out of sheer pleasure . . . and a dollop of relief.

Unexpectedly, he smiled back. He had full lips, very even white teeth, and a sturdy column of a neck.

'How often do you have to shave?' I asked, fascinated with his smoothness.

He laughed from the belly.

'Are you scared of anything?' he asked.

'So many things,' I said regretfully.

He considered that for a moment. 'Do you have an extrasensitive sense of smell?'

'Nope.'

'Do you know the blond one?'

'Never saw him before.'

'Then how did you know?'

'Sookie is a telepath,' Claude said. When he got the full weight of the big man's stare, he looked like he was sorry he'd interrupted. 'My sister is her, ah, guardian,' Claude concluded in a rush.

'Then you're doing a terrible job,' Quinn told Claudine.

'Don't you get onto Claudine,' I said indignantly. 'Claudine's saved my life a bunch.'

Quinn looked exasperated. 'Fairies,' he muttered. 'The Weres aren't going to be happy about your piece of information,' he told me. 'At least half of them are going to wish you were dead. If your safety is Claudine's top priority, she should have held your mouth shut.'

Claudine looked crushed.

'Hey,' I said, 'cut it out. I know you've got friends in there you're worried about, but don't take that out on Claudine. Or me,' I added hastily, as his eyes fixed on mine.

'I have no friends in there. And I shave every morning,' he said.

'Okay, then.' I nodded, nonplussed.

'Or if I'm going out in the evening.'

'Gotcha.'

'To do something special.'

What would Quinn consider special?

The doors opened, interrupting one of the strangest conversations I'd ever had.

'You can come back in,' said a young Were in three-inch-high fuck-me shoes. She was wearing a burgundy sheath, and when we followed her back into the big room, she gave her walk some extra sway. I wondered whom she was trying to entrance, Quinn or Claude. Or maybe Claudine?

'This is our judgment,' said Christine to Quinn. 'We'll resume the contest where it ended. According to the vote, since Patrick cheated on the second test, he is declared the loser of that test. Of the agility test, too. However, he's allowed to stay in the running. But, to win, he has to win the last test decisively.' I wasn't sure what 'decisively' meant in this context. From Christine's face, I was certain it didn't bode well. For the first time, I realized that justice might not prevail.

Alcide looked very grim, when I found his face in the crowd. This judgment seemed clearly biased in favor of his father's opponent. I hadn't realized that there were more Weres in the Furnan camp than the Herveaux camp, and I wondered when that shift had occurred. The balance had seemed more even at the funeral.

Since I had already interfered, I felt free to interfere some more. I began wandering among the pack members, listening to their brains. Though the twisted and turned brains of all Weres and shifters are difficult to decipher, I began to pick up a clue here and there. The Furnans, I learned, had followed their plan of leaking stories about Jackson Herveaux's gambling habits, talking up how unreliable that made Jackson as a leader.

I knew from Alcide that the stories about his father's gambling were true. Though I didn't admire the Furnans for playing this card, I didn't consider it stacking the deck, either.

The two competitors were still in wolf form. If I had understood correctly, they had been scheduled to fight anyway. I was standing by Amanda. 'What's changed about the last test?' I asked. The redhead whispered that now the fight was no longer a regular match, with the contestant left standing after five minutes declared the winner. Now, to win the fight 'decisively,' the loser had to be dead or disabled.

This was more than I'd bargained for, but I knew without asking that I couldn't leave.

The group gathered around a wire dome that reminded me irresistibly of *Mad Max Beyond Thunderdome*. You remember – 'Two men enter, one man leaves'. I guess this was the wolf equivalent. Quinn opened the door, and the two large wolves slunk in, casting their gazes from side to side as they counted their supporters. Or at least, that's what I guessed they were doing.

Quinn turned and beckoned to me.

Ah-oh. I frowned. The dark, purple-brown eyes were intent. The man meant business. I approached him reluctantly.

'Go read their minds again,' he told me. He laid a huge hand on my shoulder. He turned me to face him, which brought me face-to-face – well, so to speak – with his dark brown nipples. Disconcerted, I looked up. 'Listen, blondie, all you have to do is go in there and do your thing,' he said reassuringly.

He couldn't have had this idea while the wolves were outside the *cage*? What if he shut the door on me? I looked over my shoulder at Claudine, who was frantically shaking her head.

'Why do I need to? What purpose will it serve?' I asked, not being a total idiot.

'Is he gonna cheat again?' Quinn asked so softly that I knew no one else could hear him. 'Does Furnan have some means of cheating that I can't see?'

'Do you guarantee my safety?'

He met my eyes. 'Yes,' he said without hesitation. He opened the door to the cage. Though he had to stoop, he came in behind me.

The two wolves approached me cautiously. Their smell was strong; like dog, but muskier and wilder. Nervously, I laid my hand on Patrick Furnan's head. I looked in his head as hard as I could, and I could discern nothing but rage at me for costing him his win in the endurance contest. There was a glowing coal of purpose about the coming battle, which he intended to win by sheer ruthlessness.

I sighed, shook my head, moved my hand away. To be fair, I put my hand on Jackson's shoulders, which were so high I was startled all over. The wolf was literally vibrating, a faint shiver that made his fur quiver under my touch. His whole resolve was bent toward rending his rival limb from limb. But Jackson was afraid of the younger wolf.

'All clear,' I said, and Quinn turned away to open the door. He crouched to step through, and I was about to follow him when the burgundy-sheathed girl shrieked. Moving faster than I thought such a large man could move, Quinn spun on his foot, grabbed my arm with one hand, and yanked with all his might. With his other hand he slammed shut the door, and I heard something crash against it.

The noises behind me told me the battle had already started, but I was pinned against a huge expanse of smooth tan skin.

With my ear to Quinn's chest, I could hear the rumble inside as well as outside as he asked, 'Did he get you?'

I had my own shaking and quivering going on. My leg was wet, and I saw that my tights were ripped, and blood was running from an abrasion on the side of my right calf. Had my leg scraped the door when Quinn had shut it so quickly, or had I been bitten? Oh my God, if I'd been bitten . . .

Everyone else was pressed against the wire cage, watching the snarling, whirling wolves. Their spittle and blood flew in fine sprays, dotting the spectators. I glanced back to see Jackson's grip on Patrick's hind leg broken when Patrick bent himself backward to bite Jackson's muzzle. I caught a glimpse of Alcide's face, intent and anguished.

I didn't want to watch this. I would rather look at this stranger's hide than watch the two men killing each other.

'I'm bleeding,' I told Quinn. 'It's not bad.'

A high yip from the cage suggested that one of the wolves had scored a hit. I cringed.

The big man half carried me over to the wall. That was a good distance from the fight. He helped me turn and sink down into a sitting position.

Quinn lowered himself to the floor, too. He was so graceful for someone so large that I was absorbed in just watching him move. He knelt by me to pull off my shoes, and then my tights, which were ripped to shreds and dabbled with blood. I was silent and shaking as he sank down to lie on his stomach. He gripped my knee and my ankle in his huge hands as if my leg were a large drumstick. Without saying a word, Quinn began to lick the blood from my calf. I was afraid this was preparatory to taking a bite, but Dr Ludwig trotted over, looked down, and nodded. 'You'll be fine,' she said dismissively. After patting me on the head as if I were an injured dog, the tiny doctor trotted back to her attendants.

Meanwhile, though I would not have thought it was possible for me to be anything but on the knife-edge of suspense, the leg-licking thing was providing an entirely unexpected diversion. I shifted restlessly, stifling a gasp. Maybe I should remove my leg from Quinn's possession? Watching the gleaming bald head bob up and down as he licked was making me think of something worlds away from the life-and-death battle taking place across the room. Quinn was working more and more slowly, his tongue warm and a little rough as he cleaned my leg. Though his brain was the most opaque shifter brain I'd ever encountered, I got the idea he was having the same reaction that I was.

When he finished, he laid his head on my thigh. He was breathing heavily, and I was trying not to. His hands released their grip but stroked my leg deliberately. He looked up at me. His eyes had changed. They were golden, solid gold. The color filled his eyes. Whoa.

I guess he could tell from my face that I was, to put it mildly, conflicted about our little interlude.

'Not our time and place, babe,' he said. 'God, that was … great.' He stretched, and it wasn't an outward extension of arms and chest, the way humans stretch. He rippled from the base of his spine to his shoulders. It was one of the oddest things I'd ever seen, and I'd seen a lot of odd things. 'Do you know who I am?' he asked.

I nodded. 'Quinn?' I said, feeling my cheeks color.

'I've heard your name is Sookie,' he said, rising to his knees.

'Sookie Stackhouse,' I said.

He put his hand under my chin so I'd look up at him. I stared into his eyes as hard as I could. He didn't blink.

'I wonder what you're seeing,' he said finally, and removed his hand.

I glanced down at my leg. The mark on it, now clear of blood, was almost certainly a scrape from the metal of the door. 'Not a bite,' I said, my voice faltering on the last word. The tension left me in a rush.

'Nope. No she-wolf in your future,' he agreed, and flowed to his feet. He held out his hand. I took it, and he had me on my feet in a second. A piercing yelp from the cage yanked me back into the here and now.

'Tell me something. Why the hell can't they just vote?' I asked him.

Quinn's round eyes, back to their purple-brown color and properly surrounded with white, crinkled at the corners with amusement.

'Not the way of the shifter, babe. You're going to see me later,' Quinn promised. Without another word he strode back to the cage, and my little field trip was over. I had to turn my attention back to the truly important thing happening in this building.

Claudine and Claude were looking anxiously over their shoulders when I found them. They made a little space for me to ease in between them, and wrapped their arms around me when I was in place. They seemed very upset, and Claudine had two tears trailing down her cheeks. When I saw the situation in the cage, I understood why.

The lighter wolf was winning. The black wolf's coat was matted with blood. He was still on his feet, still snarling, but one of his hind legs was giving way under his weight from time to time. He managed to pull himself back up twice, but the third time the leg collapsed, the younger wolf was on him, the two spinning over and over in a terrifying blur of teeth, torn flesh, and fur.

Forgetting the silence rules, all the Weres were screaming their support of one contestant or the other, or just howling. The violence and the noise blended together to make a chaotic collage. I finally spotted Alcide pounding his hands against the metal in futile agitation. I had never felt so sorry for anyone in my life. I wondered if he'd try to break into the combat cage. But another look told me that even if Alcide's respect for pack rules broke down and he attempted to go to his father's aid, Quinn was blocking the door. That was why the pack had brought in an outsider, of course.

Abruptly, the fight was over. The lighter wolf had the darker one by the throat. He was gripping, but not biting. Maybe Jackson would have gone on struggling if he hadn't been so severely wounded, but his strength was exhausted. He lay whining, quite unable to defend himself, disabled. The room fell completely silent.

'Patrick Furnan is declared the winner,' said Quinn, his voice neutral.

And then Patrick Furnan bit down on Jackson Herveaux's throat and killed him.

Chapter 16

Quinn took over the cleanup with the sure authority of one who's supervised such things before. Though I was dull and stupid with shock, I noticed he gave clear, concise directions as to the dispersal of the testing materials. Pack members dismantled the cage into sections and took apart the agility arena with efficient dispatch. A cleanup crew took care of mopping up the blood and other fluids.

Soon the building was empty of all but the people. Patrick Furnan had reverted to his human form, and Dr Ludwig was attending his many wounds. I was glad he had every one of them. I was only sorry they weren't worse. But the pack had accepted Furnan's choice. If they would not protest such unnecessary brutality, I couldn't.

Alcide was being comforted by Maria-Star Cooper, a young Were I knew slightly.

Maria-Star held him and stroked his back, providing support by her sheer closeness. He didn't have to tell me that on this occasion, he preferred another Were's companionship to mine. I'd gone to hug him, but when I'd neared him and met his eyes, I'd known. That hurt, and it hurt bad; but today wasn't about me and my feelings.

Claudine was crying in her brother's arms. 'She's so tenderhearted,' I whispered to Claude, feeling a bit abashed that I wasn't crying myself. My concern was for Alcide; I'd hardly known Jackson Herveaux.

'She went through the second elf war in Iowa fighting with the best of them,' Claude said, shaking his head. 'I've seen a decapitated goblin stick its tongue out at her in its death throes, and she laughed. But as she gets closer to the light, she becomes more sensitive.'

That effectively shut me up. I was not about to ask for any explanation of yet another arcane supernatural rule. I'd had a bellyful this day.

Now that all the mess was cleared away (that mess included Jackson's body, which Dr Ludwig had taken somewhere to be altered, to make the story of how he'd met his death more plausible), all the pack members present gathered in front of Patrick Furnan, who hadn't resumed clothes. According to his body, victory had made him feel manly. Ick.

He was standing on a blanket; it was a red plaid stadium blanket, like you'd take to a football game. I felt my lips twitch, but I became completely sober when the new packmaster's wife led a young woman to him, a brown-haired girl who seemed to be in her late teens. The girl was as bare as the packmaster, though she looked considerably better in that state.

What the hell?

Suddenly I remembered the last part of the ceremony, and I realized Patrick Furman was going to fuck this girl in front of us. No. No way was I going to watch this. I tried to turn to walk out. But Claude hissed, 'You can't leave.' He covered my mouth and picked me up bodily to move me to the back of the crowd. Claudine moved with us and stood in front of me, but with her back to me, so I wouldn't have to see. I made a furious sound into Claude's hand.

'Shut up,' the fairy said grimly, his voice as concentrated with sincerity as he could manage. 'You'll land us all in trouble. If it makes you feel any better, this is traditional. The girl volunteered. After this, Patrick'll be a faithful husband once more. But he's already bred his whelp by his wife, and he has to make the ceremonial gesture of breeding another one. May take, may not, but it has to be done.'

I kept my eyes shut and was grateful when Claudine turned to me and placed her tear-wet hands over my ears. A shout went up from the crowd when the thing was completed. The two fairies relaxed and gave me some room. I didn't see what happened to the girl. Furnan remained naked, but as long as he was in a calm state, I could handle that.

To seal his status, the new packmaster began to receive the pledges of his wolves. They went in turn, oldest to youngest, I figured, after a moment's observation. Each Were licked the back of Patrick Furnan's hand and exposed his or her neck for a ritual moment. When it was Alcide's turn, I suddenly realized there was potential for even more disaster.

I found I was holding my breath.

From the profound silence, I knew I wasn't the only one.

After a long hesitation, Furnan bent over and placed his teeth on Alcide's neck; I opened my mouth to protest, but Claudine clapped her hand over it. Furnan's teeth came away from Alcide's flesh, leaving it unscathed.

Packmaster Furnan had sent a clear signal.

By the time the last Were had performed the ritual, I was exhausted from all the emotion. Surely this was an end to it? Yes, the pack was dispersing, some members giving the Furnans congratulatory hugs, and some striding out silently.

I dodged them myself and made a beeline for the door. The next time someone told me I had to watch a supernatural rite, I was going to tell him I had to wash my hair.

Once out in the open air, I walked slowly, my feet dragging. I had to think about things I'd put to one side, like what I'd seen in Alcide's head after the whole debacle was over. Alcide thought I'd failed him. He'd told me I had to come, and I had; I should have known he had some purpose in insisting I be present.

Now I knew that he'd suspected Furnan had some underhanded trick in mind. Alcide had primed Christine, his father's ally, ahead of time. She made sure I used my telepathy on Patrick Furnan. And, sure enough, I had found that Jackson's opponent was cheating. That disclosure should have ensured Jackson's win.

Instead, the will of the pack had gone against Jackson, and the contest had continued with the stakes even higher. I'd nothing to do with that decision. But right now Alcide, in his grief and rage, was blaming me.

I was trying to be angry, but I was too sad.

Claude and Claudine said good-bye, and they hopped into

Claudine's Cadillac and peeled out of the parking lot as if they couldn't wait to get back to Monroe. I was of the same mind, but I was a lot less resilient than the fairies. I had to sit behind the wheel of the borrowed Malibu for five or ten minutes, steadying myself for the drive home.

I found myself thinking of Quinn. It was a welcome relief from thinking of torn flesh and blood and death. When I'd looked into his head, I'd seen a man who knew his way. And I still didn't have a clue as to what he was.

The drive home was grim.

I might as well have phoned in to Merlotte's that evening. Oh, sure, I went through all the motions of taking orders and carrying them to the right tables, refilling pitchers of beer, popping my tips in the tip jar, wiping up spills and making sure the temporary cook (a vampire named Anthony Bolivar; he'd subbed for us before) remembered the busboy was off limits. But I didn't have any sparkle, any joy, in my work.

I did notice that Sam seemed to be getting around better. He was obviously restive, sitting in his corner watching Charles work. Possibly Sam was also a little piqued, since Charles just seemed to get more and more popular with the clientele. The vamp was charming, that was for sure. He was wearing a red sequined eye patch tonight and his usual poet shirt under a black sequined vest – flashy in the extreme, but entertaining, too.

'You seem depressed, beautiful lady,' he said when I came to pick up a Tom Collins and a rum and Coke.

'Just been a long day,' I said, making an effort to smile. I had so many other things to digest emotionally that I didn't even mind when Bill brought Selah Pumphrey in again. Even when they sat in my section, I didn't care. But when Bill took my hand as I was turning away to get their order, I snatched it away as if he'd tried to set me on fire.

'I only want to know what's wrong,' he said, and for a second I remembered how good it had felt that night at the hospital when he'd lain down with me. My mouth actually began to open, but then

I caught a glimpse of Selah's indignant face, and I shut my emotional water off at the meter.

'I'll be right back with that blood,' I said cheerfully, smiling wide enough to show every tooth in my head.

To heck with him, I thought righteously. *Him and the horse he rode in on.*

After that it was strictly business. I smiled and worked, and worked and smiled. I stayed away from Sam, because I didn't want to have a long conversation with yet another shifter that evening. I was afraid – since I didn't have any reason to be mad at Sam – that if he asked me what was wrong, I'd tell him; and I just didn't want to talk about it. You ever just feel like stomping around and being miserable for a while? That was the kind of mood I was in.

But I had to go over to Sam, after all, when Catfish asked if he could pay with a check for this evening's festivities. That was Sam's rule: he had to approve checks. And I had to stand close to Sam, because the bar was very noisy.

I thought nothing of it, aside from not wanting to get into my own mood with him, but when I bent over him to explain Catfish's cash-flow problem, Sam's eyes widened. 'My God, Sookie,' he said, 'Who have you been around?'

I backed off, speechless. He was both shocked and appalled by a smell I hadn't even known I carried. I was tired of supes pulling this on me.

'Where'd you meet up with a tiger?' he asked.

'A tiger,' I repeated numbly.

So now I knew what my new acquaintance Quinn turned into when the moon was full.

'Tell me,' Sam demanded.

'No,' I snapped, 'I won't. What about Catfish?'

'He can write a check this once. If there's a problem, he'll never write another one here again.'

I didn't relay this last sentence. I took Catfish's check and his alcohol-fueled gratitude, and deposited both where they belonged.

To make my bad mood worse, I snagged my silver chain on a corner of the bar when I bent over to pick up a napkin some slob had tossed to the floor. The chain broke, and I caught it up and dropped it in my pocket. Dammit. This had been a rotten day, followed by a rotten night.

I made sure to wave at Selah as she and Bill left. He'd left me a good tip, and I stuffed it in my other pocket with so much force I almost ripped the fabric. A couple of times during the evening, I had heard the bar phone ring, and when I was taking some dirty glasses to the kitchen hatch, Charles said, 'Someone keeps calling and hanging up. Very irritating.'

'They'll get tired and quit,' I said soothingly.

About an hour later, as I put a Coke in front of Sam, the busboy came to tell me there was someone at the employees' entrance, asking for me.

'What were you doing outside?' Sam asked sharply.

The boy looked embarrassed. 'I smoke, Mr Merlotte,' he said. 'I was outside taking me a break, 'cause the vamp said he'd drain me if I lit up inside, when this man walked up outta nowhere.'

'What's he look like?' I asked.

'Oh, he's old, got black hair,' the boy said, shrugging. Not long on the gift of description.

'Okay,' I said. I was glad to take a break. I suspected who the visitor might be, and if he'd come into the bar, he'd have caused a riot. Sam found an excuse to follow me out by saying that he needed a pit stop, and he picked up his cane and used it to hobble down the hall after me. He had his own tiny bathroom off his office, and he limped into it as I continued past the men's and women's to the back door. I opened it cautiously and peered outside. But then I began smiling. The man waiting for me had one of the most famous faces in the world – except, apparently, to adolescent busboys.

'Bubba,' I said, pleased to see the vampire. You couldn't call him by his former name, or he got real confused and agitated. Bubba was formerly known as ... Well, let me just put it this way. You wondered about all those sightings after his death? This was the explanation.

The conversion hadn't been a complete success because his system had been so fuddled with drugs; but aside from his predilection for cat blood, Bubba managed pretty well. The vampire community took good care of him. Eric kept Bubba on staff as an errand boy. Bubba's glossy black hair was always combed and styled, his long sideburns sharply trimmed. Tonight he was wearing a black leather jacket, new blue jeans, and a black-and-silver plaid shirt.

'Looking good, Bubba,' I said admiringly.

'You too, Miss Sookie.' He beamed at me.

'Did you want to tell me something?'

'Yessum. Mr Eric sent me over here to tell you that he's not what he seems.'

I blinked.

'Who, Bubba?' I asked, trying to keep my voice gentle.

'He's a hit man.'

I stared at Bubba's face not because I thought staring would get me anywhere, but because I was trying to figure out the message. This was a mistake; Bubba's eyes began darting from side to side, and his face lost its smile. I should have turned to stare at the wall – it would've given me as much information, and Bubba wouldn't have become as anxious.

'Thanks, Bubba,' I said, patting him on his beefy shoulder. 'You did good.'

'Can I go now? Back to Shreveport?'

'Sure,' I said. I would just call Eric. Why hadn't he used the phone for a message as urgent and important as this one seemed to be?

'I found me a back way into the animal shelter,' Bubba confided proudly.

I gulped. 'Oh, well, great,' I said, trying not to feel queasy.

'See ya later, alligator,' he called from the edge of the parking lot. Just when you thought Bubba was the worst vampire in the world, he did something amazing like moving at a speed you simply could not track.

'After a while, crocodile,' I said dutifully.

'Was that who I think it was?' The voice was right behind me.

I jumped. I spun around to find that Charles had deserted his post at the bar.

'You scared me,' I said, as though he hadn't been able to tell.

'Sorry.'

'Yes, that was him.'

'Thought so. I've never heard him sing in person. It must be amazing.' Charles stared out at the parking lot as though he were thinking hard about something else. I had the definite impression he wasn't listening to his own words.

I opened my mouth to ask a question, but before my words reached my lips I really thought about what the English pirate had just said, and the words froze in my throat. After a long hesitation, I knew I had to speak, or he would know something was wrong.

'Well, I guess I'd better get back to work,' I said, smiling the bright smile that pops onto my face when I'm nervous. And, boy, was I nervous now. The one blinding revelation I'd had made everything begin to click into place in my head. Every little hair on my arms and neck stood straight up. My fight-or-flight reflex was fixed firmly on 'flight.' Charles was between the outside door and me. I began to back down the hall toward the bar.

The door from the bar into the hall was usually left open, because people had to pass into the hall all the time to use the bathrooms. But now it was closed. It had been open when I'd come down the hall to talk to Bubba.

This was bad.

'Sookie,' Charles said, behind me. 'I truly regret this.'

'It was you who shot Sam, wasn't it?' I reached behind me, fumbled for the handle that would open that door. He wouldn't kill me in front of all those people, would he? Then I remembered the night Eric and Bill had polished off a roomful of men in my house. I remembered it had taken them only three or four minutes. I remembered what the men had looked like afterward.

'Yes. It was a stroke of luck when you caught the cook, and she confessed. But she didn't confess to shooting Sam, did she?'

'No, she didn't,' I said numbly. 'All the others, but not Sam, and the bullet didn't match.'

My fingers found the knob. If I turned it, I might live. But I might not. How much did Charles value his own life?

'You wanted the job here,' I said.

'I thought there was a good chance I'd come in handy when Sam was out of the picture.'

'How'd you know I'd go to Eric for help?'

'I didn't. But I knew someone would tell him the bar was in trouble. Since that would mean helping you, he would do it. I was the logical one to send.'

'Why are you doing all this?'

'Eric owes a debt.'

He was moving closer, though not very quickly. Maybe he was reluctant to do the deed. Maybe he was hoping for a more advantageous moment, when he could carry me off in silence.

'It looks like Eric's found out I'm not from the Jackson nest, as I'd said.'

'Yeah. You picked the wrong one.'

'Why? It seemed ideal to me. Many men there; you wouldn't have seen them all. No one can remember all the men who've passed through that mansion.'

'But they've heard Bubba sing,' I said softly. 'He sang for them one night. You'd never have forgotten that. I don't know how Eric found out, but I knew as soon as you said you'd never—'

He sprang.

I was on my back on the floor in a split second, but my hand was already in my pocket, and he opened his mouth to bite. He was supporting himself on his arms, courteously trying not to actually lie on top of me. His fangs were fully out, and they glistened in the light.

'I have to do this,' he said. 'I'm sworn. I'm sorry.'

'I'm not,' I said, and thrust the silver chain into his mouth, using the heel of my hand to snap his jaw shut.

He screamed and hit at me, and I felt a rib go, and smoke was coming out of his mouth. I scrambled away and did a little yelling of my own. The door flew open, and a flood of bar patrons thundered into the little hallway. Sam shot out of the door of his office like he'd been fired from a cannon, moving very well for a man with a broken leg, and to my amazement he had a stake in his hand. By that time, the screaming vampire was weighted down by so many beefy men in jeans you couldn't even see him. Charles was trying to bite whoever he could, but his burned mouth was so painful his efforts were weak.

Catfish Hunter seemed to be on the bottom of the pile, in direct contact. 'You pass me that stake here, boy!' he called back to Sam. Sam passed it to Hoyt Fortenberry, who passed it to Dago Guglielmi, who transferred it to Catfish's hairy hand.

'We gonna wait for the vampire police, or we gonna take care of this ourselves?' Catfish asked. 'Sookie?'

After a horrified second of temptation, I opened my mouth to say, 'Call the police.' The Shreveport police had a squad of vampire policemen, as well as the necessary special transportation vehicle and special jail cells.

'End it,' said Charles, somewhere below the heaving pile of men. 'I failed in my mission, and I can't abide jails.' 'Okeydokey,' Catfish said, and staked him.

After it was over and the body had disintegrated, the men went back into the bar and settled down at the tables where they'd been before they heard the fight going on in the hall. It was beyond strange. There wasn't much laughing, and there wasn't much smiling, and no one who'd stayed in the bar asked anyone who'd left what had happened.

Of course, it was tempting to think this was an echo of the terrible old days, when black men had been lynched if there was even a rumor they'd winked at a white woman.

But, you know, the simile just didn't hold. Charles was a different race, true. But he'd been guilty as hell of trying to kill me. I would have been a dead woman in thirty more seconds, despite my diversionary tactic, if the men of Bon Temps hadn't intervened.

We were lucky in a lot of ways. There was not one law enforcement person in the bar that night. Not five minutes after everyone resumed his table, Dennis Pettibone, the arson investigator, came in to have a visit with Arlene. (The busboy was still mopping the hall, in fact.) Sam had bound my ribs with some Ace bandages in his office, and I walked out, slowly and carefully, to ask Dennis what he wanted to drink.

We were lucky that there weren't any outsiders. No college guys from Ruston, no truckers from Shreveport, no relatives who'd dropped in for a beer with a cousin or an uncle.

We were lucky there weren't many women. I don't know why, but I imagined a woman would be more likely to get squeamish about Charles's execution. In fact, I felt pretty squeamish about it, when I wasn't counting my lucky stars I was still alive.

And Eric was lucky when he dashed into the bar about thirty minutes later, because Sam didn't have any more stakes handy. As jittery as everyone was, some foolhardy soul would have volunteered to take out Eric: but he wouldn't have come out of it relatively unscathed, as those who'd tackled Charles had.

And Eric was also lucky that the first words out of his mouth were 'Sookie, are you all right?' In his anxiety, he grabbed me, one hand on either side of my waist, and I cried out.

'You're hurt,' he said, and then realized five or six men had jumped to their feet.

'I'm just sore,' I said, making a huge effort to look okay. 'Everything's fine. This here's my friend Eric,' I said a little loudly. 'He's been trying to get in touch with me, and now I know why it was so urgent.' I met the eyes of each man, and one by one, they dropped back into their seats.

'Let's us go sit and talk,' I said very quietly.

'Where is he? I will stake the bastard myself, no matter what Hot Rain sends against me.' Eric was furious.

'It's been taken care of,' I hissed. 'Will you *chill?*'

With Sam's permission, we went to his office, the only place in the building that offered both chairs and privacy. Sam was back behind the bar, perched on a high stool with his leg on a lower stool, managing the bartending himself.

'Bill searched his database,' Eric said proudly. 'The bastard told me he came from Mississippi, so I wrote him down as one of Russell's discarded pretty boys. I had even called Russell, to ask him if Twining had worked well for him. Russell said he had so many new vampires in the mansion, he had only the vaguest recollection of Twining. But Russell, as I observed at Josephine's Bar, is not the kind of manager I am.'

I managed a smile. That was definitely true.

'So when I found myself wondering, I asked Bill to go to work, and

Bill traced Twining from his birth as a vampire to his pledge to Hot Rain.'

'This Hot Rain was the one who made him a vampire?'

'No, no,' Eric said impatiently. 'Hot Rain made the pirate's sire a vampire. And when Charles's sire was killed during the French and Indian War, Charles pledged himself to Hot Rain. When Hot Rain was dissatisfied with Long Shadow's death, he sent Charles to exact payment for the debt he felt was owed.'

'Why would killing me cancel the debt?'

'Because he decided after listening to gossip and much reconnoitering that you were important to me, and that your death would wound me the way Long Shadow's had him.'

'Ah.' I could not think of one thing to say. Not one thing. At last I asked, 'So Hot Rain and Long Shadow were doing the deed, once upon a time?'

Eric said, 'Yes, but it wasn't the sexual connection, it was the . . . the affection. That was the valuable part of the bond.'

'So because this Hot Rain decided the fine you paid him for Long Shadow's death just didn't give him closure, he sent Charles to do something equally painful to you.'

'Yes.'

'And Charles got to Shreveport, kept his ears open, found out about me, decided my death would fill the bill.'

'Apparently.'

'So he heard about the shootings, knew Sam is a shifter, and shot Sam so there'd be a good reason for him to come to Bon Temps.'

'Yes.'

'That's real, real complicated. Why didn't Charles just jump me some night?'

'Because he wanted it to look like an accident. He didn't want blame attached to a vampire at all, because not only did he not want to get caught, he didn't want Hot Rain to incur any penalty.'

I closed my eyes. 'He set fire to my house,' I said. 'Not that poor Marriot guy. I bet Charles killed him before the bar even closed that night and brought him back to my house so he'd take the blame. After all, the guy was a stranger to Bon Temps. No one would miss him. Oh my God! Charles borrowed my keys! I bet the man was in my trunk! Not dead, but hypnotized. Charles planted that card in the guy's pocket. The poor fella wasn't a member of the Fellowship of the Sun anymore than I am.'

'It must have been frustrating for Charles, when he found you were surrounded by friends,' Eric said a little coldly, since a couple of those 'friends' had just clomped by noisily, using a trip to the john as a pretext to keep an eye on him.

'Yes, must have been.' I smiled.

'You seem better than I expected,' Eric said a little hesitantly. 'Less traumatized, as they say now.'

'Eric, I'm a lucky woman,' I said. 'Today I've seen more bad stuff than you can imagine. All I can think is, I escaped. By the way, Shreveport now has a new packmaster, and he's a lying, cheating bastard.'

'Then I take it Jackson Herveaux lost his bid for the job.'

'Lost more than that.'

Eric's eyes widened. 'So the contest was today. I'd heard Quinn was in town. Usually, he keeps transgressions to a minimum.'

'It wasn't his choice,' I said. 'A vote went against Jackson; it should have helped him, but it . . . didn't.'

'Why were you there? Was that blasted Alcide trying to use you for some purpose in the contest?'

'You should talk about using.'

'Yes, but I'm straightforward about it,' Eric said, his blue eyes wide and guileless.

I had to laugh. I hadn't expected to laugh for days, or weeks, and yet here I was, laughing. 'True,' I admitted.

'So, I'm to understand that Charles Twining is no more?' Eric asked quite soberly.

'That's correct.'

'Well, well. The people here are unexpectedly enterprising. What damage have you suffered?'

'Broken rib.'

'A broken rib is not much when a vampire is fighting for his life.'

'Correct, again.'

'When Bubba got back and I found he hadn't exactly delivered his message, I rushed here gallantly to rescue you. I had tried calling the bar tonight to tell you to beware, but Charles answered the phone every time.'

'It was gallant of you, in the extreme,' I admitted. 'But, as it turns out, unnecessary.'

'Well, then . . . I'll go back to my own bar and look at my own bar patrons from my own office. We're expanding our Fangtasia product line.'

'Oh?'

'Yes. What would you think of a nude calendar? Fangtasia's Vampire Hunks' is what Pam thinks it should be called.'

'Are you gonna be in it?'

'Oh, of course. Mr January.'

'Well, put me down for three. I'll give one to Arlene and one to Tara. And I'll put one up on my own wall.'

'If you promise to keep it open to my picture, I'll give you one for free,' Eric promised.

'You got a deal.'

He stood up. 'One more thing, before I go.'

I stood, too, but much more slowly.

'I may need to hire you in early March.'

'I'll check my calendar. What's up?'

'There's going to be a little summit. A meeting of the kings and queens of some of the southern states. The location hasn't been settled, but when it is, I wonder if you can get time off from your job here to accompany me and my people.'

'I can't think that far ahead just at the moment, Eric,' I said. I winced as I began to walk out of the office.

'Wait one moment,' he said suddenly, and justlikethat he was in front of me.

I looked up, feeling massively tired.

He bent and kissed me on my mouth, as softly as a butterfly's fluttering.

'You said I told you you were the best I'd ever had,' he said. 'But did you respond in kind?'

'Don't you wish you knew?' I said, and went back to work.

Definitely Dead

Obviously, this book was finished before Hurricane Katrina struck the Gulf Coast. Since much of the plot is set in New Orleans, I struggled with whether I would leave Definitely Dead *as it was, or include the catastrophe of August and September. After much thought, since Sookie's visit takes place in the early spring of the year, I decided to let the book remain as it was originally written.*

My heart goes out to the people of the beautiful city of New Orleans and to all the people of the coastal areas of Mississippi, my home state. My thoughts and prayers will be with you as you rebuild your homes and your lives.

Chapter 1

I was draped over the arm of one of the most beautiful men I'd ever seen, and he was staring into my eyes. 'Think . . . Brad Pitt,' I whispered. The dark brown eyes still regarded me with remote interest.

Okay, I was on the wrong track.

I pictured Claude's last lover, a bouncer at a strip joint.

'Think about Charles Bronson,' I suggested. 'Or, um, Edward James Olmos.' I was rewarded by the beginnings of a hot glow in those long-lashed eyes.

In a jiffy, you would've thought Claude was going to hike up my long rustling skirt and yank down my low-cut push-up bodice and ravish me until I begged for mercy. Unfortunately for me – and all the other women of Louisiana – Claude batted for another team. Bosomy and blond was not Claude's ideal; tough, rough, and brooding, with maybe a little whisker stubble, was what lit his fire.

'Maria-Star, reach in there and pull that lock of hair back,' Alfred Cumberland directed from behind the camera. The photographer was a heavyset black man with graying hair and mustache. Maria-Star Cooper took a quick step in front of the camera to rearrange a stray strand of my long blond hair. I was bent backward over Claude's right arm, my invisible (to the camera, anyway) left hand desperately clutching the back of his black frock coat, my right arm raised to rest gently on his left shoulder. His left hand was at my waist. I think the pose was meant to suggest that he was lowering me to the ground to have his way with me.

Claude was wearing the black frock coat with black knee pants, white hose, and a white frothy shirt. I was wearing a long blue dress with a billowing skirt and a score of petticoats. As I've mentioned, the dress was scanty on the topside, with the little sleeves pushed down off my shoulders. I was glad the temperature in the studio was moderately warm. The big light (it looked to my eyes like a satellite dish) was not as hot as I'd expected.

Al Cumberland was snapping away as Claude smoldered down at me. I did my best to smolder right back. My personal life had been, shall we say, *barren* for the past few weeks, so I was all too ready to smolder. In fact, I was ready to burst into flames.

Maria-Star, who had beautiful light-toast skin and curly dark hair, was standing ready with a big makeup case and brushes and combs to perform last-minute repairs. When Claude and I had arrived at the studio, I'd been surprised to find that I recognized the photographer's young assistant. I hadn't seen Maria-Star since the Shreveport pack-leader had been chosen a few weeks before. I hadn't had much of a chance to observe her then, since the packmaster contest had been frightening and bloody. Today, I had the leisure to see that Maria-Star had completely recovered from being hit by a car this past January. Werewolves healed quickly.

Maria-Star had recognized me, too, and I'd been relieved when she smiled back at me. My standing with the Shreveport pack was, to say the least, uncertain. Without exactly volunteering to do so, I'd unwittingly thrown in my lot with the unsuccessful contestant for the packleader's job. That contestant's son, Alcide Herveaux, whom I'd counted as maybe more than a friend, felt I'd let him down during the contest; the new packleader, Patrick Furnan, knew I had ties to the Herveaux family. I'd been surprised when Maria-Star chatted away while she was zipping the costume and brushing my hair. She applied more makeup than I'd ever worn in my life, but when I stared into the mirror I had to thank her. I looked great, though I didn't look like Sookie Stackhouse.

If Claude hadn't been gay, he might have been impressed, too. He's the brother of my friend Claudine, and he makes his living stripping on ladies' night at Hooligans, a club he now owns. Claude is simply mouthwatering; six feet tall, with rippling black hair and large brown eyes, a perfect nose, and lips just full enough. He keeps his hair long to cover up his ears: they've been surgically altered to look rounded like human ears, not pointed as they originally were. If you're in the know supernaturally, you'll spot the ear surgery, and you'll know Claude is a fairy. I'm not using the pejorative term for his sexual orientation. I mean it literally; Claude's a fairy.

'Now the wind machine,' Al instructed Maria-Star, and after a little repositioning, she switched on a large fan. Now we appeared to be standing in a gale. My hair billowed out in a blond sheet, though Claude's tied-back ponytail stayed in place. After a few shots to capture that look, Maria-Star unbound Claude's hair and directed it over one shoulder, so it would blow forward to form a backdrop for his perfect profile.

'Wonderful,' Al said, and snapped some more. Maria-Star moved the machine a couple of times, causing the windstorm to strike from different directions. Eventually Al told me I could stand up. I straightened gratefully.

'I hope that wasn't too hard on your arm,' I told Claude, who was looking cool and calm again.

'Nah, no problem. You have any fruit juice around?' he asked Maria-Star. Claude was not Mr Social Skills.

The pretty Were pointed to a little refrigerator in the corner of the studio. 'Cups are on the top,' she told Claude. She followed him with her eyes and sighed. Women frequently did that after they'd actually talked to Claude. The sigh was a 'what a pity' sigh.

After checking to make sure her boss was still fiddling intently with his gear, Maria-Star gave me a bright smile. Even though she was a Were, which made her thoughts hard to read, I was picking up on the fact that she had something she wanted to tell me . . . and she wasn't sure how I was going to take it.

Telepathy is no fun. Your opinion of yourself suffers when you know what others think of you. And telepathy makes it almost impossible to date regular guys. Just think about it. (And remember, I'll know – if you are, or if you aren't.)

'Alcide's had a hard time of it since his dad was defeated,' Maria-Star said, keeping her voice low. Claude was occupied with studying himself in a mirror while he drank his juice. Al Cumberland had gotten a call on his cell phone and retreated to his office to hold his conversation.

'I'm sure he has,' I said. Since Jackson Herveaux's opponent had killed him, it was only to be expected that Jackson's son was having his ups and his downs. 'I sent a memorial to the ASPCA, and I know they'll notify Alcide and Janice,' I said. (Janice was Alcide's younger sister, which made her a non-Were. I wondered how Alcide had explained their father's death to his sister.) In acknowledgment, I'd received a printed thank-you note, the kind the funeral home gives you, without one personal word written on it.

'Well . . .' She seemed to be unable to spit it out, whatever was stuck in her throat. I was getting a glimpse of the shape of it. Pain flickered through me like a knife, and then I locked it down and pulled my pride around me. I'd learned to do that all too early in life.

I picked an album of samples of Alfred's work and began to flip through them, hardly looking at the photographs of brides and grooms, bar mitzvahs, first communions, twenty-fifth wedding anniversaries. I closed that album and laid it down. I was trying to look casual, but I don't think it worked.

With a bright smile that echoed Maria-Star's own expression, I said, 'Alcide and I weren't ever truly a couple, you know.' I might have had longings and hopes, but they'd never had a chance to ripen. The timing had always been wrong.

Maria-Star's eyes, a much lighter brown than Claude's, widened in awe. Or was it fear? 'I heard you could do that,' she said. 'But it's hard to believe.'

'Yeah,' I said wearily. 'Well, I'm glad you and Alcide are dating, and I have no right to mind, even if I did. Which I don't.' That came out kind of garbled (and it wasn't entirely true), but I think Maria-Star got my intention: to save my face.

When I hadn't heard from Alcide in the weeks following his father's death; I'd known that whatever feelings he'd had for me were quenched. That had been a blow, but not a fatal one. Realistically, I hadn't expected anything more from Alcide. But gosh darn it, I liked him, and it always smarts when you find out you've been replaced with apparent ease. After all, before his dad's death Alcide had suggested we live together. Now he was shacking up with this young Were, maybe planning to have puppies with her.

I stopped that line of thought in its tracks. Shame on me! No point in being a bitch. (Which, come to think of it, Maria-Star actually was, at least three nights a month.)

Double shame on me.

'I hope you're very happy,' I said.

She wordlessly handed me another album, this one stamped EYES ONLY. When I opened it, I realized that the Eyes were supernatural. Here were pictures of ceremonies humans never got to see ... a vampire couple dressed in elaborate costume, posed before a giant ankh; a young man in the middle of changing into a bear, presumably for the first time; a shot of a Were pack with all its members in wolf form. Al Cumberland, photographer of the weird. No wonder he had been Claude's first choice for his pictures, which Claude hoped would launch him on a cover-model career.

'Next shot,' called Al, as he bustled out of his office, snapping his phone shut. 'Maria-Star, we just got booked for a double wedding in Miss Stackhouse's neck of the woods.' I wondered if he'd been engaged for regular human work or for a supernatural event, but it would be rude to ask.

Claude and I got up close and personal again. Following Al's instructions, I pulled up the skirt to display my legs. In the era my dress represented, I didn't think women tanned or shaved their legs, and I was brown and smooth as a baby's bottom. But what the hey. Probably guys hadn't walked around with their shirts unbuttoned, either.

'Raise your leg like you're going to wrap it around him,' Alfred directed. 'Now Claude, this is your chance to shine. Look like you're going to pull your pants off at any second. We want the readers to pant when they look at you!'

Claude's portfolio of shots would be used when he entered the

Mr Romance competition, orchestrated each year by *Romantic Times Bookclub* magazine.

When he'd shared his ambition with Al (I gathered they'd met at a party), Al had advised Claude to have some pictures made with the sort of woman that often appeared on the cover of romance novels; he'd told the fairy that Claude's dark looks would be set off by a blue-eyed blonde. I happened to be the only bosomy blonde of Claude's acquaintance who was willing to help him for free. Of course, Claude knew some strippers who would have done it, but they expected to be paid. With his usual tact, Claude had told me this on our way to the photographer's studio. Claude could have kept these details to himself, which would have left me feeling good about helping out my friend's brother – but in typical Claude fashion, he shared.

'Okay, Claude, now off with the shirt,' Alfred called.

Claude was used to being asked to take off his clothes. He had a broad, hairless chest with impressive musculature, so he looked very nice indeed without his shirt. I was unmoved. Maybe I was becoming immune.

'Skirt, leg,' Alfred reminded me, and I told myself that this was a job. Al and Maria-Star were certainly professional and impersonal, and you couldn't get cooler than Claude. But I wasn't used to pulling my skirt up in front of people, and it felt pretty personal to me. Though I showed this much leg when I wore shorts and never raised a blush, somehow the pulling up of the long skirt was a little more loaded with sexuality. I clenched my teeth and hiked up the material, tucking it at intervals so it would stay in position.

'Miss Stackhouse, you have to look like you're enjoying this,' Al said. He peered at me from around his camera, his forehead creased in a definitely unhappy way.

I tried not to sulk. I'd told Claude I'd do him a favor, and favors should be done willingly. I raised my leg so my thigh was parallel with the floor, and pointed my bare toes to the floor in what I hoped was a graceful position. I put both hands on Claude's naked shoulders and looked up at him. His skin felt warm and smooth to the touch – not erotic or arousing.

'You look *bored*, Miss Stackhouse,' Alfred said. 'You're supposed to

look like you want to jump his bones. Maria-Star, make her look more
. . . more.' Maria darted over to push the little puff sleeves farther down
my arms. She got a little too enthusiastic, and I was glad the bodice
was tight.

The fact of the matter was, Claude could look beautiful and bare all
day long, and I still wouldn't want him. He was grumpy and he had
bad manners. Even if he'd been hetero, he wouldn't have been my cup
of tea – after I'd had ten minutes' conversation with him.

Like Claude earlier, I'd have to resort to fantasy.

I thought of Bill the vampire, my first love in every way. But instead
of lust, I felt anger. Bill was dating another woman, had been for a few
weeks.

Okay, what about Eric, Bill's boss, the former Viking? Eric the
vampire had shared my house and my bed for a few days in January.
Nope, that way lay danger. Eric knew a secret I wanted to keep
hidden for the rest of my days; though, since he'd had amnesia when
he'd stayed at my place, he wasn't aware it was in his memory
somewhere.

A few other faces popped into my mind – my boss, Sam Merlotte,
the owner of Merlotte's Bar. No, don't go there, thinking about your
boss naked is *bad*. Okay, Alcide Herveaux? Nope, that was a no-go,
especially since I was in the company of his current girlfriend. . . . Okay,
I was clean out of fantasy material and would have to fall back on one
of my old fictional favorites.

But movie stars seemed bland after the supernatural world I'd
inhabited since Bill came into Merlotte's. The last remotely erotic
experience I'd had, oddly enough, had involved my bleeding leg getting
licked. That had been . . . unsettling. But even under the circumstances,
it had made things deep inside me twitch. I remembered how Quinn's
bald head had moved while he cleaned my scrape in a very personal
way, the firm grip his big warm fingers had had on my leg. . . .

'That'll do,' Alfred said, and began snapping away. Claude put his
hand on my bare thigh when he could feel my muscles begin to
tremble from the effort of holding the position. Once again, a man
had a hold of my leg. Claude gripped my thigh enough to give it some
support. That helped considerably, but it wasn't a bit erotic.

'Now some bed shots,' Al said, just when I'd decided I couldn't stand it any more.

'No,' Claude and I said in chorus.

'But that's part of the package,' Al said. 'You don't need to undress, you know. I don't do that kind of picture. My wife would kill me. You just lie down on the bed like you are. Claude hikes up on one elbow and looks down at you, Miss Stackhouse.'

'No,' I said firmly. 'Take some pictures of him standing by himself in the water. That would be better.' There was a fake pond over in the corner, and shots of Claude, apparently naked, dripping water over his bare chest, would be extremely appealing (to any woman who hadn't actually met him).

'How does that grab you, Claude?' Al asked.

Claude's narcissism chimed in. 'I think that would be great, Al,' he said, trying not to sound too excited.

I started for the changing room, eager to shed the costume and get back into my regular jeans. I glanced around for a clock. I was due at work at five-thirty, and I had to drive back to Bon Temps and grab my work uniform before I went to Merlotte's.

Claude called, 'Thanks, Sookie.'

'Sure, Claude. Good luck with the modeling contracts.' But he was already admiring himself in a mirror.

Maria-Star saw me out. 'Goodbye, Sookie. It was good to see you again.'

'You, too,' I lied. Even through the reddish twisted passages of a Were mind, I could see that Maria-Star couldn't understand why I would pass up Alcide. After all, the Were was handsome in a rugged way, an entertaining companion, and a hot-blooded male of the heterosexual persuasion. Also, he now owned his own surveying company and was a wealthy man in his own right.

The answer popped into my head and I spoke before I thought. 'Is anyone still looking for Debbie Pelt?' I asked, much the same way you poke a sore tooth. Debbie had been Alcides longtime on-again, off-again lover. She'd been a piece of work.

'Not the same people,' Maria-Star said. Her expression darkened. Maria-Star didn't like thinking about Debbie any more than I did, though doubtless for different reasons. 'The detectives the Pelt family hired gave up, said they'd be fleecing the family if they'd kept on. That's what I heard. The police didn't exactly say it, but they'd reached a dead end, too. I've only met the Pelts once, when they came over to Shreveport right after Debbie disappeared. They're a pretty savage couple.' I blinked. This was a fairly drastic statement, coming from a Were.

'Sandra, their daughter, is the worst. She was nuts about Debbie, and for her sake they're still consulting people, some way-out people. Myself, I think Debbie got abducted. Or maybe she killed herself. When Alcide abjured her, maybe she lost it big-time.'

'Maybe,' I murmured, but without conviction.

'He's better off. I hope she stays missing,' Maria-Star said.

My opinion had been the same, but unlike Maria-Star, I knew exactly what had happened to Debbie; that was the wedge that had pushed Alcide and me apart.

'I hope he never sees her again,' Maria-Star said, her pretty face dark and showing a little bit of her own savage side.

Alcide might be dating Maria-Star, but he hadn't confided in her fully. Alcide knew for a fact that he would never see Debbie again. And that was my fault, okay?

I'd shot her dead.

I'd more or less made my peace with my act, but the stark fact of it kept popping back up. There's no way you can kill someone and get to the other side of the experience unchanged. The consequences alter your life.

Two priests walked into the bar.

This sounds like the opening of a million jokes. But these priests didn't have a kangaroo with them, and there was not a rabbi sitting at the bar, or a blonde, either. I'd seen plenty of blondes, one kangaroo in a zoo, no rabbis. However, I'd seen these two priests plenty of times before. They had a standing appointment to have dinner together every other week.

Father Dan Riordan, clean shaven and ruddy, was the Catholic priest who came to the little Bon Temps church once a week on Saturday to celebrate mass, and Father Kempton Littrell, pale and bearded, was the Episcopal priest who held Holy Eucharist in the tiny Episcopal church in Clarice once every two weeks.

'Hello, Sookie,' Father Riordan said. He was Irish; really Irish, not just of Irish extraction. I loved to hear him talk. He wore thick glasses with black frames, and he was in his forties.

'Evening, Father. And hi to you, Father Littrell. What can I get you all?'

'I'd like Scotch on the rocks, Miss Sookie. And you, Kempton?'

'Oh, I'll just have a beer. And a basket of chicken strips, please.' The Episcopal priest wore gold-rimmed glasses, and he was younger than Father Riordan. He had a conscientious heart.

'Sure.' I smiled at the two of them. Since I could read their thoughts, I knew them both to be genuinely good men, and that made me happy. It's always disconcerting to hear the contents of a minister's head and find out they're no better than you, and not only that, they're not trying to be.

Since it was full dark outside, I wasn't surprised when Bill Compton walked in. I couldn't say the same for the priests. The churches of America hadn't come to grips with the reality of vampires. To call their policies confused was putting it mildly. The Catholic Church was at this moment holding a convocation to decide whether the church would declare all vampires damned and anathema to Catholics, or accept them into the fold as potential converts. The Episcopal Church had voted against accepting vampires as priests, though they were allowed to take communion – but a substantial slice of the laity said that would be over their dead bodies. Unfortunately, most of them didn't comprehend how possible that was.

Both the priests watched unhappily as Bill gave me a quick kiss on the cheek and settled at his favorite table. Bill barely gave them a glance, but unfolded his newspaper and began to read. He always looked serious, as if he were studying the financial pages or the news from Iraq; but I knew he read the advice columns first, and then the comics, though he often didn't get the jokes.

Bill was by himself, which was a nice change. Usually, he brought the lovely Selah Pumphrey. I loathed her. Since Bill had been my first love and my first lover, maybe I would never be completely over him. Maybe he didn't want me to be. He did seem to drag Selah into Merlotte's every single date they had. I figured he was waving her in my face. Not exactly what you did if you didn't care any more, huh?

Without his having to ask, I took him his favorite beverage, True-Blood type O. I set it neatly in front of him on a napkin, and I'd turned to go when a cool hand touched my arm. His touch always jolted me; maybe it always would. Bill had always made it clear I aroused him, and after a lifetime of no relationships and no sex, I began walking tall when Bill made it clear he found me attractive. Other men had looked at me as if I'd become more interesting, too. Now I knew why people thought about sex so much; Bill had given me a thorough education.

'Sookie, stay for a moment.' I looked down into brown eyes, which looked all the darker in Bill's white face. His hair was brown, too, smooth and sleek. He was slim and broad-shouldered, his arms hard with muscles, like the farmer he had been. 'How have you been?'

'I'm fine,' I said, trying not to sound surprised. It wasn't often Bill passed the time of day; small talk wasn't his strong point. Even when we'd been a couple, he had not been what you'd call chatty. And even a vampire can be a workaholic; Bill had become a computer geek. 'Have things been well with you?'

'Yes. When will you go to New Orleans to claim your inheritance?'

Now I was truly startled. (This is possible because I can't read vampire minds. That's why I like vampires so much. It's wonderful to be with someone who's a mystery to me.) My cousin had been murdered almost six weeks ago in New Orleans, and Bill had been with me when the Queen of Louisiana's emissary had come to tell me about it . . . and to deliver the murderer to me for my judgment. 'I guess I'll go through Hadley's apartment sometime in the next month or so. I haven't talked to Sam about taking the time off.'

'I'm sorry you lost your cousin. Have you been grieving?'

I hadn't seen Hadley in years, and it would have been stranger than I can say to see her after she'd become a vampire. But as a person with very few living relations, I hated to lose even one. 'A bit,' I said.

'You don't know when you might go?'

'I haven't decided. You remember her lawyer, Mr Cataliades? He said he'd tell me when the will had gone through probate. He promised to keep the place intact for me, and when the queen's counselor tells you the place'll be intact, you have to believe it'll be untouched. I haven't really been too interested, to tell you the truth.'

'I might go with you when you head to New Orleans, if you don't mind having a traveling companion.'

'Gee,' I said, with just a dash of sarcasm, 'Won't Selah mind? Or were you going to bring her, too?' That would make for a merry trip.

'No.' And he closed down. You just couldn't get anything out of Bill when he was holding his mouth like that, I knew from experience. Okay, color me confused.

'I'll let you know,' I said, trying to figure him out. Though it was painful to be in Bill's company, I trusted him. Bill would never harm me. He wouldn't let anyone else harm me, either. But there's more than one kind of harm.

'Sookie,' Father Littrell called, and I hurried away.

I glanced back to catch Bill smiling, a small smile with a lot of satisfaction packed into it. I wasn't sure what it meant, but I liked to see Bill smile. Maybe he was hoping to revive our relationship?

Father Littrell said, 'We weren't sure if you wanted to be interrupted or not.' I looked down at him, confused.

'We were a tad concerned to see you consorting with the vampire for so long, and so intently,' Father Riordan said. 'Was the imp of hell trying to bring you under his spell?'

Suddenly his Irish accent wasn't charming at all. I looked at Father Riordan quizzically. 'You're joking, right? You know Bill and I dated for a good while. Obviously, you don't know much about imps from hell if you believe Bill's anything like one.' I'd seen things *much* darker than Bill in and about our fair town of Bon Temps. Some of those things had been human. 'Father Riordan, I understand my own life. I understand the nature of vampires better than you ever will. Father Littrell,' I said, 'you want honey mustard or ketchup with your chicken strips?'

Father Littrell chose honey mustard, in a kind of dazed way. I walked away, working to shrug the little incident off, wondering what the two priests would do if they knew what had happened in this bar a couple of months before when the bar's clientele had ganged up to rid me of someone who was trying to kill me.

Since that someone had been a vampire, they'd probably have approved.

Before he left, Father Riordan came over to 'have a word' with me. 'Sookie, I know you're not real happy with me at the moment, but I need to ask you something on behalf of someone else. If I've made you less inclined to listen by my behavior, please ignore that and give these people the same consideration you would have.'

I sighed. At least Father Riordan tried to be a good man. I nodded reluctantly.

'Good girl. A family in Jackson has contacted me . . .'

All my alarms started going off. Debbie Pelt was from Jackson.

'The Pelt family, I know you've heard of them. They're still searching for news of their daughter, who vanished in January. Debbie, her name was. They called me because their priest knows me, knows I serve the Bon Temps congregation. The Pelts would like to come to see you, Sookie. They want to talk to everyone who saw their daughter the night she vanished, and they feared if they just showed up on your doorstep, you might not see them. They're afraid you're angry because their private detectives have interviewed you, and the police have talked to you, and maybe you might be indignant about all that.'

'I don't want to see them,' I said. 'Father Riordan, I've told everything I know.' That was true. I just hadn't told it to the police or the Pelts. 'I don't want to talk about Debbie any more.' That was also true, very true. 'Tell them, with all due respect, there's nothing left to talk about.'

'I'll tell them,' he said. 'But I've got to say, Sookie, I'm disappointed.'

'Well, I guess it's been a bad night for me all around,' I said. 'Losing your good opinion, and all.'

He left without another word, which was exactly what I'd wanted.

Chapter 2

It was close to closing time the next night when another odd thing happened. Just as Sam gave us the signal to start telling our customers this would be their last drink, someone I thought I'd never see again came into Merlotte's.

He moved quietly for such a large man. He stood just inside the door, looking around for a free table, and I noticed him because of the quick gleam of the dim bar light on his shaven head. He was very tall, and very wide, with a proud nose and big white teeth. He had full lips and an olive complexion, and he was wearing a sort of bronze sports jacket over a black shirt and slacks. Though he would have looked more natural in motorcycle boots, he was wearing polished loafers.

'Quinn,' Sam said quietly. His hands became still, though he'd been in the middle of mixing a Tom Collins. 'What is he doing here?'

'I didn't know you knew him,' I said, feeling my face flush as I realized I'd been thinking about the bald man only the day before. He'd been the one who'd cleaned the blood from my leg with his tongue – an interesting experience.

'Everyone in my world knows Quinn,' Sam said, his face neutral. 'But I'm surprised you've met him, since you're not a shifter.' Unlike Quinn, Sam's not a big man; but he's very strong, as shifters tend to be, and his curly red-gold hair haloes his head in an angelic way.

'I met Quinn at the contest for packmaster,' I said. 'He was the, ah, emcee.' Naturally, Sam and I had talked about the change of leadership in the Shreveport pack. Shreveport isn't too far from Bon Temps, and what the Weres do is pretty important if you're any kind of a shifter.

A true shape-shifter, like Sam, can change into anything, though each shape-shifter has a favorite animal. And to confuse the issue, all those who can change from human form to animal form call themselves shape-shifters, though very few possess Sam's versatility. Shifters who can change to only one animal are were-animals: weretigers (like Quinn), werebears, werewolves. The wolves are the only ones who call themselves simply Weres, and they consider themselves superior in toughness and culture to any of the other shape-shifters.

Weres are also the most numerous subset of shifters, though compared to the total vampire population, there are mighty few of them. There are several reasons for this. The Were birthrate is low, infant mortality is higher than in the general population of humans, and only the first child born of a pure Were couple becomes a full Were. That happens during puberty – as if puberty weren't bad enough already.

Shape-shifters are very secretive. It's a hard habit to break, even around a sympathetic and strange human like me. The shifters have not come into the public view yet, and I'm learning about their world in little increments.

Even Sam has many secrets that I don't know, and I count him as a friend. Sam turns into a collie, and he often visits me in that form. (Sometimes he sleeps on the rug by my bed.)

I'd only seen Quinn in his human form.

I hadn't mentioned Quinn when I told Sam about the fight between Jackson Herveaux and Patrick Furnan for the Shreveport pack leadership. Sam was frowning at me now, displeased that I'd kept it from him, but I hadn't done it purposely. I glanced back at Quinn. He'd lifted his nose a little. He was sampling the air, following a scent. Who was he trailing?

When Quinn went unerringly to a table in my section, despite the many empty ones in the closer section that Arlene was working, I knew he was trailing me.

Okay, mixed feelings on that.

I glanced sideways at Sam to get his reaction. I had trusted him for five years now, and he had never failed me.

Now Sam nodded at me. He didn't look happy, though. 'Go see what he wants,' he said, his voice so low it was almost a growl.

I got more and more nervous the closer I came to the new customer. I could feel my cheeks redden. Why was I getting so flustered?

'Hello, Mr Quinn,' I said. It would be stupid to pretend I didn't recognize him. 'What can I get you? I'm afraid we're about to close, but I have time to serve you a beer or a drink.'

He closed his eyes and took a deep breath, as if he were inhaling me. 'I'd recognize you in a pitch-black room,' he said, and he smiled at me. It was a broad and beautiful smile.

I looked off in another direction, pinching back the involuntary grin that rose to my lips. I was acting sort of . . . shy. I never acted shy. Or maybe *coy* would be a better term, and one I disliked. 'I guess I should say thank you,' I ventured cautiously. 'That's a compliment?'

'Intended as one. Who's the dog behind the bar who's giving me the stay-away look?'

He meant *dog* as a statement of fact, not as a derogatory term.

'That's my boss, Sam Merlotte.'

'He has an interest in you.'

'I should hope so. I've worked for him for round about five years.'

'Hmmm. How about a beer?'

'Sure. What kind?'

'Bud.'

'Coming right up,' I said, and turned to go. I knew he watched me all the way to the bar because I could feel his gaze. And I knew from his mind, though his was a closely guarded shifter mind, that he was watching me with admiration.

'What does he want?' Sam looked almost . . . bristly. If he'd been in dog form, the hair on his back would have been standing up.

'A Bud,' I said.

Sam scowled at me. 'That's not what I meant, and you know it.'

I shrugged. I had no idea what Quinn wanted.

Sam slammed the full glass down on the bar right by my fingers, making me jump. I gave him a steady look to make sure he noted that I'd been displeased, and then I took the beer to Quinn.

Quinn gave me the cost of the beer and a good tip – not a ridiculously high one, which would have made me feel bought – which I slipped into my pocket. I began making the rounds of my other tables. 'You visiting someone in this area?' I asked Quinn as I passed him on my way back from clearing another table. Most of the patrons were paying up and drifting out of Merlotte's. There was an afterhours place that Sam pretended he didn't know about, way out in the country, but most of the Merlotte's regulars would be going home to bed. If a bar could be family-oriented, Merlotte's was.

'Yes,' he said. 'You.'

That left me with nowhere to go, conversationally.

I kept on going and unloaded the glasses from my tray so absently that I almost dropped one. I couldn't think of when I'd been so flustered.

'Business or personal?' I asked, the next time I was close.

'Both,' he said.

A little of the pleasure drained away when I heard about the business part, but I was left with a sharpened attention . . . and that was a good thing. You needed all your wits honed when you dealt with the supes. Supernatural beings had goals and desires that regular people didn't fathom. I knew that, since for my entire life I have been the unwilling repository for human, 'normal', goals and desires.

When Quinn was one of the few people left in the bar – besides the other barmaids and Sam – he stood and looked at me expectantly. I went over, smiling brightly, as I do when I'm tense. I was interested to find that Quinn was almost equally tense. I could feel the tightness in his brain pattern.

'I'll see you at your house, if that's agreeable to you.' He looked down at me seriously. 'If that makes you nervous, we can meet somewhere else. But I want to talk to you tonight, unless you're exhausted.'

That had been put politely enough. Arlene and Danielle were trying hard not to stare – well, they were trying hard to stare when Quinn wouldn't catch them – but Sam had turned his back to fiddle around with something behind the bar, ignoring the other shifter. He was behaving very badly.

Quickly I processed Quinn's request. If he came out to my house, I'd be at his mercy: I live in a remote place. My nearest neighbor is my ex, Bill, and he lives clear across the cemetery. On the other hand, if Quinn had been a regular date of mine, I'd let him take me home without a second thought. From what I could catch from his thoughts, he meant me no harm.

'All right,' I said, finally. He relaxed, and smiled his big smile at me again.

I whisked his empty glass away and became aware that three pairs of eyes were watching me disapprovingly. Sam was disgruntled, and Danielle and Arlene couldn't understand why anyone would prefer me to them, though Quinn gave even those two experienced barmaids pause. Quinn gave off a whiff of otherness that must be perceptible to even the most prosaic human. 'I'll be through in just a minute,' I said.

'Take your time.'

I finished filling the little china rectangle on each table with packages of sugar and sweetener. I made sure the napkin holders were full and checked the salt and pepper shakers. I was soon through. I gathered my purse from Sam's office and called good-bye to him.

Quinn pulled out to follow me in a dark green pickup truck. Under the parking lot lights, the truck looked brand spanking new, with gleaming tires and hubcaps, an extended cab, and a covered bed. I'd bet good money it was loaded with options. Quinn's truck was the fanciest vehicle I'd seen in a long time. My brother, Jason, would have drooled, and he's got pink and aqua swirls painted on the side of *his* truck.

I drove south on Hummingbird Road and turned left into my driveway. After following the drive through two acres of woods, I reached the clearing where our old family home stood. I'd turned the outside lights on before I left, and there was a security light on the electric pole that was automatic, so the clearing was well lit. I pulled around back to park behind the house, and Quinn parked right beside me.

He got out of his truck and looked around him. The security light showed him a tidy yard. The driveway was in excellent repair, and I'd recently repainted the tool shed in the back. There was a propane tank, which no amount of landscaping could disguise, but my grandmother had planted plenty of flower beds to add to the ones my family had established over the hundred-and-fifty-odd years the family had lived here. I'd lived on this land, in this house, from age seven, and I loved it.

There's nothing grand about my home. It started out as a family farmhouse and it's been enlarged and remodeled over the years. I keep it clean, and I try to keep the yard in good trim. Big repairs are beyond my skills, but Jason sometimes helps me out. He hadn't been happy when Gran left me the house and land, but he'd moved to our parents' house when he'd turned twenty-one, and I'd never made him pay me for my half of that property. Gran's will had seemed fair to me. It had taken Jason a while to admit that had been the right thing for her to do.

We'd become closer in the past few months.

I unlocked the back door and led Quinn into the kitchen. He looked around him curiously as I hung my jacket on one of the chairs pushed under the table in the middle of the kitchen where I ate all my meals.

'This isn't finished,' Quinn said.

The cabinets were resting on the floor, ready to be mounted. After that, the whole room would have to be painted and the countertops installed. Then I'd be able to rest easy.

'My old kitchen got burned down a few weeks ago,' I said. 'The builder had a cancellation and got this done in record time, but then when the cabinets didn't arrive on time, he put his crew on another job. By the time the cabinets got here, they were almost through there. I guess they'll come back eventually.' In the meantime, at least I could enjoy being back in my own home. Sam had been tremendously kind in letting me live in one of his rent houses (and gosh, I'd enjoyed the level floors and the new plumbing and the neighbors), but there was nothing like being home.

The new stove was in, so I could cook, and I'd laid a sheet of plywood over the top of the cabinets so I could use it as a work station while I was cooking. The new refrigerator gleamed and hummed quietly, quite unlike the one Gran had had for thirty years. The newness of the kitchen struck me every time I crossed the back porch – now larger and enclosed – to unlock the new, heavier back door, with its peephole and deadbolt.

'This is where the old house begins,' I said, going from the kitchen into the hall. Only a few boards had had to be replaced in the floor in the rest of the house, and everything was freshly cleaned and painted. Not only had the walls and ceilings been smoke-stained, but I'd had to eradicate the burned smell. I'd replaced some curtains, tossed out a throw rug or two, and cleaned, cleaned, cleaned. This project had occupied every extra waking moment I'd had for quite a while.

'A good job,' Quinn commented, studying how the two parts had been united.

'Come into the living room,' I said, pleased. I enjoyed showing someone the house now that I knew the upholstery was clean, there were no dust bunnies, and the glass over the pictures was simply gleaming. The living room curtains had been replaced, something I'd wanted to do for at least a year.

God bless insurance, and God bless the money I'd earned hiding Eric from an enemy. I'd gouged a hole in my savings account, but I'd had it when I needed it, and that was something for which I could be grateful.

The fireplace was laid ready for a fire, but it was just too warm to justify lighting one. Quinn sat in an armchair, and I sat across from him. 'Can I get you a drink – a beer, or some coffee or iced tea?' I asked, conscious of my role as hostess.

'No, thanks,' he said. He smiled at me. 'I've wanted to see you again since I met you in Shreveport.'

I tried to keep my eyes on him. The impulse to look down at my feet or my hands was almost overwhelming. His eyes really were the deep, deep purple I remembered. 'That was a tough day for the Herveauxes,' I said.

'You dated Alcide for a while,' he observed, in a neutral kind of voice.

I thought of a couple of possible answers. I settled for, 'I haven't seen him since the packmaster contest.'

He smiled widely. 'So he's not your steady?'

I shook my head.

'Then you're unattached?'

'Yes.'

'No toes I'd be stepping on?'

I tried to smile, but my effort was not a happy one. 'I didn't say that.' There were toes. Those toes wouldn't be happy piggies. But they didn't have any right to be in the way.

'I guess I can handle some disgruntled exes. So will you go out with me?'

I looked at him for a second or two, scouring my mind for considerations. From his brain I was getting nothing but hopefulness: I saw no deceit or self-serving. When I examined the reservations I had, they dissolved into nothing.

'Yes,' I said. 'I will.' His beautiful white smile sparked me to smile in return, and this time my smile was genuine.

'There,' he said. 'We've negotiated the pleasure part. Now for the business part, which is unrelated.'

'Okay,' I said, and put my smile away. I hoped I'd have occasion to haul it out later, but any business he would have with me would be supe-related, and therefore cause for anxiety.

'You've heard about the regional summit?'

The vampire summit: the kings and queens from a group of states would gather to confer about . . . vampire stuff. 'Eric said something about it.'

'Has he hired you to work there yet?'

'He mentioned he might need me.'

'Because the Queen of Louisiana found out I was in the area, and she asked me to request your services. I think her bid would have to cancel out Eric's.'

'You'd have to ask Eric about that.'

'I think you would have to *tell* him. The queen's wishes are Eric's orders.'

I could feel my face fall. I didn't want to tell Eric, the sheriff of Louisiana's Area Five, anything. Eric's feelings for me were confused. I can assure you, vamps don't like feeling confused. The sheriff had lost his memory of the short time he'd spent hiding in my house. That memory gap had driven Eric nuts; he liked being in control, and that meant being cognizant of his own actions every second of the night. So he'd waited until he could perform an action on my behalf, and as payment for that action he'd demanded my account of what had passed while he stayed with me.

Maybe I'd carried the frankness thing a little too far. Eric wasn't exactly surprised that we'd had sex; but he was stunned when I told him he'd offered to give up his hard-won position in the vampire hierarchy and to come live with me.

If you knew Eric, you'd know that was pretty much intolerable to him.

He didn't talk to me any more. He stared at me when we met, as if he were trying to resurrect his own memories of that time, to prove me wrong. It made me sad to see that the relationship we'd had – not the secret happiness of the few days he'd spent with me, but the entertaining relationship between a man and a woman who had little in common but a sense of humor – didn't seem to exist any more.

I knew it was up to me to tell him that his queen had superseded him, but I sure didn't want to.

'Smile's all gone,' Quinn observed. He looked serious himself.

'Well, Eric is a . . .' I didn't know how to finish the sentence. 'He's a complicated guy,' I said lamely.

'What shall we do on our first date?' Quinn asked. So he was a good subject changer.

'We could go to the movies,' I said, to start the ball rolling.

'We could. Afterward, we could have dinner in Shreveport. Maybe Ralph and Kacoo's,' he suggested.

'I hear their crawfish etouffee is good,' I said, keeping the conversational ball rolling.

'And who doesn't like crawfish etouffee? Or we could go bowling.'

My great-uncle had been an avid bowler. I could see his feet, in their bowling shoes, right in front of me. I shuddered. 'Don't know how.'

'We could go to a hockey game.'

'That might be fun.'

'We could cook together in your kitchen, and then watch a movie on your DVD.'

'Better put that one on a back burner.' That sounded a little too personal for a first date, not that I've had that much experience with first dates. But I know that proximity to a bedroom is never a good idea unless you're sure you wouldn't mind if the flow of the evening took you in that direction.

'We could go see *The Producers*. That's coming to the Strand.'

'Really?' Okay, I was excited now. Shreveport's restored Strand Theater hosted traveling stage productions ranging from plays to ballet. I'd never seen a real play before. Wouldn't that be awfully expensive? Surely he wouldn't have suggested it if he couldn't afford it. 'Could we?'

He nodded, pleased at my reaction. 'I can make the reservations for this weekend. What about your work schedule?'

'I'm off Friday night,' I said happily. 'And, um, I'll be glad to chip in for my ticket.'

'I invited you. My treat,' Quinn said firmly. I could read from his thoughts that he thought it was surprising that I had offered. And touching. Hmmm. I didn't like that. 'Okay then. It's settled. When I get back to my laptop, I'll order the tickets online. I know there are some good ones left, because I was checking out our options before I drove over.'

Naturally, I began to wonder about appropriate clothes. But I stowed that away for later. 'Quinn, where do you actually live?'

'I have a house outside Memphis.'

'Oh,' I said, thinking that seemed a long way away for a dating relationship.

'I'm partner in a company called Special Events. We're a sort of secret offshoot of Extreme(ly Elegant) Events. You've seen the Ingo, I know. E(E)E?' He made the parentheses with his fingers. I nodded. E(E)E did a lot of very fancy event designing nationally. 'There are four partners who work full-time for Special Events, and we each employ a few people full- or part-time. Since we travel a lot, we have places we use all over the country; some of them are just rooms in houses of friends or associates, and some of them are real apartments. The place I stay in this area is in Shreveport, a guesthouse in back of the mansion of a shifter.'

I'd learned a lot about him in two minutes flat. 'So you put on events in the supernatural world, like the contest for packmaster.' That had been a dangerous job and one requiring a lot of specialized paraphernalia. 'But what else is there to do? A packmaster's contest can only come up every so now and then. How much do you have to travel? What other special events can you stage?'

'I generally handle the Southeast, Georgia across to Texas.' He sat forward in his chair, his big hands resting on his knees. 'Tennessee south through Florida. In those states, if you want to stage a fight for packmaster, or a rite of ascension for a shaman or witch, or a vampire hierarchal wedding – and you want to do it right, with all the trimmings – you come to me.'

I remembered the extraordinary pictures in Alfred Cumberland's photo gallery. 'So there's enough of that to keep you busy?'

'Oh, yes,' he said. 'Of course, some of it is seasonal. Vamps get married in the winter, since the nights are so much longer. I did a hierarchal wedding in New Orleans in January, this past year. And then, some of the occasions are tied to the Wiccan calendar. Or to puberty.'

I couldn't begin to imagine the ceremonies he arranged, but a description would have to wait for another occasion. 'And you have three partners who do this full-time, too? I'm sorry. I'm just grilling you, seems like. But this is such an interesting way to make a living.'

'I'm glad you think so. You gotta have a lot of people skills, and you gotta have a mind for details and organization.'

'You have to be really, really, tough,' I murmured, adding my own thought.

He smiled, a slow smile. 'No problem there.'

Yep, didn't seem as though toughness was a problem for Quinn.

'And you have to be good at sizing up people, so you can steer clients in the right direction, leave them happy with the job you've done,' he said.

'Can you tell me some stories? Or is there a client confidentiality clause with your jobs?'

'Customers sign a contract, but none of them have ever requested a confidentiality clause,' he said. 'Special Events, you don't get much chance to talk about what you do, obviously, since the clients are mostly still traveling beneath the surface of the regular world. It's actually kind of a relief to talk about it. I usually have to tell a girl I'm a consultant, or something bogus like that.'

'It's a relief to me, too, to be able to talk without worrying I'm spilling secrets.'

'Then it's lucky we found each other, huh?' Again, the white grin. 'I'd better let you get some rest, since you just got off work.' Quinn got up and stretched after he'd reached his full height. It was an impressive gesture on someone as muscular as he was. It was just possible Quinn knew how excellent he looked when he stretched. I glanced down to hide my smile. I didn't mind one bit that he wanted to impress me.

He reached for my hand and pulled me to my feet in one easy motion. I could feel his focus centered on me. His own hand was warm and hard. He could crack my bones with it.

The average woman would not be pondering how fast her date could kill her, but I'll never be an average woman. I'd realized that by the time I became old enough to understand that not every child could understand what her family members were thinking about her. Not every little girl knew when her teachers liked her, or felt contempt for her, or compared her to her brother (Jason had an easy charm even then). Not every little girl had a funny uncle who tried to get her alone at every family gathering.

So I let Quinn hold my hand, and I looked up into his pansy-purple eyes, and for a minute I indulged myself by letting his admiration wash over me like a bath of approval.

Yes, I knew he was a tiger. And I don't mean in bed, though I was willing to believe he was ferocious and powerful there, too.

When he kissed me good night, his lips brushed my cheek, and I smiled.

I like a man who knows when to rush things . . . and when not to.

Chapter 3

I got a phone call the next night at Merlotte's. Of course, it's not a good thing to get phone calls at work; Sam doesn't like it, unless there's some kind of home emergency. Since I get the least of any of the barmaids – in fact, I could count the calls I'd gotten at work on one hand – I tried not to feel guilty when I gestured to Sam that I'd take the call back at the phone on his desk.

'Hello,' I said cautiously.

'Sookie,' said a familiar voice.

'Oh, Pam. Hi.' I was relieved, but only for a second. Pam was Eric's second in command, and she was his child, in the vampire sense.

'The boss wants to see you,' she said. 'I'm calling from his office.'

Eric's office, in the back of his club, Fangtasia, was well sound-proofed. I could barely hear KDED, the all-vampire radio station, playing in the background: Clapton's version of 'After Midnight'.

'Well, lah-de-dah. He's too lofty to make his own phone calls?'

'Yes,' Pam said. That Pam – *literal-minded* was the phrase for her.

'What's this about?'

'I am following his instructions,' she said. 'He tells me to call the telepath, I call you. You are summoned.'

'Pam, I need a little more explanation than that. I don't especially want to see Eric.'

'You are being recalcitrant?'

Uh-oh. I hadn't had that on my Word of the Day calendar yet. 'I'm not sure I understand.' It's better to just go on and confess ignorance than try to fake my way through.

Pam sighed, a long-suffering gust of sound. 'You're digging in your heels,' she clarified, her English accent making itself known. 'And you shouldn't be. Eric treats you very well.' She sounded faintly incredulous.

'I'm not giving up work *or* free time to drive over to Shreveport because Mr High and Mighty wants me to jump to do his bidding,' I protested – reasonably, I thought. 'He can haul his ass over here if he wants to tell me something. Or he can pick up the telephone his ownself.' So there.

'If he had wanted to pick up the phone "his ownself", as you put it, he would have done so. Be here Friday night by eight, he bids me tell you.'

'Sorry, no can do.'

A significant silence.

'You won't come?'

'I can't. I have a date,' I said, trying to keep any trace of smugness out of my voice.

There was another silence. Then Pam snickered. 'Oh, that's rich,' she said, abruptly switching to American vernacular. 'Oh, I'm going to love telling him that.'

Her reaction made me begin to feel uneasy. 'Um, Pam,' I began, wondering if I should backpedal, 'listen . . .'

'Oh, no,' she said, almost laughing out loud, which was very un-Pam-like.

'You tell him I did say thanks for the calendar proofs,' I said. Eric, always thinking of ways to make Fangtasia more lucrative, had come up with a vampire calendar to sell in the little gift shop. Eric himself was Mr January. He'd posed with a bed and a long white fur robe. Eric and the bed were set against a pale gray background hung with giant glittering snowflakes. He wasn't wearing the robe: oh, no. He wasn't wearing anything. He had one bent knee on the rumpled bed, and the other foot was on the floor, and he was looking directly at the camera, smoldering. (He could have taught Claude a few lessons.) Eric's blond hair fell in a tousled mane around his shoulders, and his right hand gripped the robe tossed on the bed, so the white fur rose just high enough to cover his kit 'n' kaboodle. His body was turned just slightly to flaunt the curve of his world-class butt. A light trail of dark blond hair pointed south of his navel. It practically screamed, 'Carrying concealed!'

I happened to know that Eric's pistol was more of a .357 Magnum than a snub-nose.

Somehow I'd never gotten past looking at January.

'Oh, I'll let him know,' Pam said. 'Eric said many people wouldn't like it if I were in the calendar made for women . . . so I'm in the one for men. Would you like me to send you a copy of my picture, as well?'

'That surprises me,' I told her. 'It really does. I mean, that you wouldn't mind posing.' I had a hard time imagining her participation in a project that would pander to human tastes.

'Eric tells me to pose, I pose,' she said matter-of-factly. Though Eric had considerable power over Pam since he was her maker, I have to say that I'd never known Eric to ask Pam to do anything she wasn't ready to do. Either he knew her well (which, of course, he did) or Pam was willing to do just about anything.

'I have a whip in my picture,' Pam said. 'The photographer says it'll sell a million.' Pam had wide-ranging tastes in the area of sex.

After a long moment while I contemplated the mental image that raised, I said, 'I'm sure it will, Pam. But I'll give it a pass.'

'We'll all get a percentage, all of us who agreed to pose.'

'But Eric will get a bigger percentage than the rest.'

'Well, he's the sheriff,' Pam said reasonably.

'Right. Well, bye.' I started to hang up.

'Wait, what am I to tell Eric?'

'Just tell him the truth.'

'You know he'll be angry.' Pam didn't sound at all scared. In fact, she sounded gleeful.

'Well, that's his problem,' I said, maybe a bit childishly, and this time I did hang up. An angry Eric would surely be my problem, too.

I had a nasty feeling I'd taken a serious step in denying Eric. I had no idea what would happen now. When I'd first gotten to know the sheriff of Area Five, I'd been dating Bill. Eric had wanted to use my unusual talent. He'd simply held hurting Bill over my head to get me to comply. When I'd broken up with Bill, Eric had lacked any means of coercion until I'd needed a favor from him, and then I'd supplied Eric with the most potent ammunition of all – the knowledge that I'd shot Debbie Pelt. It didn't matter that he'd hidden her body and her car and he couldn't himself remember where; the accusation would be enough to ruin the rest of my life, even if it was never proved. Even if I could bring myself to deny it.

As I carried out my duties in the bar the rest of that night, I found myself wondering if Eric really would reveal my secret. If Eric told the police what I'd done, he'd have to admit he'd had a part in it, wouldn't he?

I was waylaid by Detective Andy Bellefleur when I was on my way to the bar. I've known Andy and his sister Portia all my life. They're a few years older than me, but we'd been through the same schools, grown up in the same town. Like me, they'd been largely raised by their grandmother. The detective and I have had our ups and downs. Andy had been dating a young schoolteacher, Halleigh Robinson, for a few months now.

Tonight, he had a secret to share with me and a favor to ask.

'Listen, she's going to order the chicken basket,' he said, without preamble. I glanced over to their table, to make sure Halleigh was sitting with her back to me. She did. 'When you bring the food to the table, make sure this is in it, covered up.' He stuffed a little velvet-covered box into my hand. There was a ten-dollar bill under it.

'Sure, Andy, no problem,' I said, smiling.

'Thanks, Sookie,' he said, and for once he smiled back, a simple and uncomplicated and terrified smile.

Andy had been right on the money. Halleigh ordered the chicken basket when I went to their table.

'Make that extra fries,' I said to our new cook when I turned in the order. I wanted plenty of camouflage. The cook turned from the grill to glare at me. We've had an assortment of cooks, of every age, color, gender, and sexual preference. We even had a vampire, once. Our current cook was a middle-aged black woman named Callie Collins. Callie was heavy, so heavy I didn't know how she could get through the hours she spent standing on her feet in the hot kitchen. 'Extra fries?' Callie said, as if she'd never heard of such a thing. 'Uh-huh. People get extra fries when they pay for them, not because they friends of yours.'

It could be that Callie was so sharp-edged because she was old enough to remember the bad old days when blacks and whites had different schools, different waiting rooms, different water fountains. I didn't remember any of those things, and I was not willing to take into account Callie's bundle of baggage every time I talked to her.

'They paid extra,' I lied, not wanting to call an explanation through the service pass-through that anyone close enough could overhear. I'd put a dollar of my tip into the till, instead, to make up the money. Despite our differences, I wished Andy and his schoolteacher well. Anyone who was going to be Caroline Bellefleur's granddaughter-in-law deserved a romantic moment.

When Callie called up the basket, I trotted over to get it. Slipping the little box under the fries was harder than I imagined, and it required a bit of surreptitious rearrangement. I wondered if Andy had realized that the velvet would get greasy and salty. Oh well, this wasn't my romantic gesture, but his.

I carried the tray to the table with happy anticipation. In fact, Andy had to warn me (with a severe glance) to pull my face into more neutral lines as I served their food. Andy already had a beer in front of him, and she had a glass of white wine. Halleigh wasn't a big drinker, as befitted an elementary school teacher. I turned away as soon as the food was on the table, even forgetting to ask them if they needed anything else, like a good waitress should.

It was beyond me to try to stay detached after that. Though I tried not to be obvious, I watched the couple as closely as I could. Andy was on pins and needles, and I could hear his brain, which was simply agitated. He really wasn't sure whether he'd be accepted, and his mind was running through the list of things she might object to: the fact that Andy was almost ten years older, his hazardous profession . . .

I knew the moment when she spied the box. Maybe it wasn't nice of me to eavesdrop mentally on a very special moment, but to tell you the truth, I didn't even think of that at the time. Though ordinarily

I keep myself well guarded, I'm used to dropping into people's heads if I spy something interesting. I'm also used to believing that my ability is a minus, not a plus, so I guess I feel entitled to whatever fun I can have with it.

I had my back to them, clearing off a table, which I should have left for the busboy to do. So I was close enough to hear.

She was frozen for a long moment. 'There's a box in my food,' she said, finally, keeping her voice very low because she thought she'd upset Sam if she made a fuss.

'I know,' he said. 'It's from me.'

She knew then; everything in her brain began to accelerate, and the thoughts practically tripped over themselves in their eagerness.

'Oh, Andy,' she whispered. She must have opened the box. It was all I could do not to turn around and look right along with her.

'Do you like it?'

'Yes, it's beautiful.'

'Will you wear it?'

There was a silence. Her head was so confused. Half of it was going 'Yippee!' and half of it was troubled.

'Yes, with one stipulation,' she said slowly.

I could feel his shock. Whatever Andy had expected, it wasn't this.

'And that would be?' he asked, suddenly sounding much more like a cop than a lover.

'We have to live in our own place.'

'What?' Again, she'd surprised Andy.

'I've always gotten the idea that you assumed you'd stay in the family home, with your grandmother and your sister, even after you got married. It's a wonderful old house, and your grandmother and Portia are great women.'

That was tactful. Good for Halleigh.

'But I'd like to have a home of my own,' she said gently, earning my admiration.

And then I really had to haul ass; I had tables to tend to. But as I refilled beer mugs, cleared empty plates, and took more money to Sam at the cash register, I was filled with awe at Halleigh's stand, since the Bellefleur mansion was Bon Temps's premier residence. Most young women would give a finger or two to live there, especially since the big old house had been extensively remodeled and freshened with the influx of money from a mysterious stranger. That stranger was actually Bill, who'd discovered that the Bellefleurs were descendants of his. He'd known they wouldn't accept money from a vampire, so he'd arranged the whole 'mysterious legacy' ruse, and Caroline Bellefleur had jumped into spending it on the mansion with as much relish as Andy ate a cheeseburger.

Andy caught up with me a few minutes later. He snagged me on the way to Sid Matt Lancaster's table, so the aged lawyer had to wait a bit extra for his hamburger and fries.

'Sookie, I have to know,' he said urgently, but in a very low tone.

'What, Andy?' I was alarmed at his intensity.

'Does she love me?' There were edges of humiliation in his head, that he'd actually asked me. Andy was proud, and he wanted some kind of assurance that Halleigh didn't want his family name or his family home as he'd found other women had. Well, he'd found out about the home. Halleigh didn't want it; and he would move into some humble, small house with her, if she really loved him.

No one had ever demanded this of me before. After all the years of wanting people to believe in me, understand my freakish talent, I found I didn't enjoy being taken seriously, after all. But Andy was waiting for an answer, and I couldn't refuse. He was one of the most dogged men I'd ever met.

'She loves you as much as you love her,' I said, and he let go of my arm. I continued on my way to Sid Matt's table. When I glanced back at him, he was staring at me.

Chew on that, Andy Bellefleur, I thought. Then I felt a little ashamed of myself. But he shouldn't have asked, if he didn't want to know the answer.

There was something in the woods around my house.

I'd gotten ready for bed as soon as I'd come home, because one of my favorite moments in every twenty-four hours is when I get to put on my nightgown. It was warm enough that I didn't need a bathrobe, so I was roaming around in my old blue knee-length sleep tee. I was just thinking of shutting the kitchen window, since the March night was getting a little chilly. I'd been listening to the sounds of the night while I washed dishes; the frogs and the bugs had been filling the air with their chorus.

Suddenly, the noises that had made the night seem as friendly and busy as the day had come to a stop, cut off in midcry.

I paused, my hands immersed in the hot soapy water. Peering out into the darkness didn't help a bit, and I realized how visible I must be, standing at an open window with its curtains flung wide apart. The yard was lit up with the security light, but beyond the trees that ringed the clearing, the woods lay dark and still.

Something was out there. I closed my eyes and tried to reach out with my brain, and I found some kind of activity. But it wasn't clear enough to define.

I thought about phoning Bill, but I'd called him before when I'd been worried about my safety. I couldn't let it become a habit. Hey, maybe the watcher in the woods was Bill himself? He sometimes roamed around at night, and he came to check on me from time to time. I looked longingly over at the telephone on the wall at the end of the counter. (Well, where the counter would be when it was all put together.) My new telephone was portable. I could grab it, retreat to my bedroom, and call Bill in a snap of the fingers, since he was on my speed dial. If he answered the phone, I'd know whatever was out in the woods was something I needed to worry about.

But if he was home, he'd come racing over here. He'd hear my call like this: 'Oh, Bill, please come save me! I can't think of anything to do but call a big, strong vampire to come to my rescue!'

I made myself admit that I really knew that whatever was in the woods, it wasn't Bill. I'd gotten a brain signal of some kind. If the lurker had been a vampire, I would have sensed nothing. Only twice had I gotten a flicker of a signal from a vampire brain, and it had been like a flash of electricity in an outage.

And right by that telephone was the back door – which wasn't locked.

Nothing on earth could keep me at the sink after the fact of the open door had occurred to me. I simply ran for it. I stepped out onto the back porch, flipped the latch on the glass door there, and jumped back into the kitchen proper and locked the big wooden door, which I'd had outfitted with a thumb latch and a deadbolt.

I leaned against the door after it was safely locked. Better than anyone I could think of, I knew the futility of doors and locks. To a vampire, the physical barrier was nothing – but a vampire had to be invited in. To a Were, doors were of more consequence, but still not much of a problem; with their incredible strength, Weres could go wherever they damn well chose. The same held true of other shifters.

Why didn't I just hold an open house?

However, I felt wonderfully better with two locked doors between me and whatever was in the woods. I knew the front door was locked and bolted, since it hadn't been opened in days. I didn't get that many visitors, and I normally entered and departed through the back.

I crept back to the window, which I closed and locked. I drew the curtains, too. I'd done everything to increase my security I could do. I went back to the dishes. I got a wet circle on the front of my sleep tee because I had to lean against the edge of the sink to steady my shaking legs. But I made myself continue until all the dishes were safely in the drainer and the sink had been wiped clean.

I listened intently after that. The woods were still silent. No matter how I listened with every sense at my disposal, that faint signal did not impinge on my brain again. It was gone.

I sat in the kitchen for a while, brain still in high gear, but then I forced myself to follow my usual routine. My heart rate had returned to normal by the time I brushed my teeth, and as I climbed into bed I had almost persuaded myself that nothing had happened out there in the silent darkness. But I'm careful about being honest inside. I knew some creature had been out in my woods; and that creature had been something bigger and scarier than a raccoon.

Quite soon after I'd turned my bedside light off, I heard the bugs and the frogs resume their chorus. Finally, when it continued uninterrupted, I slept.

Chapter 4

I punched in the number of my brother's cell phone when I got up the next morning. I hadn't spent a very good night, but at least I'd gotten a bit of sleep. Jason answered on the second ring. He sounded a little preoccupied when he said, 'Hello?'

'Hi, Brother. How's it going?'

'Listen, I need to talk to you. I can't right now. I'll be there, probably in a couple of hours.' He hung up without saying good-bye, and he'd sounded pretty worried about something. Good. I needed another complication.

I glanced at the clock. A couple of hours would give me enough time to get cleaned up and run into town to go to the grocery store. Jason would be getting here about noon, and if I knew him he'd expect me to feed him lunch. I yanked my hair into a ponytail and then doubled the elastic band around it, making it into a kind of topknot. I had a little fan of the ends waving above my head. Though I tried not to admit it to myself, I thought this slapdash hairstyle was fun-looking and kind of cute.

It was one of those crisp, cool March mornings, the kind that promises a warm afternoon. The sky was so bright and sunny that my spirits rose, and I drove to Bon Temps with the window rolled down, singing along with the radio at the top of my voice. I would've sung along with Weird Al Yankovic that morning.

I drove past woods, the occasional house, and a field full of cows (and a couple of buffalo; you never know what people will raise).

The disc jockey played 'Blue Hawaii' as a golden oldie, and I wondered where Bubba was – not my own brother, but the vampire now known only as Bubba. I hadn't seen him in three or four weeks. Maybe the vamps of Louisiana had moved him to another hiding place, or maybe he'd wandered off, as he does from time to time. That's when you get your long articles in the papers they keep by the grocery check-out stand.

Though I was having a blissful moment of being happy and content, I had one of those stray ideas you get at odd moments. I thought, *How nice it would be if Eric were here with me in the car. He'd look so good with the wind blowing his hair, and he'd enjoy the moment.* Well, yeah, before he burned to a crisp.

But I realized I'd thought of Eric because it was the kind of day you wanted to share with the person you cared about, the person whose company you enjoyed the most. And that would be Eric as he'd been while he was cursed by a witch: the Eric who hadn't been hardened by centuries of vampire politics, the Eric who had no contempt for humans and their affairs, the Eric who was not in charge of many financial enterprises and responsible for the lives and incomes of quite a few humans and vampires. In other words, Eric as he would never be again.

Ding-dong, the witch was dead, and Eric was restored to his character as it was now. The restored Eric was wary of me, was fond of me, and didn't trust me (or his feelings) an inch.

I sighed heavily, and the song vanished from my lips. It was nearly quenched in my heart until I told myself to stop being a melancholy idiot. I was young, I was healthy. The day was beautiful. And I had an actual date for Friday night. I promised myself a big treat. Instead of going directly to the grocery store, I went by Tara's Togs, owned and operated by my friend Tara Thornton.

I hadn't seen Tara in a while. She'd gone on a vacation to visit an aunt in south Texas, and since she'd returned she'd been working long hours at the store. At least, that's what she'd said when I'd called her to thank her for the car. When my kitchen had burned, my car had burned with it, and Tara had loaned me her old car, a two-year-old

Malibu. She'd acquired a brand-new car (never mind how) and hadn't gotten around to selling the Malibu.

To my astonishment, about a month ago, Tara had mailed me the title and the bill of sale, with a letter telling me the car was now mine. I'd called to protest, but she had stonewalled me, and in the end, there didn't seem to be anything to do but accept the gift graciously.

She intended it as payment, since I'd extricated her from a terrible situation. But to help her, I'd had to indebt myself to Eric. I hadn't minded. Tara had been my friend all my life. Now she was safe, if she was smart enough to stay away from the supernatural world.

Though I was grateful and relieved to have the newest vehicle I'd ever owned, I would have been happier to have her uninterrupted friendship. I'd stayed away, since I assumed that I reminded her of too many bad things. But I was in the mood to try to rip down that veil. Maybe Tara had had enough time.

Tara's Togs was in a strip mall on the south side of Bon Temps. There was one other car parked in front of the store. I decided it might be good that a third party would be there; it would depersonalize the meeting.

Tara was serving Andy Bellefleur's sister Portia when I went in, so I began flicking through the size tens, and then the eights. Portia was sitting at the Isabelle table, which was extremely interesting. Tara is the local representative for Isabelle's Bridal, a national company that produces a catalog that's become the bible of all things wedding-related. You can try on samples of the bridesmaid dresses at the local outlet, so you can order the right size, and each dress comes in about twenty colors. The wedding dresses are just as popular. Isabelle's has twenty-five models. The Company also offers wedding shower invitations, decorations, garters, bridesmaids' gifts, and any bit of wedding paraphernalia you can imagine. However, Isabelle's was pretty much a middle-class phenomenon, and Portia was definitely an upper-class woman.

Since she lived with her grandmother and her brother in the Bellefleur mansion on Magnolia Street, Portia had grown up in a sort of decayed gothic splendor. Now that the mansion was repaired and her grandmother entertained more, Portia had looked noticeably happier when I'd glimpsed her around town. She didn't come into Merlotte's that much, but when she was in the bar she had more time to spare for other people, and she smiled occasionally. A plain woman just past thirty, Portia's best feature was her thick, shining chestnut hair.

Portia was thinking *wedding*, and Tara was thinking *money*.

'I have to talk with Halleigh again, but I think we'll need four hundred invitations,' Portia was saying, and I thought my jaw would drop.

'All right, Portia, if you don't mind paying the rush fee, we can have those in ten days.'

'Oh, good!' Portia was definitely pleased. 'Of course, Halleigh and I will be wearing different dresses, but we thought we might try to pick out the same bridesmaid's dress. Maybe in different colors. What do you think?'

I thought I was going to choke on my own curiosity. Portia was going to be married, too? To that stick of an accountant she'd been dating, the guy from Clarice? Tara caught a glimpse of my face over the top of the standing rack of dresses. Portia was looking at the catalog, so Tara winked at me. She was definitely pleased to have a rich customer, and we were definitely okay with each other. Relief flooded me.

'I think having the same style in different colors – coordinating colors, of course – would be really original,' Tara said. 'How many bridesmaids are there going to be?'

'Five apiece,' Portia said, her attention on the page before her. 'Can I take a copy of the catalog home? That way, Halleigh and I can look at it tonight.'

'I only have one extra copy; you know, one of the ways Isabelle's makes money is charging an arm and a leg for the darn catalog,' Tara said with a charming smile. Tara can lay it on when she needs to. 'I'll let you take it home, if you cross your heart you'll bring it back tomorrow!'

Portia made the childish gesture, and tucked the thick catalog under her arm. She was wearing one of her 'lawyer suits', a brownish tweedy-looking straight skirt and jacket with a silk blouse underneath. She had on beige hose and low-heeled pumps, and she carried a matching purse. Bo-ring.

Portia was excited, and her brain was cartwheeling with happy images. She knew she would look a little old as a bride, especially compared to Halleigh; but by God, she was finally going to be a bride. Portia would get her share of the fun, the presents, the attention, and the clothes, to say nothing of the validation of having a husband of her own. She looked up from the catalog and spied me lurking by the slacks rack. Her happiness was profound enough to encompass even me.

'Hello, Sookie!' she said, practically beaming. 'Andy told me what a help you were to him, fixing up his little surprise for Halleigh. I really appreciate it.'

'It was fun,' I said, with my own version of a gracious smile. 'Is it true that congratulations are in order for you, as well?' I know, you're not supposed to congratulate the bride, only the groom, but I didn't think Portia would mind.

Sure enough, she didn't. 'Well, I am getting married,' she confessed. 'And we decided to have a double ceremony with Andy and Halleigh. The reception will be at the house.'

Of course. Why have a mansion, if you couldn't have the reception there?

'That's going to be a lot of work, setting up a wedding by – when?' I said, trying to sound sympathetic and concerned.

'April. Tell me about it,' Portia said, laughing. 'Grandmother is already half-crazy. She's called every caterer she knows to try to book someone for the second weekend, and finally landed Extreme(ly Elegant) Events because they had a cancellation. Plus, the guy who runs Sculptured Forest in Shreveport is coming to see her this afternoon.'

Sculptured Forest was the premier landscape planning center and nursery in the area, at least if you went by their omnipresent ads. Hiring both Sculptured Forest and Extreme(ly Elegant) Events meant that this double wedding would be the primo social occasion of the Bon Temps year.

'We're thinking an outdoor wedding at the house, with tents in the back yard,' Portia said. 'In case of rain, we'll have to move it to the church, and have the reception at the Renard Parish Community Building. But we'll keep our fingers crossed.'

'Sounds wonderful.' I really couldn't think of anything else to say. 'How are you going to keep working, with all this wedding stuff to do?'

'Somehow I'll manage.'

I wondered what the rush was. Why weren't the happy couples waiting until summer, when Halleigh wouldn't be working? Why not wait, so Portia could free her calendar for a proper wedding and honeymoon? And wasn't the man she'd been dating an accountant? Surely a wedding during tax season was the worst possible scheduling.

Oooo . . . maybe Portia was pregnant. But if she was in the family way, she wasn't thinking about it, and I hardly thought she would be doing otherwise. Gosh, if I ever found out I was pregnant, I'd be so happy! If the guy loved me and would marry me, that is – because I wasn't tough enough to raise a kid by myself, and my grandmother would roll over in her grave if I was an unmarried mother. Modern thinking on that subject had completely passed my grandmother by, without even ruffling her hair with its passage.

While all these thoughts were buzzing around in my head, it took me a minute to process Portia's words: 'So try to keep the second Saturday in April free,' she said with as close to a charming smile as Portia Bellefleur could manage.

I promised I would, trying not to trip over my own tongue with astonishment. She must be high on wedding fever. Why would my presence be desired at the wedding? I was no big buddy of any of the Bellefleurs.

'We're asking Sam to bartend at the reception,' she continued, and my world realigned into a more familiar pattern. She wanted me there to assist Sam.

'An afternoon wedding?' I asked. Sam sometimes took outside bartending jobs, but Saturday was usually our heavy day at Merlotte's.

'No, night,' she said, 'but I already talked to Sam this morning, and he's agreed.'

'Okay,' I said.

She read more into my tone than I'd put there, and she flushed, 'Glen has some clients that he wants to invite,' she said, though I'd asked for no explanation. 'They can only come after dark.' Glen Vicks was the accountant. I was glad I'd retrieved his last name from my memory. Then everything clicked into place, and I understood Portia's embarrassment. Portia meant that Glen's clients were vampires. Well, well, well. I smiled at her.

'I'm sure it'll be a lovely wedding, and I look forward to being there,' I said, 'since you were kind enough to invite me.' I'd deliberately misunderstood her, and as I'd foreseen, she flushed even redder. Then a related idea occurred to me, one so important I bent one of my personal rules.

'Portia,' I said slowly, wanting to be sure she got my meaning, 'you should invite Bill Compton.'

Now Portia loathed Bill – disliked all vampires – but when she'd been forwarding one of her own plots, she'd dated Bill briefly. Which had been odd, because afterward Bill had discovered, Portia was actually his great-great-great-great-great-granddaughter, or something like that.

Bill had gone along with her pretense of interest in him. At the time, he'd just wanted to find out what her goal was. He'd realized that it made Portia's skin crawl to be around him. But when he'd discovered the Bellefleurs were his only surviving kin, he'd anonymously given them a whacking great bunch of money.

I could 'hear' that Portia thought I was purposely reminding her of the few times she'd dated Bill. She didn't want to be reminded of it, and it angered her that I'd done so.

'Why do you suggest that?' she asked coldly, and I gave her high points for not just stalking out of the shop. Tara was being studiously busy over by the Isabelle table, but I knew she could hear our conversation. Nothing wrong with Tara's hearing.

I had a ferocious internal debate. Finally, what Bill wanted prevailed over what I wanted for him. 'Never mind,' I said reluctantly. 'Your wedding, your list.'

Portia was looking at me as if she really saw me for the first time. 'Are you still dating him?' she asked.

'No, he's dating Selah Pumphrey,' I said, keeping my voice even and empty.

Portia gave me an unreadable look. Without another word, she went out to her car.

'What was all that about?' Tara asked.

I couldn't explain, so I changed the subject to one closer to Tara's retailing heart. 'I'm delighted you're getting the business,' I said.

'You and me both. If she didn't have to pull it together in such a short time, you can bet Portia Bellefleur wouldn't ever go Isabelle,' Tara said frankly. 'She'd drive to Shreveport and back a million times running errands, if she had the lead time. Halleigh is just trailing along in Portia's wake, poor thing. She'll come in this afternoon, and I'll show her the same things I've shown Portia, and she'll have to buckle under. But it's all good for me. They're getting the whole package, because the Isabelle system can deliver it all on time. Invitations, thank-you notes, dresses, garters, bridesmaids' gifts, even the mother-of-the-bride gowns – Miss Caroline will be buying one, and Halleigh's mother – they're getting it all here, either from my stock or from Isabelle's book.' She looked me up and down. 'What brought you in, by the way?'

'I need a date outfit to wear to a play in Shreveport,' I said, 'and I have to go to the grocery and get back at home to cook Jason's lunch. So, you got anything to show me?'

Tara's smile turned predatory. 'Oh,' she said, 'just a few things.'

Chapter 5

I was glad Jason was little late. I'd finished the bacon and I was putting the hamburgers in the frying pan when he arrived. I had already opened the package of buns and put two on Jason's plate, and put a bag of potato chips on the table. I'd poured him a glass of tea and set it beside his place.

Jason came in without knocking, as he always did. Jason hadn't changed that much, at least to the eyes, since he'd become a werepanther. He was still blond and attractive, and I mean attractive in the old way; he was good to look at, but he was also the kind of man that everyone looks at when he comes into a room. On top of that, he'd always had a mean streak. But since his change, he'd somehow been acting like a better person. I hadn't decided why that was. Maybe being a wild animal once a month satisfied some craving he hadn't known he had.

Since he'd been bitten, not born, he didn't change completely; he became a sort of hybrid. At first, he'd been disappointed about that. But he'd gotten over it. He'd been dating a full werepanther named Crystal for several months now. Crystal lived in a tiny community some miles out in the country – and let me tell you, out in the country from Bon Temps, Louisiana, is really *out in the country*.

We said a brief prayer and began eating. Jason didn't dig in with his usual gusto. Since the hamburger tasted good to me, I figured whatever was on his mind was important. I couldn't read it out of his brain.

Since my brother had become a Were, his thoughts had not been as clear to me.

Mostly, that was a relief.

After two bites, Jason put down his hamburger, and his body posture changed. He was ready to talk. 'I got something I got to tell you,' he said. 'Crystal doesn't want me to tell anyone, but I'm really worried about her. Yesterday, Crystal . . . she had a miscarriage.'

I shut my eyes for a few seconds. I had about twenty thoughts in that brief time, and I couldn't complete a one of them. 'I'm so sorry,' I said. 'I hope Crystal's all right?'

Jason looked at me over a plate of food he'd completely forgotten. 'She won't go to the doctor.'

I stared at him blankly. 'But she has to,' I said reasonably. 'She needs a D & C.' I wasn't sure what 'D & C' stood for, but I knew after you'd miscarried, you went to a hospital and that's what they did there. My friend and co-worker Arlene had had a D & C after her miscarriage, and she'd told me about it several times. *Several* times. 'They go in and . . .' I began, but Jason cut me off in midstream.

'Hey, I don't need to know,' he said, looking very uncomfortable. 'I just know that since Crystal's a werepanther, she didn't want to go to the hospital. She had to go when she got gored by that razorback, just like Calvin had to go when he got shot, but they both got well so fast that there was some comment in the doctors' lounge, she heard. So she won't go now. She's at my house, but she's . . . she's not doing well. She's getting worse, not better.'

'Uh-oh,' I said. 'So what's happening?'

'She's bleeding too heavy, and her legs don't work right.' He swallowed. 'She can hardly stand up, much less walk.'

'Have you called Calvin?' I asked. Calvin Norris, Crystal's uncle, is the leader of the tiny Hotshot panther community.

'She don't want me to tell Calvin. She's scared Calvin'll kill me for knocking her up. Crystal didn't want me to tell you, either, but I got to have help.'

Though her mom wasn't living, Crystal had female relatives galore in Hotshot. I'd never had a baby, I'd never even been pregnant, and

I wasn't a shifter. Any one of them would know more about the situation than I did. I told Jason this.

'I don't want her to sit up long enough to go back to Hotshot, specially in my truck.' My brother looked as stubborn as a mule.

For an awful minute, I thought that Jason's big concern was Crystal bleeding on his upholstery. I was about to hop down his throat, when he added, 'The shocks need replacing, and I'm scared the bouncing of the truck on that bad road would make Crystal worse.'

Then her kin could come to Crystal. But I knew before I spoke that Jason would find a reason to veto that, too. He had some kind of plan. 'Okay. What can I do?'

'Didn't you tell me that time when you got hurt, there was a special kind of doctor the vamps called to look at your back?'

I didn't like to think about that night. My back still bore the scars of the attack. The poison on the maenad's claws had nearly killed me. 'Yes,' I said slowly, 'Dr Ludwig.' Doctor to all that was weird and strange, Dr Ludwig was herself an oddity. She was extremely short – very, very short. And her features were not exactly regular, either. It would come as an extreme surprise to me if Dr Ludwig were at all human. I'd seen her a second time at the contest for pack-master. Both times, I'd been in Shreveport; so the chances were good that Dr Ludwig actually lived there.

Since I didn't want to overlook the obvious, I fished a Shreveport directory out of the drawer below the wall-mounted telephone. There was a listing for a Doctor Amy Ludwig. Amy? I bit back a burst of laughter.

I was very nervous about approaching Dr Ludwig on my own, but when I saw how worried Jason was, I couldn't protest over making one lousy phone call.

It rang four times. A machine picked up. A mechanical voice said, 'You have reached the telephone of Dr Amy Ludwig. Dr Ludwig is not accepting new patients, insured or uninsured. Dr Ludwig does not want pharmaceutical samples, and she does not need insurance of any kind. She is not interested in investing her money, or giving to charities she hasn't personally selected.' There was a long silence, during which time most callers presumably hung up. I didn't. After a moment, I heard another click on the line.

'Hello?' asked a gruff little voice.

'Dr Ludwig?' I asked cautiously.

'Yes? I don't accept new patients, you know! Too busy!' She sounded both impatient and cautious.

'I'm Sookie Stackhouse. Is this the Dr Ludwig who treated me in Eric's office at Fangtasia?'

'You are the young woman poisoned by the maenad's claws?'

'Yes. I saw you again a few weeks ago, remember?'

'And where was that?' She remembered quite well, but she wanted another proof of my identity.

'An empty building in an industrial park.'

'And who was running the show there?'

'A big bald guy named Quinn.'

'Oh, all right.' She sighed. 'What do you want? I'm rather busy.'

'I have a patient for you. Please come to see her.'

'Bring her to me.'

'She's too sick to travel.'

I heard the doctor muttering to herself, but I couldn't make out the words.

'Pooh,' the doctor said. 'Oh, very well, Miss Stackhouse. Tell me what the problem is.'

I explained as best I could. Jason was moving around the kitchen, because he was too worried to sit still.

'Idiots. Fools,' Dr Ludwig said. 'Tell me how to get to your house. Then you can take me where the girl is.'

'I may have to leave for work before you can get here,' I said, after glancing at the clock and calculating how long it would take the doctor to drive from Shreveport. 'My brother will be here waiting.'

'Is he the responsible party?'

I didn't know if she was talking about the bill for her services, or the pregnancy. Either way, I told her that Jason definitely was the responsible party.

'She's coming,' I told my brother, after I'd given the doctor directions and hung up. 'I don't know how much she charges, but I told her you'd pay.'

'Sure, sure. How will I know her?'

'You can't mistake her for anyone you know. She said she'd have a driver. She wouldn't be tall enough to see over the steering wheel, so I should have figured on that.'

I did the dishes while Jason fidgeted. He called Crystal to check on her, seemed okay with what he'd heard. Finally, I asked him to go outside and knock old dirt-dauber nests off the tool shed. He couldn't seem to settle down, so he might as well be useful.

I thought about the situation while I started a load of laundry and put on my barmaid outfit (black pants, white boat-neck tee with *Merlotte's* embroidered over the left breast, black Adidas). I was not a happy camper. I was worried about Crystal – and I didn't like her. I was sorry she'd lost the baby because I know that's a sad experience, but I was happy because I really didn't want Jason to marry the girl, and I was pretty sure he would have if the pregnancy had continued. I cast around for something to make me feel better. I opened the closet to look at my new outfit, the one I'd bought at Tara's Togs to wear on my date. But I couldn't even get any enjoyment out of it.

Finally, I did what I'd planned on doing before I'd heard Jason's news: I got a book and settled in a chair on the front porch, reading a few sentences every now and then in between admiring the pear tree in the front yard, which was covered in white blossoms and humming with bees.

The sun was beaming, the daffodils were just past their prime, and I had a date for Friday. And I'd already done my good deed for the day, in calling Dr Ludwig. The coil of worry in my stomach eased up a little.

From time to time, I could hear vague sounds traveling my way from the backyard; Jason had found something to keep him occupied after he'd dealt with the nests. Maybe he was pulling up weeds in the flower beds. I brightened. That would be nice, since I didn't have my grandmother's enthusiasm for gardening. I admired the results, but I didn't enjoy the whole process as she had.

After checking my watch repeatedly, I was relieved to see a rather grand pearl Cadillac pull into the front parking area. There was a tiny shape in the front passenger seat. The driver's door opened, and a Were named Amanda got out. She and I had had our differences, but we'd parted on fair terms. I was relieved to see someone I knew. Amanda, who looked exactly like a middle-class soccer mom, was in her thirties. Her red hair looked natural, quite unlike my friend Arlene's.

'Sookie, hey,' she said. 'When the doctor told me where we were going, I was relieved, since I knew how to get here already.'

'You're not her usual driver? Hey, I like the haircut, by the way.'

'Oh, thanks.' Amanda's hair was newly short, cut in a careless, almost boyish style that oddly suited her. I say oddly, because Amanda's body was definitely womanly.

'Haven't got used to it yet,' she admitted, running her hand over her neck. 'Actually, it's usually my oldest boy that drives Dr Ludwig, but he's in school today, of course. Is it your sister-in-law that's ailing?'

'My brother's fiancée,' I said, trying to put a good face on it. 'Crystal. She's a panther.'

Amanda looked almost respectful. Weres often have only contempt for other shape-shifters, but something as formidable as a panther would get their attention. 'I heard there was a cluster of panthers out here somewhere. Never met one before.'

'I have to get to work, but my brother's going to lead you over to his place.'

'So, you're not really close to your brother's fiancée?'

I was taken aback at the implication that I was less than concerned about Crystal's welfare. Maybe I should have hurried over to her bedside and left Jason here to guide the doctor? I suddenly saw my enjoyment of my moments of peace as a callous disregard for Crystal. But now was no time to wallow in guilt.

'Truthfully,' I said, 'no, I'm not that close to her. But Jason didn't seem to think there was anything I could do for her, and my presence wouldn't exactly be soothing since she's not any fonder of me than I am of her.'

Amanda shrugged. 'Okay, where is he?'

Jason came around the corner of the house just then, to my relief. 'Oh, great,' he said. 'You're the doctor?'

'No,' Amanda said. 'The doctor's in the car. I'm the driver today.'

'I'll lead you over there. I been on the phone with Crystal, and she's not getting any better.'

I felt another wave of remorse. 'Call me at work, Jason, and let me know how she's doing, okay? I can come over after work and spend the night, if you need me.'

'Thanks, Sis.' He gave me a quick hug and then looked awkward. 'Uh, I'm glad I didn't keep it a secret like Crystal wanted me to. She didn't think you'd help her.'

'I'd like to think I was at least a good enough person to help someone who needed it, no matter if we were close or not.' Surely Crystal hadn't imagined that I'd be indifferent, or even pleased, that she was ailing?

Dismayed, I watched the two very different vehicles start down the driveway on their way back to Hummingbird Road. I locked up and got in my own car in no very happy mood.

Continuing the theme of an eventful day, when I walked through the back door of Merlotte's that afternoon, Sam called to me from his office.

I went in to see what he wanted, knowing ahead of time that a few other people were waiting in there. To my dismay, I found that Father Riordan had ambushed me.

There were four people in Sam's office, besides my boss. Sam was unhappy, but trying to keep a good face on. A little to my surprise, Father Riordan wasn't happy about the people that had accompanied him, either. I suspected I knew who they were. Crap. Not only did Father Riordan have the Pelts in tow, but a young woman of about seventeen, who must be Debbie's sister, Sandra.

The three new people looked at me intently. The older Pelts were tall and slim. He wore glasses and was balding, with ears that stuck out of his head like jug handles. She was attractive, if a bit overly made up. She was wearing a Donna Karan pants set and carrying a bag with a famous logo on it. Heels, too. Sandra Pelt was more casual, her jeans and T-shirt fitting her narrow figure very tightly.

I hardly heard Father Riordan formally introduce the Pelts, I was so overwhelmed with irritation that they were intruding themselves into my life to such an extent. I'd told Father Riordan I didn't want to meet them, yet here they were. The older Pelts ate me up with their avid eyes. *Savage*, Maria-Star had termed them. *Desperate* was the word that came to my mind.

Sandra was a different kettle of fish altogether: since she was the second child, she wasn't – couldn't be – a shifter like her folks, but she wasn't altogether a regular human, either. But something caught at my brain, made me pause. Sandra Pelt *was* a shifter of some kind. I'd heard the Pelts described as much more involved with their second daughter than they'd been with Debbie. Now, getting bits of information from them, I saw why that might be. Sandra Pelt might be underage, but she was formidable. She was a full Were.

But that couldn't be, unless . . .

Okay. Debbie Pelt, werefox, had been adopted. I'd learned that the Weres were prone to fertility problems, and I assumed that the Pelts had given up on having their own little Were, and had adopted a baby that was at least some kind of shape-shifter, if not their own kind. Even a full-blooded fox must have seemed preferable to a plain human. Then the Pelts had adopted another daughter, a Were.

'Sookie,' Father Riordan said, his Irish voice charming but unhappy, 'Barbara and Gordon showed up on my doorstep today. When I told them you'd said all you wanted to say about Debbie's disappearance, they weren't content with that. They insisted I bring them here with me.'

My intense anger at the priest receded a bit. But another emotion filled its place. I was anxious enough about the encounter to feel my nervous smile spread across my face. I beamed at the Pelts, caught the backwash of their disapproval.

'I'm sorry for your situation,' I said. 'I'm sorry you're left wondering what happened to Debbie. But I don't know what else I can tell you.'

A tear ran down Barbara Pelt's face, and I opened my purse to remove a tissue. I handed it to the woman, who patted her face. 'She thought you were stealing Alcide from her,' Barbara said.

You're not supposed to speak ill of the dead, but in Debbie Pelt's case, that was just plain impossible. 'Mrs Pelt, I'm going to be frank,'

I told her. Just not too frank. 'Debbie was engaged to someone else at the time of her disappearance, a man named Clausen, if I remember correctly.' Barbara Pelt nodded, reluctantly. 'That engagement left Alcide at perfect liberty to date anyone he liked, and we did spend time together briefly.' No lies there. 'We haven't seen each other in weeks, and he's dating someone else now. So Debbie really was mistaken in what she thought.'

Sandra Pelt bit her lower lip. She was lean, with clear skin and dark brown hair. She wore little makeup, and her teeth were dazzlingly white and even. Her hoop earrings could provide a perch for a parakeet; they were that big. She had a narrow body and expensive clothes: top of the mall chain.

Her expression was angry. She didn't like what I was saying, not one little bit. She was an adolescent, and there were strong surges of emotion in the girl. I remembered what my life had been like when I'd been Sandra's age, and I pitied her.

'Since you knew both of them,' Barbara Pelt said carefully, not acknowledging my words, 'you must have known that they had – they have – a strong love-hate relationship, no matter what Debbie did.'

'Oh, *that's* true,' I said, and maybe I didn't sound respectful enough. If there was anyone I'd done a big favor to in killing Debbie Pelt, that person was Alcide Herveaux. Otherwise, he and la Pelt would have been tearing each other up for years, if not the rest of their lives.

Sam turned away when the phone rang, but I glimpsed a smile on his face.

'We just feel that there must be something you know, some tiny little thing, that would help us discover what happened to our daughter. If – if she's met her end, we want her killer to come to justice.'

I looked at the Pelts for a long moment. I could hear Sam's voice in the background as he reacted with astonishment to something he was hearing over the telephone.

'Mr and Mrs Pelt, Sandra,' I said. 'I talked to the police when Debbie vanished. I cooperated with them fully. I talked to your private investigators when they came here, to my place of work, just like you've done. I let them come into my home. I answered their questions.' Just not truthfully.

(I know, the whole edifice was a lie, but I was doing the best I could.)

'I am very sorry for your loss and I sympathize with your anxiety to discover what's happened to Debbie,' I continued, speaking slowly so I could pick my words. I took a deep breath. 'But this has got to end. Enough's enough. I can't tell you a thing other than what I've already told you.'

To my surprise, Sam edged around me and went into the bar, moving fast. He didn't say a word to anyone in the room. Father Riordan glanced after him, startled. I became even more anxious for the Pelts to leave. Something was up.

'I understand what you're saying,' Gordon Pelt said stiffly. It was the first time the man had spoken. He didn't sound happy to be where he was, or to be doing what he was doing. 'I realize we haven't gone about this in the best way, but I'm sure you'll excuse us when you think about what we've been through.'

'Oh, of course,' I said, and if that wasn't a complete truth, it wasn't a complete lie, either. I shut my purse and stowed it in the drawer in Sam's desk where all the servers kept their purses, and I hurried out to the bar.

I felt the upheaval wash over me. Something was wrong; almost every brain in the bar was broadcasting a signal combining excitement with anxiety bordering on panic.

'What's up?' I asked Sam, sidling behind the bar.

'I just told Holly that the school called. Holly's little boy is missing.'

I felt the chill start at the base of my spine and work up. 'What happened?'

'Danielle's mom usually picks up Cody from school when she picks up Danielle's little girl, Ashley.' Danielle Gray and Holly Cleary had been best friends all through high school and their friendship had continued through the failure of both their marriages. They liked to work the same shift. Danielle's mother, Mary Jane Jasper, had been a lifesaver for Danielle, and from time to time her generosity had spilled over to include Holly. Ashley must be about eight, and Danielle's son, Mark Robert, should now be four. Holly's only child, Cody, was six. He was in the first grade.

'The school let someone else pick Cody up?' I'd heard that the teachers were on the alert for unauthorized spouses picking up their kids.

'No one knows what happened to the little guy. The teacher on duty, Halleigh Robinson, was standing outside watching the kids get in their cars. She says Cody suddenly remembered he'd left a picture for his mom on his desk, and he ran back into the school to get it. She doesn't remember seeing him come out, but she couldn't find him when she went in to check.'

'So Mrs Jasper was there waiting for Cody?'

'Yes, she was the only one left, sitting there in her car with her grandchildren.'

'This is very scary. I don't suppose David knows anything?' David, Holly's ex, lived in Springhill and had remarried. I registered the departure of the Pelts: one less irritant.

'Apparently not. Holly called him at his job, and he was there and had been all afternoon, no doubt about it. He called his new wife, and she had just gotten back from picking up her own kids at the Springhill school. The local police went by their house and searched, just to be sure. Now David's on his way here.'

Holly was sitting at one of the tables, and though her face was dry, her eyes had the look of someone who'd seen inside Hell. Danielle was crouched on the floor beside her, holding her hand and speaking to Holly urgently and quietly. Alcee Beck, one of the local detectives, was sitting at the same table. A pad and pen were in front of him, and he was talking on his cell phone.

'They've searched the school?'

'Yeah, that's where Andy is now. And Kevin and Kenya.' Kevin and Kenya were two uniformed patrol officers. 'Bud Dearborn is on the phone setting up an Amber Alert.'

I spared a thought for how Halleigh must be feeling right now; she was only twenty-three or so, and this was her first teaching job. She hadn't done anything wrong, at least that I could tell – but when a kid goes missing, no one escapes blame:

I tried to think how I could help. This was a unique opportunity for my little disability to work for the greater good. I'd kept my mouth shut for years about all kinds of things. People didn't want to know what I knew. People didn't want to be around someone who could do what I could do. The way I survived was keeping my mouth shut, because it was easy for the humans around me to forget or disbelieve, when the evidence of my odd talent wasn't shoved in their face.

Would you want to be around a woman who knew you were cheating on your spouse, and with whom? If you were a guy, would you want to be around a woman who knew that you secretly wanted to wear lacy underwear? Would you want to hang with a gal who knew your most secret judgments on other people and all your hidden flaws?

No, I thought not.

But if a child was involved, how could I hold back?

I looked at Sam, and he looked back at me sadly. 'It's hard, isn't it, *cher*?' he said. 'What are you going to do?'

'Whatever I have to. But I have to do it now,' I said.

He nodded. 'Go on down to the school,' he said, and I left.

Chapter 6

I didn't know how I was going to accomplish this. I didn't know who would acknowledge that I could help.

There was a crowd at the elementary school, of course. A group of about thirty adults was standing on the grass on the street side of the sidewalk in front of the school, and Bud Dearborn, the sheriff, was talking to Andy on the front lawn. Betty Ford Elementary was the same school I'd attended. The building had been fairly new then, a straight-forward single-level brick building with a main hall containing the offices, the kindergarten, the first-grade classrooms, and the cafeteria. There was a wing to the right for the second grade, a wing to the left for the third. A small recreational building was behind the school in the large playground, attainable by a covered walkway. It was used for the children's bad-weather exercise sessions.

Of course there were flagpoles in front of the school, one for the American flag and one for the Louisiana flag. I loved driving by when they were snapping in the breeze on a day like today. I loved thinking of all the little children inside, busy being children. But the flags had been taken down for the day, and only the tied-down ropes moved in the stiff wind. The green lawn of the school was dotted with the occasional candy wrapper or crumpled notebook paper. The school custodian, Madelyn Pepper (always called 'Miss Maddy'), was sitting on a plastic chair right outside the main school doors, her rolling cart beside her. Miss Maddy had been the custodian for many years. Miss

Maddy was a very slow woman, mentally, but she was a hard worker, and absolutely reliable. She looked much the same as she had when I had gone to school there: tall, husky, and white, with a long fall of dyed platinum hair. She was smoking a cigarette. The principal, Mrs Garfield, had had a running battle with Miss Maddy for years about her habit, a battle that Miss Maddy had always won. She smoked outside, but she smoked. Today, Mrs Garfield was completely indifferent to Miss Maddy's bad habit. Mrs Garfield, the wife of a Methodist-Episcopal minister, was dressed in a mustard-color business suit, plain hose, and black pumps. She was just as strained as Miss Maddy, and a lot less guarded about showing it.

I worked my way through the front of the little crowd, not certain how to go about doing what I had to do.

Andy saw me first, and touched Bud Dearborn on the shoulder. Bud had a cell phone to his ear. Bud turned to look at me. I nodded at them. Sheriff Dearborn was not my friend. He'd been a friend of my father's, but he'd never had the time of day for me. To the sheriff, people fell into two categories: people who broke the law and could be arrested, and people who did not break the law and could not be. And most of those were people who just hadn't been caught breaking the law yet; that was what Bud believed. I fell somewhere in between. He felt sure I was guilty of something, but he couldn't figure out what it was.

Andy didn't like me much, either, but he was a believer. He jerked his head to the left, almost imperceptibly. I couldn't see Bud Dearborn's face clearly, but his shoulders stiffened in anger, and he leaned forward a little, his whole body posture saying that he was furious with his detective.

I worked my way out of the knot of anxious and curious citizens and slipped around the third-grade wing to the back of the school. The playground, about the size of half a football field, was fenced in, and the gate was ordinarily locked with a chain secured by a padlock. It had been opened, presumably for the convenience of the searchers. I saw Kevin Pryor, a thin young patrol officer who always won the 4K race at the Azalea Festival, bending over to peer into a culvert right across the street. The grass in the ditch was high, and his dark uniform pants were dusted with yellow. His partner, Kenya, who was as buxom as Kevin was thin, was across the street on the other side of the block, and I watched her head move from side to side as she scanned the surrounding yards.

The school took up a whole block in the middle of a residential area. All the houses around were modest homes on modest lots, the kind of neighborhood where there were basketball goals and bicycles, barking dogs, and driveways brightened with sidewalk chalk.

Today every surface was dusted in a light yellow powder; it was the very beginning of pollen time. If you rinsed off your car in town in your driveway, there would be a ring of yellow around the storm drain. Cats' bellies were tinged yellow, and tall dogs had yellow paws. Every other person you talked to had red eyes and carried a cache of tissues.

I noticed several thrown down around the playground. There were patches of new green grass and patches of hard-packed dirt, in areas where the children congregated the most. A big map of the United States had been painted on the concrete apron right outside the school doors. The name of each state was painted carefully and clearly. Louisiana was the only state colored bright red, and a pelican filled up its outline. The word *Louisiana* was too long to compete with the pelican, and it had been painted on the pavement right where the Gulf of Mexico would be.

Andy emerged from the rear door, his face set and hard. He looked ten years older.

'How's Halleigh?' I asked.

'She's in the school crying her eyes out,' he said. 'We have to find this boy.'

'What did Bud say?' I asked. I stepped inside the gate.

'Don't ask,' he said. 'If there's anything you can do for us, we need all the help we can get.'

'You're going out on a limb.'

'So are you.'

'Where are the people that were in the school when he ran back in?'

'They're all in here, except for the principal and the custodian.'

'I saw them outside.'

'I'll bring them in. All the teachers are in the cafeteria. It has that little stage at one end. Sit behind the curtain there. See if you can get anything.'

'Okay.' I didn't have a better idea.

Andy set off for the front of the school to gather up the principal and the custodian.

I stepped into the end of the third-grade corridor. There were bright pictures decorating the walls outside every classroom. I stared at the drawings of rudimentary people having picnics and fishing, and tears prickled my eyes. For the first time, I wished I were psychic instead of telepathic. Then I could envision what had happened to Cody, instead of having to wait for someone to think about it. I'd never met a real psychic, but I understood that it was a very uncertain talent to have, one that was not specific enough at times, and too specific at others. My little quirk was much more reliable, and I made myself believe I could help this child.

As I made my way to the cafeteria, the smell of the school evoked a rush of memories. Most of them were painful; some were pleasant. When I'd been this small, I'd had no control over my telepathy and no idea what was wrong with me. My parents had put me through the mental health mill to try to find out, which had further set me off from my peers. But most of my teachers had been kind. They'd understood that I was doing my best to learn – that somehow I was constantly distracted, but it wasn't through my own choice. Inhaling the scent of chalk, cleaner, paper, and books brought it all back.

I remembered all the corridors and doorways as if I'd just left. The walls were a peach color now, instead of the off-white I remembered, and the carpet was a sort of speckled gray in place of brown linoleum; but the structure of the school was unchanged. Without hesitation, I slipped through a back door to the little stage, which was at one end of the lunchroom. If I remembered correctly, the space was actually called the 'multipurpose room.' The serving area could be shut off with folding doors, and the picnic tables that lined the room could be folded and moved aside. Now they were taking up the floor in orderly rows, and the people sitting at them were all adults, with the exception of some teachers' children who'd been in the classrooms with their mothers when the alarm had been raised.

I found a tiny plastic chair and set it back behind the curtains on stage left. I closed my eyes and began to concentrate. I lost the awareness of my body as I shut out all stimuli and began to let my mind roam free.

It's my fault, my fault, my fault! Why didn't I notice he hadn't come back out? Or did he slip by me? Could he have gotten into a car without my noticing?

Poor Halleigh. She was sitting by herself, and the mound of tissues by her showed how she'd been spending her waiting time. She was completely innocent of anything, so I resumed my probing.

Oh my God, thank you God that it's not my son that's missing. . . .

. . . go home and have some cookies . . .

Can't go to the store and pick up some hamburger meat, maybe I can call Ralph and he can go by Sonic . . . but we ate fast food last night, not good . . .

His mom's a barmaid, how many lowlifes does she know? Probably one of them.

It went on and on, a litany of harmless thoughts. The children were thinking about snacks and television, and they were also scared. The adults, for the most part, were very frightened for their own children and worried about the effect of Cody's disappearance on their own families and their own class.

Andy Bellefleur said, 'In just a minute Sheriff Dearborn will be in here, and then we'll divide you into two groups.'

The teachers relaxed. These were familiar instructions, as they themselves had often given.

'We'll ask questions of each of you in turn, and then you can go. I know you're all worried, and we have patrol officers searching the area, but maybe we can get some information that will help us find Cody.'

Mrs Garfield came in. I could feel her anxiety preceding her like a dark cloud, full of thunder. Miss Maddy was right behind her. I could hear the wheels of her cart, loaded with its lined garbage can and laden with cleaning supplies. All the scents surrounding her were familiar. Of course, she started cleaning right after school. She would have been in one of the classrooms, and she probably hadn't seen anything. Mrs Garfield might have been in her office. The principal in my day, Mr

Heffernan; had stood outside with the teacher on duty until all the children were gone, so that parents would have a chance to talk to him if they had questions about their child's progress . . . or lack thereof.

I didn't lean out from behind the dusty curtain to look, but I could follow the progress of the two easily. Mrs Garfield was a ball of tension so dense it charged the air around her, and Miss Maddy was equally surrounded by the smell of all the cleaning products and the sounds of her cart. She was miserable, too, and above all she wanted to get back to her routine. Maddy Pepper might be a woman of limited intelligence, but she loved her job because she was good at it.

I learned a lot while I was sitting there. I learned that one of the teachers was a lesbian, though she was married and had three children. I learned that another teacher was pregnant but hadn't told anyone yet. I learned that most of the women (there were no male teachers at the elementary school) were stressed out by multiple obligations to their families, their jobs, and their churches. Cody's teacher was very unhappy, because she liked the little boy, though she thought his mother was weird. She did believe Holly was trying hard to be a good mother, and that offset her distaste for Holly's goth trappings.

But nothing I learned helped me discover Cody's whereabouts until I ventured into Maddy Pepper's head.

When Kenya came up behind me, I was doubled over, my hand over my mouth, trying to cry silently. I was not capable of getting up to look for Andy or anyone else. I knew where the boy was.

'He sent me back here to find out what you know,' Kenya whispered. She was massively unhappy about her errand, and though she'd always liked me okay, she didn't think I could do anything to help the police. She thought Andy was a fool for stalling his career by asking me to sit back there, concealed.

Then I caught something else, something faint and weak.

I jumped to my feet and grabbed Kenya by the shoulder. 'Look in the garbage can, the one loaded on the cart, right now!' I said, my voice low but (I hoped) urgent enough to light a fire under Kenya. 'He's in the can, he's still alive!'

Kenya wasn't rash enough to leap out from behind the curtain, jump down from the stage, and dash over to the custodian's cart. She gave me a hard, hard, look. I stepped out from behind the curtain to watch as Kenya made her way down the little stairs at the front of the stage, and went over to where Maddy Pepper was sitting, her fingers tapping against her legs. Miss Maddy wanted a cigarette. Then she realized that Kenya was approaching her, and a dull alarm sounded in her brain. When the custodian saw Kenya actually touch the edge of the large garbage can, she leaped to her feet and yelled, 'I didn't mean to! I didn't mean to!'

Everyone in the room turned to the commotion, and everyone's face wore identical expressions of horror. Andy strode over, his face hard. Kenya was bent over the can, rummaging, tossing a snowstorm of used tissues over her shoulder. She froze for a second when she found what she'd been looking for. She bent over, almost in danger of falling into the can.

'He's alive,' she called to Andy. 'Call 911!'

'She was mopping when he ran back into the school to get the picture,' Andy said. We were sitting in the cafeteria all by ourselves. 'I don't know if you could hear all that, there was so much noise in the room.'

I nodded. I'd been able to hear her thoughts as she'd spoken. All these years on her job, and she'd never had a problem with a student that wasn't easily resolved with a few strong words on her part. Then, today, Cody had come running into the classroom, pollen all over his shoes and pants cuffs, tracking up Maddy's freshly mopped floor. She'd yelled at him, and he'd been so startled that his feet had slipped on the wet floor. The little boy had gone over backward and hit his head on the floor. The corridor had indoor-outdoor carpeting to reduce the noise, but the classrooms did not, and his head had bounced on the linoleum.

Maddy had thought she'd killed him, and she'd hastily concealed his body in the nearest receptacle. She'd realized she'd lose her job if the child was dead, and on an impulse she'd tried to hide him. She had no plan and no idea of what would happen. She hadn't figured out how she'd dispose of his body, and she hadn't counted on how miserable she'd feel about the whole thing, how guilty.

To keep my part of it silent, which the police and I both agreed was absolutely the best idea, Andy suggested to Kenya that she'd suddenly realized the only receptacle in the school she hadn't searched was Maddy Pepper's trash can. 'That's exactly what I thought,' Kenya said. 'I should search it, at least poke around and see if an abductor had tossed something into it.' Kenya's round face was unreadable. Kevin looked at her, his brows drawn together, sensing something beneath the surface of the conversation. Kevin was no fool, especially where Kenya was concerned.

Andy's thoughts were clear to me. 'Don't ever ask me to do this again,' I told him.

He nodded in acquiescence, but he was lying. He was seeing before him a vista of cleared cases, of malefactors locked up, of how clean Bon Temps would be when I'd told him who all the criminals were and he'd found a way to charge them with something.

'I'm not going to do it,' I said. 'I'm not going to help you all the time. You're a detective. You have to find things out in a legal way, so you can build a court case. If you use me all the time, you'll get sloppy. The cases will fall through. You'll get a bad reputation.' I spoke desperately, helplessly. I didn't think my words would have any effect.

'She's not a Magic 8 Ball,' Kevin said.

Kenya looked surprised, and Andy was more than surprised; he thought this was almost heresy. Kevin was a patrolman; Andy was a detective. And Kevin was a quiet man, listening to all his co-workers, but not often offering a comment of his own. He was notoriously mother-ridden; maybe he'd learned at his mother's knee not to offer opinions.

'You can't shake her and come up with the right answer,' Kevin continued. 'You have to find out the answer on your own. It's not right to take over Sookie's life so you can do your job better.'

'Right,' said Andy, unconvinced. 'But I would think any citizen would want her town to be rid of thieves and rapists and murderers.'

'What about adulterers and people who take extra papers out of the newspaper dispensers? Should I turn those in, too? What about kids who cheat on their exams?'

'Sookie, you know what I mean,' he said, white-faced and furious.

'Yeah, 'I know what you mean. Forget it. I helped you save that child's life. Don't make me even think about regretting it.' I left the same way I'd come, out the back gate and down the side of the school property to where I'd left my car. I drove back to work very carefully, because I was still shaking with the intensity of the emotions that had flowed through the school this afternoon.

At, the bar, I found that Holly and Danielle had left – Holly to the hospital to be with her son, and Danielle to drive her there because she was so shaky.

'The police would have taken Holly, gladly,' Sam said. 'But I knew Holly didn't have anyone but Danielle here, so I thought I might as well let Danielle go, too.'

'Of course, that leaves me to serve by myself,' I said tartly, thinking I was getting punished doubly for helping Holly out.

He smiled at me, and for a second I couldn't help but smile back. 'I've called that Tanya Grissom. She said she'd like to help out, just on a fill-in basis.'

Tanya Grissom had just moved to Bon Temps, and she'd come into Merlotte's right away to put in an application. She'd put herself through college waitressing, she'd told Sam. She'd pulled down over two hundred dollars a night in tips. That wasn't going to happen in Bon Temps, and I'd told her so frankly.

'Did you call Arlene and Charlsie first?' I realized I'd overstepped my bounds, because I was only a waitress/barmaid, not the owner. It wasn't for me to remind Sam he should call the women with longer time in before he called the newcomer. The newcomer was definitely a shape-shifter, and I was afraid Sam was prejudiced in her favor.

Sam didn't look irritated, just matter-of-fact. 'Yeah, I called them first. Arlene said she had a date, and Charlsie was keeping her grand-baby. She's been hinting pretty heavily that she won't be working much longer. I think she's going to keep the baby full-time when her daughter-in-law goes back to work.'

'Oh,' I said, disconcerted. I'd have to get used to someone new. Of course, barmaids come and barmaids go, and I'd seen quite a few pass through the employee door of Merlotte's in my – gosh, now five – years of working for Sam. Merlotte's was open until midnight on weeknights and until one on Friday and Saturday. Sam had tried opening on Sunday for a while, but it didn't pay. So now Merlotte's was closed on Sunday, unless it had been rented for a private party.

Sam tried to rotate our times so everyone got a chance to work the more lucrative night shift, so some days I worked eleven to five (or six-thirty, if we became extra busy) and sometimes I worked five to closing. He'd experimented with times and days until we'd all agreed on what worked best. He expected a little flexibility from us, and in return he was good about letting us off for funerals and weddings and other milestones.

I'd had a couple of other jobs before I'd started working for Sam. He was the easiest person to work for, by far. He'd become more than my employer somewhere along the way; he was my friend. When I'd found out he was a shape-shifter, it hadn't bothered me a bit. I'd heard rumors in the shifting community that the Weres were thinking of going public, the way the vampires had. I worried about Sam. I worried about people in Bon Temps accepting him. Would they feel he'd been deceiving them all these years, or would they take it in stride? Since the vampires had made their carefully orchestrated revelation, life as we knew it had changed, all over the world. Some countries, after the initial shock had worn off, had begun working to include vampires in the mainstream of life; others had pronounced vampires nonhuman and urged their citizens to kill vampires on sight (easier said than done).

'I'm sure Tanya will be fine,' I said, but I sounded uncertain, even to my own ears. Acting on an impulse – and I can only suppose the tidal wave of emotions I'd experienced that day had something to do with this – I threw my arms around Sam and gave him a hug. I smelled clean skin and hair and the slight sweet smell of a light aftershave, an undertone of wine, a whiff of beer ... the Sam smell. I drew, it into my lungs like oxygen.

Surprised, Sam hugged me back, and for a second the warmth of his embrace made me feel almost light-headed with pleasure. Then we both backed off, because after all, this was our workplace and there were a few customers scattered around. Tanya came in, so it was good we were out of the clinch. I didn't want her to think this was routine.

Tanya was shorter than my five foot six, and she was a pleasant-looking woman in her late twenties. Her hair was short and straight and shiny, a medium brown that almost matched her eyes. She had a small mouth and a button nose and a nice figure. I had absolutely no reason to dislike her, but I wasn't happy to see her. I was ashamed of myself. I should give Tanya a fair chance to show her true character.

After all, I'd discover it sooner or later. You can't hide what you really are, not from me – not if you're a regular human person. I try not to listen in, but I can't block everything out. When I'd dated Bill, he'd helped me learn how to close my mind. Since then, life had been easier – more pleasant, more relaxed.

Tanya was a smiling woman, I'd give her that. She smiled at Sam, and she smiled at me, and she smiled at the customers. It wasn't a nervous smile, like mine, the grin that says 'I'm hearing a clamor inside my head and I'm trying to look normal on the outside'; Tanya's smile was more of a 'I'm really cute and perky and will endear myself to everyone' kind of smile. Before she picked up a tray and started working, Tanya asked a list of sensible questions, and I could tell she'd had experience.

'What's wrong?' Sam asked.

'Nothing,' I said. 'I just . . .'

'She seems nice enough,' he said. 'Do you think there's something wrong with her?'

'Nothing I know of,' I said, trying to sound brisk and cheerful. I knew I was smiling that jittery smile. 'Look, Jane Bodehouse is signaling for another round. We'll have to call her son again.'

Tanya turned around and looked at me just then, as if she felt my eyes on her back. Her own smile was gone, replaced with a look so level that my estimate of her capacity for serious action instantly upgraded. We stood for a moment, regarding each other steadily, and then she beamed at me and continued to the next table, asking the man there if he was ready for another beer.

Suddenly I thought, *I wonder if Tanya is interested in Sam*. I didn't like the way I felt when I thought about that. I decided the day had been exhausting enough without creating a new worry. And no call from Jason.

After work, I went home with a lot on my mind: Father Riordan, the Pelts, Cody, Crystal's miscarriage.

I drove down my graveled driveway through the woods, and when I pulled into the clearing and drove behind the house to park at the back door, its isolation struck me all over again. Living in town for a few weeks had made the house seem even lonelier, and though I loved being back in the old place, it didn't feel the same as it had before the fire.

I'd seldom felt worried living by myself in this isolated spot, but over the past few months my vulnerability had been impressed on me. I'd had a few close calls, and twice there'd been intruders in my house waiting for me when I'd come in. Now I had installed some really good locks on my doors, I had peepholes front and back, and my brother had given me his Benelli shotgun to keep for good.

I had some big lights on the corners of the house, but I didn't like to leave them on all night. I was considering the purchase of one of those motion-detector lights. The drawback was, since I lived in a large clearing in the middle of the woods, critters often crossed my yard at night, and the light would come on when every little possum rambled across the grass.

The second point about a light coming on was ... *So what?* The kind of thing I was scared of wasn't going to be intimidated by a light. I'd just be able to see it better before it ate me. Furthermore, there were no neighbors that a light might startle or rouse. Strange, I reflected, that I'd seldom had a frightened moment when my grandmother had been alive. She'd been a tough little lady for a woman in her late seventies, but she couldn't have defended me against a flea. Somehow, the simple fact of not being alone had made me feel safer.

After all this thinking about danger, I was in a tense state when I got out of my car. I'd passed a truck parked in front, and I unlocked the back and went through the house to open the front door with the miserable feeling that I was about to have to go through a scene. The quiet interlude on my front porch watching the bees in the pear tree seemed a week ago, instead of hours.

Calvin Norris, leader of the Hotshot werepanthers, got out of his truck and came up the steps. He was a bearded man in his early forties, and he was a serious man whose responsibilities sat squarely on his shoulders. Evidently Calvin had just gotten off work. He was wearing the blue shirt and blue jeans all the Norcross crew leaders wore.

'Sookie,' he said, nodding to me.

'Please come in,' I answered, though I was reluctant. However, Calvin had never been anything but civil to me, and he had helped me rescue my brother a couple of months ago, when Jason had been held hostage. At the least, I owed him civility.

'My niece called me when the danger had passed,' he said heavily, taking a seat on the couch after I'd waved my hand to show he was welcome to stay. 'I think you saved her life.'

'I'm real glad to hear Crystal's better. All I did was make a phone call.' I sat in my favorite old chair, and I noticed I was slumping with weariness. I forced my shoulders back. 'Dr Ludwig was able to stop her bleeding?'

Calvin nodded. He looked at me steadily, his strange eyes solemn. 'She's going to be okay. Our women miscarry a lot. That's why we were hoping . . . Well.'

I flinched, the weight of Calvin's hopes that I'd mate with him resting heavily on my shoulders. I'm not sure why I felt guilty; because of his disappointment, I guess. After all, it was hardly my fault that the idea had limited appeal for me.

'I guess Jason and Crystal will be getting hitched,' Calvin said matter-of-factly. 'I have to say, I'm not crazy about your brother, but then I'm not the one marrying him.'

I was nonplussed. I didn't know if this wedding was Jason's idea, or Calvin's, or Crystal's. Jason certainly hadn't been thinking marriage this morning, unless it was something he'd neglected to mention in the turmoil of his worry about Crystal. I said, 'Well, to be honest, I'm not crazy about Crystal. But I'm not the one marrying her.' I took a deep breath. 'I'll do my best to help them out, if they decide to . . . do that. Jason's about all I've got, as you know.'

'Sookie,' he said, and his voice was suddenly far less certain, 'I want to talk about something else, too.'

Of course he did. No way was I going to dodge this bullet.

'I know that something you got told, when you came out to the house, put you off me. I'd like to know what it was. I can't fix it, if I don't know what's broken.'

I took a deep breath, while I considered my next words very carefully. 'Calvin, I know that Terry is your daughter.' When I'd gone to see Calvin when he'd gotten out of the hospital after being shot, I'd met Terry and her mother Maryelizabeth at Calvin's house. Though they clearly didn't live there, it was equally clear that they treated the place as an extension of their own home. Then Terry had asked me if I was going to marry her father.

'Yes,' Calvin said. 'I would've told you if you'd asked me.'

'Do you have other children?'

'Yes. I have three other children.'

'By different mothers?'

'By three different mothers.'

I'd been right. 'Why is that?' I asked, to be sure.

'Because I'm pure-blooded,' he said, as if it were self- evident. 'Since only the first child of a pureblood couple turns out to be a full panther, we have to switch off.'

I was profoundly glad I'd never seriously considered marrying Calvin, because if I had, I would have thrown up right then. What I'd suspected, after witnessing the succession-to-packmaster ritual, was true. 'So it's not the woman's first child, period, that turns out to be a full-blooded shape-shifter . . . it's her first child with a specific man.'

'Right.' Calvin looked surprised that I hadn't known that. 'The first child of any given pureblood couple is the real thing. So if our population gets too small, a pureblooded male has to mate with as many pure-blooded women as he can, to increase the pack.'

'Okay.' I waited for a minute, to collect myself. 'Did you think that I would be okay with you impregnating other women, if we got married?'

'No, I wouldn't expect that of an outsider,' he answered, in that same matter-of-fact voice. 'I think it's time I settled down with one woman. I've done my duty as leader.'

I tried not to roll my eyes. If it had been anyone else I would have sniggered, but Calvin was an honorable man, and he didn't deserve that reaction.

'Now I want to mate for life, and it would be good for the pack if I could bring new blood into the community. You can tell that we've bred with each other for too long. My eyes can hardly pass for human, and Crystal takes forever to change. We have to add something new to our gene pool, as the scientists call it. If you and I had a baby, which was what I was hoping, that baby wouldn't ever be a full Were; but he or she might breed into the community, bring new blood and new skills.'

'Why'd you pick me?'

He said, almost shyly. 'I like you. And you're real pretty.' He smiled at me then, a rare and sweet expression. 'I've watched you at the bar for years. You're nice to everyone, and you're a hard worker, and you don't have no one to take care of you like you deserve. And you know about us; it wouldn't be any big shock.'

'Do other kinds of shape-shifters do the same thing?' I asked this so quietly, I could hardly hear myself. I stared down at my hands, clenched together in my lap, and I could hardly breathe as I waited to hear his answer. Alcide's green eyes filled my thoughts.

'When the pack begins to grow too small, it's their duty to,' he said slowly. 'What's on your mind, Sookie?'

'When I went to the contest for the Shreveport packmaster, the one who won – Patrick Furnan – he had sex with a young Were girl, though he was married. I began to wonder,'

'Did I ever stand a chance with you?' Calvin asked. He seemed to have drawn his own conclusions.

Calvin could not be blamed for wanting to preserve his way of life. If I found the means distasteful, that was my problem.

'You definitely interested me,' I said. 'But I'm just too human to think of having my husband's children all around me. I'd just be too . . . it would just throw me off all the time, knowing my husband had had sex with almost every woman I saw day-to-day.' Come to think of it, Jason would fit right into the Hotshot community. I paused for a second, but he remained silent. 'I hope that my brother will be welcomed into your community, regardless of my answer.'

'I don't know if he understands what we do,' Calvin said. 'But Crystal's already miscarried once before, by a full-blood. Now she's miscarried this baby of your brother's. I'm thinking this means Crystal had better not try any more to have a panther. She may not be able to have a baby of your brother's. Do you feel obliged to talk to him about that?'

'It shouldn't be up to me to discuss that with Jason ... it should be up to Crystal.' I met Calvin's eyes. I opened my mouth to remark that if all Jason wanted was babies, he shouldn't get married; but then I recognized that was a sensitive subject, and I stopped while I was ahead.

Calvin shook my hand in an odd, formal way when he left. I believed that marked the end of his courtship. I had never been deeply attracted to Calvin Norris, and I'd never seriously thought about accepting his offer. But I'd be less than honest if I didn't admit that I'd fantasized about a steady husband with a good job and benefits, a husband who came straight home after his shift and fixed broken things on his days off. There were men who did that, men who didn't change into anything other than their own form, men who were alive twenty-four/seven. I knew that from reading so many minds at the bar.

I'm afraid that what really struck me about Calvin's confession – or explanation – is what it might reveal to me about Alcide.

Alcide had sparked my affection, and my lust. Thinking of him did make me wonder what marriage to him would be like, wonder in a very personal way, as opposed to my impersonal speculation about health insurance that Calvin had inspired. I'd pretty much abandoned the secret hope Alcide had inspired in me, after I'd been forced to shoot his former fiancée; but something in me had clung to the thought, something I'd kept secret even from myself, even after I'd found out he was dating Maria-Star. As recently as this day, I'd been stoutly denying to the Pelts that Alcide had any interest in me. But something lonely inside me had nursed a hope.

I got up slowly, feeling about twice my actual age, and went into the kitchen to get something out of the freezer for my supper. I wasn't hungry, but I'd eat unwisely later if I didn't fix something now, I told myself sternly.

But I never cooked a meal for myself that night.

Instead, I leaned against the refrigerator door and cried.

Chapter 7

The next day was Friday; not only was it my day off this week, but I had a date, so it was practically a red-letter day. I refused to ruin it by moping. Though it was still cool for such a pastime, I did one of my favorite things: I put on a bikini, greased myself up, and went to lie in the sun on the adjustable chaise lounge I'd gotten at Wal-Mart on sale at the end of the previous summer. I took a book, a radio, and a hat into the front yard, where there were fewer trees and flowering plants to encourage bugs that bit. I read, sang along with the tunes on the radio, and painted my toe-nails and fingernails. Though I was goose-pimply at first, I warmed up quickly along with the sun, and there was no breeze that day to chill me.

I know sunbathing is bad and evil, and I'll pay for it later, etc., etc., but it's one of the few free pleasures available to me.

No one came to visit, I couldn't hear the phone, and since the sun was out, the vampires weren't. I had a delightful time, all by myself. Around one o'clock, I decided to run into town for some groceries and a new bra, and I stopped at the mailbox out by Hummingbird Road to see if the mail carrier had run yet. Yes. My cable bill and my electric bill were in the mailbox, which was a downer. But lurking behind a Sears sales brochure was an invitation to a wedding shower for Halleigh. Well . . . gosh. I was surprised, but pleased. Of course, I'd lived next to Halleigh in one of Sam's duplexes for a few weeks while my house was being repaired after the fire, and we'd seen each other at least once a day during that time. So it wasn't a complete stretch, her putting me on her list of invitees. Plus, maybe she was relieved that the Cody situation had been cleared up so quickly?

I didn't get many invitations, so receiving it added to my sense of well-being. Three other teachers were giving the shower, and the invitation designated kitchen gifts. How timely, since I was on my way to the Wal-Mart Supercenter in Clarice.

After a lot of thought, I bought a two-quart Corning Ware casserole dish. Those were always handy. (I also got fruit juice, sharp cheddar, bacon, gift paper, and a really pretty blue bra and matching panties, but that's beside the point.)

After I'd gotten home and unloaded my purchases, I wrapped the boxed casserole dish in some silvery paper and stuck a big white bow on it. I wrote the date and time of the shower on my calendar, and I put the invitation on top of the present. I was on top of the shower situation.

Riding high on a crest of virtue, I wiped down the inside and outside of my new refrigerator after I'd eaten lunch. I washed a load of clothes in my new washer, wishing for the hundredth time that my cabinets were in place since I was tired of looking for things in the clutter on the floor.

I walked through the house to make sure it looked nice, since Quinn was picking me up. Not even letting myself think, I changed my sheets and cleaned my bathroom – not that I had any intention of falling into bed with Quinn, but it's better to be prepared than not, right? Besides, it just made me feel good, knowing that everything was clean and nice. Fresh towels in both bathrooms, a light dusting around the living room and bedroom, a quick circuit with the vacuum. Before I got in the shower, I even swept the porches, though I knew they would be covered again in a yellow haze before I got back from my date.

I let the sun dry my hair, probably getting it full of pollen, too. I put on my makeup carefully; I didn't wear a lot, but it was fun to apply it for something more interesting than work. A little eye shadow, a lot of mascara, some powder and lipstick. Then I put on my new date underwear. It made me feel special from the skin on out: midnight blue lace. I looked in the full-length mirror to check out the effect.

I gave myself a thumbs-up. You have to cheer for yourself, right?

The outfit I'd bought from Tara's Togs was royal blue and made out of some heavy knit that hung beautifully. I zipped up the pants and put on the top. It was sleeveless and it wrapped across my breasts and tied. I experimented with the depth of cleavage, at last picking a degree of revelation I was sure toed the line between sexy and cheap.

I got my black wrap out of the closet, the one Alcide had given me to replace one Debbie Pelt had vandalized. I'd need it later in the evening. I slipped into my black sandals. I experimented with jewelry, finally settling on a plain gold chain (it had been my grandmother's) and plain ball earrings.

Hah!

There was a knock on the front door, and I glanced at the clock, a bit surprised that Quinn was fifteen minutes early. I hadn't heard his truck, either. I opened the door to find not Quinn, but Eric, standing there.

I am sure he enjoyed my gasp of surprise.

Never open your door without checking. Never assume you know who's on the other side. That's why I'd gotten the peepholes! Stupid me. Eric must have flown, since I couldn't see a car anywhere.

'May I come in?' Eric asked politely. He had looked me over. After appreciating the view, he realized it hadn't been designed with him in mind. He wasn't happy. 'I suppose you're expecting company?'

'As a matter of fact I am, and actually, I'd rather you stayed on that side of the doorsill,' I said. I stepped back so he couldn't reach me.

'You told Pam that you didn't want to come to Shreveport,' he said. Oh yes, he was angry. 'So here I am, to find out why you don't answer my call.' Usually, his accent was very slight, but tonight I noticed that it was pronounced.

'I didn't have time,' I said. 'I'm going out tonight.'

'So I see,' he said, more quietly. 'Who are you going out with?'

'Is that really any of your business?' I met his eyes, challengingly.

'Of course it is,' he said.

I was disconcerted. 'And that would be why?' I rallied a little.

'You should be mine. I have slept with you, I have cared for you, I have . . . assisted you financially.'

'You paid me money you owed me, for services rendered,' I answered. 'You may have slept with me, but not recently, and you've shown no signs of wanting to do so again. If you care for me, you're showing it in a mighty strange way. I never heard that "total avoidance aside from orders coming from flunkies" was a valid way to show caring.' This was a jumbled sentence, okay, but I knew he got it.

'You're calling Pam a flunky?' He had a ghost of smile on his lips. Then he got back to being miffed. I could tell because he began dropping his contractions. 'I do not have to hang around you to show you. I am sheriff. You . . . you are in my retinue.'

I knew my mouth was hanging open, but I couldn't help it. 'Catching flies', my grandmother had called that expression, and I felt like I was catching plenty of them. 'Your retinue?' I managed to splutter. 'Well, *up* you and your retinue. You don't tell me what to do!'

'You are obliged to go with me to the conference,' Eric said, his mouth tense and his eyes blazing. 'That was why I called you to Shreveport, to talk to you about travel time and arrangements.'

'I'm not obliged to go anywhere with you. You got outranked, buddy.'

'Buddy? *Buddy?*'

And it would have degenerated from there, if Quinn hadn't pulled up. Instead of arriving in his truck, Quinn was in a Lincoln Continental. I felt a moment of sheer snobbish pleasure at the thought of riding in it. I'd selected the pants outfit at least partly because I thought I'd be scrambling up into a pickup, but I was just as pleased to slither into a luxurious car. Quinn came across the lawn and mounted the porch with an understated speed. He didn't look as though he was hurrying, but suddenly he was there, and I was smiling at him, and he looked wonderful. He was wearing a dark gray suit, a dark purple shirt, and a tie that blended the two colors in a paisley pattern. He was wearing one earring, a simple gold hoop.

Eric had fang showing.

'Hello, Eric,' Quinn said calmly. His deep voice rumbled along my spine. 'Sookie, you look good enough to eat.' He smiled at me, and the tremors along my spine spread into another area entirely. I would never have believed that in Eric's presence I could think another man was attractive. I'd have been wrong to think so.

'You look very nice, too,' I said, trying not to beam like an idiot. It was not cool to drool.

Eric said, 'What have you been telling Sookie, Quinn?'

The two tall men looked at each other. I didn't believe I was the source of their animosity. I was a symptom, not the disease. Something lay underneath this.

'I've been telling Sookie that the queen requires Sookie's presence at the conference as part of her party, and that the queen's summons supercedes yours,' Quinn said flatly.

'Since when has the queen given orders through a shifter?' Eric said, contempt flattening his voice.

'Since this shifter performed a valuable service for her in the line of business,' Quinn answered, with no hesitation. 'Mr Cataliades suggested to Her Majesty that I might be helpful in a diplomatic capacity, and my partners were glad to give me extra time to perform any duties she might give me.'

I wasn't totally sure I was following this, but I got the gist of it.

Eric was incensed, to use a good entry from my Word of the Day calendar. In fact, his eyes were almost throwing sparks, he was so angry. 'This woman has been mine, and she will be mine,' he said, in tones so definite I thought about checking my rear end for a brand.

Quinn shifted his gaze to me. 'Babe, are you his, or not?' he asked.

'Not,' I said.

'Then let's go enjoy the show,' Quinn said He didn't seem frightened, or even concerned. Was this his true reaction, or was he presenting a facade? Either way, it was pretty impressive.

I had to pass by Eric on my way to Quinn's car. I looked up at him, because I couldn't help it. Being close to him while he was this angry was not a safe thing, and I needed to be on my guard. Eric was seldom crossed in serious matters, and my annexation by the Queen of Louisiana – his queen – was a serious matter. My date with Quinn was sticking in his throat, too. Eric was just going to have to swallow.

Then we were both in the car, belted in, and Quinn did an expert backing maneuver to point the Lincoln back to Hummingbird Road.

I breathed out, slowly and carefully. It took a few quiet moments for me to feel calm again. Gradually my hands relaxed. I realized the silence had been building. I gave myself a mental shake. 'Do you go to the theater often, as you're traveling around?' I asked socially.

He laughed, and the deep, rich sound of it filled up the car. 'Yes,' he said. 'I go to the movies and the theater and any sporting event that's going on. I like to see people do things. I don't watch much television. I like to get out of my hotel room or my apartment and watch things happen or make them happen myself.'

'So do you dance?'

He gave me a quick glance. 'I do.'

I smiled. 'I like to dance.' And I was actually pretty good at dancing, not that I got many chances to practice. 'I'm no good at singing,' I admitted, 'but I really, really enjoy dancing.'

'That sounds promising.'

I thought we'd have to see how this evening went before we made any dancing dates, but at least we knew there was something we both liked to do. 'I like movies,' I said. 'But I don't think I've ever been to any live sports besides high school games. But those, I do attend. Football, basketball, baseball . . . I go to 'em all, when my job will let me.'

'Did you play a sport in school?' Quinn asked. I confessed that I'd played softball, and he told me he'd played basketball, which, considering his height, was no surprise at all.

Quinn was easy to talk to. He listened when I spoke. He drove well; at least he didn't curse at the other drivers, like Jason did. My brother tended to be on the impatient side when he drove.

I was waiting for the other shoe to drop. I was waiting for that moment – you know the one I mean – the moment when your date suddenly confesses to something you just can't stomach: he reveals himself as a racist or homophobe, admits he'd never marry anyone but another Baptist (Southerner, brunette, marathon runner, whatever), tells you about his children by his first three wives, describes his fondness for being paddled, or relates his youthful experiences in blowing up frogs or torturing cats. After that moment, no matter how much fun you have, you know it's not going anywhere. And I didn't even have to wait for a guy to tell me this stuff verbally; I could read it right out of his head before we even dated.

Never popular with the regular guys, me. Whether they admitted it or not, they couldn't stand the idea of going out with a girl who knew exactly how often they jacked off, had a lusty thought about another woman, or wondered how their teacher looked with her clothes off.

Quinn came around and opened my door when we parked across the street from the Strand, and he took my hand as we crossed the street. I enjoyed the courtesy.

There were lots of people going into the theater, and they all seemed to look at Quinn. Of course, a bald guy as tall as Quinn is *going* to get some stares. I was trying not to think about his hand; it was very large and very warm and very dry.

'They're all looking at you,' he said, as he pulled the tickets from his pocket, and I pressed my lips together to keep from laughing.

'Oh, I don't think so,' I said.

'Why else would they be staring?'

'At you,' I said, amazed.

He laughed out loud, that deep laugh that made me vibrate inside.

We had very good seats, right in the middle and toward the front of the theater. Quinn filled up his seat, no doubt about it, and I wondered if the people behind him could see. I looked at my program with some curiosity, found I didn't recognize the names of the any of the actors in the production, and decided I didn't care at all. I glanced up to find that Quinn was staring at me. I felt my face flood with color. I'd folded my black wrap and placed it in my lap, and I had the abrupt desire to pull my top higher to cover every inch of my cleavage.

'Definitely looking at you,' he said, and smiled. I ducked my head, pleased but self-conscious.

Lots of people have seen *The Producers*. I don't need to describe the plot, except to say it's about gullible people and lovable rascals, and it's very funny. I enjoyed every minute. It was marvelous to watch people performing right in front of me on such a professional level. The guest star, the one whom the older people in the audience seemed to recognize, swashed through the lead role with this amazing assurance. Quinn laughed too, and after the intermission he took my hand again. My fingers closed around his quite naturally, and I didn't feel self-conscious about the contact.

Suddenly it was an hour later, and the play was over. We stood up along with everyone else, though we could tell it would take a while for the theater to clear out. Quinn took my wrap and held it for me, and I threw it around me. He was sorry I was covering myself up – I got that directly from his brain.

'Thank you,' I said, tugging on his sleeve to make sure he was looking at me. I wanted him to know how much I meant it. 'That was just great.'

'I enjoyed it, too. You want to go get something to eat?'

'Okay,' I said, after a moment.

'You had to think about it?'

I had actually sort of flash-thought about several different items. If I'd enumerated them, it'd have run something like, *He must be having a good time or he wouldn't suggest more of the evening. I have to get up and go to work tomorrow but I don't want to miss this opportunity. If we go to eat I have to be careful not to spill anything on my new clothes. Will it be okay to spend even more of his money, since the tickets cost so much?*

'Oh, I had to consider the calories,' I said, patting my rear end.

'There's nothing wrong with you, front or back,' Quinn said, and the warmth in his eyes made me feel like basking. I knew I was curvier than the ideal. I'd actually heard Holly tell Danielle that anything over a size eight was simply disgusting. Since a day I got into an eight was a happy day for me, I'd felt pretty forlorn for all of three minutes. I would have related this conversation to Quinn if I hadn't been sure it would sound like I was angling for a compliment.

'Let the restaurant be my treat,' I said.

'With all due respect to your pride, no, I won't.' Quinn looked me right in the eyes to make sure I knew he meant it.

We'd reached the sidewalk by that time. Surprised at his vehemence, I didn't know how to react. On one level, I was relieved, since I have to be careful with my money. On another level, I knew it was right for me to offer and I would have felt good if he'd said that would be fine.

'You know I'm not trying to insult you, right?' I said.

'I understand that you're being equal.'

I looked up at him doubtfully, but he was serious.

Quinn said, 'I believe you are absolutely as good as me in every way. But I asked you out, and I am providing the financial backup for our date.'

'What if I asked you out?'

He looked grim. 'Then I'd have to sit back and let you take care of the evening,' he said. He said it reluctantly, but he said it. I looked away and smiled.

Cars were pulling out of the parking lot at a steady pace. Since we'd taken our time leaving the theater, Quinn's car was looking lonely in the second row. Suddenly, my mental alarm went off. Somewhere close, there was a lot of hostility and evil intent. We had left the sidewalk to cross the street to the parking lot. I gripped Quinn's arm and then let it go so we could clear for action.

'Something's wrong,' I said.

Without replying, Quinn began scanning the area. He unbuttoned his suit coat with his left hand so he could move without hindrance. His fingers curled into fists. Since he was a man with a powerful protective urge, he stepped ahead of me, in front of me.

So of course, we were attacked from behind.

Chapter 8

In a blur of movement that couldn't be broken down into increments my eye could clearly recognize, a beast knocked me into Quinn, who stumbled forward a step. I was on the ground underneath the snarling half man, half wolf by the time Quinn wheeled, and as soon as he did, another Were appeared, seemingly out of nowhere, to leap on Quinn's back.

The creature on top of me was a brand-new fresh half Were, so young he could only have been bitten in the past three weeks. He was in such a frenzy that he had attacked before he had finished with the partial change that a bitten Were can achieve. His face was still elongating into a muzzle, even as he tried to choke me. He would never attain the beautiful wolf form of the full-blooded Were. He was 'bitten, not blood', as the Weres put it. He still had arms, he still had legs, he had a body covered with hair, and he had a wolf's head. But he was just as savage as a full-blood.

I clawed at his hands, the hands that were gripping my neck with such ferocity. I wasn't wearing my silver chain tonight. I'd decided it would be tacky, since my date was himself a shifter. Being tacky might have saved my life, I thought in a flash, though it was the last coherent thought I had for a few moments.

The Were was straddling my body, and I brought my knees up sharply, trying to give him a big enough jolt that he'd loosen his hold. There were shrieks of alarm from the few remaining pedestrians, and a higher, more piercing shriek from Quinn's attacker, whom I saw flying through the air as if he'd been launched from a cannon. Then a big hand grasped my attacker by his own neck and lifted him. Unfortunately, the half beast who had his hands wrapped around my throat didn't let me go. I began to rise from the pavement, too, my throat becoming more and more pinched by the grip he had on me.

Quinn must have seen my desperate situation, because he struck the Were on top of me with his free hand, a slap that rocked the Were's head back and simply knocked him for a loop so thoroughly that he let go of my neck.

Then Quinn grabbed the young Were by the shoulders and tossed him aside. The boy landed on the pavement and didn't move.

'Sookie,' Quinn said, hardly sounding out of breath. Out of breath is what I was, struggling to get my throat to open back up so I could gulp in some oxygen. I could hear a police siren, and I was profoundly thankful. Quinn slipped his arm under my shoulders and held me up. Finally I breathed in, and the air was wonderful, blissful. 'You're breathing okay?' he asked. I gathered myself enough to nod. 'Any bones broken in your throat?' I tried to raise my hand to my neck, but my hand wasn't cooperating just at the moment.

His face filled my scope of vision, and in the dim light of the corner lamp I could see he was pumped. 'I'll kill them if they hurt you,' he growled, and just then, that was delightful news.

'Bitten,' I wheezed, and he looked horrified, checking me over with hands and eyes for the bite mark. 'Not me,' I elaborated. 'Them. Not born Weres.' I sucked in a lot of air. 'And maybe on drugs,' I said. Awareness dawned in his eyes.

That was the only explanation for such insane behavior.

A heavyset black patrolman hurried up to me. 'We need an ambulance at the Strand,' he was saying to someone on his shoulder. No, it was a little radio set. I shook my head.

'You need an ambulance, ma'am,' he insisted. 'Girl over there says the man took you down and tried to choke you.'

'I'm okay,' I said, my voice raspy and my throat undeniably painful.

'Sir, you with this lady?' the patrolman asked Quinn. When he turned, the light flashed off his name pin; it said *Boling*.

'Yes, I am.'

'You . . . ah, you got these punks offa her?'

'Yes.'

Boling's partner, a Caucasian version of Boling, came up to us then. He looked at Quinn with some reservation. He'd been examining our assailants, who had fully changed to human form before the police had arrived. Of course, they were naked.

'The one has a broken leg,' he told us. 'The other is claiming his shoulder's dislocated.'

Boling shrugged. 'Got what was coming to 'em.' It might have been my imagination, but he, too, seemed a bit more cautious when he looked at my date.

'They got more than they expected,' his partner said neutrally. 'Sir, do you know either of these kids?' He tilted his head toward the teenagers, who were being examined by a patrolman from another car, a younger man with a more athletic build. The boys were leaning against each other, looking stunned.

'I've never seen them before,' Quinn said. 'You, babe?' He looked down at me questioningly. I shook my head. I was feeling better enough that I felt at a distinct disadvantage, being on the ground. I wanted to get up, and I said so to my date. Before the police officers could tell me once again to wait for an ambulance, Quinn managed to get me to my feet with as little pain as possible.

I looked down at my beautiful new outfit. It was really dirty. 'How does the back look?' I asked Quinn, and even I could hear the fear in my voice. I turned my back to Quinn and looked at him anxiously over my shoulder. Quinn seemed a little startled, but he dutifully scanned my rear view.

'No tearing,' he reported. 'There may be a spot or two where the material got a little scraped across the pavement.'

I burst into tears. I probably would have started crying no matter what, because I was feeling a powerful reaction to the adrenaline that had surged through my body when we'd been attacked, but the timing was perfect. The police got more avuncular the more I cried, and as an extra bonus, Quinn pulled me into his arms and I rested my cheek against his chest. I listened to his heartbeat when I quit sobbing. I'd gotten rid of my nervous reaction to the attack and disarmed the police at the same time, though I knew they'd still wonder about Quinn and his strength.

Another policeman called from his place by one of the assailants, the one Quinn had thrown. Our two patrolmen went to answer the summons, and we were briefly alone.

'Smart,' Quinn murmured into my ear.

'Mmmm,' I said, snuggling against him.

He tightened his arms around me. 'You get any closer, we're going to have to excuse ourselves and get a room,' he whispered.

'Sorry.' I pulled back slightly and looked up at him. 'Who you reckon hired them?'

He may have been surprised I'd figured that out, but you couldn't tell by his brain. The chemical reaction that had fueled my tears had made his mental snarl extra complicated. 'I'm definitely going to find out,' he said. 'How's your throat?'

'Hurts,' I admitted, my voice raspy. 'But I know there's nothing really wrong with it. And I don't have health insurance. So I don't want to go to the hospital. It would be a waste of time and money.'

'Then we won't go.' He bent and kissed my cheek. I turned my face up to him, and his next kiss landed in exactly the right spot. After a gentle second, it flared into something more intense. We were both feeling the aftereffects of the adrenalin rush.

The sound of a throat clearing brought me back into my right mind as effectively as if Officer Boling had thrown a bucket of cold water on us. I disengaged and buried my face against Quinn's chest again. I knew I couldn't move away for a minute or two, since his excitement was pressed right up against me. Though these weren't the best circumstances for evaluation, I was pretty sure Quinn was proportional. I had to resist the urge to rub my body against his. I knew that would make things worse for him, from a public viewpoint – but I was in a much better mood than I had been, and I guess I was feeling mischievous. And frisky. Very frisky. Going through this ordeal together had probably accelerated our relationship the equivalent of four dates.

'Did you have other questions for us, Officer?' Quinn asked, in a voice that was not perfectly calm.

'Yes, sir, if you and the lady will come down to the station, we need to take your statements. Detective Coughlin will do that while we take the prisoners to the hospital.'

'All right. Does that have to be tonight? My friend needs to rest. She's exhausted. This has been quite an ordeal for her.'

'It won't take long,' the officer said mendaciously. 'You sure you've never seen these two punks before? Because this seems like a real personal attack, you don't mind me saying so.'

'Neither of us knows them.'

'And the lady still refuses medical attention?'

I nodded.

'Well, all right then, folks. Hope you don't have no more trouble.'

'Thank you for coming so quickly,' I said, and turned my head a little to meet Officer Boling's eyes. He looked at me in a troubled way, and I could hear in his head that he was worried about my safety with a violent man like Quinn, a man who could throw two boys several feet in the air. He didn't realize, and I hoped he never would, that the attack had been personal. It had been no random mugging.

We went to the station in a police car. I wasn't sure what their thinking was, but Boling's partner told us that we'd be returned to Quinn's vehicle, so we went along with the program. Maybe they didn't want us to have a chance to talk to each other alone. I don't know why; I think the only thing that could have aroused their suspicion was Quinn's size and expertise in fighting off attackers.

In the brief seconds we had alone before an officer climbed into the driver's seat, I told Quinn, 'If you think something at me, I'll be able to hear you – if you need me to know something urgently.'

'Handy,' he commented. The violence seemed to have relaxed something inside him. He rubbed his thumb across the palm of my hand. He was thinking he'd like to have thirty minutes in a bed with me, right now, or even fifteen; hell, even ten, even in the backseat of a car, would be fantastic. I tried not to laugh, but I couldn't help it, and when he realized that I'd read all that clearly, he shook his head with a rueful smile.

We have somewhere to go after this, he thought deliberately. I hoped he didn't mean he was going to rent a room or take me to his place for sex, because no matter how attractive I found him, I wasn't going to do that tonight. But his brain had mostly cleared of lust, and I perceived his purpose was something different. I nodded.

So don't get too tired, he said. I nodded again. How I was supposed to prevent exhaustion, I wasn't sure, but I'd try to hoard a little energy.

The police station was much like I expected it to be. Though there's a lot to be said for Shreveport, it has more than its fair share of crime. We didn't excite much attention at all, until officers who'd been on the scene put their heads together with police in the building, and then there were a few stolen glances at Quinn, some surreptitious evaluations. He was formidable-looking enough for them to credit ordinary strength as the source of his defeat of the two muggers. But there was just enough strangeness about the incident, enough peculiar touches in the eyewitness reports . . . and then my eye caught a familiar weathered face. Uh-oh.

'Detective Coughlin,' I said, remembering now why the name had sounded familiar.

'Miss Stackhouse,' he responded, with about as much enthusiasm as I had shown. 'What you been up to?'

'We got mugged,' I explained.

'Last time I saw you, you were engaged to Alcide Herveaux, and you'd just found one of the most sickening corpses I've ever seen,' he said easily. His belly seemed to have gotten even bigger in the few months since I'd met him at a murder scene here in Shreveport. Like many men with a disproportionate belly, he wore his khaki pants buttoned underneath the overhang, so to speak. Since his shirt had broad blue and white stripes, the effect was that of a tent overhanging packed dirt.

I just nodded. There was really nothing to say.

'Mr Herveaux doing okay after the loss of his father?' Jackson Herveaux's body had been found half-in, half-out of a feed tank filled with water on an old farm belonging to the family. Though the newspaper had tap-danced around some of the injuries, it was clear wild animals had chewed at some of the bones. The theory was that the older Herveaux had fallen into the tank and broken his leg when he hit the bottom. He had managed to get to the edge and haul himself halfway

out, but at that point he had passed out. Since no one knew he'd visited
the farm, no one came to his rescue, the theory went, and he'd died
all by himself.

Actually, a large crowd had witnessed Jackson's demise, among them
the man beside me.

'I haven't talked to Alcide since his dad was found,' I said truthfully.

'My goodness, I'm sure sorry that didn't work out,' Detective
Coughlin said, pretending he didn't see that I was standing with my
date for the evening. 'You two sure made a nice-looking couple.'

'Sookie is pretty no matter who she's with,' Quinn said. I smiled up
at him, and he smiled back. He was sure making all the right moves.

'So if you'll come with me for a minute, Miss Stackhouse, we'll get
your story down on paper and you can leave.'

Quinn's hand tightened on mine. He was warning me. Wait a
minute, who was the mind reader around here? I squeezed right back.
I was perfectly aware that Detective Coughlin thought I must be guilty
of *something*, and he'd do his best to discover what. But in fact, I was
not guilty.

We had been the targets, I'd picked that from the attackers' brains.
But why?

Detective Coughlin led me to a desk in a roomful of desks, and he
fished a form out of a drawer. The business of the room continued;
some of the desks were unoccupied and had that 'closed for the night'
look, but others showed signs of work in progress. There were a few
people coming in and out of the room, and two desks away, a younger
detective with short white-blond hair was busily typing on his computer. I was being very careful, and I'd opened my mind, so I knew he
was looking at me when I was looking in another direction, and I knew
he'd been positioned there by Detective Coughlin, or at least prodded
to get a good hard look at me while I was in the room.

I met his eyes squarely. The shock of recognition was mutual. I'd
seen him at the packmaster contest. He was a Were. He'd acted as
Patrick Furnan's second in the duel. I'd caught him cheating. Maria-
Star had told me his punishment had been having his head shaved.
Though his candidate won, this punishment had been exacted, and his
hair was just now growing in. He hated me with the passion of the

guilty. He half rose from his chair, his first instinct being to come over to me and beat the crap out of me, but when he absorbed the fact that someone had already tried to do that, he smirked.

'Is that your partner?' I asked Detective Coughlin.

'What?' He'd been peering at the computer through reading glasses, and he glanced over at the younger man, then back at me. 'Yeah, that's my new partner. The guy I was with at the last crime scene I saw you at, he retired last month.'

'What's his name? Your new partner?'

'Why, you going after him next? You can't seem to settle on one man, can you, Miss Stackhouse?'

If I'd been a vampire, I could have made him answer me, and if I were really skilled, he wouldn't even know he'd done it.

'It's more like they can't settle on me, Detective Coughlin,' I said, and he gave me a curious look. He waved a finger toward the blond detective.

'That's Cal. Cal Myers.' He seemed to have called up the right form, because he began to take me through the incident once again, and I answered his questions with genuine indifference. For once, I had very little to hide.

'I did wonder,' I said, when we'd concluded, 'if they'd taken drugs.'

'You know much about drugs, Miss Stackhouse?' His little eyes went over me again.

'Not firsthand, but of course, from time to time someone comes into the bar who's taken something they shouldn't. These young men definitely seemed . . . influenced by something.'

'Well, the hospital will take their blood, and we'll know.'

'Will I have to come back?'

'To testify against them? Sure.'

No way out of it. 'Okay,' I said, as firmly and neutrally as I could. 'We through here?'

'I guess we are.' He met my eyes, his own little brown eyes full of suspicion. There was no point in my resenting it; he was absolutely right, there was something fishy about me, something he didn't know. Coughlin was doing his best to be a good cop. I felt suddenly sorry for him, floundering through a world he only knew the half of.

'Don't trust your partner,' I whispered, and I expected him to blow up and call Cal Myers over and ridicule me to him. But something in my eyes or my voice arrested that impulse. My words spoke to a warning that had been sounding surreptitiously in his brain, maybe from the moment he'd met the Were.

He didn't say anything, not one word. His mind was full of fear, fear and loathing ... but he believed I was telling him the truth. After a second, I got up and left the squad room. To my utter relief, Quinn was waiting for me in the lobby.

A patrolman – not Boling – took us back to Quinn's car, and we were silent during the drive. Quinn's car was sitting in solitary splendor in the parking lot across from the Strand, which was closed and dark. He pulled out his keys and hit the keypad to open the doors, and we got in slowly and wearily.

'Where are we going?' I asked.

'The Hair of the Dog,' he said.

Chapter 9

The Hair of the Dog was off Kings Highway, not too far from Centenary College. It was an old brick storefront. The large windows facing the street were covered with opaque cream curtains, I noticed, as we turned in to the left side of the building to lurch through an alley that led to a parking area at the back. We parked in the small, weedy lot. Though it was poorly lit, I could see that the ground was littered with empty cans, broken glass, used condoms, and worse. There were several motorcycles, a few of the less expensive compact cars, and a Suburban or two. The back door had a sign on it that read NO ENTRANCE – STAFF ONLY.

Though my feet were definitely beginning to protest the unaccustomed high heels, we had to pick our way through the alley to the front entrance. The cold creeping down my spine intensified as we grew close to the door. Then it was like I'd hit a wall, the spell gripped me that suddenly. I stopped dead. I struggled to go forward, but I couldn't move. I could smell the magic. The Hair of the Dog had been warded. Someone had paid a very good witch a handsome amount of money to surround the door with a go-away spell.

I fought not to give in to a compulsion to turn and walk in another direction, any other direction.

Quinn took a few steps forward, and turned to regard me with some surprise, until he realized what was happening. 'I forgot,' he said, that same surprise sounding in his voice. 'I actually forgot you're human.'

'That sounds like a compliment,' I said, with some effort. Even in the cool night, my forehead beaded with sweat. My right foot edged forward an inch.

'Here,' he said, and scooped me up, until he was holding me just like Rhett carried Scarlett O'Hara. As his aura wrapped around me, the unpleasant go-away compulsion eased. I drew a deep breath of relief. The magic could no longer recognize me as human, at least not decisively. Though the bar still seemed unattractive and mildly repellent, I could enter without wanting to be sick.

Maybe it was the lingering effects of the spell, but after we'd entered it, the bar *still* seemed unattractive and mildly repellent. I wouldn't say all conversation ceased when we walked in, but there was a definite lull in the noise that filled the bar. A jukebox was playing 'Bad Moon Rising', which was like the Were national anthem, and the motley collection of Weres and shifters seemed to reorient themselves.

'Humans are not allowed in this place!' A very young woman leaped across the bar in one muscular surge and strode forward. She was wearing fishnet stockings and high- heeled boots, a red leather bustier – well, a bustier that wished it was made of red leather, it was probably more like Naugahyde – and a black band of cloth that I supposed she called a skirt. It was like she'd pulled a tube top on, and then worked it down. It was so tight I thought it might roll up all at once, like a window shade.

She didn't like my smile, correctly reading it as a comment on her ensemble.

'Get your human ass out of here,' she said, and growled. Unfortunately, it didn't sound too threatening, since she hadn't had any practice at putting the menace into it, and I could feel my smile widen. The dress-challenged teen had the poor impulse control of the very new Were, and she pulled her hand back to punch me.

Then Quinn snarled.

The sound came from deep in his belly, and it was thunderous, the deep sound of it penetrating every corner of the bar. The bartender, a biker type with beard and hair of considerable length and tattoos that covered his bare arms, reached down below the bar. I knew he was pulling out a shotgun.

Not for the first time, I wondered if I shouldn't start going armed everywhere I went. In my law-abiding life, I had never seen the need until the past few months. The jukebox cut off just then, and the silence of the bar was just as deafening as the noise had been.

'Please don't get the gun out,' I said, smiling brightly at the bartender. I could feel it stretching my lips, that too-bright grin that made me look a little nuts. 'We come in peace,' I added, on a crazy impulse, showing them my empty palms.

A shifter who'd been standing at the bar laughed, a sharp bark of startled amusement. The tension began to ratchet down a notch. The young woman's hand dropped to her side, and she took a step back. Her gaze flickered from Quinn to me and back again. Both the bartender's hands were in sight now.

'Hello, Sookie,' said a familiar voice. Amanda, the red-haired Were who'd been chauffeuring Dr Ludwig the day before, was sitting at a table in a dark corner. (Actually, the room seemed to be full of dark corners.)

With Amanda was a husky man in his late thirties. Both were supplied with drinks and a bowl of snack mix. They had company at the table, a couple sitting with their backs to me. When they turned, I recognized Alcide and Maria-Star. They turned cautiously, as if any sudden movement might trigger violence. Maria-Star's brain was a motley jumble of anxiety, pride, and tension. Alcide's was just conflicted. He didn't know how to feel.

That made two of us.

'Hey, Amanda,' I said, my voice as cheerful as my smile. It wouldn't do to let the silence pile up.

'I'm honored to have the legendary Quinn in my bar,' Amanda said, and I realized that, whatever other jobs she might have, she owned the Hair of the Dog. 'Are you two out for an evening on the town, or is, there some special reason for your visit?'

Since I had no idea why we were there, I had to defer to Quinn for an answer, which didn't make me look too good, in my opinion.

'There's a very good reason, though I've long wanted to visit your bar,' Quinn said in a courtly, formal style that had come out of nowhere.

Amanda inclined her head, which seemed to be a signal for Quinn to continue.

'This evening, my date and I were attacked in a public place, with civilians all around us.'

No one seemed awfully upset or astonished by this. In fact, Miss Fashion-Challenged shrugged her bare skinny shoulders.

'We were attacked by Weres,' Quinn said.

Now we got the big reaction. Heads and hands jerked and then became still. Alcide half rose to his feet and then sat down again.

'Weres of the Long Tooth pack?' Amanda asked. Her voice was incredulous.

Quinn shrugged. 'The attack was a killing one, so I didn't stop to ask questions. Both were very young bitten Weres, and from their behavior, they were on drugs.'

More shocked reaction. We were creating quite the sensation.

'Are you hurt?' Alcide asked me, as if Quinn weren't standing right there.

I tilted my head back so my neck would be visible. I wasn't smiling anymore. By now the bruises left by the boy's hands would be darkening nicely. And I'd been thinking hard. 'As a friend of the pack, I didn't expect anything to happen to me here in Shreveport,' I said.

I figured my status as friend of the pack hadn't changed with the new regime, or at least I hoped it hadn't. Anyway, it was my trump card, and I played it.

'Colonel Flood did say Sookie was a friend of the pack,' Amanda said unexpectedly. The Weres all looked at each other, and the moment seemed to hang in the balance.

'What happened to the cubs?' asked the biker behind the bar.

'They lived,' Quinn said, giving them the important news first. There was a general feeling that the whole bar gave a sigh; whether of relief or regret, I couldn't tell you.

'The police have them,' Quinn continued. 'Since the cubs attacked us in front of humans, there was no way around police involvement.' We'd talked about Cal Myers on our way to the bar. Quinn had caught only a glimpse of the Were cop, but of course he'd known him for what he was. I wondered if my companion would now raise the issue of Cal Myers's presence at the station, but Quinn said nothing. And truthfully, why comment on something the Weres were sure to already know? The Were pack would stand together against outsiders, no matter how divided they were among themselves.

Police involvement in Were affairs was undesirable, obviously. Though Cal Myers's presence on the force would help, every scrutiny raised the possibility that humans would learn of the existence of creatures that preferred anonymity. I didn't know how they'd flown (or crawled, or loped) under the radar this long. I had a conviction that the cost in human lives had been considerable.

Alcide said, 'You should take Sookie home. She's tired.'

Quinn put his arm around me and pulled me to his side. 'When we've received your assurance that the pack will get to the bottom of this unprovoked attack, we'll leave.'

Neat speech. Quinn seemed to be a master of expressing himself diplomatically and firmly. He was a little overwhelming, truthfully. The power flowed from him in a steady stream, and his physical presence was undeniable.

'We'll convey all this to the packmaster,' Amanda was saying. 'He'll investigate, I'm sure. Someone must have hired these pups.'

'Someone converted them to start with,' Quinn said. 'Unless your pack has degraded to biting street punks and sending them out to scavenge?'

Okay, hostile atmosphere now. I looked up at my large companion and discovered that Quinn was nearasthis to losing his temper.

'Thank you all,' I said to Amanda, my bright smile again yanking at the corners of my mouth. 'Alcide, Maria-Star, good to see you. We're going to go now. Long drive back to Bon Temps.' I gave Biker Bartender and Fishnet Girl a little wave. He nodded, and she scowled. Probably she wouldn't be interested in becoming my best friend. I wriggled out from under Quinn's arm and linked his hand with mine.

'Come on, Quinn. Let's hit the road.'

For a bad little moment, his eyes didn't recognize me. Then they cleared, and he relaxed. 'Sure, babe.' He said good-bye to the Weres, and we turned our backs on them to walk out. Even though the little crowd included Alcide, whom I trusted in most ways, it was an uncomfortable moment for me.

I could feel no fear, no anxiety, coming from Quinn. Either he had great focus and control, or he really wasn't scared of a bar full of werewolves, which was admirable and all, but kind of . . . unrealistic.

The correct answer turned out to be 'great focus and control'. I found out when we got to the dim parking lot. Moving quicker than I could track, I was against the car and his mouth was on mine. After a startled second, I was right in the moment. Shared danger does that, and it was the second time – on our first date – that we'd been in peril. Was that a bad omen? I dismissed that rational thought when Quinn's lips and teeth traveled down to find that vulnerable and sensitive place where the neck curves into the shoulder. I made an incoherent noise, because along with the arousal I always felt when kissed there, I felt undeniable pain from the bruises that circled my neck. It was an uncomfortable combination.

'Sorry, sorry,' he muttered into my skin, his lips never stopping their assault. I knew if I lowered my hand, I'd be able to touch him intimately. I'm not saying I wasn't tempted. But I was learning a little caution as I went along . . . probably not enough, I reflected with the sliver of my mind that wasn't getting more and more involved with the heat that surged up from my lowest nerve bundle to meet the heat generated by Quinn's lips. Oh, geez. Oh, oh, oh.

I moved against him. It was a reflex, okay? But a mistake, because his hand slipped under my breast and his thumb began stroking. I shuddered and jerked. He was doing a little gasping, too. It was like jumping onto the running board of a car that was already speeding down the dark road.

'Okay.' I breathed, pulled away a little. 'Okay, let's stop this now.'

'Ummm,' he said in my ear, his tongue flicking. I jerked.

'I'm not doing this,' I said, trying to sound definite. Then my resolve gathered. 'Quinn! I'm not having sex with you in this nasty parking lot!'

'Not even a little bit of sex?'

'No. Definitely not!'

'Your mouth' (here he kissed it) 'is saying one thing, but your body' (he kissed my shoulder) 'is saying another.'

'Listen to the mouth, buster.'

'Buster?'

'Okay. Quinn.'

He sighed, straightened. 'All right,' he said. He smiled ruefully. 'Sorry. I didn't plan on jumping you like that.'

'Going into a place where you're not exactly welcome, and getting out unhurt, that's some excitement,' I said.

He expelled a deep breath. 'Right,' he said.

'I like you a lot,' I said. I could read his mind fairly clearly, just at this instant. He liked me, too; right at the moment, he liked me a whole bunch. He wanted to like me right up against the wall.

I battened my hatches. 'But I've had a couple of experiences that have been warnings for me to slow down. I haven't been going slow with you tonight. Even with the, ah, special circumstances.' I was suddenly ready to sit down in the car. My back was aching and I felt a slight cramp. I worried for a second, then thought of my monthly cycle. That was certainly enough to wear me out, coming on top of an exciting, and bruising, evening.

Quinn was looking down at me. He was wondering about me. I couldn't tell what his exact concern was, but suddenly he asked, 'Which of us was the target of that attack outside the theater?'

Okay, his mind was definitely off sex now. Good. 'You think it was just one of us?'

That gave him pause. 'I had assumed so,' he said.

'We also have to wonder who put them up to it. I guess they were paid, in some form – either drugs or money, or both. You think they'll talk?'

'I don't think they'll survive the night in jail.'

Chapter 10

They didn't even rate the front page. They were in the local section of the Shreveport paper, below the fold. JAILHOUSE HOMICIDES, the headline read. I sighed.

> Two juveniles awaiting transport from the holding cells to the Juvenile Facility were killed last night sometime after midnight.

The newspaper was delivered every morning to the special box at the end of my driveway, right beside my mailbox. But it was getting dark by the time I saw the article, while I was sitting in my car, about to pull out onto Hummingbird Road and go to work. I hadn't ventured out today until now. Sleeping, laundry, and a little gardening had taken up my day. No one had called, and no one had visited, just like the ads said. I'd thought Quinn might phone, just to check up on my little injuries . . . but not.

> The two juveniles, brought into the police station on charges of assault and battery, were put in one of the holding cells to wait for the morning bus to arrive from the Juvenile Facility. The holding cell for juvenile offenders is out of sight from that for adult offenders, and the two were the only juveniles incarcerated during the night. At some point, the two were strangled by a person or persons unknown. No other prisoners were harmed,

and all denied seeing any suspicious activity. Both the youths had extensive juvenile records. 'They had had many encounters with the police,' a source close to the investigation said.

'We're going to look into this thoroughly,' said Detective Dan Coughlin, who had responded to the original complaint and was heading the investigation of the incident for which the youths were apprehended. 'They were arrested after allegedly attacking a couple in a bizarre manner, and their deaths are equally bizarre.' His partner, Cal Myers, added, 'Justice will be done.'

I found that especially ominous.

Tossing the paper on the seat beside me, I pulled my sheaf of mail out of the mailbox and added it to the little pile. I'd sort through it after my shift at Merlotte's.

I was in a thoughtful mood when I got to the bar. Preoccupied with the fate of the two assailants of the night before, I hardly flinched when I found that I would be working with Sam's new employee. Tanya was as bright-eyed and efficient as I'd found her previously. Sam was very happy with her; in fact, the second time he told me how pleased he was, I told him a little sharply that I'd already heard about it.

I was glad to see Bill come in and sit at a table in my section. I wanted an excuse to walk away, before I would have to respond to the question forming in Sam's head: *Why don't you like Tanya?*

I don't expect to like everyone I meet, any more than I expect everyone to like me. But I usually have a basis for disliking an individual, and it's more than an unspecified distrust and vague distaste. Though Tanya was some kind of shape-shifter, I should have been able to read her and learn enough to either confirm or disprove my instinctive suspicion. But I couldn't read Tanya. I'd get a word here and there, like a radio station that's fading out. You'd think I'd be glad to find someone my own age and sex who could perhaps become a friend. Instead, I was disturbed when I realized she was a closed book. Oddly, Sam hadn't said a word about her essential nature. He hadn't said, 'Oh, she's a weremole,' or 'She's a true shifter, like me,' or anything like that.

I was in a troubled mood when I strode over to take Bill's order. My bad mood compounded when I saw Selah Pumphrey standing in the doorway scanning the crowd, probably trying to locate Bill. I said a few bad words to myself, turned on my heel, and walked away. Very unprofessional.

Selah was staring at me when I glanced at their table after a while. Arlene had gone over to take their order. I simply listened to Selah; I was in a rude mood. She was wondering why Bill always wanted to meet her here, when the natives were obviously hostile. She couldn't believe that a discerning and sophisticated man like Bill could ever have dated a barmaid. And the way she'd heard it, I hadn't even gone to college, and furthermore, my grandmother had gotten *murdered*.

That made me sleazy, I guess.

I try to take things like this with a grain of salt. After all, I could have shielded myself pretty effectively from these thoughts. People who eavesdrop seldom hear good about themselves, right? An old adage, and a true one. I told myself (about six times in row) that I had no business listening to her, that it would be too drastic a reaction to go slap her upside the head or snatch her baldheaded. But the anger swelled in me, and I couldn't seem to get it under control. I put three beers down on the table in front of Catfish, Dago, and Hoyt with unnecessary force. They looked up at me simultaneously in astonishment.

'We do something wrong, Sook?' Catfish said. 'Or is it just your time of the month?'

'You didn't do anything,' I said. And it wasn't my time of the month – oh. Yes, it was. I'd had the warning with the ache in my back, the heaviness in my stomach, and my swollen fingers. My little friend had come to visit, and I felt the sensation even as I realized what was contributing to my general irritation.

I glanced over at Bill and caught him staring at me, his nostrils flaring. He could smell the blood. A wave of acute embarrassment rolled over me, turning my face red. For a second, I glimpsed naked hunger on his face, and then he wiped his features clean of all expression.

If he wasn't weeping with unrequited love on my doorstep, at least he was suffering a little. A tiny pleased smile was on my lips when I glimpsed myself in the mirror behind the bar.

A second vampire came in an hour later. She looked at Bill for a second, nodded to him, and then sat at a table in Arlene's section. Arlene hustled over to take the vamp's order. They spoke for a minute, but I was too busy to check in on them. Besides, I'd just have heard the vamp filtered through Arlene, since vampires are silent as the grave (ho ho) to me. The next thing I knew, Arlene was wending her way through the crowd to me.

'The dead gal wants to talk to you,' she said, not moderating her voice in the least, and heads turned in our direction. Arlene is not long on subtlety – or tact, for that matter.

After I made sure all my customers were happy, I went to the vamp's table. 'What can I do for you?' I asked, in the lowest voice I could manage. I knew the vamp could hear me; their hearing is phenomenal, and their vision is not far behind in acuity.

'You're Sookie Stackhouse?' asked the vamp. She was very tall, just under six feet, and she was of some racial blend that had turned out awfully well. Her skin was a golden color, and her hair was thick and coarse and dark. She'd had it cornrowed, and her arms were weighed down with jewelry. Her clothes, in contrast, were simple; she wore a severely tailored white blouse with long sleeves, and black leggings with black sandals.

'Yes,' I said. 'Can I help you?' She was looking at me with an expression I could only identify as doubtful.

'Pam sent me here,' she said. 'My name is Felicia.' Her voice was as lilting and exotic as her appearance. It made you think about rum drinks and beaches.

'How-de-do, Felicia,' I said politely. 'I hope Pam is well.'

Since vampires don't have variable health, this was a stumper for Felicia. 'She seems all right,' the vamp said uncertainly. 'She has sent me here to identify myself to you.'

'Okay, I know you now,' I said, just as confused as Felicia had been.

'She said you had a habit of killing the bartenders of Fangtasia,' Felicia said, her lovely doe eyes wide with amazement. 'She said I must come to beg your mercy. But you just seem like a human, to me.'

That Pam. 'She was just teasing you,' I said as gently as I could. I didn't think Felicia was the sharpest tool in the shed. Super hearing and super strength do not equal super intelligence. 'Pam and I are friends, sort of, and she likes to embarrass me. I guess she likes to do the same thing to you, Felicia. I have no intention of harming anyone.' Felicia looked skeptical. 'It's true, I have a bad history with the bartenders of Fangtasia, but that's just, ah, coincidence,' I babbled on. 'And I am really, truly just a human.'

After chewing that over for a moment, Felicia looked relieved, which made her even prettier. Pam often had multiple reasons for doing something, and I found myself wondering if she'd sent Felicia here so I could observe her attractions – which of course would be obvious to Eric. Pam might be trying to stir up trouble. She hated a dull life.

'You go back to Shreveport and have a good time with your boss,' I said, trying to sound kind.

'Eric?' the lovely vampire said. She seemed startled. 'He's good to work for, but I'm not a lover of men.'

I glanced over at my tables, not only checking to see if anyone urgently needed a drink, but to see who'd picked up on that line of dialogue. Hoyt's tongue was practically hanging out, and Catfish looked as though he'd been caught in the headlights. Dago was happily shocked. 'So, Felicia, how'd you end up in Shreveport, if you don't mind me asking?' I turned my attention back to the new vamp.

'Oh, my friend Indira asked me to come. She said servitude with Eric is not so bad.' Felicia shrugged, to show how 'not so bad' it was. 'He doesn't demand sexual services if the woman is not so inclined, and he asks in return only a few hours in the bar and special chores from time to time.'

'So he has a reputation as a good boss?'

'Oh, yes.' Felicia looked almost surprised. 'He's no softie, of course.'

Softie was not a word you could use in the same sentence as *Eric*.

'And you can't cross him. He doesn't forgive that,' she continued thoughtfully. 'But as long as you fulfill your obligations to him, he'll do the same for you.'

I nodded. That more or less fit with my impression of Eric, and I knew Eric very well in some respects . . . though not at all in others.

'This will be much better than Arkansas,' Felicia said.

'Why'd you leave Arkansas?' I asked, because I just couldn't help it. Felicia was the simplest vampire I'd ever met.

'Peter Threadgill,' she said. 'The king. He just married your queen.

Sophie-Anne Leclerq of Louisiana was by no means *my* queen, but out of curiosity, I wanted to continue the conversation.

'What's so wrong with Peter Threadgill?'

That was a poser for Felicia. She mulled it over. 'He holds grudges,' she said, frowning. 'He's never pleased with what he has. It's not enough that he's the oldest, strongest vampire in the state. Once he became king – and he'd schemed for years to work his way up to it – he still wasn't content. There was something wrong with the state, you see?'

'Like, 'Any state that would have me for a king isn't a good state to be king of'?'

'Exactly,' Felicia said, as if I were very clever to think of such a phrase. 'He negotiated with Louisiana for months and months, and even Jade Flower got tired of hearing about the queen. Then she finally agreed to the alliance. After a week of celebrating, the king grew sullen again. Suddenly, that wasn't good enough. She had to love him. She had to give up everything for him.' Felicia shook her head at the vagaries of royalty.

'So it wasn't a love match?'

'That's the last thing vampire kings and queens marry for,' Felicia said. 'Now he is having his visit with the queen in New Orleans, and I'm glad I'm at the other end of the state.'

I didn't grasp the concept of a married couple visiting, but I was sure that sooner or later I'd understand.

I would have been interested in hearing more, but it was time for me to get back to my section and work. 'Thanks for visiting, Felicia, and don't worry about a thing. I'm glad you're working for Eric,' I said.

Felicia smiled at me, a dazzling and toothy experience. 'I'm glad you don't plan on killing me,' she said.

I smiled back at her, a bit hesitantly.

'I assure you, now that I know who you are, you won't get a chance to creep up on me,' Felicia continued. Suddenly, the true vampire looked out from Felicia's eyes, and I shivered. It could be fatal to underestimate Felicia. Smart, no. Savage, yes.

'I don't plan on creeping up on anyone, much less a vampire,' I said.

She gave me a sharp nod, and then she glided out the door as suddenly as she'd come in.

'What was all that about?' Arlene asked me, when we happened to be at the bar waiting for orders at the same time. I noticed Sam was listening, as well.

I shrugged. 'She's working at Fangtasia, in Shreveport, and she just wanted to make my acquaintance.'

Arlene stared at me. 'They got to check in with you, now? Sookie, you need to shun the dead and involve yourself more with the living.'

I stared right back. 'Where'd you get an idea like that?'

'You act like I can't think for myself.'

Arlene had never worked out a thought like that in her life. Arlene's middle name was *tolerance*, mostly because she was too easygoing to take a moral stance.

'Well, I'm surprised,' I said, sharply aware of how harshly I'd just evaluated someone I'd always looked on as a friend.

'Well, I been going to church with Rafe Prudhomme.'

I liked Rafe Prudhomme, a very quiet man in his forties who worked for Pelican State Title Company. But I'd never had the chance to get to know him well, never listened in to his thoughts. Maybe that had been a mistake. 'What kind of church does he go to?' I said.

'He's been attending that Fellowship of the Sun, that new church.'

My heart sank, almost literally. I didn't bother to point out that the Fellowship was a collection of bigots who were bound together by hatred and fear. 'It's not really a church, you know. There's a branch of the Fellowship close to here?'

'Minden.' Arlene looked away, the very picture of guilt. 'I knew you wouldn't like that. But I saw the Catholic priest, Father Riordan, there. So even the ordained people think it's okay. We've been the past two Sunday evenings.'

'And you believe that stuff?'

But one of Arlene's customers yelled for her, and she was definitely glad to walk away.

My eyes met Sam's, and we looked equally troubled. The Fellowship of the Sun was an antivampire, antitolerance organization, and its influence was spreading. Some of the Fellowship enclaves were not militant, but many of them preached hatred and fear in its most extreme form. If the Fellowship had a secret underground hit list, I was surely on it. The Fellowship founders, Steve and Sarah Newlin, had been driven out of their most lucrative church in Dallas because I'd interfered with their plans. I'd survived a couple of assassination attempts since then, but there was always the chance the Fellowship would track me down and ambush me. They'd seen me in Dallas, they'd seen me in Jackson, and sooner or later they'd figure out who I was and where I lived.

I had plenty to worry about.

Chapter 11

The next morning, Tanya showed up at my house. It was Sunday, and I was off work, and I felt pretty cheerful. After all, Crystal was healing, Quinn seemed to like me, and I hadn't heard any more from Eric, so maybe he would leave me alone. I try to be optimistic. My gran's favorite saying from the Bible was, 'Sufficient unto the day is the evil thereof'. She had explained that that meant that you don't worry about tomorrow, or about things you can't change. I tried to practice that philosophy, though most days it was hard. Today it was easy.

The birds were tweeting and chirping, the bugs were buzzing, and the pollen-heavy air was full of peace as if it were yet another plant emission. I was sitting on the front porch in my pink robe, sipping my coffee, listening to *Car Talk* on Red River Radio, and feeling really good, when a little Dodge Dart chugged up my driveway. I didn't recognize the car, but I did recognize the driver. All my peacefulness vanished in a puff of suspicion. Now that I knew about the proximity of a new Fellowship conclave, Tanya's inquisitive presence seemed even more suspicious. I was not happy to see her at my home. Common courtesy forbade me from warning her off, with no more provocation than I'd had, but I wasn't giving her any welcoming smile when I lowered my feet to the porch and stood.

'Good morning, Sookie!' she called as she got out of her car.

'Tanya,' I said, just to acknowledge the greeting.

She paused halfway to the steps. 'Um, everything okay?'

I didn't speak.

'I should have called first, huh?' She tried to look winsome and rueful.

'That would have been better. I don't like unannounced visitors.'

'Sorry, I promise I'll call next time.' She resumed her progress over the stepping stones to the steps. 'Got an extra cup of coffee?'

I violated one of the most basic rules of hospitality. 'No, not this morning,' I said. I went to stand at the top of the steps to block her way onto the porch.

'Well ... Sookie,' she said, her voice uncertain. 'You really are a grump in the morning.'

I looked down at her steadily.

'No wonder Bill Compton's dating someone else,' Tanya said with a little laugh. She knew immediately she'd made an error. 'Sorry,' she added hastily, 'maybe I haven't had enough coffee myself. I shouldn't have said that. That Selah Pumphrey's a bitch, huh?'

Too late now, Tanya. I said, 'At least you know where you stand with Selah.' That was clear enough, right? 'I'll see you at work.'

'Okay. I'll call next time, you hear?' She gave me a bright, empty smile.

'I hear you.' I watched her get back into the little car. She gave me a cheerful wave and, with a lot of extra maneuvering, she turned the Dart around and headed back to Hummingbird Road.

I watched her go, waiting until the sound of the engine had completely died away before I resumed my seat. I left my book on the plastic table beside my lawn chair and sipped the rest of my coffee without the pleasure that had accompanied the first few mouthfuls.

Tanya was up to something.

She practically had a neon sign flashing above her head. I wished the sign would be obliging enough to tell me what she was, who she worked for, and what her goal might be, but I guessed I'd just have to find that out myself. I was going to listen to her head every chance I got, and if that didn't work – and sometimes it doesn't, because not only was she a shifter, but you can't make people think about what you need them to, on demand – I would have to take more drastic action.

Not that I was sure what that would be.

In the past year, somehow I'd assumed the role of guardian of the weird in my little corner of our state. I was the poster girl for inter-species tolerance. I'd learned a lot about the other universe, the one that surrounded the (mostly oblivious) human race. It was kind of neat, knowing stuff that other people didn't. But it complicated my already difficult life, and it led me into dangerous byways among beings who desperately wanted to keep their existence a secret.

The phone rang inside the house, and I stirred myself from my unhappy thoughts to answer it.

'Hey, babe,' said a warm voice on the other end.

'Quinn,' I said, trying not to sound too happy. Not that I was emotionally invested in this man, but I sure needed something positive to happen right now, and Quinn was both formidable and attractive.

'What are you doing?'

'Oh, sitting on my front porch drinking coffee in my bathrobe.'

'I wish I was there to have a cup with you.'

Hmmm. Idle wish, or serious 'ask me over'?

'There's plenty in the pot,' I said cautiously.

'I'm in Dallas, or I'd be there in a flash,' he said. Deflation. 'When did you leave?' I asked, because that seemed the safest, least prying question.

'Yesterday. I got a call from the mother of a guy who works for me from time to time. He quit in the middle of a job we were working on in New Orleans, weeks ago. I was pretty pissed at him, but I wasn't exactly worried. He was kind of a free-floating guy, had a lot of irons in the fire that took him all over the country. But his mom says he still hasn't shown up anywhere, and she thinks something's happened to him. I'm looking around his house and going through his files to help her out, but I'm reaching a dead end. The track seems to have ended in New Orleans. I'll be driving back to Shreveport tomorrow. Are you working?'

'Yes, early shift. I'll be off around five-ish.'

'So can I invite myself over for dinner? I'll bring the steaks. You got a grill?'

'As a matter of fact, I do. It's pretty old, but it works.'

'Got coals?'

'I'd have to check.' I hadn't cooked out since my grandmother had died.

'No problem. I'll bring some.'

'Okay,' I said. 'I'll fix everything else.'

'We have a plan.'

'See you at six?'

'Six it is.'

'Okay, good-bye then.'

Actually, I would have liked to talk to him longer, but I wasn't sure what to say, since I'd never had the experience of much idle chitchat with boys. My dating career had begun last year, when I'd met Bill. I had a lot of catching up to do. I was not like, say, Lindsay Popken, who'd been Miss Bon Temps the year I graduated from high school. Lindsay was able to reduce boys to drooling idiots and keep them trailing after her like stunned hyenas. I'd watched her at it often and still could not understand the phenomenon. It never seemed to me she talked about anything in particular. I'd even listened to her brain, but it was mostly full of white noise. Lindsay's technique, I'd concluded, was instinctive, and it was based on never saying anything serious.

Oh well, enough of reminiscence. I went into the house to see what I needed to do to get it ready for Quinn's visit the next evening and to make a list of necessary purchases. It was a happy way to spend a Sunday afternoon. I'd go shopping. I stepped into the shower contemplating a pleasurable day.

A knock at my front door interrupted me about thirty minutes later as I was putting on some lipstick. This time I looked through the peephole. My heart sank. However, I was obliged to open the door.

A familiar long black limo was parked in my drive. My only previous experience with that limo led me to expect unpleasant news and trouble.

The man – the being – standing on my front porch was the personal representative and lawyer for the vampire queen of Louisiana, and his name was Mr Cataliades, emphasis on the second syllable. I'd first met Mr Cataliades when he'd come to let me know that my cousin Hadley had died, leaving her estate to me. Not only had Hadley died, she'd been murdered, and the vampire responsible had been punished right before my eyes. The night had been full of multiple shocks: discovering not only that Hadley had left this world, but she'd left it as a vampire, and she'd been the favorite of the queen, in a biblical sense.

Hadley had been one of the few remaining members of my family, and I felt her loss; at the same time, I had to admit that Hadley, in her teenage years, had been the cause of much grief to her mother and much pain to my grandmother. If she'd lived, maybe she'd have tried to make up for that – or maybe she wouldn't. She hadn't had the chance.

I took a deep breath. I opened the door. 'Mr Cataliades,' I said, feeling my anxious smile stretch my lips unconvincingly. The queen's lawyer was a man composed of circles, his face round and his belly rounder, his eyes beady and circular and dark. I didn't think he was human – or perhaps not wholly human – but I wasn't sure what he could be. Not a vampire; here he was, in broad daylight. Not Were, or shifter; no red buzz surrounding his brain.

'Miss Stackhouse,' he said, beaming at me. 'What a pleasure to see you again.'

'And you also,' I said, lying through my teeth. I hesitated, suddenly feeling achy and jumpy. I was sure Cataliades, like all the other supes I encountered, would know I was having my time of the month. Just great. 'Won't you come in?'

'Thank you, my dear,' he said, and I stepped aside, filled with misgivings, to let this creature enter my home.

'Please, have a seat,' I said, determined to be polite. 'Would you care for a drink?'

'No, thank you. You seem to be on your way somewhere.' He was frowning at the purse I'd tossed on my chair on my way to the door.

Okay, something I wasn't understanding, here. 'Yes,' I said, raising my eyebrows in query. 'I had planned on going to the grocery store, but I can put that off for an hour or so.'

'You're not packed to return to New Orleans with me?'

'What?'

'You received my message?'

'What message?'

We stared at each other, mutually dismayed.

'I sent a messenger to you with a letter from my law office,' Mr Cataliades said. 'She should have arrived here four nights ago. The letter was sealed with magic. No one but you could open it.'

I shook my head, my blank expression telling him what I needed to say.

'You are saying that Gladiola didn't get here? I expected her to arrive here Wednesday night, at the latest. She wouldn't have come in a car. She likes to run.' He smiled indulgently for just a second. But then the smile vanished. If I'd blinked, I would have missed it. 'Wednesday night,' he prompted me.

'That was the night I heard someone outside the house,' I said. I shivered, remembering how tense I'd been that night. 'No one came to the door. No one tried to break in. No one called to me. There was only the sense of something moving, and all the animals fell silent.'

It was impossible for someone as powerful as the supernatural lawyer to look bewildered, but he did look very thoughtful. After a moment he rose ponderously and bowed to me, gesturing toward the door. We went back outside. On the front porch, he turned to the car and beckoned.

A very lean woman slid from behind the wheel. She was younger than me, maybe in her very early twenties. Like Mr Cataliades, she was only partly human. Her dark red hair was spiked, her makeup laid on with a trowel. Even the striking outfit of the girl in the Hair of the Dog paled in comparison to this young woman's. She wore striped stockings, alternating bands of shocking pink and black, and her ankle boots were black and extremely high-heeled. Her skirt was transparent, black, and ruffled, and her pink tank top was her sole upper garment.

She just about took my breath away.

'Hi, howareya?' she said brightly, her smile revealing very sharp white teeth a dentist would fall in love with, right before he lost a finger.

'Hello,' I said. I held out my hand. 'I'm Sookie Stackhouse.'

She covered the ground between us very speedily, even in the ridiculous heels. Her hand was tiny and bony. 'Pleasedtameetya,' she said. 'Diantha.'

'Pretty name,' I said, after I figured out it wasn't another run-on sentence.

'Thankya.'

'Diantha,' Mr Cataliades said, 'I need to you to conduct a search for me.'

'To find?'

'I'm very afraid we are looking for Glad's remains.'

The smile fell from the girl's face.

'No shit,' she said quite clearly.

'No, Diantha,' the lawyer said. 'No shit.'

Diantha sat on the steps and pulled off her shoes and her striped tights. It didn't seem to bother her at all that without the tights, her transparent skirt left nothing to the imagination. Since Mr Cataliades's expression didn't change in the least, I decided I could be worldly enough to ignore it, too.

As soon as she'd disencumbered herself, the girl was off, moving low to the ground, sniffing in a way that told me she was even less human than I'd estimated. But she didn't move like the Weres I'd observed, or the shape-shifting panthers. Her body seemed to bend and turn in a way that simply wasn't mammalian.

Mr Cataliades watched her, his hands folded in front of him. He was silent, so I was, too. The girl darted around the yard like a demented hummingbird, vibrating almost visibly with an unearthly energy.

For all that movement, I couldn't hear her make a sound.

It wasn't long before she stopped at a clump of bushes at the very edge of the woods. She was bent over looking at the ground, absolutely still. Then, not looking up, she raised her hand like a schoolchild who'd discovered the correct answer.

'Let us go see,' Mr Cataliades suggested, and in his deliberate way he strode across the driveway, then the grass, to a clump of wax myrtles at the edge of the woods. Diantha didn't look up as we neared, but remained focused on something on the ground behind the bushes. Her face was streaked with tears. I took a deep breath and looked down at what held her attention.

This girl had been a little younger than Diantha, but she too was thin and slight. Her hair had been dyed bright gold, in sharp contrast with her milk chocolate skin. Her lips had drawn back in death, giving her a snarl that revealed teeth as white and sharp as Diantha's. Oddly enough, she didn't seem as worse for wear as I would have expected, given the fact that she might have been out here for several days. There were only a few ants walking over her, not at all the usual insect activity ... and she didn't look bad at all for a person who'd been cut in two at the waist.

My head buzzed for a minute, and I was little scared I would go down on one knee. I'd seen some bad stuff, including two massacres, but I'd never seen anyone divided like this girl had been. I could see her insides. They didn't look like human insides. And it appeared the two halves had been separately seared shut. There was very little leakage.

'Cut with a steel sword,' Mr Cataliades said. 'A very good sword.'

'What shall we do with her remains?' I asked. 'I can get an old blanket.' I knew without even asking that we would not be calling the police.

'We have to burn her,' Mr Cataliades said. 'Over there, on the gravel of your parking area, Miss Stackhouse, would be safest. You're not expecting any company?'

'No,' I said, shocked on many levels. 'I'm sorry, why must she be ... burned?'

'No one will eat a demon, or even a half demon like Glad or Diantha,' he said, as if explaining that the sun rises in the east. 'Not even the bugs, as you see. The ground will not digest her, as it does humans.'

'You don't want to take her home? To her people?'

'Diantha and I are her people. It's not our custom to take the dead back to the place where they were living.'

'But what killed her?'

Mr Cataliades raised an eyebrow.

'No, of course she was killed by something cutting through her middle, I'm seeing that! But what wielded the blade?'

'Diantha, what do you think?' Mr Cataliades said, as if he were conducting a class.

'Something real, real strong and sneaky,' Diantha said. 'It got close to Gladiola, and she weren't no fool. We're not easy to kill.'

'I have seen no sign of the letter she was carrying, either.' Mr Cataliades leaned over and peered at the ground. Then he straightened. 'Have you got firewood, Miss Stackhouse?'

'Yessir, there's a good bit of split oak in the back by the toolshed.' Jason had cut up some trees the last ice storm had downed.

'Do you need to pack, my dear?'

'Yes,' I said, almost too overwhelmed to answer. 'What? What for?'

'The trip to New Orleans. You can go now, can't you?'

'I . . . I guess so. I'll have to ask my boss.'

'Then Diantha and I will take care of this while you are getting permission and packing,' Mr Cataliades said, and I blinked.

'All right,' I said. I didn't seem to be able to think very clearly.

'Then we need to leave for New Orleans,' he said. 'I'd thought I'd find you ready. I thought that Glad had stayed to help you.'

I wrenched my gaze from the body to stare up at the lawyer. 'I'm just not understanding this,' I said. But I remembered something. 'My friend Bill wanted to go to New Orleans when I went to clean out Hadley's apartment,' I said. 'If he can, if he can arrange it, would that be all right with you?'

'You want Bill to go,' he said, and there was a tinge of surprise in his voice. 'Bill is in favor with the queen, so I wouldn't mind if he went.'

'Okay, I'll have to get in touch with him when it's full dark,' I said. 'I hope he's in town.'

I could have called Sam, but I wanted to go somewhere away from the strange funeral on my driveway. When I drove off, Mr Cataliades was carrying the limp small body out of the woods. He had the bottom half.

A silent Diantha was filling a wheelbarrow with wood.

Chapter 12

'Sam,' I said, keeping my voice low, 'I need a few days off.' When I'd knocked on his trailer door, I'd been surprised to find he had guests, though I'd seen the other vehicles parked by Sam's truck. JB du Rone and Andy Bellefleur were perched on Sam's couch, beer and potato chips set handily on the coffee table. Sam was engaging in a male bonding ritual. 'Watching sports?' I added, trying not to sound astonished. I waved over Sam's shoulder to JB and Andy, and they waved back: JB enthusiastically, and Andy less happily. If you can be said to wave ambivalently, that was what he did.

'Uh, yeah, basketball. LSU's playing . . . oh, well. You need the time off right now?'

'Yes,' I said 'There's kind of an emergency.'

'Can you tell me about it?'

'I have to go to New Orleans to clean out my cousin Hadley's apartment,' I said.

'And that has to be right now? You know Tanya is still new, and Charlsie just quit, she says for good. Arlene's not as reliable as she used to be, and Holly and Danielle are still pretty shaky since the school incident.'

'I'm sorry,' I said. 'If you want to let me go and get someone else, I'll understand.' It broke my heart to say that, but in fairness to Sam, I had to.

Sam shut the trailer door behind him and stepped out on the porch.

He looked hurt. 'Sookie,' he said, after a second, 'you've been completely reliable for at least five years. You've only asked for time off maybe two or three times total. I'm not going to fire you because you need a few days.'

'Oh. Well, good.' I could feel my face redden. I wasn't used to praise. 'Liz's daughter might be able to come help.'

'I'll call down the list,' he said mildly. 'How are you getting to New Orleans?'

'I have a ride.'

'Who with?' he asked, his voice gentle. He didn't want me to get mad at his minding my business. (I could tell that much.)

'The queen's lawyer,' I said, in an even quieter voice. Though tolerant of vampires in general, the citizens of Bon Temps might get a little excitable if they knew that their state had a vampire queen, and that her secret government affected them in many ways. On the other hand, given the disrepute of Louisiana politics, they might just think it was business as usual.

'You're going to clean out Hadley's apartment?'

I'd told Sam about my cousin's second, and final, death.

'Yes. And I need to find out about whatever she left me.'

'This seems real sudden.' Sam looked troubled. He ran a hand over his curly red-gold hair until it stood out from his head in a wild halo. He needed a haircut.

'Yes, to me, too. Mr Cataliades tried to tell me earlier, but the messenger was killed.'

I heard Andy yelling at the television as some big play roused his excitement. Strange, I'd never thought of Andy as a sports guy, or JB either, for that matter. I'd never added up all the time I'd heard men thinking about assists and three-pointers when the women with them were talking about the need for new kitchen drapes or Rudy's bad grade in algebra. When I did add it up, I wondered if the purpose of sports wasn't to give guys a safe alternative to thornier issues.

'You shouldn't go,' Sam said instantly. 'It sounds like it could be dangerous.'

I shrugged. 'I have to,' I said. 'Hadley left it to me; I have to do it.'

I was far from as calm as I was trying to look, but it didn't seem to me like it would do any good to kick and scream about it.

Sam began to speak, then reconsidered. Finally, he said, 'Is this about money, Sook? Do you need the money she left you?'

'Sam, I don't know if Hadley had a penny to her name. She was my cousin, and I have to do this for her. Besides . . .' I was on the verge of telling him the trip to New Orleans had to be important in some way, since someone was trying so hard to keep me from going.

But Sam tended to be a worrier, especially if I was involved, and I didn't want to get him all worked up when nothing he could say would dissuade me from going. I don't think of myself as a stubborn person, but I figured this was the last service I could perform for my cousin.

'What about taking Jason?' Sam suggested, taking my hand. 'He was Hadley's cousin, too.'

'Evidently, he and Hadley were on the outs toward the end,' I said. 'That's why she left her stuff to me. Besides, Jason's got a lot on his plate right now.'

'What, something besides bossing Hoyt around and screwing every woman who'll stand still long enough?'

I stared at Sam. I'd known he was not a big fan of my brother's, but I hadn't known his dislike went this deep.

'Yes, actually,' I said, my voice as cold and frosty as a beer mug. I wasn't about to explain my brother's girlfriend's miscarriage while I was standing on a doorstep, especially given Sam's antagonism.

Sam looked away, shaking his head in disgust with himself. 'I'm sorry, Sookie, I'm really sorry. I just think Jason should pay more attention to the only sister he's got. You're so loyal to him.'

'Well, he wouldn't let anything happen to me,' I said, bewildered. 'Jason would stand up for me.'

Before Sam said, 'Of course,' I caught the flicker of doubt in his mind.

'I have to go pack,' I said. I hated to walk away. No matter his feelings about Jason, Sam was important to me, and leaving him with this unhappiness between us shook me a bit. But I could hear the men roaring at some play inside the trailer, and I knew I had to let him get back to his guests and his Sunday afternoon pleasure. He gave me a kiss on the cheek.

'Call me if you need me,' he said, and he looked as if he wanted to say a lot more. I nodded, turned away, and went down the steps to my car.

'Bill, you said you wanted to go to New Orleans with me when I went to close out Hadley's estate?' Finally it was full dark, and I was able to call Bill. Selah Pumphrey had answered the phone and called Bill to talk to me in a very chilly voice.

'Yes.'

'Mr Cataliades is here, and he wants to leave real shortly.'

'You could have told me earlier, when you knew he was coming.' But Bill didn't sound truly angry, or even surprised.

'He sent a messenger, but she was killed in my woods.'

'You found the body?'

'No, a girl who came with him did. Her name's Diantha.'

'Then it was Gladiola who died.'

'Yes,' I said, surprised. 'How did you know?'

Bill said, 'When you come into a state, it's only polite to check in with the queen or king if you're staying for any length of time. I saw the girls from time to time, since they function as the queen's messengers.'

I looked at the telephone in my hands with as much thoughtfulness as if it'd been Bill's face. I couldn't help but think all these thoughts in quick succession. Bill wandered in my woods . . . Gladiola had been killed in my woods. She'd been killed without noise, efficiently and accurately, by someone well versed in the lore of the supernatural, someone who'd known to use a steel sword, someone who'd been strong enough to sweep a sword through Gladiola's entire body.

These were characteristics of a vampire – but any number of super-natural creatures could do the same.

To get close enough to wield the sword, the killer had been super quick or quite innocuous-looking. Gladiola hadn't suspected she was going to be killed.

Maybe she had known the murderer.

And the way Gladiola's little body had been left, tossed in the bushes carelessly . . . the killer hadn't cared if I found her body or not, though of course the demonic lack of putrefaction had played a role there. Her *silence* was all the killer had wanted. Why had she been killed? Her message, if I was getting the whole story from the heavy lawyer, had simply been for me to prepare for my trip to New Orleans. I was going, anyway, though she hadn't had a chance to deliver it. So what had been gained by silencing her? Two or three more days of ignorance on my part? It didn't seem to me that was much motivation.

Bill was waiting for me to end the long pause in our conversation, one of the things I'd always liked about him. He didn't feel the need to fill conversational pauses.

'They burned her in the driveway,' I said.

'Of course. It's the only way to dispose of anything with demon blood,' Bill said, but absently, as if he'd been thinking deep thoughts about something else.

'"Of course"? How was I supposed to know that?'

'At least you know now. Bugs won't bite them, their bodies won't corrupt, and sex with them is corrosive.'

'Diantha seems so perky and obedient.'

'Of course, when she's with her uncle.'

'Mr Cataliades is her uncle,' I said. 'Glad's uncle, too?'

'Oh, yes. Cataliades is mostly demon, but his half brother Nergal is a full demon. Nergal's had several half-human children. All by different mothers, obviously.'

I wasn't sure why this was so obvious, and I wasn't about to ask him.

'You're letting Selah listen to all this?'

'No, she's in the bathroom showering.'

Okay, still feeling jealous. And envious: Selah had the luxury of ignorance, while I did not. What a nicer world it was when you didn't know about the supernatural side of life.

Sure. Then you just had to worry about famine, war, serial killers, AIDS, tsunamis, old age, and the Ebola virus.

'*Can* it, Sookie,' I said to myself, and Bill said, 'Pardon me?'

I shook myself. 'Listen, Bill, if you want to go to New Orleans with me and the lawyer, be over here in the next thirty minutes. Otherwise,

I'll assume you have other fish to fry.' I hung up. I would have a whole drive to the Big Easy to think about all this.

'He'll be here, or not, in the next thirty minutes,' I called out the front door to the lawyer.

'Good to hear,' Mr Cataliades called back. He was standing by Diantha while she was hosing the black smudge off my gravel.

I trotted back to my room and packed my toothbrush. I ran down my mental checklist. I'd left a message on Jason's answering machine, I'd asked Tara if she'd mind running out to get my mail and my papers every day, I'd watered my few houseplants (my grandmother believed that plants, like birds and dogs, belonged outside; ironically enough, I'd gotten some houseplants when she died, and I was trying hard to keep them alive).

Quinn!

He wasn't with his cell phone, or wasn't answering it, at any rate. I left a voice mail message. Only our second date, and I had to cancel it.

I found it hard to figure out exactly how much to tell him. 'I have to go to New Orleans to clean out my cousin's apartment,' I said. 'She lived in a place on Chloe Street, and I don't know if there's a phone or not. So I guess I'll just call you when I get back? I'm sorry our plans changed.' I hoped he would at least be able to tell I was genuinely regretful that I wouldn't be able to eat dinner with him.

Bill arrived just as I was carrying my bag out to the car. He had a backpack, which struck me as funny. I suppressed my smile when I saw his face. Even for a vampire, Bill looked pale and drawn. He ignored me.

'Cataliades,' he said, with a nod. 'I'll hitch a ride with you, if that suits you. Sorry about your loss.' He nodded to Diantha, who was alternating long, furious monologues in a language I didn't understand with the sort of frozen-faced stare I associated with deep shock.

'My niece died an untimely death,' Cataliades said, in his deliberate way. 'She will not go unavenged.'

'Of course not,' Bill said, in his cool voice. While Diantha reached in to pop the trunk, Bill moved to the back of the car to toss his backpack into its depths. I locked my front door behind me and hurried down the steps to put my bag in with his. I caught a glimpse of his face before he registered my approach, and that glimpse shook me.

Bill looked desperate.

Chapter 13

There were moments on the drive south when I felt like sharing all my thoughts with my companions. Mr Cataliades drove for a couple of hours, and then Diantha took the wheel. Bill and the lawyer didn't have a lot of small talk, and I had too many things on my mind for social chitchat, so we were a silent bunch.

I was as comfortable as I'd ever been in a vehicle. I had the rear-facing seat all to myself, while Bill and the lawyer sat opposite me. The limo was the last word in automotive luxury, at least in my eyes. Upholstered in leather and padded to the nth degree, the limo boasted lots of leg room, bottles of water and synthetic blood, and a little basket of snacks. Mr Cataliades was real fond of Cheetos.

I closed my eyes and thought for a while. Bill's brain, naturally, was a null to me, and Mr Cataliades's brain was very nearly so. His brain emitted a low-level buzz that was almost soothing, while the same emanation, from Diantha's brain, vibrated at a higher pitch. I'd been on the edge of a thought when I'd been talking with Sam, and I wanted to pursue it while I could still catch hold of its tail. Once I'd worked it through, I decided to share it.

'Mr Cataliades,' I said, and the big man opened his eyes. Bill was already looking at me. Something was going on in Bill's head, something weird. 'You know that Wednesday, the night your girl was supposed to appear on my doorstep, I heard something in the woods.'

The lawyer nodded. Bill nodded.

'So we assume that was the night she was killed.'

Again with the double nods.

'But why? Whoever did it had to know that sooner or later you would contact me, or come to see me, to find out what had happened. Even if the killer didn't know the message Gladiola was bringing, they'd figure that she'd be missed sooner rather than later.'

'That's reasonable,' Mr Cataliades said.

'But on Friday night, I was attacked in a parking lot in Shreveport.'

I got my money's worth out of that statement, I can tell you. If I'd hooked both the men up to electroshock machines and given them a jolt, the reaction couldn't have been more dynamic.

'Why didn't you tell me?' Bill demanded. His eyes were glowing with anger, and his fangs were out.

'Why should I? We don't date any more. We don't see each other regularly.'

'So this is your punishment for my dating someone else, keeping something so serious from me?'

Even in my wildest fantasies (which had included such scenes as Bill breaking up with Selah in Merlotte's, and his subsequent public confession to me that Selah had never measured up to my charms), I'd never envisioned such a reaction. Though it was very dark in the car's interior, I thought I saw Mr Cataliades roll his eyes. Maybe he thought that was over the top, too.

'Bill, I never set out to punish you,' I said. At least I didn't think I had. 'We just don't share details of our lives any more. Actually, I was out on a date when the attack occurred. I believe I'm used to us not being part of the scenery.'

'Who was your date?'

'Not that it's actually your business, but it is pertinent to the rest of the story. I'm dating Quinn.' We'd had one date and planned another. That counted as 'dating', right?

'Quinn the tiger,' Bill said expressionlessly.

'Hats off to you, young lady!' Mr Cataliades said. 'You are courageous and discerning.'

'I'm not really asking for approval,' I said as neutrally as I could manage. 'Or disapproval, for that matter.' I waved my hand to show that topic was off the table. 'Here's what I want you to know. The attackers were very young Weres.'

'Weres,' Mr Cataliades said. As we sped through the darkness, I couldn't decipher his expression or his voice. 'What kind of Weres?'

Good question. The lawyer was on the ball. 'Bitten Weres,' I said. 'And I believe they were on drugs, as well.' That gave them pause.

'What happened during the attack and afterward?' Bill said, breaking a long silence.

I described the attack and its aftermath.

'So Quinn took you to the Hair of the Dog,' Bill said. 'He thought that was an appropriate response?'

I could tell Bill was furious, but as usual, I didn't know why.

'It may have worked,' Cataliades said. 'Consider. Nothing else has happened to her, so apparently Quinn's threat took root.'

I tried not to say 'Huh?' but I guess Bill's vampire eyes could see it on my face.

'He challenged them,' Bill said, sounding even colder than usual. 'He told them you were under his protection, and that they harmed you at their peril. He accused them of being behind the attack, but at the same time reminded them that even if they didn't know of it, they were responsible for bringing the one who planned it to justice.'

'I got all that on the spot,' I said patiently. 'And I think Quinn was warning them, not challenging them. Big difference. What I didn't get was ... nothing should happen in the pack without Patrick Furnan's knowledge, right? Since he's the grand high poobah now. So why not go straight to Patrick? Why go to the local watering hole?'

'What a very interesting question,' Cataliades said. 'What would your answer be, Compton?'

'The one that springs to mind ... Quinn might know there's a rebellion fomenting against Furnan already. He's added fuel to it by letting the rebels know that Furnan is trying to kill a friend of the pack.'

We're not talking armies here. There might be thirty-five members of the pack, maybe a little more with servicemen from Barksdale Air Force Base added in. It would take only five people to make a rebellion.

'Why don't they just take him out?' I asked. I'm not politically minded, as I guess you can tell.

Mr Cataliades was smiling at me. It was dark in the car, but I just knew it. 'So direct, so classic,' he said. 'So American. Well, Miss Stackhouse, it's like this. The Weres can be savage, oh yes! But they do have rules. The penalty for killing the packleader, except by open challenge, is death.'

'But who would, ah, enact that penalty, if the pack kept the killing secret?'

'Unless the pack is willing to kill the whole Furnan family, I think the Furnan family would be delighted to inform the Were hierarchy of Patrick's murder. Now maybe you know the Shreveport Weres better than most. Are there ruthless killers among them who wouldn't mind slaughtering Furnan's wife and children?'

I thought about Amanda, Alcide, and Maria-Star. 'That's a whole different kettle of fish. I see that.'

'Now vampires, you'd find many more who were up for that kind of treachery,' the lawyer said. 'Don't you think so, Mr Compton?'

There was a curious silence. 'Vampires have to pay a price if they kill another vampire,' Bill said stiffly.

'If they're affiliated with a clan,' Mr Cataliades said mildly.

'I didn't know vampires had clans,' I said. Learning something new all the time, that was me.

'It's a fairly new concept. It's an attempt to regularize the vampire world so it looks more palatable to humans. If the American model catches on, the vampire world will resemble a huge multinational corporation more than a loosely ruled collection of vicious bloodsuckers.'

'Lose some of the color and tradition, gain some of the profits,' I murmured. 'Like Wal-Mart versus Dad's Downtown Hardware.' Mr Cataliades laughed.

'You're right, Miss Stackhouse. Exactly. There are those in both camps, and the summit we'll attend in a few weeks will have this item high on the agenda.'

'To get from what's going to take place weeks from now and get back to something a little more on topic, why would Patrick Furnan try to kill me? He doesn't like me, and he knows I'd stand with Alcide if I had to make a choice between 'em, but so what? I'm not important. Why would he plan all this – find the two boys who would do it, bite them, send them out to get me and Quinn – if there wasn't some big payoff?'

'You have a knack for asking good questions, Miss Stackhouse. I wish my answers were as good.'

Well, I might as well keep my thoughts to myself if I wasn't going to get any information out of my companions.

The only reason to kill Gladiola, at least the only reason that this direct human could see, was to delay my getting the message that I needed to be ready to leave for New Orleans. Also, Gladiola would have provided some buffer between me and anything that came after me, or at the least she would have been more alert to the attack.

As it was, she'd been lying dead in the woods when I'd gone on my date with Quinn. Whoa. How had the young wolves known where to find me? Shreveport isn't that big, but you couldn't guard every road into town on the off chance I'd show up. On the other hand, if a Were had spotted Quinn and me going into the theater, they'd have known I'd be there for a couple of hours, and that was time enough to arrange something.

If this mastermind had known even earlier, it would have been even easier . . . if someone, say, had known beforehand that Quinn had asked me to go the theater. Who'd known I had a date with Quinn? Well, Tara: I'd told her when I bought my outfit. And I'd mentioned it to Jason, I thought, when I'd called him to inquire after Crystal. I'd told Pam I had a date, but I didn't remember telling her where I was going.

And then there was Quinn himself.

I was so grieved by this idea that I had to suppress tears. It was not like I knew Quinn that well or could judge his character based on the time I'd spent with him. . . . I'd learned over the past few months that you couldn't really know someone that quickly, that learning a person's true character might take years. It had shaken me profoundly, since I'm used to knowing people very well, very quickly. I know them better than they ever suspect. But making mistakes about the character of a few supernaturals had caught me flatfooted, emotionally. Used to the quick assessment my telepathy made possible, I'd been naive and careless.

Now I was surrounded by such creatures.

I snuggled into a corner of the broad seat and shut my eyes. I had to be in my own world for a while, with no one else allowed inside. I fell asleep in the dark car, with a semi-demon and a vampire sitting across from me and a half demon in the driver's seat.

When I woke up, I had my head in Bill's lap. His hand was gently stroking my hair, and the familiar touch of his fingers brought me peace and a stirring of that sensual feeling that Bill had always been able to rouse in me.

It took a second for me to remember where we were and what we were doing, and then I sat up, blinking and tousled. Mr Cataliades was quite still on the opposite seat, and I thought he was asleep, but it was impossible to be sure. If he'd been human, I would've known.

'Where are we?' I asked.

'Almost there,' Bill said. 'Sookie . . .'

'Hmm?' I stretched and yawned and longed for a toothbrush.

'I'll help you go through Hadley's apartment if you want me to.'

I had a feeling he'd changed his mind about what he was going to say, at the last minute.

'If I need help, I know where to go,' I answered. That should be ambiguous enough. I was beginning to get a mighty bad feeling about Hadley's apartment. Maybe Hadley's legacy to me was more in the nature of a curse than a blessing. And yet she'd pointedly excluded Jason, because he had failed her when she'd needed help, so Hadley presumably had meant her bequest to be a boon. On the other hand, Hadley had been a vampire, no longer human, and that would have changed her. Oh, yeah.

Looking out the window, I could see streetlights and a few other cars moving through the gloom. It was raining, and it was four in the morning. I wondered if there was an IHOP anywhere nearby. I'd been to one, once. It had been wonderful. That had been on my only previous trip to New Orleans, when I'd been in high school. We'd been to the aquarium and the slave museum and the church on Jackson Square, the St. Louis Cathedral. It had been wonderful to see something new, to think about all the people who had passed through the same area, what they must have looked like in the clothes of their time. On the other hand, a telepath with poor shielding is not going to have a great time with a bunch of teenagers.

Now my companions were much less easy to read, and quite a bit more dangerous.

We were on a quiet residential street when the limousine pulled to a curb and stopped.

'Your cousin's apartment,' Mr Cataliades said as Diantha opened the door. I was out and on the sidewalk while Mr Cataliades maneuvered himself into the right position to exit, and Bill was stuck behind him.

I was facing a six-foot wall with an opening for the driveway. It was hard to tell, in the uncertain glow of a streetlight, what lay within, but it seemed to be a small courtyard with a very tight circular drive. In the middle of the drive was an explosion of greenery, though I couldn't discern the individual plants. In the right front corner was a tool shed. There was a two-storey building forming an L. To take advantage of the depth of the lot, the building was oriented with the L inverted. Right next door was a similar building, at least as far as I could tell. Hadley's was painted white, with dark green shutters.

'How many apartments are here, and which one is Hadley's?' I asked Mr Cataliades, who was steaming along behind me.

'There's the bottom floor, where the owner lives, and the top floor, which is yours now for as long as you want it. The queen has been paying the rent until the estate was probated. She didn't think it fair that Hadley's estate should do so.' Even for Mr Cataliades, this was a formal speech.

My reaction was muted by my exhaustion, and I could only say, 'I can't think why she didn't just put Hadley's stuff into storage. I could have gone through it all at one of the rental places.'

'You'll get used to way the queen does things,' he said.

Not if I had anything to say about it. 'For right now, can you just show me how to get into Hadley's apartment, so I can unpack and get some sleep?'

'Of course, of course. And dawn is coming, so Mr Compton needs to go to the queen's headquarters to gain shelter for the day.' Diantha had already started up the stairs, which I could just make out. They curved up the short part of the L, which lay to the back of the lot. 'Here is your key, Miss Stackhouse. As soon as Diantha comes down, we'll leave you to it. You can meet the owner tomorrow.'

'Sure,' I said, and trudged up the stairs, holding to the wrought-iron handrail. This wasn't what I had envisioned at all. I thought Hadley would have a place like one of the apartments at the Kingfisher Arms, the only apartment building in Bon Temps. This was like a little bitty mansion.

Diantha had put my sports bag and my big carryall by one of two doors on the second floor. There was a broad, roofed gallery running below the windows and doors of the second floor, which would provide shade for people sitting inside on the ground floor. Magic trembled around all those French windows and the doors. I recognized the smell and feel of it, now. The apartment had been sealed with more than locks.

I hesitated, the key in my hand.

'It will recognize you,' called the lawyer from the courtyard. So I unlocked the door with clumsy hands, and pushed the door open. Warm air rushed out to meet me. This apartment had been closed for weeks. I wondered if anyone had come in to air it out. It didn't smell actively bad, just stale, so I knew the climate control system had been left on. I fumbled around for the switch of the nearest light, a lamp on a marble-topped pedestal to the right of the door. It cast a pool of golden light on the gleaming hardwood floors and some faux antique furniture (at least I was assuming it was faux). I took another step inside the apartment, trying to imagine Hadley here, Hadley who'd worn black lipstick to have her senior picture made and bought her shoes at Payless.

'Sookie,' Bill said behind me, by way of letting me know that he was standing right outside the doorway. I didn't tell him he could come in.

'I have to get to bed now, Bill. I'll see you tomorrow. Do I have the queen's phone number?'

'Cataliades stuck a card in your purse while you were sleeping.'

'Oh, good. Well, night.'

And I shut the door in his face. I was rude, but he was hovering, and I just wasn't up for talking to him. It had shaken me, finding my head in his lap when I woke; it was like we were still a couple.

After a minute I heard his footsteps going back down the stairs. I was never more relieved to be alone in my life. Thanks to the night spent in a car and the brief sleep I'd had, I felt disoriented, rumpled, and desperately in need of a toothbrush. Time to scope out the place, with emphasis on bathroom discovery.

I looked around carefully. The shorter segment of the upside-down L was the living room, where I now stood. Its open plan included a kitchen against the far right wall. On my left, forming the long side of the L, was a hall lined with French windows that opened directly onto the gallery. The wall that formed the other side of the hall was punctuated with doors.

Bags in hand, I started down the hall, peering into each open door. I didn't find the light switch that would illumine the hall, though there must be one, since there were fixtures at regular intervals on the ceiling.

But enough moonlight streamed through the windows of the rooms to enable me to see as much as I needed. The first room was a bathroom, thank God, though after a second I realized it wasn't Hadley's. It was very small and very clean, with a narrow shower stall, a toilet and sink; no toiletries, no personal clutter. I passed it by and glanced in the next doorway, discovering that it opened into a small room that had probably been intended as the guest bedroom. Hadley had set up a computer desk loaded with computer gear, not items of great interest to me.

In addition to a narrow daybed, there was a bookshelf crammed full with boxes and books, and I promised myself I'd go through that tomorrow. The next door was shut, but I cracked it open to peer inside for a second. It was the door to a narrow, deep, walk-in closet lined with shelves full of items that I didn't take the time to identify.

To my relief, the next door was that of the main bathroom, the one with the shower and the tub and a large sink with a dressing table built in. The surface of the surround was littered with cosmetics and an electric curler, still plugged in. Five or six bottles of perfume were lined up on a shelf, and there were crumpled towels in the hamper, spotted with dark blotches. I put my face right down to them; at that range, they emitted an alarming reek. I couldn't understand why the smell hadn't pervaded the entire apartment. I picked up the whole hamper, unlocked the French window on the other side of the hall, and set it outside. I left the light on in the bathroom, because I intended to revisit it shortly.

The last door, set at right angles to all the others and forming the end of the hall, led into Hadley's bedroom. It was big enough, though not as big as my bedroom at home. It held another large closet, crammed full with clothes. The bed was made, not a Hadley trademark, and I wondered who'd been in the apartment since Hadley had been killed. Someone had entered before the place had been sealed by magic. The bedroom, of course, was completely darkened. The windows had been covered by beautifully painted wood panels, and there were two doors to the room. There was just enough space between them for a person to stand.

I set my bags on the floor by Hadley's chest of drawers, and I rooted around until I found my cosmetics bag and my tampons. Trudging back into the bathroom, I extricated my toothbrush and toothpaste from the small bag and had the delight of brushing my teeth and washing my face. I felt a little more human after that, but not much. I switched out the bathroom light and pulled back the covers on the bed, which was low and broad. The sheets startled me so much that I stood there with my lips curled. They were disgusting: black satin, for God's sake! And not even real satin, but some synthetic. Give me percale or 100% cotton, any day. However, I wasn't going to hunt down another set of sheets at this hour of the morning. Besides, what if this was all she had?

I climbed into the king-size bed – well, I slithered into the king-size bed – and after an uneasy wiggle or two to get used to the feel of them, I managed to fall asleep between those sheets just fine.

Chapter 14

Someone was pinching my toe and saying 'Wake up! Wake up!' I roared back to consciousness in a terrified rush, my eyes opening on the unfamiliar room streaming with sunshine. A woman I didn't know was standing at the foot of the bed.

'Who the hell are you?' I was irritated, but not scared. She didn't look dangerous. She was about my age, and she was very tan. Her chestnut hair was short, her eyes a bright blue, and she was wearing khaki shorts and a white shirt that hung open over a coral tank top. She was rushing the season a little.

'I'm Amelia Broadway. I own the building.'

'Why are you in here waking me up?'

'I heard Cataliades in the courtyard last night, and I figured he'd brought you back to clean out Hadley's apartment. I wanted to talk to you.'

'And you couldn't wait until I woke up? And you used a key to get in, instead of ringing the doorbell? What's wrong with you?'

She was definitely startled. For the first time, Amelia Broadway looked as if she realized she could have handled the situation better. 'Well, see, I've been worried,' she said in a subdued way.

'Yeah? Me, too,' I said. 'Join the club. I'm plenty worried right now. Now get out of here and wait for me in the living room, okay?'

'Sure,' she said. 'I can do that.'

I let my heart rate get back to normal before I slid out of bed. Then

I made the bed quickly and pulled some clothes out of my bag. I shuffled into the bathroom, catching a quick glimpse of my uninvited guest as I went from bedroom to bath. She was dusting the living room with a cloth that looked suspiciously like a man's flannel shirt. O-kay.

I showered as quickly as I could, slapped on a little makeup, and came out barefoot but clad in jeans and a blue T-shirt.

Amelia Broadway stopped her housecleaning and stared at me. 'You don't look a thing like Hadley,' she said, and I couldn't decide by her tone if she thought that was a good thing or a bad thing.

'I'm not at all like Hadley, all the way through,' I said flatly.

'Well, that's good. Hadley was pretty awful,' Amelia said unexpectedly. 'Whoops. Sorry, I'm not tactful.'

'Really?' I tried to keep my voice level, but a trace of sarcasm may have leaked through. 'So if you know where the coffee is, can you point me in that direction?' I was looking at the kitchen area for the first time in the daylight. It had exposed brick and copper, a stainless steel food preparation area and a matching refrigerator, and a sink with a faucet that cost more than my clothes. Small, but fancy, like the rest of the place.

All this, for a vampire who didn't really need a kitchen in the first place.

'Hadley's coffeepot is right there,' Amelia said, and I spotted it. It was black and it kind of blended in. Hadley had always been a coffee freak, so I'd figured that even as a vampire she'd kept a supply of her favorite beverage. I opened the cabinet above the pot, and behold – two cans of Community Coffee and some filters. The silvery seal was intact on the first one I opened, but the second can was open and half full. I inhaled the wonderful coffee smell with quiet pleasure. It seemed amazingly fresh.

After I fixed the pot and punched a button to set it perking, I found two mugs and set them beside it. The sugar bowl was right by the pot, but when I opened it, I found only a hardened residue. I pitched the contents into the trash can, which was lined but empty. It had been cleaned out after Hadley's death. Maybe Hadley had had some powdered creamer in the refrigerator? In the South, people who don't use it constantly often keep it there.

But when I opened the gleaming stainless steel refrigerator, I found nothing but five bottles of TrueBlood.

Nothing had brought home to me so strongly the fact that my cousin Hadley had died a vamp. I'd never known anyone before and after. It was a shock. I had so many memories of Hadley, some of them happy and some of them unpleasant – but in all of those memories, my cousin was breathing and her heart was beating. I stood with my lips compressed, staring at the red bottles, until I'd recovered enough to shut the door very gently.

After a vain search in the cabinets for Cremora, I told Amelia I hoped she took her coffee black.

'Yes, that'll be fine,' Amelia said primly. She was obviously trying to be on her better behavior, and I could only be grateful for that. Hadley's landlady was perched on one of Hadley's spindle-legged armchairs. The upholstery was really pretty, a yellow silky material printed with dark red and blue flowers, but I disliked the fragile style of the furniture. I like chairs that look as though they could hold big people, heavy people, without a creak or a groan. I like furniture that looks as though it won't be ruined if you spill a Coke on it, or if your dog hops up on it to take a nap. I tried to settle myself on the loveseat opposite the landlady's. Pretty, yes. Comfortable, no. Suspicion confirmed.

'So what are you, Amelia?'

'Beg pardon?'

'What are you?'

'Oh, a witch.'

'Figured.' I hadn't caught the sense of the supernatural that I get from creatures whose very cells have been changed by the nature of their being. Amelia had acquired her 'otherness'. 'Did you do the spells to seal off the apartment?'

'Yes,' she said rather proudly. She gave me a look of sheer evaluation. I had known the apartment was warded with spells; I had known she was a member of the other world, the hidden world. I might be a regular human, but I was in the know. I read all these thoughts as easily as if Amelia had spoken them to me. She was an exceptional broadcaster, as clear and clean as her complexion. 'The night Hadley died, the queen's lawyer phoned me. Of course, I was asleep. He told me to shut this sucker up, that Hadley wouldn't be coming back, but the queen wanted her place kept intact for her heir. I came up and began cleaning early the next morning.' She'd worn rubber gloves, too; I could see that in her mental picture of herself the morning after Hadley had died.

'You emptied the trash and made the bed?'

She looked embarrassed. 'Yes, I did. I didn't realize 'intact' meant 'untouched'. Cataliades got here and let me have it. But I'm glad I got the trash out of here, anyway. It's strange, because someone went through the garbage bin that night, before I could put it out for pickup.'

'I don't guess you know if they took anything?'

She cast me an incredulous look. 'It's not like I inventory the trash,' she said. She added, reluctantly, 'It had been treated with a spell, but I don't know what the spell was for.'

Okay, that wasn't good news. Amelia wasn't even admitting it to herself; she didn't want to think about the house being the target for supernatural assault. Amelia was proud because her wards had held, but she hadn't thought to ward the garbage bin.

'Oh, I got all her potted plants out and moved them down to my place for easier care, too. So if you want to take 'em back to Hole-in-the-Road with you, you're welcome.'

'Bon Temps,' I corrected. Amelia snorted. She had the born city dweller's contempt for small towns. 'So you own this building, and you rented the upstairs to Hadley when?'

'About a year ago. She was a vamp already,' Amelia said. 'And she was the queen's girlfriend, had been for quite a while. So I figured it was good insurance, you know? No one's going to attack the queen's honeybun, right? And no one's going to break into her place, either.'

I wanted to ask how come Amelia could afford such a nice place herself, but that was just too rude to get past my lips. 'So the witch business supports you?' I asked instead, trying to sound only mildly interested.

She shrugged, but looked pleased I'd asked. Though her mother had left her a lot of money, Amelia was delighted to be self-supporting.

I heard it as clearly as if she'd spoken it out loud. 'Yeah, I make a living,' she said, aiming for a modest tone and just missing. She'd worked hard to become a witch. She was proud of her power.

This was just like reading a book.

'If things get slow, I help out a friend who has a magic shop right off Jackson Square. I read fortunes there,' she admitted. 'And sometimes I do a magic tour of New Orleans for the tourists. That can be fun, and if I scare 'em enough, I get big tips. So between one thing and another, I do okay.'

'You perform serious magic,' I said, and she nodded happily. 'For who?' I asked. 'Since the regular world doesn't admit it's possible.'

'The supes pay real well,' she said, surprised I had to ask. I didn't really need to, but it was easier to direct her thoughts to the right information if I asked her out loud. 'Vamps and Weres, especially. I mean, they don't like witches, but vamps especially want every little advantage they can gain. The rest aren't as organized.' With a wave of her hand she dismissed the weaker ones of the supernatural world, the werebats and the shape-shifters and so on. She discounted the power of the other supes, which was a mistake.

'What about fairies?' I asked curiously.

'They have enough of their own magic,' she said, shrugging. 'They don't need me. I know someone like you might have a hard time accepting that there's a talent that's invisible and natural, one that challenges everything you were taught by your family.'

I stifled a snort of disbelief. She sure didn't know anything about me. I didn't know what she and Hadley had talked about, but it hadn't been Hadley's family, for sure. When that idea crossed my mind, a bell rang in the back of my head, one that said that avenue of thought should be explored. But I put it aside to think of later. Right now, I needed to deal with Amelia Broadway.

'So you would say you have a strong supernatural ability?' I said.

I could feel her stifle the rush of pride. 'I have some ability,' she said modestly. 'For example, I laid a stasis spell on this apartment when I couldn't finish cleaning it. And though it's been shut up for months, you don't smell anything, do you?'

That explained the lack of odor wafting from the stained towels.

'And you do witchcraft for supernaturals, you read fortunes off Jackson Square, and you lead tour groups sometimes. Not exactly regular office jobs,' I said.

'Right.' She nodded, happy and proud.

'So you make up your own schedule,' I said. I could hear the relief bouncing through Amelia's mind, relief that she didn't have to go into an office any more, though she'd done a stint at the post office for three years until she'd become a full-fledged witch.

'Yes.'

'So will you help me clean out Hadley's apartment? I'll be glad to pay you.'

'Well, sure I'll help. The sooner all her stuff is out, the sooner I can rent the place. As for your paying me, why don't we wait to see how much time I can give it? Sometimes I get, like, emergency calls.' Amelia smiled at me, a smile suitable for a toothpaste ad.

'Hasn't the queen been paying the rent since Hadley passed?'

'Yeah, she has. But it's given me the creeps, thinking of Hadley's stuff up here. And there've been a couple of break-in attempts. The last one was only a couple of days ago.' I gave up any pretense of smiling.

'I thought at first,' Amelia burbled on, 'that it might be like when someone dies and their death notice is in the paper, you get break-ins during the funeral. Course, they don't print obituaries for vampires, I guess because they're already dead or because the other vampires just don't send one to the paper ... that would be interesting, to see how they handled it. Why don't you try sending in a few lines about Hadley? But you know how vamps gossip, so I guess a few people heard she was definitely dead, dead for the second time. Especially after Waldo vanished from the court. Everyone knows he didn't care for Hadley. And then, too, vamps don't have funerals. So I guess the break-in wasn't related. New Orleans does have a pretty high crime rate.'

'Oh, you knew Waldo,' I said, to interrupt the flow. Waldo, once the queen's favorite – not in bed, but as a lackey, I thought – had resented being supplanted by my cousin Hadley. When Hadley remained in favor with the queen for an unprecedented length of time,

Waldo lured her to St. Louis Cemetery Number One with the ruse of pretending they were going to raise the spirit of Marie Laveau, the notorious voodoo queen of New Orleans. Instead, he'd killed Hadley and blamed it on the Fellowship of the Sun. Mr Cataliades had nudged me in the right direction until I'd figured out Waldo's guilt, and the queen had given me the opportunity to execute Waldo myself – that was the queen's idea of a big favor. I'd taken a pass on that. But he was finally, definitely dead, now, just like Hadley. I shuddered.

'Well, I know him better than I want to,' she said, with the frankness that seemed to be Amelia Broadway's defining characteristic. 'I hear you using the past tense, though. Dare I hope that Waldo has gone to his final destination?'

'You can,' I said. 'Dare, that is.'

'Oo-wee,' she said happily. 'My, my, my.'

At least I'd brightened someone's day. I could see in Amelia's thoughts how much she'd disliked the older vampire, and I didn't blame her. He'd been loathsome. Amelia was a single-minded kind of woman, which must make her a formidable witch. But right now she should have been thinking about other possibilities involving me, and she wasn't. There's a downside to being focused on a goal.

'So you want to clear out Hadley's apartment because you think your building won't be targeted any more? By these thieves who've learned that Hadley's dead?'

'Right,' she said, taking a final gulp of her coffee. 'I kind of like knowing someone else is here, too. Having the apartment empty just gives me the creeps. At least vampires can't leave ghosts behind.'

'I didn't know that,' I said. And I'd never thought about it, either.

'No vamp ghosts,' Amelia said blithely. 'Nary a one. Got to be human to leave a ghost behind. Hey, you want me to do a reading on you? I know, I know, it's kind of scary, but I promise, I'm good at it!' She was thinking that it would be fun to give me a touristy-type thrill, since I wouldn't be in New Orleans long; she also believed that the nicer she was to me, the quicker I'd clean out Hadley's place so she could have the use of it back.

'Sure,' I said slowly. 'You can do a reading, right now, if you want.' This might be a good measure of how gifted a witch Amelia really was. She sure didn't bear any resemblance to the witch stereotype. Amelia looked scrubbed and glowing and healthy, like a happy suburban housewife with a Ford Explorer and an Irish setter. But quick as a wink, Amelia extricated a Tarot pack from a pocket of her cargo shorts and leaned over the coffee table to deal them out. She did this in a quick and professional way that didn't make a bit of sense to me.

After poring over the pictures for a minute, her gaze stopped roaming over the cards and fixed on the table. Her face reddened, and she closed her eyes as if she were feeling mortified. Of course, she was.

'Okay,' she said at last, her voice calm and flat. 'What are you?'

'Telepath.'

'I'm always making assumptions! Why don't I learn!'

'No one thinks of me as scary,' I said, trying to sound gentle, and she winced.

'Well, I won't make that mistake again,' she said. 'You did seem more knowledgeable about supes than the ordinary person.'

'And learning more every day.' Even to myself, my voice sounded grim.

'Now I'll have to tell my advisor that I blew it,' my landlady said. She looked as gloomy as it was possible for her to look. Not very.

'You have a . . . mentor?'

'Yeah, an older witch who kind of monitors our progress the first three years of being a professional.'

'How do you know when you're a professional?'

'Oh, you have to pass the exam,' Amelia explained, getting to her feet and going over to the sink. In a New York minute, she had washed the coffeepot and the filter apparatus, put them neatly in the drainer, and wiped out the sink.

'So we'll start packing up stuff tomorrow?' I said.

'What's wrong with right now?'

'I'd like to go through Hadley's things by myself, first,' I said, trying not to sound irritated.

'Oh. Well, sure you would.' She tried to look as if she'd thought of that already. 'And I guess you have to go over to the queen's tonight, huh?'

'I don't know.'

'Oh, I'll bet they're expecting you. Was there a tall, dark, and handsome vamp out there with you last night? He sure looked familiar.'

'Bill Compton,' I said. 'Yes, he's lived in Louisiana for years and he's done some work for the queen.'

She looked at me, her clear blue eyes surprised. 'Oh, I thought he knew your cousin.'

'No,' I said. 'Thanks for getting me up so I could start work, and thanks for being willing to help me.'

She was pleased that she was leaving, because I hadn't been what she'd expected, and she wanted to think about me some and make some phone calls to sisters in the craft in the Bon Temps area. 'Holly Cleary,' I said. 'She's the one I know best.'

Amelia gasped and said a shaky good-bye. She left as unexpectedly as she'd arrived.

I felt old all of a sudden. I'd just been showing off, and I'd reduced a confident, happy young witch to an anxious woman in the space of an hour.

But as I got out a pad and pencil – right where they should be, in the drawer closest to the telephone – to figure out my plan of action, I consoled myself with the thought that Amelia had needed the mental slap in the face pretty badly. If it hadn't come from me, it might have come from someone who actually meant her harm.

Chapter 15

I needed boxes, that was for sure. So I'd also need strapping tape, lots of it, and a Magic Marker, and probably scissors. And finally, I'd need a truck to take whatever I salvaged back to Bon Temps. I could ask Jason to drive down, or I could rent a truck, or I could ask Mr Cataliades if he knew of a truck I could borrow. If there was a lot of stuff, maybe I would rent a car and a trailer. I'd never done such a thing, but how hard could it be? Since I didn't have a ride right now, there was no way to obtain the supplies. But I might as well start sorting, since the sooner I finished, the sooner I could get back to work and away from the New Orleans vampires. I was glad, in a corner of my mind, that Bill had come, too. As angry as I sometimes felt with him, he was familiar. After all, he'd been the first vampire I'd ever met, and it still seemed almost miraculous to me how it had happened.

He'd come into the bar, and I'd been fascinated with the discovery that I couldn't hear his thoughts. Then later the same evening, I'd rescued him from drainers. I sighed, thinking how good it had been until he'd been recalled by his maker, Lorena, now also definitely dead.

I shook myself. This wasn't the time for a trip down memory lane. This was the time for action and decision. I decided to start with the clothes.

After fifteen minutes, I realized that the clothes were going to be easy. I was going to give most of them away. Not only was my taste radically different from my cousin's, but her hips and breasts had been smaller and her coloring had been different from mine. Hadley had liked dark, dramatic clothes, and I was altogether a lower-key person. I did sort of wonder about one or two of the black wispy blouses and skirts, but when I tried them on, I looked just like one of the fang-bangers who hung around Eric's bar. Not the image I was going for. I put only a handful of tank tops and a couple of pairs of shorts and sleep pants in the 'keep' pile.

I found a large box of garbage bags and used those to pack the clothes away. As I finished with each bag, I set it out on the gallery to keep the apartment clear of clutter.

It was about noon when I started to work, and the hours passed quickly after I found out how to operate Hadley's CD player. A lot of the music she had was by artists who'd never been high on my list, no big surprise there – but it was interesting listening. She had a horde of CDs: No Doubt, Nine Inch Nails, Eminem, Usher.

I'd started on the drawers in the bedroom when it just began turning dark. I paused for a moment to stand on the gallery in the mild evening, and watch the city wake up for the dark hours ahead. New Orleans was a city of the night now. It had always been a place with a brawling and brazen nightlife, but now it was such a center for the undead that its entire character had changed. A lot of the jazz on Bourbon Street was played these days by hands that had last seen sunlight decades before. I could catch a faint spatter of notes on the air, the music of faraway revels. I sat on a chair on the gallery and listened for a while, and I hoped I'd get to see some of the city while I was here. New Orleans is like no other place in America, both before the vampire influx and after it. I sighed and realized I was hungry. Of course, Hadley didn't have any food in the apartment, and I wasn't about to start drinking blood. I hated to ask Amelia for anything else. Tonight, whoever came to pick me up to go to the queen's might be willing to take me to the grocery store. Maybe I should shower and change?

As I turned to go back into the apartment, I spotted the mildewed towels I'd set out the night before. They smelled much stronger, which surprised me. I would have thought the smell would have diminished by now. Instead, my breath caught in the back of my throat in disgust as I picked up the basket to bring it inside. I intended to wash them.

In a corner of the kitchen was one of those washer/dryer sets with the dryer on top. Like a tower of cleanliness.

I tried to shake out the towels, but they'd dried in a stiff crumpled mass. Exasperated, I jerked at the protruding edge of one towel, and with a little resistance, the clots of stuff binding the folds together gave, and the medium blue terrycloth spread out before my eyes.

'Oh, *shit*,' I said out loud in the silent apartment. 'Oh, *no*.'

The fluid that had dried and clumped on the towels was blood.

'Oh, Hadley,' I said. 'What did you do?'

The smell was as awful as the shock. I sat down at the small dining table in the kitchen area. Flakes of dried blood had showered onto the floor and clung to my arms. I couldn't read the thoughts of a towel, for God's sake. My condition was of no help to me whatsoever. I needed . . . a witch. Like the one I'd chastened and sent away. Yep, just like that one.

But first I needed to check the whole apartment, see if it held any more surprises.

Oh, yeah. It did.

The body was in the walk-in closet in the hall.

There was no odor at all, though the corpse, a young man, had probably been there for the whole time my cousin had been dead. Maybe this young man had been a demon? But he didn't look anything like Diantha or Gladiola, or Mr Cataliades, for that matter. If the towels had started to smell, you would think . . . oh well, maybe I'd just gotten lucky. This was something that I would have to find the answer to, and I suspected it lay downstairs.

I knocked on Amelia's door. She answered it immediately, and I saw over her shoulder that her place, though of course laid out exactly like Hadley's, was full of light colors and energy. She liked yellow, and cream, and coral, and green. Her furniture was modern and heavily cushioned, and the wooden bits were polished to the nth degree. As I'd suspected, Amelia's place was spotless.

'Yes?' she said, in a subdued kind of way.

'Okay,' I said, as if I were laying down an olive branch. 'I've got a problem, and I suspect you do, too.'

'Why do you say that?' she asked. Her open face was closed now, as if keeping her expression blank would keep me out of her mind.

'You put a stasis spell on the apartment, right? To keep everything exactly as it was. Before you warded it against intruders?'

'Yes,' she said cautiously. 'I told you that.'

'No one's been in that apartment since the night Hadley died?'

'I can't give you my word on it, because I suppose a very good witch or wizard could have breached my spell,' she said. 'But to the best of my knowledge, no one's been in there.'

'So you don't know that you sealed a body in there?'

I don't know what I expected in the way of reaction, but Amelia was pretty cool about it. 'Okay,' she said steadily. She may have gulped. 'Okay. Who is it?' Her eyelids fluttered up and down a few extra times.

Maybe she wasn't quite so cool.

'I really don't know,' I said carefully. 'You'll have to come see.' As we went up the stairs, I said, 'He was killed there, and the mess was cleaned up with towels. They were in the hamper.' I told her about the condition of the towels.

'Holly Cleary tells me you saved her son's life,' Amelia said.

That took me aback. It made me feel awkward, too. 'The police would have found him,' I said. 'I just accelerated it a little.'

'The doctor told Holly if the little boy hadn't gotten to the hospital when he did, the bleeding in his brain might not have been stopped in time,' Amelia said.

'That's good then,' I said, uncomfortable in the extreme. 'How's Cody doing?'

'Well,' the witch said. 'He's going to be well.'

'In the meantime, we got a problem right here,' I reminded her.

'Okay, let's see the corpse.' Amelia worked hard to keep her voice level.

I kind of liked this witch.

I led her to the closet. I'd left the door open. She stepped inside. She didn't make a sound. She came back out with a slightly green tinge to her glowing tan and leaned against the wall.

'He's a Were,' she said, a moment later. The spell she'd put on the apartment had kept everything fresh, as part of the way it worked. The blood had begun to smell a little before the spell had been cast, and when I'd entered the apartment, the spell had been broken. Now the towels reeked of decay. The body didn't have an odor yet, which surprised me a little, but I figured it would any minute. Surely the body would decompose rapidly now that it had been released from Amelia's magic, and she was obviously trying not to point out how well that had worked.

'You know him?'

'Yes, I know him,' she said. 'The supernatural community, even in New Orleans, isn't that big. It's Jake Purifoy. He did security for the queen's wedding.'

I had to sit down. I exited the walk-in closet and slid down the wall until I was sitting propped up, facing Amelia. She sat against the opposite wall. I hardly knew where to start asking questions.

'That would be when she married the King of Arkansas?' I recalled what Felicia had said, and the wedding photo I'd seen in Al Cumberland's album. Had that been the queen, under that elaborate headdress? When Quinn had mentioned making the arrangements for a wedding in New Orleans, was this the wedding he'd meant?

'The queen, according to Hadley, is bi,' Amelia told me. 'So yes, she married a guy. Now they have an alliance.'

'They can't have kids,' I said. I know, that was obvious, but I wasn't getting this alliance thing.

'No, but unless someone stakes them, they'll live forever, so passing things on is not a big issue,' Amelia said. 'It takes months, even years, of negotiations to hammer out the rules for such a wedding. The contract can take just as long. Then they both gotta sign it. That's a big ceremony, takes place right before the wedding. They don't actually have to spend their lives together, you know, but they have to visit a couple of times a year. Conjugal-type visit.'

Fascinating as this was, it was beside the point right now. 'So this guy in the closet, he was part of the security force.' Had he worked for Quinn? Hadn't Quinn said that one of his workers had gone missing in New Orleans?

'Yeah, I wasn't asked to the wedding, of course, but I helped Hadley into her dress. He came to pick her up.'

'Jake Purifoy came to pick Hadley up for the wedding.'

'Yep. He was all dressed up that night.'

'And that was the night of the wedding.'

'Yeah, the night before Hadley died.'

'Did you see them leave?'

'No, I just . . . No. I heard the car pull up. I looked out my living room window and saw Jake coming in. I knew him already, kind of casually. I had a friend who used to date him. I went back to whatever I was doing, watching TV I think, and I heard the car leave after a while.'

'So he may not have left at all.'

She stared at me, her eyes wide. 'Could be,' she said at last, sounding as if her mouth were dry.

'Hadley was by herself when he came to pick her up . . . right?'

'When I came down from her apartment, I left her there alone.'

'All I came to do,' I said, mainly to my bare feet, 'was clean out my cousin's apartment. I didn't much like her anyway. Now I'm stuck with a body. The last time I got rid of a body,' I told the witch, 'I had a big strong helper, and we wrapped it in a shower curtain.'

'You did?' Amelia said faintly. She didn't look too happy to be the recipient of this information.

'Yes.' I nodded. 'We didn't kill him. We just had to get rid of the body. We thought we'd be blamed for the death, and I'm sure we would have been.' I stared at my toenail polish some more. It had been a good job when it started out, a nice bright pink, but now I needed to refresh the paint job or remove it. I stopped trying to think about other things and resumed my gloomy contemplation of the body. He was lying in the closet, stretched out on the floor, pushed under the lowest shelf. He'd been covered with a sheet. Jake Purifoy had been a handsome man, I suspected. He'd had dark brown hair, and a muscular build. Lots of body hair. Though he'd been dressed for a formal wedding, and Amelia had said he looked very nice, now he was naked. A minor question: where were his clothes?

'We could just call the queen,' Amelia said. 'After all, the body's been here, and Hadley either killed him or hid the body. No way could he have died the night she went out with Waldo to the cemetery.'

'Why not?' I had a sudden, awful thought.

'You got a cell phone?' I asked, rising to my feet as I spoke. Amelia nodded. 'Call the queen's place. Tell them to send someone over *right now*.'

'What?' Her eyes were confused, even as her fingers were punching in numbers.

Looking into the closet, I could see the fingers of the corpse twitch.

'He's rising,' I said quietly.

It only took a second for her to get it. 'This is Amelia Broadway on Chloe Street! Send an older vampire over here *right now*,' she yelled into the phone. 'New vamp rising!' She was on her feet now, and we were running for the door.

We didn't make it.

Jake Purifoy was after us, and he was hungry.

Since Amelia was behind me (I'd had a head start) he dove to grab her ankle. She shrieked as, she went down, and I spun around to help her. I didn't think at all, because I would have kept on going out the door if I had. The new vamp's fingers were wrapped around Amelia's bare ankle like a shackle, and he was pulling her toward him across the smooth laminated-wood floor. She was clawing at the floor with her fingers, trying to find something to stop her progress toward his mouth, which was wide open with the fangs extended full length, oh God! I grabbed her wrists and began pulling. I hadn't known Jake Purifoy in life, so I didn't know what he'd been like. And I couldn't find anything human left in his face, anything I could appeal to. 'Jake!' I yelled. 'Jake Purifoy! Wake up!' Of course, that didn't do a damn bit of good. Jake had changed into something that was not a nightmare but a permanent otherness, and he could not be roused from it: he was it. He was making a kind of *gnarr-gnarr-gnarr* noise, the hungriest sound I'd ever heard, and then he bit down on the calf of Amelia's leg, and she screamed.

It was like a shark had hold of her. If I yanked at her any more, he might take out the bit his teeth had clamped on. He was sucking on the leg wound now, and I kicked him in the head with my heel, cursing my lack of shoes. I put everything I had behind it, and it didn't faze the new vampire in the least. He made a noise of protest, but continued sucking, and the witch kept shrieking with pain and shock. There was a candlestick on the table behind one of the loveseats, a tall glass candlestick with lots of heft to it. I plucked the candle from it, grasped it with both hands, and brought it down as hard as I could on Jake Purifoy's head. Blood began to run from his wound, very sluggishly; that's how vampires bleed. The candlestick came apart with the blow, and I was left with empty hands and a furious vampire. He raised his blood-smeared face to glare at me, and I hope I'm never on the receiving end of another look like that again in my life. His face held the mindless rage of a mad dog.

But he'd let go of Amelia's leg, and she began to scramble away. It was obvious she was hurt, and it was kind of a slow scramble, but she made the effort. Tears were streaming down her face and her breathing was all over the place, harsh in the night's silence. I could hear a siren drawing closer and I hoped it was coming here. It would be too late, though. The vampire launched himself from the floor to knock me down, and I didn't have time to think about anything.

He bit down on my arm, and I thought the teeth would penetrate the bone. If I hadn't thrown up the arm, those teeth would have gripped my neck, and that would have been fatal. The arm might be preferable, but just at this moment the pain was so intense I nearly passed out, and I'd better not do that. Jake Purifoy's body was heavy on top of mine, and his hands were pressing my free arm to the floor, and his legs were on top of mine. Another hunger was wakening in the new vampire, and I felt its evidence pressing against my thigh. He freed a hand to begin yanking at my pants.

Oh, no . . . this was so bad. I would die in the next few minutes, here in New Orleans in my cousin's apartment, far away from my friends and my family.

Blood was all over the new vampire's face and hands.

Amelia crawled awkwardly across the floor toward us, her leg trailing blood behind her. She should have run, since she couldn't save me. No more candlesticks. But Amelia had another weapon, and she reached out with a violently shaking hand to touch the vampire. '*Utinam hic sanguis in ignem commutet!*' she yelled.

The vampire reared back, screaming and clawing at his face, which was suddenly covered by tiny licking blue flames.

And the police came through the door.

They were vampires, too.

For an interesting moment, the police officers thought we had attacked Jake Purifoy. Amelia and I, bleeding and screaming, were shoved up against the wall. But in the meantime, the spell Amelia had cast on the new undead lost its efficacy and he leaped on the nearest uniformed cop, who happened to be a black woman with a proud straight back and a high-bridged nose. The cop whipped out her nightstick and used it with a reckless disregard for the new vamp's teeth. Her partner, a very short man whose skin was the color of butterscotch, fumbled to open a bottle of TrueBlood that was stuck in his belt like another tool. He bit off the tip, and stuck the rubber cap in Jake Purifoy's questing mouth. Suddenly, all was silence as the new vamp sucked down the contents of the bottle. The rest of us stood panting and bleeding.

'He will be quiet now,' said the female officer, the cadence of her voice letting me know that she was far more African than American. 'I think we have subdued him.'

Amelia and I sank onto the floor, after the male cop gave us a nod to let us know we were off the hook. 'Sorry we got confused about who was the bad guy,' he said in a voice as warm as melted butter. 'You ladies okay?' It was a good thing his voice was so reassuring, since his fangs were out. I guess the excitement of the blood and the violence triggered the reaction, but it was kind of disconcerting in a law enforcement officer.

'I think not,' I said. 'Amelia here is bleeding pretty bad, and I guess I am, too.' The bite didn't hurt as badly as it was going to. The vamp's saliva secretes a tiny bit of anesthetic, along with a healing agent. But the healing agent was meant for sealing the pinpricks of fangs, not for actual large tears in human flesh. 'We're going to need a doctor.' I'd met a vamp in Mississippi who could heal large wounds, but it was a rare talent.

'You both human?' he asked. The female cop was crooning in a foreign language to the new vampire. I didn't know if the former werewolf, Jake Purifoy, could speak the language, but he recognized safety when he saw it. The burns on his face healed as we sat there.

'Yes,' I said.

While we waited for the paramedics to come, Amelia and I leaned against each other wordlessly. Was this the second body I'd found in a closet, or the third? I wondered why I even opened closet doors any more.

'We should have known,' Amelia said wearily. 'When he didn't smell at all, we should have known.'

'Actually, I figured that out. Since it was only thirty seconds before he woke up, it didn't do a hell of a lot of good,' I said. My voice was just as limp as hers.

Everything got very confusing after that. I kept thinking it would be a good time to faint if I was ever going to, because this was really not a process I wanted to be in on, but I just couldn't pass out. The paramedics were very nice young men who seemed to think we'd been partying with a vamp and it had gotten out of hand. I guessed neither of them would be calling Amelia or me for a date any time soon.

'You don't want to be messing with no vampires, *cherie*,' said the man who was working on me. His name tag read DELAGARDIE. 'They supposed to be so attractive to women, but you wouldn't believe how many poor girls we've had to patch up. And that was the lucky ones,' Delagardie said grimly. 'What's your name, young lady?'

'Sookie,' I said. 'Sookie Stackhouse.'

'Pleased to meet you, Miss Sookie. You and your friend seem like nice girls. You need to hang with better people, live people. This city's overrun with the dead, now. It was better when everyone here was breathing, I tell you the truth. Now let's get you to the hospital and get you stitched up. I'd shake your hand if you wasn't all bloody,' he said. He gave me a sudden smile, white-toothed and charming. 'I'm giving you good advice for free, pretty lady.'

I smiled, but it was the last time I was going to be doing that for a while. The pain was beginning to make itself felt. Very quickly, I became preoccupied with coping.

Amelia was a real warrior. Her teeth were gritted as she fought to keep herself together, but she managed all the way to the hospital. The emergency room seemed to be packed. By a combination of bleeding, being escorted by cops, and the friendly Delagardie and his partner putting in a word for us, Amelia and I got put in curtained cubicles right away. We weren't adjacent to each other, but we were in line to see a doctor. I was grateful. I knew that had to be quick, for an urban emergency room.

As I listened to the bustle around me, I tried not to swear at the pain in my arm. In moments when it wasn't throbbing as much, I wondered what had happened to Jake Purifoy. Had the vampire cops taken him to a vampire cell at the jail, or was everything excused since he was a brand new vamp with no guidance? There'd been a law passed about that, but I couldn't remember the terms and strictures. It was hard for me to be too concerned. I knew the young man was a victim of his new state; that the vampire who had made him should have been there to guide him through his first wakening and hunger. The vampire to blame was most likely my cousin Hadley, who had hardly expected to be murdered. Only Amelia's stasis spell on the apartment had kept Jake from rising months ago. It was a strange situation, probably unprecedented even in vampire annals. And a werewolf who'd become a vampire! I'd never heard tell of such a thing. Could he still change?

I had a while to think about that and quite a few other things, since Amelia was too far away for conversation, even if she'd been up to it. After about twenty minutes, during which time I was disturbed only by a nurse who wrote down some information, I was surprised to see Eric peer around the curtain.

'May I come in?' he asked stiffly. His eyes were wide and he was speaking carefully. I realized that to a vampire, the smell of blood in the emergency room was enchanting and pervasive. I caught a glimpse of his fangs.

'Yes,' I said, puzzled by Eric's presence in New Orleans. I wasn't really in an Eric mood, but there was no point in telling the former Viking he couldn't come into the curtained area. This was a public building, and he wasn't bound by my words. Anyway, he could simply stand outside and talk to me through the cloth until he found out whatever he'd come to discover. Eric was nothing if not persistent. 'What on earth are you doing here in town, Eric?'

'I drove down to bargain with the queen for your services during the summit. Also, Her Majesty and I have to negotiate how many of my people I can bring with me.' He smiled at me. The effect was disconcerting, what with the fangs and all. 'We've almost reached an agreement. I can bring three, but I want to bargain up to four.'

'Oh, for God's sake, Eric,' I snapped. 'That's the lamest excuse I've ever heard. Modern invention, known as the telephone?' I moved restlessly on the narrow bed. I couldn't find a comfortable position. Every nerve in my body was jangling with the aftermath of the fear of my encounter with Jake Purifoy, new child of the night. I was hoping that when I finally saw a doctor, he or she would give me an excellent painkiller. 'Leave me alone, okay? You don't have a claim on me. Or a responsibility to me.'

'But I do.' He had the gall to look surprised. 'We have a bond. I've had your blood, when you needed strength to free Bill in Jackson. And we've made love often, according to you.'

'You *made* me tell you,' I protested. And if I sounded a little on the whiny said, well, dammit, I thought it was okay to whine a little. Eric had agreed to save a friend of mine from danger if I'd spill the truth to him. Is that blackmail? Yes, I think so.

But there wasn't any way to untell him. I sighed. 'How'd you get here, anyway?'

'The queen monitors what happens to vampires in her city very closely, of course. I thought I'd come provide moral support. And, of course, if you need me to clean you of blood . . .' His eyes flashed as he inspected my arm. 'I'd be glad to do it.'

I almost smiled, very reluctantly. He never gave up.

'Eric,' said Bill's cool voice, and he slipped around the curtain to join Eric at my bedside.

'Why am I not surprised to see you here?' Eric said, in a voice that made it clear he was displeased.

Eric's anger wasn't something Bill could ignore. Eric outranked Bill, and he looked down his substantial nose at the younger vampire. Bill was around one hundred thirty-five years old: Eric was perhaps over a thousand. (I had asked him once, but he honestly didn't seem to know.) Eric had the personality for leadership. Bill was happier on his own. The only thing they had in common was that they'd both made love to me: and just at the moment, they were both pains in my butt.

'I heard over the police band radio at the queen's headquarters that the vampire police had been called in to subdue a fresh vampire, and I recognized the address,' Bill said by way of explanation. 'Naturally, I found out where Sookie had been brought, and came here as fast as I could.'

I closed my eyes.

'Eric, you're tiring her out,' Bill said, his voice even colder than usual. 'You should leave Sookie alone.'

There was a long moment of silence. It was fraught with some big emotion. My eyes opened and went from one face to another. For once, I wished I could read vampire minds.

As much as I could read from his expression, Bill was deeply regretting his words, but why? Eric was looking at Bill with a complex expression compounded of resolve and something less definable; regret, maybe.

'I quite understand why you want to keep Sookie isolated while she's in New Orleans,' Eric said. His r's became more pronounced, as they did when he was angry.

Bill looked away.

Despite the pain pulsing in my arm, despite my general exasperation with the both of them, something inside me sat up and took notice. There was an unmistakable significance to Eric's tone. Bill's lack of response was curious . . . and ominous.

'What?' I said, my eyes flicking from one to the other. I tried to prop myself up on my elbows and settled for one when the other arm, the bitten one, gave a big throb of pain. I pressed the button to raise the head of the bed. 'What's all the big hinting about, Eric? Bill?'

'Eric should not be agitating you when you've got a lot to handle already,' Bill said, finally. Though never known for its expressiveness, Bill's face was what my grandmother would have described as 'locked up tighter than a drum.'

Eric folded his arms across his chest and looked down at them.

'Bill?' I said.

'Ask him why he came back to Bon Temps, Sookie,' Eric said very quietly.

'Well, old Mr Compton died, and he wanted to reclaim his ...' I couldn't even describe the expression on Bill's face. My heart began to beat faster. Dread gathered in a knot in my stomach. 'Bill?'

Eric turned to face away from me, but not before I saw a shade of pity cross his face. Nothing could have scared me more. I might not be able to read a vampire's mind, but in this case his body language said it all. Eric was turning away because he didn't want to watch the knife sliding in.

'Sookie, you would find out when you saw the queen ... Maybe I could have kept it from you, because you won't understand ... but Eric has taken care of that.' Bill gave Eric's back a look that could have drilled a hole through Eric's heart. 'When your cousin Hadley was becoming the queen's favorite ...'

And suddenly I saw it all, knew what he was going to say, and I rose up on the hospital bed with a gasp, one hand to my chest because I felt my heart shattering. But Bill's voice went on, even though I shook my head violently.

'Apparently, Hadley talked about you and your gift a lot, to impress the queen and keep her interest. And the queen knew I was originally from Bon Temps. On some nights, I've wondered if she sent someone to kill the last Compton and hurry things along. But maybe he truly died of old age.' Bill was looking down at the floor, didn't see my left hand extended to him in a 'stop' motion.

'She ordered me to return to my human home, to put myself in your way, to seduce you if I had to ...'

I couldn't breathe. No matter how my right hand pressed to my chest, I couldn't stop the decimation of my heart, the slide of the knife deeper into my flesh.

'She wanted your gift harnessed for her own use,' he said, and he opened his mouth to say more. My eyes were so blurred with tears that I couldn't see properly, couldn't see what expression was on his face and didn't care anyway. But I could not cry while he was anywhere near me. I would not.

'Get out,' I said, with a terrible effort. Whatever else happened, I could not bear for him to see the pain he had caused.

He tried to look me straight in the eyes, but mine were too full.

Whatever he wanted to convey, it was lost on me. 'Please let me finish,' he said.

'I never want to see you again, ever in my life,' I whispered. 'Ever.'

He didn't speak. His lips moved, as if he were trying to form a word or phrase, but I shook my head. 'Get out,' I told him, in a voice so choked with hatred and anguish that it didn't sound like my own. Bill turned and walked past the curtain and out of the emergency room. Eric did not turn around to see my face, thank God. He reached back to pat me on the leg before he left, too.

I wanted to scream. I wanted to kill someone with my bare hands.

I had to be by myself. I could not let anyone see me suffer this much. The pain was tied up with a rage so profound that I had never felt its like. I was sick with anger and hurt. The snap of Jake Purifoy's teeth had been nothing compared to this.

I couldn't stay still. With some difficulty, I eased off the bed. My feet were still bare, of course, and I noticed with an odd detached part of my mind that they were extraordinarily dirty. I staggered out of the triage area, spotted the doors to the waiting room, and aimed myself in that direction. Walking was a problem.

A nurse bustled up to me, a clipboard in her hand. 'Miss Stackhouse, a doctor's going to be with you in just a minute. I know you've had to wait, and I'm sorry, but . . .'

I turned to look at her and she flinched, took a step backward. I kept on toward the doors, my steps uncertain but my purpose clear. I wanted out of there. Beyond that, I didn't know. I made it to the doors and pushed and then I was dragging myself through the waiting room thronged with people. I blended in perfectly with the mix of patients and relatives waiting to see a doctor. Some were dirtier and bloodier than I was; and some were older – and some were way younger. I supported myself with a hand against a wall and kept moving to the doors, to the outside.

I made it.

It was much quieter outside, and it was warm. The wind was blowing, just a little. I was barefoot and penniless, standing under the glaring lights of the walk-in doors. I had no idea where I was in relation to the house, and no idea if that was where I was going, but I wasn't in the hospital any more.

A homeless man stepped in front of me. 'You got any change, sister?' he asked. 'I'm down on my luck, too.'

'Do I *look* like I have *anything*?' I asked him, in a reasonable voice.

He looked as unnerved as the nurse had. He said, 'Sorry,' and backed away. I took a step after him.

I screamed, '*I HAVE NOTHING!*' And then I said, in a perfectly calm voice, 'See, I never had anything to start with.'

He gibbered and quavered and I ignored him. I began my walk. The ambulance had turned right coming in, so I turned left. I couldn't remember how long the ride had been. I'd been talking to Delagardie. I had been a different person. I walked and I walked. I walked under palm trees, heard the rich rhythm of music, brushed against the peeling shutters of houses set right up to the sidewalk.

On a street with a few bars, a group of young men came out just as I was passing, and one of them grabbed my arm. I turned on him with a scream, and with a galvanic effort I swung him into a wall. He stood there, dazed and rubbing his head, and his friends pulled him away.

'She crazy,' one of them said softly. 'Leave her be.' They wandered off in the other direction.

After a time, I recovered enough to ask myself why I was doing this. But the answer was vague. When I fell on some broken pavement, scraping my knee badly enough to make it bleed, the new physical pain called me back to myself a little bit more.

'Are you doing this so they'll feel sorry they hurt you?' I asked myself out loud. 'Oh my God, poor Sookie! She walked out of the hospital all by herself, driven crazy with grief, and she wandered alone through the dangerous streets of the Big Easy because Bill made her so crazy!'

I didn't want my name to cross Bill's lips ever again. When I was a little more myself – just a little – the depth of my reaction began to surprise me. If we'd still been a couple when I learned what I'd learned this evening, I'd have killed him; I knew that with crystal clarity. But the reason I'd had to get away from the hospital was equally clear; I couldn't have stood dealing with anyone in the world just then. I'd been blindsided with the most painful knowledge: the first man to ever say he loved me had never loved me at all.

His passion had been artificial.

His pursuit of me had been choreographed.

I must have seemed so easy to him, so gullible, so ready for the first man who devoted a little time and effort to winning me. Winning me! The very phrase made me hurt worse. He'd never thought of me as a prize.

Until the structure had been torn down in a single moment, I hadn't realized how much of my life in the past year had been built on the false foundation of Bill's love and regard.

'I saved his life,' I said, amazed. 'I went to Jackson and risked my life for his, because he loved me.' One part of my brain knew that wasn't entirely accurate. I'd done it because I had loved him. And I was amazed, at the same moment, to realize that the pull of his maker, Lorena, had been even stronger than the orders of his queen. But I wasn't in the mood to split emotional hairs. When I thought of Lorena, another realization socked me in the stomach. 'I killed someone for him,' I said, my words floating in the thick dark night. 'Oh, my God. I killed someone for *him*.'

I was covered in scrapes, bruises, blood, and dirt when I looked up to see a sign reading CHLOE STREET. That was where Hadley's apartment was, I realized slowly. I turned right, and began to walk again.

The house was dark, up and down. Maybe Amelia was still at the hospital. I had no idea what time it was or how long I had walked.

Hadley's apartment was locked. I went downstairs and picked up one of the flowerpots Amelia had put around her door. I carried it up the stairs and smashed in a glass pane on the door. I reached inside, unlocked the door, and stepped in. No alarm shrieked. I'd been pretty sure the police wouldn't have known the code to activate it when they'd left after doing whatever it was they'd done.

I walked through the apartment, which was still turned upside down by our fight with Jake Purifoy. I had some more cleaning to do in the morning, or whenever ... whenever my life resumed. I went into the bathroom and stripped off the clothes I'd been wearing. I held them and looked at them for a minute, at the state they were in. Then I stepped across the hall, unlocked the closest French window, and threw the clothes over the railing of the gallery. I wished all problems were that easily disposed of, but at the same time my real personality was waking up enough to trigger a thread of guilt that I was leaving a mess that someone else would have to clean up. That wasn't the Stackhouse way. That thread wasn't strong enough to make me go back down the stairs to retrieve the filthy garments. Not then.

After I'd wedged a chair under the door I'd broken, and after I'd set the alarm system with the numbers Amelia had taught me, I got into the shower. The water stung my many scrapes and cuts, and the deep bite in my arm began bleeding again. Well, shit. My cousin the vampire hadn't needed any first aid supplies, of course. I finally found some circular cotton pads she'd probably used for removing makeup, and I rummaged through one of the bags of clothes until I found a ludicrously cheerful leopard-patterned scarf. Awkwardly, I bound the pads to the bite and got the scarf tight enough.

At least the vile sheets were the least of my worries. I climbed painfully into my nightgown and lay on the bed, praying for oblivion.

Chapter 16

I woke up unrefreshed, with that awful feeling that in a moment I would remember bad things.

The feeling was right on the money.

But the bad things had to take a backseat, because I had a surprise to start the day with. Claudine was lying beside me on the bed, propped up on one elbow looking down at me compassionately. And Amelia was at the end of the bed in an easy chair, her bandaged leg propped up on an ottoman. She was reading.

'How come you're here?' I asked Claudine. After seeing Eric and Bill last night, I wondered if everyone I knew followed me around. Maybe Sam would come in the door in a minute.

'I told you, I'm your fairy godmother,' Claudine said. Claudine was usually the happiest fairy I knew. Claudine was just as lovely for a woman as her twin Claude was for a man; maybe lovelier, because her more agreeable personality shone through her eyes. Her coloring was the same as his; black hair, white skin. Today she was wearing pale blue capris and a coordinating black-and-blue tunic. She looked ethereally lovely, or at least as ethereal as you can look in capris.

'You can explain that to me right after I go to the bathroom,' I said, remembering all the water I'd chugged down when I'd gotten to the sink the night before. All my wanderings had made me thirsty. Claudine swung gracefully from the bed, and I followed her awkwardly.

'Careful,' Amelia advised, when I tried to stand up too quickly.

'How's your leg?' I asked her, when the world had righted itself. Claudine kept a grip on my arm, just in case. It felt good to see Claudine, and I was surprisingly glad to see Amelia, even limping.

'Very sore,' she said. 'But unlike you, I stayed at the hospital and had the wound treated properly.' She closed her book and put it on the little table by the chair. She looked a little better than I suspected I did, but she was not the radiant and happy witch she'd been the day before.

'Had a learning experience, didn't we?' I said, and then my breath caught when I remembered just how much I'd learned.

Claudine helped me into the bathroom, and when I assured her I could manage, she left me alone. I did the necessary things and came out feeling better, almost human. Claudine had gotten some clothes out of my sports bag, and there was a mug on the bedside table with steam rising from it. I carefully sat against the headboard, my legs crossed in front of me, and held the mug to my face so I could breathe in the smell.

'Explain the fairy godmother thing,' I said. I didn't want to talk about anything more urgent, not just yet.

'Fairies are your basic supernatural being,' Claudine said. 'From us come elves and brownies and angels and demons. Water sprites, green men, all the natural spirits . . . all are some form of fairy.'

'So you're what?' Amelia asked. It hadn't occurred to Amelia to leave, and that seemed to be okay with Claudine, too.

'I'm trying to become an angel,' Claudine said softly. Her huge brown eyes looked luminous. 'After years of being . . . well, a good citizen, I guess you'd call it, I got a person to guard. The Sook, here. And she's really kept me busy.' Claudine looked proud and happy.

'You're not supposed to prevent pain?' I asked. If so, Claudine was doing a lousy job.

'No, I wish I could.' The expression on Claudine's oval face was downcast. 'But I can help you recover from disasters, and sometimes I can prevent them.'

'Things would be *worse* without you around?'

She nodded vigorously.

'I'll take your word for it,' I said. 'How come I rated a fairy god-mother?'

'I'm not allowed to say,' Claudine said, and Amelia rolled her eyes.

'We're not learning a lot, here,' she said. 'And in view of the problems we had last night, maybe you're not the most competent fairy god-mother, huh?'

'Oh, right, Miss I-Sealed-Up-The-Apartment-So-It-Would-Be-All-Fresh,' I responded, irrationally indignant at this assault on my god-mother's competence.

Amelia scrambled out of her chair, her skin flushed with anger. 'Well, I did seal it up! He would have risen like that no matter when he rose! I just delayed it some!'

'It would have helped if we had known he was in there!'

'It would have helped if your ho of a cousin hadn't killed him in the first place!'

We both screeched to a halt in our dialogue. 'Are you sure that's what happened?' I asked. 'Claudine?'

'I don't know,' she said, her voice placid. 'I'm not omnipotent or omniscient. I just pop in to intervene when I can. You remember that time you fell asleep at the wheel and I got there in time to save you?'

And she'd nearly given me a heart attack in the process, appearing in the front seat of the car in the blink of an eye. 'Yes,' I said, trying to sound grateful and humble. 'I remember.'

'It's really, really hard to get somewhere that fast,' she said. 'I can only do that in a real emergency. I mean, a life-or-death emergency. Fortunately, I had a bit more time when your house was on fire. . . .'

Claudine was not going to give us any rules, or even explain the nature of the rule maker. I'd just have to muddle through on my belief system, which had helped me out all my life. Come to think of it, if I was completely wrong, I didn't want to know.

'Interesting,' said Amelia. 'But we have a few more things to talk about.'

Maybe she was being so hoity-toity because she didn't have her own fairy godmother.

'What do you want to talk about first?' I asked.

'Why'd you leave the hospital last night?' Her face was tight with resentment. 'You should have told me. I hauled myself up these stairs last night to look for you, and there you were. And you'd barricaded the door. So I had to go back down the damn stairs again to get my keys, and let myself in the French windows, and hurry – on *this leg* – to the alarm system to turn it off. And then this doofus was sitting by your bed, and she could have done all of that.'

'You couldn't open the windows with magic?' I asked.

'I was too tired,' she said with dignity. 'I had to recharge my magical batteries, so to speak.'

'So to speak,' I said, my voice dry. 'Well, last night, I found out . . .' and I stopped dead. I simply couldn't speak of it.

'Found out what?' Amelia was exasperated, and I couldn't say as I blamed her.

'Bill, her first lover, was planted in Bon Temps to seduce her and gain her trust,' Claudine said. 'Last night, he admitted that to her face, and in front of her only other lover, another vampire.'

As a synopsis, it was flawless.

'Well . . . that sucks,' Amelia said faintly.

'Yeah,' I said. 'It does.'

'Ouch.'

'Yeah.'

'I can't kill him for you,' Claudine said. 'I'd have to take too many steps backward.'

'That's okay,' I told her. 'He's not worth your losing any brownie points.'

'Oh, I'm not a brownie,' Claudine explained kindly. 'I thought you understood. I'm a full-blooded fairy.'

Amelia was trying not to laugh, and I glared at her. 'Just let it go, witch,' I said.

'Yes, telepath.'

'So what next?' I asked, in general. I would not talk any more about my broken heart and my demolished self-worth.

'We figure out what happened,' the witch said.

'How? Call CSI?'

Claudine looked confused, so I guessed fairies didn't watch television.

'No,' Amelia said, with elaborate patience. 'We do an ectoplasmic reconstruction.'

I was sure that my expression matched Claudine's, now.

'Okay, let me explain,' Amelia said, grinning all over. 'This is what we do.'

Amelia, in seventh heaven at this exhibition of her wonderful witch powers, told Claudine and me at length about the procedure. It was time- and energy-consuming, she said, which was why it wasn't done more often. And you had to gather at least four witches, she estimated, to cover the amount of square footage involved in Jake's murder.

'And I'll need real witches,' Amelia said. 'Quality workers, not some hedgerow Wiccan.' Amelia went off on Wiccans for a good long while. She despised Wiccans (unfairly) as tree-hugging wannabes – that came out of Amelia's thoughts clearly enough. I regretted Amelia's prejudice, as I'd met some impressive Wiccans.

Claudine looked down at me, her expression doubtful. 'I'm not sure we ought to be here for this,' she said.

'You can go, Claudine.' I was ready to experiment with anything, just to take my mind off the big hole in my heart. 'I'm going to stay to watch. I have to know what happened here. There are too many mysteries in my life, right now.'

'But you have to go to the queen's tonight,' Claudine said. 'You missed last night. Visiting the queen is a dress-up occasion. I have to take you shopping. You don't want to wear any of your cousin's clothes.'

'Not that my butt could get into them,' I said.

'Not that your butt should want to,' she said, equally harshly. 'You can cut that out right now, Sookie Stackhouse.'

I looked up at her, letting her see the pain inside me.

'Yeah, I get that,' she said, her hand patting me gently on the cheek. 'And that sucks big-time. But you have to write it off. He's only one guy.'

He'd been the first guy. 'My grandmother served him lemonade,' I said, and somehow that triggered the tears again.

'Hey,' Amelia said. 'Fuck him, right?'

I looked at the young witch. She was pretty and tough and off-the-wall nuts, I thought. She was okay. 'Yeah,' I said. 'When can you do the ecto thing?'

She said, 'I have to make some phone calls, see who I can get together. Night's always better for magic, of course. When will you go pay your call to the queen?'

I thought for a moment. 'Just at full dark,' I said. 'Maybe about seven.'

'Should take about two hours,' Amelia said, and Claudine nodded. 'Okay, I'll ask them to be here at ten, to have a little wiggle room. You know, it would be great if the queen would pay for this.'

'How much do you want to charge?'

'I'd do it for nothing, to have the experience and be able to say I'd done one,' Amelia said frankly, 'but the others will need some bucks. Say, three hundred apiece, plus materials.'

'And you'll need three more witches?'

'I'd like to have three more, though whether I can get the ones I want on this short notice . . . well, I'll do the best I can. Two might do. And the materials ought to be . . . She did some rapid mental calculations. 'Somewhere in the ballpark of sixty dollars.'

'What will I need to do? I mean, what's my part?'

'Observe. I'll do the heavy lifting.'

'I'll ask the queen.' I took a deep breath. 'If she won't pay for it, I will.'

'Okay, then. We're set.' She limped out of the bedroom happily, counting off things on her fingers. I heard her go down the stairs.

Claudine said, 'I have to treat your arm. And then we need to go find you something to wear.'

'I don't want to spend money on a courtesy call to the vampire queen.' Especially since I might have to foot the bill for the witches.

'You don't have to. It's my treat.'

'You may be my fairy godmother, but you don't have to spend money on me.' I had a sudden revelation. 'It's you who paid my hospital bill in Clarice.'

Claudine shrugged. 'Hey, it's money that came in from the strip club, not from my regular job.' Claudine co-owned the strip club in Ruston, with Claude, who did all the day-to-day running of the place.

Claudine was a customer service person at a department store. People forgot their complaints once they were confronted with Claudine's smile.

It was true that I didn't mind spending the strip club money as much as I would have hated using up Claudine's personal savings. Not logical, but true.

Claudine had parked her car in the courtyard on the circular drive, and she was sitting in it when I came down the stairs. She'd gotten a first aid kit from the car, and she'd bandaged my arm and helped me into some clothes. My arm was sore but it didn't seem to be infected. I was weak, as if I'd had the flu or some other illness involving high fever and lots of fluids. So I was moving slowly.

I was wearing blue jeans and sandals and a T-shirt, because that was what I had.

'You definitely can't call on the queen in that,' she said, gently but decisively. Whether she was very familiar with New Orleans or just had good shopping karma, Claudine drove directly to a store in the Garden District. It was the kind of shop I'd dismiss as being for more sophisticated women with lots more money than I had, if I'd been shopping by myself. Claudine pulled right into the parking lot, and in forty-five minutes we had a dress. It was chiffon, short-sleeved, and it had lots of colors in it: turquoise, copper, brown, ivory. The strappy sandals that I wore with it were brown.

All I needed was a membership to the country club.

Claudine had appropriated the price tag.

'Just wear your hair loose,' Claudine advised. 'You don't need fancy hair with that dress.'

'Yeah, there is a lot going on in it,' I said. 'Who's Diane von Furstenburg? Isn't it real expensive? Isn't it a little bare for the season?'

'You might be a little cool wearing it in March,' Claudine conceded. 'But it'll be good to wear every summer for years. You'll look great. And the queen will know you took the time to wear something special to meet her.'

'You can't go with me?' I asked, feeling a little wistful. 'No, of course, you can't.' Vampires buzz around fairies like hummingbirds around sugar water.

'I might not survive,' she said, managing to sound embarrassed that such a possibility would keep her from my side.

'Don't worry about it. After all, the worst thing has already happened, right?' I spread my hands. 'They used to threaten me, you know? If I didn't do thus and such, they'd take it out on Bill. Hey, guess what? *I don't care any more.*'

'Think before you speak,' Claudine advised. 'You can't mouth off to the queen. Even a goblin won't mouth off to the queen.'

'I promise,' I said. 'I really appreciate your coming all this way, Claudine.'

Claudine gave me a big hug. It was like an embrace with a soft tree, since Claudine was so tall and slim. 'I wish you hadn't needed me to,' she said.

Chapter 17

The queen owned a block of buildings in downtown New Orleans, maybe three blocks from the edge of the French Quarter. That tells you what kind of money she was pulling in, right there. We had an early dinner – I realized I was really hungry – and then Claudine dropped me off two blocks away, because the traffic and tourist congestion were intense close to the queen's headquarters. Though the general public didn't know Sophie-Anne Leclerq was a queen, they knew she was a very wealthy vampire who owned a hell of a lot of real estate and spent lots of money in the community. Plus, her bodyguards were colorful and had gotten special permits to carry arms in the city limits. This meant her office building/living quarters were on the tourist list of things to see, especially at night.

Though traffic did surround the building during the day, at night the square of streets around it was open only to pedestrians. Buses parked a block away, and the tour guides would lead the out-of-towners past the altered building. Walking tours and gaggles of independent tourists included what the guides called 'Vampire Headquarters' in their plans.

Security was very evident. This block would be a natural target for Fellowship of the Sun bombers. A few vampire-owned businesses in other cities had been attacked, and the queen was not about to lose her life-after-death in such a way.

The vampire guards were on duty, and they were scary-looking as hell. The queen had her own vampire SWAT team. Though vampires were simply lethal all on their own, the queen had found that humans paid more attention if they found the silhouettes recognizable. Not only were the guards heavily armed, but they wore black bulletproof armor over black uniforms. It was lethal-killer *chic*.

Claudine had prepared me for all this over dinner, and when she let me out, I felt fully briefed. I also felt as if I were going to the Queen of England's garden party in all my new finery. At least I didn't have to wear a hat. But my brown high heels were a risky proposition on the rough paving.

'Behold the headquarters of New Orleans's most famous and visible vampire, Sophie-Anne LeClerq,' a tour guide was telling his group. He was dressed colorfully in a sort of colonial outfit: tricorn hat, knee breeches, hose, buckled shoes. My goodness. As I paused to listen, his eyes flickered over to me, took in my outfit, and sharpened with interest.

'If you're calling on Sophie-Anne, you can't go in casual,' he told the group, and gestured to me. 'This young lady is wearing proper dress for an interview with the vampire ... one of America's most prominent vampires.' He grinned at the group, inviting them to enjoy his reference.

There were fifty other vampires just as prominent. Maybe not as publicly oriented or as colorful as Sophie-Anne Leclerq, but the public didn't know that.

Rather than being surrounded with the appropriate air of exotic deadliness, the queen's 'castle' was more of a macabre Disneyland, thanks to the souvenir peddlers, the tour guides, and the curious gawkers. There was even a photographer. As I approached the first ring of guards, a man jumped in front of me and snapped my picture. I was frozen by the flash of light and stared after him – or in what I thought was his direction – while my eyes adjusted. When I was able to see him clearly, I found he was a small, grubby man with a big camera and a determined expression. He bustled off immediately to what I guessed was his accustomed station, a corner on the opposite side of the street. He didn't offer to sell me a picture or tell me where I could purchase one, and he didn't give me any explanation.

I had a bad feeling about this incident. When I talked to one of the guards, my suspicion was confirmed.

'He's a Fellowship spy,' said the vampire, nodding in the little man's direction. He'd located my name on a checklist clamped to a clipboard. The guard himself was a sturdy man with brown skin and a nose as curved as a rainbow. He'd been born somewhere in the Middle East, once-upon a time. The name patch attached with Velcro to his helmet said RASUL.

'We're forbidden to kill him,' Rasul said, as if he were explaining a slightly embarrassing folk custom. He smiled at me, which was kind of disconcerting, too. The black helmet came down low on his face and the chinstrap was the kind that actually rounded his chin, so I could see only a little bit of his face. At the moment, that bit was mostly sharp, white teeth. 'The Fellowship photographs everyone who goes in and out of this place, and there doesn't seem to be anything we can do about it, since we want to keep the goodwill of the humans.'

Rasul correctly assumed I was a vampire ally, since I was on the visitors list, and was treating me with a camaraderie that I found relaxing. 'It would be lovely if something happened to his camera,' I suggested. 'The Fellowship is hunting me already.' Though I felt pretty guilty, asking a vampire to arrange an accident to another human being, I was fond enough of my own life to want it saved.

His eyes gleamed as we passed under a streetlight. The light caught them so that for a moment they shone red, like people's eyes sometimes do when the photographer is using a flash.

'Oddly enough, a few things have happened to his cameras already,' Rasul said. 'In fact, two of them have been smashed beyond repair. What's one more accident? I'm not guaranteeing anything, but we'll do our best, lovely lady.'

'Thank you so much,' I said. 'Anything you can do will be much appreciated. After tonight, I can talk to a witch who could maybe take care of that problem for you. Maybe she could make all the pictures turn out overexposed, or something. You should give her a call.'

'That's an excellent idea. Here is Melanie,' he said, as we reached the main doors. 'I'll pass you on to her, and return to my post. I'll see you when you exit, get the witch's name and address?'

'Sure,' I said.

'Did anyone ever tell you that you smell enchantingly like a fairy?' Rasul said.

'Oh, I've been with my fairy godmother,' I explained. 'She took me shopping.'

'And the result was wonderful,' he said gallantly.

'You flatterer.' I couldn't help but smile back at him. My ego had taken a blow to the solar plexus the night before (but I *wasn't thinking about that*), and a little thing like the guard's admiration was just what I needed, even if it was really Claudine's smell that had triggered it.

Melanie was a delicate woman, even in the SWAT gear. 'Yum, yum, you do smell like fairy,' she said. She consulted her own clipboard. 'You are the Stackhouse woman? The queen expected you last night.'

'I got hurt.' I held my arm out, showing the bandage. Thanks to a lot of Advil, the pain was down to a dull throb.

'Yes, I heard about it. The new one is having a great night tonight. He received instructions, he has a mentor, and he has a volunteer donor. When he feels more like his new self, he may tell us how he came to be turned.'

'Oh?' I heard my voice falter when I realized she was talking about Jake Purifoy. 'He might not remember?'

'If it's a surprise attack, sometimes they don't remember for a while,' she said, and shrugged. 'But it always comes back, sooner or later. In the meantime, he'll have a free lunch.' She laughed at my inquiring look. 'They register for the privilege, you know. Stupid humans.' She shrugged. 'There's no fun in that, once you've gotten over the thrill of feeding, in and of itself. The fun was always in the chase.' Melanie really wasn't happy with the new vampire policy of feeding only from willing humans or from the synthetic blood. She clearly felt the lack of her former diet.

I tried to look politely interested.

'When the prey makes the first advance, it's just not the same,' she grumped. 'People these days.' She shook her little head in weary exasperation. Since she was so small that her helmet almost wobbled on her head, I could feel myself smiling.

'So, he wakes up and you all herd the volunteer in? Like dropping a live mouse into a snake's tank?' I worked to keep my face serious. I didn't want Melanie to think I was making fun of her personally.

After a suspicious moment, Melanie said, 'More or less. He's been lectured. There are other vampires present.'

'And the volunteer survives?'

'They sign a release beforehand,' Melanie said, carefully.

I shuddered.

Rasul had escorted me from the other side of the street to the main entrance to the queen's domain. It was a three-storey office building, perhaps dating from the fifties, and extending a whole city block. In other places, the basement would have been the vampires' retreat, but in New Orleans, with its high water table, that was impossible. All the windows had received a distinctive treatment. The panels that covered them were decorated in a Mardi Gras theme, so the staid brick building was pepped up with pink, purple, and green designs on a white or black background. There were iridescent patches on the shutters, too, like Mardi Gras beads. The effect was disconcerting.

'What does she do when she throws a party?' I asked. Despite the shutters, the prosaic office rectangle was simply not festive.

'Oh, she owns an old monastery,' Melanie said. 'You can get a brochure about it before you go. That's where all the state functions are held. Some of the old ones can't go into the former chapel, but other than that . . . it's got a high wall all around, so it's easy to patrol, and it's decorated real nice. The queen has apartments there, but it's too insecure for year-round living.'

I couldn't think of anything to say. I doubted I would ever see the queen's state residence. But Melanie seemed bored and inclined to chat. 'You were Hadley's cousin, I hear?' she asked.

'Yes.'

'Strange, to think of having living relatives.' For a moment, she looked far away, and as wistful as a vampire can look. Then she seemed to kind of shake herself mentally. 'Hadley wasn't bad for one so young. But she seemed to take her vampire longevity a little too much for granted.' Melanie shook her head. 'She should never have crossed someone as old and wily as Waldo.'

'That's for damn sure,' I said.

'Chester,' Melanie called. Chester was the next guard in line, and he was standing with a familiar figure clothed in the (what I was coming to think of as) usual SWAT garb.

'Bubba!' I exclaimed, as the vampire said, 'Miss Sookie!' Bubba and I hugged, to the vampires' amusement. Vampires don't shake hands, in the ordinary course of things, and hugging is just as outré in their culture.

I was glad to see they hadn't let him have a gun, just the accoutrements of the guards. He was looking fine in the military outfit, and I told him so. 'Black looks real good with your hair,' I said, and Bubba smiled his famous smile.

'You're mighty nice to say so,' he said 'Thank you very much.'

Back in the day, everyone in the world had known Bubba's face and smile. When he'd been wheeled into the morgue in Memphis, a vampire attendant had detected the tiniest flicker of life. Since the attendant was a huge fan, he had taken on the responsibility for bringing the singer over, and a legend had been born. Unfortunately, Bubba's body had been so saturated with drugs and physical woes that the conversion hadn't been entirely successful, and the vampire world passed Bubba around like the public relations nightmare he was.

'How long have you been here, Bubba?' I asked.

'Oh, a couple of weeks, but I like it real well,' he said. 'Lots of stray cats.'

'Right,' I said, trying not to think about that too graphically. I really like cats. So did Bubba, but not in the same way.

'If a human catches a glimpse of him, they think he's an impersonator,' Chester said quietly. Melanie had gone back to her post, and Chester, who'd been a sandy-haired kid from the backwoods with poor dentition when he was taken, was now in charge of me. 'That's fine, most often. But every so now and then, they call him by his used-to-be name. Or they ask him to sing.'

Bubba very seldom sang these days, though every now and then he could be coaxed into belting out a familiar song or two. That was a memorable occasion. Most often, though, he denied he could sing a note, and he usually got very agitated when he was called by his original name.

He trailed along after us as Chester led me further into the building. We had turned, and gone up a floor, encountering more and more vampires – and a few humans – heading here or there with a purposeful air. It was like any busy office building, any weekday, except the workers were vampires and the sky outside was as dark as the New Orleans sky ever got. As we walked, I noticed that some vampires seemed more at ease than others. I observed that the wary vamps were all wearing the same pins attached to their collars, pins in the shape of the state of Arkansas. These vamps must be part of the entourage of the queen's husband, Peter Threadgill. When one of the Louisiana vampires bumped into an Arkansas vampire, the Arkansan snarled and for a second I thought there would be a fight in the corridor over a slight accident.

Jeesh, I'd be glad to get out of here. The atmosphere was tense.

Chester stopped before a door that didn't look any different from all the other closed doors, except for the two whacking big vampires outside it. The two must have been considered giants in their day, since they stood perhaps six foot three. They looked like brothers, but maybe it was just their size and mien, and the color of their chestnut hair, that sparked the comparison: big as boulders, bearded, with ponytails that trailed down their backs, the two looked like prime meat for the pro wrestling circuit. One had a huge scar across his face, acquired before death, of course. The other had had some skin disease in his original life. They weren't just display items; they were absolutely lethal.

(By the way, some promoter had had the idea for a vampire wrestling circuit a couple of years before, but it went down in flames immediately. At the first match, one vamp had ripped another's arm off, on live TV. Vamps don't get the concept of exhibition fighting.)

These two vampires were hung with knives, and each had an ax in his belt. I guess they figured if someone had penetrated this far, guns weren't going to make a difference. Plus their own bodies were weapons.

'Bert, Bert,' Chester said, nodding to each one in turn. 'This here's the Stackhouse woman; the queen wants to see her.'

He turned and walked away, leaving me with the queen's bodyguards.

Screaming didn't seem like a good idea, so I said, 'I can't believe you both have the same name. Surely he made a mistake?'

Two pairs of brown eyes focused on me intently. 'I am Sigebert,' the scarred one said, with a heavy accent I couldn't identify. He said his name as *See-ya-bairt*. Chester was using a very Americanized version of what must be a very old name. 'Dis my brodder, Wybert.'

This is my brother, Way-bairt? 'Hello,' I said, trying not to twitch. 'I'm Sookie Stackhouse.'

They seemed unimpressed. Just then, one of the pinned vampires squeezed past, casting a look of scarcely veiled contempt at the brothers, and the atmosphere in the corridor became lethal. Sigebert and Wybert watched the vamp, a tall woman in a business suit, until she rounded a corner. Then their attention switched back to me.

'The queen is . . . busy,' Wybert said. 'When she wants you in her room, the light, it will shine.' He indicated a round light set in the wall to the right of the door.

So I was stuck here for an indefinite time – until the light, it shone. 'Do your names have a meaning? I'm guessing they're, um, early English?' My voice petered out.

'We were Saxons. Our fadder went from Germany to England, you call now,' Wybert said. 'My name mean Bright Battle.'

'And mine, Bright Victory,' Sigebert added.

I remembered a program I'd seen on the History Channel. The Saxons eventually became the Anglo-Saxons and later were overwhelmed by the Normans. 'So you were raised to be warriors,' I said, trying to look intelligent.

They exchanged glances. 'There was nothing else,' Sigebert said. The end of his scar wiggled when he talked, and I tried not to stare. 'We were sons of war leader.'

I could think of a hundred questions to ask them about their lives as humans, but standing in the middle of a hallway in an office building in the night didn't seem the time to do it. 'How'd you happen to become vampires?' I asked. 'Or is that a tacky question? If it is, just forget I said anything. I don't want to step on any toes.'

Sigebert actually glanced down at his feet, so I got the idea that colloquial English wasn't their strong suit. 'This woman . . . very beautiful ... she come to us the night before battle,' Wybert said haltingly. 'She say ... we be stronger if she ... have us.'

They looked at me inquiringly, and I nodded to show I understood that Wybert was saying the vampire had implied her interest was in bedding them. Or had they understood she meant to bleed them? I couldn't tell. I thought it was a mighty ambitious vampire who would take on these two humans at the same time.

'She did not say we only fight at night after that,' Sigebert said, shrugging to show that there had been a catch they hadn't understood. 'We did not ask plenty questions. We too eager!' And he smiled. Okay, nothing so scary as a vampire left with only his fangs. It was possible Sigebert had more teeth in the back of his mouth, ones I couldn't see from my height, but Chester's plentiful-though-crooked teeth had looked super in comparison.

'That must have been a very long time ago,' I said, since I couldn't think of anything else to say. 'How long have you worked for the queen?'

Sigebert and Wybert looked at each other. 'Since that night,' Wybert said, astonished I hadn't understood. 'We are hers.'

My respect for the queen, and maybe my fear of the queen, escalated. Sophie-Anne, if that was her real name, had been brave, strategic, and busy in her career as a vampire leader. She'd brought them over and kept them with her, in a bond that – the one whose name I wasn't going to speak even to myself – had explained to me was stronger than any other emotional tie, for a vampire.

To my relief, the light shone green in the wall.

Sigebert said, 'Go now,' and pushed open the heavy door. He and Wybert gave me matching nods of farewell as I walked over the threshold and into a room that was like any executive's office anywhere.

Sophie-Anne Leclerq, Queen of Louisiana, and a male vampire were sitting at a round table piled with papers. I'd met the queen once before, when she'd come to my place to tell me about my cousin's death. I hadn't noticed then how young she must have been when she died, maybe no more than fifteen. She was an elegant woman, perhaps four inches shorter than my height of five foot six, and she was groomed down to the last eyelash. Makeup, dress, hair, stockings, jewelry – the whole nine yards.

The vampire at the table with her was her male counterpart. He wore a suit that would have paid my cable bill for a year, and he was barbered and manicured and scented until he almost wasn't a guy any more. In my neck of the woods, I didn't often see men so groomed. I guessed this was the new king. I wondered if he'd died in such a state; actually, I wondered if the funeral home had cleaned him up like that for his funeral, not knowing that his descent below ground was only temporary. If that had been the case, he was younger than his queen. Maybe age wasn't the only requirement, if you were aiming to be royalty.

There were two other people in the room. A short man stood about three feet behind the queen's chair, his legs apart, his hands clasped in front of him. He had close-cut white-blond hair and bright blue eyes. His face lacked maturity; he looked like a large child, but with a man's shoulders. He was wearing a suit, and he was armed with a saber and a gun.

Behind the man at the table stood a woman, a vampire, dressed all in red; slacks, T-shirt, Converses. Her preference was unfortunate, because red was not her color. She was Asian, and I thought she'd come from Vietnam – though it had probably been called something else then. She had very short unpainted nails, and a terrifying sword strapped to her back. Apparently, her hair had been cut off at chin length by a pair of rusty scissors. Her face was the unenhanced one God had given her.

Since I hadn't had a briefing on the correct protocol, I dipped my head to the queen, said, 'Good to see you again, ma'am,' and tried to look pleasantly at the king while doing the head-dip thing again. The two standees, who must be aides or bodyguards, received smaller nods. I felt like an idiot, but I didn't want to ignore them. However, they didn't have a problem with ignoring me, once they'd given me an all-over threat assessment.

'You've had some adventures in New Orleans,' the queen said, a safe lead-in. She wasn't smiling, but then I had the impression she was not a smiley kind of gal.

'Yes, ma'am.'

'Sookie, this is my husband. Peter Threadgill, King of Arkansas.' There was not a trace of affection on her face. She might as well have been telling me the name of her pet cockapoo.

'How-de-do,' I said, and repeated my head-bob, adding, 'Sir,' hastily. Okay, already tired of this.

'Miss Stackhouse,' he said, turning his attention back to the papers in front of him. The round table was large and completely cluttered with letters, computer printouts, and an assortment of other papers – bank statements?

While I was relieved not to be an object of interest to the king, I was wondering exactly why I was there. I found out when the queen began to question me about the night before. I told her as explicitly as I could what had happened.

She looked very serious when I talked about Amelia's stasis spell and what it had done to the body.

'You don't think the witch knew the body was there when she cast the spell?' the queen asked. I noticed that though the king's gaze was on the papers in front of him, he hadn't moved a one of them since I'd begun talking. Of course, maybe he was a very slow reader.

'No, ma'am. I know Amelia didn't know he was there.'

'From your telepathic ability?'

'Yes, ma'am.'

Peter Threadgill looked at me then, and I saw that his eyes were an unusual glacial gray. His face was full of sharp angles: a nose like a blade, thin straight lips, high cheekbones.

The king and the queen were both good-looking, but not in a way that struck any chord in me. I had an impression that the feeling was mutual. Thank God.

'You're the telepath that my dear Sophie wants to bring to the conference,' Peter Threadgill said.

Since he was telling me something I already knew, I didn't feel the need to answer. But discretion won over sheer irritation. 'Yes, I am.'

'Stan has one,' the queen said to her husband, as if vampires collected telepaths the way dog fanciers collected springer spaniels.

The only Stan I knew was a head vampire in Dallas, and the only other telepath I'd ever met had lived there. From the queen's few words, I guessed that Barry the Bellman's life had changed a lot since I'd met him. Apparently he worked for Stan Davis now. I didn't know if Stan was the sheriff or even a king, since at the time I hadn't been privy to the fact that vampires had such.

'So you're now trying to match your entourage to Stan's?' Peter Threadgill asked his wife, in a distinctly unfond kind of way. From the many clues thrown my way, I'd gotten the picture that this wasn't a love match. If you asked me to cast a vote, I would say it wasn't even a lust match. I knew the queen had liked my cousin Hadley in a lusty way, and the two brothers on guard had said she'd rocked their world. Peter Threadgill was nowhere near either side of that spectrum. But maybe that only proved the queen was omnisexual, if that was a word. I'd have to look it up when I went home. If I ever got home.

'If Stan can see the advantage in employing such a person, I can certainly consider it – especially since one is easily available.'

I was in stock.

The king shrugged. Not that I had formed many expectations, but I would have anticipated that the king of a nice, poor, scenic state like Arkansas would be less sophisticated and folksier, with a sense of humor. Maybe Threadgill was a carpetbagger from New York City. Vampire accents tended to be all over the map literally – so it was impossible to tell from his speech.

'So what do you think happened in Hadley's apartment?' the queen asked me, and I realized we'd reverted to the original subject.

'I don't know who attacked Jake Purifoy,' I said. 'But the night Hadley went to the graveyard with Waldo, Jake's drained body landed in her closet. As to how it came there, I couldn't say. That's why Amelia is having this ecto thing tonight.'

The queen's expression changed; she actually looked interested. 'She's having an ectoplasmic reconstruction? I've heard of those, but never witnessed one.'

The king looked more than interested. For a split second, he looked extremely angry.

I forced my attention back to the queen. 'Amelia wondered if you would care to, ah, fund it?' I wondered if I should add, 'My lady,' but I just couldn't bring myself to do it.

'That would be a good investment, since our newest vampire might have gotten us all into a great deal of trouble. If he had gotten loose on the populace . . . I will be glad to pay.'

I drew a breath of sheer relief.

'And I think I'll watch, too,' the queen added, before I could even exhale.

That sounded like the worst idea in the world; I thought the queen's presence would flatten Amelia until all the magic was squished out. However, there was no way I was going to tell the queen she was not welcome.

Peter Threadgill had looked up sharply when the queen had announced she'd watch. 'I don't think you should go,' he said, his voice smooth and authoritative. 'It will be hard for the twins and Andre to guard you out in the city in a neighborhood like that.'

I wondered how the King of Arkansas had any idea what Hadley's neighborhood was like. Actually, it was a quiet, middle-class area, especially compared to the zoo that was vampire central headquarters, with its constant stream of tourists and picketers and fanatics with cameras.

Sophie-Anne was already preparing to go out. That preparation consisted of glancing in a mirror to make sure the flawless façade was still flawless and sliding on her high, high heels, which had been below the edge of the table. She'd been sitting there barefoot. That detail suddenly made Sophie-Anne Leclerq much more real to me. There was a personality under that glossy exterior.

'I suppose you would like Bill to accompany us,' the queen said to me.

'No,' I snapped. Okay, there was a personality – and it was unpleasant and cruel.

But the queen looked genuinely startled. Her husband was outraged at my rudeness – his head shot up and his odd gray eyes fixed me with a luminous anger – but the queen was simply taken aback by my reaction. 'I thought you were a couple,' she said, in a perfectly even voice.

I bit back my first answer, trying to remember who I was talking to, and said, almost in a whisper, 'No, we are not.' I took a deep breath and made a great effort. 'I apologize for being so abrupt. Please excuse me.'

The queen simply looked at me for a few seconds longer, and I still could not get the slightest indication of her thoughts, emotions, or intentions. It was like looking at an antique silver tray – a shining surface, an elaborate pattern, and hard to the touch. How Hadley could have been adventurous enough to bed this woman was simply beyond my comprehension.

'You are excused,' she said finally.

'You're too lenient,' her husband said, and his surface, at least, began to thin somewhat. His lips curled in something closely approaching a snarl, and I discovered I didn't want to be the focus of those luminous eyes for another second. I didn't like the way the Asian gal in red was looking at me, either. And every time I looked at her haircut, it gave me the heebie-jeebies. Gosh, even the elderly lady who'd given my gran a permanent three times a year would have done a better job than the Mad Weed Whacker.

'I'll be back in an hour or two, Peter,' Sophie-Anne said, very precisely, in a tone that could have sliced a diamond. The short man, his childish face blank, was by her side in a jiffy, extending his arm so she could have his assistance in rising. I guessed he was Andre.

The atmosphere was cuttable. Oh, I so wished I were somewhere else.

'I would feel more at ease if I knew Jade Flower was with you,' the king said. He motioned toward the woman in red. Jade Flower, my ass: she looked more like Stone Killer. The Asian woman's face didn't change one iota at the king's offer.

'But that would leave you with no one,' the queen said.

'Hardly true. The building is full of guards and loyal vampires,' Peter Threadgill said.

Okay, even I caught that one. The guards, who belonged to the queen, were separate from the loyal vampires, whom I guessed were the ones Peter had brought with him.

'Then, of course, I would be proud to have a fighter like Jade Flower accompany me.'

Yuck. I couldn't tell if the queen was serious, or trying to placate her new husband by accepting his offer, or laughing up her sleeve at his lame strategy to ensure that his spy was at the ectoplasmic reconstruction. The queen used the intercom to call down – or up, for all I knew – to the secure chamber where Jake Purifoy was being educated in the ways of the vampire. 'Keep extra guards on Purifoy,' she said. 'And let me know the minute he remembers something.' An obsequious voice assured Sophie-Anne that she'd be the first to know.

I wondered why Jake needed extra guards. I found it hard to get real concerned about his welfare, but obviously the queen was.

So here we went – the queen, Jade Flower, Andre, Sigebert, Wybert, and me. I guess I've been in company just as assorted, but I couldn't tell you when. After a lot of corridor tromping, we entered a guarded garage and piled into a stretch limo. Andre jerked his thumb at one of the guards, indicating that the guard should drive. I hadn't heard the baby-faced vampire utter a word, so far. To my pleasure, the driver was Rasul, who felt like an old friend compared to the others.

Sigebert and Wybert were uncomfortable in the car. They were the most inflexible vampires I'd ever met, and I wondered if their close association with the queen hadn't been their undoing. They hadn't had to change, and changing with the times was the key vampire survival technique before the Great Revelation. It remained so in countries that hadn't accepted the existence of vampire with the tolerance America had shown. The two vampires would have been happy wearing skins and hand-woven cloth and would have looked perfectly at home in handmade leather boots, carrying shields on their arms.

'Your sheriff, Eric, came to speak to me last night,' the queen told me.

'I saw him at the hospital,' I said, hoping I sounded equally off-handed.

'You understand that the new vampire, the one that was a Were – he had no choice, you understand?'

'I get that a lot with vampires,' I said, remembering all the times in the past when Bill had explained things by saying he couldn't help himself. I'd believed him at the time, but I wasn't so sure any more. In fact, I was so profoundly tired and miserable I hardly had the heart to continue trying to wrap up Hadley's apartment and her estate and her affairs. I realized that if I went home to Bon Temps, leaving unfinished business here, I'd just sit and brood when I got there.

I knew this, but at the moment, it was hard to face.

It was time for one of my self-pep talks. I told myself sternly I'd already enjoyed a moment or two of that very evening, and I would enjoy a few more seconds of every day until I built back to my former contented state. I'd always enjoyed life, and I knew I would again. But I was going to have to slog through a lot of bad patches to get there.

I don't think I've ever been a person with a lot of illusions. If you can read minds, you don't have many doubts about how bad even the best people can be.

But I sure hadn't seen this coming.

To my horror, tears began sliding down my face. I reached into my little purse, pulled out a Kleenex, and patted my cheeks while all the vamps stared at me, Jade Flower with the most identifiable expression I'd seen on her face: contempt.

'Are you in pain?' the queen asked, indicating my arm.

I didn't think she really cared; I was sure that she had schooled herself to give the correct human response for so long that it was a reflex.

'Pain of the heart,' I said, and could have bitten my tongue off.

'Oh,' she said. 'Bill?'

'Yes,' I said, and gulped, doing my best to stop the display of emotion.

'I grieved for Hadley,' she said unexpectedly.

'It was good she had someone to care.' After a minute I said, 'I would have been glad to know she was dead earlier than I did,' which was as cautiously as I could express it. I hadn't found out my cousin was gone until weeks after the fact.

'There were reasons I had to wait to send Cataliades down,' Sophie-Anne said. Her smooth face and clear eyes were as impenetrable as a wall of ice, but I got the definite impression that she wished I hadn't raised the subject. I looked at the queen, trying to pick up on some clue, and she gave a tiny flick of the eye toward Jade Flower, who was sitting on her right. I didn't know how Jade Flower could be sitting in her relaxed position with the long sword strapped to her back. But I definitely had the feeling that behind her expressionless face and flat eyes, Jade Flower was listening to everything that transpired.

To be on the safe side, I decided I wouldn't say anything at all, and the rest of the drive passed in silence.

Rasul didn't want to take the limo into the courtyard, and I recalled that Diantha had parked on the street, too. Rasul came back to open the door for the queen, and Andre got out first, looked around for a long time, then nodded that it was safe for the queen to emerge. Rasul stood at the ready, rifle in his hands, sweeping the area visually for attackers. Andre was just as vigilant.

Jade Flower slithered out of the backseat next and added her eyes to those scanning the area. Protecting the queen with their bodies, they moved into the courtyard. Sigebert got out next, ax in hand, and waited for me. After I'd joined him on the sidewalk, he and Wybert took me through the open gateway with less ceremony than the others had taken the queen.

I'd seen the queen at my own home, unguarded by anyone but Cataliades. I'd seen the queen in her own office, guarded by one person. I guess I didn't realize until that moment how important security was for Sophie-Anne, how precarious her hold on power must be. I wanted to know against whom all these guards were protecting her. Who wanted to kill the Louisiana queen? Maybe all vampire rulers were in this much danger – or maybe it was just Sophie-Anne. Suddenly the vampire conference in the fall seemed like a much scarier proposition than it had before.

The courtyard was well lit, and Amelia was standing on the circular driveway with three friends. For the record, none of them were crones with broomsticks. One of them was a kid who looked just like a Mormon missionary: black pants, white shirt, dark tie, polished black shoes. There was a bicycle leaning up against the tree in the center of the circle. Maybe he *was* a Mormon missionary. He looked so young that I thought he might still be growing. The tall woman standing beside him was in her sixties, but she had a Bowflex body. She was wearing a tight T-shirt, knit slacks, sandals, and a pair of huge hoop earrings. The third witch was about my age, in her mid- to late twenties, and she was Hispanic. She had full cheeks, bright red lips, and rippling black hair, and she was short and had more curves than an S turn. Sigebert admired her especially (I could tell by his leer), but she ignored all the vampires as if she couldn't see them.

Amelia might have been startled by the influx of vampires, but she handled introductions with aplomb. Evidently the queen had already identified herself before I approached. 'Your Majesty,' Amelia was saying, 'These are my co-practitioners.' She swept her hand before them as if she were showing off a car to the studio audience. 'Bob Jessup, Patsy Sellers, Terencia Rodriguez – Terry, we call her.'

The witches glanced at each other before nodding briefly to the queen. It was hard to tell how she took that lack of deference, her face was so glass-smooth – but she nodded back, and the atmosphere remained tolerable.

'We were just preparing for our reconstruction,' Amelia said. She sounded absolutely confident, but I noticed that her hands were trembling. Her thoughts were not nearly as confident as her voice, either. Amelia was running over their preparations in her head, frantically itemizing the magic stuff she'd assembled, anxiously reassessing her companions to satisfy herself they were up to the ritual, and so on. Amelia, I belatedly realized, was a perfectionist.

I wondered where Claudine was. Maybe she'd seen the vamps coming and prudently fled to some dark corner. While I was looking around for her, I had a moment when the heartache I was staving off just plain ambushed me. It was like the moments I had after my grandmother died, when I'd be doing something familiar like brushing my teeth, and all of a sudden the blackness would overwhelm me. It took a moment or two to collect myself and swim back to the surface again.

It would be like that for a while, and I'd just have to grit my teeth and bear it.

I made myself take notice of those around me. The witches had assumed their positions. Bob settled himself in a lawn chair in the courtyard, and I watched with a tiny flare of interest as he drew powdered stuff from little snack-size Ziploc bags and got a box of matches out of his chest pocket. Amelia bounded up the stairs to the apartment, Terry stationed herself halfway down the stairs, and the tall older witch, Patsy, was already standing on the gallery looking down at us.

'If you all want to watch, probably up here would be best,' Amelia called, and the queen and I went up the stairs. The guards gathered in a clump by the gate so they'd be as far away from the magic as they could be; even Jade Flower seemed respectful of the power that was about to be put to use, even if she did not respect the witches as people.

As a matter of course, Andre followed the queen up the stairs, but I thought there was a less than enthusiastic droop to his shoulders.

It was nice to focus on something new instead of mulling over my miseries, and I listened with interest as Amelia, who looked like she should be out playing beach volleyball, instead gave us instructions on the magic spell she was about to cast.

'We've set the time to two hours before I saw Jake arrive,' she said. 'So you may see a lot of boring and extraneous stuff. If that gets old, I can try to speed up the events.'

Suddenly I had a thought that blinded me by its sheer serendipity. I would ask Amelia to return to Bon Temps with me, and there I would ask her to repeat this procedure in my yard; then I would know what had happened to poor Gladiola. I felt much better once I'd had this idea, and I made myself pay attention to the here and now.

Amelia called out 'Begin!' and immediately began reciting words, I suppose in Latin. I heard a faint echo come up from the stairs and the courtyard as the other witches joined in.

We didn't know what to expect, and it was oddly boring to hear the chanting continue after a couple, of minutes. I began to wonder what would happen to me if the queen got very bored.

Then my cousin Hadley walked into the living room.

I was so shocked, I almost spoke to her. When I looked for just a second longer, I could tell it wasn't really Hadley. It had the shape of her, and it moved like her, but this simulacrum was only washed with color. Her hair was not a true dark, but a glistening impression of dark. She looked like tinted water, walking. You could see the surface's shimmer. I looked at her eagerly: it had been so long since we'd seen each other. Hadley looked older, of course. She looked harder, too, with a sardonic set to her mouth and a skeptical look to her eyes.

Oblivious to the presence of anyone else in the room, the reconstruction went over to the loveseat, picked up a phantom remote control, and turned on the television. I actually glanced at the screen to see if it would show anything, but of course, it didn't.

I felt a movement beside me and I glanced at the queen. If I had been shocked, she was electrified. I had never really thought the queen could have truly loved Hadley, but I saw now that she had, as much as she was able.

We watched Hadley glance at the television from time to time while she painted her toenails, drank a phantom glass of blood, and made a phone call. We couldn't hear her. We could only see, and that within a limited range. The object she reached for would appear the minute her hand touched it, but not before, so you could be sure of what she had only when she began to use it. When she leaned forward to replace the glass of blood on the table, and her hand was still holding the glass, we'd see the glass, the table with its other objects, and Hadley, all at once, all with that glistening patina. The ghost table was imposed over the real table, which was still in almost exactly the same space as it had been that night, just to make it weirder. When Hadley let go of the glass, both glass and table winked out of existence.

Andre's eyes were wide and staring when I glanced back at him, and it was the most expression I'd seen on his face. If the queen was grieving and I was fascinated and sad, Andre was simply freaked out.

We stood through a few more minutes of this until Hadley evidently heard a knock at the door. (Her head turned toward the door, and she looked surprised.) She rose (the phantom loveseat, perhaps two inches to the right of the real one, became nonexistent) and padded across the floor. She stepped through my sneakers, which were sitting side by side next to the loveseat.

Okay, that was weird. This whole thing was weird, but fascinating.

Presumably the people in the courtyard had watched the caller come up the outside stairs, since I heard a loud curse from one of the Berts – Wybert, I thought. When Hadley opened a phantom door,

Patsy, who'd been stationed outside on the gallery, pushed open the real door so we could see. From Amelia's chagrined face, I could tell she hadn't thought that one through ahead of time.

Standing at the door was (phantom) Waldo, a vampire who had been with the queen for years. He had been much punished in the years before his death, and it had left him with permanently wrinkled skin. Since Waldo had been an ultrathin albino before this punishment, he'd looked awful the one and only night I'd known him. As a watery ghost creature, he looked better, actually.

Hadley looked surprised to see him. That expression was strong enough to be easily recognizable. Then she looked disgusted. But she stepped back to let him in.

When she strolled back to the table to pick up her glass, Waldo glanced around him, as if to see if anyone else was there. The temptation to warn Hadley was so strong it was almost irresistible.

After some conversation, which of course we couldn't understand, Hadley shrugged and seemed to agree to some plan. Presumably, this was the idea Waldo had told me about the night he'd confessed to killing my cousin. He'd said it had been Hadley's idea to go to St. Louis Cemetery Number One to raise the ghost of voodooienne Marie Laveau, but from this evidence it seemed Waldo was the one who had suggested the excursion.

'What's that in his hand?' Amelia said, as quietly as she could, and Patsy stepped in from the gallery to check.

'Brochure,' she called to Amelia, trying to use equally hushed tones. 'About Marie Laveau.'

Hadley looked at the watch on her wrist and said something to Waldo. It was something unkind, judging by Hadley's expression and the jerk of her head as she indicated the door. She was saying 'No,' as clearly as body language could say it.

And yet the next night she had gone with him. What had happened to change her mind?

Hadley walked back to her bedroom and we followed her. Looking back, we watched Waldo leave the apartment, putting the brochure on the table by the door as he departed.

It felt oddly voyeuristic to stand in Hadley's bedroom with Amelia, the queen, and Andre, watching Hadley take off a bathrobe and put on a very fancy dress.

'She wore that to the party the night before the wedding,' the queen said quietly. It was a skintight, cut-down-to-here red dress decked with darker red sequins and some gorgeous alligator pumps. Hadley was going to make the queen regret what she was losing, evidently.

We watched Hadley primp in the mirror, do her hair two different ways, and mull her choice of lipsticks for a very long time. The novelty was wearing off the process, and I was willing to fast-forward, but the queen just couldn't get enough of seeing her beloved again. I sure wasn't going to protest, especially since the queen was footing the bill.

Hadley turned back and forth in front of her full-length mirror, appeared satisfied with what she saw, then burst into tears.

'Oh, my dear,' the queen said quietly. 'I am so sorry.'

I knew *exactly* how Hadley felt, and for the first time I felt the kinship with my cousin I'd lost through the years of separation. In this reconstruction, it was the night before the queen's wedding, and Hadley was going to have to go to a party and watch the queen and her fiancé be a couple. And the next night she would have to attend their wedding; or so she thought. She didn't know that she'd be dead by then; finally, definitely dead.

'Someone coming up,' called Bob the witch. His voice wafted through the open French windows onto the gallery. In the phantom, ghostly world, the doorbell must have rung, because Hadley stiffened, gave herself a last look in the mirror (right through us, since we were standing in front of it) and visibly braced herself. When Hadley walked down the hall, she had a familiar sway to her hips and her watery face was set in a cold half smile.

She pulled open the door. Since the witch Patsy had left the actual door open after Waldo had 'arrived', we could see this happening. Jake Purifoy was dressed in a tux, and he looked very good, as Amelia had said. I glanced at Amelia when he stepped into the apartment, and she was eyeing the phantasm regretfully.

He didn't care for being sent to pick up the queen's honeybun, you could tell, but he was too politic and too courteous to take that out on Hadley. He stood patiently while she got a tiny purse and gave her hair a final combing, and then the two were out the door.

'Coming down out there,' Bob called, and we went out the door and across the gallery to look over the railing. The two phantoms were getting into a glistening car and driving out of the courtyard. That was where the area affected by the spell came to an end. As the ghost car passed through the gate area, it winked out of existence right by the group of vampires who were clustered by the opening. Sigebert and Wybert were wide-eyed and solemn, Jade Flower appeared disgruntled, and Rasul looked faintly amused, as if he were thinking of the good stories he'd have to tell in the guards' mess hall.

'Time to fast-forward,' Amelia called. She was looking tired now, and I wondered how great a strain coordinating this act of witchcraft was placing on the young witch.

Patsy, Terry, Bob, and Amelia began to say another spell in unison. If there was a weak link in this team effort, it was Terry. The round-faced little witch was sweating profusely and shaking with the effort of keeping her magical end up. I felt a little worried as I saw the strain on her face.

'Take it easy, easy!' Amelia exhorted her team, having read the same signs. Then they all resumed chanting, and Terry seemed to be pacing herself a bit better; she didn't look so desperate.

Amelia said, 'Slow ... down ... now,' and the chanting eased its pace.

The car appeared again in the gate, this time running right through Sigebert, who'd taken a step forward, the better to watch Terry, I suspected. It lurched to an abrupt stop half-in, half-out of the aperture.

Hadley threw herself out of the car. She was weeping, and from the looks of her face, she'd been weeping for some time. Jake Purifoy emerged from his side and stood there, his hands on the top of his door, talking across the roof of the car at Hadley.

For the first time, the queen's personal bodyguard spoke. Andre said, 'Hadley, you have to cut this out. People will notice, and the new king will do something about it. He's the jealous kind, you know? He doesn't care about—' Here Andre lost the thread, and shook his head. 'He cares about keeping face.'

We all stared at him. Was he channeling?

The queen's bodyguard switched his gaze to the ectoplasmic Hadley. Andre said, 'But Jake, I can't stand it. I know she has to do this politically, but she's sending me away! I can't take it.'

Andre could read lips. Even ectoplasmic lips. He began speaking again.

'Hadley, go up and sleep on it. You can't go to the wedding if you're going to create a scene. You know that would embarrass the queen, and it would ruin the ceremony. My boss will kill me if that happens. This is the biggest event we've ever worked.'

He was talking about Quinn, I realized. Jake Purifoy *was* the employee Quinn had told me was missing.

'I can't stand it,' Hadley repeated. She was shrieking, I could tell from the way her mouth moved, but luckily Andre saw no need to imitate that. It was eerie enough hearing the words come out of his mouth. 'I've done something terrible!' The melodramatic words sounded very strange in Andre's monotone.

Hadley ran up the stairs, and Terry automatically moved out of the way to let her pass. Hadley unlocked the (already open) door and stormed into her apartment. We turned to watch Jake. Jake sighed, straightened up, and stepped away from the car, which vanished. He flipped open a cell phone and punched in a number. He spoke into the phone for less than a minute, with no pause for an answer, so it was safe to assume he'd gotten voice mail.

Andre said, 'Boss, I have to tell you I think there's going to be trouble. The girlfriend won't be able to control herself on the day.'

Oh my God, tell me Quinn didn't have Hadley killed! I thought, feeling absolutely sick at the thought. But even as the idea formed fully, Jake wandered over to the rear of the car, which appeared again as he brushed against it. He ran his hand lovingly along the line of the trunk, stepping closer and closer to the area outside the gate, and suddenly a hand reached out and grabbed him. The witches' area did not extend beyond the walls, so the rest of the body was absent, and the effect of a hand materializing from nowhere and seizing the unsuspecting Were was as scary as anything in a horror movie.

This was exactly like one of those dreams where you see danger approaching, but you can't speak. No warnings on our part could alter what had already happened. But we were all shocked. The brothers Bert cried out, Jade Flower drew her sword without my even seeing her hand move, and the queen's mouth fell open.

We could see only Jake's feet, thrashing. Then they lay still.

We all stood and looked at each other, even the witches, their concentration wavering until the courtyard began to fill with mist.

'Witches!' Amelia called harshly. 'Back to work!' In a moment, everything had cleared up. But Jake's feet were still, and in a moment, their outline grew still more faint; he was fading out of sight like all the other lifeless objects. In a few seconds, though, my cousin appeared on the gallery above, looking down. Her expression was cautious and worried. She'd heard something. We registered the moment when she saw the body, and she came down the stairs with vampiric speed. She leaped through the gate and was lost to sight, but in a moment she was back in, dragging the body by the feet. As long as she was touching it, the body was visible as a table or chair would have been. Then she bent over the corpse, and now we could see that Jake had a huge wound in his neck. The wound was sickening, though I have to say that the vamps watching did not look sickened, but enthralled.

Ectoplasmic Hadley looked around her, hoping for help that didn't come. She looked desperately uncertain. Her fingers never left Jake's neck as she felt for his pulse.

Finally she bent over him and said something to him.

'It's the only way,' Andre translated. 'You may hate me, but it's the only way.' We watched Hadley tear at her wrist with her own fangs and then put her bleeding wrist to Jake's mouth, watched the blood trickle inside, watched him revive enough to grip her arms and pull her down to him. When Hadley made Jake let go of her, she looked exhausted, and he looked as if he were having convulsions.

'The Were does not make a good vampire,' Sigebert said in a whisper. 'I've never before seen a Were brought over.'

It was sure hard for poor Jake Purifoy. I began to forgive him the horror of the evening before, seeing his suffering. My cousin Hadley gathered him up and carried him up the stairs, pausing every now and then to look around her. I followed her up one more time, the queen right behind me. We watched Hadley pull off Jake's ripped clothes, wrap a towel around his neck until the bleeding stopped, and stow him in the closet, carefully covering him and closing the door so the morning sun wouldn't burn the new vampire, who would have to lie in the dark for three days. Hadley crammed the bloody towel into her hamper. Then she stuffed another towel into the open space at the bottom of the door, to make sure Jake was safe.

Then she sat in the hall and thought. Finally she got her cell phone and called a number.

'She asks for Waldo,' Andre said. When Hadley's lips began moving again, Andre said, 'She makes the appointment for the next night. She says she must talk to the ghost of Marie Laveau, if the ghost will really come. She needs advice, she says.' After a little more conversation, Hadley shut her phone and got up. She gathered up the former Were's torn and bloody clothing and sealed it in a bag.

'You should get the towel, too,' I advised, in a whisper, but my cousin left it in the hamper for me to find when I arrived. Hadley got the car keys out of the trouser pockets, and when she went down the stairs, she got into the car and drove away with the garbage bag.

Chapter 18

'Your Majesty, we have to stop,' Amelia said, and the queen gave a flick of her hand that might have been agreement.

Terry was so exhausted she was leaning heavily against the railing of the stairs, and Patsy was looking almost as haggard out on the gallery. The nerdy Bob seemed unchanged, but then he'd wisely seated himself in a chair to start with. At Amelia's wordless signal, they began undoing the spell they'd cast, and gradually the eerie atmosphere lessened. We became an ill-assorted bunch of weird people in a courtyard in New Orleans, rather than helpless witnesses to a magical reenactment.

Amelia went to the corner storage shed and pulled out some folding chairs. Sigebert and Wybert did not understand the mechanism, so Amelia and Bob set the chairs out. After the queen and the witches sat, there was one remaining seat, and I took it after a silent to and fro between me and the four vampires.

'So we know what happened the next night,' I said wearily. I was feeling a little silly in my fancy dress and high-heeled sandals. It would be nice to put on my regular clothes.

'Uh, 'scuse me, you might, but the rest of us don't, and we want to know,' Bob said. He seemed oblivious to the fact that he ought to be shaking in his sandals in the queen's presence.

There was something kind of likable about the geeky witch. And all four had worked so hard; if they wanted to know the rest of the story, there wasn't any reason they couldn't hear it. The queen raised no objection. Even Jade Flower, who had resheathed her sword, looked faintly interested.

'The next night, Waldo lured Hadley to the cemetery with the story of the Marie Laveau grave and the vampire tradition that the dead can raise the dead – in this case, the voodoo priestess Marie Laveau. Hadley wanted Marie Laveau to answer her questions, which Waldo had told Hadley the ghost could, if the correct ritual was followed. Though Waldo gave me a reason Hadley agreed to do this on the night I met him, now I know he was lying. But I can think of several other reasons she might have agreed to go with Waldo to St. Louis Cemetery,' I said. The queen nodded silently. 'I think she wanted to find out what Jake would be like when he rose,' I said. 'I think she wanted to find out what to do with him. She couldn't let him die, you saw that, but she didn't want to admit to anyone that she had created a vampire, especially one that had been a Were.'

I had quite an audience. Sigebert and Wybert were squatting on either side of the queen, and they were wrapped up in the story. This must be like going to the movies, for them. All the witches were interested in hearing the backstory on the events they'd just witnessed. Jade Flower had her eyes fixed on me. Only Andre seemed immune, and he was busy doing his bodyguard job, constantly scanning the courtyard and the sky for attack.

'It's possible, too, that Hadley might have believed the ghost could give her advice on how to regain the queen's affections. No offense, ma'am,' I added, remembering too late that the queen was sitting three feet away from me in a folding lawn chair with the Wal-Mart price label still hanging on a plastic loop.

The queen waved her hand in a negligent gesture. She was sunk in thought, so deeply that I wasn't even sure she heard me.

'It wasn't Waldo who drained Jake Purifoy,' the queen said, to my amazement. 'Waldo could not have imagined that when he succeeded in killing Hadley and reported it to me, blaming it on the Fellowship of the Sun, this clever witch would obey the order to seal the apartment very literally, including a stasis spell. Waldo already had a plan. Whoever killed Jake had a separate plan – perhaps to blame Hadley for Jake's death and his rebirth . . . which would condemn her to jail in a vampire cell. Perhaps the killer thought that Jake would kill Hadley when he rose in three days . . . and possibly, he would have.'

Amelia tried to look modest, but it was an uphill battle. It should have been easy, since the only reason she'd cast the spell was to prevent the apartment from smelling like garbage when it finally was reopened. She knew it, and I knew it. But it had been a pretty piece of witchcraft, and I wasn't about to burst her bubble.

Amelia burst it all by herself.

'Or maybe,' she said blithely, 'someone paid Waldo to get Hadley out of the picture, by one means or another.'

I had to shut down my shields immediately, because all the witches began broadcasting such strong panic signals that being around them was unbearable. They knew that what Amelia had said would upset the queen, and when the Queen of Louisiana was agitated, those around her tended to be even more agitated.

The queen shot out of her chair, so we all scrambled to our feet, hastily and clumsily. Amelia had just gotten her legs tucked underneath her, so she was especially awkward, which served her right. Jade Flower took a couple steps away from the rest of the vampires, but maybe she wanted more room in case she had to swing her sword. Andre was the only one who noticed that, besides me. He kept his gaze fixed on the king's bodyguard.

I don't know what would have happened next if Quinn hadn't driven through the gate.

He got out of the big black car, ignored the tense tableau as if it didn't even exist, and strode across the gravel to me. He casually draped an arm over my shoulders and bent to give me a light kiss. I don't know how to compare one kiss to another. Men all kiss differently, don't they? And it says something about their character. Quinn kissed me as if we were carrying on a conversation.

'Babe,' he said, when I'd had the last word. 'Did I get here at a good time? What happened to your arm?'

The atmosphere relaxed a bit. I introduced him to the people standing in the courtyard. He knew all the vampires, but he hadn't met the witches. He moved away from me to meet and greet. Patsy and Amelia had obviously heard of him and tried hard not to act too impressed at meeting him.

I had to get the rest of the evening's news off my chest. 'My arm got bitten, Quinn,' I began. Quinn waited, his eyes intent on my face. 'I got bitten by a ... I'm afraid we know what happened to your employee. His name was Jake Purifoy, wasn't it?' I said.

'What?' In the bright lights of the courtyard, I saw that his expression was guarded. He knew something bad was coming; of course, seeing the assembled company, anyone would guess that.

'He was drained and left here in the courtyard. To save his life, Hadley turned him. He's become a vampire.'

Quinn didn't comprehend, for a few seconds. I watched as realization dawned as he grasped the enormity of what had happened to Jake Purifoy. Quinn's face became stony. I found myself hoping he never looked at me like that.

'The change was without the Were's consent,' the queen said. 'Of course, a Were would never agree to become one of us.' If she sounded a little snarky, I wasn't too surprised. Weres and vamps regarded each other with scarcely concealed disgust, and only the fact that they were united against the normal world kept that disgust from flaring into open warfare.

'I went by your house,' Quinn said to me, unexpectedly. 'I wanted to see if you'd gotten back from New Orleans before I drove down here to look for Jake. Who burned a demon in your driveway?'

'Someone killed Gladiola, the queen's messenger, when she came to deliver a message to me,' I said. There was a stir among the vampires around me. The queen had known about Gladiola's death, of course; Mr Cataliades would have been sure to tell her. But no one else had heard about it.

'Lots of people dying in your yard, babe,' Quinn said to me, though his tone was absent, and I didn't blame him for that being on his back burner.

'Just two,' I said defensively, after a quick mental rundown. 'I would hardly call that a lot.' Of course, if you threw in the people who'd died in the house ... I quickly shut off that train of thought.

'You know what?' Amelia said in a high, artificially social voice.

'I think we witches will just mosey on down the street to that pizza place on the corner of Chloe and Justine. So if you need us, there we'll be. Right, guys?' Bob, Patsy, and Terry moved faster than I'd thought they were able to the gate opening, and when the vampires didn't get any signal from their queen, they stood aside and let them by. Since Amelia didn't bother retrieving her purse, I hoped she had money in one pocket and her keys in another. Oh well.

I almost wished I were trailing along behind them. Wait a minute! Why couldn't I? I looked longingly at the gate, but Jade Flower stepped into the gap and stared at me, her eyes black holes in her round face. This was a woman who didn't like me one little bit. Andre, Sigebert, and Wybert could definitely take me or leave me, and Rasul might think I wouldn't be a bad companion for an hour on the town – but Jade Flower would enjoy whacking off my head with her sword, and that was a fact. I couldn't read vampire minds (except for a tiny glimpse every now and then, which was a big secret) but I could read body language and I could read the expression in her eyes.

I didn't know the reason for this animosity, and at this point in time I didn't think it mattered a heck of a lot.

The queen had been thinking. She said, 'Rasul, we shall go back to the house very shortly.' He bowed and walked out to the car.

'Miss Stackhouse,' she said, turning her eyes on me. They shone like dark lamps. She took my hand, and we went up the stairs to Hadley's apartment, Andre trailing behind us like something tied to Sophie-Anne's leg with string. I kept having the unwise impulse to yank my hand from the queen's, which of course was cold and dry and strong, though she was careful not to squeeze. Being so close to the ancient vampire made me vibrate like a violin string. I didn't see how Hadley had endured it.

She led me into Hadley's apartment and shut the door behind us. I didn't think even the excellent ears of the vampires below us could hear our conversation now. That had been her goal, because the first thing she said was, 'You will not tell anyone what I am about to tell you.'

I shook my head, mute with apprehension.

'I began my life in what became northern France, about . . . one thousand, one hundred years ago.'

I gulped.

'I didn't know where I was, of course, but I think it was Lotharingia. In the last century I tried to find the place I spent my first twelve years, but I couldn't, even if my life depended on it.' She gave a barking laugh at the turn of phrase. 'My mother was the wife of the wealthiest man in the town, which meant he had two more pigs than anyone else. My name then was Judith.'

I tried hard not to look shocked, to just look interested, but it was a struggle.

'When I was about ten or twelve, I think, a peddler came to us from down the road. We hadn't seen a new face in six months. We were excited.' But she didn't smile or look as if she remembered the feeling of that excitement, only the fact of it. Her shoulders rose and fell, once. 'He carried an illness that had never come to us before. I think now that it was some form of influenza. Within two weeks of his stay in our town, everyone in it was dead, excepting me and a boy somewhat older.'

There was a moment of silence while we thought about that. At least I did, and I suppose the queen was remembering. Andre might have been thinking about the price of bananas in Guatemala.

'Clovis did not like me,' the queen said. 'I've forgotten why. Our fathers . . . I don't remember. Things might have gone differently if he had cared for me. As it was, he raped me and then he took me to the next town, where he began offering me about. For money, of course, or food. Though the influenza traveled across our region, we never got sick.'

I tried to look anywhere but at her.

'Why will you not meet my eyes?' she demanded. Her phrasing and her accent had changed as she spoke, as if she'd just learned English.

'I feel so bad for you,' I said.

She made a sound that involved putting her top teeth on her lower lip and making the extra effort to intake some air so she could blow it out. It sounded like '*ffft!*' 'Don't bother,' the queen said. 'Because what happened next was, we were camped in the woods, and a vampire got him.' She looked pleased at the recollection. What a trip down memory lane. 'The vampire was very hungry and started on Clovis first, because he was bigger, but when he was through with Clovis, he could take a minute to look at me and think it might be nice to have a companion. His name was Alain. For three years or more I traveled with Alain. Vampires were secret then, of course. Their existence was only in stories told by old women by the fire. And Alain was good at keeping it that way. Alain had been a priest, and he was very fond of surprising priests in their beds.' She smiled reminiscently.

I found my sympathy diminishing.

'Alain promised and promised to bring me over, because of course I wanted to be as he was. I wanted the strength.' Her eyes flicked over to me.

I nodded heartily. I could understand that.

'But when he needed money, for clothes and food for me, he would do the same thing with me that Clovis had, sell me for money. He knew the men would notice if I was cold, and he knew I would bite them if he brought me over. I grew tired of his failing in his promise.'

I nodded to show her I was paying attention. And I was, but in the back of my mind I was wondering where the hell this monologue was heading and why I was the recipient of such a fascinating and depressing story.

'Then one night we came into a village where the headman knew Alain for what he was. Stupid Alain had forgotten he had passed through before and drained the headman's wife! So the villagers bound him with a silver chain, which was amazing to find in a small village, I can tell you . . . and they threw him into a hut, planning to keep him until the village priest returned from a trip. Then they meant to put him in the sun with some church ceremony. It was a poor village, but on top of him they piled all the bits of silver and all the garlic the people possessed, in an effort to keep him subdued.' The queen chuckled.

'They knew I was a human, and they knew he had abused me,' she said. 'So they didn't tie me up. The headman's family discussed taking me as a slave, since they had lost a woman to the vampire. I knew what that would be like.'

The expression on her face was both heartbreaking and absolutely chilling. I held very still.

'That night, I pulled out some weak planks from the rear of the hut and crawled in. I told Alain that when he'd brought me over, I'd free him. We bargained for quite a time, and then he agreed. I dug a hole in the floor, big enough for my body. We planned that Alain would drain me and bury me under the pallet he lay on, smoothing the dirt floor over as best he could. He could move enough for that. On the third night, I would rise. I would break his chain and toss away the garlic, though it would burn my hands. We would flee into the darkness.' She laughed out loud. 'But the priest returned before three days were up. By the time I clawed my way out of the dirt, Alain was blackened ash in the wind. It was the priest's they'd stored Alain in. The old priest was the one who told me what had happened.'

I had a feeling I knew the punch line to this story. 'Okay,' I said quickly, 'I guess the priest was your first meal.' I smiled brightly.

'Oh, no,' said Sophie-Anne, formerly Judith. 'I told him I was the angel of death, and that I was passing him over since he had been so virtuous.'

Considering the state Jake Purifoy had been in when he'd risen for the first time, I could appreciate what a gut-wrenching effort that must have been for the new vampire.

'What did you do next?' I asked.

'After a few years, I found an orphan like me; roaming in the woods, like me,' she said, and turned to look at her bodyguard. 'We've been together ever since.'

And I finally saw an expression in Andre's unlined face: utter devotion.

'He was being forced, like I had been,' she said gently. 'And I took care of that.'

I felt a cold shiver run down my spine. I couldn't have picked something to say if you had paid me.

'The reason I've bored you with my ancient history,' the queen said, shaking herself and sitting up even straighter, 'is to tell you why I took Hadley under my wing. She, too, had been molested, by her great-uncle. Did he molest you, too?'

I nodded. I'd had no idea he'd gotten to Hadley. He hadn't progressed to actual penetration, only because my parents had died and I'd gone to live with my grandmother. My parents hadn't believed me, but I'd convinced my grandmother I was telling the truth by the time he would have felt I was ripe, when I was about nine. Of course, Hadley had been older. We'd had much more in common than I'd ever thought. 'I'm sorry, I didn't know,' I said. 'Thanks for telling me.'

'Hadley talked about you often,' the queen said.

Yeah, thanks, Hadley. Thanks for setting me up for the worst . . . no, wait, that was unfair. Finding out about Bill's massive deception was *not* the worst thing that had ever happened to me. But it wasn't too far down on my personal list, either.

'That's what I've found out,' I said, my voice as cold and crisp as a celery stick.

'You are upset that I sent Bill to investigate you, to find out if you could be of use to me,' the queen said.

I took a deep breath, forced my teeth to unclench. 'No, I'm not upset with you. You can't help being the way you are. And you didn't even know me.' Another deep breath. 'I'm *upset* with Bill, who *did* know me and went ahead with your whole program in a very thorough and calculated way.' I had to drive away the pain. 'Besides, why would you care?' My tone was bordering on insolent, which was not wise when you're dealing with a powerful vampire. She'd touched me in a very sore spot.

'Because you were dear to Hadley,' Sophie-Anne said unexpectedly.

'You wouldn't have known it from the way she treated me, after she became a teenager,' I said, having apparently decided that reckless honesty was the course to follow.

'She was sorry for that,' the queen said 'once she became a vampire, especially, and found out what it was like to be a minority. Even here in New Orleans, there is prejudice. We talked about her life often, when we were alone.'

I didn't know which made me more uncomfortable, the idea of the queen and my cousin Hadley having sex, or having pillow talk about me afterward.

I don't care if consenting adults have sex, no matter what that sex consists of, as long as both parties agree beforehand. But I don't necessarily need to hear any details, either. Any prurient interest I might have had has been flooded over the years with images from the minds of the people in the bar.

This was turning out to be a long conversation. I wanted the queen to get to the point.

'The point is,' the queen said, 'I am grateful that you – through the witches – gave me a better idea of how Hadley died. And also you have let me know there is a wider plot against me than just Waldo's jealous heart.'

I had?

'So I am in your debt. Tell me what I can do for you now.'

'Ah. Send over a lot of boxes so I can pack up Hadley's stuff and get back to Bon Temps? Get someone to take the stuff I don't want to a charity drop-off?'

The queen looked down, and I swear she was smothering a smile. 'Yes, I think I can do that,' she said. 'I'll send some human over tomorrow to do those things.'

'If someone could pack the stuff I want into a van and drive it up to Bon Temps, that would be real good,' I said. 'Maybe I could ride back in that van?'

'Also not a problem,' she said.

Now for the big favor. 'Do I actually have to go with you to this conference thing?' I asked, which I knew was kind of pushing it.

'Yes,' she said.

Okay, stonewall there.

She added, 'But I'll pay you handsomely.'

I brightened. Some of the money I'd gotten for my previous vampire services was still in my savings account, and I'd gotten a big financial break when Tara 'sold' me her car for a dollar, but I was so used to living close to the financial bone that a cushion was always welcome. I was always scared I'd break my leg, or my car would throw a rod, or my house would burn down . . . wait, that had already happened . . . well, that some disaster would happen, like a high wind would blow off the stupid tin roof my grandmother had insisted on, or something.

'Did you want something of Hadley's?' I asked her, my train of thought having veered away from money. 'You know, a remembrance?'

Something flashed in her eyes, something that surprised me.

'You took the words right out of my mouth,' said the queen, with an adorable hint of a French accent.

Uh-oh. It couldn't be good that she'd switched on the charm.

'I did ask Hadley to hide something for me,' she said. My bullshit meter was beeping like an alarm clock. 'And if you come across it in your packing, I'd like to have it back.'

'What does it look like?'

'It's a jewel,' she said. 'My husband gave it to me as an engagement gift. I happened to leave it here before I got married.'

'You're welcome to look in Hadley's jewelry box,' I said immediately. 'If it belongs to you, of course you have to have it back.'

'That's very kind of you,' she said, her face back to its regular glassy smoothness. 'It's a diamond, a large diamond, and it's fixed on a platinum bracelet.'

I didn't remember anything like that in Hadley's stuff, but I hadn't looked carefully. I'd planned to pack Hadley's jewelry box intact so I could pick through it at my leisure in Bon Temps.

'Please, look now,' I suggested. 'I know that it would be like a faux pas to lose a present from your husband.'

'Oh,' she said gently, 'you have no idea.' Sophie-Anne closed her eyes for just a second, as if she were too anxious for words. 'Andre,' she said, and with that word he took off for the bedroom – didn't need any directions, I noticed – and while he was gone, the queen looked oddly incomplete. I wondered why he hadn't accompanied her to Bon Temps, and on an impulse, I asked her.

She looked at me, her crystalline eyes wide and blank. 'I was not supposed to be gone,' she said. 'I knew if Andre showed himself in New Orleans, everyone would assume I was here, too.' I wondered if the reverse would be true. If the queen was here, would everyone assume Andre was; also? And that sparked a thought in me, a thought that had gone before I could quite grasp hold of it.

Andre came back at that moment, the tiniest shake of his head telling the queen he hadn't found what she wanted to reclaim. For a moment, Sophie-Anne looked quite unhappy. 'Hadley did this in a minute of anger,' the queen said, and I thought she was talking to herself. 'But she may bring me down from beyond the veil.' Then her face relaxed into its usual emotionless state.

'I'll keep an eye open for the bracelet,' I said. I suspected that the value of the jewelry did not lie in its appraisal. 'Would that bracelet have been left here the last night before the wedding?' I asked cautiously.

I suspected my cousin Hadley had stolen the bracelet from the queen out of sheer pique that the queen was getting married. That seemed like a Hadley thing to do. If I'd known about Hadley's concealment of the bracelet, I would have asked the witches to roll the clock back on the ectoplasmic reconstruction. We could have watched Hadley hide the thing.

The queen gave one short nod. 'I must have it back,' the queen said. 'You understand, it's not the value of the diamond that concerns me? You understand, a wedding between vampire rulers is not a love match, where much can be forgiven? To lose a gift from your spouse, that's a very grave offense. And our spring ball is scheduled for two nights from now. The king expects to see me wearing his gifts. If I'm not . . .' Her voice trailed away, and even Andre looked almost worried.

'I'm getting your point,' I said. I'd noticed the tension already rolling through the halls at Sophie's headquarters. There'd be hell to pay, and Sophie-Anne would be the one to pay it. 'If it's here, you'll get it back. Okay?' I spread my hands, asking her if she believed me.

'All right,' she said. 'Andre, I can't spend any more time here. Jade Flower will report the fact that I came up here with Sookie. Sookie, we must pretend to have had sex.'

'Sorry, anyone who knows me knows I don't do women. I don't know who you expect Jade Flower's reporting to . . .' (Of course I did, and that would be the king, but it didn't seem tactful to say 'I know your business', just then.) 'But if they've done any homework, that's just a fact about me.'

'Perhaps you had sex with Andre, then,' she said calmly. 'And you let me watch.'

I thought of several questions, the first one being, 'Is that the usual procedure with you?' followed by, 'It's not okay to misplace a bracelet, but okay to bump pelvises with someone else?' But I clamped my mouth shut. If someone were holding a gun to my head, I'd actually have to vote for having sex with the queen rather than with Andre, no matter what my gender preference, because Andre creeped me out big-time. But if we were just pretending . . .

In a businesslike way, Andre removed his tie, folded it, put it in his pocket, and undid a few shirt buttons. He beckoned to me with a crook of his fingers. I approached him warily. He took me in his arms and held me close, pressed against him, and bent his head to my neck. For a second I thought he was going to bite, and I had a flare of absolute panic, but instead he inhaled. That's a deliberate act for a vampire.

'Put your mouth on my neck,' he said, after another long whiff of me. 'Your lipstick will transfer.'

I did as he told me. He was cold as ice. This was like . . . well, this was just weird. I thought of the picture-taking session with Claude; I'd spent a lot of time lately *pretending* to have sex.

'I love the smell of fairy. Do you think she knows she has fairy blood?' he asked Sophie-Anne, while I was in the process of transferring my lipstick.

My head snapped back then. I stared right into his eyes, and he stared right back at me. He was still holding me, and I understood that he was ensuring I would smell like him and he would smell like me, as if we'd actually done the deed. He definitely wasn't up for the real thing, which was a relief.

'I what?' I hadn't heard him correctly, I was sure. 'I have what?'

'He has a nose for it,' the queen said. 'My Andre.' She looked faintly proud.

'I was hanging around with my friend Claudine earlier in the day,' I said. 'She's a fairy. That's where the smell is coming from.' I really must need to shower.

'You permit?' Andre asked, and without waiting for an answer, he jabbed my wounded arm with a fingernail, right above the bandage.

'Yow!' I said in protest.

He let a little blood trickle onto his finger, and he put it in his mouth. He rolled it around, as if it were a sip of wine, and at last he said, 'No, this smell of fairy is not from association. It's in your blood.' Andre looked at me in a way that was meant to tell me that his words made it a done deal. 'You have a little streak of fairy. Maybe your grandmother or your grandfather was half-fey?'

'I don't know anything about it,' I said, knowing I sounded stupid, but not knowing what else to say. 'If any of my grandparents were other than a hundred percent human, they didn't pass that information along.'

'No, they wouldn't,' the queen said, matter-of-factly. 'Most humans of fairy descent hide the fact, because they don't really believe it. They prefer to think their parents are mad.' She shrugged. Inexplicable! 'But that blood would explain why you have supernatural suitors and not human admirers.'

'I don't have human admirers because I don't want 'em,' I said, definitely piqued. 'I can read their minds, and that just knocks them out of the running. If they're not put off from the get-go by my reputation for weirdness,' I added, back into my too-much-honesty groove.

'It's a sad comment on humans that none of them are tolerable to one who can read their minds,' the queen said.

I guess that was the final word on the value of mind-reading ability. I decided it would be better to stop the conversation. I had a lot to think about.

We went down the stairs, Andre leading, the queen next, and me trailing behind. Andre had insisted I take off my shoes and my earrings so it could be inferred that I had undressed and then just slipped back into the dress.

The other vampires were waiting obediently in the courtyard, and they sprang to attention when we began making our way down. Jade Flower's face didn't change at all when she read all the clues as to what we'd been up to in the past half hour, but at least she didn't look skeptical. The Berts looked knowing but uninterested, as if the scenario of Sophie-Anne watching her bodyguard engaging in sex (with a virtual stranger) were very much a matter of routine.

As he stood in the gateway waiting for further driving instructions, Rasul's face expressed a mild ruefulness, as if he wished he had been included in the action. Quinn, on the other hand, was pressing his mouth in such a grim line that you couldn't have fed him a straight pin. There was a fence to mend.

But as we'd walked out of Hadley's apartment, the queen had told me specifically not to share her story with anyone else, emphasis on the *anyone*. I would just have to think of a way to let Quinn know, without letting him *know*.

With no discussion or social chitchat, the vampires piled into their car. My brain was so crowded with ideas and conjectures and every-thing in between that I felt punch-drunk. I wanted to call my brother, Jason, and tell him he wasn't so irresistible after all, it was the fairy blood in him, just to see what he'd say. No, wait, Andre had implied that humans weren't affected by the nearness of fairies like vampires were. That is, humans didn't want to consume fairies, but did find them sexually attractive. (I thought of the crowd that always surrounded Claudine at Merlotte's.) And Andre had said that other supernaturals were attracted by fairy blood too, just not in the eat-'em-up way that vamps were. Wouldn't Eric be relieved? He would be so glad to know he didn't really love me! It was the fairy blood all along!

I watched the royal limo drive away. While I was fighting a wave compounded of about six different emotions, Quinn was fighting only one.

He was right in front of me, his face angry. 'How'd she talk you into it, Sookie?' he asked. 'If you'd yelled, I'd have been right up there. Or maybe you wanted to do that? I would have sworn you weren't the type.'

'I haven't gone to bed with anyone this evening,' I said. I looked him straight in the eyes. After all, this wasn't revealing anything the queen had told me, this was just . . . correcting an error. 'It's fine if others think that,' I said carefully. 'Just not you.'

He looked down at me for a long moment, his eyes searching mine as if he were reading some writing on the back of my eyeballs.

'Would you *like* to go to bed with someone this evening?' he asked. He kissed me. He kissed me for a long, long time, as we stood glued together in the courtyard. The witches did not return; the vampires stayed gone. Only the occasional car going by in the street or a siren heard in the distance reminded me we were in the middle of a city. This was as different from being held by Andre as I could imagine. Quinn was warm, and I could feel his muscles move beneath his skin. I could hear him breathe, and I could feel his heartbeat. I could sense the churn of his thoughts, which were mostly now centered on the bed he knew must be somewhere upstairs in Hadley's apartment. He loved the smell of me, the touch of me, the way my lips felt . . . and a large part of Quinn was attesting to that fact. That large part was pressed between us right at this very moment.

I'd gone to bed with two other males, and both times it hadn't worked out well. I hadn't known enough about them. I'd acted on impulse. You should learn from your mistakes. For a second, I wasn't feeling especially smart.

Luckily for my decision-making ability, Quinn's phone chose that moment to ring. God bless that phone. I'd been within an ace of chucking my good resolutions right out the window, because I'd been scared and lonely throughout the evening, and Quinn felt relatively familiar and he wanted me so much.

Quinn, however, was not following the same thought processes – far from it – and he cursed when the phone rang a second time.

'Excuse me,' he said, fury in his voice, and answered the damn phone.

'All right,' he said, after listening for a moment to the voice on the other end. 'All right, I'll be there.'

He snapped the tiny phone shut. 'Jake is asking for me,' he said.

I was so at sea with a strange combination of lust and relief that it took me a moment to connect the dots. Jake Purifoy, Quinn's employee, was experiencing his second night as a vampire. Having been fed some volunteer, he was enough himself to want to talk to Quinn. He'd been in suspended animation in a closet for weeks, and there was a lot he would need to catch up on.

'Then you have to go,' I said, proud that my voice was practically rock steady. 'Maybe he'll remember who attacked him. Tomorrow, I have to tell you about what I saw here tonight.'

'Would you have said yes?' he asked. 'If we'd been undisturbed for another minute?'

I considered for a minute. 'If I had, I would've been sorry I did,' I said. 'Not because I don't want you. I do. But I had my eyes opened in the past couple of days. I know that I'm pretty easy to fool.' I tried to sound matter-of-fact, not pitiful, when I said that. No one likes a whiny woman, least of all me. 'I'm not interested in starting that up with someone who's just horny at the moment. I never set out to be a one-night-stand kind of woman. I want to be sure, if I have sex with you, that it's because you want to be around for a while and because you like me for who I am, not what I am.'

Maybe a million women had made approximately the same speech. I meant it as sincerely as any one of those million.

And Quinn gave a perfect answer. 'Who would want just one night with you?' he said, and then he left.

Chapter 19

I slept the sleep of the dead. Well, probably not, but as close as a human would ever come. As if in a dream, I heard the witches come carousing back into the courtyard. They were still congratulating one another with alcohol-lubricated vigor. I'd found some real, honest cotton sheets among the linens (Why are they still called linens? Have you seen a linen sheet in your life?) and I'd tossed the black silky ones into the washer, so it was very easy to slip back into sleep.

When I got up, it was after ten in the morning. There was a knocking at the door, and I stumbled down the hall to unlock it after I'd pulled on a pair of Hadley's spandex exercise pants and a hot pink tank top. I saw boxes through the peephole, and I opened the door feeling really happy.

'Miss Stackhouse?' said the young black man who was holding the flattened boxes. When I nodded, he said, 'I got orders to bring you as many boxes as you want. Will thirty do to start with?'

'Oh, yes,' I said. 'Oh, that'll be great.'

'I also got instructions,' he said precisely, 'to bring you anything related to moving that you might need. I have here strapping tape, masking tape, some Magic Markers, scissors, and stick-on labels.'

The queen had given me a personal shopper.

'Did you want colored dots? Some people like to put living room things in boxes with an orange dot, bedroom things in boxes with a green dot, and so on.'

I had never moved, unless you counted taking a couple of bags of clothes and towels over to Sam's furnished duplex after the kitchen burned, so I didn't know the best way to go about it. I had an intoxicating vision of rows of neat boxes with colored dots on each side, so there couldn't be any mistake from any angle. Then I snapped back to reality. I wouldn't be taking that much back to Bon Temps. It was hard to form an estimate, since this was unknown territory, but I knew I didn't want much of the furniture.

'I don't think I'll need the dots, thanks anyway,' I said. 'I'll start working on these boxes, and then I can call you if I need any more, okay?'

'I'll assemble them for you,' he said. He had very short hair and the curliest eyelashes I'd ever seen on a person. Cows had eyelashes that pretty, sometimes. He was wearing a golf-type shirt and neatly belted khakis, along with high- end sneakers.

'I'm sorry, I didn't catch your name,' I said, as he whipped a roll of strapping tape from a large lumpy plastic shopping bag. He set to work.

'Oh, 'scuse me,' he said, and it was the first time he'd sounded natural. 'My name is Everett O'Dell Smith.'

'Pleasure to meet you,' I said, and he paused in his work so we could shake hands. 'How did you come to be here?'

'Oh, I'm in Tulane Business School, and one of my professors got a call from Mr Cataliades, who is, like, *the* most famous lawyer in the vampire area. My professor specializes in vampire law. Mr Cataliades needed a day person; I mean, he can come out in the day, but he needed someone to be his gofer.' He'd gotten three boxes done, already.

'And in return?'

'In return, I get to sit in court with him on his next five cases, and I get to earn some money I need real bad.'

'Will you have time this afternoon to take me to my cousin's bank?'

'Sure will.'

'You're not missing a class now, are you?'

'Oh, no, I got two hours before my second class.'

He'd already been to a class and accumulated all this stuff before I'd even gotten up. Well, he hadn't been up half the night watching his dead cousin walk around.

'You can take these garbage bags of clothes to the nearest Goodwill or Salvation Army store.' That would clear the gallery and make me feel productive all at the same time. I'd gone over the garments quite carefully to make sure Hadley hadn't hidden anything in them, and I wondered what the Salvation Army would make of them. Hadley had been into Tight and Skimpy; that was the nicest way to put it.

'Yes, ma'am,' he said, whipping out a notebook and scribbling in it. Then he waited attentively. 'Anything else?' he prompted me.

'Yes, there's no food in the house. When you come back this afternoon, can you bring me something to eat?' I could drink tap water, but I couldn't create food out of nothing.

Just then a call from the courtyard made me look over the railing. Quinn was down there with a bag of something greasy. My mouth began watering.

'Looks like the food angle is covered,' I told Everett, waving Quinn up.

'What can I do to help?' Quinn asked. 'It struck me your cousin might not have coffee and food, so I brought some beignets and some coffee so strong it'll make you grow hair on your chest.'

I'd heard that quite a few times, but it still made me smile. 'Oh, that's my goal,' I said. 'Bring it on. There's actually coffee here, but I didn't have a chance to make it because Everett here is such a take-charge kind of guy.'

Everett smiled up from his tenth box. 'You know that's not true, but it's good to hear you say it,' he said. I introduced the two men, and after Quinn handed me my bag, he began to help Everett assemble boxes. I sat at the glass-topped dining table and ate every crumb of the beignets that were in the bag and drank every drop of the coffee. I got powdered sugar all over me, and I didn't care a bit. Quinn turned to look at me and tried to hide his smile. 'You're wearing your food, babe,' he said,

I looked down at the tank top. 'No hair on my chest, though,' I said, and he said, 'Can I check?'

I laughed and went to the back to brush my teeth and hair, both essential tasks. I checked out Hadley's clothes that I'd wriggled into. The black spandex workout pants came to midthigh. Hadley probably had never worn them, because they would have been too big, to her taste. On me, they were very snug; but not the snug Hadley liked, where you could count the ... oh, never mind. The hot pink tank top left my pale pink bra straps showing, to say nothing of a couple of inches of my middle, but thanks to Peck's Tan-a-Lot (located inside Peck's Bunch-o-Flicks, a video rental place in Bon Temps), that middle was nice and brown. Hadley would have put a piece of jewelry in her belly button. I looked at myself in the mirror, trying to picture myself with a gold stud or something. Nah. I slipped on some sandals decorated with crystal beads and felt quite glamorous for about thirty seconds.

I began talking to Quinn about what I planned to do that day, and rather than yell, I stepped from the bedroom into the hall with my brush and my elastic band. I bent over at the waist, brushed my hair while I was inverted, and gathered it into a ponytail on top of my head. I was sure it was centered, because the movements were just automatic after all these years. My ponytail came down past my shoulder blades now. I looped the band, ran the ponytail through, and I straightened, ponytail flying back over my shoulders to bounce in the middle. Quinn and Everett had stopped their task to stare. When I looked back at them, the two men hastily bent back to their tasks.

Okay, I didn't get that I'd done anything interesting, but apparently I had. I shrugged and vanished into the master bathroom to slap on some makeup. After another glance in the mirror, it occurred to me that maybe anything I did in that outfit was fairly interesting, if you were a fully functional guy.

When I came out, Everett had gone and Quinn gave me a slip of paper with Everett's cell number on it. 'He says to call him when you need some more boxes,' Quinn said. 'He took all the bagged clothes. Looks like you don't need me at all.'

'No comparison,' I said, smiling. 'Everett didn't bring me grease and caffeine this morning, and you did.'

'So what's the plan, and how can I help?'

'Okay, the plan is ...' I didn't exactly have one more specific than

'go through this stuff and sort it out,' and Quinn couldn't do that for
me.

'How's this?' I asked. 'You get everything out of the kitchen cabinets,
and set it out where I can see it all, and I'll make a 'keep or toss'
decision. You can pack what I want to keep, and put what I want to
toss out on the gallery. I hope the rain stays away.' The sunny morning
was clouding over, fast. 'While we work, I'll fill you in on what happened here last night.'

Despite the threat of bad weather, we worked all morning, called
in a pizza for lunch, and resumed work in the afternoon. The stuff
I didn't want went into garbage bags, and Quinn furthered his muscular development by carrying all the garbage bags down to the courtyard and putting them in the little shed that had held the lawn chairs,
still set up on the grass. I tried to admire his muscles only when he
wasn't looking, and I think I was successful. Quinn was very interested
to hear about the ectoplasmic reconstruction, and we talked about
what it might all mean without reaching any conclusions. Jake didn't
have any enemies among the vampires that Quinn knew of, and Quinn
thought that Jake must have been killed for the embarrassment it
would cause Hadley, rather than for any sin of Jake's own.

I saw neither hide nor hair of Amelia, and I wondered if she'd gone
home with the Mormonish Bob. Or maybe he'd stayed with her, and
they were having a fabulous time in Amelia's apartment. Maybe he
was a real ball of fire under that white shirt and those black pants.
I looked around the courtyard. Yes, Bob's bicycle was still propped
against the brick wall. Since the sky was getting darker by the minute,
I put the bike in the little shed, too.

Being with Quinn all day was stoking my fire a bit hotter every
moment. He was down to a tank top and jeans, and I found myself
wondering what he'd look like without those. And I didn't think
I was the only one conjecturing about what people would look like
naked. I could catch a flash from Quinn's mind every now and then
as he was toting a bag down the stairs or packing pots and pans
into a box, and those flashes weren't about opening his mail or
doing his laundry.

I had enough practical presence of mind left to switch on a lamp when I heard the first peal of thunder in the distance. The Big Easy was about to be drenched.

Then it was back to flirting with Quinn wordlessly – making sure he had a good view when I stretched up to get a glass down from the cabinets or bent down to wrap that glass in newspaper. Maybe a quarter of me was embarrassed, but the rest of me was having fun. Fun had not been a big factor in my life recently – well, ever – and I was enjoying my little toddle on the wild side.

Downstairs, I felt Amelia's brain click on, after a fashion. I was familiar with the feel of this, from working in a bar: Amelia had a hangover. I smiled to myself as the witch thought of Bob, who was still asleep beside her. Aside from a basic, 'How could I?' Amelia's most coherent thought was that she needed coffee. She needed it bad. She couldn't even turn on a light in the apartment, which was darkening steadily with the approach of the storm. A light would hurt her eyes too much.

I turned with a smile on my lips, ready to tell Quinn we might be hearing from Amelia soon, only to find he was right behind me, and his face was intent with a look I could not mistake. He was ready for something entirely different.

'Tell me you don't want me to kiss you, and I'll back off,' he said, and then he was kissing me.

I didn't say a word.

When the height difference became an issue, Quinn just picked me up and put me on the edge of the kitchen counter. A clap of thunder sounded outside as I parted my knees to let him get as close to me as he could. I wrapped my legs around him. He pulled the elastic band out of my hair, not a totally pain-free process, and ran his fingers through the tangles. He crushed my hair in his hand and inhaled deeply, as if he were extracting the perfume from a flower.

'This is okay?' he asked raggedly, as his fingers found the bottom back edge of my tank top and sneaked up under it. He examined my bra tactilely and figured out how to open it in record time.

'Okay?' I said, in a daze. I wasn't sure whether I meant, 'Okay? Hell, yes, hurry up!' or 'Which part of this is okay, you want to know?' but Quinn naturally took it as a green light. His hands pushed the bra aside and he ran his thumbs across my nipples, which were already hard. I thought I was going to explode, and only the sure anticipation of better things to come kept me from losing it right then and there. I wriggled even further to the edge of the counter, so the big bulge in the front of Quinn's jeans was pressed against the notch in my pants. Just amazing, how they fit. He pressed against me, released, pressed again, the ridge formed by the stretch of the jeans over his penis hitting just the right spot, so easy to reach through the thin and stretchy spandex. Once more, and I cried out, holding on to him through the blind moment of orgasm when I could swear I'd been catapulted into another universe. My breathing was more like sobbing, and I wrapped myself around him like he was my hero. In that moment, he certainly was.

His breathing was still ragged, and he moved against me again, seeking his own release, since I had so loudly had mine. I sucked on his neck while my hand went down between us, and stroked him through his jeans, and suddenly he gave a cry as ragged as mine had been, and his arms tightened around me convulsively. 'Oh, God,' he said, 'oh, God.' His eyes closed tight with his release, he kissed my neck, my cheek, my lips, over and over. When his breathing – and mine – was a little more even, he said, 'Babe, I haven't come like that since I was seventeen, in the backseat of my dad's car with Ellie Hopper.'

'So, that's a good thing,' I mumbled.

'You bet,' he said.

We stayed clinched for a moment, and I became aware that the rain was beating against the windows and the doors, and the thunder was booming away. My brain was thinking of shutting down for a little nap, and I was lazily aware of Quinn's brain going equally drowsy as he rehooked my bra at my back. Downstairs, Amelia was making coffee in her dark kitchen and Bob the witch was waking up to the wonderful smell and wondering where his pants were. And in the courtyard, swarming silently up the stairs, enemies were approaching.

'Quinn!' I exclaimed, just in the moment his sharp hearing picked up the shuffle of the footsteps. Quinn went into fighting mode. Since I hadn't been home to check the calendar symbols, I'd forgotten we were close to the full moon. There were claws on Quinn's hands now, claws at least three inches long, instead of fingers. His eyes slanted and became altogether gold, with dilated black pupils. The change in the bones of his face had made him alien. I'd made a form of love with this man in the past ten minutes, and now I would hardly have known him if I'd passed him on the street.

But there wasn't time to think about anything but our best defense. I was the weak link, and I had better depend on surprise. I slid off the counter, hurried past him to the door, and lifted the lamp from its pedestal. When the first Were burst through the door, I bashed him upside the head, and he staggered, and the one coming in right after him tripped over his flailing predecessor, and Quinn was more than ready for the third one.

Unfortunately, there were six more.

Chapter 20

It took just two of them to subdue me, and I was kicking and scream-ing, biting and hitting, with every bit of energy I had. It took four for Quinn, but those four succeeded only because they used a stun gun. Otherwise, I'm sure he could have taken six or eight of them out of action, instead of the three he took care of before they got him.

I knew I would be overcome, and I knew I could save myself some bruises and maybe a broken bone if I just assented to be taken. But I have my pride. More practically, I wanted to be sure that Amelia heard what was happening above her. She'd do something. I wasn't sure what she'd do, but she'd act.

I was hustled down the stairs, my feet hardly touching them, by two husky men I'd never seen before. These same two men had bound my wrists together with duct tape. I'd done my best to arrange for a little slack, but I was afraid they'd done a fair job of it.

'Mmm, smells like sex,' the shorter one said as he pinched my butt. I ignored his tacky leer and took some satisfaction in eyeing the bruise I'd given him on his cheekbone with my fist. (Which, by the way, was aching and smarting over the knuckles. You can't hit someone without paying for it yourself.)

They had to carry Quinn, and they weren't gentle about it. He got banged around against the stairs, and once they dropped him. He was a big guy. Now he was a bleeding big guy, since one of the blows had cut the skin above his left eye. He'd had the duct tape treatment, too, and I wondered how the fur would react to the tape.

We were being held side by side in the courtyard, briefly, and Quinn looked over at me as if he desperately wanted to speak to me. The blood was running down his cheek from the wound over his eyes, and he looked *groggy* from the stun gun. His hands were changing back to regular hands. I lunged toward him, but the Weres kept us apart.

Two vans drove into the circular drive, two vans that said BIG EASY ELECTRIC on the side. They were white and long and windowless in the back, and the logo on the side had been covered up with mud, which looked highly suspicious. A driver jumped out of the cab of each van, and the first driver threw open the doors to the rear of the first vehicle.

While our captors were hustling Quinn and me over to that van, the rest of the raiding party was being brought down the stairs. The men Quinn had managed to hurt were damaged far worse than Quinn, I'm glad to say. Claws can do an amazing amount of damage, especially wielded with the force a tiger can exert. The guy I'd hit with the lamp was unconscious, and the one who'd reached Quinn first was possibly dead. He was certainly covered with blood and there were things exposed to the light that should have been neatly packed in his belly.

I was smiling with satisfaction when the men holding me shoved me into the back of the van, which I discovered was awash with trash and absolutely filthy. This was a high-class operation. There was a wide-mesh screen between the two front seats and the open rear, and the shelves in the rear had been emptied, I supposed for our occupancy.

I was crammed into the narrow aisle between the shelves, and Quinn was jammed in after me. They had to work hard because he was still so stunned. My two escorts were slamming the rear van doors on the two of us as the hors de combat Weres were loaded into the other van. I was guessing the vans had been parked out on the street briefly so we wouldn't hear the vehicles pulling into the driveway. When they were ready to load us up, our captors had pulled into the courtyard. Even the people of a brawling city like New Orleans would notice some battered bodies being loaded into vans . . . in the pouring rain.

I hoped the Weres wouldn't think of grabbing Amelia and Bob, and

I prayed that Amelia would think cleverly and hide herself, rather than do some impulsive and brave witch thing. I know it's a contradiction, right? Praying for one thing (asking God a favor) while at the same time hoping your enemies would be killed. All I can say is, I have a feeling Christians have been doing that from the get go – at least bad ones, like me.

'Go, go, go,' bellowed the shorter man, who'd hopped into the front seat. The driver obliged with a completely unnecessary squealing of tires, and we lurched out of the courtyard as if the president had just been shot and we had to get him to Walter Reed.

Quinn came to completely as we turned off Chloe Street to head for our final destination, wherever it might be. His hands were bound behind him, which is painful, and he hadn't quit bleeding from the head. I'd expected him to remain groggy and shocked. But when his eyes focused on my face, he said, 'Babe, they beat you bad.' I must not look too good.

'Yeah, well, you seem to be in the same boat,' I said. I knew the driver and his companion could hear us, and I didn't give a damn.

With a grim attempt at a smile, he said, 'Some defender I turned out to be.'

In the Weres' estimation, I wasn't very dangerous, so my hands had been bound in front. I squirmed until I was able to put pressure on the cut on Quinn's forehead. That had to have hurt even more, but he didn't say a word in protest. The motion of the van, the effects of the beating, and the constant shifting and smell of the trash all around us combined to make the next ten minutes very unpleasant. If I'd been very clever, I could have told which way we were going – but I wasn't feeling very clever. I marveled that in a city with as many famed restaurants as New Orleans had, this van was awash with Burger King wrappers and Taco Bell cups. If I got a chance to rummage through the debris, I might find something useful.

'When we're together, we get attacked by Weres,' Quinn said.

'It's my fault,' I said. 'I'm so sorry I dragged you into this.'

'Oh, yeah,' he said. 'I'm known for hanging with a desperate crowd.'

We were lying face to face, and Quinn sort of nudged me with his leg. He was trying to tell me something, and I wasn't getting it.

The two men in the front seat were talking to each other about a cute girl crossing the street at a traffic light. Just listening to the conversation was almost enough to make you swear off men, but at least they weren't listening to us.

'Remember when we talked about my mental condition?' I said carefully. 'Remember what I told you about that?'

It took him a minute because he was hurting, but he got the hint. His face squinched up as if he were about to chop some boards in half, or something else requiring all his concentration, and then his thought shoved into my head. *Phone in my pocket*, he told me. The problem was, the phone was in his right pocket, and he was lying on that side. There was hardly room for him to turn over.

This called for a lot of maneuvering, and I didn't want our captors to see it. But I managed, finally, to work my fingers into Quinn's pocket, and made a mental note to advise him that, under this set of circumstances, his jeans were too tight. (Under other circumstances, no problem with the way they fit.) But extricating that phone, with the van rocking, while our Were assailants checked on us every minute or so, that was difficult.

Queen's headquarters on speed dial, he told me when he felt the phone leave his pocket. But that was lost on me. I didn't know how to access speed dial. It took me a few moments to make Quinn understand that, and I'm still not sure how I did it, but finally he *thought* the phone number at me, and I awkwardly punched it in and pressed SEND. Maybe we hadn't thought that through all the way, because when a tiny voice said, 'Hello?' the Weres heard it.

'You didn't search him?' the driver asked the passenger incredulously.

'Hell no, I was trying to get him in the back and get myself out of the rain,' the man who had pinched me snarled right back. 'Pull over, dammit!'

Has someone had your blood? Quinn asked me silently, though this time he could have spoken, and after a precious second, my brain kicked in. 'Eric,' I said, because the Weres were out their doors and running to open the rear doors of the van.

'Quinn and Sookie have been taken by some Weres,' Quinn said into the phone I was holding to his mouth. 'Eric the Northman can track her.'

I hoped Eric was still in New Orleans, and I further hoped whoever answered the phone at the queen's headquarters was on the ball. But then the two Weres were yanking open the van doors and dragging us out, and one of them socked me while the other hit Quinn in the gut. They yanked the phone from my swollen fingers and tossed it into the thick undergrowth at the side of the road. The driver had pulled over by an empty lot, but up and down the road were widely spaced houses on stilts in a sea of grasses. The sky was too overcast for me to get a fix on our direction, but I was sure now we'd driven south into the marshes. I did manage to read our driver's watch, and was surprised to find out it was already past three in the afternoon.

'You dumb shit, Clete! Who was he calling?' yelled a voice from the second van, which had pulled over to the side of the road when we did. Our two captors looked at each other with identical expressions of consternation, and I would have been laughing if I hadn't been hurting so badly. It was as if they'd practiced looking stupid.

This time Quinn was searched very thoroughly, and I was, too, though I had no pockets or anywhere else to conceal anything, unless they wanted to do a body cavity check. I thought Clete – Mr Pinch-Ass – was going to, just for a second, as his fingers jabbed the spandex into me. Quinn thought so, too. I made an awful noise, a choked gasp of fear, but the sound that came from Quinn's throat was beyond a snarl. It was a deep, throaty, coughing noise, and it was absolutely menacing.

'Leave the girl alone, Clete, and let's get back on the road,' the tall driver said, and his voice had that 'I'm done with you' edge to it. 'I don't know who this guy is, but I don't think he changes into a nutria.'

I wondered if Quinn would threaten them with his identity – most Weres seemed to know him, or know of him – but since he didn't volunteer his name, I didn't speak.

Clete shoved me back into the van with a lot of muttering along the lines of 'Who died and made you God? You ain't the boss of me,' and so on. The taller man clearly *was* the boss of Clete, which was a good thing. I wanted someone with brains and a shred of decency between me and Clete's probing fingers.

They had a very hard time getting Quinn into the van again. He didn't want to go, and finally two men from the other van came over, very reluctantly, to help Clete and the driver. They bound Quinn's legs with one of those plastic things, the kind where you run the pointed tip through a hole and then twist it. We'd used something similar to close the bag when we'd baked a turkey last Thanksgiving. The tie they used on Quinn was black and plastic and it actually locked with what looked like a handcuff key.

They didn't bind my legs.

I appreciated Quinn's getting angry at their treatment of me, angry enough to struggle to be free, but the end result was that my legs were free and his weren't – because I still didn't present a threat to them, at least in their minds.

They were probably right. I couldn't think of anything to do to prevent them from taking us wherever we were going. I didn't have a weapon, and though I worried at the duct tape binding my hands, my teeth didn't seem to be strong enough to make a weak spot. I rested for a minute, shutting my eyes wearily. The last blow had opened a cut on my cheek. A big tongue rasped over my bleeding face. Then again.

'Don't cry,' said a strange, guttural voice, and I opened my eyes to check that it was, indeed, coming from Quinn. Quinn had so much power that he could stop the change once it had begun. I suspected he could trigger it, too, though I'd noticed that fighting could bring it on in any shape-shifter. He'd had the claws during the fight in Hadley's apartment, and they'd almost tipped the balance in our favor. Since he'd gotten so enraged at Clete during the episode by the side of the road, Quinn's nose had flattened and broadened. I had a close-up view of the teeth in his mouth, teeth that had altered into tiny daggers.

'Why didn't you change fully?' I asked, in a tiny whisper.

Because there wouldn't be enough room for you in this space, babe. After I change, I'm seven feet long and I weigh about four hundred fifty pounds.

That will make any girl gulp. I could only be grateful he'd thought that far ahead. I looked at him some more.

Not grossed out?

Clete and the driver were exchanging recriminations about the phone incident. 'Why, grandpa, what big teeth you have,' I whispered. The upper and lower canines were so long and sharp they were really scary. (I called them *canines;* to cats, that might be an insult.)

Sharp . . . they were sharp. I worked my hands up close to his mouth, and begged him with my eyes to understand. As much as I could tell from his altered face, Quinn was worried. Just as our situation aroused his defensive instincts, the idea I was trying to sell to him excited other instincts. I *will make your hands bleed*, he warned me, with a great effort. He was partially animal now, and the animal thought processes didn't necessarily travel the same paths as the human.

I bit my own bottom lip to keep from gasping as Quinn's teeth bit into the duct tape. He had to exert a lot of pressure to get the three-inch canines to pierce the duct tape, and that meant that those shorter, sharp incisors bit into my skin, too, no matter how much care he took. Tears began rolling down my face in an unending stream, and I felt him falter. I shook my bound hands to urge him on, and reluctantly he bent back to his task.

'Hey, George, he's biting her,' Clete said from the passenger's seat. 'I can see his jaw moving.'

But we were so close together and the light was so poor that he couldn't see that Quinn was biting the binding on my hands. That was good. I was trying hard to find good things to cling to, because this was looking like a bleak, bleak world just at this moment, lying in the van traveling through the rain on an unknown road somewhere in southern Louisiana.

I was angry and bleeding and sore and lying on my already injured left arm. What I wanted, what would be ideal, would be to find myself clean and bandaged in a nice bed with white sheets. Okay, clean and bandaged and in a clean nightgown. And then Quinn would be in the bed, completely in his human form, and he would be clean and bandaged, too. And he'd have had some rest, and he'd be wearing nothing at all. But the pain of my cut and bleeding arms was becoming too demanding to ignore any longer, and I couldn't concentrate enough to cling to my lovely daydream. Just when I was on the verge of whimpering – or maybe just out-and-out screaming – I felt my wrists separate.

For a few seconds I just lay there and panted, trying to control my reaction to the pain. Unfortunately Quinn couldn't gnaw on the binding on his own hands, since they'd been bound behind him. He finally succeeded in turning over so I could see his wrists.

George said, 'What are they doing?'

Clete glanced back at us, but I had my hands together. Since the day was dark, he couldn't see very clearly. 'They're not doing anything. He quit biting her,' Clete said, sounding disappointed.

Quinn succeeded in getting a claw hooked into the silvery duct tape. His claws were not sharp-edged along their curve like a scimitar; their power lay in the piercing point backed by a tiger's huge strength. But Quinn couldn't get the purchase to exercise that strength. So this was going to take time, and I suspected the tape was *going* to make a ripping noise when he succeeded in slicing it open.

We didn't have much time left. Any minute even an idiot like Clete would notice that all was not well.

I began the difficult maneuvering to get my hands down to Quinn's feet without giving away the fact that they weren't bound any longer. Clete glanced back when he glimpsed my movement, and I slumped against the empty shelves, my hands clasped together in my lap. I tried to look hopeless, which was awfully easy. Clete got more interested in lighting a cigarette after a second or two, giving me a chance to look at the plastic strap binding Quinn's ankles together. Though it had reminded me of the bag tie we used last Thanksgiving, this plastic was black and thick and extra tough, and I didn't have a knife to cut it or a key to unlock it. I did think Clete had made a mistake putting the restraint on, however, and I hurried to try to take advantage of it. Quinn's shoes were still on, of course, and I unlaced them and pulled them off. Then I held one foot pointed down. That foot began to slide up inside the circle of the tie. As I'd suspected, the shoes had held his feet apart and allowed for some slack.

Though my wrists and hands were bleeding onto Quinn's socks (which I left on so the plastic wouldn't scrape him) I was managing pretty well. He was being stoic about my drastic adjustments to his foot. Finally I heard his bones protest at being twisted into a strange position, but his foot slid up out of the restraint. Oh, thank God.

It had taken me longer to think about than to do. It had felt like hours.

I pulled the restraint down and shoved it into the debris, looked up at Quinn, and nodded. His claw, hooked in the duct tape, ripped at it. A hole appeared. The sound hadn't been loud at all, and I eased myself back full length beside Quinn to camouflage the activity.

I stuck my thumbs in the hole in the duct tape and yanked, achieving very little. There's a reason duct tape is so popular. It's a reliable substance.

We had to get out of that van before it reached its destination, and we had to get away before the other van could pull up behind ours. I scrabbled around through the chalupa wrappers and the cardboard french fry cartons on the floor of the van and finally, in a little gap between the floor and the side, I found an overlooked Phillips screwdriver. It was long and thin.

I looked at it and took a deep breath. I knew what I had to do. Quinn's hands were bound and he couldn't do it. Tears rolled down my face. I was being a crybaby, but I just couldn't help it. I looked at Quinn for a moment, and his features were steely. He knew as well as I did what needed to be done.

Just then the van slowed and took a turn from a parish road, reasonably well paved, onto what felt like a graveled track running into the woods. A driveway, I was sure. We were close to our destination. This was the best chance, maybe the last chance, we would have.

'Stretch your wrists,' I murmured, and I plunged the Phillips head into the hole in the duct tape. It became larger. I plunged again. The two men, sensing my frantic movement, were turning as I stabbed at the duct tape a final time. While Quinn strained to part the perforated bindings, I pulled myself to my knees, gripping the latticed partition with my left hand, and I said, 'Clete!'

He turned and leaned between the seats, closer to the partition, to see better. I took a deep breath and with my right hand I drove the screwdriver between the crosshatched metal. It went right into his cheek. He screamed and bled and George could hardly pull over fast enough. With a roar, Quinn separated his wrists. Then Quinn moved like lightning, and the minute the van slammed into Park, he and I were out the back doors and running through the woods. Thank God they were right by the road.

Beaded thong sandals are not good for running in the woods, I just want to say here, and Quinn was only in his socks. But we covered some ground, and by the time the startled driver of the second van could pull over and the passengers could leap out in pursuit, we were out of sight of the road. We kept running, because they were Weres, and they would track us. I'd pulled the screwdriver out of Clete's cheek and had it in my hand, and I remember thinking that it was dangerous to run with a pointed object in my hand. I thought about Clete's thick finger probing between my legs, and I didn't feel so bad about what I'd done. In the next few seconds, while I was jumping over a downed tree snagged in some thorny vines, the screwdriver slipped from my hand and I had no time to search for it.

After running for some time, we came to the swamp. Swamps and bayous abound in Louisiana, of course. The bayous and swamps are rich in wildlife, and they can be beautiful to look at and maybe tour in a canoe or something. But to plunge into on foot, in pouring rain, they suck.

Maybe from a tracking point of view this swamp was a good thing, because once we were in the water we wouldn't be leaving any scent. But from my personal point of view, the swamp, was awful, because it was dirty and had snakes and alligators and God knows what else.

I had to brace myself to wade in after Quinn, and the water was dark and cool since it was still spring. In the summer, it would feel like wading through warm soup. On a day so overcast, once we were under the overhanging trees, we would be almost invisible to our pursuers, which was good; but the same conditions also meant that any lurking wildlife would be seen approximately when we stepped on it, or when it bit us. Not so good.

Quinn was smiling broadly, and I remembered that some tigers have lots of swamps in their natural habitat. At least one of us was happy.

The water got deeper and deeper, and soon we were swimming. There again, Quinn swam with a large grace that was kind of daunting to me. I was trying with all my might just to be quiet and stealthy. For a second, I was so cold and so frightened I began to think that . . . no, it wouldn't be better to still be in the van . . . but it was a near thing, just for a second.

I was so tired. My muscles were shaking with the aftermath of the adrenalin surge of our escape, and then I'd dashed through the woods, and before that there'd been the fight in the apartment, and before that . . . oh my God, I'd had sex with Quinn. Sort of. Yes, definitely sex. More or less.

We hadn't spoken since we'd gotten out of the van, and suddenly I remembered I'd seen his arm bleeding when we'd burst out of the van. I'd stabbed him with the Phillips head, at least once, while I was freeing him.

And here I was, whining. 'Quinn,' I said. 'Let me help you.'

'Help me?' he asked. I couldn't read his tone, and since he was forging through the dark water ahead of me, I couldn't read his face. But his mind, ah, that was full of snarled confusion and anger that he couldn't find a place to stuff. 'Did I help you? Did I free you? Did I protect you from the fucking Weres? No, I let that son of a bitch stick his finger up you, and I watched, I couldn't do anything.'

Oh. Male pride. 'You got my hands free,' I pointed out. 'And you can help me now.'

'How?' he turned to me, and he was deeply upset. I realized that he was a guy who took his protecting very seriously. It was one of God's mysterious imbalances, that men are stronger than women. My grandmother told me it was his way of balancing the scales, since women are tougher and more resilient. I'm not sure that's true, but I knew that Quinn, perhaps because he was a big, formidable guy and, perhaps because he was a weretiger who could turn into this fabulously beautiful and lethal beast, was in a funk because he hadn't killed all our attackers and saved me from being sullied by their touch.

I myself would have preferred that scenario a lot, especially considering our present predicament. But events hadn't fallen out that way. 'Quinn,' I said, and my voice was just as weary as the rest of me, 'they have to have been heading somewhere around here. Somewhere in this swamp.'

'That's why we turned off,' he said in agreement. I saw a snake twined around a tree branch overhanging the water right behind him, and my face must have looked as shocked as I felt, because Quinn whipped around faster than I could think and had that snake in his hand and snapped it once, twice, and then the snake was dead and floating away in the sluggish water. He seemed to feel a lot better after that. 'We don't know where we're going, but we're sure it's away from them. Right?' he asked.

'There aren't any other brains up and running in my range,' I said, after a moment's checking. 'But I've never defined how big my range is. That's all I can tell you. Let's try to get out of the water for a minute while we think, okay?' I was shivering all over.

Quinn slogged through the water and gathered me up. 'Link your arms around my neck,' he said.

Sure, if he wanted to do the man thing, that was fine. I put my arms around his neck and he began moving through the water.

'Would this be better if you turned into a tiger?' I asked.

'I might need that later, and I've already partially changed twice today. I better save my strength.'

'What kind are you?'

'Bengal,' he said, and just then the pattering of the rain on the water stopped.

We heard voices calling then, and we came to a stop in the water, both of our faces turned to the source of the sound. As we were standing there stock-still, I heard something large slide into the water to our right. I swung my eyes in that direction, terrified of what I'd see – but the water was almost still, as if something had just passed. I knew there were tours of the bayous south of New Orleans, and I knew locals made a good living out of taking people out on the dark water and letting them see the alligators. The good thing was, these natives made money, and out-of-staters got to see something they'd never have seen otherwise. The bad thing was, sometimes the locals threw treats to attract the gators. I figured the gators associated humans with food.

I laid my head on Quinn's shoulder and I closed my eyes. But the voices didn't get any closer, and we didn't hear the baying of wolves, and nothing bit my leg to drag me down. 'That's what gators do, you know,' I told Quinn. 'They pull you under and drown you, and stick you somewhere so they can snack on you.'

'Babe, the wolves aren't going to eat us today, and neither will the gators.' He laughed, a low rumble deep in his chest. I was so glad to hear that sound. After a moment, we began moving through the water again. The trees and the bits of land became close together, the channels narrow, and finally we came up on a piece of land large enough to hold a cabin.

Quinn was half supporting me when we staggered out of the water.

As shelter, the cabin was poor stuff. Maybe the structure had once been a glorified hunting camp, three walls and a roof, no more than that. Now it was a wreck, halfway fallen. The wood had rotted and the metal roof had bent and buckled, rusting through in spots. I went over to the heap of man-tailored material and searched very carefully, but there didn't seem to be anything we could use as a weapon.

Quinn was occupied by ripping the remnants of the duct tape off his wrists, not even wincing when some skin went with it. I worked on my own more gently. Then I just gave out.

I slumped dismally to the ground, my back against a scrubby oak tree. Its bark immediately began making deep impressions in my back. I thought of all the germs in the water, germs that were doubtless speeding through my system the moment they'd gained entry through the cuts on my wrists. The unhealed bite, still covered by a now-filthy bandage, had doubtless received its share of nasty particles. My face was swelling up from the beating I'd taken. I remembered looking in the mirror the day before and seeing that the marks left by the bitten Weres in Shreveport had finally almost faded away. Fat lot of good that had done me.

'Amelia should have done something by now,' I said, trying to feel optimistic. 'She probably called vampire HQ. Even if our own phone call didn't reach anyone who'd do something about it, maybe someone's looking for us now.'

'They'd have to send out human employees. It's still technically daylight, even though the sky's so dark.'

'Well, at least the rain's over with,' I said. At that moment, it began to rain again.

I thought about throwing a fit, but frankly, it didn't seem worth using up the energy. And there was nothing to do about it. The sky was going to rain, no matter how many fits I threw. 'I'm sorry you got caught up in this,' I said, thinking that I had a lot for which to apologize.

'Sookie, I don't know if *you* should be telling me *you're* sorry.' Quinn emphasized the pronouns. 'Everything has happened when we were together.'

That was true, and I tried to believe all this wasn't my fault. But I was convinced that somehow, it really was.

Out of the blue, Quinn said 'What's your relationship with Alcide Herveaux? We saw him in the bar last week with some other girl. But the cop, the one in Shreveport, said you'd been engaged to him.'

'That was bullshit,' I said, sitting slumped in the mud. Here I was, deep inside a southern Louisiana swamp, the rain pelting down on me . . .

Hey, wait a minute. I stared at Quinn's mouth moving, realized he was saying something, but waited for the trailing end of a thought to snag on something. If there'd been a lightbulb above my head, it would have been flashing. 'Jesus Christ, Shepherd of Judea,' I said reverently. 'That's who's doing this.'

Quinn squatted in front of me. 'You've picked who's been doing what? How many enemies do you have?'

'At least I know who sent the bitten Weres, and who had us kidnapped,' I said, refusing to be sidetracked. Crouched together in the downpour like a couple of cave people, Quinn listened while I talked.

Then we discussed probabilities.

Then we made a plan.

Chapter 21

Once he knew what he was doing, Quinn was relentless. Since we couldn't be any more miserable than we already were, he decided we might as well be moving. While I did little more than follow him and stay out of his way, he began to scour the area for smells. Finally he got tired of crouching, and he said, 'I'm going to change.' He stripped quickly and efficiently, rolling the clothes into a compact (but sopping) bundle and handing them to me to carry. Every conjecture I'd had about Quinn's body was absolutely on target, I was pleased to note. He'd begun taking off his clothes without a single hesitation, but once he noticed I was looking, he held still and let me look. Even in the dark, dripping rain, he was worth it. Quinn's body was a work of art, though a scarred work of art. He was one large block of muscle, from his calves to his neck.

'Do you like what you see?' he asked.

'Oh, *boy*,' I said. 'You look better than a Happy Meal to a three-year-old.'

Quinn gave me a broad, pleased smile. He bent to crouch on the ground. I knew what was coming. The air around Quinn began to shimmer and tremble, and then within that envelope Quinn began to change. Muscles rippled and flowed and reformed, bones reshaped, fur rolled out of somewhere inside him – though I knew that couldn't be, that was the illusion. The sound was dreadful. It was a kind of gloppy, sticky sound, but with hard notes in it, as if someone were stirring a pot of stiff glue that was full of sticks and rocks.

At the end of it, the tiger stood across from me.

If Quinn had been a gorgeous naked man, he was an equally beautiful tiger. His fur was a deep orange slashed with black stripes, and there were touches of white on his belly and face. His eyes slanted, and they were golden. He was maybe seven feet long and at least three feet tall at the shoulder. I was amazed at how big he was. His paws were fully developed and as big as some dinner plates. His rounded ears were just plain cute. He walked over to me silently, with a grace unusual in such a massive form. He rubbed his huge head against me, almost knocking me down, and he purred. He sounded like a happy Geiger counter.

His dense fur was oily to the touch, so I figured he was pretty well waterproofed. He gave a barking cough, and the swamp went silent. You wouldn't think Louisiana wildlife would recognize the sound of a tiger, right? But it did, and it shut its mouth and hid.

We don't have the same special space requirements with animals that we do with people. I knelt beside the tiger that had been Quinn, in some magical way was still Quinn, and I put my arms around his neck, and I hugged him. It was a little disturbing that he smelled so much like an actual tiger, and I forced my mind around the fact that he was a tiger, that Quinn was inside him. And we set out through the swamp.

It was a little startling to see the tiger mark his new territory – this is not something you expect to see your boyfriend do – but I decided it would just be ridiculous to mind the display. Besides, I had enough to think about, keeping up with the tiger. He was searching for scents, and we covered a lot of ground. I was growing more and more exhausted. My sense of wonder faded, and I was simply wet and chilly, hungry and grumpy. If someone had been thinking right under my feet, I'm not sure my mind would have picked the thoughts up.

Then the tiger froze, nose testing the air. His head moved, ears twitching, to search in a particular direction. He turned to look at me. Though tigers can't smile, I got the definite wave of triumph from the huge cat. The tiger turned his head back to the east, rotated his massive head to look at me, and turned his head to the east again. *Follow me*, clear as a bell.

'Okay,' I said, and put my hand on his shoulder.

Off we went. The trip through the swamp lasted an eternity, though later I estimated that 'eternity', in this case, was probably about thirty minutes. Gradually the ground grew firmer, the water scarcer. Now we were in forest, not swamp.

I'd figured we'd gotten close to our abductors' destination when the van had turned off onto the side road. I'd been right. When we came to the edge of the clearing surrounding the little house, we were to the west side of the north-facing house. We could see both front and back yards. The van that had held us captive was parked in the back. In the tiny clearing at the front was a car, some kind of GMC sedan.

The little house itself was like a million other houses in rural America. It was a box of a place: wooden, painted tan, with green shutters on the windows and green uprights to support the roof over the tiny front porch. The two men from the van, Clete and George, were huddled on the concrete square because of that bit of shelter, however inadequate it was.

The matching structure at the rear of the house was a little deck outside the back door, scarcely large enough to hold a gas grill and a mop. It was open to the elements. By the way, the elements were really going to town.

I stowed Quinn's clothes and shoes at the foot of a mimosa tree. The tiger's lips pulled back when he scented Clete. The long teeth were as frightening as a shark's.

The afternoon of rain had lowered the temperature. George and Clete were shivering in the damp cool of the evening. They were both smoking. The two Weres, in human form and smoking, would not have a better sense of smell than regular people. They showed no sign of being aware of Quinn at all. I figured they would react pretty dramatically if they caught the scent of tiger in southern Louisiana.

I worked my way through the trees around the clearing until I was very close to the van. I eased my way around it and crept up to the passenger side. The van was unlocked, and I could see the stun gun. That was my goal. I took a deep breath and opened the door, hoping the light that came on wasn't interesting to anyone who could see out the back window. I grabbed the stun gun from the jumble of stuff between the front seats. I shut the door as quietly as a van door can be shut. Luckily, the rain seemed to muffle the noise. I gave a shaky sigh of relief when nothing happened. Then I duckwalked back into the edge of the woods and knelt by Quinn.

He licked my cheek. I appreciated the affection in the gesture, if not the tiger breath, and I scratched his head. (Somehow, kissing his fur had no appeal.) That done, I pointed to the left west window, which should belong to a living room. Quinn didn't nod or give me a high five, both of which would have been untigerlike gestures, but I guess I had expected him to give me some kind of green light. He just looked at me.

Picking up my feet carefully, I stepped out into the little open space between the forest and the house, and very carefully I made my way to the lit window.

I didn't want to pop into view like a jack-in-the-box, so I hugged the side of the house and inched sideways until I could peer in at the very corner of the glass. The older Pelts, Barbara and Gordon, were sitting on an 'early American' loveseat dating from the sixties, and their body language clearly proclaimed their unhappiness. Their daughter Sandra paced back and forth in front of them, though there wasn't much room for such an exhibtion. It was a very small family room, a room that would be comfortable only if you had a family of one. The older Pelts looked as if they were going to a Lands' End photo shoot, while Sandra was more adventurously clad in skintight stretch khakis and a bright striped short-sleeved sweater. Sandra was dressed for trolling for cute guys at the mall, rather than torturing a couple of people. But torturing was what she'd been planning to do. There was a straight-backed chair crammed into the room, too, and it had straps and handcuffs already attached.

On a familiar note, there was a roll of duct tape sitting ready beside it.

I'd been pretty calm until I saw the duct tape.

I didn't know if tigers could count, but I held up three fingers in case Quinn was watching. Moving slowly and carefully, I squatted down and moved south until I was below the second window. I was feeling pretty proud of my sneaking ability, which should have alerted me to potential disaster. Pride goeth before a fall.

Though the window was dark, when I eased up into position, I was looking through the glass right into the eyes of a small swarthy man with a mustache and goatee. He was sitting at a table right by the window, and he'd been holding a cup of coffee in his hand. In his shock, he let it drop to the table and the hot backsplash hit his hands and chest and chin.

He shrieked, though I wasn't sure he was using actual words. I heard a commotion at the front door and in the front room.

Well . . . eff.

I was around the corner of the house and up the steps to the little deck faster than you could say Jack Robinson. I yanked open the screen door and pushed in the wooden door, and I leaped into the kitchen with the stun gun on. The small guy was still patting at his face with a towel while I zapped him, and he went down like a sack of bricks. Wow!

But the stun gun had to recharge, I discovered, when Sandra Pelt, who'd had the advantage of already being on her feet, charged into the kitchen, teeth bared. The stun gun didn't do a damn thing to her, and she was on me like an – well, like an enraged wolf.

However, she was still in the form of a girl, and I was desperate and desperately angry.

I've seen at least two dozen bar fights, ranging from halfhearted punches to rolling-on-the-ground biting, and I know how to fight. Right now I was willing to do whatever it took. Sandra was mean, but she was lighter and less experienced, and after some wrestling and punching and hair pulling that went by in a flash, I was on top of her and had her pinned to the floor. She snarled and snapped but she couldn't reach my neck, and I was prepared to head-butt her if I had to.

A voice in the background bellowed, 'Let me in!' and I assumed it was Quinn behind some door. 'Come on now!' I yelled in answer. 'I need help!'

She was squirming underneath me, and I dared not let go to shift my grip. 'Listen, Sandra,' I panted, 'hold still, dammit!'

'Fuck you,' she said bitterly, and her efforts redoubled.

'This is actually kind of exciting,' a familiar voice said, and I glanced up to see Eric looking down at us with wide blue eyes. He looked immaculate: neat as a pin in blue jeans that had a crease and a starched blue-and-white striped dress shirt. His blond hair was shining clean and (here was the most enviable part) dry. I hated his guts. I felt nasty to the nth degree.

'I could use some help here,' I snapped, and he said, 'Of course, Sookie, though I'm enjoying the wiggling around. Let go of the girl and stand up.'

'Only if you're ready for action,' I said, my breathing ragged with the effort of holding Sandra down.

'I'm always ready for action,' Eric said, with a glowing smile. 'Sandra, look at me.'

She was too smart for that. Sandra squeezed her eyes shut and fought even harder. In a second, she freed one of her arms and swung it back to get momentum for her punch. But Eric dropped to his knees and caught the hand before it could fly at my head.

'That's enough,' he said in an entirely different tone, and her eyes flew open in surprise. Though he still couldn't catch her with his eyes, I figured he had charge of her now. I rolled off the Were to lie on my back in what remained of the floor in the tiny kitchen. Mr. Small and Dark (and Burned and Stunned), who I figured owned this house, was crumpled by the table.

Eric, who was having almost as much trouble with Sandra as I'd had, took up a lot more of the available space. Exasperated with the Were, he adopted a simple solution. He squeezed the fist he'd caught, and she screamed. And shut up – and quit struggling.

'That's just not fair,' I said, fighting a wave of weariness and pain.

'All's fair,' he said quietly.

I didn't like the sound of that. 'What are you talking about?' I asked. He shook his head. I tried again. 'Where's Quinn?'

'The tiger has taken care of your two abductors,' Eric said, with an unpleasant smile. 'Would you like to go see?'

'Not particularly,' I said, and closed my eyes again. 'I guess they're dead?'

'I'm sure they wish they were,' Eric said. 'What did you do to the little man on the floor?'

'You wouldn't believe me if I told you,' I said.

'Try me.'

'I scared him so bad he spilled hot coffee on himself. Then I hit him with a stun gun that I got out of the van.'

'Oh.' There was a kind of breathy sound, and I opened my eyes to see that Eric was laughing silently.

'The Pelts?' I asked.

'Rasul has them covered,' Eric said. 'You have another fan, it seems.'

'Oh, it's because of the fairy blood,' I said irritably. 'You know, it's not fair. Human guys don't like me. I know about two hundred of 'em who wouldn't want to date me if I came with a Chevy truck. But because supes are attracted to the fairy smell, I get accused of being a guy magnet. How wrong is that?'

'You have fairy blood,' Eric said, as if his own lightbulb had just lit up. 'That explains a lot.'

That hurt my feelings. 'Oh no, you couldn't just like me,' I said, tired and hurting beyond coherence. 'Oh no, gosh, there has to be a *reason*. And it's not gonna be my sparkling personality, oh no! It's gonna be my blood, because it's *special*. Not me, *I'm* not special . . .'

And I would have gone on and on, if Quinn hadn't said, 'I don't give a damn about fairies, myself.' Any available room left in the kitchen vanished.

I scrambled to my feet. 'You okay?' I asked in a wobbly voice.

'Yes,' he said, in his deepest rumble. He was altogether human again, and altogether naked. I would've hugged him, but I felt a little embarrassed about embracing him in the altogether, in front of Eric.

'I left your clothes out there in the woods,' I said. 'I'll go get 'em.'

'I can.'

'No, I know where they are, and I couldn't get any wetter.' Besides, I'm not sophisticated enough to be comfortable in a room with a naked guy, an unconscious guy, a real horrible girl, and another guy who's been my lover.

'Fuck you, bitch,' the charming Sandra called after me, and shrieked again, as Eric made it clear he didn't care for name calling.

'Right back at you,' I muttered, and trudged out into the rain.

Oh, yes, it was still raining.

I was still brooding over the fairy-blood thing as I scooped up the bundle of Quinn's sodden clothes. It would be easy to slide into a depressed trough if I thought the only reason anybody ever liked me was because I had fairy blood. Of course, there was always the odd vampire who had been ordered to seduce me . . . I was sure the fairy blood had just been a bonus, in that case . . . no, no, no, *wasn't going there.*

If I looked at it in a reasonable way, the blood was just as much a part of me as my eye color or the thickness of my hair. It hadn't done a thing for my half-fairy grandmother, assuming the gene had come to me through her and not one of my other grandparents. She'd married a human man who hadn't treated her any differently than he would have if her blood had been plain old grade A human. And she'd been killed by a human who hadn't known anything about her blood other than the color of it. Following the same assumption, fairy blood hadn't made a bit of difference to my father. He'd never in his life encountered a vampire who might be interested in him because of it – or if he had, he'd kept it mighty close. That didn't seem likely. And the fairy blood hadn't saved my father from the flash flood that had washed my parents' truck off the bridge and into the swollen stream. If the blood had come to me through my mother, well, she'd died in the truck, too. And Linda, my mother's sister, had died of cancer in her midforties, no matter what kind of heritage she had.

I didn't believe this wonderful fairy blood had done all that much for me, either. Maybe a few vampires had been a little more interested in me and friendly to me than they would have been otherwise, but I couldn't say that had been much of an advantage.

In fact, many people would say the vampire attention had been a big negative factor in my life. I might be one of those people. Especially since I was standing out here in the pouring rain holding someone else's wet clothes and wondering what the hell to do with them.

Having come full circle, I slogged back to the house. I could hear a lot of moaning coming from the front yard: Clete and George, presumably. I should have gone to check, but I couldn't muster up the energy.

Back in the kitchen, the small dark man was stirring a little, his eyes opening and shutting and his mouth twitching. His hands were tied behind him. Sandra was bound with duct tape, which cheered me up quite a bit. It seemed a neat piece of poetic justice. She even had a neat rectangle squarely over her mouth, which I presumed was Eric's work. Quinn had found a towel to secure around his waist, so he looked very . . . preppy.

'Thanks, babe,' he said. He took his clothes and began squeezing them out over the sink. I dripped on the floor. 'I wonder if there's a dryer?' he asked, and I opened another door to find a little pantry/utility room with shelves on one wall and on the other a water heater and a tiny washer and dryer.

'Pass 'em in here,' I called, and Quinn came in with his clothes. 'Yours need to go in there, too, babe,' he said, and I noticed he sounded as tired as I felt. Changing into and out of tiger form without the full moon, in such a short space of time, must have been very difficult. 'Maybe you can find me a towel?' I asked, pulling off the wet pants with great effort. Without a single joke or leer, he went to see what he could find. He returned with some clothes, I assumed from the small man's bedroom: a T-shirt, shorts, socks. 'This is the best I could do,' he said.

'It's better than I hoped for,' I said. After I'd used the towel and I had pulled on the clean, dry clothes, I almost wept with gratitude. I gave Quinn a hug and then went to find out what we were going to do with our hostages.

The Pelts were sitting on the floor, securely handcuffed, in the living room, watched by Rasul. Barbara and Gordon had looked so mild when they'd come to Merlotte's to meet with me in Sam's office. They looked mild no longer. Rage and malice sat oddly on their suburban faces.

Eric brought Sandra in, too, and dumped her by her parents. Eric stood in one doorway, Quinn in another (which a glance told me led into Small and Dark's bedroom). Rasul, gun in hand, relaxed his vigilance a little now that he had such formidable backup. 'Where's the little guy?' he asked. 'Sookie, I'm glad to see you looking so well, even though your ensemble falls below your usual standards.'

The shorts were baggy cargo shorts, the shirt was big, and the white socks were the capper. 'You really know how to make a girl feel beautiful, Rasul,' I said, scraping together maybe half a smile to offer him. I sat down in the straight-backed chair and I asked Barbara Pelt, 'What were you going to do with me?'

'Work on you until you told us the truth, and Sandra was satisfied,' she said. 'Our family couldn't be at peace until we knew the truth. And the truth lies in you, I just know it.'

I was troubled. Well, beyond troubled. Because I didn't know what to say to her just yet, I looked from Eric to Rasul. 'Just the two of you?' I asked.

'Any time two vampires can't handle a handful of Weres is the day I become human again,' Rasul said, with an expression so snooty I was tempted to laugh. But he'd been exactly right (though of course he'd had a tiger who helped). Quinn was propped in the doorway looking picturesque, though just at the moment his great expanse of smooth skin didn't interest me at all.

'Eric,' I said, 'what should I do?'

I don't think I'd ever asked Eric for advice before. He was surprised. But the secret wasn't only mine.

After a moment, he nodded.

'I'll tell you what happened to Debbie,' I said to the Pelts. I didn't ask Rasul and Quinn to leave the room. I was getting rid of this right now, both the lingering guilt and the hold Eric had on me.

I'd thought about that evening so often that my words came automatically. I didn't cry, because all my tears had been shed months ago, in private.

Once I'd finished the story, the Pelts sat and stared at me, and I stared back.

'That sounds like our Debbie,' said Barbara Pelt. 'This has the ring of truth.'

'She did have a gun,' said Gordon Pelt. 'I gave it to her for Christmas two years ago.' The two Weres looked at each other.

'She was . . . proactive,' Barbara said, after a moment. She turned to Sandra. 'Remember when we had to go to court, when she was in high school, because she put superglue in that cheerleader's hairbrush? The one that was dating her ex-boyfriend? That does sound like Debbie, huh?'

Sandra nodded, but the duct tape wouldn't permit her speech. Sandra had tears rolling down her cheeks.

'You still don't remember where you put her?' Gordon asked Eric.

'I would tell you if I did,' Eric said. *Not that I care*, his tone implied.

'You guys hired the two kids who attacked us in Shreveport,' Quinn said.

'Sandra did,' Gordon admitted. 'We didn't know about it until Sandra had already bitten them. She'd promised them . . .' He shook his head. 'She'd sent them to Shreveport on her errand, but they would have returned home to collect their reward. Our Jackson pack would have killed them. Mississippi doesn't permit bitten Weres. They kill them on sight. The boys would have named Sandra as their maker. The pack would have abjured her. Barbara's dabbled with witchcraft, but nothing of the level that would have sealed the boys' mouths. We hired an out-of-state Were to track them when we found out. He couldn't stop them, couldn't prevent their arrest, so he had to be arrested and go into the jail system with them, to take care of the problem.' He looked up at us, shook his head sternly. 'He bribed Cal Myers to put him in the cell with them. Of course, we punished Sandra for that.'

'Oh, did you take away her cell phone for a week?' If I sounded sarcastic, I thought I had a right to be. Even cooperative, the Pelts were pretty horrible. 'We were both hurt,' I said, nodding toward Quinn, 'and those two kids are dead now. Because of Sandra.'

'She's our daughter,' Barbara said. 'And she believed she was avenging her murdered sister.'

'And then you hired all the Weres that were in the second van, and the two Weres lying out in the front yard. Are they going to die, Quinn?'

'If the Pelts don't take them to a Were doctor, they may. And they sure can't go to any human hospital.'

Quinn's claws would have left distinctive marks.

'Will you do that?' I asked skeptically. 'Take Clete and George to a Were doctor?'

The Pelts looked at each other and shrugged. 'We figured you were going to kill us,' Gordon said. 'Are you going to let us walk away? With what assurances?'

I'd never met anyone quite like the Pelts before, and it was easier and easier to see where Debbie had gotten her charming personality, adopted or not.

'With assurances that I never hear of this again,' I said. 'Neither I nor Eric.'

Quinn and Rasul had been listening silently.

'Sookie is a friend of the Shreveport pack,' Quinn said. 'They are very upset she was attacked, in their own city, and now we know you're responsible for that attack.'

'We heard she was no favorite of the new packleader.' Barbara's voice held a trace of contempt. She was reverting to her own personality, since she no longer feared her own death. I liked them better when they were scared.

'He may not be packleader for long,' Quinn said, his voice a quiet threat. 'Even if he stays in office, he can't rescind the pack's protection, since it was guaranteed by the previous packleader. The honor of the pack would be destroyed.'

'We'll make reparations to the Shreveport pack,' Gordon said wearily.

'Did you send Tanya to Bon Temps?' I asked.

Barbara looked proud of herself. 'Yes, I did that. You know our Debbie was adopted? She was a werefox.'

I nodded. Eric looked quizzical; I didn't think he'd met Tanya.

'Tanya is a member of Debbie's birth family, and she wanted to do something to help. She thought if she went to Bon Temps and began working with you, you might let something spill. She said you were too suspicious to warm up to her offer of friendship. I think she might stay in Bon Temps. I understand finding the bar owner so attractive was an unexpected bonus.'

It was kind of gratifying to discover Tanya was as untrustworthy as

I'd suspected. I wondered if I had the right to tell Sam this whole story, by way of warning. I'd have to think about that later.

'And the man who owns this house?' I could hear him groaning and moaning from the kitchen.

'He's a former high school buddy of Debbie's,' Gordon said. We asked him if we could borrow his house for the afternoon. And we paid him. He won't talk after we leave.'

'What about Gladiola?' I asked. I remembered the two burning body sections on my driveway. I remembered Mr Cataliades's face, and Diantha's grief.

They all three stared at me blankly. 'Gladiola? The flower?' Barbara said, looking genuinely puzzled. 'It's not even the right season for glads, now.'

That was a dead end.

'Do you agree we're square on this?' I asked baldly. 'I've hurt you, you've hurt me. Even?'

Sandra shook her head from side to side, but her parents ignored her. Thank God for duct tape. Gordon and Barbara nodded at each other.

Gordon said, 'You killed Debbie, but we do believe that you killed her in self-defense. And our living daughter took extreme and unlawful methods to attack you. . . . It goes against my grain to say this, but I think we have to agree to leave you alone, after this day.'

Sandra made a lot of weird noises.

'With these stipulations.' Gordon's face suddenly looked hard as a rock. The yuppie man took a backseat to the Were. 'You won't come after Sandra. And you stay out of Mississippi.'

'Done,' I said instantly. 'Can you control Sandra enough to make her keep to this agreement?' It was a rude but valid question. Sandra had enough balls for an army, and I doubted very much if the Pelts had ever really had control over either of their daughters.

'Sandra,' Gordon said to his daughter. Her eyes blazed at him from her forcibly mute face. 'Sandra, this is law. We are giving our word to this woman, and our word is binding on you. If you defy me, I'll challenge you at the next full moon. I'll take you down in front of the pack.'

Both mother and daughter looked shocked, Sandra more so than her mother. Sandra's eyes narrowed, and after a long moment, she nodded.

I hoped Gordon lived a long time and enjoyed good health while he lived. If he grew ill, or if he died, Sandra wouldn't feel bound by this agreement, I felt pretty darn sure. But as I walked out of the little house in the swamp, I thought I had a reasonable chance of not seeing the Pelts again in my life, and that was absolutely okay with me.

Chapter 22

Amelia was rummaging through her walk-in closet. It was just after dark the next day. Suddenly the hangers quit sliding across the rack at the very back of the closet.

'I think I have one,' she called, sounding surprised. I waited for her to emerge, sitting on the edge of her bed. I'd had at least ten hours' sleep, I'd had a careful shower, I'd had some first aid, and I felt a hundred times better. Amelia was glowing with pride and happiness. Not only had Bob the Mormony witch been wonderful in bed, they'd been up in time to watch Quinn's and my abduction, and to have the brilliant idea of calling the vampire queen's mansion instead of the regular police. I hadn't told her yet that Quinn and I had made our own call, because I didn't know which one had been more effective, and I enjoyed seeing Amelia so happy.

I hadn't wanted to go to the queen's shindig at all until after my trip to the bank with Mr Cataliades. After I'd returned to Hadley's apartment, I'd resumed packing my cousin's stuff and heard a strange noise when I'd put the coffee into a box. Now if I wanted to avert disaster, I had to go to the queen's spring party, the supernatural event of the year. I'd tried getting in touch with Andre at the queen's headquarters, but a voice had told me he was not to be disturbed. I wondered who was answering the phones at Vampire Central that day. Could it be one of Peter Threadgill's vamps?

'Yes, I do!' Amelia exclaimed. 'Ah, it's kind of daring. I was the bridesmaid at an extreme wedding.' She emerged from the closet with her hair disheveled, her eyes lit with triumph. She rotated the hanger so I could get the full effect. She'd had to pin the dress to the hanger because there was so little to hang.

'Yikes,' I said, uneasily. Made mostly of lime-green chiffon, it was cut in a deep V almost down to the waist. A single narrow strap ran around the neck.

'It was a movie star wedding,' Amelia said, looking as if she had a lot of memories of the service. Since the dress was also backless, I was wondering how those Hollywood women kept their boobs covered. Double-sided tape? Some kind of glue? As I hadn't seen Claudine since she vanished from the courtyard before the ectoplasmic recon-struction, I had to assume she'd gone back to her job and her life in Monroe. I could have used her special services just about now. There had to be a fairy spell that would make your dress stay still.

'At least you don't need a special bra to wear under it,' Amelia said helpfully. That was true; it wasn't possible to wear a bra at all. 'And I've got the shoes, if you can wear a seven.'

'That's a big help,' I said, trying to sound pleased and grateful. 'I don't suppose you can do hair?'

'Nah,' Amelia said. She waved a hand at her own short 'do'. 'I wash it, brush it, and that's that. But I can call Bob.' Her eyes glowed happily. 'He's a hairdresser.'

I tried not to look too astonished. *At a funeral home?* I thought, but I was smart enough to keep that to myself. Bob just looked no way like any hairdresser I'd ever seen.

After a couple of hours, I was more or less into the dress, and fully made up.

Bob had done a good job with my hair, though he'd reminded me several times to keep very still, in a way that had made me a little nervous.

And Quinn had shown up on time in his car. When Eric and Rasul had dropped me off at about two in the morning, Quinn had just gotten in his car and driven away to wherever he was staying, though he'd put a light kiss on my forehead before I started up the stairs. Amelia had come out of her apartment, all happy I was safely back, and I'd had to return a call from Mr Cataliades, who wondered if I was quite all right; and who wanted me to go to the bank with him to finalize Hadley's financial affairs. Since I'd missed my chance to go with Everett, I'd been grateful.

But when I'd returned to Hadley's apartment after the bank trip, I'd found a message on Hadley's answering machine telling me that the queen expected to see me at the party at the old monastery tonight. 'I don't want you to leave the city without seeing me again,' the queen's human secretary had quoted her as saying, before informing me that the dress code was formal. After my discovery, when I realized I'd have to attend the party, I'd gone down the stairs to Amelia's in a panic.

The dress caused another kind of panic. I was better-endowed than Amelia, though a bit shorter, and I had to stand really straight.

'The suspense is killing me,' said Quinn, eyeing my chest. He looked wonderful in a tux. My wrist bandages stuck out against my tan like strange bracelets; in fact, one of them was acutely uncomfortable, and I was anxious to take it off. But the wrist would have to stay covered a while, though the bite on my left arm could remain uncovered. Maybe the suspense about my boobs would distract partygoers from the fact that my face was swollen and discolored on one side.

Quinn, of course, looked as though nothing had ever happened to him. Not only did he have the quick-healing flesh of most shape-shifters, but a man's tux covers up a lot of injuries.

'Don't you make me feel any more self-conscious than I already do,' I said. 'For about a dime, I'd go crawl back into bed and sleep for a week.'

'I'm up for that, though I'd reduce the sleep time,' Quinn said sincerely. 'But for our peace of mind, I think we better do this first. By the way, my suspense was about the trip to the bank, not your dress. I figure, with your dress, it's a win-win situation. If you stay in it, good. If you don't, even better.'

I looked away, trying to control an involuntary smile. 'The trip to the bank.' That seemed like a safe topic. 'Well, her bank account didn't have a lot in it, which I figured would be the case. Hadley didn't have much sense about money. Hadley didn't have much sense, period. But the safe-deposit box . . .'

The safe-deposit box had held Hadley's birth certificate, a marriage license, and a divorce decree dated more than three years ago – both naming the same man, I was glad to see – and a laminated copy of my aunt's obituary. Hadley had known when her mother had died, and she'd cared enough to keep the clipping. There were pictures from our shared childhood, too: my mother and her sister; my mother and Jason, me, and Hadley; my grandmother and her husband. There was a pretty necklace with sapphires and diamonds (which Mr Cataliades had said the queen had given to Hadley), and a pair of matching earrings. There were a couple more things that I wanted to think about.

But the queen's bracelet was not there. That was why Mr Cataliades had wanted to accompany me, I think; he half expected the bracelet would be there, and he seemed quite anxious when I held the lockbox out to him so he could see its contents for himself.

'I finished packing the kitchen stuff this afternoon after Cataliades took me back to Hadley's apartment,' I said to Quinn, and watched his reaction. I would never again take the disinterestedness of my companions for granted. I found myself fairly convinced Quinn had not been helping me pack the day before in order to search for something, after I saw that his reaction was perfectly calm.

'That's good,' he said. 'Sorry I didn't make it over to help you today. I was closing out Jake's dealings with Special Events. I had to call my partners, let them know. I had to call Jake's girlfriend. He wasn't steady enough to be around her, if she even wants to see him again. She's not a vamp lover, to put it mildly.'

At the moment, I wasn't either. I couldn't fathom the true reason the queen wanted me at the party, but I had found another reason to see her. Quinn smiled at me, and I smiled back at him, hoping that some good would come out of this evening. I had to admit to myself that I was a bit curious about seeing the queen's party barn, so to speak – and I was also kind of glad to dress up and be pretty after all the swamp slogging.

As we drove, I almost opened a conversation with Quinn at least three times – but on every occasion, when it got to the point, I kept my mouth shut.

'We're getting close,' he told me when we'd reached one of the oldest neighborhoods in New Orleans, the Garden District. The houses, set in beautiful grounds, would cost many times what even the Bellefleur mansion would fetch. In the middle of these marvelous homes, we came to a high wall that extended for a whole block. This was the renovated monastery that the queen used for entertaining.

There might be other gates at the back of the property, but tonight all the traffic was moving through the main front entrance. It was heavily protected with the most efficient guards of all: vampires. I wondered if Sophie-Anne Leclerq was paranoid, or wise, or simply did not feel loved (or safe) in her adopted city. I was sure the queen also had the regular security provisions – cameras, infrared motion detectors, razor wire, maybe even guard dogs. There was security out the ying-yang here, where the elite vampires occasionally partied with the elite humans. Tonight the party was supes only, the first large party the newlyweds had given since they'd become a couple.

Three of the queen's vampires were at the gate, along with three of the Arkansas vampires. Peter Threadgill's vampires all wore a uniform, though I suspected the king called it livery. The Arkansas bloodsuckers, male and female, were wearing white suits with blue shirts and red vests. I didn't know if the king was ultrapatriotic or if the colors had been chosen because they were in the Arkansas state flag as well as the U.S. flag. Whichever, the suits were beyond tacky and into some fashion hall of shame, all on their own. And Threadgill had been dressed so conservatively! Was this some tradition I'd never heard of? Gosh, even I knew better than that, tastewise, and I bought most of my clothes at Wal-Mart.

Quinn had the queen's card to show to the guards at the gate, but still they called up to the main house. Quinn looked uneasy, and I hoped he was as concerned as I was about the extreme security and the fact that Threadgill's vampires had worked so hard to distinguish themselves from the queen's adherents. I was thinking hard about the queen's need to offer the king's vamps a reason she would go upstairs with me at Hadley's. I thought of the anxiety she displayed when she asked about the bracelet. I thought of the presence of both camps of vampires at the main gate. Neither monarch trusted the spouse to provide protection.

It seemed like a long time before we were given leave to pass through. Quinn was as quiet as I while we waited.

The grounds seemed to be beautifully landscaped and kept, and they were certainly well lit.

'Quinn, this is just wrong,' I said. 'What's going on here? Do you think they'd let us leave?' Unfortunately, it seemed as though all my suspicions were true.

Quinn didn't look any happier than I was. 'They won't let us out,' he said. 'We have to go on now.' I clutched my little evening bag closer to me, wishing there was something more lethal in it than a few small items like a compact and a lipstick, and a tampon. Quinn drove us carefully up the winding drive to the front of the monastery.

'What did you do today, besides work on your outfit?' Quinn asked.

'I made a lot of phone calls,' I said. 'And one of them paid off.'

'Calls? Where to?'

'Gas stations, all along the route from New Orleans to Bon Temps.'

He turned to stare at me, but I pointed just in time for Quinn to apply the brakes.

A lion strolled across the drive.

'Okay, what's that? Animal? Or shifter?' I was edgier by the minute.

'Animal,' Quinn said.

Scratch the idea of dogs roaming the enclosure. I hoped the wall was high enough to keep the lion in.

We parked in front of the former monastery, which was a very large two-storey building. It hadn't been built for beauty, but for utility, so it was a largely featureless structure. There was one small door in the middle of the facade, and small windows placed regularly. Again, fairly easy to defend.

Outside the small door stood six more vampires, three in fancy but unmatching clothes – surely Louisiana bloodsuckers – and three more from Arkansas, in their glaringly garish outfits.

'That's just butt-ugly,' I said.

'But easy to see, even in the dark,' Quinn said, looking as if he were thinking deep, significant thoughts.

'Duh,' I said. 'Isn't that the point? So they'll instantly . . . oh.' I mulled it over. 'Yeah,' I said. 'No one would wear anything close to that, on purpose or by accident. Under any circumstances. Unless it was really important to be instantly identifiable.'

Quinn said, 'It's possible that Peter Threadgill is not devoted to Sophie-Anne.'

I gave a squawk of laughter just as two Louisiana vampires opened our car doors in a move so coordinated it must have been rehearsed. Melanie, the guard vampire I'd met at the queen's downtown head-quarters, took my hand to help me from the car, and she smiled at me. She looked a lot better out of the overwhelming SWAT gear. She was wearing a pretty yellow dress with low heels. Now that she wasn't wearing a helmet, I could see her hair was short, intensely curly, and light brown.

She took a deep, dramatic breath as I passed, and then made an ecstatic face. 'Oh, the odor of the fairy!' she exclaimed. 'It makes my heart sing!'

I swatted at her playfully. To say I was surprised would be an understatement. Vampires, as a whole, are not noted for their sense of humor.

'Cute dress,' Rasul said. 'Kind of on the daring side, huh?'

Chester said, 'Can't be too daring for me. You look really tasty.'

I thought it couldn't be a coincidence that the three vampires I'd met at the queen's headquarters were the three vampires on door duty tonight. I couldn't figure out what that could mean, though. The three Arkansas vampires were silent, regarding the to-and-fro between us with cold eyes. They were not in the same relaxed and smiling mood as their fellows.

Something definitely off-kilter here. But with the acute vampire hearing all around, there wasn't anything to say about it.

Quinn took my arm. We walked into a long hall that seemed to run nearly the length of the building. A Threadgill vampire was standing at the door of a room that seemed to serve as a reception area.

'Would you like to check your bag?' she asked, obviously put out at being relegated to a hat-check girl.

'No, thanks,' I said, and thought she was going to pull it out from under my arm.

'May I search it?' she asked. 'We screen for weapons.'

I stared at her, always a risky thing to do to a vampire. 'Of course not. I have no weapons.'

'Sookie,' Quinn said, trying not to sound alarmed. 'You have to let her look in your purse. It's procedure.'

I glared at him. 'You could have told me,' I said sharply.

The door guard, who was a svelte young vamp with a figure that challenged the cut of the white pants, seized my purse with an air of triumph. She turned it out over a tray, and its few contents clattered to the metal surface: a compact, a lipstick, a tiny tube of glue, a handkerchief, a ten-dollar bill, and a tampon in a rigid plastic applicator, completely covered in plastic wrap.

Quinn was not unsophisticated enough to turn red, but he did glance discreetly away. The vampire, who had died long before women carried such items in their purses, asked me its purpose and nodded when I explained. She repacked my little evening bag and handed it to me, indicating with a hand gesture that we should proceed down the hall. She'd turned to the people who'd come in behind us, a Were couple in their sixties, before we'd even exited the room.

'What are you up to?' Quinn asked, in the quietest possible voice, as we moved along the corridor.

'Do we have to pass through any more security?' I asked, in a voice just as hushed.

'I don't know. I don't see any up ahead.'

'I have to do something,' I said. 'Excuse me, while I find the nearest ladies' room.' I tried to tell him, with my eyes, and with the pressure of my hand on his arm, that in a few minutes everything would be all right, and I sincerely hoped that was the truth. Quinn was clearly not happy with me, but he waited outside the ladies' room (God knows what that had been when the building was a monastery) while I ducked into one of the stalls and made a few adjustments. When I came out, I'd tossed the tampon container into the little bin in the stall, and one of my wrists had been rebandaged. My purse was a little heavier.

The door at the end of the corridor led into the very large room

that had been the monks' refectory. Though the room was still walled
with stone and large pillars supported the roof, three on the left and
three on the right, the rest of the decor was considerably different now.
The middle of the room was cleared for dancing, and the floor was
wooden. There was a dais for musicians close to the refreshments
table, and another dais at the opposite end of the room for the royalty.

Around the sides of the room were chairs in conversational grou-
pings. The whole room was decorated in white and blue, the colors of
Louisiana. One of the walls had murals depicting scenes from around
the state: a swamp scene, which made me shudder; a Bourbon Street
montage; a field being plowed and lumber being cut; and a fisherman
hoisting up a net in the Gulf Coast. These were all scenes featuring
humans, I thought, and wondered what the thinking was behind that.
Then I turned to look at the wall surrounding the doorway I'd just
entered, and I saw the vampire side of Louisiana life: a group of happy
vampires with fiddles under their chins, playing away; a vampire police
officer patrolling the French Quarter; a vampire guide leading tourists
through one of the Cities of the Dead. No vamps snacking on humans,
no vamps drinking anything, I noticed. This was a statement in public
relations. I wondered if it really fooled anyone. All you had to do was
sit down at a supper table with vampires, and you'd be reminded how
different they were, all right.

Well, this wasn't what I'd come to do. I looked around for the queen,
and I finally saw her standing by her husband. She was wearing a long-
sleeved orange silk dress, and she looked fabulous. Long sleeves maybe
seemed a little strange in the warm evening, but vampires didn't notice
such things. Peter Threadgill was wearing a tux, and he looked equally
impressive. Jade Flower was standing behind him, sword strapped to
her back even though she was wearing a red sequined dress (in which,
by the way, she looked awful). Andre, also fully armed, was at his
station behind the queen. Sigebert and Wybert couldn't be far off.
I spotted them on either side of a door that I assumed led to the queen's
private apartments. The two vampires looked acutely uncomfortable
in their tuxes; it was like watching bears who'd been made to wear
shoes.

Bill was in the room. I caught a glimpse of him in the far corner, in the opposite direction from the queen, and I shivered with loathing.

'You have too many secrets,' Quinn complained, following the direction of my gaze.

'I'll be glad to tell you a few of 'em, real soon,' I promised, and we joined the tail end of the reception line. 'When we reach the royals, you go ahead of me. While I'm talking to the queen, you distract the king, okay? Then I will tell you everything.'

We reached to Mr Cataliades first. I guess he was sort of the queen's secretary of state. Or maybe attorney general would be more appropriate?

'Good to see you again, Mr Cataliades,' I said, in my most correct social tone. 'I've got a surprise for you,' I added.

'You may have to save it,' he said with a kind of stiff cordiality. 'The queen is about to have the first dance with her new king. And we're all so looking forward to seeing the present the king gave her.'

I glanced around but I didn't see Diantha. 'How's your niece?' I asked.

'My surviving niece,' he said grimly, 'is at home with her mother.'

'That's too bad,' I said. 'She should be here this evening.'

He stared at me. Then he looked interested.

'Indeed,' he said.

'I heard that someone from here stopped to get gas a week ago Wednesday, on her way to Bon Temps,' I said. 'Someone with a long sword. Here, let me tuck this in your pocket. I don't need it any more.' When I stepped away from him and faced the queen, I had one hand over my injured wrist. The bandage had vanished.

I held out my right hand, and the queen was forced to take it in her own. I had counted on obliging the queen to follow the human custom of shaking hands, and I was mighty relieved when she did. Quinn had passed from the queen to the king, and he said, 'Your Majesty, I'm sure you remember me. I was the event coordinator at your wedding. Did the flowers turn out like you wanted?'

Somewhat startled, Peter Threadgill turned his large eyes on Quinn, and Jade Flower kept her eyes on what her king did.

Trying very hard to keep my movements swift but not jerky, I pressed my left hand and what was in it onto the queen's wrist. She didn't flinch, but I think she thought about it. She glanced down at her wrist to see what I'd put on it, and her eyes closed in relief.

'Yes, my dear, our visit was lovely,' she said, at random. 'Andre enjoyed it very much, as did I.' She glanced back over her shoulder, and Andre picked up his cue, and inclined his head to me, in tribute to my supposed talents in the sack. I was so glad to get the ordeal over with that I smiled at him radiantly, and he looked a shade amused. The queen raised her arm slightly to beckon him closer, and her sleeve rode up. Suddenly Andre was smiling as broadly as I was.

Jade Flower was distracted by Andre's movement forward, and her eyes followed his. They widened, and she was very much not smiling. In fact, she was enraged. Mr Cataliades was looking at the sword on Jade Flower's back with a completely blank face.

Then Quinn was dismissed by the king and it was my turn to pay homage to Peter Threadgill, King of Arkansas.

'I hear that you had an adventure in the swamps yesterday,' he said, his voice cool and indifferent.

'Yes, sir. But it all worked out okay, I think,' I said.

'Good of you to come,' he said. 'Now that you have wrapped up your cousin's estate, I am sure you will be returning to your home?'

'Oh, yes, quick as can be,' I said. It was the absolute truth. I would go home providing I could just survive this evening, though at the moment the chances weren't looking too good. I had counted, as well as I was able in a throng like this. There were at least twenty vampires in the room wearing the bright Arkansas outfit, and perhaps the same number of the queen's homies.

I moved away, and the Were couple that had entered after Quinn and me took my place. I thought he was the lieutenant governor of Louisiana, and I hoped he had good life insurance.

'What?' Quinn demanded.

I led him over to a place against the wall, and gently maneuvered him until his back was against it. I had to face away from any lip-readers in the room.

'Did you know the queen's bracelet was missing?' I asked.

He shook his head. 'One of the diamond bracelets the king gave her as a wedding present?' he asked, his head ducked to baffle any watchers.

'Yes, missing,' I said. 'Since Hadley died.'

'If the king knew the bracelet was missing, and if he could force the queen to acknowledge that she'd given it to a lover; then he would have grounds for divorce.'

'What would he get then?'

'What *wouldn't* he get! It was a vampire hierarchical marriage, and you don't get any more binding than that. I think the wedding contract was thirty pages.'

I understood much better now.

A beautifully dressed vampire woman wearing a gray-green gown strewn with gleaming silver flowers raised her arm to get the attention of the crowd. Gradually the assembled people fell silent.

'Sophie-Anne and Peter welcome you to their first joint enter-tainment,' the vamp said, and her voice was so musical and mellow that you wanted to listen to her for hours. They should get her to do the Oscars. Or the Miss America pageant. 'Sophie-Anne and Peter invite all of you to have a wonderful evening of dancing, eating, and drinking. To open the dancing, our host and hostess will waltz.'

Despite his glitzy surface, I thought Peter might be more com-fortable doing a square dance, but with a wife like Sophie-Anne, it was waltz or nothing. He advanced on his wife, his arms at the ready to receive her, and in his carrying vampire voice he said, 'Darling, show them the bracelets.'

Sophie-Anne swept the crowd with a smile and raised her own arms to make the sleeves slide back, and a matching bracelet on each wrist shone at the guests, the two huge diamonds winking and blinking in the chandelier lights.

For a moment Peter Threadgill was absolutely still, as if someone had zapped him with a freeze gun. He altered his stance as he moved forward, after that, and took one of her hands in both of his. He stared down at one bracelet, then released her hand to take the other. That bracelet, too, passed his silent test.

'Wonderful,' he said, and if it was through his fangs you'd only think they'd extended because he was horny for his beautiful wife. 'You're wearing both of them.'

'Of course,' Sophie-Anne said. 'My darling.' Her smile was just as sincere as his.

And away they danced, though something about the way he swung her let me know the king was letting his temper get the better of him. He'd had a big plan, and now I'd spoiled it . . . but thankfully, he didn't know my part. He just knew that somehow Sophie-Anne had managed to retrieve her bracelet and save her face, and he had nothing to justify whatever he'd plotted to do. He would have to back down. After this, he'd probably think of another way to subvert his queen, but at least I'd be out of the fray.

Quinn and I retreated to the refreshments table, located to the south side of the large room, beside one of the thick pillars. Servers were there with carving knives to shave off ham or roast beef. There were yeasty rolls to pile the meat on. It smelled wonderful, but I was too nervous to think of eating. Quinn got me a cup of ginger ale from the bar. I stared at the dancing couple and waited for the ceiling to fall in.

'Don't they look lovely together?' a well-dressed gray-haired woman said. I realized she was the one who'd come in after me.

'Yes, they do,' I agreed.

'I'm Genevieve Thrash,' she said. 'This is my husband, David.'

'Pleased to meet you,' I said. 'I'm Sookie Stackhouse, and this is my friend, John Quinn.' Quinn looked surprised. I wondered if that was actually his first name.

The two men, tiger and Were, shook hands while Genevieve and I watched the couple dance a bit longer.

'Your dress is so pretty,' Genevieve said, giving every indication she was speaking sincerely. 'It takes a young body to show off a gown like that.'

'I appreciate your saying so,' I said. 'I'm showing a bit more of that body than I'm comfortable with, so you've made me feel better.'

'I know your date appreciates it,' she said. 'And so does that young man over there.' She nodded her head subtly, and I glanced in the direction she was indicating. Bill. He looked very good in his tuxedo, but even being in the same room made something within me twist with pain.

'I believe your husband is the lieutenant governor?' I said.

'You're absolutely correct.'

'And how do you like being Mrs Lieutenant?' I asked.

She told some amusing stories about people she'd met while she followed David's political career. 'And what does your young man do?' she asked, with that eager interest that must have helped her husband up that ladder.

'He's an events coordinator,' I said, after a moment's hesitation.

'How interesting,' Genevieve said. 'And yourself, you have a job?'

'Oh, yes ma'am,' I said. 'I'm a barmaid.'

That was a bit startling to the politician's wife, but she grinned at me. 'You're the first I've ever met,' she said cheerfully.

'You're the first Mrs Lieutenant Governor I've ever met,' I said. Damn, now that I'd met her and liked her, I felt responsible for her. Quinn and David were just chatting away, and I think fishing was their topic.

'Mrs Thrash,' I said, 'I know you're a Were and that means you're tough as tough can be, but I'm going to give you a piece of advice.'

She looked at me quizzically.

'This advice is pure gold,' I said.

Her eyebrows flew up. 'Okay,' she said, slowly. 'I'm listening.'

'Something very bad is going to happen here in the next hour or so. It's going to be so bad that it might get a lot of people killed. Now you can stay and have a good time until it happens, and then you'll wonder why you didn't listen to me, or you can leave now after acting like you've been taken ill, and you can save yourself a lot of unhappiness.'

Her gaze was intent. I could hear her wondering whether to take me seriously. I didn't seem like a weirdo or a crazy person. I seemed like a normal, attractive, young woman with a heck of a handsome date.

'Are you threatening me?' she asked.

'No, ma'am. I'm trying to save your ass.'

'We'll get one dance in first,' Genevieve Thrash said, making up her mind. 'David, honey, let's take a spin around the dance floor and then make our excuses. I've got the worst headache you ever felt.' David obligingly broke off his conversation with Quinn to take his wife to the clear space and begin waltzing along with the royal vampire couple, who looked relieved to have company.

I was beginning to relax my posture again, but a glance from Quinn reminded me to stand very straight. 'I *love* the dress,' he said. 'Shall we dance?'

'You can waltz?' I hoped my jaw hadn't dropped too far.

'Yep,' he said. He didn't ask if I could, though as a matter of fact I'd been watching the queen's steps intently. I can dance – can't sing, but I love a dance floor. I'd never waltzed, but I figured I could do it.

It was wonderful to have Quinn's arm around me, to be moving so gracefully around the floor. For a moment, I just forgot everything and enjoyed looking up at him, feeling the way a girl feels when she's dancing with a guy she expects she'll make love with, sooner or later. Quinn's fingers touching my bare back just made me tingle.

'Sooner or later,' he said, 'we're gonna be in a room with a bed, no phones, and a door that will lock.'

I smiled up at him and spied the Thrashes easing out of the door. I hoped their car had been brought around. And that was the last normal thought I had for some time.

A head flew past Quinn's shoulder. It was moving too fast for me to pin down whose head it was, but it looked familiar. A spray of blood created a ruddy cloud in the head's wake.

I made a sound. It wasn't a scream or a gasp; more like 'Eeeeep.'

Quinn stopped dead, though the music didn't for a long moment. He looked in all directions, trying to analyze what was happening and how we could survive it. I'd thought one dance would be okay, but we should have gone with the Were couple. Quinn began pulling me over to the side of the ballroom, and he said, 'Backs against the wall.' We'd know from which direction the danger was coming: good thinking. But someone cannoned into us and Quinn's hold on my hand was broken.

There was a lot of screaming and a lot of movement. The screaming was all from the Weres and other supes who'd been invited to the party, and the movement was mostly from the vampires, who were looking for their allies amid the chaos. This was where the horrible outfits worn by the king's followers came into their own. It was instantly easy to see who belonged to the king. Of course, that made them an easy target, too, if you didn't happen to like the king and his minions.

A thin black vampire with dreadlocks had whipped a sword with a curved blade out of nowhere, apparently. The blade was bloody, and I thought Dreadlocks was the head-topper. He was wearing the awful suit, so he was someone I wanted to dodge. If I had any allies here, it wasn't anyone working for Peter Threadgill. I'd gotten behind one of the pillars holding up the ceiling of the west end of the refectory, and I was trying to figure out the safest way from the room when my foot bumped something that shifted. I looked down to see the head. It belonged to Wybert. I wondered for a fraction of a second if it would move or speak, but decapitation is pretty final, no matter what species you are.

'Oh,' I moaned, and decided I'd better get a good hold on myself, or I was gonna look just like Wybert, at least in one important respect.

Fighting had broken out throughout the room. I hadn't seen the precipitating incident, but on some pretext the black vampire had attacked Wybert and cut off his head. Since Wybert was one of the queen's bodyguards and Dreadlocks was one of Peter's attendants, the beheading was a pretty decisive act.

The queen and Andre were standing back to back in the middle of the floor. Andre was holding a gun in one hand and a long knife in the other, and the queen had acquired a carving knife from the buffet. There was a circle of white coats surrounding them, and when one fell, another would take its place. This was like Custer's last stand, with the queen standing in for Custer. Sigebert was equally besieged on the bandstand, and the orchestra, part Were or shifter and part vampire, had separated into its various components. Some were joining in the combat, while others were trying to flee. Those who were doing their best to get the hell out of there were clogging the door leading to the long corridor. The effect was a log jam.

The king was under attack from my three friends Rasul, Chester, and Melanie. I was sure I'd find Jade Flower at his back, but she was having her own problems, I was glad to see. Mr Cataliades was doing his best to – well, it looked like he was just trying to touch her. She was parrying his attempts with her whacking big sword, the sword that had sliced Gladiola in two, but neither of them looked like they were giving up any time soon.

Just then I was knocked flat to the floor, losing my breath for a minute. I struck out, only to have my hand trapped. I was smushed under a big body. 'I've got you,' Eric said.

'What the hell are you doing?'

'Protecting you,' he said. He was smiling with the joy of battle, and his blue eyes were glittering like sapphires. Eric loved a brawl.

'I don't see anybody coming after me,' I said. 'It seems to me like the queen needs you more than I do. But I appreciate it.'

Carried away on a wave of excitement, Eric kissed me long and hard and then scooped up Wybert's head. 'Bowling for vampires,' he said happily, and flung the disgusting object at the black vampire with an accuracy and force that knocked the sword out of the vampire's hand. Eric was on it with a great leap, and the sword swung on its owner with deadly force. With a war cry that had not been heard in a thousand years, Eric attacked the circle around the queen and Andre with a savagery and abandon that was almost beautiful in its way.

A shifter trying to find another way out of the room knocked against me with enough force to dislodge me from behind my comparatively secure position. Suddenly, there were too many people between me and the pillar, and the way back was blocked. Damn! I could see the door Wybert and his brother had been guarding. The door was across the room, but it was the only empty passage. Any way out of this room was a good way. I began sidling around the walls to reach it, so I wouldn't have to cross the dangerous open spaces.

One of the whitecoats leaped in front of me.

'We're supposed to find you!' he bellowed. He was a young vampire; there were clues, even at such a moment. This vamp had known the amenities of modern life. He had all the signs – superstraight teeth that had known braces, a husky build from modern nutrition, and he was big-boned and tall.

'Look!' I said, and pulled one side of my bodice away. He did, God bless him, and I kicked him in the balls so hard I thought they'd come out through his mouth. That's gonna get a man on the floor, no matter what their nature is. This vampire was no exception. I hurried around him and reached the east wall, the one with the door.

I had maybe a yard to go when someone grabbed my foot, and down I went. I slipped in a pool of blood and landed on my knees in it. It was vamp blood, I could tell by the color.

'Bitch,' said Jade Flower. 'Whore.' I didn't think I'd ever heard her talk before. I could have done without it now. She began dragging me, hand over hand, toward her extended fangs. She wasn't getting up to kill me, because one of her legs was missing. I almost threw up but became more concerned with getting away than with ralphing. My hands scrabbled at the smooth wood floor, and my knees tried to get purchase so I could pull away from the vampire. I didn't know if Jade Flower would die of this terrible wound or not. Vampires could survive so many things that would kill a human, which of course was a big part of the attraction ... *Snap to, Sookie!* I told myself fiercely.

The shock must be getting to me.

I threw out my hand and managed to get a grip on the door frame. I pulled and pulled, but I couldn't break free from Jade Flower's hold, and her fingers were digging into the flesh of my ankle. Soon she would snap the bones, and then I wouldn't be able to walk.

With my free foot I kicked the little Asian woman in the face. I did it again and again. Her nose was bleeding, and her lips were, too, but she would not let go. I don't think she even felt it.

Then Bill jumped on her back, landing with enough force to break her spine, and her hold on my ankle relaxed. I scrambled away while he raised a carving knife very like the one the queen had had. He sank it into Jade Flower's neck, over and over, and then her head was off and he was looking at me.

He didn't speak, just gave me that long, dark look. Then he was up and gone, and I had to get the hell out of there.

The queen's apartments were dark. That wasn't good. Beyond where the light penetrated from the ballroom, who knew what could be lurking?

There just had to be an outside door through here. The queen wouldn't leave herself bottled up. She'd have a way to get outside. And if I was remembering the orientation of the building, I needed to walk straight ahead to reach the correct wall.

I gathered myself and decided I'd just stride right on through. No more of this skulking around the wall. The hell with it.

And to my surprise, it worked, up to a point. I went through one room – a sitting room, I figured – before I ended up in what must have been the queen's bedroom. A whisper of movement in the room retriggered my fear switch, and I fumbled along the wall for the light. When I flipped it, I found I was in the room with Peter Threadgill. He was facing Andre. A bed was between them, and on the bed was the queen, who had been badly wounded. Andre didn't have his sword, but then neither did Peter Threadgill. Andre did have a gun, and when I turned on the light, he shot the king right in the face. Twice.

There was a door beyond the body of Peter Threadgill. It had to lead to the grounds. I began to sidle around the room, my back pressed against the wall. No one paid a bit of attention to me.

'Andre, if you kill him,' the queen said quite calmly, 'I'll have to pay a huge fine.' She had a hand pressed to her side, and her beautiful orange dress was dark and wet with her blood.

'But wouldn't it be worth it, lady?'

There was a thoughtful silence on the queen's part, while I unlocked about six locks.

'On the whole, yes,' Sophie-Anne said. 'After all, money isn't everything.'

'Oh, *good*,' Andre said happily, and raised the gun. He had a stake in the other hand, I saw. I didn't stick around to see how Andre did the deed.

I set off across the lawn in my green evening shoes. Amazingly, the evening shoes were still intact. In fact, they were in better shape than my ankle, which Jade Flower had hurt pretty badly. I was limping by the time I'd taken ten steps. 'Watch out for the lion,' called the queen, and I looked behind me to see that Andre was carrying her out of the building. I wondered whose side the lion was on.

Then the big cat appeared right in front of me. One minute my escape route was clear, and the next it was filled by a lion. The outside security lights were off, and in the moonlight the beast looked so beautiful and so deadly that fear pulled the air right out of my lungs.

The lion made a low, guttural sound.

'Go away,' I said. I had absolutely nothing to fight a lion with, and I was at the end of my rope. 'Go away!' I yelled. 'Get out of here!'

And it slunk into the bushes.

I don't think that is typical lion behavior. Maybe it smelled the tiger coming, because a second or two later, Quinn appeared, moving like a huge silent dream across the grass. Quinn rubbed his big head against me, and we went over to the wall together. Andre laid down his queen and leaped up on top with grace and ease. For his queen, he pulled apart the razor wire with hands just barely cushioned with his torn coat. Then down he came and carefully lifted Sophie-Anne. He gathered himself and cleared the wall in a bound.

'Well, I can't do that,' I said, and even to my own ears, I sounded grumpy. 'Can I stand on your back? I'll take my heels off.' Quinn snugged up to the wall, and I ran my arm through the sandal straps. I didn't want to hurt the tiger by putting a lot of weight on his back, but I also wanted to get out of there more than I've wanted anything, just about. So, trying to think light thoughts, I balanced on the tiger's back and managed to pull myself, finally, to the top of the wall. I looked down, and it seemed like a very long way to the sidewalk.

After all I'd faced this evening, it seemed stupid to balk at falling a few feet. But I sat on the wall, telling myself I was an idiot, for several long moments. Then I managed to flip over onto my stomach, let myself down as far as I could reach, and said out loud, 'One, two, three!' Then I fell.

For a couple of minutes I just lay there, stunned at how the evening had turned out.

Here I was, lying on a sidewalk in historical New Orleans, with my boobs hanging out of my dress, my hair coming down, my sandals on my arm, and a large tiger licking my face. Quinn had bounded over with relative ease.

'Do you think it would be better to walk back as a tiger, or as a large naked man?' I asked the tiger. 'Because either way, you might attract some attention. I think you stand a better chance of getting shot if you're a tiger, myself.'

'That will not be necessary,' said a voice, and Andre loomed above me. 'I am here with the queen in her car, and we will take you where you need to go.'

'That's mighty nice of you,' I said, as Quinn began to change back.

'Her Majesty feels that she owes you,' Andre said.

'I don't see it that way,' I said. Why was I being so frank, now? Couldn't I just keep my mouth shut? 'After all, if I hadn't found the bracelet and given it back, the king would have . . .'

'Started the war tonight anyway,' Andre said, helping me to my feet. He reached out and quite impersonally pushed my right breast under the scanty lime-green fabric. 'He would have accused the queen of breaking her side of the contract, which held that all gifts must be held in honor as tokens of the marriage. He would have brought suit against the queen, and she would have lost almost everything and been dishonored. He was ready to go either way, but when the queen was wearing the second bracelet, he had to go with violence. Ra Shawn set it off by beheading Wybert for bumping against him.' Ra Shawn had been Dreadlock's name, I assumed.

I wasn't sure I got all that, but I was equally sure Quinn could explain it to me at a time when I had more brain cells to spare for the information.

'He was so disappointed when he saw she had the bracelet! And it was the right one!' Andre said merrily. He was turning into a babbling brook, that Andre. He helped me into the car. 'Where was it?' asked the queen, who was stretched across one of the seats. Her bleeding had stopped, and only the way she was holding her lips indicated what pain she was in.

'It was in the can of coffee that looked sealed,' I said. 'Hadley was real good with arts and crafts, and she'd opened the can real carefully, popped the bracelet inside, and resealed it with a glue gun.' There was a lot more to explain, about Mr Cataliades and Gladiola and Jade Flower, but I was too tired to volunteer information.

'How'd you get it past the search?' the queen asked. 'I'm sure the searchers were checking for it.'

'I had the bracelet part on under my bandage,' I said. 'The diamond stood out too far, though, so I had to prize it out. I put it in a tampon holder. The vampire who did the searching didn't think of pulling out the tampon, and she didn't really know how it was supposed to look, since she hadn't had a period in centuries.'

'But it was put together,' the queen said.

'Oh, I went into the ladies room after I'd had my purse searched. I had a little tube of superglue in my purse, too.'

The queen didn't seem to know what to say. 'Thank you,' she told me, after a long pause. Quinn had climbed into the back with us, quite bare, and I leaned against him. Andre got into the driver's seat, and we glided off.

He dropped us off in the courtyard. Amelia was sitting on the pavement in her lawn chair, a glass of wine in her hand.

When we emerged, she set the glass down very carefully on the ground and then looked us over from head to toe.

'Okay, don't know how to react,' she said, finally. The big car glided out of the courtyard as Andre took the queen to some safe hideaway. I didn't ask, because I didn't want to know.

'I'll tell you tomorrow,' I said. 'The moving truck will be here tomorrow afternoon, and the queen promised me people to load it and drive it. I have to get back to Bon Temps.'

The prospect of going home seemed so sweet I could taste it on my tongue.

'So you got lots to do at home?' Amelia asked, as Quinn and I began going up the stairs. I guessed Quinn could sleep in the same bed. We were both too tired to plunge into anything; tonight was not the night to begin a relationship, if I hadn't already begun one. Maybe I had.

'Well, I have a lot of weddings to go to,' I said. 'I have to get back to work, too.'

'Got an empty guest bedroom?'

I stopped about halfway up the stairs. 'I might. Would you be needing one?'

It was hard to tell in the poor light, but Amelia might be looking embarrassed. 'I tried something new with Bob,' she said. 'And it didn't exactly work out right.'

'Where is he?' I asked. 'In the hospital?'

'No, right there,' she said. She was pointing at a garden gnome.

'Tell me you're joking,' I said.

'I'm joking,' she said. 'This is Bob.' She picked up a big black cat with a white chest that had been curled up in an empty planter. I hadn't even noticed him. 'Isn't he cute?'

'Sure, bring him along,' I said. 'I've always been fond of cats.'

'Babe,' said Quinn, 'I'm glad to hear you say that. I was too tired to completely change.'

For the first time, I really looked at Quinn.

Now he had a tail.

'You're definitely sleeping on the floor,' I said.

'Ah, babe.'

'I mean it. Tomorrow you'll be able to be all human, right?'

'Sure. I've changed too many times lately. I just need some rest.'

Amelia was looking at the tail with wide eyes. 'See you tomorrow, Sookie,' she said. 'We'll have us a little road trip. And then I'll get to stay with you for a while!'

'We'll have such fun,' I said wearily, trudging up the rest of the stairs and feeling profoundly glad I'd stuck my door key in my underwear. Quinn was too tired to watch me retrieve it. I let the remnants of the dress fall back into place while I unlocked the door. 'Such fun.'

Later, after I'd showered and while Quinn was in the bathroom himself, I heard a tentative knock on the door. I was decent enough in my sleep pants and tank top. Though I wanted to ignore it more than anything, I opened the door.

Bill was looking pretty good for someone who'd fought in a war. The tuxedo would never be functional again, but he wasn't bleeding, and whatever cuts he might have sustained had already healed over.

'I have to talk to you,' he said, and his voice was so quiet and limp that I took a step out of the apartment. I sat down on the gallery floor, and he sat with me.

'You have to let me say this, just once,' he said. 'I loved you. I love you.'

I raised a hand to protest, and he said, 'No, let me finish. She sent me there, true. But when I met you – after I came to know you – I really . . . loved you.'

How long after he'd taken me to bed had this supposed love come about? How could I possibly believe him, since he'd lied so convincingly from the very moment I'd met him – playing disinterested because he could read my fascination with the first vampire I'd ever met?

'I risked my life for you,' I said, the words coming out in a halting sequence. 'I gave Eric power over me forever, for your sake, when I took his blood. I killed someone for you. This is not something I take for granted, even if you do . . . even if that's everyday existence for you. It's not, for me. I don't know if I can ever not hate you.'

I got up, slowly and painfully, and to my relief he didn't make the mistake of trying to help me. 'You probably saved my life tonight,' I said, looking down at him. 'And I thank you for that. But don't come into Merlotte's any more, don't hang around in my woods, and don't do anything else for me. I don't want to see you again.'

'I love you,' he said stubbornly, as if that fact were so amazing and such an undeniable truth that I should believe him. Well, I had, and look at where it had gotten me.

'Those words are not a magical formula,' I said. 'They're not going to open my heart to you.'

Bill was over a hundred and thirty years old, but at that moment I felt I could match him. I dragged myself inside, shut the door behind me and locked it, and made myself go down the hall to the bedroom.

Quinn was drying himself off, and he turned around to show me his muscular derriere. 'Fur-free,' he said. 'Can I share the bed?'

'Yes,' I said, and crawled in. He got in the other side, and he was asleep in thirty seconds. After a minute or two, I slid over in the bed and put my head on his chest.

I listened to his heartbeat.

Chapter 23

What was the deal with Jade Flower?' Amelia asked the next day. Everett was driving the U-Haul, and Amelia and I were following in her little car. Quinn had left the next morning by the time I'd gotten up, leaving me a note telling me he was going to call me after he'd hired someone to take Jake Purifoy's place and after his next job, which was in Huntsville, Alabama – a Rite of Ascension, he said, though I had no idea what that was. He ended the note with a very personal comment about the lime-green dress, which I won't repeat here.

Amelia had her bags packed by the time I'd dressed, and Everett was directing two husky men in loading up the boxes I wanted to take back to Bon Temps. When he returned, he would take the furniture I didn't want to Goodwill. I'd offered it to him, but he'd looked at the fake antiques and politely said they weren't his style. I'd tossed my own stuff in Amelia's trunk, and off we'd driven. Bob the cat was in his own cage on the backseat. It was lined with towels and also held a food and water bowl, which was kind of messy. Bob's litter box was on the floorboard.

'My mentor found out what I'd done,' Amelia said gloomily. 'She's very, very unhappy with me.'

I wasn't surprised, but it didn't seem tactful to say so, when Amelia had been such a help to me.

'He is missing his life now,' I pointed out, as mildly as I could manage.

'Well, true, but he's having a hell of an experience,' Amelia said, in the voice of someone determined to look on the bright side. 'I'll make it up to him. Somehow.'

I wasn't sure this was something you could 'make up' to someone. 'I'll bet you can get him back to himself soon,' I said, trying to sound confident. 'There are some really nice witches in Shreveport who might help.' If Amelia could conquer her prejudice against Wiccans.

'Great,' the witch said, looking more cheerful. 'In the meantime, what the hell happened last night? Tell me in detail.'

I figured it was all over the supernatural community today, so I might as well spill the beans. I told Amelia the whole story.

'So how did Cataliades know Jade Flower had killed Gladiola?' Amelia asked.

'Um, I told him,' I said, my voice small.

'How'd you know?'

'When the Pelts told me they hadn't hired anyone to watch the house, I figured the murderer was someone sent by Peter Threadgill to delay my getting the message from Cataliades. Peter Threadgill knew all along that the queen had lost the bracelet to Hadley. Maybe he had spies among the queen's own people, or maybe one of her dumber followers, like Wybert, let it slip. It wouldn't be hard to watch the movements of the two goblin girls the queen used as messengers. When one of them came to deliver the queen's message to me, Jade Flower followed her and killed her. The wound was pretty drastic, and after I saw Jade Flower's sword and watched her whip it out so fast I couldn't see it move, I figured she was a likely candidate for the designated killer. Plus, the queen had said if Andre was in New Orleans, everyone had to assume she was, too . . . so the reverse had to be true, right? If the king was in New Orleans, everyone would assume Jade Flower was, too. But she was outside my house, in the woods.' I shuddered all over at the memory. 'I found out for sure after calling a lot of gas stations. I talked to a guy who definitely remembered Jade Flower.'

'So why did Hadley steal the bracelet?'

'Jealousy, I guess, and the desire to put the queen in a bad spot. I don't think Hadley understood the implications of what she'd done, and by the time she did, it was too late. The king had laid his plans.

Jade Flower watched Hadley for a while, snatched the opportunity to take Jake Purifoy and kill him. They hoped it would be blamed on Hadley. Anything that would discredit Hadley would discredit the queen. They had no way of knowing she would turn him.'

'What will happen to Jake now?' Amelia looked troubled. 'I liked him. He was a nice guy.'

'He still may be. He's just a vampire nice guy.'

'I'm not sure there's such a thing,' my companion said quietly.

'Some days, I'm not sure either.' We rode for a while in silence.

'Well, tell me about Bon Temps,' Amelia said, to get us out of our conversational doldrums.

I began to tell her about the town, and the bar where I worked, and the wedding shower I'd been invited to attend, and all the upcoming weddings.

'Sounds pretty good,' Amelia said. 'Hey, I know I kind of asked myself along. Do you mind, I mean, really?'

'No,' I said, with a speed that surprised even me. 'No, it'll be nice to have company . . . for a while,' I added cautiously. 'What will you do about your house in New Orleans while you're gone?'

'Everett said he wouldn't mind living in the upper apartment, because his mom was getting kind of hard to take. Since he's got such a good job with Cataliades, he can afford it. He'll watch my plants and stuff until I get back. He can always e-mail me.' Amelia had a laptop in her trunk, so for the first time there'd be a computer in the Stackhouse home. There was a pause, and then she said, her voice tentative, 'How are you feeling now? I mean, with the ex and all?'

I considered. 'I have a big hole in my heart,' I said. 'But it'll close over.'

'I don't want to sound all Dr Phil,' she said. 'But don't let the scab seal the pain in, okay?'

'That's good advice,' I said. 'I hope I can manage it.'

I'd been gone a few days, and they'd been eventful ones. As we drew closer to Bon Temps, I wondered if Tanya had succeeded in getting Sam to ask her out. I wondered if I'd have to tell Sam about Tanya's role as spy. Eric didn't have to be confused about me any more, since our big secret was out. He didn't have a hold on me. Would the Pelts stick to their word? Maybe Bill would go on a long trip. Maybe a stake would accidentally fall on his chest while he was gone:

I hadn't heard from Jason while I was in New Orleans. I wondered if he was still planning on getting married. I hoped Crystal had recovered. I wondered if Dr Ludwig accepted insurance payments. And the Belle-fleur double wedding should be an interesting event, even if I was working while I was there.

I took a deep breath. My life was not so bad, I told myself, and I began to believe that was true. I had a new boyfriend, maybe; I had a new friend, surely; and I had events to look forward to. This was all good, and I should be grateful.

So what if I was obliged to attend a vampire conference as part of the queen's entourage? We'd stay in a fancy hotel, dress up a lot, attend long boring meetings, if everything other people had told me about conferences was true.

Gosh, how bad could that be?

Better not to think about it.

Acknowledgments – Dead to the World

My thanks to Wiccans who answered my call for knowledge with more information than I could use – Maria Lima, Sandilee Lloyd, Holly Nelson, Jean Hontz, and M. R. 'Murv' Sellars. I owe further thanks to other experts in different fields: Kevin Ryer, who knows more about feral hogs than most people do about their own pets; Dr D. P. Lyle, who is so gracious about answering medical questions; and, of course, Doris Ann Norris, reference librarian to the stars.

If I have made mistakes in the use of the knowledge these kind people imparted, I'll do my best to somehow blame it on them.

Acknowledgments – Dead as a Doornail

I didn't thank Patrick Schulz for loaning me his Benelli for the last book – sorry, Son. My friend Toni L. P. Kelner, who pointed out some problems in the first half of the book, is due a big hats-off. My friend Paula Woldan gave me moral support and some information on pirates, and was willing to endure me on Talk Like a Pirate Day. Her daughter Jennifer saved my life by helping me prepare the manuscript. Shay, a Faithful Reader, had the great idea for the calendar. And in thanking the Woldan family, I have to include Jay, a volunteer firefighter for many years, who shared his knowledge and expertise with me.

Acknowledgments – Definitely Dead

My thanks to so many people: Jerrilyn Farmer's son's Latin teacher; Toni L.P. Kelner and Steve Kelner, friends and sounding boards; Ivan Van Laningham, who has both knowledge and opinions about many, many subjects; Dr. Stacy Clanton, about whom I can say the same; Alexandre Dumas, author of the fabulous *The Three Musketeers*, which everyone ought to read; Anne Rice, for vampirizing New Orleans; and to the reader at Uncle Hugo's who guessed the plot of this book in advance . . . hats off to you all!

*Hungry for more Sookie? Turn the page for the
first chapter of* All Together Dead,
the next book in the Sookie Stackhouse series.

Available now from Gollancz.

Chapter 1

The Shreveport vampire bar would be opening late tonight. I was running behind, and I'd automatically gone to the front door, the public door, only to be halted by a neatly lettered sign, red Gothic script on white cardboard: WE'LL BE READY TO GREET YOU WITH A BITE TONIGHT, AT EIGHT O'CLOCK. PLEASE EXCUSE OUR DELAYED OPENING. It was signed 'The Staff of Fangtasia'.

It was the third week in September, so the red neon FANGTASIA sign was already on. The sky was almost pitch-black. I stood with one foot inside my car for a minute, enjoying the mild evening and the faint, dry smell of vampire that lingered around the club. Then I drove around to the back and parked beside several other cars lined up at the employee entrance. I was only five minutes late, but it looked like everyone else had beaten me to the meeting. I rapped on the door. I waited.

I'd raised my hand to knock again when Pam, Eric's second-in-command, opened the door. Pam was based at the bar, but she had other duties in Eric's various business dealings. Though vampires had gone public five years ago and turned their best face to the world, they were still pretty secretive about their moneymaking methods, and sometimes I wondered how much of America the undead actually owned. Eric, the owner of Fangtasia, was a true vampire in the keeping-things-to-himself department. Of course, in his long, long existence he'd had to be.

'Come in, my telepathic friend,' Pam said, gesturing dramatically. She was wearing her work outfit: the filmy, trailing black gown that all the tourists who came into the bar seemed to expect from female vampires. (When Pam got to pick her own clothing, she was a pastels-and-twinset kind of woman.) Pam had the palest, straightest blond hair you ever saw; in fact, she was ethereally lovely, with a kind of deadly edge. The deadly edge was what a person shouldn't forget.

'How you doing?' I asked politely.

'I am doing exceptionally well,' she said. 'Eric is full of happiness.'

Eric Northman, the vampire sheriff of Area Five, had made Pam a vampire, and she was both obliged and compelled to do his bidding. That was part of the deal of becoming undead: you were always in sway to your maker. But Pam had told me more than once that Eric was a good boss to have, and that he would let her go her own way if and when she desired to do so. In fact, she'd been living in Minnesota until Eric had purchased Fangtasia and called her to help him run it.

Area Five was most of northwestern Louisiana, which until a month ago had been the economically weaker half of the state. Since Hurricane Katrina, the balance of power in Louisiana had shifted dramatically, especially in the vampire community.

'How is that delicious brother of yours, Sookie? And your shape-shifting boss?' Pam said.

'My delicious brother is making noises about getting married, like everyone else in Bon Temps,' I said.

'You sound a bit depressed.' Pam cocked her head to one side and regarded me like a sparrow eyeing a worm.

'Well, maybe a tad wee bit,' I said.

'You must keep busy,' Pam said. 'Then you won't have time to mope.'

Pam *loved* 'Dear Abby'. Lots of vampires scrutinized the column daily. Their solutions to some of the writers' problems would just make you scream. Literally. Pam had already advised me that I could only be imposed on if I permitted it, and that I needed to be more selective in picking my friends. I was getting emotional-health counseling from a vampire.

'I am,' I said. 'Keeping busy, that is. I'm working, I've still got my roommate from New Orleans, and I'm going to a wedding shower tomorrow. Not for Jason and Crystal. Another couple.'

Pam had paused, her hand on the doorknob of Eric's office. She considered my statement, her brows drawn together. 'I am not remembering what a wedding shower is, though I've heard of it,' she said. She brightened. 'They'll get married in a bathroom? No, I've heard the term before, surely. A woman wrote to Abby that she hadn't gotten a thank-you note for a large shower gift. They get . . . presents?'

'You got it,' I said. 'A shower is a party for someone who's about to get married. Sometimes the shower is for the couple, and they're both there. But usually only the bride is the honoree, and all the other people at the party are women. Everyone brings a gift. The theory is that this way the couple can start life with everything they need. We do the same thing when a couple's expecting a baby. Course, then it's a baby shower.'

'Baby shower,' Pam repeated. She smiled in a chilly way. It was enough to put frost on your pumpkin, seeing that up-curve of the lips. 'I like the term,' she said. She knocked on Eric's office door and then opened it. 'Eric,' she said, 'maybe someday one of the waitresses will get pregnant, and we can go to a *baby shower*!'

'That would be something to see,' said Eric, lifting his golden head from the papers on his desk. The sheriff registered my presence, gave me a hard look, and decided to ignore me. Eric and I had issues.

Despite the fact that the room was full of people waiting for his attention, Eric lay down his pen and stood to stretch his tall and magnificent body, perhaps for my benefit. As usual, Eric was in tight jeans and a Fangtasia T-shirt, black with the white stylized fangs that the bar used as its trademark. 'Fangtasia' was written in jazzy red script across the white points in the same style as the neon sign outside. If Eric turned around, the back would read 'The Bar with a Bite'. Pam had given me one when Fangtasia first got into marketing its own stuff.

Eric made the shirt look good, and I remembered all too well what was underneath it.

I tore my gaze away from Eric's stretch to look around the room. There were lots of other vampires crammed into the smallish space, but till you saw them you didn't know they were there, they were so still and silent. Clancy, the bar manager, had claimed one of the two visitor chairs before the desk. Clancy had just barely survived the previous year's Witch War, but he hadn't come out unscathed. The witches had drained Clancy near to the point of no return. By the time Eric discovered Clancy, tracing his smell to a Shreveport cemetery, Clancy was one Vacutainer short of dead. During his long recovery, the red-haired vamp had grown bitter and snappish. Now he grinned at me, showing some fang. 'You can sit in my lap, Sookie,' he said, patting his thighs.

I smiled back, but not like my heart was in it. 'No, thanks, Clancy,' I said politely. Clancy's flirting had always had an edge to it, and now that edge was razor sharp. He was one of those vamps I'd rather not be alone with. Though he ran the bar capably, and he had never laid a finger on me, he still set off warning bells. I can't read vampire minds, which was why I found it refreshing to hang with them, but when I felt that tingle of warning, I did find myself wishing I could just dip into Clancy's head and find out what was going on in there.

Felicia, the newest bartender, was sitting on the couch, along with Indira and Maxwell Lee. It was like the vampire Rainbow Coalition meeting. Felicia was a happy mixture of African and Caucasian, and she was almost six feet tall, so there was more loveliness to appreciate. Maxwell Lee was one of the darkest men I'd ever seen. Little Indira was the daughter of Indian immigrants.

There were four more people in the room (using the term 'people' loosely), and each one of them upset me, though in varying degrees.

One of them was someone I didn't acknowledge. I'd taken a page from the Were rule book and treated him like an outlawed member of my pack: I abjured him. I didn't speak his name, I didn't speak to him, I didn't recognize his existence. (Of course, this was my ex, Bill Compton – not that I recognized that he was in the room, brooding away in a corner.)

Leaning against the wall next to him was ancient Thalia, who was possibly even older than Eric. She was as small as Indira and very pale, with tightly waving black hair – and she was extremely rude.

To my amazement, some humans found that a complete turn-on.

Thalia actually had a devoted following who seemed thrilled when she used her stilted English to tell them to fuck off. I'd discovered she even had a website, established and maintained by fans. Go figure. Pam had told me that when Eric had agreed to let Thalia live in Shreveport, it was the equivalent of keeping a badly trained pit bull tethered in the yard. Pam had not approved.

These undead citizens all lived in Area Five. To live and work under Eric's protection, they'd all sworn fealty to him. So they were required to devote a certain amount of their time to doing his bidding, even if they didn't work at the bar. There were a few extra vampires in Shreveport these days, since Katrina; just like a lot of humans, they had to go somewhere. Eric hadn't decided what to do about the undead refugees, and they hadn't been invited to the meeting.

Tonight there were two visitors in Fangtasia, one of whom out-ranked Eric.

Andre was the personal bodyguard of Sophie-Anne Leclerq, the Queen of Louisiana. The queen, at present, was an evacuee in Baton Rouge. Andre looked very young, maybe sixteen; his face was baby smooth, his pale hair was thick and heavy. Andre had lived a long existence caring only for Sophie-Anne, his maker and saviour. He was not wearing his saber tonight, because he wasn't acting as her bodyguard, but I was sure Andre was armed with something – knife or gun. Andre himself was a lethal weapon, with or without an aid.

Just as Andre was about to speak to me, from beyond his chair a deep voice said, 'Hey, Sookie.' Our second visitor, Jake Purifoy. I made myself hold still when every impulse I had was telling me to get out of the office. I was being an idiot. If I hadn't run screaming at the sight of Andre, Jake shouldn't make me think of bolting. I forced myself to nod to the nice-looking young man who still looked alive. But I knew my greeting didn't look natural. He filled me with a terrible blend of pity and fear.

Jake, born a Were, had been attacked by a vampire and bled to the point of death. In what had been perhaps a mistaken gesture of mercy, my cousin Hadley (another vampire) had discovered Jake's nearly lifeless body and brought Jake over. This might have been considered a good deed; but as it turned out, no one had really appreciated Hadley's kindness . . . not even Jake himself. No one had ever heard of a turned Were before: Weres disliked and distrusted vampires, and the feeling was heartily reciprocated. The going was very rough for Jake, who occupied a lonely no-man's-land. The queen had given him a place in her service, since no one else had stepped forward.

Jake, blind with bloodlust, had gone after me as his first vampire snack. I had a still-red scar on my arm as a result.

What a wonderful evening this was turning out to be.

'Miss Stackhouse,' said Andre, rising from Eric's second guest chair. He bowed. This was a true tribute, and it lifted my spirits a bit.

'Mr Andre,' I said, bowing back. Andre swept his hand to indicate his politely vacated seat, and since that solved my placement problem, I accepted.

Clancy looked chagrined. He should have given me his chair, since he was the lower-ranked vampire. Andre's action had pointed that out as clearly as a blinking neon arrow. I tried hard not to smile.

'How is Her Majesty?' I asked, trying to be just as courteous as Andre had been. It would be stretching it to say I liked Sophie-Anne, but I sure respected her.

'That's part of the reason I am here tonight,' he said. 'Eric, can we get started now?' A gentle chiding for Eric's time-wasting tactics, I thought. Pam folded to the floor beside my chair, crouched on the balls of her feet.

'Yes, we're all here. Go ahead, Andre. You have the floor,' Eric said with a little smile at his own modern terminology. He slumped back down into his chair, extending his long legs to rest his feet on the corner of his desk.

'Your queen is living in the Area Four sheriff's house in Baton Rouge,' Andre said to the little assemblage. 'Gervaise was very gracious in extending his hospitality.'

Pam cocked an eyebrow at me. Gervaise would have lost his head if he *hadn't* extended his hospitality.

'But staying at Gervaise's place can only be a temporary solution,' Andre continued. 'We've been down to New Orleans several times since the disaster. Here's a report of our property's condition.'

Though none of the vampires moved, I felt their attention had heightened.

'The queen's headquarters lost most of its roof, so there was extensive water damage on the second floor and in the attic area. Furthermore, a large piece of someone else's roof landed inside the building, causing a pileup of debris and some holes in walls – problems like that. While we're drying the inside, the roof is still covered with blue plastic. One reason I came up this way is to find a contractor who will start reroofing immediately. So far, I haven't had any luck, so if any of you have personal influence with some human who does this kind of work, I need your help. On the ground floor, there was a lot of cosmetic damage. Some water came in. We had some looters, too.'

'Maybe the queen should remain in Baton Rouge,' Clancy said maliciously. 'I'm sure Gervaise would be overwhelmed with delight at the prospect of hosting her permanently.'

So Clancy was a suicidal idiot.

'A delegation of New Orleans leaders came to visit our queen in Baton Rouge to ask that she return to the city,' Andre said, ignoring Clancy completely. The human leaders think that if the vampires will return to New Orleans, tourism will pick up again.' Andre fixed Eric with a cold gaze. In the meantime, the queen has talked to the four other sheriffs about the financial aspect of restoring the New Orleans buildings.'

Eric gave an almost imperceptible inclination of the head. Impossible to say what he felt about being taxed for the queen's repairs.

New Orleans had been the place to go for vampires and those who wanted to be around them ever since Anne Rice had been proven right about their existence. The city was like Disneyland for vamps. But since Katrina, all that had gone to hell, of course, along with so much else. Even Bon Temps was feeling the storm's effect, and had been ever since Katrina had hit land. Our little town was still crowded with people who had fled from the south.

'What about the queen's entertainment estate?' asked Eric. The queen had bought an old monastery at the edge of the Garden District for entertaining large numbers of people, both vamp and non-vamp. Though surrounded by a wall, the estate was not considered easily defensible (since it was a registered building, historic and unchange-able, the windows couldn't be blocked up), so the queen couldn't actually live there. I thought of it as her party barn.

'It didn't suffer much damage,' Andre said 'There were looters there, too. Of course, they left a trace of their smell.' Vampires were second only to Weres in their tracking abilities. 'One of them shot the lion.'

I felt sorry for that. I'd liked the lion, sort of.

'Do you need help with the apprehension?' Eric asked.

Andre arched an eyebrow.

'I only ask because your numbers are low,' Eric said.

'No, already taken care of,' Andre said, and smiled just a tad.

I tried not to think about that.

'Aside from the lion and the looting, how was the estate?' Eric said to get the discussion of the storm damage back on track.

'The queen can stay there while she views the other properties,' Andre continued, 'but at the most for a night or two only.'

There were tiny nods all around.

'Our loss of personnel,' Andre said, moving on in his agenda. All the vampires tensed a bit, even Jake, the newbie. 'Our initial assessment was modest, as you know. We assumed some would come forward after the impact of the storm was absorbed. But only ten have surfaced: five here, three in Baton Rouge, two in Monroe. It seems that we have lost thirty of our number just in Louisiana. Mississippi has lost at least ten.'

There were tiny sounds and movements all over the room as the Shreveport vampires reacted to the news. The concentration of vamps, both resident and visiting, had been high in New Orleans. If Katrina had visited Tampa with that much force, the number of dead and missing would have been much lower.

I raised my hand to speak. 'What about Bubba?' I asked when Andre nodded at me. I hadn't seen or heard of Bubba since Katrina. You'd know Bubba if you saw him. Anyone on earth would know him; at least, anyone over a certain age. He hadn't quite died on that bathroom floor in Memphis. Not quite. But his brain had been affected before he was brought over, and he wasn't a very good vampire.

'Bubba's alive,' said Andre. 'He hid in a crypt and survived on small mammals. He isn't doing too well mentally, so the queen has sent him up to Tennessee to stay with the Nashville community for a while.'

'Andre has brought me a list of those that are missing,' Eric said. 'I'll post it after the meeting.'

I'd known a few of the queen's guards, too, and I would be glad to find out how they'd fared.

I had another question, so I waved my hand.

'Yes, Sookie?' Andre asked. His empty gaze fixed me in place, and I was sorry I'd asked to speak.

'You know what I wonder, y'all? I wonder if one of the kings or queens attending this summit, or whatever you all call it, has a – like a weather predictor, or something like that on staff.'

Plenty of blank stares were aimed my way, though Andre was interested.

'Because, look, the summit, or conference, or whatever, was supposed to take place in late spring originally. But – delay, delay, delay, right? And then Katrina hit. If the summit had started when it was supposed to, the queen could have gone in a powerful position. She would have had a big war chest and a full quiver of vamps, and maybe they wouldn't have been so anxious to prosecute her for the king's death. The queen would have gotten anything she asked for, probably. Instead, she's going in as' – I started to say 'a beggar,' but I considered Andre just in time – 'much less powerful.' I'd been afraid they'd laugh or maybe ridicule me, but the silence that followed was intensely thoughtful.

'That's one of the things you'll need to look for at the summit,' Andre said. 'Now that you've given me the idea, it seems oddly possible. Eric?'

'Yes, I think there is something in that,' Eric said, staring at me. 'Sookie is good at thinking outside the box.'

Pam smiled up at me from beside my elbow.

'What about the suit filed by Jennifer Cater?' Clancy asked Andre. He'd been looking increasingly uncomfortable in the chair he'd thought he was so clever to snag.

You could have heard a pin drop. I didn't know what the hell the red-haired vampire was talking about, but I thought it would be better to find out from the conversation than to ask.

'It's still active,' Andre said.

Pam whispered, 'Jennifer Cater was in training to become Peter Threadgill's lieutenant. She was in Arkansas managing his affairs when the violence erupted.'

I nodded to let Pam know I appreciated her filling me in. The Arkansas vampires, though they hadn't gone through a hurricane, had undergone quite a reduction in their own ranks, thanks to Louisiana's group.

Andre said, 'The queen has responded to the suit by testifying that she had to kill Peter to save her own life. Of course, she offered reparation to the common fund.'

'Why not to Arkansas?' I whispered to Pam.

'Because the queen maintains that since Peter is dead, Arkansas goes to her, according to the marriage contract,' Pam murmured. 'She can't make reparation to herself. If Jennifer Cater wins her suit, not only will the queen lose Arkansas, she'll have to pay Arkansas a fine. A huge one. And make other restitution.'

Andre began to drift around the room soundlessly, the only indication that he was unhappy about the topic.

'Do we even have that much money after the disaster?' Clancy asked. It was an unwise question.

'The queen hopes the suit will be dismissed,' Andre said, again ignoring Clancy. Andre's permanently teenage face was quite blank. 'But apparently the court is prepared to hear a trial. Jennifer is charging that our queen lured Threadgill to New Orleans, away from his own territory, having planned all along to start the war and assassinate him.' This time Andre's voice came from behind me.

'But that wasn't what happened at all,' I said. And Sophie-Anne hadn't killed the king. I'd been present at his death. The vampire standing behind me right at this moment had killed Threadgill, and I'd thought at the time he was justified.

I felt Andre's cold fingers brush my neck as I sat there. How I knew the fingers were Andre's, I couldn't tell you; but the light touch, the second of contact, made me suddenly focus on an awful fact: I was the only witness to the death of the king, besides Andre and Sophie-Anne.'

I'd never put it to myself in those terms, and for a moment, I swear, my heart stopped beating. At that skipped beat, I drew the gaze of at least half the vamps in the room. Eric's eyes widened as he looked at my face. And then my heart beat again, and the moment was over as if it never had been. But Eric's hand twitched on the desk, and I knew that he would not forget that second, and he would want to know what it meant.

'So you think the trial will be held?' Eric asked Andre.

'If the queen had been going to the summit as the ruler of New Orleans – New Orleans as it was – I believe the sitting court would have negotiated some kind of settlement between Jennifer and the queen. Maybe something involving Jennifer being raised to a position of power as the queen's deputy and getting a large bonus; something like that. But as things are now . . .' There was a long silence while we filled in the blanks. New Orleans wasn't as it had been, might never be so again. Sophie-Anne was a lame duck right now. 'Now, because of Jennifer's persistence, I think the court will pursue it,' Andre said, and then fell silent.

'We know there's no truth to the allegations,' a clear, cold voice said from the corner. I'd been doing a good job of ignoring the presence of my ex, Bill. But it didn't come naturally to me. 'Eric was there. I was there. Sookie was there,' the vampire (Nameless, I told myself) continued.

That was true. Jennifer Cater's allegation, that the queen had lured her king to her party barn in order to kill him, was completely bogus. The bloodbath had been precipitated by the decapitation of one of the queen's men by one of Peter Threadgill's.

Eric smiled reminiscently. He'd enjoyed the battle. 'I accounted for the one who started it,' he said. 'The king did his best to trap the queen in an indiscretion, but he didn't, thanks to our Sookie. When his plot didn't work, he resorted to a simple frontal attack.' Eric added, 'I haven't seen Jennifer in twenty years. She's risen fast. She must be ruthless.'

Andre had stepped to my right and within my line of vision, which was a relief. He nodded. Again, all the vampires in the room made a little group movement, not quite in unison but eerily close. I had seldom felt so alien: the only warmblood in a room full of animated dead creatures.

'Yes,' Andre said. 'Ordinarily the queen would want a full contingent there to support her. But since we're forced to practice economy, the numbers going have been cut.' Again, Andre came near enough to touch me, just a brush of my cheek.

The idea triggered a kind of mini-revelation: *This was how it felt to be a normal person.* I hadn't the slightest idea of the true intentions and plans of my companions. This was how real people lived every day of their lives. It was frightening but exciting; a lot like walking through a crowded room blindfolded. How did regular people stand the suspense of day-to-day living?

'The queen wants this woman close to her in meetings, since other humans will be there,' Andre continued. He was speaking strictly to Eric. The rest of us might as well not have been in the room. 'She wants to know their thoughts. Stan is bringing his telepath. Do you know the man?'

'I'm sitting right here,' I muttered, not that anyone paid any attention but Pam, who gave me a sunny smile. Then, with all those cold eyes fixed on me, I realized that they were waiting for me, that Andre had been addressing me directly. I'd become so used to the vamps talking over and around me that I'd been taken by surprise. I mentally replayed Andre's remarks until I understood he was asking me a question.

'I've only met one other telepath in my life, and he was living in Dallas, so I'm supposing it's the same guy – Barry the Bellboy. He was working at the vamp hotel in Dallas when I picked up on his, ah, gift.'

'What do you know about him?'

'He's younger than me, and he's weaker than me – or at least he was at the time. He'd never accepted what he was, the way that I had.' I shrugged. That was the sum total of my knowledge.

'Sookie will be there,' Eric told Andre. 'She is the best at what she does.'

That was flattering, though I faintly recalled Eric saying he'd encountered only one telepath previously. It was also infuriating, since he was implying to Andre that my excellence was to Eric's credit instead of my own.

Though I was looking forward to seeing something outside of my little town, I found myself wishing I could think of a way to back out of the trip to Rhodes. But months ago I'd agreed to attend this vampire summit as a paid employee of the queen's. And for the past month, I'd been working long hours at Merlotte's Bar to bank enough time so the other barmaids wouldn't mind covering for me for a week. My boss, Sam, had been helping me keep track of my overage with a little chart.

'Clancy will stay here to run the bar,' Eric said.

'This human gets to go while I have to remain?' the red-haired manager said. He was really, really unhappy with Eric's decision. 'I won't get to see any of the fun.'

'That's right,' Eric said pleasantly. If Clancy had thought of saying something else negative, he took one look at Eric's face and clamped down on it. 'Felicia will stay to help you. Bill, you will stay.'

'No,' said that calm, cool voice from the corner. 'The queen requires me. I worked hard on that database, and she's asked me to market it at the summit to help recoup her losses.'

Eric looked like a statue for a minute, and then he moved, a little lift of his eyebrows. 'Yes, I'd forgotten your computer skills,' he said. He might have been saying, 'Oh, I'd forgotten you can spell *cat*,' for all the interest or respect he showed. 'I suppose you need to be with us, then. Maxwell?'

'If it's your will, I will stay.' Maxwell Lee wanted to make it clear that he knew a thing or two about being a good underling. He glanced around at the assemblage to underscore his point.

Eric nodded. I guessed that Maxwell would get a nice toy for Christmas, and Bill – whoops, Nameless – would get ashes and switches. 'Then you'll remain here. And you, too, Thalia. But you must promise me that you will be good in the bar.' Thalia's required tour of duty in the bar, which simply consisted of sitting around being mysterious and vampiric a couple of evenings a week, did not always go by without incident.

Thalia, perpetually sullen and broody, gave a curt nod. 'I don't want to go, anyway,' she muttered. Her round black eyes showed nothing but contempt for the world. She had seen too much in her very long life, and she hadn't enjoyed herself in a few centuries, was the way I read it. I tried to avoid Thalia as much as possible. I was surprised she'd even hang with the other vamps; she seemed like a rogue to me.

'She has no desire to lead,' Pam breathed into my ear. 'She only wants to be left in peace. She was thrown out of Ilinois because she was too aggressive after the Great Revelation.' The Great Revelation was the vampire term for the night that they'd gone on television all over the world to let us know that they actually existed and, furthermore, that they wanted to come out of the shadows and into the economic and social flow of human society.

'Eric lets Thalia do what she wants as long as she follows the rules and shows up on time for her hours at the bar,' Pam continued in her tiny whisper. Eric was ruler of this little world, and no one was forgetting it. 'She knows what the punishment will be if she steps out of line. Sometimes she seems to forget how little she would like that punishment. She should read Abby, get some ideas.'

If you weren't getting any joy out of your life, you needed to . . . oh, do something for others, or take up a new hobby, or something like that, right? Wasn't that the usual advice? I flashed on Thalia volunteering to take the night shift at a hospice, and I shuddered. The idea of Thalia knitting, with two long, sharp needles, gave me another frisson of horror.

To heck with the therapy.

'So, the only ones attending the summit are Andre, our queen, Sookie, myself, Bill, and Pam,' Eric said. 'Cataliades the lawyer and his niece as his runner. Oh, yes, Gervaise from Four and his human woman, a concession since Gervaise has been hosting the queen so generously. Rasul, as driver. And Sigebert, of course. That's our party. I know some of you are disappointed, and I can only hope that next year will be a better year for Louisiana. And for Arkansas, which we now consider part of our territory.'

'I think that's all that we needed to talk about with all of you present,' Andre said. The rest of the stuff he and Eric had to discuss would be done in private. Andre didn't touch me again, which was a good thing. Andre scared me down to my polished pink toenails. Of course, I should feel that way about everyone in the room. If I'd had good sense, I would move to Wyoming, which had the lowest vamp population (two; there'd been an article about them in *American Vampire)*. Some days I was sorely tempted.

I whipped a little notepad out of my purse as Eric went over the date of our departure, the date of our return, the time our chartered Anubis Airline plane, was arriving from Baton Rouge to pick up the Shreveport contingent, and a rundown of the clothes we would need. With some dismay, I realized I would have to go borrowing from my friends again. But. Eric added, 'Sookie, you wouldn't need these clothes if it wasn't for the trip. I've called your friend's store and you have credit there. Use it.'

I could feel my cheeks redden. I felt like the poor cousin until he added, 'The staff has an account at a couple of stores here in Shreveport, but that would be inconvenient for you.' My shoulders relaxed, and I hoped he was telling the truth. Not one flicker of an eyelid told me any different.

'We may have suffered a disaster, but we won't go in looking poor,' Eric said, being careful to give me only a fraction of his stare.

'Don't look poor,' I made a note.

'Is everyone clear? Our goals for this conference are to support the queen as she tries to clear herself of these ridiculous charges, and to let everyone know that Louisiana is still a prestigious state. None of the Arkansas vampires who came to Louisiana with their king survived to tell the tale.' Eric smiled, and it wasn't a pleasant smile.

I hadn't known that before this night.

Gosh, wasn't that convenient.